Petra Croft writes extensively in other genres and is the pen name for this piece of period literature. She has written contemporary fiction but this is her first period novel. She has an interest and knowledge of this circa of British life – the 1800s. *The Preference* was inspired by private family diaries. She lives and works in the U.K.

The sequel to *The Preference* is *The Entitlement* and follows the lives of the main characters – due out soon.

This book is dedicated to P.M & S.S who inspired me to write it.

Petra Croft

THE PREFERENCE

AUSTIN MACAULEY PUBLISHERS

LONDON * CAMBRIDGE * NEW YORK * SHARJAH

A CIP catalogue record for this title is available from the British Library.

ISBN 9781035844913 (Paperback)
ISBN 9781035844920 (ePub e-book)

www.austinmacauley.com

First Published 2024
Austin Macauley Publishers Ltd®
1 Canada Square
Canary Wharf
London
E14 5AA

Introduction

The Preference is a work of historical fiction which defies much of the stereotypes of the time. It is both a love story and an erotic journey. It encompasses the strong emotions of love and loathing and the interface which binds the two: the journey through contempt to the reconciling of causes and possibilities. It begins with two girls of advantaged background in their comparative innocence and continues into their blossoming maturity. Seeing the world through the eyes of young women, and men, from an age where self-expression was perhaps more strongly desired because it was not encouraged. In the arena of emotion some things never change. Human nature clothes its desires and needs in different ways from era to era but there remains a similarity in the way we set about achieving fulfilment. Language and manners and fashion change with the decades, but some desires are innate and ephemeral. *The Preference* is written with humour and with a view to entertain. It has a variance of characters which might have stepped from Austen or Dickens, or other historical writers, but always the emphasis is on the reality of human nature.

Table of Contents

Part One January 1839   11

    Little Acorns   13

    The Lion's Den   18

    Enter the Lionesses   27

    Old Love in New Eras   38

    Correct by Default   48

    Probability and Possibility   57

    All Girls Together   66

    Wallflowers and Summer Blooms   83

    Time and Tide   93

    Ebb, Flow and Consequences   108

    Flights of Fancy and Rude Awakenings   119

    Era's End   140

Part Two October 1844   155

    High Teas and Low Tactics   157

    Touche   182

    From Bad to Worse   191

    Needs Must   210

    Fear of Blind Alleys   222

    Illusions and Stark Realities   252

Ace of Diamonds and King of Swords   267

Chance, the Fickle Companion   303

Frayed Ends and Floral Gatherings   323

The Wise and the Willing   339

Sensitivities Like Harp Strings   364

Secrets, Lies and Modifications   380

The Circular Motion of Life   415

Scoundrels, Saviours and Sensible Folk   435

Serious and More Serious   459

Tides Turning and Winds Changing   488

Sofas and Solicitude   506

Visitors and Variants   534

The Levelling   569

Part One
January 1839

Little Acorns

The winter was as bleak and harsh as only January could be, the first time Anthony Fairchild rode into the grounds of Barton Grange Academy for Girls. He dismounted his horse on the lawn in front of the house and looked at the lower windows wherein sat a classroom of female pupils. The blanket of blinding white snow covering the lawns threw up a deflective light which obscured a lot of the inner scene he was attempting to scan.

In front of one of the four low windows was a girl, staring at him with a languid expression, not disguising her grave interest. He stared back, a steady and unreadable gaze he hoped was off-putting. It was not and she stared longer and turned her head to one side to contemplate him, as if a slight change in angle might give her the information she sought.

Melissa Shaw was surprised at his appearance on this freezing January day. She was less curious about who he may be than the fact that he should appear at all when no disruption to the boring and familiar surroundings was usually to be had.

Standing slightly to one side of the pane, she put her hand behind her and tugged the sleeve of her friend so that she might also share in this sudden apparition. Melanie Petersham turned at once and leaned forwards so that her head was next to Melissa's. "Who is that?" she asked. "How long has he been there?"

"I do not know," said Melissa. "And I only just now spotted him."

The playing of the harpsichord halted and Miss Madeley's voice called out, "What are you two staring at out there?"

"A gentleman has appeared, Miss Madeley. On the lawn," Melanie informed her.

Henrietta Madeley was mortified. "Well, do not stare at him in that way! We do not stare at gentlemen we have not been introduced to…" she said, quelling her note of anxiety as she tried hard to follow their line of vision. "We do not stare at gentlemen at all unless we are engaged in conversation with them."

A groom had now entered the scene outside and was taking the gentleman's horse and he was moving with the groom, thus bringing him closer to the window so as to follow the trajectory of the path leading to the stables.

"Come away from the window this instant," snapped Miss Madeley in her most threatening tone, which was really not threatening to anyone.

They could not look away; they were glued to the scene. Then the visitor lifted his head from the deep collar of his greatcoat as he came nearer. The window was elevated a little with the lie of the land; his tread audible as his boots crunched virgin snow. And now he was visible to them in clearer lines. No older, Melissa thought, than her eldest brother who was five and twenty. Clean shaven with pale hair the length of his neck and swept behind his ears. No hat, despite the cold, but a muffler of beige wool about his chin so that his lower face was not much discernible below his nose.

Miss Madeley's harpsichord accompanied the stitching they were meant to be doing in the embroidery lesson, and had slowed considerably until it screeched to a halt, painful on the ears. "Come away from the window!" Miss Madeley repeated. "I shall not ask you again."

In one last gesture of much needed frivolity, Melanie leaned into the glass and fixed his gaze with her own and put out her tongue—a semi-darting movement like that of a lazy snake—and then followed it with a face of general disdain. She was rewarded immediately by his look of appalled astonishment. They giggled softly and bent their heads over their embroidery frames while Miss Madeley resumed playing in the most vehement of tones. She too had seen the visitor, advantaged by position and so less of the sun's glare on glass, and had viewed him briefly in all his glory. He was around her own age, if she were not mistaken, and pleasing to the eye in all usual ways. She had a vague idea of his professional identity and motivation for coming and was exhilarated: she was forever on the alert for a prospective husband.

* * *

This was a day school, not a boarding school, and took only girls from the best families. Allied to a boys' academy which was larger but ran on the same principles. It was a notable place of excellence and had been established for some fifty or so years. It took pupils from twelve to sixteen years at the girls' school but this was extended in the boys' academy to eighteen, for university aspirants. The girls entered on becoming exactly twelve years of age, not a moment before, and left on becoming sixteen, literally at the end of the week of their birthday—unless that fell during a holiday, in which case they left at the end of the term. It was a rigid and unusual method, but was deemed the only way to suit the academy's guidelines. Fourteen pupils per class and no more. Exact numbers must be adhered to, the governors had decided at its inception, and this had never varied. The waiting list to enter saw that there was never a problem with this regime.

Miss Tongs led him to her sitting room where the maid had been instructed to bring hot scones and tea. He followed her in absolute silence and noted the small things about the headmistress that any man might note. Her slight and quite short stature—she may be mistaken for one of her own pupils at a distance from the rear surely! Her dark hair wound in a plaited affair at the nape of her neck. It must, he conjectured, be extremely long when released from its pins. Her brusque and direct way of speaking, punctuated occasionally with little witty asides.

Anthony Fairchild seldom spoke a lot with females he had just met in formal circumstances, until he had their measure. Meticulous in his conduct, he did not venture words without thought.

"I believe you have not taught girls before?" she queried and indicated the arm chair opposite the one she intended to take.

"That is correct," he told her.

"Well, then, it may take you some time to adjust."

He paused in reaching for the cup and saucer, glazed in exquisite eggshell blue and powder pink. "It surely cannot be much different than teaching boys," he said.

She laughed quite raucously, like a youth in a tavern, he thought, not a headmistress in her office.

"I am glad you think not," she said at length.

He was a little taken aback. "Please correct me if I am mistaken."

"'tis not for me to correct you..." she said. "'tis for you to discover these things for yourself."

He heaved a deep breath and sipped some of the hot tea, scalding his tongue. "Anatomically, they may be different, but surely their brains cannot be so different."

15

Again, she laughed, lifting her own cup for something to occupy herself while she conjectured. "Let me put it to you this way, Anthony… I may call you Anthony, may I?"

He was again taken aback and did not respond.

"And you may call me Judith."

He surveyed her as she prepared her words, a woman of about thirty-five to eight. Single, perhaps widowed, or perhaps not. Plain but striking in a manner which may please some men and displease others. "I will call you Miss Tongs, if you do not mind," he announced eventually, disliking familiarity of this nature in professional settings.

"Please yourself… I shall continue to call you Anthony, though obviously not in front of the girls."

"I would hope not," he replied in low calm tones.

She laughed once more—this time as if he had been in jest. "You are mostly accustomed to the orderly and attentive classroom of young males, no doubt. That is obvious from your working experience to date, notwithstanding the awful place you were last employed…"

"The less said about it the better…" he murmured.

"Indeed…but the attitude of these girls who are from the better class of society…some of them from very wealthy homes where they are…"

"Yes, yes…" intervened Fairchild, too abruptly he knew. "I saw for myself what kind of brats they are…" He had said it without thinking, without his usual self-control. But she maintained her previous amusement and showed no sign of misgiving at his appraisal.

"No doubt you saw them behaving in a less than decorous manner in Henrietta's classroom."

"I believe I did…" he said, and was not about to report the foolery involving the pulling of faces. He would deal with their more precocious habits in his own way, in his own time. "… If her classroom is directly in front of the central tree on the lawn!"

Miss Tongs smiled in a sardonic way. "She has as much notion of classroom discipline as I have of the compositions of Scarlatti… She allows them to do just as they wish, on the pretext of not noticing anything…"

His turn to smile. It was a very old and tired excuse for lack of classroom order, he had been told by other men in the profession, though he was as yet unfamiliar with the ruse.

"And of course Mistress Sulivan was scarcely awake…she nodded off at the odd moment in mid-sentence and the lesson often concluded without her noting the fact."

"God's Teeth!" he muttered, despite himself.

"Quite! And of course Mr Stringer is nearly as bad. He feels that as girls they should be given huge laxity and not expected to labour at anything."

He drained his tea cup and sat back in the chair and then surveyed the ceiling so as not to have to offer comment or criticism.

"Not that I am trying to put you off…" said Judith Tongs with irony. "The post is already yours…this interview is merely a formality. The boys' school has accepted you, and who are we poor women to say you nay!"

It being a rhetorical question he gazed at Miss Tongs directly and Miss Tongs gazed back with something approaching a hungry look. She was in the habit of bedding the young male teachers when she could, and when she thought it safe. And she was quite sure she wanted it to be safe and convenient to bed this latest one.

Reading her mind—in the way he had become adept in the company of some females—he thought to deter her train of thought. She was not pleasing to his senses in any way. "I will cope, Ma'am," he announced and stood.

"Good," said Miss Tongs. "I am sure you will, Anthony! I am sure you are the sort of young man who always copes in most circumstances."

He said nothing and took out his timepiece to emphasise the need for a speedy departure. "I have to leave before the darkness sets in… I have a good ride ahead. Some twenty miles."

"You have come on horseback?"

"Indeed… I always ride when I can… 'tis far quicker when covering distances."

"Then I shall not detain you…" She held out her dainty hand and he took it in his chilly hand. His hands had barely had time to thaw from the cold, but he was anxious to be away before she ate him alive.

The Lion's Den

The first day at the girls' academy for Anthony Fairchild was fraught with frustration. He expected some turbulence within the schedule, but not the kind of disruption which emerged in the feminine world they inhabited. They looked at him as he entered, all of them variously standing, lolling and sitting about as if in a place of recreation. He looked back at them, almost afraid to enter their midst. He assessed them with one swift eye movement. "What are you waiting for?" he asked evenly as he made quickly for his desk at the front towards the side of the room nearest the window.

"I expect it might be you… Sir!" responded one of them whom he soon knew to be called Abigail Grimwell. She had added the appellation of 'Sir' as an afterthought with a slight tone of irony, and he paused a second to consider if this was in fact a facetious slur upon his authority and looked at her with his shrewd and careful gaze. It was nothing, he deduced, beyond their usual careless attitude towards teachers. She looked back at him, bright eyed and expectant and somewhat amused by proceedings.

"Then sit down…" he said as he pulled out the chair from behind the large expensive desk allotted to him. "I do not expect to see you all mulling around the room before lessons as if you are at the market or the town square."

This caused them to giggle surreptitiously as they moved unhurriedly to their places—though he failed to see how his comment had been amusing—then the hilarity became somewhat contagious as they sat, taking in his appearance and demeanour with a rapacious shared appraisal which was unnerving in the extreme. Did they imagine he had been hired as a court jester or an entertaining diversion in their tedious day? For he could not have enjoyed a more appreciative response to his warning! He was less than pleased.

They looked not at his face when he spoke, but at his clothing, which was of the greatest interest to them; his utterances were boredom itself next to his attire—of the finest and most fashionable—and they drank in its detail with undisguised delight. He wore no gown, unlike Mr Stringer or Mr Stevenson, and was not obliged too except in morning assemblies or at meetings with parents and governors. Accustomed from many occasions in his life to being surveyed with appreciation by members of the opposite sex, he was not foolish enough to allow his vanity to get the better of him amid a bunch of young girls. "Kindly look at me," he told them, "When I am speaking…and not at what I am wearing."

This honesty shocked them, this shrewd noting of their reaction; they were too used to the false and distant manner of more indifferent scholars of learning, some of whom dressed in an appalling way. It caused more giggling, of the stifled and covert kind, and he began to rue his decision to accept the post. He could not for a moment or two rid himself of the mood.

The heat in the room was unbearable, the fire stoked to capacity and burning evidently for some hours. It was only just past nine o'clock, but apparently Mistress Sullivan—owing to her advanced age—had long since given instructions, and her instructions were always adhered to.

He rummaged in the desk drawers and deliberated while now and then glancing from the window to his right and wishing he might change places with the groom whom he had already engaged in conversation, he being perhaps the only other young male he would encounter in the place. The groom was friendly and of a lively wit. They had talked of horses and in particular the one he rode which was much admired generally.

The groom had told him of the overall tone of the place and the eccentricities of Miss Tongs; her sudden tempers, her cleverness, her gin drinking, her penchant for bedding young male staff. The groom had evaded her clutches some months back, only by inventing a betrothal which did not really exist.

Anthony Fairchild moved to the fire in the classroom holding the decanter of drinking water left for his refreshment, and he threw half the contents onto the coals, thus dousing the flames. Then he threw open a window wide enough to admit a draft.

Immediately there was consternation, expressed quite loudly and without a view to respect for his position.

"Be silent…" he told them. "No-one can work if they are falling to sleep… 'tis far too warm in here."

The temperature dropped rapidly. They were mortified. Murmurings began, and tuttings and sighings and other expressions of insolence he found hard to countenance. But he summoned patience and reminded himself that this was foreign territory to him. He allowed their shock and dismay to subside while opening text books and perusing pages.

They began shivering theatrically. He ignored them. Until one of them said in a stage whisper audible to the room. "Now I shall no doubt have earache."

He looked up from his books and directed his gaze towards the direction of the errant voice. "Your name?" he asked of her.

"Abigail Grimwell," she replied, not bothering to add the expected appellation at all.

He frowned at her before speaking and she looked back at him with a tired and curious expression he was never forced to endure while teaching boys. "Well, let me assure you, Miss Grimwell, you will have more than earache if you make such audacious commentary in my classroom again!"

There was silence and then they glanced at each other, their faces masks of tepid wariness. They could not at all reconcile his sartorial elegance, youthful appearance and urbane air of success with his autocratic manner. Mr Stringer never opened windows or doused fires or made them uncomfortable in such a way. Nor did Miss Madeley, and certainly not Mistress Sullivan.

His second shocking announcement came at the end of the lesson when he told them that there would be homework. There was a collective gasp of shock. He looked around at them all. "Is this an unheard-of event? Homework?" Nothing would surprise him now, he felt.

They looked at one another, until another of their fold, Melanie Petersham, informed him. "We never have homework on Tuesdays, Sir!"

He turned from the blackboard and sought the source of the announcement. "Who said that?"

"I did!" said Melanie.

He appraised her without recognition, while she coloured a little and waited for him to remember her from the tongue-pulling exercise of a few days ago. She gripped Melissa under cover of the shared desk and pinched her hard to denote the fact that he would now probably remember. Melissa squealed and smothered it, causing herself to cough excruciatingly.

He did not immediately remember them—distracted by the coughing and squealing and other sounds from immediate recognition. He enquired in his smooth deep tones. "Is it a superstition or some such…no homework on Tuesday? Or what is it?"

No-one spoke. And then Lucinda began to giggle, in a soft and subdued way, for she was the *chief giggler,* and soon several others caught the bug and there was a cacophony of merriment. He paced at the front of the room, his hands beneath the back folds of his expensively tailored jacket, and waited for the amusement to cease.

Then Melanie found her voice. "We know not...but Granny never set homework on Tuesdays."

He wheeled about in a full circle, a show of complete surprise. "Granny? Who is Granny? Are you referring to Mistress Sullivan, by any chance?"

"Of course!" chirruped the irrepressible Abigail Grimwell cheerfully.

"Then award her, her proper title...and do not refer to any teacher in that disrespectful manner in my hearing... I set homework on Tuesdays and other days when I teach here...and I expect to see it completed. So, I will expect the first on Friday when I return... Do I make myself understood?"

They made general noises that might or might not infer compliance. He inhaled a long breath to assume a former calm which had slowly deserted him during the hour's lesson. "I will repeat the question... Do I make myself understood?"

"Yes, Sir!" they muttered in low desolate tone.

"Good! And let me also add that I do not accept excuses for homework not completed...short of plague and fire and major catastrophe, I always punish people for that offence, without exception."

He surveyed their faces. They were fourteen and fifteen, ripening into early womanhood but bearing the traces still of childhood. Some were plain, some were pretty and some were simply unmemorable. He wondered for the umpteenth time if he had not been mistaken in engaging the post at Barton Grange, and how long it would take them to see him as a respected member of staff and not a credulous imposter, or some kind of curious addition they could take with a pinch of salt. "And one more thing..." he pronounced in a perfunctory fashion as he packed his satchel of equipment ready for the next lesson with the younger female pupils of twelve and thirteen. "I do not wish to hear a continuance of that hideous giggling. There is no hilarity to be found in learning English and French. I expect not to hear any more of it."

This was perhaps the most onerous of commands set so far. To expect them not to giggle now and then was like asking them not to draw breath.

"You may go…" he told them, but left the room first and went straight out to the grounds to light a small cigar.

They sat in complete silence for several seconds after his departure, until Lucinda Harvey, the *chief giggler*, said to her companions. "Well! What do you make of *him*?"

"Peas-above-sticks with himself!" Abigail Grimwell said.

"Not a sociable person," offered Mary Hampshire, usually the quietest member of the class.

"He is not actually here to be sociable," commented Millicent Bromley sensibly, and against the odds.

"Simply odious!" Melissa Shaw said and withdrew her sweet tin from her bag to be rid of the taste of tedium.

"Beautiful clothes, betimes," mused Miranda Moreton. "What does he want with working here if he can afford those clothes?"

"Phooey…" said Melanie. "He could have pawned something to pay for them and obtain the position, or borrowed them. He may not have two farthing to his name. He may be all show."

"He will mellow in time perhaps…" said Miranda who loved to pen satirical poems about people and already had the first lines of something about Fairchild in her head. "We will have him wrapped around our fingers in a little while."

"I would not count on it," said the omniscient Mary who often fell asleep against her will with a little-known condition called narcolepsy.

"Neither would I!" Melissa agreed.

They considered matters individually and in silence before rising from their seats, various impressions and thoughts occurring to them. Miss Tongs had alluded in her sardonic manner to the fact that he was not to be mistaken for Mr Stringer…or to Mr Frondley, the current head of the academy, or any other of the hapless teaching staff who wandered in and out of the classrooms of the Girls' school. She had warned that there was to be excellent conduct and application to work, hinting at dire consequences in the absence of such from this language teacher whose pedigree and reputation was such as to make him god-like. *They had regarded her with little seriousness.* It was the kind of expected rhetoric which lacked imagination and they were totally unprepared. Whatever Anthony Fairchild was, or was not, he was certainly not set to be much fun.

* * *

In 'The Four Horsemen', the next evening he drank with his closest friend, Timothy Trimingham. They had known each other since early childhood. Trimingham was also a teacher of languages—although only possessed three besides English and not five—at a boys' school on the other side of the town. Neither of them had entered the teaching profession from a sense of vocation but for differing reasons of financial pressure and convenience of qualification.

"How did it go so far?" Trim asked, half way into their first tankard of ale.

"Which part in particular?" Fairchild replied, "Otherwise it may take all night."

"The girls' place…" said Trimingham succinctly.

Fairchild swilled the ale around and considered. "Let us put it this way, I may have been better off joining the Foreign Legion as a less tortuous means of recouping losses."

Trim erupted into laughter. "You exaggerate or jest…obviously."

"I do neither!" His friend said. "They are mostly insolent brats…they look at me as if I am the hired help who has stepped above his station…"

"Very galling!" Trim said. "But you will get the situation in hand with time."

They drank in silence for several minutes and watched the rest of the customers, ranging from towns' people to overnight visitors and the looser type of women preying on likely looking men. A silence ensued between them. The tavern being a fascinating scenario of everyday life.

"Have you seen Lottie in these past days?" Trimingham enquired casually and at length.

"Not until this Saturday evening. We plan to borrow her cousin Kate's cottage while she is away."

Trim stared at him and hesitated.

"Why do you ask?" said Fairchild.

"She is planning to go away…and I wondered if you knew…"

"Go away!" he echoed, thinking he had misheard. "Where the hell to?"

"Well, I…" Trimingham looked flustered. "I perhaps should let her tell you herself."

"The devil you should!" Fairchild uttered. "Tell me now what you know."

"According to Susan, who saw her yesterday, she is signing on with a travelling theatre company."

Fairchild swallowed ale the wrong way and coughed for a time, winded and too shocked to regain his breath. When he did, he swore vehemently and stared at Trimingham. "For the love of God! What a damn foolish notion."

Trimingham shrugged. "She can certainly act well enough…and she needs an escape route…"

"Phipps, I take it?" said Fairchild, he had paled considerably and looked sick to the stomach.

"Her father is pressing for the suit…she has no option but to go away, she says. Unless…" Trimingham paused and took up his tankard and watched his friend in silence. Fairchild shook his head, seeming ready to drop. They were both weary, following a long day. "I cannot wed her, Trim! I have not the funds as yet. I have told her all this. Why am I doing this blasted teaching if not to be able to wed her!"

"Can you not borrow?" Trim said. "I will loan you some and surely Richard will grant you a loan if you ask him…"

"I will not borrow money…" Fairchild said with heat. "I have lost enough money as it is. And no, I will not ask Richard for a bean ever again. I tried him last month and he flatly refused…and made me feel like an idiot."

Trim did not pursue the topic, he knew that if Fairchild went to his brother, Richard, it would be as a very last resort.

"Do you not think I would attain the money if I could…rather than see her travelling the country and flaunting herself on a stage."

"She is performing Shakespeare and the classics…not in Music Hall," said Trimingham carefully. They had all been friends since childhood: Susan, Trim's fiancé, and Lottie and he and Fairchild.

Fairchild shrugged impatiently. "Makes little difference to me…other men will stare at her, try to seduce her."

"Then let me loan you some blunt…you will have funds in the bank soon…and I am sure my father will help you out if I ask him."

"No!" Fairchild said in a louder voice than he had intended. "I have not been raised to borrow and beg money… 'tis entirely against my principles."

Trimingham sighed in annoyance and ordered more ale. "Then your principles must risk you losing her, for what is the girl to do? She will be forced into marrying Phipps!"

Fairchild wheeled around at the bar counter and then thumped the top of it with his fist. He swore again, lengthy cursings that were out of character for him in public places, even the ale house. "Perhaps she could come and stay at your parents' house?" he suggested desperately on becoming calmer.

"That my father would not countenance," replied Trim. "He knows full well what Fitzwilliam is capable of. Besides, he will not aid and abet a young woman on this kind of matter…though I am sure he will loan you money to wed her…he's not unsympathetic."

"I sometimes suspect…" Fairchild confided, ignoring the character summary of Trim's father. "I sometimes have the feeling that she wishes secretly to go off and act…*to tread the boards,* as they say. She may want it more than marrying me."

"Not according to Susan."

Fairchild again ignored him, his spirits plummeting to the bottom of the empty tankard. "I mean, what am I but a humble schoolmaster!"

"Do you know how many great men of the past began as humble schoolmasters?" Trim attested.

"No, and I imagine you do…but I do not wish you to recount them for me now, Timothy, if you do not mind."

Trimingham sighed loudly and summoned the barmaid. They were well on their way to inebriation, having previously avowed to stay sober on a mid-week evening, but their need for solace through drink and the sombre tone of the evening was driving them.

"She will have to leave her home if Phipps persist… Fitzwilliam will lock her away or remove her to some place where she cannot escape…" Fairchild declared in mounting desperation.

"What of your uncles?" Trim suggested. "Surely one of them might help…"

He made a face of disdain and then cursed again. "Frederick is out of the country…and Felix is mortgaged to the hilt after the collapse of his roof last month… 'twill be a fool's errand."

"What of your cousins?" Fairchild's male cousins were somewhat older than they were and quite prosperous. "Isaac has the legacy from his grandmother does he not? And besides, he is successful himself now you tell me!"

"No," snapped the other. "I cannot and will not raise funds within the family just now."

"Exactly why she has accepted this touring engagement, I perceive. She knows your mind on this," said Trim reasonably. "And not because she wants so badly to be in the theatre."

"Once she has a taste for it though?"

"It will be out of her blood…" persisted Trimingham.

"Are you sure that is the way it always goes?" Fairchild asked.

"No, I am not sure!" Trimingham admitted with candour.

"Why does she not discuss things with me first!" he said in a rising bout of anger.

Trim swallowed ale and looked at him sidelong. "Pride, Tony! Do you imagine she wants to coerce you into wedlock? What woman wants that start to marriage! She has her pride in the matter the way you do over the borrowing of the money…"

He stared into the distance. Across the counter at the other side of the room two doxies were watching them and making lewd faces of lustful desire, when the landlord did not observe them. He slammed the tankard onto the counter top, slopping the ale. "Checkmate," he told Trim in finality. "You have just taken the advantage…for I cannot gainsay your point."

Enter the Lionesses

On Friday afternoon at the girls' academy, he hoped for a better view of matters resulting from their more respectful conduct and a more attentive attitude. But he was disappointed. The giggling began early on, caused by his confusion over just where they were up to in written French. There were no clues left by Miss Sullivan and scanning their books showed only a dismal progress attained since the beginning of last term. He asked them questions to try to ascertain their advancement. They were obstinately unhelpful.

The desks were in two rows, with a central aisle. The right side of the aisle housing four desks on each row and the other side housing three. Fourteen pupils in all. It was an easy number to manage, or should have been, considering he had been recently managing classes of twenty-five boys and more in state grammar schools and classes of larger rotating numbers in the last privately owned school. This present consignment should be easy he had reasoned.

Presently he looked at the books of both Melissa Shaw and Melanie Petersham who sat directly in front of his desk in the second row and saw that one had copied from the other. "Who has copied from whom?" he demanded.

Melanie was truthful in a brazen manner which set his teeth on edge. "I copied from Melissa…" she told him quite proudly. "For I cannot understand the half of it… 'tis like a foreign language to me."

This was perhaps meant to be a witticism. He was not amused, though it gave him pause; that a fourteen-year-old laid claim to such wit was somewhat impressive. He stared at her until she assumed a look of near contrition and said with false humility. "'tis the same when I speak it… I cannot get my tongue around the words."

He turned and then turned back. "Oh indeed! But I perceive you have no problem at all with your tongue when pulling faces through windows at complete strangers!"

He had recognised her. She froze, as did Melissa next to her. While Lucinda found this so hilarious her giggling took on new heights of absurdity, resembling a door on rusty hinges. He shifted his position to stare at her. "Leave the room," he said. "And do not return until you have composed yourself."

Lucinda fled; her kerchief held against her mouth.

More covert merriment began in sporadic places.

"I believe I warned you of this random amusement on Tuesday!" he said to them. "Cease it at once!"

But Melanie was determined to right matters and broke his emphasis on the hilarity. "I am very sorry about that day, Sir. I did not know then who you were."

"Evidently not, though 'tis a poor excuse," he said.

He moved his penetrating gaze to the girl next to her, the one called Melissa, whose other name he had not yet memorised. "And you are?"

"Melissa Shaw," she replied and looked at him with an equally penetrating stare—she had lively intelligent eyes full of undisclosed meaning—and then she partially closed them in the dismissive way of females who were less than enthralled with someone—and then she turned away and looked from the window to the outer world. Melanie had nudged her sharply as a reminder to add the word 'Sir' for politeness, but she had taken no notice.

He had scarcely met with such subtle insolence and he breathed deeply to summon patience, pausing to see if she would return her attention to him. She did not. "Miss Shaw, do not gaze out of the window when I am speaking to you. I am liable to take it as an insult," he said evenly. He appraised her for a few moments more with a neutral expression while she sealed her lips tightly, no doubt to stop herself from showing amusement. He frowned to let her see the full strength of his displeasure. She lifted her brows slightly in acknowledgement of his continued attention. He could barely believe he was in a classroom and he turned once more to Melanie Petersham. "Write out this passage again…and do not look at her book…"

Presently he came upon Mary Hampshire who sat on the second row beyond the aisle. She appeared to be dozing or asleep, her head on her arms. He stepped in front of her, waiting for her to open her eyes.

Melanie was exchanging looks of desperate frustration with Melissa over the French exercise and Melissa was pencilling her a note telling her not to worry; she would watch and silently offer correction. Melanie did not think they would get away with this, nothing seemed to escape his notice, but she thought it worth a try.

"And who is Sleeping Beauty here?" he enquired calmly of Miranda, seated next to Mary in the left hand first row.

"Mary Hampshire!" Miranda said in a condescending tone, reminiscent of a duchess receiving annoying guests who were unexpected.

"Miss Hampshire?" Fairchild said, not raising his voice but speaking plainly and waiting for a reaction.

"'twill not do any good speaking to her while she is like that!" Abigail Grimwell informed him from the row behind.

He turned to address her. "I have not asked for your opinion. Be silent."

Abigail sighed in a manner expressing piteous contempt for people who would not take advice.

Some covert merriment ensued once more and moments passed in near tranquillity as he waited. Then Mary opened her eyes suddenly and looked at him in a startled daze.

"I beg your pardon…" he told her facetiously. "Do I disturb your slumber?"

Mary did not respond and looked ashamed.

"She often does it…she cannot help it and we are all accustomed to it," Abigail daringly ventured with aplomb.

He moved his opaque green eyes, shielded somewhat behind his blonde lashes, and surveyed Abigail who watched him in fascination and grinned and folded her arms in a gesture of satisfaction against her plump body. He frowned, this time with serious intent, and her grin faded like sunlight over a lake. He was not someone to be grinned at, it was rapidly becoming apparent. Abigail Grimwell was beyond impertinent, he surmised, and would induce those around her to lose concentration from any task.

"Perhaps you did not hear me the first time…when I want your opinion, I will ask for it," he told her in his unruffled voice. "Until then you will do well to hold your tongue."

"I was simply being helpful…" responded Abigail, much affronted.

Possibly this was true and his own manners were now being called into question, though he doubted it. He was out of his depth and at a loss. Mary, meanwhile, watched him and he returned to her problem. "What does she mean, you cannot help it? Is this correct?"

"Yes, Sir… I fall asleep without warning and cannot prevent it."

"I see," he said, bereft of opinion. He would have to take it up with Judith Tongs, and he made a mental note of how to express what he had witnessed in Mary Hampshire.

At this moment Lucinda came back into the room looking sheepish and baleful, the very opposite of the mood in which she had departed. She stared at him mournfully and took her seat. What curious little creatures they were—this example of upper-class adolescent femininity! Why had he imagined he could handle these girls? The lower form, twelve to thirteen year olds, were hardly any trouble, being an ocean away from their older sisters in attitude. They simply watched him with wary expressions and waited to hear what he would say next. How did they make the leap almost overnight and grow into the brats he saw before him, with so little chronological difference in age!

Moving back to his desk and wondering if he might reasonably take a few moments and go out to the stables and smoke, he became aware that Melanie Petersham was again taking tuition from Melissa Shaw. It was beyond belief.

"If you dare to copy from her any further, I shall take the matter to serious heights of misconduct!" he said and grabbed the exercise book and ripped out the page. "Begin again, at once!"

Melanie was quashed but assumed the facial expression of someone surprised by another's temper while making allowances for them. Melissa Shaw made a low sound of contempt and shifted her omniscient grey eyes to the window. He was close to exploding. "As for you…if you make any more of your derisive sounds and expressions you are sure to fall foul of my temper."

They settled immediately into biddable demeanours, like members of a church congregation awaiting Vespers, and looked demurely at their books. He was not fooled and continued to survey them for a further minute or so.

After the lesson and on his way along the corridor to make swift exit, he encountered Henrietta Madeley leaving her sewing room. She called him back and said, "Anthony…do you mind if I have a word with you?"

He bridled somewhat at the use of his first name, but no doubt Judith Tongs had encouraged her into such familiarity and no doubt they all called each other by first names—it was in keeping with the laxity and casual tone of the conduct.

"Yes, *Miss Madeley*…?" he said pointedly, hoping she would take his meaning.

"I thought you might be a little perturbed by Mary Hampshire's problem…" she said anxiously.

"Indeed." He paused, startled by her reading of his mind on the subject so soon after the exchange with the girl in question. Henrietta was shorter than him by three or four inches, even in her low flared heels, and he gazed down on her as she leaned against the wall, her skirts so full they bordered on a crinoline, but not quite. She held them to herself so that she could be nearer to him. She was more enamoured of him close up, so good-looking was he, so clean shaven and fine boned. He caught sight of the flush on her throat above her neckline and gleaned that she wished to know him more intimately but he showed no sign of having noticed.

"Do not be alarmed by Mary's sleeping… 'tis some kind of disorder and she cannot help it. So, I do not want you to be annoyed with her or harsh or…" she faltered.

"Harsh?" he repeated.

"She does not disrupt the class in any way…or cause you trouble as a teacher…does she?"

"No but…" he faltered.

"But what?" the charming music mistress persevered.

"It is not appropriate in a classroom…" he said dully.

Miss Madeley smiled, displaying dimples just below her cheeks, her face flushing a little. "That hardly matters here…her fees are paid and she may as well be among her peers as at home and lonely…she may as well take the benefit of being young with others…"

There was really no answer to this statement. He was completely thrown by it. It made sense in some humane and benevolent world of its own—a world no doubt inhabited constantly by Henrietta Madeley. "She means and does no harm!" she affirmed, as if he may have misunderstood her previous sentiments.

He sighed and hung on to his already ragged patience. "Next to the rest of the insolent little madams I perceive her to be quite harmless!" he confirmed and watched Henrietta's eyelids droop upon his perusal of her face.

"They do not mean to be insolent," she told him fondly, "'tis just their way…"

He sighed again and then, taken up with her charms, he partially grinned but tightened his jaw to conceal it. His jawline was perfection, Miss Madeley noted, his bone structure remarkable, and the overall effect on her was compelling.

"I see…" he said, smiling openly now to put her at ease. "Well, unfortunately 'tis not my way…so they will have to mend *their way* or reap the consequences."

31

His breath seemed to cool her agitation on his every word. He was quite splendid in all aspects and she was astonished by how much he influenced her senses. Her search for a husband did not usually, or so easily, take in her more sensual desires. She sought to reconcile the exact meaning of his last words; what sort of consequences did he intend! She recalled Judith Tongs telling her that his classroom methods would tend towards strictness not lenience. Henrietta floundered, she did not know whether this repelled or intrigued her. She was quite undone.

"As to Miss Hampshire, you may have no fear…" he said, seeing her in some confusion and struggling for the right response. "I shall let this sleeping matter pass until I have spoken with Miss Tongs."

She inclined her head in the most modest and respectful of ways and rolled her eyes to look up to his. "Thank you," she said in a whisper. "I am grateful."

He perceived that she was a gentle soul and that she genuinely cared about her pupils. She was a good woman, a young one of around his own age, and had not yet found herself properly. He made her a semi-bow and moved on and then had a second thought. She was extremely pretty and he was experiencing hard times in the personal sense. He needed something, or someone, to soften his mood. He was losing his long-term sweetheart to the wider world; he was not intending to delude himself: the pain may just be in abeyance but then would grow worse. He needed to numb it a little, and her gentle female company would be soothing. He turned again. "Miss Madeley?"

"Yes? You may call me Henrietta…"

He came back to stand before her. "Would you care to go walking with me one Sunday?"

She flushed more deeply and then her eyes sparkled for a mere second and she looked down at the floor to take control of herself. "Yes, I should like that."

"Splendid!" he said. "I am away this weekend, but perhaps the Sunday following?"

She nodded, unable to believe that she had made such a favourable impression on him in so short an interlude. He gave her another semi-bow and went on his way.

* * *

He paused outside the side door leading directly to the stables and lit a small cigar. What had he done? To form an intimacy with a female colleague was surely the height of foolishness! He paced a little and smoked and fretted. And then he saw that all they need do was meet and chat and stroll, perhaps take afternoon refreshment. Though he could see she would ultimately wish more progress than that. She was out for a husband; it was written all over her. She was the very opposite sort of woman from Judith Tongs and it was obvious that she did not have casual liaisons just by listening to her. Too late now! He would not worry about it, for she might change her mind or dislike him on closer acquaintance. He stubbed the cigar out underfoot and stepped from the doorway as Miss Tongs came around the corner of the building, having alighted from the trap driven by the groom.

"Anthony!" she said, her small dark eyes shaded by the brim of a fur trimmed bonnet to keep away the chill of the day.

"Yes, Miss Tongs?"

"I am glad I have seen you…step inside please while I have a few words."

He saw little choice but to do as she asked, hoping this was not a prelude to the seduction the groom had warned him of.

"I am in something of a hurry, Miss Tongs," he told her briskly. "I am due in a meeting with Mr Frondley."

She gave a trilling laugh and turned to eye him as she walked, expecting automatically that he would be following behind. She was that rare thing: a woman with complete power, and she took it for granted and used it. "Martin will not mind if you explain to him," she said.

Secondary to his noting her familiar use of the headmaster's first name was his relief at the fact that she obviously had no personal intentions or she would not make such a remark.

"What is this problem with Mary Hampshire!" he began at once, as they entered her office, to seize the lead in any conversation. "This propensity to dropping off to sleep?"

"Oh that…" said Judith airily, "'tis nothing…we do not let it concern us."

"But why does she do it?" he demanded, his patience now teetering on the brink of an abyss. He had had enough of all of them.

"Why does it concern you so much?" she countered as she took off her bonnet and cloak and walked to her chair.

He looked at her with amazement. "Why?" he echoed, and she nodded and watched him keenly. "Because…because 'tis obviously of concern. A child who drops to sleep without being able to prevent it! She is either suffering from some ailment or is deprived of sleep during the night. Do you not think so yourself?"

She raised her dark brows and patted her immaculate shiny black hair, the pristine plaits today wound around her ears. "I do not really think about it."

He gritted his teeth and refused the chair she offered.

"What would you like me to do?" she said next, fluffing out her skirts and seating herself.

"Has there been a doctor's report?" he enquired.

"No, her guardian, who is her grandmother…or her aunt… I forget now which…say 'tis something she has done for quite a while."

"Have they not sought the root of the problem through medical opinion?"

"Obviously not…" said Judith tartly. "And it is their business whether they do… Not all things are solvable through medical opinion, Anthony."

He did not trust himself to speak but stared towards the window and wondered how to express his grave annoyance. Judith jumped into the silence. "Would you like me to order a doctor to attend here? I can do so to please you…there is one whom we summon when emergencies arise… I am sure he will come and look at her."

"Yes… I think that should be done. As to it not being our business, I disagree…if 'tis affecting her school work," he added as he moved to leave. "Thank you, Miss Tongs."

"Call me Judith," she said in her off-duty voice.

He ignored her. The cloying familiarity in the female establishment was beginning to grate on him. "And how are you getting along in general?" she queried, coming after him to prevent his departure so hurriedly. She was taking his cold attitude personally now.

He paused, seeing that it would be rude not to, and considered his next statements which might be damning or set a tone of discord. He did not wish to be at odds with her—his financial stability depended on the job for the next six months or so. Unless he went to the trouble of attaining a fresh post.

"You may be entirely honest with me," she added and placed herself next to him and peered up at him.

"I am finding things gradually easing…" he offered. "Although I have to say they are in general very insolent, prone to bad manners and often quite lax in their attitudes."

"I did try to warn you… If you recall."

"I do recall," he said in what he hoped was finality. She did not move and continued to look at him, making it difficult for him to leave her presence.

"Are you saying they are deliberately rude to you?" she pursued.

"Not rude perhaps…more lacking due respect…they think it amusing to lead me down blind alleys, to divert the subject in hand, to make irreverent comments…and I shall not even mention the hideous giggling which ensues…" He stopped mid-sentence. Any moment now it would turn into a liturgy of moaning complaints that may weaken her opinion of his professional capability.

Miss Tongs found it hard not to dissolve into pure laughter, but smiled warmly instead and then said in mock seriousness. "We cannot have that…we take good manners and respect very seriously, and their parents are informed of it at the start of the engagement they make with us…" She moved to a corner cupboard and then beckoned with her uplifted forefinger for him to follow.

He watched as she opened the door of the cabinet and searched. "You may when necessary, use this…" she said and produced a short thin cane, handing it to him across the desk.

He hesitated, staring at it with cautious foreboding. She waited a moment or two and surveyed him. "Surely you have used a cane before? In your three or four years' experience of teaching!" she said archly.

"Certainly…but never before on girls!"

"Obviously, as you have never before had to work with girls. But as long as you use it discriminately and not to excess it is quite permissible…"

He had not expected to resort to such measures with female pupils. He deplored the misuse of corporal punishment, but did not scruple to use it when necessary.

"Of course…" continued Miss Tongs. "If you are squeamish about it, you can always send them to me when they are testing your patience, and I will deal with them."

He cleared his throat and straightened his posture and took the cane. "I do not think I can find it in myself to hide behind you in times of duress," he announced.

"I am sure you cannot," she said and smiled at him through her complex assortment of meanings.

She watched the door after he left the room and deliberated, before taking the bottle of gin from the same cabinet and adding some to the existing glass of tonic water on her desk. Fairchild was, according to Frondley and Stevenson, part of a growing band of zealous young men who were intent upon reforming the state of education in the country—from the point of view of poor teaching methods and lack of structure in learning, and of the callous treatment meted out to pupils in the worst establishments. Miss Tongs had no opinion one way or another…the world was a gruesome place and if they believed they could change it then that was their affair. It did, however, explain his concern for Mary Hampshire's health condition. Charity always began at home.

Both the groom and Fairchild were currently bent on evading her advances, though they were surely aware of what she silently proposed. It did not displease her—rather it fascinated her, for both of them had their positions at the school to consider, albeit at differing levels of responsibility, both as indispensable to the running of the place in their individual ways. It was interesting to think how long it might take to have one of them weaken. The groom of course had been employed for much longer and she had all but given up on him. But Anthony Fairchild was as yet unknown territory…

Her cogitation was interrupted by the abrupt entrance of Henrietta Madeley who dashed in with her vermillion velvet cloak in her hand and tossed the key to the supplies room onto the desk.

"What are you looking so smug about? Have you come into money or some such?" said Judith. She was always patronising with Henrietta for Henrietta was no more worldly than the girls she instructed in needlework, deportment and dancing.

Henrietta smiled modestly and then threw her cloak about her shoulders. "He has asked me to go walking with him next weekend."

"Who has?" said Judith, deliberately obtuse, for she knew there could be only one man Henrietta was referring to.

"Anthony Fairchild."

"Of course he has!" Judith drained the last of the gin with the tonic water and smiled in her sardonic fashion. "What a perfect match…both of you the children of vicars, possessed of beguiling faces and perfect manners!"

Henrietta wheeled around as she tied the strings of her cloak. "What? He is the son of a vicar? Are you sure?" she queried.

"So Martin Frondley tells me…" confirmed Judith. "And of latter years the man became a bishop…"

Henrietta's look of pure joy could not have been greater had she been told he had descended from the sky in a chariot of fire. "Just think how much in common there will be!" enthused the head mistress. "You can talk all afternoon about choirs and bell-ringing and what you got up to in the vestry while your fathers were discussing Harvest Festivals elsewhere!"

Henrietta's mood was not daunted by Judith's sarcasm. No more than Judith's was daunted by the news of Henrietta and he walking out together. They were the same sort of age and he would doubtless like to be seen with a young woman of her ilk; utterly feminine and biddable and every man's idea of an English rose. Whether she would succeed in the wifely ambition was something Judith had doubts about. "How pleasing he is to the feminine eye…" she continued for Henrietta's benefit. "And with a brain to boot…he is charisma personified, is he not?"

"Well…he is certainly very…" Henrietta floundered, unsure if this was one of the older woman's verbal traps. "He is very eligible, it has to be said…though, of course, before I know him better, I cannot tell if he has hidden character flaws…beauty is only skin deep, Judith."

Judith replenished her drink in the obscured depth of the drawer. "And even his hidden flaws will be irresistible…to women of discernment," she uttered.

Miss Madeley knew that Judith was insinuating her lack of such discernment, and she cared not. It was she whom he had asked to go walking. Not Judith. She tutted to show vague disgust with such a claim, and glanced at the headmistress with a modest yet sanctimonious air. Judith tossed back more of the gin. She cared little about Henrietta's walking with him of a Sunday afternoon. What a waste of time and effort all that nonsense was, when they might just as easily be lying down.

Old Love in New Eras

He met with Lottie on the Saturday evening in a dark and damp clearing of the wood nearest the cottage she sometimes borrowed for their trysts. She was wearing her brother's clothes so as to not be recognised as she rode. It irked him to see her dressed like this, although she would look good in anything she wore.

The clearing was a few hundred yards away from the cottage itself and she had dismounted from her horse and stood at the top of the incline up which he cantered from the lower bridal path to reach her.

"I should think so…you are very late… I thought you were not coming!" she said in agitation as he drew near. "I have been standing here nearly frozen to death."

He turned his horse around while she mounted her own to join him. "Do not begin with your berating after I have ridden hours to get here," he replied testily.

They rode in silence to the cottage where they tethered the horses and as soon as it was done, she launched herself on him and kissed him with a fury and a passion which always amazed him, even after the five years of their adult relationship.

He put her away from him and looked at her long and she pulled the cap off her head and her brunette hair billowed about her shoulders, irradiated by the light from the lantern he carried. She could tell immediately by his eyes and his expression that he knew of her imminent departure. She had told Susan knowing she would confide in Trim who would feel honour bound to tell him. She needed to have him absorb it before they met.

She moved around the one low room of the cottage, tending the fire she had laid earlier, pouring wine from a flagon she had brought from home into two cups. Setting out cold food on the low table.

"Kate is not back for another day…" she told him. "She is at her sister's confinement over Lichfield way."

He murmured a response to the statement and did not speak further, warming his hands at the fire. The room was not cold, she had been tending the grate since four in the afternoon and there was a slight mist of smoke in the air where the fire had blown back down the chimney. It was a perpetual hazard and one he had become accustomed to. This was not refined living, it was a far cry from the comfort he enjoyed in Mrs Anstey's lodgings, with maid and laundry services and cooked meals when necessary. And far from his childhood home. He had been raised to comfortable standards of living, though not to great opulence.

"You can stay until morning?" she asked of him.

"Certainly, I am not intending to ride back in the freezing dead of night!" he replied, pulling off his boots.

Beneath her brother's discarded trousers and loose shirt, she wore meagre silk underwear; a chemise and drawers and silk stockings. He looked over at her and felt his arousal begin. She came to him and fell onto him on the narrow bed. He devoured her almost as she pulled him further and further into herself and wrapped her legs around his waist, limp with longing and gradual satiation.

Nearer to midnight and eating the bread and the cheese and the grapes they came finally around to conversation.

"Tell me about this last post you left in a hurry. What was the school like? Bad enough for you to have moved to Barton Grange in such a hurry?"

He lit one of his cigars and passed it to her. "I do not want to talk of it…it will ruin my mood…let us just say, we will have the place shut down within this next year, or we will die in the attempt."

"You are determined in this Foundation then? You and the rest?"

"We are!" he said. "Education in some parts of this country needs huge reform."

She pressed her face into his and chewed his earlobe and kissed his neck and did all manner of things that only women who loved wished to do following union. "I adore the way you see life, Tony!" she said and he thought about the words and what they meant. His way of seeing life was constantly with him and not something he viewed from another's perspective. "You see, you have your passions and I have mine… I believe that theatre is as important to life as education."

"I do not think I have ever denied that," he said, "But if we are to wed you cannot go off around the country appearing in plays…"

"Can I not?" she replied in a way that he could not rightly read. "Are you telling me or asking me?"

"I certainly would not like it…what happens when we have a family?"

"Then I would give it up and stay at home."

He thought twice before responding but could not prevent himself. "But I am not enough myself to make you stay home…even in wedlock!"

He felt her bristle and stiffen. "Now you are being childish…"

"No, I am being honest."

"In your terms perhaps…but I could earn money for us as I reach more critical acclaim for myself and the group."

Gritting his teeth, he closed his eyes and sought sensible inoffensive words. "I do not want my wife forced into earning money…if I cannot provide then I cannot marry you…"

She laughed in a high and what he thought of as a theatrical manner. "Now that is not practical at all."

"No, 'tis ethically traditional… I have integrity and self-respect."

She rose and tended the fire—what a useful distraction was a fire grate!

"And now you teach young girls?" She posed at length, changing the subject, a teasing note rising in her voice.

"Some part of the time, yes!"

Her chin lifted as she surveyed him, her throat a smooth glow in the firelight. "Little wonder you come with so much passion…a parcel of wenches to kindle your ardour."

"For God's sake, Lottie, they are children…twelve to fifteen."

She moved towards him, much amused but on her metal. "You forget I was merely fifteen when you first took me…"

"And I was only seventeen myself…there is a world of difference."

She drew on the cigar and blew the smoke into the distance of the room. "I am very jealous! You are obliged to give them your full attention for long bouts of time!" In the surrounding tranquillity of the wood, the only sound of life was an owl. "I would not bother," he intoned. "They see me as the devil incarnate. They fear and detest me… I am severe and demanding. I compel them to behave properly and pay heed. They have only apparently ever read of ogres like me in fairy tales…"

She found this amusing and laughed cheerfully for several seconds, but then sobered again rapidly.

"I am still very jealous," she pronounced in a sombre tone.

He was silent and looked at her with intent. "No more than I shall be soon when I think of men in theatres watching you…" he said.

She grew serious in her turn. "You know then?"

"I do," he said. "Trim told me, though why you could not tell me first I do not know…"

"I did not tell Trim, I told Susan…"

"'tis practically the same thing!" he rejoined.

"'tis the only way…given that you will not wed me."

"Charlotte, listen…" He left the narrow bed, put on his shirt. "I cannot marry you. We have been into all this… I have not the funds. It will take me a year or more to get to that point."

"I care not about money."

"You say that because you have never been without what it buys."

"No, but I have been without other things which matter more!" she flared. "And you insult me!" Her temper was always quick but not lasting. He came back to the bed and lay beside her. "I am simply telling you that you will not like to live in straitened circumstances with me… It would kill the marriage before it had properly begun."

She was silent and chewed her thumb and he took her hand away from her mouth, as he always had since she could remember. He kissed her thumb. "Your father would hound me to death…he would probably have me horse whipped…he would ruin our lives."

"Not if we went away!"

"Where to?"

"I do not know…anywhere…abroad or somewhere! How many languages do you have at your command? They could be put to good use!"

"It might take an age before I found the right connections. 'tis unrealistic fantasy," he told her. "Besides, I am committed to the Foundation for a while…"

"And there we have it…" she said. "You may have your commitments elsewhere but I cannot have mine."

"I have not said that…but they are quite different in nature and requirement."

She lay back and was quiet. He had upset her, but he could not delude her or himself at this stage.

"I will be back on track in one to two years…" he said, "We can wed then!"

"When is that to be?" She sat upright and leaned against the rough plaster wall, "When Phipps agrees to divorce me, you mean! Now who is unrealistic?" She rose and paced the room, her temper rising. "If I stay, I have to marry him. I have no choice. My father will force me into it. He desires some of his land in return!"

"We should have gone away directly I returned from Oxford. I had the money then," he opined.

"I know…and 'twas my fault we did not. I did not want to…"

"You did not," he confirmed in a flat voice. "Obviously because the lure of the theatre was too great!"

"No, not just that…because I was not sure…but now I am! I am certain! I will wed no-one but you…your ring, your bed, your babies… I will have no other man."

It was some consolation to her going away, the fact that she felt so strongly, and he pondered for an hour or so while she dozed. He thought of the aristocrats, and the titled nobility who famously coveted actresses and dancers and the like…the temptation she would be under as she roamed the greater world. And when she woke, he ventured a suggestion. He took her hands in his and lay next to her. "Lottie, I know this is difficult, but perhaps…perhaps you should consider accepting Phipps for now. Agree to a long engagement…insist on it…and I will endeavour to make money enough. Then when I have it you can break the engagement off…"

"No!" she cried and suddenly she was wide awake with anger and misery. "He would be coming near me and mauling me and trying to make love to me…how can you want to throw me to another man…and one like Gerald Phipps?"

"It would keep your father at bay!" he said, his agitation rising with hers. "Until we can wed…"

"How would you like it if I suggested you give yourself to some horrible woman you did not like…" she wailed, and he thought of Judith Tongs and her suggestive ways and seduction of younger men. He was silent, partially ashamed of himself and partially angry with her. It was different for women. Worse in all ways. "But surely, Phipps would not touch you before wedlock if you did not wish it… Your father would not accept that, surely."

Her face was a mask of fury, her eyes vibrant with mixed emotions. "Gerald Phipps is a licentious man…like my father! They are neither of them honourable men. They will not care what I think or want…"

He watched her pace around the low room, swathed now and then by the billows of smoke blown about by the back draft, like an apparition or a ghost. He was heart-sore and desperate.

"And there is this…" she said, turning to look at him. "Phipps will discover I am not a virgin…which is what he and my father both believe presently. What do you think will happen then?"

"There are endless possibilities," he said wearily.

"Yes, there are!" She poured herself more wine and grew calmer. "I have to go with this company, Tony. You must see that…'tis the only way."

Lost for a suitable reply and beyond hope he nodded.

"There are other things you could do…" he said at length.

"Not as well as I will do this…and not as well paid." She heartened a little. "But I shall return. Of course I shall. Then we will wed, then we can go somewhere miles away and be wed."

"Yes…we can be wed then," he concurred, his tone desultory; he had given up on the argument. She thought he sounded like a child. Meekly agreeing for lack of stronger opinion of his own. He held her and she talked more of the future, of the fine things they would buy and install in their home. Of the children they would have. He let her ramble on, half asleep with exhaustion. He felt exactly like a child listening to bedtime stories.

In his own mind, he believed she may get a taste for the travelling life, for the theatre itself, and not wish to settle or marry. Least not to him. He would be unable to offer her a colourful enough existence. She would forget him and outgrow him and he would be only a part of her growing up and her early womanhood. He did not say any of these things to her. To voice them would be unbearable for both of them. They needed to believe, they needed to feel the future and themselves together within it.

Soon, amid her talking, she realised he was asleep. He had ridden in freezing weather and made virile love to her; he was tired out. In repose, he was so good to look at she could not take her eyes from him. She thought that if he took to the stage as an actor, he would never be short of work. But he would not do so, he was not cut out for that kind of life. He preferred less flamboyant pursuits; books, languages, educational reform…apart from the festive occasions he enjoyed while about town drinking with friends, he did not crave adulation or excitement.

They slept for several hours and she woke first and then roused him with coffee and bread, holding the timepiece in front of his face. He rubbed his eyes and stared at it blearily and then sat up in the bed.

"I need to ride back before I am missed…" she said. "Later this morning I will ride back here and tidy up the cottage and change the linen…" She talked of the domestic itinerary and it was painful for him to hear, sounding as she did so much like a wife. He ceased to listen and as he washed in the water, she had heated on the fire he asked her. "When do you leave with this theatre?"

"Tuesday?" she replied.

He gaped at her. "That is a mere two days away."

"I know, but I cannot risk my father discovering my plans…so 'tis best to go very soon before he finds out…or he will prevent me."

"How long will you be gone and how will I contact you?"

She deliberated for what seemed an age. "Perhaps three months at first…we go to York then to Scotland. I will write to you with addresses where we are to stay and agendas…and then you may forward me letters which I will receive when I arrive."

"You have thought it through then?" he said.

"Of course I have thought it through… Tony, you have to keep the faith now. Life is nothing without faith."

She sounded like his elder brother and his late father, both clergymen. He did not know what he felt about faith. He had experienced only hope and fortitude so far. Faith was another matter.

They walked to the horses and he helped her mount.

"I will ride with you to the turnpike and then turn back," he told her.

"There is no need…'tis not on your way."

"I will ride with you, Charlotte!" he said adamantly. "'tis not yet fully light and there are dangers, so do not argue with me on the point."

She laughed. "Whatever you wish, Anthony!" She turned her horse. "But when we are wed, I am sure to argue with you on lots of things…so you are warned."

"Do not jest about it," he said. He was morose and could not face the separation.

"Which part of it? The marrying or the fact that I will argue with you?"

"Either!" Then he had other cautionary thoughts: "And take great care when you go into strange cities and towns…make sure you are with others of your troop or whatever they are called."

"They are not called a troop…" she laughed. "We are not acrobats, or soldiers…"

He ignored the humour. "You comprehend my meaning even so," he said impatiently. "Take good care…and don't go out after dark unless accompanied by someone…and be careful of eating and drinking in places of which you know nothing…"

She smiled and looked in the other direction while the list of *do's and don'ts* continued. "I know you are concerned for me, but try to be less didactic. Save your bossier tendencies for your darling girls…"

"Which darling girls?" he demanded.

"The female pupils in your classroom!" she said airily.

"They are not *'darling girls'*…they are irritating little wretches." He thought of the week ahead and the unknown trials he faced as yet.

"If you say so," she retorted with levity.

He did not feel in a humorous frame of mind and did not welcome her skittish way. He dealt with things differently than she. He looked ahead solidly as they rode, and then at the turnpike he kissed her.

"I love you, Tony! Remember, I shall always love you."

He closed his eyes and murmured assent. He was wiser than her, he thought, and minded of the wisdom that at times in life love was not enough.

* * *

On the ride home, he was not in his full senses, his mind haunted by past and future errors of judgement. He would worry now that they had conceived a child, so unrestrained were they in their love making. If it were to happen, he would have no choice but to go cap-in-hand to all his relatives and beg loans to begin married life. But then, it would also bring her home sooner surely. He was tormented by diversity of mind, wretched with uncertainty.

Charlotte Fitzwilliam was the only woman he had loved, the first and possibly the last. She had not had his secure childhood. Her mother had left when she was small, fleeing from an abusive marriage. And then there had been a succession of governesses who never stayed, fleeing from similar abuse at the

45

hands of her father: wealthy and influential and feared, the squire of the district. So, she had soothed her loneliness and neglect with fairy tales and flights of fancy. She loved to dress up and move her imagination to another world. She was a million miles from his own outlook and temperament. But he loved her and she him. It was the *'attraction of opposites'* his mother had once told him.

The ride back was one which he had done many times before and his horse knew the way even though it was uphill and down and hazardous in forested areas. The mare took him amiss twice and it was a good quarter hour each time before he realised it. He had to turn around and find his bearings again. It added an hour or more onto his journey. He cared little, it was Sunday.

Passing by a village he knew vaguely he stopped at the only inn and saw the landlord about his yard at a little after eight o'clock. He pulled in his horse and enquired whether the man would be good enough to sell him a bottle of gin, or rum, or any strong liquor. The landlord obliged with rum and he rode the rest of the way home in an increasingly alcoholic daze, during which he allowed the horse free rein. Losing your way when sober was annoying and full of anxieties. Losing it while intoxicated was a matter for happenstance.

He reached the steps of Mrs Anstey's lodging house—a four storey building in a row of six in the residential area of the town—having stabled his horse at the ostlers around the corner. The morning was now progressing, sunny and crisp in mid-February. Swilling down the front steps was the landlady's daughter who worked also as a barmaid at the tavern in the next street. She was a bonny girl, in the manner of popular barmaids, and about his own age. She did not care for standing on ceremony but was generous and helpful to her mother's clientele. She straightened her posture and glanced at him as he passed. "Good morn, Mr Fairchild!" she said cheerily.

He mumbled something incoherent and lurched a little on the second step, gripping the railing and becoming somewhat embarrassed.

"Worst for wear today, are we?" she enquired in her forthright and familiar manner, borne of years of being around gentlemen in the guest house.

"Unfortunately, we are!" he agreed and attempted a grin that emerged more as a grimace. He looked haggard and somewhat broken. Though he could grimace like a gargoyle and still look good: Miss Anstey had been admiring him since his arrival in the house, now and then serving him his breakfast or his supper in the downstairs dining room. He drank often in her tavern with others of his ilk. She felt she knew him quite well, even without much acquaintance.

He was a treat for the senses of any woman. She was due to be wed soon, to a drayman from the brewery, to whom she had been engaged for a while, and she therefore felt determined to sew her final wild oats, if a female could be said to do such a thing. Although Miss Anstey cared little herself about semantics and grammar, she had a partiality for educated young men with excellent manners who dressed fine and spoke well. "There's breakfast still on the hob if you wish it."

"I cannot face it…" he told her and managed a more mellow smile. "Thank you though, Miss Anstey…for your consideration."

Clara Anstey pushed out her generously rounded bosom with a long breath, her decolletage deep and revealing over the lace edged bodice, and she winked at him. "You be welcome to my consideration any time, my duck."

He went on up the steps and she went on with her mopping. It would not be long, he perceived, before she was in his bed, or he hers'. Convenience and emotional pain would hold sway with him and he would accept her careful seduction.

Correct by Default

Friday mornings he was expected at the girls' school, teaching there every Tuesday and Friday for half a day. He was resigned to the task now of working with these girls, it was the only way through the next couple of years financially.

In the classroom allotted to him and ten minutes before the lesson, Abigail announced proudly to her peers that she had not completed the homework he had set on Tuesday—the French grammar—and she boasted of it as they lolled about and gossiped, taking things easy as always before a lesson. Miranda Moreton keeping watch from the doorway in case he arrived without warning. Melissa keeping her eye on the lawn to see his horse come by.

"I would not be so ready to brag about the homework issue…" Millicent Bromley said to Abigail. "He will not take it well."

"He can take it any way he wishes," retorted Abigail. "I am leaving in three weeks."

"That will make little or no difference to him," cautioned Melanie. "Does he seem to you like someone who accepts excuses of that nature?"

"Leave her to her own devices," commented Melissa. "We all know she enjoys playing these dangerous games…"

"Dangerous!" derided Abigail. "What is dangerous about it? My mother was in childbirth and I had other things to be doing…"

"You had better copy from me while you can," said Jane Reynolds, generous of spirit despite her haughty ways. Abigail scoffed but accepted the offer and had begun to transcribe into her book when Miranda waved at them frantically. "He is coming up the staircase!"

"What?" Melissa was disbelieving. "He cannot be… I have not seen his horse."

"Obviously he was here very early," offered Lucinda.

Miranda took her seat swiftly. "And he walks very rapidly," she retorted, as if he had made the entire journey on foot. This allusion set Lucinda off giggling;

the slightest thing tending to trigger her hilarity. Mary nudged her sharply. "Do not start, Lucy, remember what happened last week!"

Abigail shut her book and passed Jane's back with an almost triumphant look. She was quite enjoying the thought of going into conflict with him, to see his reaction—scathing and self-important as he appeared to be so far. The fact that he had the right to be did not enter her thinking, accustomed as she was to Henrietta Madeley and Mr Stringer; only Judith Tongs managed to acquire their obedient respect, with ways as didactical and abrasive as his.

He entered hastily. "Good day!" he said as they rose to their feet.

"Good day, Sir!" a handful of them responded.

He sat at his desk and surveyed them as they surveyed him. His mood had not improved during the week, even though he had received the first of Lottie's letters with an address in York—or perhaps because of her letter. It underlined their separation and made him taciturn. "Be seated," he said and began to remove books from his satchel which held an enormous amount of them. Mr Stringer never carried such a case, and did not seem to own such a library of text books and literature. Of course, he was ancient and perhaps too feeble to shoulder such a heavy load, they reasoned to one another in times of casual gossip.

They noted his every article of clothing, as if perusing the front window of a clothing emporium—yet a different jacket and shirt this day, and the fact that his hair seemed to be not as lustrous: combed back behind his ears and lacking its curl and wave, as if unwashed for several days. He looked decidedly defeated by life, despite his sartorial elegance. Melanie, at once, penned a note to Melissa informing her that his private life was obviously not going well, it was evident in all his features. She kicked Melissa twice under the desk to signal that a note was forthcoming. They employed this code all the time with Judith Tongs, but not with other teachers who were indifferent to their note writing.

Meanwhile, he studied them all from beneath his lashes which shielded his expression, and found them as disparaging and indifferent as they had been since his initial arrival. Seated on the second row but directly in his line of vision, Melissa Shaw seemed just to wait upon his next wrong move with her lively and humorous eyes. While Melanie Petersham had acquired an almost parodied expression of doting attention—her lashes fluttering over an idiotic stare of rapt concentration. It set his teeth on edge. He breathed in and out a couple of times, feeling sick through lack of food and too little sleep.

Lucinda was giggling and making intermittent spluttering which she turned into coughs. He ignored it for now. When she was not able to laugh out loud in rich tones she was giggling and when she could not giggle, she tittered; a sound she could easily turn into a ticklish cough.

He then noticed that Melanie Petersham had lost her intense concentration upon him and he saw her covertly pass a piece of paper to Melissa Shaw. It was done in an instant, but nothing much escaped him even on bad days. "What has she just written to you?" he demanded of Melissa.

"I beg your pardon?" Melissa said, a little too huffily, surprised out of her wits by his alertness.

"The paper she has just passed to you…what is on it?" he snapped.

"I do not know to what you refer… Sir."

Now they were playing him for a complete fool. He felt his heart rate begin to increase with anger. He would be dead inside two years if this carried on. "Bring it out here!" he said evenly.

"Bring what?" Melissa said quietly.

"The note she has just passed to you."

Melissa was frozen in apprehension, despite her apparent calm. Melanie was rapidly thinking; she leaned slightly into Melissa's side and slid a piece of blank paper in front of her—below his eye line she hoped—sliding the offending written note to the floor at her feet. He loosely followed the movements but did not see the continuity adding up. Melissa looked at Melanie who raised her eyebrows and tilted her head minutely in his direction. Melissa rose and took the blank paper out to him while Melanie stretched her arm downwards—seeming not to move her upper body—and retrieved the written note, and then she stuffed it into her shoe. If he managed to read the note, all hell would explode. It was unthinkable.

He gazed at the blank paper and drew breath and gazed at Melissa. "Where is the actual note?" he demanded.

"Which note, Sir?" said Melissa obtusely.

"Come out here…" he told Melanie and she rose and obeyed.

"What did you just write to her?" he enquired of her evenly.

"Nothing whatever, Sir!" said Melanie blithely.

He sprang to his feet, startling them, so that they moved back a few paces, and then he strolled between the first and second row desks, searching for the note by lifting up their books and scanning the floor. Behind his back Melissa pulled a face at Melanie who shook her head and frowned, to denote that nothing could come of it. The entire class was breathless with anticipation, guessing what had transpired.

Eventually he gave up and came back to his desk. He knew instinctively that Melissa Shaw was not as brazen as her friend—despite her variety of silent disdainful faces—and would confess more easily, given time. Time, he did not have if he was to make any advancement this day.

"There is no note!" Melanie said with almost arch impatience, then added. "Sir."

"No…but the question is, what you have done with it."

They looked at him and then at each other in a parody of hapless ignorance after the fact. He lost his calm somewhat, which he did not like to do ever in the classroom, for to do so was to lose ultimate control. How he wished they were boys; he would have caned them without more ado or further evidence, simply for wasting valuable time. But they were not boys. Boys seldom went in for penning notes to each other.

"Sit down!" he said in a doom-laden voice. "And do not try playing me for a fool… I am not Mistress Sullivan and there is nothing at all wrong with my eyesight."

They sat, with the greatest of dignity, and Lucinda began a crescendo of uncontrollable mirth.

"Be quiet!" he told her. "Or leave the room."

He sat in his chair and cleared his throat. Not ten in the morning and he already needed a strong drink. He set them to reading passages from popular literature, and all was silent for a while. It was an English lesson and he soon had them parsing sentences. All was peaceful but there was now a cloying smell in the air, the cause of which he hesitated to trace, in case it was something he felt unequal to dealing with, something arcane and hugely feminine which might disconcert a man unduly. He opened the letter from Lottie to distract himself from his temper and placed it between the pages of the textbook on his desk, and then he read it for the third time all the way through.

It had arrived this morning early and was waiting on the hall table in Mrs Anstey's, along with mail for the other guests. In it, Lottie assured him that her journey had gone well and her departure unnoticed until too late. They were beginning rehearsals for two plays opening in a fortnight to be performed bi-nightly. 'Othello' and 'A Comedy of Errors'. His temper, if anything, worsened.

He put the letter in his inside pocket and stood and began walking about the room looking at the progress they were making and examining their books. He paused at Melissa's book and commented. "I hope your writing is not always this appalling…"

She waited until he had lost interest and then tutted and sighed and gazed from the window. He turned back quickly and glared at her. "I suggest you do not make such expressions of disdain, Miss Shaw, lest you regret it."

"I beg your pardon, Sir," said Melissa without sincerity and he moved on before his patience gave out totally and betrayed him.

He strolled in silence. Then the cloying smell grew worse and he traced its source to Miranda. She was clutching a blue lace kerchief which seemed to emit the offending odour. "Is that item you are holding responsible for the odious smell in here?" he asked her.

"It is otto of roses, Sir…" she informed him in sententious defence. "All the best people wear it."

"Not in my classes they do not…and the correct term, Miss Moreton, is 'attar'…'attar of roses'…" He felt tempted to grin but stifled it by tightening his jaw; their ignorance was quite amusing of course, were it not so flagrantly impudent. "Give it to me…" He held out his hand for the kerchief and waited.

Miranda clutched it, crumpling it like an illusionist performing a vanishing trick. "'tis not mine, Sir…it belongs to my sister!"

"I do not care if it belongs to Her Majesty the Queen. Give it to me now."

Miranda slowly opened her hand and he took the kerchief between his thumb and forefinger and walked to the fire and dropped it onto the flames.

Miranda gasped audibly, accompanied by Abigail and Jane and Millicent, while Lucinda felt she might explode at any second from having to cope with so much comedy.

"Do not bring such frivolities into my classroom in the future…" said Fairchild to Miranda who was near to tears at the thought of her oldest sister's wrath. "This is not a drawing room soiree…"

He strolled once more to his desk and sat.

They glanced at each other, like mourners at a funeral, their sympathy was for Miranda at this moment but also for themselves in the future.

"What a very heartless act," commented Jane in a stage whisper which carried through the still room.

He looked over to where he thought the voice had come from. "Who said that?" he enquired.

"I did," said Jane fearlessly.

He paused. Jane was usually silent and therefore unmemorable. "Stand up," said Fairchild and Jane rose. "Your name?"

"Jane Reynolds, Sir!"

"Miss Reynolds, please refrain from making those kinds of inflammatory asides in future…have the manners to wait until I have left the room."

Lucinda found this last remark hilarious beyond reason. His irony and sarcasm was too much for anyone with a sense of humour. She dived under the desk to cough and splutter and pretended to retrieve a dropped nib.

"I beg your pardon, Sir," retorted Jane. "I did not realise I had said it aloud."

He wondered whether he was meant to take this seriously or if it were yet more insolence. Their outlandish comments were hard to decipher and taxed him more than the teaching itself.

The lesson proceeded in silence. Until the matter of the homework arose. "Pass the French homework from Tuesday to the front," he instructed. And they passed their books along to where Annabelle collected them and placed them in a pile on his desk.

"Thank you!" he said and then after a few moments went through them and compared names to a list in front of him. He had not yet fully memorised their names and had to be reminded. He spoke in ominous tones. "Who is Abigail Grimwell?"

Abigail stood up, as if nominated for a vital task. "'tis I…" she announced importantly.

He looked over and said in a low voice. "I might have guessed," and then in a louder tone. "Your homework, Miss Grimwell, it seems to be missing!"

"'tis here…" She waved the book in the air.

"Why is it not with the rest?" he enquired wearily.

"Well… I…'tis not…" Now that the moment of confrontation had arrived, she was losing confidence.

"Out with it, Miss Grimwell, we do not have all day…" he said wearily.

Everyone stared at Abigail with expressions of curiosity and then back at him with similar faces. Lucinda stuffed her kerchief into her mouth and chewed it, preparing to dive beneath the desk if the scene took more comedic turns.

"Why is it not with the rest?" Fairchild queried again.

"'tis not quite finished… Sir," replied Abigail.

He leaned back in his chair and took his ease, closing his eyes and sucking his front teeth until he had a grip on his mood. "What do you mean, not quite finished?"

"'tis here…" said Abigail in a cheerful voice.

"Indeed…but why is it not completed?"

"Because my mother was in childbirth and last night I had to run up and down the stairs doing my aunt's bidding and fetching things…and then my grandmother wanted me to…"

He interjected abruptly into what was becoming a monologue. "Have you a note to this effect?"

"No, Sir!"

He rose again from his seat. "Do you recall what I said about homework and how seriously I view its omission?"

"Well, 'twill not matter…" offered Abigail in haste. "I am leaving in three weeks, so I shall not learn much in that time."

"Oh, shall you not?" he said in a deadlier tone of voice. "We shall see about that."

The silence now was ominous and a pin might be heard to drop. "Perhaps you will learn not to be so insolent, for one thing! Why did you not do the homework?"

"I have just explained that…" said Abigail in near exasperation. "My mother was in her confinement last night and I…"

"And the nights before that? You have had three nights to finish the homework."

Abigail paused, realising her error and trying to recalculate the days quickly. "Yes, but as I have said, I am leaving soon, so you need not trouble yourself on my account…"

Lucinda fell to her knees and began to scrabble around on the floor searching for non-existent items, her laughter preventing her almost from breathing, while one or two others could not prevent themselves from joining in. Once more he might have been on a stage entertaining them with comedy sketches—it was beyond galling. He ignored the subdued hilarity and sauntered over to Abigail who sat on the second row of desks on the right-hand side. He stood with his head back and regarded her, a hollow expression on his face which aged him some ten years. He had decided in the last days that he could either overlook their more facile antics and hope for the best. Or he could become a tyrant of mammoth proportions and terrify them into submission; there was no middle ground as yet.

"Unfortunately, Miss Grimwell, I have to trouble myself. The school pays me to educate you…and your father pays the school good money to have me do so. Your leaving in three weeks is purely hypothetical," he intoned in a tired monotone.

Abigail gazed around the ceiling above him to avoid his overbearing presence. "'tis not hypothetical. I am certainly leaving," claimed the obstinate Miss Grimwell. He continued to watch her with his omniscient green eyes. "And I am certain my father will not mind if the homework is not completed…" gabbled Abigail in a more civil tone, a desperate attempt to have the matter done with, despite her previous bravado. "You have done your very best and I…"

"Miss Grimwell, be silent," said Fairchild. "Your leaving in three weeks is not of interest to me. Whereas your impertinence and disrespect is…come with me!"

He walked to the front of the room and opened his desk drawers and rummaged. Abigail trailed after him, a feeling of foreboding in her stomach.

"I have had just about enough of these insolent remarks…these indifferent attitudes and comments. I have had enough of all of you!" he announced at large. "At times I find it hard to comprehend I am in a classroom at all. I have so far tolerated disrespect, trickery and sheer disobedience…and your audacity in particular, Miss Grimwell, is staggering. Your confounded insolence would win prizes."

Lucinda squeaked beneath the desk; a noise reminiscent of the woodland. The atmosphere had become dire with undisclosed threat.

He found what he searched for and retrieved from the drawer the cane Miss Tongs had given him. There was at once a collective murmur of consternation and Abigail turned pale. They had no idea he possessed a cane, much less that he could use it. A horrified silence descended and even Lucinda rose partially to look over the desk lid to stare, her amusement turning to dismay.

"I will tolerate no more of it…" he said, and then to Abigail. "Hold out your hand…the one you do not write with…"

Instinctively, Abigail put her hands behind her back and glared at him. "Can you not send me to Miss Tongs!" she cried.

"No, I cannot…" he replied casually. "I do not intend to trouble Miss Tongs every five minutes. If 'tis me you offend, 'tis me you will answer too…now hold out your hand."

Abigail—the daughter of a prosperous farmer—raced through a range of thoughts; if she were to be caned, she preferred it to be by Miss Tongs: it was less of an indignity. But if she refused to comply now the row would escalate, her parents might be informed, and only her mother would be sympathetic, her father would not. Especially as he intended to send her two young brothers for education at Barton Grange. And her mother always liked to please her father for fear of his not being generous enough with the housekeeping. She was in the grip of a shocking dilemma. She put out her left hand, cautiously, holding it only a little way from her body in line with her hip.

He gauged things; he had never caned anyone on the hand before and judged it to be a precision-filled procedure, lest it damage the fingers or break small bones or other accidental consequences he heard about in appalling schools he knew of via the Foundation. But he could not allow his authority and self-respect to be any further undermined by these girls. He took Abigail's arm and raised it and pulled it straight, then held it below her wrist so that she could not move it…

Some of the class had closed their eyes—it was too awful to contemplate. Like witnessing a public execution or torture in the Tower of London. The remainder felt compelled to watch and could not take their eyes away.

He lifted the cane and delivered three moderately hard strokes to Abigail's left hand in rapid succession as she let out strangulated and agonised sounds which struggled to leave her throat. "Return to your seat!" he told her, and she did so with a hang-dog and mute expression.

He addressed them in general. "Now a precedent is set! From hereon I shall not bother warning you about your misbehaviour, I shall simply cane you."

Abigail cradled her hand between her knees to lessen the stinging of her palm and stared at him with incredible loathing and unswerving animosity. No-one took any notice, least of all Anthony Fairchild.

A new mood had descended, one of sombre silence and reluctant acquiescence.

Probability and Possibility

The afternoon lesson was Miss Madeley's deportment and dance class. At which Millicent played either the harpsichord or the piano, so that Miss Madeley might move about and dance and instruct. Millicent was far and away Henrietta Madeley's favourite pupil. Not just because she played beautifully, but because she was modest and quiet of nature. It was always a popular lesson of course, because merriment was to be had, and much enjoyment and upliftment of the spirit.

Abigail was sulking near the windows and Miss Madeley was at a loss to understand her reluctance to join the square. "Abigail, do come along…'twas you who requested this particular set last time. What is the matter with you? Why are you holding your arm in that manner?"

Abigail pushed her arm defensively under her armpit and turned her face away.

"Abigail!" commanded Miss Madeley more sharply.

Then Miranda danced into range with her imaginary partner, for proceedings had not properly begun. "The matter with her is that she was caned this morning, by Mr Fairchild," she informed Miss Madeley in a prosaic tone.

"What?" Miss Madeley wheeled around to look at Miranda and then wheeled back again to stare at Abigail. "What on earth did you do, Child?"

Abigail lifted her chin and pulled her mouth into a malicious expression.

"She did not complete his homework," supplied Annabelle on Abigail's behalf.

"Then she spoke to him as if he were a servant," Lucinda added.

Miss Madeley had let her mouth drop open somewhat before clamping it shut while moving to Abigail and seizing her injured hand and inspecting the rapidly fading red lines on her palm. She gasped, having not until then quite believed the tale. "How very disgraceful and mortifying, Abigail!"

"'twas not my fault!" the petulant Abigail cried.

"'twas all your fault!" Jane said, suddenly speaking out on the matter. "Telling him you will not learn more in the next three weeks and not to trouble himself…"

Miss Madeley gasped again.

"Yes, and then arguing with him about the hypothetical whatnots…" said Lucinda, dancing alone in a circle…

Miss Madeley stared at Abigail. "I wonder you did not faint from the shame!"

Abigail turned; her eyes defiant. She was beginning to enjoy the attention. "I almost fainted from the pain," she flared. "Except I would not give him the satisfaction."

Quite overcome, Miss Madeley relapsed into a chair and took a phial of smelling salts from the folds of her dress. She thought of the intended tryst with Anthony Fairchild on the coming Sunday, yet another in a series of their assignations to go walking. She did not wish to have to think of him in this draconian way at all, could not reconcile it with the pleasant visage of manhood she had so far held fast to. Her romantic glow of things to come was dissolving under this pragmatic and distasteful news.

"Your precious hand will be better by tonight…" Miranda was saying to Abigail. "But my sister's kerchief is lost forever."

"What has that to do with anything?" Miss Madeley lisped in a near whisper.

"He burnt it on the fire because he did not care for the perfume," Miranda retorted.

"Phooey…" Melanie danced into view, her satin dance slippers making no noise at all as she glided. "'twas all about him not wishing frivolities to be present in his lessons."

"And your secret notes did not help matters…" Miranda told her. "Nor your conjuring tricks with the paper. So do not pretend you are innocent."

"I fear we annoy him greatly, Miss Madeley," announced Jane in her level headed approach.

"Everything annoys him," sneered Melissa. "He is the most easily annoyed person imaginable."

"Of course he is not!" Miss Madeley stated in aggravation. "He is simply used to teaching boys…and they are different altogether than girls."

Overcome by this stating of the obvious, Lucinda let out peals of laughter to rival Millicent's music.

"Your sister can well afford a new kerchief..." Abigail was saying to Miranda, not wishing for irrelevance to enter the topic and detract from her suffering. "So, do not go on as if hard done by."

"She will be absolutely furious," Miranda moaned. "She will pull my hair until I scream."

"Serves you right for bringing it out in the classroom in the first place..." Melanie scoffed, dancing by herself to the accompaniment of Millicent's playing. "Besides, she can have her beau buy her twenty more..." and turning to Miss Madeley. "Her sister is betrothed to young whatshisname of Netherfield Hall...they are as rich as Croesus."

"'tis beside the point!" Miranda screamed. "How dare he do such a thing! Burning other peoples' property!"

"He is foul tempered and too odious for words," Abigail wailed. "Who does he imagine he is! And scarcely beyond his twenty first year."

Miss Madeley had heard enough. "He is twenty-five!" she amended snappily, then put her hand over her mouth upon realising her faux pas. "And do not tell anyone I told you that. 'twas indelicate of me."

"The worst of it is, Miss Madeley..." Miranda announced, "Because of all Abigail's *staggering audacity and insolence...*" she deepened her voice in imitation of Fairchild's.

"And don't forget his intolerance to *disrespect and trickery and incomplete homework...*" put in Melanie using the same kind of baritone.

"...because of all that," Miranda repeated amid the peals of laughter, "He is threatening to use the cane whenever he pleases."

Millicent paused in her recital. "No, Miranda, when we offend him...there is a difference."

The laughter died as they all stared at Millicent and, Millicent being of a shy and retiring nature, retreated beneath the lid of the piano and sought out a fresh sheet of music.

"Oh, do speak in his defence, Millie..." cried Abigail petulantly. "He is so in need of your support where we are not."

"I am just saying, he has a job to do..." Millicent lifted her head, flushing a little. "He is a very good teacher; you must admit that... I always understand what he is saying...and you have to admit that you are all very outre at times..."

"I admit no such thing, little goody-two-shoes!" Melanie objected. "We are merely engaging and adopt a light-hearted stance to welcome people."

"You are not here to be engaging and adopt stances…you are here to be educated and do as you are told," Miss Madeley cried. "He does not know what to make of your behaviour and outspoken ways. He thinks of it as insolence."

Melanie rolled her eyes. "Only because he is completely lacking a sense of humour."

"I do not know about that…" Lucinda interjected. "Some of his remarks are so hilarious I think I may wet myself."

"Lucinda, we do not speak of wetting ourselves in company…" Miss Madeley retrieved her salts and sniffed them. "He does not set out to entertain you, he is being sarcastic…as are a lot of gentlemen. It releases their anger without them appearing vulgar."

Finding this too amusing Lucinda fell again into paroxysms of mirth and then fell against Elspeth with whom she was paired in the chaotic dancing.

"He causes her such hilarity…" remarked the beleaguered Elspeth to Miss Madeley, "That she is hardly ever upright these days."

"She spends all the time under the desk," supplied Miranda to the music mistress. "Hiding from exposure…because naturally giggling is forbidden also."

"Naturally it is," rejoined Miss Madeley. "The subjects he teaches call for concentration and seriousness."

"'tis not the teaching or the subjects…" Jane told Miss Madeley. "'tis the way he views us in general…everything we do upsets him, or disgusts him or throws him into freakish moods."

"Stop exaggerating, Jane. You do not behave as pupils in school should…" Miss Madeley waved at Millicent to go on playing and for them all to begin movement. She was in need of some water, her senses reeling as she rose to leave the room. Once more she did not know what she felt; caught between fascination and revulsion on hearing of this harsher side to his nature. "You will simply have to mind your manners and do as you are bidden, and most of all stop answering him back with such impertinence…he is not Mr Stringer."

"He will not get the better of me…" declared Abigail, relapsing to her default nature. "I do not care how many languages he speaks or what he did at Oxford University… I shall do as I please in these last weeks, I am not afraid of him!"

"Abigail, you are quite incorrigible… I wash my hands of you." Miss Madeley turned on her heel. "Do not say I have not warned you… I shall have no sympathy when things worsen for you."

Lucinda's imagination threw up visions of it all and the set she danced within fell apart utterly as she lost her step and careered clumsily into the others.

"I do not want your sympathy, Miss Madeley, thank you kindly!" chirruped the incorrigible Abigail as she joined the rightful set. "I can fend for myself. I am simply saying that he will not get the better of me…"

"Of course he will get the better of you!" yelled Miss Madeley in shrill and unbecoming tones which pained her own ears as she paused at the door. "You are a pupil here and he is a master. Do you think he will allow himself to be bested by the likes of you?"

"I shall tell my father, who will write to the school governors," lied Abigail, relishing the situation now that the worst was over.

"He was within his rights, Abigail! If you are so naughty you must be corrected…" Henrietta was at the end of her tether. "I wonder how you can wish to tell your father anything so shameful…and you may be sure that if the governors hear they will take Mr Fairchild's side, not yours."

"Foolish girl!" opined Melissa. "You are your own worst enemy, Abi."

"And possibly ours!" Annabelle claimed, "Abi, if you antagonise him in the next three weeks and then leave us to his mercy I will never speak to you again in any society."

"I care not…" Abigail said loftily.

More noisy arguing ensued as Miss Madeley left the room. Once in the corridor she leant against the closed double doors and breathed; her corset which facilitated her unnaturally tiny waist restraining the air to her lungs. Now her class was in complete disarray, as was often the case, and any insurrection caused by Abigail would only highlight her own lack of classroom control.

Judith Tongs was teaching maths to the lower form in the classroom above and could not fail to hear the noise. If Anthony Fairchild learned of her lack of professionalism (and Judith would delight in telling him) he would think her weak and negligent and his opinion of her would be vastly lowered. Her marriage plans may dissolve into ashes.

* * *

On his way to his first class of the afternoon at the boys' academy he met with Nicholas Stevenson, the deputy head. A man his senior by fourteen or fifteen years and one of his best allies in the school. Someone with whom he could connect at a mental level. "Tony…" said Stevenson. "How is it going in the henhouse?"

Fairchild paused, his cumbersome satchel of books balanced between his hip and his arm, and he shrugged and looked mournful. "I do not really know… I am unsure."

"What!!" claimed Stevenson in fake surprise and jocular tone. "I hear you are making progress there…"

Stevenson was a tall and angular man with patrician features denoting his greater intelligence and his suitability for positions of authority. He had straight dark hair which he wore quite long and swept back from his forehead and behind his ears. He was an imposing figure and something of a mathematical genius.

Fairchild dropped the satchel to the ground and looked pained, worn out now after only half a day, due to the demands of the female pupils. His lunch was always a good one, proffered by the cooks at either of the schools, and it had sustained him a little, but his mood was not something to be mended easily.

"What on earth has gone wrong?" said Stevenson, becoming earnest.

"I am not cut out for teaching these girls… I am not the man for the job," he told Stevenson who laughed immediately and straightened his shoulders beneath the scholarly robe he wore as one of the heads.

"They scarcely take me seriously…" continued the younger man. "They are complacent…and impudent in their remarks to the point of… I feel I could throttle them."

Stevenson laughed a second time, but briefly. "You must not let them get you down…they will do so if they can. That is the nature of girls."

Fairchild thought about Lottie; everything at the moment made him think of her. Nicholas Stevenson himself was a careful but prolific womaniser, a bachelor, insatiably curious about the private romantic lives of others. "You have a fiancé? Or a beloved?" he queried cautiously.

"I have a long-term sweetheart whom I hope to wed one day…"

"And are you betrothed to her?"

"No," said Fairchild shortly. "Not officially…she is away with a theatre company, acting in Shakespeare and other classics."

Stevenson stepped back. He was not expecting that from this son of an erstwhile Anglican bishop. "Is she, by God! And you do not mind?"

"I have little choice… I am unable to wed her as yet…her father is someone of influence in the county…" he faltered, feeling overwhelmed by confusion and embarrassment. "He is pressing her to wed elsewhere…and I have not the funds at present…'tis impossible!" he concluded.

"You need say no more," Stevenson assured. "I have the gist of it! But these girls, they are the very devil for…"

"For goading people like me." Fairchild cut him off in a morose and bitter voice. "I had the need to cane one of them this morning."

The deputy raised his brows and showed dawning amusement.

"I am not proud of it…resorting to corporal punishment with girls."

Stevenson drew breath and said in his hearty tones. "Neither is there any need to be ashamed of it…do you think other male teachers before you have not resorted to it?"

"I was hoping my strength of character would be enough…"

Stevenson laughed silently, he felt he was in danger any moment of being seen as smug or flippant. "But you are reckoning without *their* strength of character…" he said philosophically in an off-hand way. "They do possess such a thing, you know…and you have to take a firm stand with them or they will bring you to your knees before you know it…they are famous for it."

Fairchild remained silent. He had the vague and distracted look seen many times by Stevenson in male staff when leaving the *henhouse*. "You must know how females are at their worst! They are testing you and…"

"And I failed."

"Nonsense! They will not be happy until they have pushed you to the limits of your tolerance…which has now happened. Which one of them was it?"

"Abigail Grimwell!" Fairchild said with consummate distaste.

"Oh yes, the farmer's daughter! Wealthy farmers it has to be said. Now you see why we call it the *henhouse*!" Stevenson was fond of using wit on every occasion where possible. "And she is leaving in a couple of weeks, or so I hear?"

"Indeed…and has the nerve to tell me she will not learn more in that time…"

"Then now perhaps she will rethink her resolve," joked the deputy. He clapped Fairchild on the shoulder. "They are lax and ill-managed, but we hesitated to tell you that for fear of deterring you."

"Obviously!" said the morose young teacher.

"You will bring them around. They need to be reminded of where they are." Stevenson made as if to move and then thought better of it. "For heaven's sake, dear boy, remember your authority. They cannot be allowed to disrespect staff and do as they want…and they have a choice do they not?" He paused for effect, "They can simply behave themselves!"

Fairchild smiled thinly and picked up his satchel. "They are lucky to have such an erudite tutor as yourself."

Realising he was being flattered with ulterior motive, he cleared his throat and remained silent and Stevenson suggested, "We will have a draught or two perhaps, at the end of the week, one of the local hostelries…the one near your lodgings will do. I shall invite Mr Carmichael and Mr McCarthy…they are very good company and your age. I will book a private room and order a good supper and we can imbibe." Nicholas Stevenson would go to great lengths not to lose able teaching staff of good calibre, especially ones willing to teach girls.

"Yes, that will be acceptable…thank you," Fairchild murmured in the distracted haze that had befallen him.

"Excellent!" said the deputy head.

He thought of Clara Anstey working in the tavern designated by Stevenson, and of being in her bed at weekend, where he would no doubt be again before too long. Although he perceived that she was discretion itself where her work might clash with her private life.

The deputy was about to take his leave when a further thought struck him. He turned back. "By the by, Tony…be very careful around Judith Tongs…you are just the kind of prime specimen she likes to prey upon…"

Fairchild looked directly into the older man's eyes for the first time in the impromptu meeting. "I know…the groom warned me."

"And has she tried to lure you yet?"

"A little…but I saw which way the wind was blowing… I wonder she keeps her position here."

"My dear fellow…" said Nicholas Stevenson with heavy patience. "Have you any idea how hard it is to find women interested in teaching mathematics, let alone excel at it? She sometimes teaches the boys on occasions of my absence, you know! And she fits the bill of headmistress betimes! She would be very hard to replace… Try not to upset her but beware falling into her clutches…or her bed!"

"The thought is exceedingly distressing…" said Fairchild and Stevenson grinned. "'tis far more difficult to lay hold of good language teachers than grooms… I am quite safe from her myself, of course…too old to be of interest to her." He went on his way, smiling at his own wit.

Fairchild continued to his classroom: advanced Latin grammar with the senior boys, most of whom were as tall as himself and had begun shaving their faces. All of them present because they wanted to enter university. They stood up immediately on his entrance and paid him due respect and he felt himself relax amid the placid male ambience. He smiled at them as he removed his jacket for comfort and he began at once to talk of the complexities of the designated language.

All Girls Together

In the staff room at the girls' academy the next day, Judith and Henrietta took their ease in the last of the lunchtime break. Henrietta busily making lace edging for one of her bodices while Judith watched, sipping a small sherry to fortify herself.

"I suppose that is for Sunday's little jaunt, is it? That thing you are crocheting?" she ventured.

"It is tatting, not crocheting," replied Henrietta evasively.

"Whatever…" said Judith. "I do not know one form of needlework from another…"

"Nor I a fraction from an equation," said Henrietta, not about to be railroaded by Miss Tongs in her discursive dialogue. "But it would not do for us all to be the same!" she added quaintly, softening her remark.

"Oh, certainly it would not!" agreed Judith, mellowed somewhat by the sherry—just enough to make the day bearable. "And what do you plan to wear when you go walking with him?"

Henrietta paused, thought about telling her to mind her own business, but then not brave enough at the last moment. "I have not quite decided…of course it depends a lot on the weather."

"Well, if it rains, he will need to bring a horse and carriage! I believe he keeps one…or hires one or some such…"

"Does he?" asked Henrietta with some eagerness. "How do you know?"

"The groom mentioned it…he converses with him regularly about horses…"

Henrietta went back to her tatting, her thoughts overflowing with the possibilities, both fortunate and unfortunate, for Sunday and the weather being only one of them. If it were to become bitter cold again, then they would certainly need a conveyance. Otherwise, they could walk briskly around the park or the town and then repair to a tea shop.

Judith broke the silence by saying. "As long as you do not pin your hopes on his marrying you…"

Henrietta raised her head sharply and stared at the older woman.

"For I can lay good money that he will not."

"He might," said Henrietta almost petulantly, "You cannot know that."

"But I can…" contradicted Judith. "Simply by looking at him…by his features and his expressions."

"What? is it some kind of fortune telling gift?" said Henrietta in the same tone.

"No…'tis my knowledge of men," replied Judith.

"Why would he not marry me if he likes me?" Henrietta bemoaned.

"What a simpleton you are at heart, Henrietta," claimed Judith. "For men it has little to do with how much they like you, 'tis mostly about passion and he wants more than you have to give…passion, I mean."

"How do you know how much passion I can give!" Henrietta felt herself becoming riled, she felt herself becoming giddily unsettled and nauseated.

"I have been teaching girls for a long time, and I know how to gauge them…just as I know how to gauge men," said Judith smoothly.

"But I am not a girl!" claimed the music mistress in near distress.

"Yes, but 'twas not so long ago that you were! You are more like to one of the pupils here than you think."

Henrietta sprang from her chair and crossed to the tea table where the tea pot had only cool tea to offer. But it gave her something to do.

"Walk out with him certainly…he will enjoy that… You both will enjoy that, being of an age…but do not hope for marriage."

"You are simply jealous, Judith!" claimed Henrietta.

Judith laughed and then tapped the delicate rim of the sherry glass gently against her front teeth—a habit she had to stop herself swigging the contents too quickly.

"You want him for yourself. For your lecherous needs…then you will cast him aside when you are bored… If he consents to go with you in the first place," claimed Henrietta. "We all know what you do! The whole place knows of your capers!"

"What a parochial and narrow view you have of life," said Judith. "But it will be a lot easier for me to get his consent to what I have in mind than it will for you to get him to the altar."

"So you say!"

"When he weds it will be to someone of greater depth than yours…someone with a greater sense of her own spirit and her own needs. You have no more knowledge of your needs than the girls you teach. You think walking with him is the height of desire, as if it will entrance him into loving you. 'twill not…he asks you because you are convenient, and he is new to the post, that is all."

Henrietta replaced the tea cup and marched back to her chair—the faded green fabric one which had seen better days but was just the right size for her. "You are malevolent, Judith! You cannot bear to see anyone happy…you…" Henrietta stopped suddenly as the door opened and Mr Stringer entered, bringing in the cold air on his clothes and his reddened face, telling the edge of winter, which was often the coldest part. "It may snow!" he said cheerily.

"Henry, do not say that to your female namesake here…" chirruped Judith. "She is desirous of clement weather for weekend, when she walks out with Mr Fairchild."

Henrietta blushed and Henry turned from the tea table and looked at her kindly. "Ahh, yes…a very decent young fellow…very genial…and proficient at the job too, so I hear…you could do worse, Henrietta…"

"Do not get her hopes up, Henry, please! She is already planning her wedding gown and they have scarce exchanged any conversation beyond 'good morning'… Do not fill her with false hope…just because they were both the children of the clergy, she thinks it a perfect match." Judith paused and stared provocatively at Henrietta. "But he has left the vicarage behind long ago in his mind, where she has not."

The two teachers stared at Miss Tongs as one united thought. She was contrary and bitter, and they could not adequately find the words. Mr Stringer patted Miss Madeley's arm reassuringly on his way to ring for hot tea.

* * *

He received another letter from Lottie in the middle of the following week. Telling him that the time at York had gone well and that two more bookings were procured—they were on their way to Carlisle and then to Edinburgh. The plays had changed; this time it was 'Much Ado' and 'King Lear'.

Another address appeared as a footnote, at which he might write to her and she receive it after Wednesday next. He sat on the bottom stair of Mrs Anstey's main staircase, the house very quiet in the early morning. Lost was his keen sense of focus, his invisible compass for navigating the day without too much thought or stress. Lottie gave him a kind of brain fog and he recognised it as his emotional self. It made a mockery at times of all he held important.

Mrs Anstey came by and stopped. Mrs Anstey was a very dignified woman whom he suspected had originated from a genteel background. He thought she might have had a raw deal when younger, as many women did, and been forced to make her own way in the world. Perhaps after an unwanted pregnancy or being disowned by her family, cast off with some small inheritance. She was well-bred and cultured. Her daughter, Clara, quite different in all ways. Mrs Anstey had struggled and succeeded. He rose and inclined his head to her respectfully.

"Are you quite well, Mr Fairchild?" she asked in her capable tone.

"Quite well, Mrs Anstey, thank you…" he straightened his clothing. "I was simply checking my boot strap…it catches in the stirrup often when I ride."

"Oh, well then…" smiled Mrs Anstey, not entirely convinced—he had been staring at the front door for entire moments before she approached. "We can't have that! Lamb stew with dumplings for supper tonight…" she informed him in a brightened voice, her arms full of clean laundry. "The maid or Clara will leave it on your grate hob if you have not sat downstairs to dine before seven-thirty…"

"Thank you…" he said. "That is most obliging of you."

"We try to be obliging to our guests…" said Mrs Anstey pleasantly before going on her way to the upper regions of the building.

He smiled and partially bowed and thought of how *obliging* her daughter was in his bed and whether Mrs Anstey was in any way aware. And then he thought of Clara's fiancé, the drayman, and the dangers if he found out what was going on. The fact that Clara was not virginal or prudish was evident from her uninhibited ways in the bedroom. She was not of his class, of course, and the mores and dictates were different. He glanced through the early mail indifferently, and presently Clara herself came by, her hair down about her shoulders, buttoning her bodice which currently revealed her chemise and the top part of a corselette holding her fulsome bosom in check. He flushed slightly at this nakedness in the hall of the guest house, for anyone may appear from anywhere, though she cared little it seemed. "You had breakfast?" she asked.

"No, I do not have the time today…" he told her.

He had not slept in her bed for five nights and she looked at him with barely disguised longing.

"I can cook you bacon…if you want?"

"Thank you, but I will be late…" he said and gave her the same kind of bow he had given her mother, which made her smile. It pleased her, this kind of 'toff' behaviour he exhibited towards her. She moved closer to him. "I could kiss you…" she said in dusky tones. "But mayhap it not be wise."

"Indeed, it would not…" he replied. "You must not think of it right now."

"Oh, must I not!" said Clara in seductive mode with sarcastic undertones. "I shall think what I will when I will…"

"I did not mean… I meant not to consider it of this moment," he faltered. The language difference between them was immense, the way they used words and their meanings; it was in part what separated their walks of life. "Never mind!" he told her. He would end up giving her a lecture on comprehension and grammar if it continued. She waited to see what would ensue next, his speech and manner fascinating her as usual. But nothing else was forthcoming from him as he fastened buttons on his greatcoat.

"I'll see you tomorrow eve," said she, sending him the kind of look mixing motive with desire.

He did not reply but raised his brows a little. He was not used to being at the beck and call of women three doors away who lured him with sensuality. Since the departure of Lottie, he seemed to be besieged by female attention; he wondered why and thought of it in a philosophical way and then an abstract way and then a practical way as he rode to work. But still his thoughts went always back to Lottie and the latest letter. At this rate she could be gone months, and even years.

Perhaps never returning at all if life took her on a tangent. It was a ridiculous state of affairs, not to be countenanced. He did not yet know what he would do about it or exactly what he wanted to do about it. She might herself be enjoying dalliances, or the odd bedroom caper, with men who took her fancy, although he perceived it to be a more serious matter with women of her ilk. Clara Anstey was of a different class entirely to Lottie. And even so, the theatre world was notorious for its lax morals.

Loose morals became a prolonged mental theme as he went through his day. How loose were his own? Could he use his masculinity to excuse them? Men did so all the time, but did that mean it was excusable? And excusable by whom? He came as always to the unanswerable question of a Higher Being, or a divine principle within the universe. His background was devoutly Christian but his intellect was explorative.

Abigail Grimwell had just over one and a half weeks to go and grew worse in her reckless behaviour. He had already caned her twice more. She seemed not to care. He had of course met with this attitude before, in boys, but he expected girls to have different feelings on the matter. Therefore, he was at a loss and still floundering. He was sick of her staring at him constantly in a warlike way and watching his every move and not attempting to complete lessons. He petitioned Judith Tongs to send her from the school early, expelling her if necessary, and writing to inform her parents of why.

Miss Tongs refused. It would be unprecedented and difficult to explain. It would look very odd, and her parents might tell other parents, and they might wonder why he could not keep order in his classroom.

He did not think that would occur and suspected Miss Tongs of being obdurate on the issue, simply to get back at him for not succumbing to her advances.

Her only suggestion was that he cane Abigail Grimwell harder. He was loath to do so, and told her of his views on excessive corporal punishment. Miss Tongs paid scant attention, glancing at him with an almost pitying expression: she had heard all that reformist rhetoric before from other young male teachers in the past. It was not a new ideology!

"I can tell you who will fill Abigail's shoes once she has gone…in terms of insolence and disrespect," she said. They were in the staffroom as they took afternoon refreshments. He waited patiently, his attention on the distant hills beyond the window. Where he longed to be right now, riding free in the pastoral pleasures of England.

He avoided Judith Tongs' eye contact where possible, it was a veritable crucible of menacing and dark intentions which unnerved him. *If Lottie was the Holy Grail, Judith Tongs might well be his Nemesis.*

"Melanie Petersham or Melissa Shaw…both of them perhaps," announced the head mistress, pursuing her theme.

"Indeed?" he said lightly with apparent disinterest.

"Indubitably! Have you not noticed them yet? Their intelligence does them credit…but they are in no way meekly compliant…they come from wealthy and prestigious homes."

"Do they!" he said, with consummate boredom.

"Their fathers are extremely successful men of business," she told him.

"Are they!" he said in yet the same tone.

Miss Tongs was about to become irritated by his monotone, it bordered on rudeness. "What I am trying to tell you, Anthony, is that they will not be easily managed if you allow them to get the better of you."

"I shall not allow it," said he in what he hoped was finality. "But there are other ways of control besides corporal punishment."

"Perhaps…that is your affair, but one does not always have time for all these *other ways*…"

"Had I wanted to use a cane all day, I would have trained as a lion tamer!" he said and glared at her.

She was tempted to laugh, his wit was unquestionably a breath of fresh air, and she decided to take it as a dawning interest in her personally; she had wished to have a reaction. Even so, his remarks now were almost abrasive.

Then Miss Madeley entered and saved the day.

Having nodded to her, he continued in a new vein to the head mistress. "I do not care what sort of backgrounds they derive from; I am confirming that they will behave themselves in my classroom."

Judith was a little mollified and held her own council.

"Who are you speaking of?" enquired Henrietta, taking her usual chair, conveniently opposite the one he was occupying.

"Melanie Petersham and Melissa Shaw…" Judith said. "I am telling him how they will fill Abigail's shoes when she has gone."

"Not necessarily, Judith…" said Henrietta sweetly, and then fixed her attention on him with her china blue eyes. She was very pretty and he looked at her steadfastly. She did not know this yet about men; that they simply liked to admire and look, and it did not necessarily lead anywhere beyond appreciation. She did not heed Miss Tongs' previous philosophy.

"They are good girls in the main…" she told him. "Melanie is a little headstrong and…"

"Ha!" Judith cut in with a derogatory hoot of laughter. "That is an understatement…she is a veritable force of nature… I have seldom witnessed such spirit in a female, though it is disguised beneath her apparent femininity…"

"Take little notice of her!" Henrietta told him. "Judith is quite critical about a lot of the pupils."

"I am simply truthful," said Judith with mock humility.

"Melissa is less strident in nature than Melanie, quite reserved in fact, but both of them are very bright indeed." Henrietta went on. "Had they been boys they would quickly rise to positions of prominence in society."

Judith exclaimed again in derisive tone, while they ignored her.

"Melissa does not engage with many people…apart from one or two of her classmates. Whereas Melanie engages with everyone and knows everything that is going on. Melissa is less interested in the world at large…she is becoming a very talented artist, I hear. Melanie is protective of Melissa to a large degree and will often take the blame for both of them. For together they can be quite naughty, and it might appear that Melanie is the stronger character, but she is simply the more colourful…she likes to be the centre of attention whereas Melissa does not. But they are not spiteful or nasty…they will grow into good women, I think…"

He listened carefully to all this. Henrietta clearly had the kind of wisdom which was inspired by affection, or even love. She came from the heart. Like his mother and his sister-in-law and, of course, Lottie. He looked away at the thought of Lottie and gazed at the window. Then he stood. "Your insights are most welcome, Miss Madeley…thank you." He smiled at her and bowed briefly in the direction of both women and left the room.

"Well, done, Henrietta," said Judith once the door had closed, clapping her hands in rapid soft movements, like an excited child. "Now he sees that there may be a side to you other than threading needles and sitting at the pianoforte."

Henrietta rose to pour tea and did not reply; she had scored over Judith in this brief skirmish and needed to be careful.

* * *

Walking into the classroom minutes later he looked immediately at Melanie and Melissa, thinking of Henrietta's words. They were chattering in quiet voices as they stood for his entrance, they were always chattering, along with the rest of them. But they stopped abruptly as he reached his desk, and Melissa Shaw watched him with a wary and humorous curiosity, as if he were a slightly mad aged relation whom she was obliged to tolerate for some enforced period.

Melanie Petersham performed her ridiculous eyelid fluttering, as if surprised from something more important and forced into his ludicrous presence but willing anyway to hear him out. It was galling in the extreme, it was an offensive behaviour he could not call out, for lack of suitable description. In his imagination, he saw himself move from his desk and slap both their faces to put them in their proper place and perspective. It soothed him a little. Miss Madeley was right about them; they were bright and clever and cunning, possibly too much so for his dull-witted male mind. "Sit down!" he announced.

Abigail Grimwell cleared her throat and began coughing noisily, and Lucinda began to giggle for no obvious reason; all was as expected.

They were again doing English grammar, parsing sentences, and there was quiet and a false tranquillity. At length, he took out some paper and began to pen a swift letter to Lottie. He had purchased for her a small gold pin, about the size of a halfpenny, inlaid with a coloured crystal made into the shape of a butterfly wing. It was the sort of thing she would wear on a blouse or a collar, and it was quite exquisite. It was presently in his inside jacket pocket, next to his timepiece, and wrapped in velvet by the jeweller in the high street from whom he had purchased it.

He wanted badly to take it out and examine it again, to look at it the way her eyes would look at it. But he contented himself by writing the letter. He could see it later in private, it would not need to be dispatched until tomorrow.

The pin was in part a balm to his own conscience; he had slept with Clara Anstey on two occasions and he felt guilty. In addition, he was walking out with Henrietta Madeley, and had agreed to more strolling the Sunday next. He was not faithful in body or mind to Lottie. Though his heart was a different territory completely.

He turned his attention to the letter and wrote: *'My dearest Lottie, I am heartened to hear of your safe arrival in...'* He got no further because of a knock on the door. The maid entered and informed him that Miss Tongs needed to see him at once in her office. He was immediately on the defensive and rose. Miss Tongs was with the doctor who had examined Mary Hampshire.

"I can find nothing amiss with the child," he told Fairchild.

"Nothing whatever?"

"No. Perhaps she is malingering!"

"I doubt that somehow...it has gone on for too long." He looked at Miss Tongs for confirmation and then at the doctor with cool disdain but remained silent. Most doctors were in his opinion quacks and snake oil salesmen. And he could not put confidence in those of them who drank sherry at this hour of the day when supposedly on professional missions, as this one was doing now. "Then I do not understand it at all…" he announced eventually.

"My dear young man," said the doctor unctuously, "I no more understand the intricacies of the French language…but there we are!"

Back in the classroom the letter had been noticed by Miranda on the front row.

"Well, go and read it…" said Melanie in hushed tones.

Miranda dithered. "Why do I have to?"

"You are nearest!" said Jane.

"Be careful indeed…" cautioned Millicent. "Imagine if he comes back and finds you reading his private correspondence…"

"Make a decision for heaven's sake…" said Abigail. "In fact, do not bother… I will do it."

"No, you will not," said Melanie. "You will spoil it or not be able to decipher it or something…and it will all take too long."

"How dare you!" said Abigail with asperity.

"I shall do it myself," said Miranda decidedly. "He will be back before it has been read at this rate…" She proceeded to read the aborted first line of his letter.

"Who is this Lottie?" entreated Lucinda.

"Obviously his sweetheart…" ventured Melissa.

"Surely he does not have one," said Lucinda, "Who would want him, with his foul temper and even fouler moods?"

"Of course he will have one…he will be different entirely outside of this school," Jane offered.

"Will he?" Miranda had doubts.

"One would hope so," Annabelle said. "And he is appealing to the eye, if one looks beyond his other flaws."

"Lottie could be his sister…" said Jane sensibly. "Or his cousin or someone."

"Unlikely," said Melissa.

"Quickly, he is coming back…" cried Lucinda from the doorway. And placing the letter back on the wrong part of the desk, Miranda took her seat.

He re-entered and realised at once that he had left the letter exposed, and that it was now in the wrong place from where he had dropped it, and that they had read it most probably. Nothing to be done and, besides, he did not much care, he had barely begun it. Thank God. Or he would feel seriously compromised. He began on the letter where he had left off.

At length, he glanced up and saw Melissa Shaw watching him from beneath her lashes, the sort of up tilted gaze that children give to adults they do not trust or like, but one which was not in itself offensive. He stared back at her, a neutral kind of gaze, and she continued to watch him, her eyes fastening on his with avid candour and no trace of mendacity. Perhaps she was planning to begin the staring game, just as Abigail relinquished it. "Is there something wrong, Miss Shaw?" he asked her sharply.

"Nothing, Sir," she said, her eyes still on his own.

"Then why are you staring at me in that manner?"

She altered her gaze to one of perplexity. "I did not realise I was doing so…my mind was elsewhere… Sir."

This was obviously a lie, but he let it pass, and as he looked away a small involuntary smile swept his mouth. He had thought of Lottie referring to them as *'his darling girls'* in jealousy. He looked out of the window to his right and soon his mind was reprising that whole conversation before she left and her reminding him of their being teenagers.

He had taken her virginity—and broken his own—the first time in the belfry of the church where his father was vicar. She had been three weeks from being sixteen and he seventeen. He scarcely thought of it, but when he did, he saw the foolhardy risks they had taken from then on. It was mostly his need, his desire to do so, in their younger years. It would have been his crime had she fallen pregnant. But would that have been better than what had transpired? Clearly not!

His parents and family would have suffered the shame, the child would have been taken, or his parents forced to raise it and pretend it was a late baby: the usual deceit and subterfuge that went on in good families more often than was documented. It would have been raised as his sibling, never perhaps knowing the truth. And God only knew what other consequences to Lottie…

He had utterly lost his concentration on the letter, the room, and his role in general. He emerged from his memories to become aware of the rustling and murmuring in the row which held Melanie Petersham and Melissa Shaw. He saw lightning movement and some reaction and murmuring from Jane Reynolds who sat next to Melanie, and then more furtive shuffling and more of Melanie's silly eye fluttering, obviously to distract him from the nub of things. They were penning notes again, he could sense it. This time he would not allow himself to be made a fool of, even without evidence. He was between Henrietta's wisdom and Judith's warnings. "What have you been writing to one another?" he demanded of them, switching his gaze between Melanie and Melissa and Jane.

They stared back at him with vacant expressions in which the terror was dormant like a contrary undercurrent in calm water. They feared him now and of course he must maintain that. It was a necessary evil; it was better than failure in the job. "Well?" he said in a louder voice.

"Nothing whatever, Sir," said the fearless Miss Petersham. "Beyond the lesson we have written nothing."

"You are lying, Miss Petersham...come out here...and you Miss Shaw!"

They rose, but Jane still sat, unsure; her uncertainty an artifice, and as the other two moved she swept the notes from her own desk where Melanie had placed them for her perusal and into her shoe. Her footwear, like the rest of their footwear, was an ankle boot—the manoeuvre was easy and meant reaching to just below her calf to secrete the notes.

The first note—for there were in all three—had been penned by Melanie to Melissa, it read: *'He likes you better than most of us...he almost smiled at you.'*

"Utter nonsense..." Melissa had scribbled in reply. *"'twas probably wind."*

This was terribly humorous of course, and Melanie had then allowed Jane to read them. The third note read: *'He has fallen into some kind of agonised reverie now...no doubt regarding Lottie...'* But Jane had put her book over it and pulled it back to her own desk.

Melissa stood with Melanie and stared at the deep red and blue carpet. He could not know the content of these notes, even if she had to run haring out of the building and down the driveway and home. She would run all the way so no-one could catch her, and then hide for two days. She cast about the floor for clever things to throw him off the scent and he watched her in particular—her guilt being all about her face and not in question. "Are you prepared to tell me where the notes are presently?" he asked in a quiet voice.

There was no reply until Melanie offered in a near whisper and a humble tone. "They do not exist, Sir!"

"Do not lie to me, Miss Petersham...you are not yet that clever."

Lucinda could not contain her pent-up amusement any longer and gave into spluttering and squeaking.

"And you may come out here as well…" he told her, "I have had enough of your random hilarity."

Lucinda joined them and lost the urge to giggle. The class sat in mesmerised silence.

"Do you wish to tell me what they contained, these missives?"

Melissa and Melanie spoke at one and the same time.

"No…" said Melissa bluntly. "There is nothing to tell," uttered Melanie.

He surveyed them both and then looked to Lucinda. "Perhaps you know…being that the content renders you prey to such merriment?"

"I do not know, Sir," said Lucinda.

"Then what is so amusing?"

"I do not know that either, enough to explain…many things cause me to laugh, Sir."

"Very well…" he pronounced. "If you recall, I did warn you that such misdemeanours would bear consequences…all three of you shall be caned."

He moved to the window ledge where he had placed the cane and took it up, then stood in the centre front of the room. Miss Tongs was right; he did not have time for convoluted methods of discipline.

The class gasped as one, like an audience in a melodrama. Melissa blanched and was as pale as death, and Lucinda bit her lip and tried not to show her fear. Melanie sighed and arched her brows. "But we have done nothing wrong, Sir."

He looked at her for seconds and drew breath. "Miss Petersham, if you say one more contradictory false word, I shall double the punishment.…now step forwards and hold out your hand, whichever one you do not write with."

Melissa was trembling hard and Melanie pushed against her with her hip as a means of comforting her. They might have been standing on the scaffold in Elizabethan England. "'twas me who wrote the note!" volunteered Melanie next. "So, you may let Melissa go…"

He drew a deeper breath, remembering Henrietta's words about her protective attitude to Melissa Shaw. "I shall decide who goes and when…and I will ask you only once more, Miss Petersham, hold out your hand."

Melanie held out her arm and he took it and straightened it then held it below her wrist, as he had with Abigail, and administered three strokes of the cane. "Sit down," he said on completion.

He moved onto Melissa and then Lucinda, following the exact procedure, not varying it by the slightest degree.

He stared at them in their seats for several moments afterwards, so that they would understand his intention to be respected. Lucinda had begun to weep, and given her penchant for hysterical amusement he was unsurprised—one intense emotion mirroring the other. Melissa dabbed at her eyes with the back of her hand but was otherwise silent. While Melanie sat with a stony expression and stared back at him. She was not going to succumb to vulnerability in any way, but still he knew she had taken the action seriously. He looked at Jane. "Miss Reynolds, I am unsure what your part in all this was, but you may be assured that if I find out you will also be caned."

Jane regarded him with her cool aloofness, her usual haughty disdain. Her parents were distressed aristocrats and she lived in faded grandeur with her family but did not speak of it to anyone. She knew not where he had attained his autocratic superiority of manner, only that it was certainly more impressive than her own.

He took his assiduous scrutiny away from her and viewed the class in general. "Now cease the note writing, and all other distraction, and get on with your work."

Abigail, on the second row to the left, sat like a statue, her nib on the desk and untouched that afternoon as she stared at him with a menacing and unflinching glower. She had just lost her position of *Agent Provocateur* three or four days too soon and was displeased. He ignored her. He saw that as Judith had said, she was a lesser worry. And as Nicholas Stevenson had cautioned him, he needed to take a strong stand if he was not to be brought down by them all.

* * *

At the end of the lesson, Melissa hurried into the cloakroom, followed shortly by Melanie and several others. She was holding her hand beneath the faucet and allowing the water to ease her stinging palm. Her fingers felt cold and numb by comparison, and she wondered how he could do such a thing to them.

She removed her hand from the stream of water and dried it on her skirt hastily as Jane entered. She rushed to her and took her hands. "Lady Jane!" she said, using the nickname they gave her courtesy of her heritage. "I am entirely indebted to you, thank you with all my heart."

Jane looked pleasantly surprised. "'twas nothing, Melissa."

"Oh, but it was," said Melissa. "Only imagine if he had found what was penned…" She put her arms around Jane and Jane suffered herself to be embraced. "We are eternally grateful, are we not, Melanie?"

"I expect we may be," said Melanie in more casual manner, running her hand calmly beneath the faucet.

Jane was pragmatic as usual. "It was the logical thing to do."

"Yes, but you risked yourself to do it. I shall buy you cakes and dainties at the tea shop, if you will allow it, tomorrow afternoon perhaps," offered Melissa.

Jane looked reticent. "My mother does not like me to go into the town…not unescorted at any rate. So, I doubt I can attend."

"Then I shall bring you chocolate or other confectionery on Monday!" Melissa said.

Melanie added in a placatory manner. "Yes, yes…we will buy you something pleasing, Jane. Your quick wittedness is to be applauded."

"And your foolishness is not…" retorted Jane. "Your droll notes will be the death of us…you should cease them now."

Abigail appeared, her outdoor clothes in one hand. "Anyone would think she had saved you from execution," she said peevishly.

"You say that only because you lack sensitivity and self-respect…" Miranda told her. "You were the one who provoked him to such tempers in the first instance."

"Cowards, all of you!" said Abigail with spirit and Melanie moved towards her angrily. "Do not call me a coward! Or I will hold your head beneath the faucet until you gasp for breath."

"I should like to see you try, Miss know-it-all. You do not have the strength."

"We will see about that, you ignorant little milk-maid…" threatened Melanie.

Lucinda had barely stopped weeping and Abigail turned on her. "And as for you, *cry-baby,* you are playing right into his hands…"

Melanie grabbed Abigail's hair, "Shut your large farmyard mouth…you are leaving and we are here for another year or more… I will drown you alive, Abi, if you say anything else."

"Is that not a contradiction in terms?" asked Elspeth in passing.

"And you can shut up too," Melanie told her.

"Do stop!" said Jane. "You are giving me a headache, we have had enough strain for one day."

Melissa turned the faucet back on. "He is a perfidious tyrant! I loathe and detest him."

"He is bound to lose sleep over that..." said Miranda facetiously.

"And to think Miss Madeley has been seen walking with him," remarked Annabelle, and everything stopped abruptly.

"Has she?" enquired Millicent, newly arriving on the scene.

"She is silly enough to walk with any man possessing two legs." Melanie released the struggling Abigail, diverted by the gossip "She will see only his marriageable status...before it is too late."

"But what about Lottie of today's letter?" queried Miranda. "Where does she come into it?"

"He is probably just dallying with Madeley," declared Jane.

"Just imagine being wed to him!" Annabelle speculated. "One would have no peace for fear of what he may do next in temper..."

"Or who he might dally with behind one's back," said Miranda.

"Do not be so theatrical..." Millicent spoke earnestly and they stared at her, astonished at her further display in his defence. "He was simply doing what many school teachers would do under the circumstances..."

"Do not dare to defend him!" cried Melanie, incensed. "Millie, this is not the time and place for your insipid and saintly fairness...he is an unspeakable monster."

"Of course he is not!" declared Millicent. "You should behave with more sense. You have simply become used to doing as you wish with Mistress Sullivan and Mr Stringer."

"Millie, I warn you, I will lose my patience if you continue," Melanie warned.

Lucinda joined Melissa at the large sink and Melissa said: "Lucy, put your hand beneath this water, it will feel better..."

"I doubt it!" said Lucinda in barely contained misery.

"Stop being such a ninny..." Melanie was exasperated. "If you want him to get the better of you in this way then I do not."

"I cannot help it..." Lucinda wailed.

"Of course you can...you muster something called self-*control*...and do not be such a mardy little milksop..."

"And think on this…" Abigail pushed past Melanie's strident presence to hold the centre of the floor. "Were you boys he would cane you on the opposite end, and then it would be your arses you needed to hold beneath the faucet."

"Well, you would have a problem, Abigail…your fat arse would not fit over the sink…" shrilled Melanie. "And we are not boys, so it is a moot point."

"Must we have such coarse vulgarity?" Jane cried in grave revulsion, remembering to fish the secreted notes from her shoe and hand them to Melissa.

Millicent, in her quiet way, made a last-ditch attempt at reason. "Try to see things from his point of view, I beg of you, and improve your behaviour."

"Oh, she begs of us on his account," said Annabelle. "How absolutely Christian of you, Millie."

Melissa turned off the faucet and said more gently. "I do not think it is the time to make that suggestion, Millie…"

"Certainly not if she wants to go home with dry hair!" remarked Melanie.

Millicent took on a pained air and wrapped her cloak around her and left them to it. Jane watched her go. "We must forgive her… I believe she may be in love with him."

"What?" Melanie screeched. "She cannot be…"

"She can indeed," Jane offered. "She is beloved of Miss Madeley for her musical talents, remember! She imitates what Madeley does and says all the time…and Madeley is enamoured of him, it seems."

The cloakroom was quiet for a moment or two while this was digested, and then Miranda began to laugh. "'tis too comical for words…just consider it… Millicent Bromley in competition with Henrietta Madeley for the worst despot known to education! It may come down to who can play Beethoven's Fifth the loudest…"

Burblings of mirth arose and soon there were peals of laughter: the shared camaraderie in times of crisis was a priceless thing.

Wallflowers and Summer Blooms

Millicent realised she was alone now in the class in most senses. They almost hated her for defending Fairchild, for trying to get them to be more mature and reasonable. She did not fully understand herself but knew that she had some kind of strange feeling for him, some abiding fascination with everything he did and said. Orphaned at a very young age from parents dying together in a coach accident, she was raised by her paternal grandmother and her aunt, both of whom were very austere and strict. Beyond her musical abilities which her aunt encouraged—being of that bent herself—she had no outlet for her feelings on life, and no male relatives to speak of. She knew not that she missed a patriarchal figure, or a protective elder brother, and Fairchild in his comparative youthfulness and authority represented both those things, filling the gap she did not realise existed. He was well-dressed, handsome and clever. He shone radiantly at the blackboard and Millicent found it hard some days to distinguish between the sun's rays and his magnificence at the front of the room.

Being possessed of a timid disposition she hesitated to stare at him overlong, or to ask questions that might occur to her about his tutoring—which she thought excellent—but felt it was her responsibility to take his corner against the rest of her classmates, the majority of them, who had turned into catty and spiteful creatures where he was concerned. He could not now do right for doing wrong, and they were determined not to see themselves as they were, so that more trouble and insurrection was almost inevitable.

Millicent felt she could not bear it for him; he might stop being such an erudite teacher…and worse than that: he might up and leave. She secretly thought it right that he had begun to cane people for their misbehaviour—they deserved it—and although she knew this was singularly disloyal to the classmates who had been mostly fair to her, she knew that in his position she might do the same. And it was altogether better than his resigning from the post.

That Miss Madeley was now taken with him she did not mind. She adored Miss Madeley, the only adult she knew who showed her warmth and considerable kindness. She and Miss Madeley were of a kind, though Miss Madeley was decidedly prettier, she thought. They both had sensitive dispositions, given to their music mostly. Miss Madeley naturally had the advantage, being an adult. She was his equal, his colleague, and appropriate for him to pay court to. She would share him with Miss Madeley willingly, and Miss Madeley would never know how she felt so it did not matter.

Her peers cared more about their ridiculous vendetta, even at their own expense. It was a war and he had no choice but to fight it.

Abigail had left and Melanie was the brightest star of the rebellion, arriving late to his lessons with arguably valid excuses. Asking him stupid questions, as if she were dim or he inept. Followed closely by Miranda who had taken to staring from the window as he taught, and when reprimanded claiming she had developed an eye condition which caused her to squint from her side vision. Then writing awful rhymes about him in her satirical and talented manner.

These odes were considered riotously funny and were always discarded after being read for fear of his finding them, (except for the ones Melanie gave to her sometime beau, James Harcourt at the boys' academy, so he might share the humour with his peers. Harcourt being the male equivalent of herself in terms of unstoppable spirit and boldness and also inviting enmity with Fairchild, though succeeding less).

Millicent watched on one Friday morning as Melissa Shaw was encouraged into sketching his likeness with chalk fifteen minutes before a lesson. She agreed to it, reluctantly, but only with Prescilla watching from the door and Jane surveying the grounds from the window to note his untimely arrival. The likeness was very good, considering it was done in minutes: his bone structure and the outline of his eyes and his splendiferous hair. And Millie told her this. "'tis just like him, Lissy!" she said with pleasure.

Jane arched her brows and kicked Melanie beneath the table. They smiled at Millie with irony, like fond parents, but she knew not why.

Then Melanie said. "Well, Millie, that is only his outer visage…inwardly he is monstrous."

"Yes, like this…" declared Melissa and she began rapidly going over her lines and making his nose into an ugly shape and his hair and brows like something from the forest and his mouth a snarling cavern with wolverine teeth.

Gales of laughter ensued and Millie exclaimed with impatience. "Childish, Lissy! And spiteful…not worthy of you."

"I beg your pardon, goody-two-shoes?" said Melissa, only mildly put out. "Did you say something?"

Millie was about to add other brave comments, dredged from she knew not where in her being, when Prescilla hissed at them. "He is coming up the stairs, I hear him."

"Quickly…wipe the board!" instructed Jane.

Melissa looked about for the muslin cloth with which the board was cleaned and could not find it. Several of them leapt up to help her. It was nowhere.

"Stop him…" Melanie called out. "Someone hold him off…"

Lucinda danced on the spot with anxiety and then ran along the corridor to where he was ascending the stairs and rounding the passageway, telling him the first thing she thought of. "Mr Fairchild! How fortunate you have come…there is a fox…"

"What?" he stopped, abruptly shaken from his thoughts of Lottie. "A fox?"

"Indeed, Sir…it was chasing us around the room."

He stared at her uncomprehendingly in the morning light from the passage window. "Foxes do not chase people, Miss Harvey…'tis the other way around."

Meanwhile, Melanie was ripping a piece from her petticoat with which to clean the board.

"Be quick, be quick…" Melissa was squealing, feeling faint with tension.

"Then perhaps it was a wolf…" Lucinda said to him, walking backwards in front of him so that it was difficult for him to move at his normal pace.

"You do not know the difference?" he enquired smoothly. "Where is it now?"

"We chased it off and it went that way and to the back stairs…" Lucinda leaned forwards with an outstretched arm to detain him from any movement whatsoever and pointed, as if he did not know the location of the said stairs. He watched her sceptically. Some kind of a prank perhaps! He stared in the direction indicated but did not attempt to follow this legendary animal. Then taking her upper arm, he pulled her to one side and walked briskly on. "Well, 'tis evidently gone now, so you may return."

"But what if the fox…or the wolf, or whatever it is, returns?" she said in false and dramatic alarm.

He thought of what he knew of foxes, but all the while smelled a rat. He carried on to the classroom and ignored her as she scurried after him, raising her voice unnecessarily and uttering nonsense.

"I am not deaf, Miss Harvey…" he said as he made his long strides. "Kindly lower your voice."

By the time he entered the classroom, they were all seated, like statues. It was the clue he needed. Melanie Petersham seemed to be fiddling with the underwear beneath her dress. Mary Hampshire had fallen asleep on her arms as usual, although he ignored this nowadays, for he could do little in the face of inept medical diagnosis. "You are all remarkably quiet considering the presence of this wild animal," he announced sardonically.

The blackboard was smeared white with recent chalk, but the markings were indecipherable. They had been chalking on the board, it was evident. He decided to let it pass, he could not be bothered at this hour of the day to become derailed by their antics. Melissa Shaw was looking at him directly for the first time in weeks since the occasion he had caned her; a look of consummate satisfaction. He recalled Henrietta Madeley telling him of her being an aspiring artist. She had caricatured him in chalk, he knew it as sure as he saw the hills beyond the window pane.

They looked at each other eventually with faces of smug delight. And after the lesson, they wallowed; it was too rich an escapade to go without greater dissection.

"Very well played, Lucy," said Melanie. "An expert distraction…the fox or wolf…"

"He did not believe it," said Lucinda stupidly.

"Of course he did not," cried Annabelle, "Whatever else he is, he is not an idiot."

"Who cares!" declared Melanie. "He knows we have the better of him…"

"Perhaps he has better things to worry about," put in Millicent; a lone dissenting voice in a political rally.

"Too, too amusing…" declared Miranda. "Lissy, that was quite wonderful…and very quick witted of you, Melanie, to think of tearing your petticoat in time."

"What will you say about it at home…the petticoat?" enquired the practical Jane.

"I shall say I tore it on thorn bushes…" replied Melanie.

"But where would you have encountered those?" queried Melissa.

"I have no idea…but you know me, Lissy, I shall think of something betimes."

Lucinda took out her sweet tin and shared peppermints. "Your turn to write more odes to him…" she said to Miranda.

"I really need his first name," Miranda claimed after some perusal of the matter. "Does no-one know it?"

They did not, and several suggestions were made, all of them derogatory and unflattering. Melanie proposed then a kitty, to which they would all contribute by some coins twice a week, until one of them discovered his name and won the money. It was readily agreed and Melissa supplied a kerchief into which the first offerings were placed and handed it to Melanie who volunteered to keep it safe and make the tally. Millicent refused to participate and left the room in mournful disapproval.

"*My heart is sore all upon his sake…*" quoted Jane as she departed. They shook their heads and tutted and wondered how they could harbour such a viper in their midst.

* * *

He had not heard from Lottie in over three weeks. He was between anger and concern. He suspected her of just putting him out of her mind, while she was never that far from his. He was bitterly upset. His moods were more vexatious as the days passed. He slept with Clara Anstey on a regular basis but assiduously avoided the attentions of Judith Tongs. He continued to walk with Henrietta on Sundays and she began to be more and more anxious that he should kiss her or make some move displaying affection for her. He did neither.

Beyond taking her hand to help her over styles and up steps, he did not touch her. She began to ache for him to do so. He sensed this and saw that things were going too far with her: something had to be done. Then one afternoon she suggested they call on her parents. This alarmed him greatly, but he saw not the means to refuse. Her father was a vicar and knew his brother, Rupert, also a clergyman. He agreed, and suffered himself to drink afternoon tea with her family and answer the questions her father put to him about his own late father, who was known to the gentleman years previously.

They were nice people, good people. He felt like an imposter, for they were obviously convinced he would bid for Henrietta's hand in marriage at some point, and he knew he would never do that.

The next time he walked with Henrietta early May had arrived, with sunshine and clement weather. Henrietta said she needed to rest and sat on a bench overlooking the river and she removed her light silk shawl and revealed her short-sleeved silk dress. Her arms gleaming smooth as marble in the bright light.

When he was seated beside her, she placed her hand on his and without looking at him uttered: "Anthony, you may kiss me if you wish, you know…"

He considered this for some seconds and gazed at the water, and she looked at him sidelong to gauge his thoughts. Eventually he had what he considered the perfectly balanced response. "I shall if you wish it…" he said.

"I do wish it," she told him in a small voice. "I have wished it for some time now."

"But first I must tell you something, and then you may decide afresh…"

Henrietta put her hand on her ribs, her heart rate was increasing and she thought to still it with her fingers as she tried to control her racing mind.

He turned slightly towards her. "Henrietta, I cannot marry you…and you must know that before we kiss…you are not the sort of lady I would wish to trifle with, or show disrespect…" He paused and she began to shiver, with fear and untold misgivings.

"There is a girl in my life, a woman… I have known her since I was a young boy…and we are unofficially engaged but I…"

"Where is she?" demanded Henrietta, cutting in on him clumsily in her anxiety. "Where is this person?" She believed him to be lying.

"Precisely where at this moment I know not… I have not heard of her exact whereabouts for a while…"

"Do you mean she is missing?" She turned to him, frowning with intent and annoyance. "How can she be missing?"

"She had to leave home…her father is pressing her into a suit she does not wish for."

"And why do you not wed her?"

"Because I do not have sufficient funds at present…and because he does not want it, her father…and he would hound us to death…"

"And why do you not know her whereabouts?"

He was patient with her sharp question, more so than with the curiosity of others; she warranted his honesty. He was not known for treating women badly, nor would he begin now. "She is with a theatre company…she is an actress…"

"What?" shrieked Henrietta. This was getting worse by the second, this treatise of miserable love.

"A Shakespearian actress…" he said.

Henrietta paused in her interrogation and rose from the bench and he watched her walk a little way to the river's edge. She strolled and he lit a cigar, allowing her time to think. When she returned, she asked, "Then why did you ask me to walk out with you?"

He saw that his having done so was a potential act of cruelty. He was embarrassed and annoyed with himself. "Because you are a lovely woman…"

"So you thought you would entertain yourself with me?"

Her inexperience or her unworldliness was like a small wounded animal one would rescue and then not know what to do with. "No… I thought I would enjoy your company," he said simply. "But I did not think you would take it so seriously."

She turned onto him her light blue eyes which were full of tears. He sighed inwardly and stubbed out his small cigar. "Why ever not?" she cried.

"Well, …because…because ladies do not always do so."

"I think they do, Anthony…with men like yourself."

"Men like myself! I know not what you mean."

She gazed at him, her tears spilling onto her cheeks.

"Eligible and attractive men of standing, I mean."

He let this pass and said, "Henrietta, you are extremely eligible yourself…which is why I am being honest with you. There are many men who would fall over themselves to marry you. But I cannot!"

"And what if she does not return, this girl? Would you marry me then?"

The sun went in suddenly, and it seemed like a timely measure of the impasse he was at. He opened his mouth and attempted words and then closed it again.

"I do not know…" he lied, unable to flatly insult her.

There were occasions when a lie was better than the truth, when the truth would be an unnecessary evil. "If she does not return, I do not know if I will ever marry anyone."

She looked at him directly and he looked back at her. His honesty and integrity had now made her desire him more.

"So, perhaps we had better not kiss…" he said. "It might not be wise."

She was carrying a reticule and a parasol and she took hold of them as a prelude to leaving. "You must love her a lot…this girl!"

"I do," he said.

"Then I hope she returns, for your sake," said Henrietta with majesty, though she did not really mean it and did not care. "And no, I no longer wish you to kiss me."

He watched her prepare to leave. "Henrietta, allow me to at least escort you home."

"No thank you… I can go by myself, 'tis perfectly safe at this time of day."

He did not protest or insist, and thought that had she been Lottie he would have insisted. But to do so with this woman would be to add insult to injury perhaps. She walked slowly and gracefully back along the river bank and he watched her progress until the first turning on to the road which led by a mere three-minute walk to the vicarage. It was better, he thought, to let her down at this stage than to have her carry on hoping, especially having kissed her.

Women like Henrietta were careful of their virtue to the point of celibacy. She was the diametrically opposed female to Clara Anstey. And she was not someone he would wed, although her inclination to chastity and obedience and all the other wifely virtues were probably not in doubt.

He walked by himself along the edge of the river and thought about Lottie. It had been weeks now and no letter or communication of any kind. She had been recently in Ireland, according to her itinerary of almost two months ago. She had probably left there already, but he had not heard from her since she had left Carlisle, though she had written to say she received the gold pin and how much she liked it. And how much she missed him. Did she miss him? She was an actress, and had about her that ability to pretence—even with herself. Perhaps especially with herself.

The worst thing now, after the longing to hear from her, was the not knowing what he could do about it. How he could go about tracing her, or if she really wanted to be traced. Perhaps, like himself with Henrietta, she had been loath to let him down badly and did not really feel the things she said she felt. The only difference perhaps was the length of their relationship—which would make her proclamations more meaningful, or her denials more serious.

He was morose and beyond hope, beyond anyone's comfort or anyone's worldly wisdom. He thought he might talk to his mother, an expert on such matters courtesy of her work in the parish. He considered riding over to see her, but then it would be gone midnight when he got back to his lodgings and he would be awake all night thinking of what they had talked of. And he had work in the morning at the Boys' Academy.

By the time he reached the lodgings, it was getting dark. He had called at one of the taverns in the town and drank a few glasses of rum, but he felt the need for more. He was not averse to drinking heavily at any suitable time. It was—his brother Rupert told him—a thorn in his side. It would be the undoing of him if he did not control it at his age, in the same way it was for many people of his years.

He took his horse from the stables and rode to Trim's house where Susan was enjoying Trim's company but was soon to leave. Mondays were her busiest days; she assisted her father, a local doctor, in the surgery and also made up herbal tinctures for people taken ill over the weekend. When she was not occupied in the medical sense, she was busy teaching the children at the alms schools—she was a veritable whirlwind of good works. He grinned at her as he entered Trim's parlour, she reminded him of better days and their childhood.

"Have you heard from Lottie by any chance?" he enquired of her lightly.

"No…not since about two months ago when she left York… I thought you may have heard."

"I have not," he said on a downwards inflection.

"Oh!" said Susan in a similar tone. "What a naughty girl."

"Indeed… I shall lose no time in telling her so when I see her…if I see her."

Susan tied her bonnet and laughed. "She will be back, Tony, you may be sure…"

"But what has befallen her, is the question…for her not to have written?" Trim said.

"Timothy!" Susan adopted a matriarchal tone. "We do not need a harbinger of doom at this point…'tis perhaps a dispatch error…letters often go missing."

"That had better be the excuse!" Fairchild said. "I shall not take kindly to any other."

"Come…" said Susan to her fiancé who was a good foot taller than herself. "'tis late," she smiled at Fairchild, her small pointed features softening into affectionate lines as she pulled Trim towards the door. She was bossier than any female he knew, but Trim seemed not to care. And perhaps that was anyway preferable to her having theatrical aspirations.

Trimingham lived with his family, in rooms of his own in the copious mansion, enjoying his bachelor life but engaged to Susan for some interminable time. Had it not been for his father's stricture on his doing some kind of honourable work, and therefore deciding to teach, his life may have been idyllic. His father was aware, as was Rupert, of the dissipated and prodigal habits young men were prey to.

At length Trim returned, with a bottle of best brandy in hand. They drank and talked for a good while and he slept on the couch—to which he was no stranger—and then rode back to his lodgings early morning to bathe and change his clothes for work.

Time and Tide

Henrietta shunned him now or avoided him, though he treated her exactly as he had treated her always in their working days. Miss Tongs was the first to notice. "You seem to be avoiding Anthony Fairchild!" she said one afternoon as she helped herself to gin and perused the class registers in the staff room. "Or is it my imagination?"

"We are no longer walking out," said Henrietta in a dignified tone. "But I am not avoiding him…well, perhaps a little…to save embarrassment."

Judith laughed loudly and briefly. She had been proven right. "What on earth has gone wrong?" she enquired, looking up from the registers. "You two so suited, such a beautiful young couple…he has not tried to ravish you prematurely, has he!"

Henrietta paused before replying. "He has a woman he is betrothed to…"

"I did try to warn you…weeks ago," claimed the headmistress with barely disguised satisfaction. "I told you he was not in the business of marrying."

Henrietta ignored this gloating. "She is off somewhere being an actress, this girl…and I cannot continue under that knowledge."

Judith stared at the window, where rain threatened the recent clement weather. "I expect he has invented her…so that he may dally with all the women he likes in safety."

"I do not think so, Judith," said Henrietta with sincerity. "He is not that sort of man."

"They are all that sort of man, given the opportunity!" said Judith darkly, returning to her work.

* * *

Millicent had been practising for a recital she was delivering with Miss Madeley for the Mayoral Inauguration at the Guild Hall, to represent the school.

On the day of this conversation between Henrietta Madeley and Judith Tongs, she was hard at rehearsal and consequently arrived ten minutes late for his class.

"And where the devil have you been?" he demanded as she crept in, trying not to disturb anyone.

"In Miss Madeley's room rehearsing for the Town's Guild Ceremony, Sir," she told him in a small voice.

He stared at her, the chalk in his hand, and she stared back with a timid face. He wondered whether it was Henrietta's way of showing him contempt, as if ignoring him were not enough. Then he shook himself mentally and realised how ridiculous the thought was. "I beg your pardon?" he said, meaning he did not like or believe what he heard. "This lesson began ten minutes ago. Did you not hear the caretaker ring the bell?"

"I did, Sir…" said Millie, "But Miss Madeley had gone from the room and I did not like to leave without her permission…it seemed impolite."

"So you thought you would seem impolite to me instead? Is that it?"

"No, Sir…that is not it at all…she said she would return before the next lesson and I waited and…"

"Miss Bromley, I do not wish to hear a repeat of these excuses…"

"They are not excuses!" said Millicent in what for her was a brave voice. "'tis simply that—"

"Simply that you do not think my lesson important enough to arrive punctually!" he interjected.

"No that is not it…but the harpsichord at the town hall is new to us and we must get this piece at the right note or—"

"Miss Bromley…" he intoned in a louder voice. "Be quiet. I do not wish to hear any more of this diatribe on harpsichords."

Millicent was speechless with confusion. The class watched her, between amusement and sympathy. Lucinda felt she may not be able to control her laughter and she tucked in her chin and pulled up the front of her dress so that her nose and mouth were covered and she could release the merriment silently. Miranda was making a wagging motion with her forefinger at Millie, out of his line of vision. And Jane was displaying a silencing gesture to Millie by tapping her lips, concerned for Millicent's position.

Millie ignored all this and stared at him like a supplicant in a court of law. She had gone this far, there was no point in stopping now. "Sir, if you ask Miss Madeley, I am sure she will explain."

"Sit down, Miss Bromley! I have no intention of asking Miss Madeley. I have better things to do…in future use your common sense…and if you dare to walk into my lessons ten minutes late again on such a flimsy excuse you will be caned."

Millicent sat, utterly crushed and near to tears. Miranda wagged a finger at her again as he turned to the board and Melanie made soft tutting noises. Annabelle leaned into Jane, whom she was seated next to, and passed her a note which she read hastily and then passed to Melanie.

'He seems to have fallen from Millie's pedestal… I wonder if he can ever climb back again? Or shall he need a ladder!'

Melanie grinned and passed it to Melissa who frowned and immediately stuffed it into her pocket without reading it, in case he turned unexpectedly and saw her with it.

Having written on the board, Fairchild turned and caught sight of Lucinda's partially hidden face. "Miss Harvey, what do you think you are doing?"

Lucinda took a few seconds to withdraw her face from her dress and emerged with an exaggeratedly pursed mouth and a stupid expression to denote seriousness. She wondered if she could speak without the amusement getting the better of her. There was little choice. "I was drawing warm breath to ease my toothache," she replied in a tight voice.

He glared at her but thought it best not to pursue this claim. "Then arrange your clothing and pay attention…enough time has been wasted."

Millicent felt betrayed. How could he speak to her in that way when all she had done was to defend him and hold him in the highest esteem! She could not concentrate on her work and felt the overwhelming need to cry. On leaving the classroom later, some of the girls clustered around her.

"You see what a heartless despot he is now, Millie, I hope," said Melanie. "A callous beast, not worthy of your kind words and consideration."

"I think… I think he…" Millicent could not rightly frame her sentiments, floundering between several emotions.

"At least you stood up to him…," said Elspeth. "Well done!"

"He would not listen to me!" cried Millie, quite incensed.

"Of course he would not…" trilled Lucinda merrily. "He listens only to his own voice."

"But at least you tried," said Melissa. "Though take care not to push him too far…you will not like it if he canes you, 'tis unpleasant and painful."

"There you are Millie, you have learned something," drawled Melanie satirically. "'tis unpleasant and painful! State the obvious, Lissy, the reminder is helpful…"

Miranda and Lucinda began giggling as they trooped out. "I shall write a malefic ode to him later," Miranda said, pulling Millie by the arm to move her from her miserable torpor. "I have the start of it already in mind… I shall bring it in tomorrow. We can pass it around during Mr Stringer's lesson…he will not notice. Then Melanie may give it to Harcourt. He can distribute it over there."

"And even if Mr Stringer sees, he will not care!" put in Elizabeth, who had recently come up from the lower form.

Millicent listened to them comment on Fairchild disparagingly as they went to the cloakroom. They had brought her back into their fold somewhat: she was one of them again courtesy of his disapproval. Whose side should she take!

* * *

The next time she was with Miss Madeley, she ventured a very forward question.

"Miss Madeley?" she said and Henrietta replied. "Yes, Millie?"

"What is Mr Fairchild's first name?"

Miss Madeley looked up, puzzled. "Why do you want to know that?" she asked suspiciously.

"Because I thought I heard the caretaker call him 'Arthur'…and that does not suit him at all," replied Millie cunningly, amazing herself with her own artifice.

Miss Madeley allowed herself a small laugh, not something she had wanted to do recently. "That is not his name," she returned to the sorting of sheet music, distracted and listless, then adding casually. "'tis Anthony!"

Only realising too late her indiscretion; the caretaker would not be so above his station as to address one of the masters by his first name. It had been some kind of trick question. But she let the worry go; disregarding protocol at this juncture with someone as innocuous as Millicent Bromley was quite easy.

"Thank you, Miss Madeley," said Millicent and played with more gusto as she savoured the information. She would keep it to herself for now, like a stolen token he did not know she had taken.

* * *

Three more weeks went by and still no word from Lottie. He was growing very anxious. He rode to see his brother Rupert and his family, and on the way stopped off at the mansion owned by the Fitzwilliam family. A very grand estate in many acres but somewhat dilapidated these days. A lack of funds due to the squire's profligate spending habits while drinking and gaming.

Once there he bribed the stable boy to take him into the stable where her horse stood. The horse was a stallion of young years and he made a fuss of him, savouring the horse's closeness to Lottie, and then lifted his back hooves. They were clean, he had not been well ridden since persistent summer rain had set in a week ago.

He came from the stable where the boy was holding his own horse. "Hark, lad," he said in his authoritative classroom voice. "Have you seen Miss Charlotte of late?"

"Not lately, Sir," said the boy. "Folk has it she's left for good…months ago!"

"And she has not once returned, even briefly?"

The boy squinted up at him, the sun making brief appearance between grey and black clouds. "I dunna think so…you'd best ask at the kitchen, Sir…"

"Thank you," said Fairchild and gave him generous coinage for his service. "I may be back…but tell no-one of my visit today."

"I shonna, Sir," promised the lad, delighted with his earnings for five minutes work.

He would not ask at the kitchen, though he sorely wanted to, but to make himself known was to invite trouble.

"You can do nothing…" said Rupert as they sat in his study and drank coffee. "I shall make some enquiries of the parish clerk to see if she is by chance in either of the infirmaries…but if the stable lad has not seen her then I would take it she is still away…you must wait…and pray!"

He rolled his eyes; the praying part was too annoying for words. *God helped those who helped themselves!* It was one of his mother's favourite sayings, and he heartily agreed with it.

"I will leave that to you, Rupert!" he said. "You excel at it while I do not."

"Poor excuse, Tony!" said his brother. "Even discounting your sarcasm."

"I am often sarcastic, as you know…it gets me through life!" he replied.

"Stay for dinner at least!" entreated Rupert. "You have not seen your nephews and nieces in an age…not to mention Bella. I will be in trouble if she thinks I let you leave without pressing you to dine."

He liked Rupert's wife, Bella, a vicar's wife like his mother but with a more wicked sense of humour—they always shared laughter at the world in general whenever he called. "Tell her I will see her at Mother's birthday party next week…as long as Richard is not present."

Rupert maintained his composure, as he did in all situations. "He is our brother, Tony! And her middle son. Naturally he will be at her birthday party, I would imagine." He watched his youngest brother with a wary look. "And there must not…must not, I repeat, be any altercation between you."

"Tell him that…he starts them."

"Of course he does," said Rupert patiently, and then smiled. "That is what my five-year-old twin sons say of their older brother!"

He rose to leave, grinning a little despite the trials and tribulations. "Well, Ru, it actually goes to show how little the world changes, does it not!"

* * *

At his mother's birthday and despite his best efforts, he met with his brother Richard and his lady companion—who claimed to be thirty-five but was realistically more like fifty. A painted jade with social aspirations and a title which was inherited from a prior marriage. His brother had in the last year refused him a loan he badly needed, knowing full well that he was now able to repay it and was earning good money.

"Tony! Are you well?" chorused Richard, the 'painted jade' hanging on his arm.

"I am tolerably well, Richard," he replied, not able to dredge up any false or heartier response.

Richard moved in closer to him, necessitating Caroline to move with him, and lowered his voice. "Did you hear that Gerald Phipps is serving Fitzwilliam with a Breach of Promise suit?"

"What?" said Fairchild. "You jest!"

"I do not…tell him, Caroline…she knows the ins and outs…"

He moved his attention to Caroline Wentworth's face—his opaque green eyes immediately captivating her. She smiled sweetly, knowing even so that he would not return her smile; he disliked her, she knew…all Richard's family disliked her, but it did not deter her from liking him.

"Well?" he demanded, "What is it?"

Richard drew breath irritably. "I would not now tell him Caro, until he asks in a more polite fashion…and not as if addressing one of his blasted pupils…"

Caroline waved her closed fan at Richard and then obliged in a bored voice "My aunt is close with Phipps' mother, and she had the information from her…but don't ask me for more detail because I do not have it."

He paused while wondering if it was the truth, allowing Caroline's casual and hungry gaze to remain on his, and then after a second or two exclaimed, "Preposterous!"

"Phipps is claiming the betrothal was agreed between them and she has now run off," said Caroline Wentworth in the same bored voice.

"Inaccurate! Her father promised for her and was forcing her into it…'twill never stand in any court. She has run away to avoid Phipps…she wants nothing of him. 'tis common knowledge," said Anthony Fairchild.

"Nevertheless, he is suing," said Richard.

"Well, he is an idiot then…making himself look a bigger fool than he already is." He made a semi-bow to Caroline Wentworth and said coldly. "Thank you, Ma'am, for your insight!"

She smiled again and he did not. He turned to go and Richard followed him while Caroline let her attention move elsewhere in the hallway, thronged with guests for their mother's birthday celebration.

"Where is the chit anyway?" asked his brother in a whisper.

"I know not," he said. "And do you imagine I would tell you if I did!"

Richard heaved a sigh of contempt. "Tony, there is no need to be so damned sensitive on the subject."

"What?" He swung around and advanced towards Richard. "Sensitive! The woman I love has fled and I am not to be sensitive about your *insensitive* curiosity."

"You are well rid of the chit!" claimed Richard. "She is a fly-by-night floozy, obviously…she would—"

Fairchild silenced him by suddenly seizing him and pushing him against the wall, holding one arm against his upper chest. "If you talk about her in that way any further, I will knock your filthy teeth down your throat. If you had loaned me the money, I asked for… If you had shown one ounce of generosity, she might not have had to do what she has done…"

Rupert became aware of the fracas from further along the hall and broke away from his own conversation with guests and moved in quickly to pull his youngest brother away. "Stop this now! Have some respect." It was too late, of course, the hall had fallen silent as people watched.

Richard and Anthony Fairchild ignored Rupert and glared at one another. "And my teeth are not filthy…" said Richard airily, playing the buffoon to deflect the social awkwardness. "I pay a fortune to a fellow in Stafford who cleans and polishes them with some miracle potion."

"Well, I can save you your money, when I knock them out of your head," said Anthony Fairchild in a near whisper, straightening the cuffs of his jacket.

"You see, this is what he is like…" Richard said to no-one in particular and to anyone listening. "No wonder she has fled…between him and Phipps she cannot decide which of them might be the sanest."

He lunged at Richard but Rupert moved swiftly between them and pushed Richard away. "You are antagonising him purposely, Dick…"

"Take his side, Rupert! You usually do."

"'tis not a question of sides…" declared Rupert, "But of manners and decency. We do not need talk of Phipps tonight."

Then their mother came into the hall, weaving adroitly between guests. The butler having discreetly informed her. "You two are fighting," she said in despondent anger. "Tonight, of all nights, on my birthday!"

"Don't worry, Mama," said Rupert. "'twas just a spat."

"Whatever it was, it must stop immediately…" declared Mrs Fairchild, soon to change her last name on her second marriage.

"Mama, be easy and go into the drawing room and enjoy the party…nothing else will transpire here." Her youngest son assured her, taking her elbow to guide her, and Mrs Fairchild allowed herself to be steered in the direction of the large drawing room and then stopped and pulled her arm free. "Tony, I hope you do realise…" she said in a quiet mutinous voice, "that you hold a position of responsibility within the larger community now?"

"I do!" he said soothingly.

"Parents entrust their children to your care to be educated! A few of them present here tonight…they will not take kindly to seeing you brawling."

"Richard was goading him about Lottie Fitzwilliam…" Rupert said in his younger brother's defence.

"He has always goaded him, Rupert…" stated their mother. "And I would have hoped he could manage it all with more maturity these days…"

Both Rupert and Anthony looked at her in silence, they never argued with her wherever possible. She moved backwards to where Richard stood and said in a lower voice than before. "And you, Richard, appal me! Your malevolence grows worse with the years. Can you not see he is heartbroken about that girl? Do you have no sensibility that you ride roughshod through his finer feelings."

"Does he have any?" said Richard in unctuously gracious tones.

Mrs Fairchild looked askance at Caroline Wentworth as she joined them— bewigged and bejewelled and more painted than ever, like something from a doll factory—and then she looked again at Richard. "Were we not in such a crowd, I would slap your face."

She moved off to return to the drawing room and Lady Caroline said to Richard. "You should not have brought the subject up…you might have known what would happen!"

Richard, much displeased, swigged more of his wine. "For God's sake, not you too! The pair of them can do no wrong in her eyes, whereas I can do nothing right."

"No…really!" murmured Caroline sardonically.

"I must leave…" Anthony told Rupert and retrieved from his inside pocket a thin velvet package containing a silver filigree bookmark, purchased from the town jeweller supplying all the gifts he bought for his womenfolk. "Give her this for me, would you?"

Rupert held his arm to prevent him. "Wait until she has cut the cake…you can give it to her yourself. She will be upset if you go right away, straight after such upset."

"I have embarrassed myself, Rupert…and you and her…"

"They will soon lose interest…it will look worse if you leave…" Rupert was six or seven years his senior and he was long in the habit of deferring to his instructions. So he stayed where he was and suffered himself to be stared at from several directions. Women murmured and fluttered their fans, and the men raised their brows and smiled vaguely. Then the bishop (their future stepfather) loomed up suddenly and gripped his shoulder as a gesture to the room. "Come, Anthony, do not take this so hard…" he cajoled gently.

The bishop was a different sort of man altogether than their father, a different sort of cleric; a genial and sociable man with many influential connections in high places. Anthony Fairchild was yet to decide whether he liked him or not.

"I must apologise, Sir!" Fairchild told him. "My mother must enjoy her party and I will leave presently."

"No, no, there is no need…you are under pressure of the worst kind from this young woman's absence…and you may be forgiven for your temper loss…" The bishop said, and dropped his voice. "Besides, a little drama always adds to the occasion…people enjoy it, especially when it ends well."

He acquiesced to the bishop—soon to be stepfather—and the bishop was content. Hildegarde's sons had impeccable manners, with the exception perhaps of the middle one. He knew their heritage and their history, of course, having been at clerical college with Joseph Fairchild and a close friend of his.

Meantime the general gossip and ululation of the crowd returned to normal, rising like the low cry of gulls on the shore.

"He needs to grow up," Richard said in a furious tone to Caroline, "does little brother!"

"Oh, I do not know," she replied in her sanguine manner, having seen some of the female reaction. "He seems to be doing quite well as he is."

Richard closed his eyes in disdain and turned away from her before he said something else to bring him into disrepute. He was extremely jealous of his younger brother's effect on women.

* * *

Riding home he was even more desolate. He seethed about Richard, plus his own inability in these adult years to control his anger towards him. His inability to progress his life on lines he wished it to go was worsened by his brother's words and recent refusal of a loan he could well afford. He seethed too about his powerlessness to hold onto the woman he loved. Trapped in a job he did not really wish to be doing, perhaps for a long time. He was educated and seemingly with the world at his feet. But he could not get his life back on track.

By the time he had reached his lodgings, he had decided to employ an enquiry agent to trace Lottie, a hired sleuth to find the whereabouts of the theatre company. Before it was too late. But in his heart, he had this sense of foreboding that it was already too late.

By the Monday evening, he had contacted such an agent and waited for the man's reply regarding availability. Then on the Wednesday evening, while eating his evening meal in the dining room at Mrs Anstey's, a maid came to tell him there was someone in the communal parlour wanting to see him. This room was for the use of guests should they require it. "He thinks he needs to speak with you…" the maid told him.

"He thinks?" echoed Fairchild. "Is he not sure?"

"He is unsure of your identity…"

He finished his meal hurriedly, disturbed by the announcement, and went into the designated room. The man was about thirty, with the reserved air of someone charged with sensitive business.

"Forgive me…but I do not know yet if you are the person I am looking for. I am informed by your landlady that you are known often as Tony?" He extended his hand and introduced himself.

Fairchild smiled doubtfully; a curious opening to a conversation. "Yes, that is so. I am Anthony Fairchild, to be precise!"

The visitor retrieved from an envelope a tattered piece of paper—much faded…water-logged then dried, it seemed. The name 'Tony' was written in the top left corner and the address of the lodging house below it. He recognised Lottie's handwriting and stared at it for a few seconds, bracing himself before speaking. Then he looked into the man's face with a calm expression and raised his brows to invite explanation.

"It was taken up last week with a lady's purse, from the wreckage of the 'Countess of Galway'…" the man told him, "One of our passenger vessels… I am sorry to tell you it went down over a month ago in the Irish Sea in very bad weather."

"Went down?" he repeated dumbly.

"We are only now able to go through the items salvaged. This may have belonged to a Miss Charlotte Fitzwilliam, sailing with an English theatre company, we believe…"

He could not comprehend; his mind would not process the information. He stared at the clerk who returned the stare with a blank face, having encountered many reactions in similar circumstances.

"It is her handwriting," Fairchild confirmed. "But where is she now?"

The man bowed his head to dignify his next statement. "We believe she drowned, my good Sir, with most of the other passengers…"

The world tipped and tilted as if the building in which they stood was itself a floundering ship.

"There were only a very few survivors and she was sadly not one of them…"

He fell into a chair and stared at the wall. The clerk waited in respectful silence then offered a further envelope containing the gold pin he had sent her which had been also in the purse, the only thing of value. Anthony Fairchild held it and rubbed two fingers over its surface as if he might conjure her from the gold. "She is dead then!" he whispered.

Unsure whether this was a query or a statement the clerk cleared his throat and spoke carefully. "We should like to extend our deepest condolences to you in your loss…"

He wanted to exclaim, to yell…'*and what good does that do me?*' but he did not, he could not speak. It was not this man's fault.

"Was she related to you?" ventured the man with gentle diplomacy.

"My fiancé."

The clerk again left a silence; words, he had discovered, were nothing short of clumsy in these moments. "Perhaps you could inform others of her family or associates?"

He blinked acknowledgement and the man again waited, in case there were more questions, then said, "I shall leave you to your grief, my dear Sir." He placed a hand on the other's shoulder and left the room without a sound. Not even the tread of his boots.

The shock and devastation were colossal. Unparalleled with anything he had experienced in life to date. Some unfathomable time later Mrs Anstey came at his side where he still sat, her skirts rustling to announce her arrival. "My dear boy," she intoned. "Can I get you anything? A brandy perhaps?"

He shook his head, not removing his eyes from a fixed point on the far wall.

"You may be better off upstairs resting…" declared the landlady. "You have had a terrible shock…"

He stood. "Thank you, I do not require anything."

A terrible shock was when you discovered all your money had been stolen, or you had lost your horse in a card game. This was beyond shock. It was a mortifying impasse which rendered near paralysis of the limbs and the mind.

He drank for ten hours in places he lost count of and could not recall entering. And eventually, Clara Anstey found him slumped against the wall at the top of the front steps in the early morning, staring and incoherent. She helped him rise and enlisted the porter's aid. "Come on, my duck," she said brightly. "Whatever this is, 'tis better dealt with in private…let's go up the stairs."

They helped him to his room. *He had been taken ill,* she informed two other guests encountered on the stairway, although the smell of strong drink belied the fact. They laid him on his bed and the porter took off his boots. Left alone with him, she pulled off his clothes and sat beside him. His eyes were wide open and glazed and occasionally he blinked. She knew it to be a state of terror amid the alcoholic daze. "What is it, Anthony?" she enquired softly after a quarter hour, placing damp cloths on his forehead and making him drink water. "What has happened?" She had not seen her mother the previous night to ascertain the news.

He remained mute, time had ceased to exist in any reality. Some fifteen minutes later he suddenly told her. "Lottie is dead…drowned…in the Irish Sea."

Clara Anstey shifted on the chair beside his bed and searched her mind before realising who Lottie was. He had talked to her of his fiancé, just as she had talked to him of her own. She said nothing, holding his hand—lifeless and cold. "I'll fetch the physic."

"Do not…" he said. "I have no wish to live…so do not trouble!"

She held his hand tighter and shook it a little. "Listen, you ain't to say that nor think it. This dreadful hurting will pass…all things pass…you must be braver."

He turned his head and looked at her. "Braver!" he muttered.

"Wishing death on yourself is a kind of cowardice…"

"Oh!" he said, without feeling or reaction.

"You are stronger than that Anthony Francis Fairchild…" She had seen other people before wish for death and knew that often it passed soon enough.

He stared at her longer, distracted from the misery for a moment by her use of his middle name. She smiled. "I saw your name on the banker's draft when you first arrived… If that is what you're wondering… I was curious about you so I stuck my nose into the paperwork…you know how I am! Never backwards at coming forwards, to quote my ma."

He turned his face away. There was an insipid pause, a sort of lull in the reality he had left behind since the news. Clara felt it too; awful and leaden and not to be quantified or dismissed.

"Do you think she would want you to die too?" she continued. "… A'fore your time? And you only five and twenty!"

"She was only just three and twenty!" he said.

"What was she doing getting drowned?" asked Clara, grasping the nettle in a matter-of-fact way.

"She was sailing from Ireland where she had been performing…"

"Well, then…she died an honourable death, in the service of what she did best."

"Honourable?" he echoed feebly. "Yes, perhaps she did!"

"And she would not want you dying a dishonourable one…"

He looked at this girl, not much more than Lottie's age herself, daughter of his landlady, capable and down-to-earth. This comely barmaid whose bed he shared on certain nights…and he wondered at her wisdom.

She began to tell him of her thoughts on the afterlife and God, or whatever ruled the earthly world and beyond… *She was not sure if it was God or some other kind of force, like the county council and the town hall, only bigger of course, and mightier. How there must be such a body because weird things happened that could not be explained. Not even by chemists and philosophers and the like…*

He listened to her in semi-fascination, and he might have smiled had he the energy. How easily one was diverted in his weakened state, mentally, emotionally and physically.

Afterwards in the days and the weeks following he saw that she had saved his life. She had brought to it a sense of proportion, some strange sort of momentary order to the chaos that had no name. He began to understand what his brother Rupert often told him: the proof of the divine was in the small inconsequential things, in the impromptu occurrences.

She talked to him for hours that morning as he went in and out of some melancholy alcohol fuelled delirium. She spoke quietly and endlessly as the day lengthened into afternoon, ignoring all the other duties she no doubt needed to attend to. Until eventually he squoze her hand weakly, and she knew then he would live. Knew that she was safe to leave him. His skin was icy cold and beads of sweat stood on his forehead. He needed medical assistance of a discreet kind.

The physician who attended the guest house was summoned, and he came within the hour.

He took to his bed for four days and Clara brought him food and saw to his needs or arranged for the two maids to do so in her absence. Occasionally she climbed into the bed beside him and held him.

He thought her a marvellous woman. Had she been of his class in society he would have wanted to wed her. But she was not of his class and she did not wish it either. She would wed her drayman and he would…he knew not! Nevertheless, the time she devoted to his recovery was a miracle of some kind.

* * *

He returned to work the week after, looking like someone recovering from illness, or an upset of great magnitude.

Barton Grange upper form girls noted it right away after his first five minutes in the classroom.

"He has a sickness of the soul…" Melissa told them in the afternoon break. "He has suffered a tragedy or similar…"

"How do you know?" asked Miranda.

"Just by looking at him," replied Melissa. "And I can feel his pain when he walks by…"

Melanie sighed extravagantly. "How touching!"

"Positively holy!" agreed Lucinda.

"You will be telling us next you feel sorry for him," said Annabelle.

"I do," said Melissa. "One can feel sorry for someone without actually liking them, you know."

"Can one?" queried Lucinda. "Surely one has to be sainted for that?"

"No, one does not…" corrected Jane. "One has merely to be humane."

"Indeed," agreed Melissa. "'tis a matter of sensitivity."

"Well, Joan of Arc…" said Melanie skittishly. "I am not about to be swayed by his suffering, whatever it has been…tyrants and monsters become ill and upset as others do, but it does not mean they are any less tyrannical and monstrous…"

Ebb, Flow and Consequences

Time went by, days without end, monotonous in their repetition. He ceased to note the passing of them. By the start of the new school term, Melissa and Melanie had just turned fifteen within a month of each other. Henrietta Madeley handed in her resignation, on the first day of her return from the holiday. Nicholas Stevenson told him of it in his capacity as deputy head—soon to take the headship when Martin Frondley retired.

"Has this something to do with your attentions upon her?" Stevenson asked casually as he played chess with William Rudlow, the other maths master besides himself. Stevenson studied women as he studied numbers and chess. He was an expert and could have written many books, were he inclined to sharing his findings with other mortals. Only certain men, he perceived, were suited to appreciating his arcane wisdom. Women were drawn to him with ease, and he caused in them a reaction similar to the one Fairchild evoked. He was impressive in demeanour, distinguished from the mediocre by the arrangement of all his bodily features and his character within them.

Fairchild paused before answering. "I am no longer paying her attention," he replied wearily, marking exercise books.

"That will be an affirmative then!" said Rudlow, as unremarkable in appearance as his two colleagues were distinctive.

"Lord above, Tony!" Stevenson opined. "What have you done to the girl?"

"Nothing whatever… I simply implied I would not be able to marry her."

Stevenson had vivid blue eyes radiating strength and he raised them sharply above the steel rimmed spectacles worn for close scrutiny. Rudlow, a married man of middle age, let out a hoot of laughter. "That will do it!"

"I was simply being honest!" he told them flatly.

"There is honesty and then there is sheer lack of subtlety," countered Rudlow humorously.

Fairchild groaned softly and stared at the far wall. Not about to defend himself and his private life when he knew he had no other choice, given the sort of woman Henrietta was.

"They are not like us, Tony…they do not just shake hands and agree to differ, as we do. They take these things badly. Now we have to find another needlework and music teacher for the henhouse," remarked Stevenson.

"Should not be so difficult, surely?" he commented, finishing the last of the marking. "There must be more of them around the region."

"S'truth!" muttered Rudlow. "The boy has become a callous rake in next to no time." The older members of staff were fond of ragging him, as with all the young teachers who joined, and Rudlow was enjoying the opportunity while he surveyed the pieces on the board.

Stevenson said, "Yes, perhaps they are not so hard to come by, but not sweet little things like Henrietta…the girl is a plum and you have to admit it."

"You should not have dallied with her!" added Rudlow.

"I did not dally with her. I merely took her walking…" he said calmly.

Rudlow ignored him. "She is quite fragile…anyone can see it. She is not cut from the same cloth as Judith Tongs."

"I have not dallied with Judith Tongs either…" he told Rudlow.

"Not yet perhaps…but watch out…you are just her kind of fellow…"

"So they all keep telling me… I did not lay a finger on Henrietta, beyond holding her hand to assist her over stiles and so on…" persisted Fairchild.

Stevenson concentrated on the chess as he spoke. "That is quite enough for genteel women like Henrietta…there does not have to be any more than that to induce them into falling in love and hoping for marriage."

"I did not encourage her affections in any way. I was merely…" he broke off in exasperation.

"Merely what?" enquired Rudlow. "Entertaining yourself?"

"Perhaps," he admitted, "And her also…"

Some laughter erupted from both the older men so that he felt callow and naive.

"If you wish to entertain ladies, you should look to Nick for contacts…" Rudlow said, his eyes on Stevenson's knight. "He knows more of them than the Town's Women's' Guild…"

"Yes, with discernment! And there speaks the envy of a married man!" replied Stevenson airily.

"Quite possibly!" concurred Rudlow.

"And if this wench of yours does not reappear…" continued Stevenson, "You may look differently upon Miss Madeley. She is wifely material if ever there was such a thing."

Fairchild flung the pencil down to the table and rose. "I am not in the way of wanting a wife, thank you." He strode to the door before he lost his temper.

"And when a replacement is found…" Rudlow called after him, "take care not to dally with her…or take her walking…or any other of the pastimes which may be construed as romantic overtures…" This was meant as further comedy but fell wide off the mark.

Fairchild paused at the door and bristled, "You have my word, Mr Rudlow. I shall not even engage her in conversation when our paths cross."

"Oh, for God's sake," said Stevenson. "From the sublime to the ridiculous! Then she will think you are being churlish…whoever she might be."

"Better that than a *callous rake,*" he retorted and both men stared, unable to believe he was taking it so seriously. "And just so you are aware, Nick, the wench you refer to will not reappear…she is dead!" he announced flatly, lingering in the doorway, embarrassed by his personal tragedy.

Stevenson dropped his knight in surprise and Rudlow and he exchanged looks uncomfortably—they had been playing with him, employing banter for the hell of it.

"Dead?" repeated Stevenson. "Your fiancé is dead?"

"She drowned off a passenger ship from Ireland…the reason I was indisposed before the holidays."

Stevenson stood quickly. "Tony, I am most sincerely sorry."

"As am I…" Rudlow was flummoxed and embarrassed himself now…"My dear boy… I do not know what to say…"

"Why did you not tell us sooner?" queried Stevenson.

"Because I could not bring myself to speak of it…"

Before anything further could be added, he left the staff room and went out into the grounds to stroll and smoke a cigar before teaching.

In his wake, Rudlow said, "Well, I'll be eternally damned! Who was this young woman? Do you know?"

"I have heard from the gossips…" Stevenson cleared his throat and lowered his voice confidentially, even though they were alone in the room, "that she was Bartholmew Fitzwilliam's daughter…"

"You jest!" said Rudlow, shocked. "No wonder she fled from home, having that bastard for a father."

"Just so!" said Stevenson. "But pray, do not quote me on it."

"Naturally not," responded the other.

"And I believe he cared greatly for her," added the deputy head.

Rudlow pondered, then rallied in spirit. "But he is young...he will find another to love..."

Stevenson held a chess piece aloft. "Perhaps, but a man may search for years..." he said in the voice of experience, neatly clipping his opponent's bishop. "'tis not like hiring a housemaid, you know, Will! One does not order one's heart the way one orders his mind..."

Rudlow reflected: he had many offspring and a lot of years in the service of wedlock. Rumour had it that Mrs Rudlow was a veritable gorgon and ruled the household with a rod of iron. He had forgotten what it was to recognise romance and desire. "Well, Nick," he concluded, lamenting the loss of his bishop. "I must bow to your greater knowledge on the matter."

Stevenson inclined his head with feigned humility and said, "At any rate, try not to tell him he's a *callous rake* when broaching the matter with him..."

"Oh, I shan't be broaching the matter with him... I am far too long in the tooth. I shall leave it to you aficionados of the female gender..." said Rudlow in jocularity.

* * *

Following her epiphany, Millie viewed life somewhat differently, especially in the classroom. She now yearned to be seen utterly as one of the rest of them, not the prim and prudish nonentity they held her as—setting aside her musical gift which everyone acknowledged but which had nothing to do with her person, she felt; it was not enough. She had been brooding on it over the holiday, in her loneliness, in her grandmother's austere house with its foreboding atmosphere of sterile life.

On the following week as soon as the conversation turned to Fairchild (whom Melanie named '*Atilla the Hun*' owing to his facial features and blonde hair) she listened for her cue.

"... Madeley has only resigned because of him," Lucinda was saying in the interim after the lesson and before they departed for luncheon.

"Then more fool her!" proclaimed Melanie. "I would not let him drive me from my position…no matter how badly he treated me."

"He may not have treated her badly!" said Jane, the voice of reason as always. "He may just have refused to speak of marriage."

"That will be it," agreed Melissa. "She is quite desperate to procure a husband."

"She must indeed be desperate to consider him suitable," said Miranda. "I shall write another ode to honour the happening… I have something meaty to go on now." The first lines already in her mind.

"And I have more to add," said Millicent, standing and moving to the front of the room.

They watched her in surprise. There were only about half of the class still lingering, while the rest had gone to eat. Some of the former girls had left at the summer break, as near as possible to their sixteenth birthday. The departed pupils were replaced by girls from the lower form who had now reached fourteen, and there were currently three of these.

"I have his first name?" announced Millie into the expectant pause.

"Are you sure?" queried Melissa.

"Quite certain… Miss Madeley told me. I tricked her into it."

The room was filled with an almost palpable disbelief at the change in Millicent Bromley and the idea of her tricking Miss Madeley. "Well, do not keep us in suspense…" Melanie cried. "What is it?"

"'tis Anthony!" Millicent proclaimed with muted relish.

"Anthony?" echoed Jane. "As in the saint?"

"No!" snorted Melanie. "The Roman General!"

"Give her the kitty," sanctioned Prescilla.

Melanie took the kerchief containing the money from her bag and tossed it to Millicent who merely looked at it—it was not the money that had inspired her to act.

"Do cheer up," Lucinda said, "You have won it fairly and squarely…"

Millicent was heartened, it was what she had wanted—to be included as one of them. But she still felt like Judas. "I did not contribute to the kitty…" she said warily.

"That matters not, Millie!" Melanie reassured her. "You have earned it."

"Wait before you open it…" Miranda cautioned. "Let us be sure he has left the building first."

"He has left, I saw him from this window ride from the stables," announced Annabelle.

Melissa sprang from her seat and took the chalk and wrote on the board in large letters—ANTONY.

"It has an aitch," Lucinda amended.

She rubbed it out and put in the aitch, and then after a second or two added AND CLEOPATRA next to it. There was much frivolity and exhilaration. So, Melanie seized the duster and erased the Egyptian queen's name and, in its place, wrote HENRIETTA.

It now read: 'ANTHONY AND HENRIETTA.'

And then Melissa took up the chalk again and drew a heart around the names and stuck an arrow through the whole of it.

"That may bring her the luck she needs," said Lucinda.

"'tis more like to be a curse," said Annabelle.

They admired the handiwork on the board for moments and Miranda had completely forgotten her surveillance of the corridor and started as if he were an apparition on his appearance in the doorway. She turned suddenly in shock and gave a loud, almost blood curdling squeal.

Immediately out of the gates, he had remembered he had left books needed for the lesson with the lower form boys on his desk and had ridden back to the house.

He was for a second bemused by her squeal—even though the silence was now deafening. He entered the room a little way, as surprised as Miranda was as he almost collided with her. Miranda froze. Melanie froze also—standing near the board. The rest hurried to their places and sat.

He surveyed them in bland curiosity and seeming ignorance of the fact, and then Melanie came to life and darted for the duster. But he was quicker and intercepted her, catching her arm in mid-air, taking the duster from her hand and turning to view the board.

They were paralysed in unified shock, as in the seconds following a disaster.

"Sit down," he told Melanie in his usual low and even tone.

They looked at each other, there were but eight of them present and they watched his double careful perambulation of the room, deep in thought, his trajectory going from left to right, around the desks and back again, his head bowed, his hands behind him and concealed beneath the folds of his cutaway up-to-the-minute jacket. He was completely mortified. His heavy grief for Lottie, the recent comments by male staff on his liaison with Henrietta, her resignation, Clara's departure from the lodging house. Even his mother's forthcoming second marriage… In his inner turmoil he saw this chalking almost as a personal attack.

"Who is responsible for this?" he enquired at length, still in a calm voice; he must keep his patient and controlled approach to misdemeanour now. It was vital if he were not to lose all control and throttle one of them. "Well?" he repeated in a more brittle tone.

Melanie and Melissa rose slowly to their feet.

"I might have guessed," he murmured.

Then Millicent rose also and he spun around in disbelief to see her. "Miss Bromley, are you telling me you had a hand in this?" He was unable to credit the fall from grace of the usually shy and model pupil.

"Yes, Sir," said Millie miserably. "'twas all my fault…without me it would never have happened."

Melanie made a loud gasp of incredulity at this martyrdom and he flashed her a dark look, forbidding her to speak. "You are sure?" he said to Millicent.

"Yes, I am, Sir!" said Millie, close to tears.

He circled the room again in its entire periphery, unable all at once to deal with the incident. "You may go," he said to the other five girls present. "If you are sure you had nothing to do with this chalking on the board."

Lucinda looked hesitant and was about to speak, but Melanie shook her head at her and indicated for her to leave, confident that she could manage the confrontation and get it to blow over.

"You will deliver me one hundred lines for Thursday… '*Manners maketh man and procrastination is the thief of time*'…and if there is but one mistake in any of it or one ink blot, you will do it all again…" Fairchild announced.

The five girls filed out slowly, looking back at the guilty three; Millicent, Melissa and Melanie, who shared the blame, and the same first initial to their names.

As the door closed Melanie shut her eyes tight and blurted the only excuse she could think of. "They are characters from a novel, Sir!" she told him, her voice sounding odd in the quiet room where nothing stirred.

He came to a standstill and said, "What was that?" She blinked rapidly. Melissa kicked her under the desk—she was liable to make everything worse now with her vivid imagination.

"Anthony and Henrietta…they are characters in a novel I read…"

"And what is the title of this novel?" he asked with the greatest scepticism.

She swept her eyes along the desk tops in desperation, her mind blank. "It escapes me for the moment."

"Of course it does!" he said darkly. "Can you produce this book?"

"No, 'tis not mine… I have returned it."

"Have you indeed?"

"Yes…but it is about a girl who goes as governess to a duke in Scotland and she—"

He slammed the flat of his hand down on the desk in front of them and they jumped at the sound and Melanie tailed off. "Miss Petersham, if you add one more layer to this elaborate tissue of lies, I shall arrange for your expulsion from this school before the day is out! Do you take me for a complete idiot?"

"No, Sir, we…" but for once Melanie was unable to find words and fell silent.

Melissa had wanted the lavatory since the lesson ended and felt that if she did not go soon, she would have an accident. She crossed her legs and squirmed in her seat. Sensing this movement, he turned to her. "And what have you to say for yourself?"

She fixed her intelligent grey eyes on him, filled with abject terror. "Nothing whatever, Sir… I cannot think of anything," she added in her usual direct manner, so open to misunderstanding.

"I am not surprised, Miss Shaw…for there is nothing to say… I have never met with such flagrant vulgarity and insolence in my entire life."

Millicent had begun to cry; rasping dry sobs which rent the air and disturbed the stillness.

"Stop that immediately," he told her. "It will do you no good whatever."

She endeavoured to stop, swallowed hard several times and spluttered, her shoulders shaking convulsively in this her first experience of serious trouble. She had ruined her life and things would not be the same ever again.

"Do you realise how grave this breach of conduct and protocol is? Were you trying to get yourselves expelled?" he enquired, leaning against the wall next to the blackboard.

Melissa thought of being expelled; of being free of him and his demands and his wretched criticism of her work and handwriting. Then she thought of the scandal that would ensue after expulsion and of her parents' anger, especially her father's. She would never hear the last of it. "No, Sir, we were not!" She looked at Melanie to support this and Melanie nodded, her eyes blank and wide and fixed on Melissa's face as if she did not fully understand but was agreeing for the sake of it. He turned to Millicent in an almost gracious manner, and she said, "I do not wish to be expelled either, Sir!" Although she felt that nothing could matter now and that death would be preferable.

He cleared his throat and became resolved, straightening up from the wall. "I shall see the three of you at five minutes past four today in this classroom. I shall return and expect to find you here. Then I will deal with the matter."

He picked up the pile of exercise books and left the classroom.

No-one spoke until Melissa said in a hushed tone. "What do you think he will do?"

"Cane us," replied Millicent.

"Then why did he not just do so now?" said Melanie.

"Because he is short of time," Millicent replied and began again to cry.

"Shut up, you ninny…" snapped Melanie. "You and your morbid confession have made matters worse. Without that I may have thought of something to tell him which he couldn't disprove."

"No, Melanie," said Melissa from her well of despair, "There is nothing you can think of to say. We have gone too far and he has caught us out."

"'twas my fault," reiterated Millie.

"I was the one who wrote his name on the board, Millie, stop blaming yourself," Melissa intoned.

"Oh, that is right…" Melanie leapt to her feet. "Fight between you about the blame, but I will have none of it. He is too full of his own importance. If he had a heart, he would see that what we wrote was quite endearing."

"Of course he would not," Melissa objected. "He is a man. He sees only the embarrassment."

"Well, I am not being bested by him," cried Melanie. "I will think of something."

"I doubt you will." Millicent held her drenched kerchief like a wet rag from her hand.

"She will not," concurred Melissa. "Though she will spend the afternoon wracking her brains…we must just face the consequences."

"Consequences my eye! What is he going to do? Organise our execution?" Melanie began gathering her belongings. "He has said he will not expel us, or as good as…what can he do that is so bad?" She made for the door and the other

116

two followed her. Her mind was conjuring possibilities for getting them home free. "And do not say anything about the kitty!" she advised. "Whatever he threatens us with, say nothing about where we had his name from, or everything will spin out of control."

"Can it be any more out of control than it is?" asked Melissa drearily.

"Of course it can…" Melanie marched ahead and ran down the stairs and waited for them. "You two are so weak-kneed! Just because we have written his name and Henrietta's does not necessitate him enacting a Cheltenham tragedy… Say nothing to damn us more."

"I shall say nothing!" promised Millicent. "I am too ashamed… I have let him down."

"For God's sake…" Melanie spun around on Millie and hissed at her. "What about us? I suppose you will tell us next that he is just doing his job."

"I do not need to state the obvious," said Millie. "He *is* doing his job."

"I think you've gone potty, Millicent Bromley! There is no other explanation!"

"Except the one where she is in love with him…" sighed Melissa. "As Jane has suggested."

"Are you?" demanded Melanie. "Are you in love with him, Millie?"

"Of course not," said Millicent stoically, and broke down into fresh gales of weeping.

* * *

In the staffroom Henrietta Madeley, Judith Tongs and Henry Stringer, having finished their luncheon, were taking their ease in armchairs. The maid had brought Fairchild a dish of something, even though he had not asked for it. The maid too had a partiality for him which consisted of fantasy and rendering him unsolicited kindnesses.

"I have no time to eat it," he told them as he dashed in and hurriedly downed some coffee. "I must leave now, I am very late… Judith, I will see you in your office at just after four. I have a serious incident of misconduct among the upper form girls and I must talk to you of it today…it cannot wait."

Judith looked at him with interest, they all looked at him with interest. Then Henrietta swept her eyes from him as if he were an annoying presence she was glad to look away from. When he had gone, Henry Stringer said merrily, "Have they tied him up and relieved him of his wallet, do you think?"

"'twill be nothing," said Henrietta. "They will have dared to talk in his lesson or something similar. He is very severe with them, you know, Mr Stringer."

Judith tutted, "She means he is strict."

"I mean what I say," snapped Henrietta. "I do know the difference."

"I doubt you do…you cannot even bring yourself to raise your voice to them, so I doubt you know the difference."

"I expect he is so because he is still afraid of them," said Stringer. "It is quite a test of character for someone his age, dealing with teenage girls in a classroom."

Judith replied in an imperial tone, "Left to you two, the place would be an utter shambles, for neither of you have the first idea of discipline. I am sick and tired of being the only one here to command any respect. I welcome the presence of someone like him."

Mr Stringer ignored this attack upon his professionalism and Henrietta barely heard it. "You will tell us what he has said?" she queried.

"I might!" said Judith. "It depends what it is. I might not wish to disclose it…if it is of a confidential nature."

"It cannot be anything so bad, surely," said Henry Stringer. "They are little girls, when all is said and done."

Henrietta stood up and shook her head at him. "Of course they are, but she is simply drunk with her own power… I am glad I am leaving this place."

"Or you are just peeved because he would not move to marriage with you," sniped Judith.

"You know nothing of it," Henrietta retorted with asperity. "He is not the kind of husband I am seeking."

"And what kind is that? Someone with most of his faculties and below the age of eighty!" said Judith nastily as Henrietta swept from the room, her taffeta dress rustling in the air around her like the leaves of the lilac bushes in the gardens.

* * *

Flights of Fancy and Rude Awakenings

In the afternoon dancing lesson, Miss Madeley had problems with her harpsichord and did not at first notice that Millicent was absent. She had removed her dancing shoes and was standing on the music stool attempting to look into the depth of the instrument, being unable to locate the caretaker who was usually able to fix all these kinds of problems.

"Where is Millie?" enquired Jane into the babble of voices. They looked around and saw no sign of Millie who was normally near Miss Madeley, preparing music to be played or seated at either the piano or the harpsichord.

"Perhaps she is in the cloakroom!" said Lucinda.

"She is not… I have only just come from it," rejoined Prudence, one of the recent lower form pupils to come up. Several of them looked out of the window to the lavatory, located away from the main building, housed in a square brick structure some twenty-five yards to the right. They watched for her coming out but saw no movement.

"Millicent is missing…" chirped Miranda to Henrietta and Henrietta climbed down from the stool, puffing out her breath and blowing the hair from her face. "What? Where is she?"

"If we knew that she would not be missing," said Melanie.

Miss Madeley made an exasperated noise and shook out her voluminous skirts. "Melanie, do not be so impertinent…that is just the kind of statement which gets you into trouble."

Melanie smirked and momentarily forgot the main problem of the day.

"Go and find her…" said Henrietta, "'tis most unlike her…she may be unwell…"

"She will not be quite well, Miss Madeley…" began Annabelle importantly, "Because this morning, she—" The tale-telling was cut short by Melanie who came behind Annabelle and dug her sharply in the back with her elbow. Annabelle squealed.

"Do not breathe a word of it," hissed Melanie. "We have enough to deal with without Madeley falling into a fit of the vapours."

"Go and find Millie…" the music teacher said to anyone listening. "Time is getting on…do not all stand there like statues."

"I will go…" said Melanie and looked to Melissa and indicated the door with her head.

"Yes… I shall come too." Melissa took up her pelisse, for the day was very cool.

"Me too," said Lucinda.

Others leapt forwards but Miss Madeley sanctioned: "No, three is quite enough…there are not many places she can be…the rest of you take your positions to dance. I will play and then Miranda can play after ten minutes…"

Miranda hated playing and pulled faces at Melissa and Lucinda as they stared at her and warned her with looks and hand gestures not to say anything of the board chalking. Melanie was striding already along the passageway.

They caught up after a few minutes with Millicent—scurrying through the low trees close to the main gates. Her cloak wrapped around her and her bonnet pulled forwards. She was carrying her satchel which bulged in all the wrong places. Melanie caught her arm to stop her movement. "Where are you going, Millie?"

Millicent did not reply, she was beside herself with terror and it was evident from her face and her swollen eyes.

"Millie, where do you think you are going?" Melissa took her other arm to turn her back towards the school, Melanie holding tight to the arm carrying the satchel.

"I am going away," pronounced Millicent, unintentionally melodramatic.

"Away where?" scoffed Lucinda.

"Anywhere… I cannot face the consequences of my actions." She began to pull herself free from their grip but Lucinda caught hold of her shoulder, obstructing her further.

"Millie, you are being ridiculous," said Melanie. "This will be over by tomorrow…what can he do that is so bad?"

"He can cane you until you faint…" said Lucinda, as dramatic as Millie. "If he so chooses."

"Of course he cannot…" Melanie took Millie's satchel and began to undo the fastenings to see inside, all the while giving her summary of the pending proceedings. "He is bound by certain restraints and protocols. He can cane us certainly, but not to some dangerous degree as you are suggesting…where do you imagine we are!"

"I cannot face what he will think of me," said Millicent. "For I will have to tell him all."

"You will not tell him all!" cried Melanie fiercely. "Tell him nothing at all…beyond what he imagines he knows. 'tis better that way…or Madeley will become embroiled and there will be more trouble."

"She is leaving!" declared Millicent in childish turmoil. "'tis all very well for her." *How could Henrietta Madeley just leave the school and desert her like that! Millicent was bereft at the thought.*

"Millicent!" Melissa said more gently. "Retract what you have told him and say you really had no part in it beyond passing me the chalk…then he will let you off with lines or something."

"'tis not punishment I fear!" Millie was slowly sinking to the ground. "I deserve that!"

"Here she goes again with this ridiculous martyrdom in her own head." Melanie's voice was rising, until Melissa nudged her to quieten her. "Then what is it?"

"'tis other things," said Millicent inaudibly.

"'tis she is in love with him!" said Lucinda carelessly and Melissa shot her a furious look. But for once Millicent did not deny it. Her satchel containing bread and cold meats and hastily wrapped in cheesecloth fell to the ground as Melanie pulled it open. "Is this from the kitchen?" she asked.

Millicent nodded. "To eat while I travel."

"You will get no further than the turnpike," said Melissa. "They will send out a search for you…the constabulary will be summoned."

"Yes," said Lucinda with glee. "Then they will add theft to your tarnished reputation."

"Shut up!" said Melanie and Lucinda made to reply tartly but Melissa intervened. "'tis true you have stolen food…but they will not hang you even if they find out… Millie, come back with us…and do as I suggest and tell him you were not actually involved. He will punish us but not you."

"Yes, but he will then punish you two twice as badly…" added Lucinda with relish.

Hitting the ground hard with a stick she was using to push back bushes and stalks, Melanie finally exploded. "Lucinda, if you say another thing, I shall rip up my petticoat and use the material to bind your mouth and tie you to a tree. And do not think I will not….if you are not actually a Judas in a frock, then you are a Job's Comforter, and I do not know which is worse…"

"I am only stating the truth!" said the hapless Lucinda, "And if you lift one finger to me, I shall bite you and claw you, Melanie Petersham…until they think wolves have been at you."

"Stop it!" cried Melissa stridently. "The gibberish you talk." She began lifting Millie from the ground where she had fallen to her knees in almost blind hysteria. "Come now, Millie…see the greater trouble you will cause us if you do not…think about it for a moment…you will leave us to face the music alone and that is not like you at heart."

Millie let out an anguished cry and then became still. "Yes, you are right. I am a coward."

"Come!" Melissa encouraged, like the mother Millie had hardly known, and Millicent allowed herself to be led towards the school. "Throw the food down into the bushes for the wildlife," she called to Lucinda, "And conceal the muslin…and don't say anything else, either of you…"

Melanie and Lucinda allowed themselves to be subdued by Melissa's wiser guidance as they walked back to the main building. Melissa with her arm around Milicent, patting her now and then as if she were a distressed infant. And calmed by this in her loveless and bleak existence, Millicent fell into some kind of stupor as she moved.

"We shall take her to the sick-room where she can lie down," instructed Melissa. "Lucy, you must go and tell Madeley we found her unwell and have left her to recover…and do not say anything else to her about any of it."

"No, no…" Melanie became animated, snapping out of the spell. "I will tell Madeley…blabbermouth here cannot be trusted to say only that… Lucinda, you go with them to the sick-room and then return to Madeley's lesson."

"What if she tries to run away again…or faints? 'twill need three of us to carry her," Lucinda argued.

"I shall not run away again…" said Millie. "I see now that it was quite wrong…and I shall not faint. I cannot leave you to face him alone."

They entered the building by the side door, hesitating for a few seconds before rounding the corridor to the sick-room. The colour was returning slightly to Millicent's waxen face—she was naturally very pale and often looked as if she might fade away within the hour.

Melissa told them. "I am quite terrified myself…but I have come to see over the course of the day that there is nothing so terrible in what we did. 'tis only in his mind."

"You are right!" whispered Millicent. "But that does not make me feel better."

"'tis his arrogant self-importance…" said Lucinda blithely.

Melissa was covering Millie with a blanket. "'tis the torment of his soul…we have worsened it."

"Good," said Lucinda. "I hope he dies from it."

"He will not die from it," said Melissa.

"And that is a very wicked thing to say, Lucy…" whispered Millie, falling deeper into an exhausted doze.

* * *

Meantime Nicholas Stevenson was searching for Anthony Fairchild in the grounds surrounding the vicinity of the boys school during the afternoon recess. He feared yet another resignation, which would stretch staffing levels beyond what was reasonable and cause chaos in the schedule, or worse—complaints about poor grades. He was determined to talk him out of such a move and convinced he could succeed.

Fairchild was not to be found. He had seen Stevenson striding around the lawns and had stepped back deeper into an enclave of low overhanging willow and cedar trees, obscured and out of sight. He felt like one of the pupils; skulking and guilty and avoiding consequences.

It had occurred to him that he could actually just ignore this morning's incident by the upper form girls. Put it from his mind totally. He could simply see it as a good reason to resign. Hand in his notice, pretend it never happened and carry on to the end of the term without another worry. It was the easy way out, he felt, and it would solve all his problems. It would draw a line under this part of his career and he would resolve never to teach girls again, least not girls of their age and ilk. In fact, he could saddle his horse now and ride out of the place and never ride back…

They would be waiting for him after four, sitting in the classroom, and he could not simply go in and hand them some lines and a strong telling off and expect them not to feel victorious. And then expect them not to believe in their own inviolability—until they attempted something similar the next time. He either left at the end of the week or he made now, this day, significant gesture to his authority. He watched the lit end of his cigar and contemplated.

He could not just walk away from this now as if it had not occurred; he was not that type of man! If he left at the half term, three weeks away, he could take office as a clerk somewhere. Perhaps adding a few more pounds to his salary by using his language skills where required. The thought of it was dreary. He did not mind teaching, certainly not the boys; he was a good teacher, a good communicator, it came easily to him. He was not a defeatist, nor a coward.

Why should he allow a group of girls to get the better of him! How could he look himself in the mirror if he simply walked out and did not come back? Leaving Stevenson and the rest of his colleagues to fill in the void!

And besides all that…if he walked away now the upper form girls had won. Defeated by a group of teenage girls!

He straightened his back from the tree and dropped the cigar but onto the soil. He would make sure that Misses Petersham, Shaw and Bromley bethought themselves before they again toyed with the chalk—and his name.

* * *

Miss Madeley had looked in on Millicent in the sick-room to find her not there. Something had gone very wrong in Anthony Fairchild's lesson that morning, but none of them would tell her what it was—she had informed them all some days ago that she did not care to hear about their misdemeanours in his classes and the consequences. It pained her greatly, even having his name mentioned, now that her hopes were dashed. But she thought that in dire circumstances it would not deter them from informing her. Obviously, she was wrong and they were not telling her of something so dreadful it could not be countenanced.

She went to the cloakroom and found Millie not there either. So, she hurried to Judith's office where Judith sat drinking gin from a glass she had placed in her opened drawer for discretion. Henrietta watched her with muted dislike concealed behind her kerchief as she sniffled and blew her nose daintily.

"Millicent has been taken ill…she was resting in the sick-room but now she is not there…" she told Judith who licked her lips in the way of someone having imbibed something delicious. "She is behaving oddly today."

"She is not ill…" said the headmistress at length. "She is involved in the trouble from this morning which Anthony is on his way to deal with."

"What?" Henrietta tripped nearer to Judith's desk. "You must be mistaken… Millicent is never in trouble."

"Have you heard the saying about there being a first time for everything, Henrietta?" Judith took another small sip of her drink and eyed the younger woman. "The sickness is a ruse, no doubt, to get her out of the disgrace she is in."

"How do you know this?" said Henrietta in great scepticism.

"The cook…she tells me everything!" said Judith, pausing for another sip and then savouring it on her tongue. "She overheard them talking at dinner… Melanie Petersham, Melissa Shaw and your darling Millicent…they are the ones who have offended him."

"Offended him how?" asked Henrietta. "'tis hard to see Millie offending him."

"I am not at liberty to say…" Judith harboured the kind of muted delight of people who hold privileged information and careless power. "No doubt you may hear tomorrow…should he or I care to tell you. But let us say, 'tis your lack of due discretion that has brought them to this."

"What?" Henrietta dropped to the chair beside the desk. "Judith, stop playing games and tell me at once what I have done."

The gin glass to her lips in a caressing manner, Judith watched the skyline beyond the window pane. A little knowledge would do no harm; indeed, it was the most satisfying thing to both giver and receiver. "You have somehow allowed them to learn of his first name and they have abused it…"

"Abused it!" Henrietta stood once more and took small fluttering movements about the office. "Is it a state secret, his first name?"

"I am saying no more…he has asked me not to." Judith locked the empty glass in the drawer and then pocketed the key. "And now you must leave. Millicent will be taken care of…but her feigned illness will be of little meaning to him. She has grievously erred, as have the other two. I am pretending to know nothing about any of it. I will wait to let him tell me in his own words."

"Yes, and how you will enjoy it," said Henrietta with heat and heart.

"Leave please, Henrietta! You will be in the way. We shall deal with the matter…you will no doubt attempt to soften him with your charms and your pleas for clemency…and I will not allow it."

Henrietta ran along the corridor to see if she could find the three girls, never thinking to look in the classroom he used but running straight back to her own and encountering him in the entrance hall.

"Anthony!" she said, addressing him for the first time in many weeks and aware suddenly of how ridiculous she had been.

He stopped. "Yes, Miss Madeley?"

"I hear I have inadvertently got Melanie, Melissa and Millicent into trouble…your Christian name or something!"

He froze and looked at her, his eyes finding her's and displaying the cloud of confusion which all the same had some resolve in them. "Never mind now," he said. "'tis done. I will deal with this."

"But what did they say to offend you so?"

He was statuesque in his stillness and she longed for the days when they were walking out, before she had so precipitously suggested kissing. His male containment and dignity were an aphrodisiac to her. She moved nearer to him. "I do not wish to go into it here," he asserted. "I am on my way to see them." She would weaken his resolve if he allowed it.

"But if it were my fault then I feel I should intervene."

He remained silent and she went on hurriedly, "I fear I may have accidentally let your name slip…'tis my doing."

"*Accidentally*?" he repeated sardonically, controlling his greater anger. "How does one manage to let someone's name slip accidentally to pupils?"

"Because the caretaker thought you were called *Arthur*, apparently, and he told one of the girls who—"

He cut in on her. "The caretaker? What has he to do with this? No, never mind, don't bother with the explanation…" Getting to the bottom of things may take forever, for it undoubtedly concerned the conjugated ploys of the upper form whose scheming was both exhausting and multi-layered. His time would be further wasted.

"Allow me to explain, Anthony, please! On their behalf!"

"No, Henrietta…" He turned suddenly and looked her in the eye, without emotion, and her heart ached with painfully immediate reaction to him. "You do too much excusing of their faults and misbehaviour. Your error over my name was unfortunate, but 'tis only one part of the equation. I am dealing with them as I see fit."

He was quite as bad as Judith with his self-appointed need to be autocratic, but still she ached to have his attention once more. "I implore you…please do not blame them entirely." Millicent Bromley had duped her, as she suspected.

"Henrietta!" he said in a stronger voice. "Do not alarm yourself unduly…you should not become involved. They must learn respect and better conduct, and I intend to remind them of that in no uncertain terms."

"I am aware that you think me very lacking as a teacher…perhaps 'tis a good thing I am leaving."

"Perhaps you are not cut out to teach in a school," he said more gently. "Or perhaps you should teach younger children…or find more…" he hesitated and searched for words, "…more soothing work. If you must work." If he informed her now of the chalking and her name within the heart, she would be overcome with embarrassment and he could not cope with that and remain determined in what he intended.

"I do not have to work… I live as you know with my parents and they do not mind whether I work or not. I choose to work," said Henrietta with a regal lift of her chin.

"That is admirable…" he told her sincerely and began to mount the stairs. She caught his sleeve between two of her fingers—barely a touch and more a reminder to stay. "Please do not be too harsh with them… I feel so guilty about it. And I am sorry for not speaking to you these past weeks."

He inclined his head to her graciously but did not look her in the eye. "Miss Tongs will give you a full report tomorrow, I am sure," he said in finality, then continued to the classroom.

* * *

They had been waiting for him for fifteen or more minutes and Millicent was again crying, while Melissa was stoney faced and Melanie sat thinking still of ways to extricate them from the dilemma. "Let us say we want to be expelled…" she said into the silence of the room. "We can retract it again tomorrow when he has become less vexed."

"Do not be ridiculous!" Melissa asserted. "He will no doubt reject the retraction and we will be back where we started and in worse trouble."

"Why will we?" said Melanie in curiosity, her head to one side in listening mode but staring out of the window. She looked almost angelic, the late afternoon sunlight glistening in her honey blonde hair.

"Because letters will go out to our parents today if we accept expulsion. He will instruct the clerk who works until six…"

"Not without Miss Tongs, surely?"

"She has not yet left," said Millicent in a faint little voice. "She is in the office… I heard the maid speaking to the housekeeper about the tea she has ordered for half after four."

"Yes, perhaps 'tis not a good plan." Melanie stood up and walked around the room. "If my father hears of it, it will be a never-ending saga…"

"Naturally!" cried Melissa in great disdain. "Do you imagine any of our parents will take it well? This suggested expulsion!"

"My grandmother will lock me in my room forever," cried Millicent in dire distress.

"Why is he taking so long?" asked Melissa almost to herself.

"To make us suffer…why do you think!" expostulated Melanie, "He is, after, all, the worst possible kind of tyrant…"

"I doubt you have met many tyrants," remarked Melissa scornfully, and they were tempted for a split second to giggle, for it was a truism, and only Millie was immune to the wit. "Be quiet, I think he is coming up the stairs," she hissed and attempted to wipe her tears which flowed without sound down her cheeks.

He entered in his usual calm manner and caught sight of Millicent first and looked swiftly away; yet more female emotion to deter him from action. He looked at Melissa Shaw—her face was impassive and her eyes quite defiant and this gave him renewed resolve. Melanie Petersham was batting her eyelids in the ludicrous manner she employed to steer life on the course she wanted it to go, especially with authority figures. "Go to the waiting room next to Miss Tongs' office…" he instructed without further ado. "I shall join you presently."

They rose as one and Melanie hesitated and said, "Sir, if I may just explain that we—"

"You may not explain anything, Miss Petersham," he said. "Now go where I have told you to go immediately."

The waiting room was a small room furnished in the mode of a drawing room at the end of the last century, then considered to be the height of fashion. It was uncluttered and shining spotlessly—a place for visiting dignitaries and parents and other important persons to wait if necessary.

There was a large solid round oaken table in the centre and a bookcase on the wall opposite the large window, several upholstered and generally stylish chairs dotted here and there. Off this room was an identical room of smaller proportions with an identical table and fewer chairs: another design fad from previous decades.

The girls entered slowly, the door opening to admit them into the silent opulence of the space which none of them had seen previously. They stood in a line before the table and facing the marble mantlepiece where a grate was housed with a fire set but unlit. They expected him to enter almost at once, which he did not, and Melanie said: "I am not standing here while he pleases himself…" and she sat on the chesterfield sofa nearest the door.

Melissa began walking around looking at the pictures on the walls. Millicent warily sat in a chair much too large for her and seemed to shrink into it and reduce in size.

"Millie, do not fear anything," said Melanie.

"Ha!" scoffed Melissa. "Who would not be in fear? She has not been caned by him before…whereas we have, so we know what to expect."

"Or you think you do!" Millicent said ominously.

"What do you mean by that?" demanded Melanie.

"I have a bad feeling about it," Millie replied.

"Of course you do…" Melanie sucked a peppermint and then concealed it beneath her tongue to see if she could hide it quickly enough should he appear before it was finished. "We are not going to a country fayre, Millie! Naturally you have a bad feeling."

"I just wish I was in my grave!" Millie said dramatically. "I really do."

"Millicent!" Melissa said sharply. "You are being melodramatic and morbid…*over-egging-the-pudding* is after all Melanie's prerogative."

Melanie was again tempted to giggle but could not get the sound to pass her lips. "I suppose next she will be asking for the last rites," she supplied in a contrived wilting voice.

"I am not Catholic," pronounced Millicent dourly.

Melanie disclaimed and said, "How many parties are you invited to, Millie?"

"None…" said the unsocialised Millicent, missing the point. "Only to play music for people."

"Do not taunt her," said Melissa. "She is entitled to be terrified…so am I…"

"The pair of you are so infuriatingly docile…he will see it at once and exploit it."

"We are not all Amazonian women…" opined Melissa. "It will make no odds to him what we are and are not, he will do what he wants to do…and Melanie, I implore you, do not make matters worse by inventing things to infuriate him…" and then to Millicent. "What did you mean, you have a bad feeling?"

Millie considered the words without replying, so that Melissa went on, "…and remember to tell him you only passed me the chalk and he will doubtless let you off…" Again Millie did not speak.

"She will not tell him that…" Melanie avowed. "She is determined to be a martyr…if she cannot have his love, she will accept the suffering he inflicts."

"For heaven's sake!" Melissa said. "We are not in a Gothic novel."

Then he strode past the opened door and merely glanced in. Melanie and Millicent stood quickly and he passed on into Miss Tongs' office.

"Another delay I suppose…" Melanie sank into the nearest chair and sucked the mint furiously to be rid of it. "Why is he informing Tongs of all this…he once said he would not trouble her with our misbehaviour…if you recall…"

The length of time, the eeriness of the waiting room in its untouched splendour, the suspended activity—it was as if they were part of a tableau and not in reality. Then Miss Tongs entered alone, wearing her light brown cotton dress with the white broderie-angle collar, her long black hair shining in coils around her head. She looked at them; self-satisfied smugness mingled with fake displeasure. She resembled a disingenuous witness at a murder trial.

"Stand up at once!" she commanded. "How dare you sit about as if you were at home…"

They got to their feet and watched her.

"You have gone too far this time with your mischief…and no doubt you will soon regret it. Quite utterly disgraceful behaviour. You are fortunate not to be expelled."

"Miss Tongs…" began Melanie and Melissa nudged her to silence her.

"Be quiet, girl," snapped Miss Tongs. "I do not wish to hear from you… I am used to your lies and manipulations and they will not wash here."

Then Fairchild sauntered in, his cane held loosely in one hand behind his back, and the headmistress took an armchair near the mantlepiece and acquired a waiting pose, her hands folded in her lap and her full attention upon him.

He moved over the room and looked out from the window which gave a view over the side of the school and onto a small hedge of hawthorn bordering the larger grounds. He wandered back and stood with his back to the bookcases. "I do not wish a long-winded deposition of the reasons and motives behind this escapade…" he said in his calm level tones. "Suffice it to say, I will not tolerate that kind of vulgarity concerning my private life and my first name…"

"Sir…" said Melanie once more. "If I might just explain…"

"Be silent!" yelled Miss Tongs. "How dare you interrupt."

"Miss Petersham," he continued, his voice unnaturally low next to that of Miss Tongs. "I am aware that you think life a matter of mere cleverness with words, which you believe you can use to talk your way out of every situation…but you will find that it does not work with all people on every occasion…and I am one of those people…perhaps your first ever experience of one…" He paused to look at Melanie who had averted her gaze and was watching the window, her mouth pursed in what he took to be exasperation but was actually caused by the remains of the mint. "And look at me when I am speaking to you…" He waited for her attention before continuing. "Perhaps your parents have different views from my own, but how you have been allowed thus far to have so little respect for authority and to imagine your opinions are of interest to all and sundry is quite beyond me…"

Melanie drew breath, the last of the sweet dispensed with, but did not take the risk of commenting.

"I am surprised at your presence here, Miss Bromley…" He switched his gaze to Millicent who sniffed and blinked away her tears. "Your behaviour is normally so exemplary…but if you are foolish enough to be led by these two, who are adept at disruption and artifice, then that is your choice…"

"She is quite innocent…" interceded Melissa in a strong voice. "She merely passed me the chalk when I asked her to."

Miss Tongs chirruped laughter of incredulity and he moved his weight from one foot to the other, looking from Melissa with suspicion and back to Millicent. "Is this true, Miss Bromley?"

There was a pause of a second or two and Millie said. "No, Sir, 'tis not."

"So, you did not pass her the chalk when she asked? Is that what you mean?"

This was very cunning questioning and Millie glanced at Melissa as Melanie sighed and he watched the three of them. "You refused to pass her the chalk? Or she is lying when she says she asked you to?" he persevered in a slow tone laced with undertones of impatience. He felt duty bound to establish the innocence alleged of Millicent Bromley who had never previously caused him concern. His integrity demanded it.

Melissa stared at Millie in subtle encouragement, then looked at him directly and said, "'tis very complicated to explain, Sir, but Millicent is innocent of chalking your names."

He moved to the right of the room in deeper thought, his head bowed as he followed the rose pattern of the carpet. "And I am now asking her to explain," he said in a sharper tone. "Complicated or not."

He was too clever for them and thought in devious ways, like a lawyer, which even Melanie could not get ahead of.

"I did not pass her the chalk, and I do not recall her asking it of me," replied Millicent, forestalling greater scrutiny of meaning by more of his verbal ploys.

"Then what was your part in all of this?" he enquired.

"I would rather not say," answered Millie faintly.

"But you admit to being part of it?" He watched Millicent flush, her face a picture of woebegone misery. She frowned and conjured thoughts to explain without incriminating Miss Madeley or anyone else. Nothing occurred to her and she felt his waiting as an excruciating pain screaming in the silence.

"Very well then," he said, "We will take it that Miss Bromley is part of this misbehaviour."

"I am," said Millicent bravely.

He paced a little and thought of inherent possibilities and was somewhat at a loss. "I do not entirely believe you..." he told Millicent.

Millie looked away and Melissa said. "Sir, she is on the whole blameless in the chalking of your names."

He flicked his gaze to Melissa and Miss Tongs stirred but refrained from intervening; he did not need or welcome interference in his interrogative tactics.

"I think she must speak for herself," he said. "And if she cannot or will not do that then she must take the consequences...unless she is being coerced by you in some way..." He looked at Millie.

"I am not being coerced," said Millicent in her quivering little voice.

"Protected then?" he said.

None of them spoke. Melissa turned her face in the direction of the window but watched him from her side vision. She had never before encountered anyone with such steady and piercing skills of enquiry: authority was usually posturing and false, she had found, made of importance without the wisdom or the means to penetrate fuller truths. Here was someone who could rise above that effortlessly. She was on the verge of admiration then brought her mind quickly to the idea of her pride and reverted again to mere loathing and disapproval. The enemy was still the enemy!

"If you will prevaricate in this way, Miss Bromley, I have no choice but to punish you…"

"I do not mind," said Millicent stoically.

Now he was faced with sheer stupidity under the guise of some kind of martyrdom. He looked at Melanie Petersham, who had about her the kind of pained intolerance of one who found themselves among idiots. And then at Melissa Shaw, who was displaying her usual dismissive eye movement away from him. She had never sought to placate or persuade him one way or the other on any controversial or inflammatory issue: she was continually the same and steadfastly impenetrable. Of the three of them only Millicent was showing any contrition or humility. The attitude of the other two incensed him. Though they obviously wished to do the right thing by Milicent Bromley, and it spoke of some kind of better characteristic. He looked at Millie who was heaving silent sobs, then quickly away again before his resolve deserted him utterly.

"Am I meant to take this denial of Miss Bromley's part as your personal integrity?" he enquired of the other two. They thought very little about integrity of any kind generally, it was not in their vocabulary, and therefore there was silence. "For there is no integrity in lying…none whatever. Unless for a much worthier cause than this…"

Moments passed and the room was still, almost tranquil. Melissa was again gazing at the window and watching him from the corner of her eye. "As for you Miss Shaw…if you imagine your variety of insolence is not noticeable because it is silent then you are mistaken…'tis perhaps worse for all that…look at me directly when I am speaking to you…"

She could not get her face to obey her and although she turned her face towards him, her mouth was frozen in a square of tight exasperation and her eyes would not open and her chin would not sink to a lowered position of deference, and she felt that if she altered even a fraction of her face she would crumble inwardly and run from the room or begin yelling objections at him.

He watched this frozen mask of sullen haughtiness with distaste and fascination and seconds passed and her eyes flickered as if to open but refused at the last minute to do so. She smiled vaguely instead—against her own volition—which he took for a worse form of disrespect. "Very well…we will continue…" he said, as if he were conducting an English lesson. He moved to the back of the room where three matching mahogany dining chairs stood. He hooked his foot beneath one of them and pulled it forwards to the centre of the floor. The chair had rounded wooden arms which spanned and comprised the backrest in an open framed design, with a pink and ivory satin upholstered seat. It had been part of a set of dining chairs in its heyday, expensive and elegant.

The girls stared at it quite uncomprehendingly, until he gave further instruction. "You will in turn kneel on the chair and lift up your skirts, leaving your petticoats in place, and lean over the back of the chair and receive six strokes of the cane…you will not move until the punishment is complete… Miss Petersham, you may go first."

They could not believe what they heard and felt ill with fear. Melanie moved forwards as if in a dream and faltered before the chair. She looked at him in distress. "Must we do this?" she implored. "'tis so undignified."

He raised his brows a little. "I am surprised you know the meaning of the word…but 'tis perhaps the only way you will learn respect…kneel on the chair."

Still Melanie faltered, genuinely afraid and unable to move. He had encountered this sort of reluctance before even in boys and considered it to be not unnatural and knew from experience that it was a fleeting obstinacy which soon passed. Miss Tongs was never so forbearing. "Hurry up, girl, we do not have time to waste with you all day!" Then she dropped her voice to its most sardonic. "Or do you prefer that the matter be referred to your parents prior to your expulsion?"

Melanie considered things and her cornflower blue irises were huge with dismay.

"Is that what you want?" asked Miss Tongs briskly.

"No, 'tis not," she replied.

"Then do as you are told," said Fairchild. "And if you delay any longer, I shall add two more strokes to the punishment."

Melanie knelt tentatively on the chair and pulled up the outer blue woven cotton skirt of her summer uniform.

"Lean over the back and grip the centre rail," he commanded.

She complied shakily and felt her skirt slip back into place with her hip movement. Wearied by the delays he took a handful of her skirt at the hem and threw it back over her haunches, revealing her white cotton petticoat which afforded little protection from what was to happen but modestly covered her anatomy to just above her knees. A lull in motion and time, and only the birds were audible in the trees outside. Melissa closed her eyes and heard the punishment without seeing it, praying that some divine intervention would happen to spare her.

Of course it did not and her turn came next. How she wished she had the knack of fainting at will. She trembled and her teeth chattered and her throat was so dry she could not swallow. "On the chair!" he said in the cold neutral way he used for the execution of discipline. Boys, of course, did not require these theatrical props and niceties to corporal punishment and he strove to remain patient in new and sensitive territory.

Melissa did exactly as Melanie had done but also forgot her skirt and he repeated the same removal of its obstacle, flinging the garment back swiftly. She gritted her teeth so hard her jaw ached. She felt the cane rest against her behind a mere second and then heard it glide through the air with the thinnest of sounds before she felt the first stroke.

It sent a shock through her whole body and she was stunned to lack of thought. The blood sang in her ears and the second stroke came as an even greater surprise, obliterating the memory of the first. The third stroke seemed to render her numb to all sensation and the fourth was an echo of all that had gone before while the fifth and sixth brought renewed discomfort.

Suddenly it was over and a few moments elapsed before she could bring herself to normality and move from the chair. She stood carefully, as if she might fall apart, then went to stand next to Melanie who was quite still under the callous gaze of Miss Tongs—sitting with great composure like a theatre audience of one. Melissa let her tears flow soundlessly and closed her eyes so as not to have to witness Millicent giving little cries of anguish on each stroke.

Eventually it was done with and he surveyed them from the centre of the floor, the cane discarded on the oak table, his expression showing nothing of any feeling beneath its neutrality. "Now harken to this…my first name is not for your use, no more than is Miss Madeley's, and I do not wish to see or hear it again. You will show more respect and you will not treat my lessons as some kind of entertaining diversion… Or you will be back in here for a repeat of this correction." He moved to open the door. "And if your parents or guardians wish to know the reason for your lateness and seek verification, we shall write to them. Now you may go…"

* * *

"Well!" said Miss Tongs in their wake, rising and shaking out her dress. "That is something they will remember when they are old ladies…"

He sank onto the sofa and leaned back, quite drained by the tension of the whole process. "I tend to doubt it," he said. "I merely flicked them…they will feel next to nothing after a quarter hour."

Miss Tongs pushed back the chair he had used. "Such modesty…they are not boys, you know."

"That is why I exercised restraint," he said.

"Do you think the pain of it is everything to them? 'tis nothing next to the indignity. You may take my word for it…" replied the headmistress smoothly.

"I shall have to," he said, "For I am not a female."

"You certainly are not!" crooned Miss Tongs, testing the furniture for dust with her finger tip. "Perhaps you would care for some sherry…to revive you a little?"

He stared at the headmistress, masking his repugnance behind his lowered lashes. From all he had learned about her it was not a surprising overture, but nonetheless he had seldom heard anything so inappropriate in his life to date.

* * *

In the cloakroom the girls lingered, pulling themselves together and swilling their faces with water.

"Do not talk of it…" warned Melissa. "…do not say a word, Mel!"

"What is there to say?" said Melanie but then went on to contradict herself by pronouncing, "He is an utter swine… I always knew it…"

"He was reluctant to do it, I think…" put in Millicent softly.

"He was reluctant where you were concerned, such a model pupil, because he thought you were innocent…which you were in practise," said Melanie. "I hope you are pleased with your ability to persuade him otherwise, despite our best efforts…"

Millicent did not reply, but turned her face away in bitter resolve to they knew not what.

"Millie!" warned Melanie, "Please do not say again that he was only doing his job… I cannot bear to hear it."

"I shall not do so," appeased Millicent, fastening her bonnet.

They were always given money to retain a Hansom cab near the gates where coaches lingered to bring home older pupils each day, those who were not collected by family or servants. This was a quarter hour after the lower form left, to avoid a deluge of conveyances clogging the driveway and the road outside. The time being now well past four thirty all waiting cabs had dispersed and they had a small trek to the nearest location where they might be found. Millicent sometimes walked home, when her aunt neglected to give her the necessary fare. Like this day. "I will go on foot!" she told them, "And get a head start by setting off now."

"You may come into my coach…" said Melanie, guessing the reason behind her words. "We will ask them to drop you off first. I have money enough…"

"That is very good of you," said Millicent with dignity.

"Not at all," Melanie said in similar vein. "We do not want you fainting with delayed shock on the way home, Millie!"

"Are you quite alright, Millie?" enquired Melissa as they set off down the driveway.

"Do not be ridiculous, Lissy…" declared Melanie striding ahead. "How can she be quite alright with her behind on fire!"

"I am quite alright…" said Millie bravely. "The effects are wearing off now."

They continued for several moments and then Melissa added. "And Melanie, do not speak of it to anyone—ever! I do not wish anyone to know! Nor you, Millie."

"I shall not," said Millie in revulsion. "I could not bring myself to do so."

"'twas the worst ordeal I have ever been through," Melissa said calmly.

Melanie took on a careless tone. "Perhaps on a par with having a tooth pulled?"

"Far, far worse," said Melissa.

Melanie was scathing. "I think not, though it was very unpleasant indeed!"

"What an understatement!" Melissa stated. "Only you could phrase it so…"

"Wait until you birth a child!" concluded her closest friend, already back to something of her usual self. The cool September air was pleasant, hazy sun and a light breeze. More moments passed as their feet crunched the gravel driveway. Until Melanie felt bound to comment: "How dare he speak of my parents in that manner!"

Millicent rallied in spirit to summarise. "He was merely suggesting they had not raised you to standards he considers important…"

"I know what he was *merely* suggesting," snapped Melanie, "And how dare he! I don't care a fig for his standards."

"But he is right…" continued Millicent bravely, "There is no integrity in lies."

"Here she goes again…defending him!" Melanie was moving quickly and stopping every few yards to watch the other two.

"I am not defending him; I am defending what he said. 'tis different…"

"Oh, is it?" cried Melanie, then addressing Melissa. "And don't you now mention the sadness of his soul as a reason for this…"

Melissa was not listening but looking at Millie—taken by a new idea: timid and retiring though Millicent's temperament was, she had her own brand of strength and integrity. She and Fairchild were both strong in their different genders and individual ways. This notion struck her quite forcibly and she halted to consider it. She had witnessed two people with principle and character play opposing roles. In a few days she might sketch them both from the side angle during the interrogation stage: Millie standing before Fairchild, but alone, so that her character would dominate the impression along with his. She would attempt it in charcoal first and then perhaps in watercolour, if it was any good.

In later years, she could display it and title it *'Conscience and Consequence'… It might be donated to a public gallery. By then, she would be accomplished enough as an artist and many people would relate to it from their own schooldays. Though she would need the permission of Millicent before offering it for public viewing. She would waiver his permission, she cared not what he might think.*

Then suddenly she saw that somehow, he was right; she was an expert in *deceit and subterfuge.* She deceived everyone at home all the time…her father when she told him she had only been as far as the land end sketching, when really, she had been a few miles beyond it, tramping relentlessly to catch the light or the right views. And her mother, who believed she sat sociably with her grandmother or her cousins, when in reality she was out somewhere forbidden with Melanie. Or in the woods with Roger Braithwaite, drinking small beer he had taken from their family cellar. She was disingenuous and sly. She was what Fairchild had accused them of.

Melanie began edging her along the footpath, supposing her to be in some kind of aftershock. Melissa moved automatically like one in a trance, and being possessed of the ability for contemplative thought, she saw that he penetrated truths with his mind and spoke them in words while she sought to depict the truth of what she saw on paper and canvas.

"What are you refining on now, Lissy?" enquired Melanie, pausing stride herself.

"Nothing…perhaps this question of integrity," she replied.

"Oh piffle! 'tis mere rhetoric he uses to verbally triumph in matters where he might otherwise flounder."

"I think he believes it…" said Millie. "It distresses him to think people can be so without moral honesty."

"Well, of course you would think that of him," Melanie said. "You would most likely have him knighted if you could."

Melissa knew the question that now haunted her was whether one had a right to one's own version of integrity or whether there was a generally agreed version which should always hold sway. It was a very vexing question. It marked the beginning of a long road to greater maturity.

They found the first coach. Melanie urged Melissa to board it by herself so she would not be waiting alone. Millicent smiled and waved at Melissa through the coach window as it rolled off; she was happier now, for she felt she was at last one of them and part of an enclave. Their suffering had truly bonded them.

Era's End

Judith lost no time in the staffroom the next day giving Henrietta chapter and verse on the crime and the retribution. Henrietta turned several shades of pink. "I do not believe you could sanction it, Judith!" she claimed. "'twas so unnecessary..."

"I did not have any choice. He would have resigned otherwise and Stevenson would have flown into a temper and blamed me..." She looked with highly arched brows at Henrietta who had the decency to look guilty. "How many resignations do you think we need at any one time? Stevenson gave Fairchild leave to take any disciplinary measure he thought appropriate...short of hanging them from a tree...obviously to deter him from resignation. Anyone with common sense would endorse his actions...except you, of course," she concluded blithely.

"But there was no need to encourage him in such...such..."

"Such what?" said Judith, pouring tea. "Such a time honoured and effective method of chastisement?"

"Such cruelty!" amended Henrietta.

Judith laughed in high falsetto. "Do not be so feeble, Henrietta! We are not talking about the cat o'nine tails! Can you imagine what would happen to them in one of the city institutions if they dared such a measure of impertinence?"

"We are not in one of those places, Judith, we are a civilised establishment," argued Henrietta, her face more suffused with colour and her throat dry and parched.

"The correction was civilised...he knows exactly what he is doing...and that is why Stevenson wants him for deputy when he takes headship next year...he is counting on that, in fact, and it was my duty to make sure Anthony Fairchild did not resign." Judith regarded Henrietta a moment or two in her glow of sanctimonious satisfaction, then said. "Of course, had you stepped forwards sooner and admitted your faux pas with his name, you might have saved them…you could have asked him to cane you instead and he might have agreed…you may both have been thrilled by the experience and rekindled your friendship!”

Henrietta turned quite pale by contrast to her recent flush and looked askance at the other woman. “What? Why would you pose such a ridiculous notion! Why would you even think it?”

Judith paused for seconds in the light of Henrietta’s puritanical innocence, then recovered and waved her hand dismissively. “Never mind! Suffice it to say justice prevailed.”

“Justice! How you do like to pontificate!” retorted Henrietta. She was glad she was leaving at the end of the term, all things considered, and at the same time saddened that she had given up a romantic option. She had realised now that after the mourning period of his sweetheart he may relent his affirmed bachelor status and there was no reason why she should not have been considered suitable as his wife. She was overwhelmed by tormented mixed feelings and irreversible facts.

Reading her mind, Judith offered: “And before you go off on a valiant excursion of guilt, imagining yourself to be utterly to blame, remember that they may well have discovered his name from somewhere else eventually…” She set down a cup and saucer in front of Henrietta. “Stop being so melodramatic, you are leaving, he is not. He has to bear with their disagreeable and insolent ways in the future…”

Henrietta pushed the saucer away. “I expect you enticed him into your bedroom?” she suggested, not looking at the other woman as she spoke.

“Mind your own business,” said Judith, which told Henrietta that Judith had failed in any attempt to seduce him.

* * *

He met with Trimingham on the following evening for a Friday night drinking bout. Other men they knew joined them briefly and conversed and left again, some to wives or fiancés, others to mistresses or to places of recreation. The death of Lottie was becoming more bearable. It no longer woke him in the night in nightmares of her in deep sea currents—her face a mask of death as she floated, hair billowing in the water, himself swimming to save her, never reaching her. Waking, tangled in sheets and drenched in sweat. The effects of the tragedy were receding, but with it came a bitter sort of empty resolve to just

141

get through the days. Perhaps it was better to feel the pain than to feel nothing at all. *It would pass,* his mother told him, and his brother Rupert, and even Trimingham. But what was it that had to pass? He did not know and because he could not define it, he was lost in the midst of it.

McCarthy soon joined Trim and he in the 'Broken Broom' tavern, a boisterous place full of people from various walks of life. Smoke laden air from the two fires and the pipes and cigars and cigarettes, and the rowdy rise and fall of laughter and voice.

A few doxies circled the place, watched by the landlord, some of the girls no older than the upper form pupils at Barton Grange. They made grotesque and appalling faces for ones so young; painted lips and cheeks, eyes heavily ringed in charcoal like theatrical masks. They fixed on younger men of higher class because that was where they knew the money to be—and the manners that made their job more bearable. Two of them latched onto Dominic McCarthy's rich accent and came near, one tickling his ear with a long red feather. He flicked the feather away with his hand rather than break stride in his conversation. They resumed after a pause and the feather tickled his nose.

"Be gone!" he told them in a stern tone.

They mimicked his accent. "He's from the old country…" said one of them, no taller than his elbow. "Let me sing you some folk songs, my duck…"

McCarthy turned to her. "I'll sing you a different song if you don't leave us…you are too young to be in here."

They ignored this and the smaller girl moved on to Fairchild and the tickling began on his cheek. "This 'un's pretty…look at his hair. Be that your true colour or be it dyed? I want hair that colour."

Eventually, in his smooth tone, he addressed them. "Go from our vicinity or we will have you removed…"

"Toffs!" said the first one provocatively, bigger than her sister but childlike in figure. "Dandies and toffs!"

"See the length of this gent…" said the younger of the two, leaning against Trimingham's tall physique. "He be some'at to look up to."

Trimingham put her away from him without looking at her and they lost interest momentarily and moved on to a group of soldiers home on leave. One of the barmaids whispered in the landlord's ear and the landlord watched them keenly as he worked.

"They are more like children playing!" commented Trimingham. "No older than your troublesome schoolgirls…"

"They are not playing though," said McCarthy. "Their intent and purpose is not to be contemplated in ones so young…it turns my stomach!"

"The abysmal state of this country!" muttered Fairchild.

McCarthy laughed. "Let it put into perspective the positions of two kinds of young female in our orbit then…one overly privileged and forced to learn…and the other underprivileged and forced to whore. But which one is deserving of most sympathy?"

"The latter?" Trim said.

"Undoubtedly!" agreed McCarthy.

"The system fails them badly…" remarked Trimingham.

Fairchild rallied himself to object. "There is no system, and no redress for children of their ilk…the workhouse is not a system which advantages anyone but the merchants and the wealthy…"

"Now see what I've begun…" said McCarthy merrily to Trim. "There'll be a lecture on reform next."

"There will not," declared Fairchild, swigging ale. "I am not in the mood."

The two girls had returned, spurned by the soldiers who saw their true age and the potential jailbait. The feather was aimed again at Fairchild and tickled his neck with undeterred fervour. "You are likely to get yourselves taken into charge," he told them, "If you carry on this way…"

"We been taken into that a'fore," said the small one cockily.

"And what was the outcome?" enquired Trim with his usual curiosity for the lives of others.

"The workhouse," said the older girl, "But we escaped!"

Trim looked at Fairchild with meaning; his opinion being so verified within a short space of minutes. Fairchild nodded but did not comment.

"It were brutal in there…" the little one told Trim. "We weren't for staying and we escaped."

"Well, you are likely to be returning unless you mend your ways…" Trimingham said. "So, why do you not show common sense?"

"We can show you something else…" said the feather-wielder. "If you show us your blunt first…"

"Cease being so damnably brazen…" demanded McCarthy with heat, and they grinned delightedly, the feather then placed in Fairchild's ear. He turned to grab it as it was whisked away.

"I'll wager you can read and write…" stated the youngest to Fairchild with glib satisfaction.

"Perhaps a little…" Fairchild replied in droll fashion. She smirked at him. "Thought so…" she told her sister proudly, as if producing some amazing insight. "Talking so posh an' all. You could write us a letter…"

"To whom?" he asked, a little intrigued. "And to what purpose?"

"Any folk who might read it…saying you know us and what good people we be."

He frowned at her while Trimingham and McCarthy entered into subdued laughter. "Utterly absurd!" he thought of his mother's good works and clerical ministries, and he told them quickly of a church hall a few streets away where they could obtain food and a bed for the night—hoping to be rid of them.

"What will we have to do for it?" said the eldest.

"Perhaps just behave yourselves!" he rejoined.

"I 'spect they may try to bring us to Jesus," commented the elder importantly and McCarthy and Trimingham laughed quite soundlessly, their shoulders shaking with mirth.

"I do not think they perform those kind of miracles…" Fairchild said. "But they may be able to seek work for you in service somewhere…"

The girls looked at each other, bewildered and wary. "How do you know?" demanded the elder suspiciously.

He hesitated, unable to deflect or lie. "My mother has involvement…" he said, simplifying things.

"Your ma is a mission lady!" The girl's astonishment transformed her face to its correct age.

"In a manner of speaking, yes."

"What's her name then?" the smaller one asked.

"That is not your concern…she will not attend you personally…there are others there who will help you. Now be off…you are quite beyond annoying!"

The feather was produced once more but this time to provoke Trimingham. whose demeanour of kindly interest was worth pursuing. The landlord, having seen enough nuisance to customers, gave a piercing whistle and two men arrived;

employed to mind the door and keep order, they hauled the girls away to the door.

The landlord was contrite. "Sorry gents…we summoned the henchmen five minutes ago but they were dealing with a brawl outside…"

A rousing group of musicians played in one corner of the tavern; jigs and popular tunes so that the clientele could sing and dance in a space no bigger than a pantry, bumping into travellers making their way upstairs for overnight beds. McCarthy sometimes begged a fiddle from them and joined in the renditions, unable to resist the music from his homeland. Tonight though he controlled the urge, and Fairchild wondered why.

The landlord's wife, with two helpers, wove in and out of the crowd with plates of food. A room devoted to cards and table skittles and dominoes lay to the left of the front door. The fires were encircled by men talking and swapping stories. This was just the place to escape the worries of the world and customers would willingly contend with waiting half an hour to be served—prompting the buying of more liquor than was needed at any one time. The place was understaffed, and consequently prosperous.

One of the henchmen was back. "Check your money and valuables, gents! Before we release 'em…very light fingered some of 'em."

Trimingham and Fairchild were already basking in the early stages of inebriation where life seemed rosier. Dominic McCarthy, having arrived later, had some way to go to catch up. "Talking of irritating females, I hear you dealt with those three girls at yonder place…" he said to Fairchild.

"I did!" the other confirmed.

"'twas the talk of the staffroom," McCarthy added. "When Nick informed them of what had occurred there were ringing endorsements…"

"I fail to understand why he had to inform the whole staff," Fairchild said dully.

"Because he believed you may resign…" McCarthy was incredulous. "The relief in the staffroom was immense…"

"I'm flattered!" he returned in the same dull tone.

Trimingham naturally enquired after the nature of these comments and was told of recent events at the girls school. "Fairchild, you heartless fiend!" he proclaimed.

"Am I not!" agreed his friend, unperturbed.

"No more than they deserved," asserted McCarthy in his defence.

145

Trimingham was of a softer disposition. "No doubt they would have removed this offensive chalking in time, had you not returned when you did…"

"Beside the point…" Fairchild replied.

"I expect they meant no harm…'tis how girls go on…" Trimingham had younger sisters.

"Trim," began Fairchild, reigning in his impatience. "I do not care how they meant it! I am not tolerating that kind of insolence… I turn a blind eye often enough to their ridiculous antics…and I am not ignoring that manner of vulgarity."

"No, no," McCarthy insisted. "Or else what might come next!"

"My meaning was that they did not intend you to see it, most likely!" said Trimingham.

"Obviously not…" sighed Fairchild.

"You could have pretended not to notice," persevered Trimingham.

"No, he could not…" defended McCarthy. "That is what Henry Stringer does and look at the result."

"And do you imagine they would not know I was doing so!" Fairchild said to Trimingham. "They would think me a weak-kneed idiot…"

"I doubt that very much," Trimingham finished half the ale in his tankard in one go. "They would merely think you could not be bothered with such minor mischief…"

"So that the next *minor mischief* would then occur at an interval," he countered.

"Just so! And I would not agree it was a minor mischief…" McCarthy put in diplomatically.

"Dominic, just disregard his comments…he has taught only boys and has not the first clue of how these wenches go on…" said Fairchild, then added in a milder tone. "Though I had to steel myself to go through with it… I am not naturally a monster."

"I expect you will be wanting a medal next!" remarked Trim blithely. McCarthy found this hilarious and was forced to lean against the counter. Having recovered, he then thought to enquire. "By the by, what was Miss Tongs' reaction to it all?"

Fairchild made a disparaging shape to his mouth and rolled his eyes to the old smoke dappled ceiling. "She is another story entirely…one I do not want to go into presently…"

McCarthy laughed louder and Trim said: "I hope you did not let her prevail on your good nature after this debacle…"

"Of course not, Timothy!" Fairchild retorted. "I do have moral standards; the woman is a freak of nature! I would sooner enter a monastery."

McCarthy was now in a paroxysm of mirth, the euphemisms made richer by the drink, and he rapped the counter top with his knuckles to remind himself to be serious. He put his arms around both men and pulled them in closer to him so that they were in a conclave of conspirators. He lowered his voice and said, "Turning the subject to more acceptable female company… I have an invite to a house soiree tonight where we may find women very biddable to men like ourselves, and very amenable to being entertained."

Trim looked dubious. "They are ladies of easy virtue, I presume?"

"They are certainly not in holy orders," laughed McCarthy. "But they are of the highest calibre…exquisite manners and versed in good conversation…and pristine in cleanliness…"

"You have previous experience of this event?" asked Fairchild curiously.

"I do!"

"How so?"

"One of the proprietors is a distant cousin, an Irishman like myself. His father is the Marquis of Dunleoghrie, but has disinherited him…"

"Vastly inconvenient!" Trimingham said, slurring his words slightly. "How did that come about?"

"I would not get him started on this kind of family history…" interjected Fairchild. "Else we'll be detained all night…"

Dominic McCarthy cleared his throat and became intense. "These are some of the most beautiful and captivating women you will ever find…from all across the globe…scrupulously vetted by…well…by my second cousin whose real name I dare not use…we will just call him Rory, for that is one of his given names. He owns the house and maintains their health and welfare for the time they are with him…he employs one of the finest medics in the county on a weekly basis…"

Fairchild gazed over to the musical corner which was abuzz now with antics of one kind and another. He thought of the reasons why women would take up that kind of life. It was only perhaps as demanding—but maybe less so—than the plight of a lot of women living conventional lives. Then he thought of Lottie escaping from an enforced marriage and was lost to his surroundings for whole minutes. McCarthy and Trim spoke in quiet tones about the venue for this vivifying excursion and of the visitors one might meet there.

"Are you joining me or not?" enquired Dominic eventually into Fairchild's silent vacuum. "We must set off shortly…'tis more than a half hour's ride in a coach and we cannot gain entrance after ten of the clock."

"Are you sure it lives up to your description?" Fairchild asked. "We know how your countrymen love to embellish matters!"

McCarthy widened his eyes. "I would not be encouraging you otherwise! Would I want to have the repercussions raining down on me for the rest of the working term? now, would I?"

"I am walking straight out of the door again if it does not fit your glowing review," said Fairchild.

"'twould do him no good though…" McCarthy said to Trimingham in an undertone. "*Out of the door* leads straight into the countryside…the middle of nowhere…the back of beyond…so secluded is the mansion!"

Trim emitted his own brand of quiet mirth, his light brown hair falling over his light brown eyes.

"I heard some of that," Fairchild said, "And I am telling you now, if these women are cheap harlots or doxies I am not staying."

McCarthy went on doggedly, "Even if we don't partake of the goods, which we are not obliged to do, we can at least look at them…"

Trimingham said he would decline; he was engaged to Susan Darnley for some years and not inclined to carousing. McCarthy looked at Fairchild who confirmed his own willingness and then excused himself to use the outside lavatorial facilities in readiness for the journey. In his absence, McCarthy told Trimingham. "I'll tell you, Timothy, 'twas paid for by Nicholas Stevenson…" he paused for Trim to follow the gist. "He wants me to take Tony along. He is concerned about his low state and his perpetual gloom since his sweetheart passed away…and of course he is anxious to avert his resignation."

Trim listened attentively, bringing out his pipe and lighting it successfully only on the third attempt. McCarthy continued. "You know how Nick adores the ladies…and these events are bespoke…men wager for introductions. You are more than welcome to join us… I have told Rory there might be a third person with us…and supper is included. Though I implore you not to tell Tony what I have said… Nick wants him to think 'twas my idea and my invitation."

"Of course he does," concluded Trimingham. "They do not come much shrewder than Old Nick..."

Fairchild was returning and they stopped the conversation.

"Are you joining me or not?" Dominic asked.

"I am joining you," Fairchild confirmed and straightened his shoulders and looked resolved. He was not in the habit of paying for the company of women, he had never had need, but it was perhaps the best option given that serious romantic encounters were off the agenda. There were no desirable single women at Mrs Anstey's currently looking for nocturnal company, and he had no time to go looking. Aside from the ever-predatory Judith Tongs, there was no likely female companionship. He might well become a confirmed celibate; a dried-up academic before he was thirty.

"I invited Nick too, but he declined..." said Dominic for effect.

"He does not go in for this kind of thing these days..." replied Fairchild. "He is looking to settle with a widow who has taken his fancy and he wishes to be more discreet...especially with his headship looming."

McCarthy had a diverting thought. "That reminds me...he has warned us not to mention where we're employed to anyone present there, unless they already know...we must pretend to be lawyers or businessmen or similar...so as not to bring disrepute to the academy."

Trimingham, on finishing his drink, rejoined, "Not to bring blackmail threats is what he means."

Again finding the remark hilarious, McCarthy took a few moments before being able to count his loose change efficiently.

"I am betimes leaving Barton Grange," announced Fairchild with gravity. "So the pretence will not be hard."

"No, Tony, you are not!" McCarthy objected.

"I may go abroad," supplied Fairchild.

"Take it with a pinch of salt..." interposed Trim dismissively, "He says this all the time while in his cups. 'tis a lot like my proposed marriage...it tends not to happen."

"Where abroad?" asked McCarthy.

"Perhaps Copenhagen...where my mother is from, or Norway...she has relations in business over there...and I speak the language."

"But Nick has you earmarked for deputy next year...he has his heart set on it."

"That is too bad! I have had enough." He was unsteady on his feet and resolved to stop drinking immediately.

"What you need is a good bout of revelry!" McCarthy slapped him on the back suddenly so that he had to grip hold of Trimingham to remain upright.

"If he goes in this state, he will not be able to stand...the ladies will be obliged to prop him up," Trim said airily.

"I shall be stone cold sober in less than a quarter hour," Fairchild called to the pot boy and gave him generous coinage to bring strong coffee. "Are you joining us, Trim?"

"I think not!" Trim said. "I am betrothed, you know."

Fairchild turned to McCarthy and informed him in the sententious tone of the inebriated. "He has been betrothed to her since he was eleven...he put down the claiming suit then...but the denouement never occurs..."

"I was thirteen actually," said Trim in good humour. "And she twelve..."

Fairchild went on in festive manner. "It is not even clear whether she has ever said yes..."

"You have a good woman in your life... I envy you!" McCarthy opined.

Trim was silent and somewhat diffident and Fairchild supplied an answer. "She is certainly a good woman...her goodness is legendary! She makes the large decisions and orders his soul..."

"'tis somewhat true..." admitted Trimingham, grinning.

"But you love her?" asked McCarthy.

"He does!" Fairchild said.

"I do," confirmed Trim.

"He is a one-woman man, Dominic..."

"I am!" Trim affirmed, and then turned to Fairchild. "You used to be so yourself, of course, at one time." This was a risky statement and Trimingham knew it, but knew also it was an appropriate reminder of what could be again, with time.

"I did," Fairchild confirmed, his eternal grief soothed minimally by the surroundings and the alcohol. There was a ponderous silence and McCarthy had not long joined the staff when the tragedy of his sweetheart had been talked of. He longed to enquire more into his personal history, but knew it to be imprudent. "Ah God! To love a woman and know she loves you in return," he lamented instead.

"You have experience of that yourself?" Trimingham asked as Fairchild took the coffee from the pot boy and scalded his mouth trying to drink it…

"I do…but our families are mortal enemies and she will not leave them. It caused us to part. I keep thinking to find a woman to love over here but so far it has not happened…and that is another thing…" McCarthy watched Fairchild pour milk into the coffee. "…the one rule at this occasion is not to seek assignation with the ladies in the outside world…"

"That is easy enough," said Fairchild.

"You are sure you will not come?" McCarthy asked Trimingham.

"I am sure," Trim replied.

"The good woman awaits you, no doubt?"

"She does, at a later hour!"

"I would willingly change places with you, Timothy. There is nothing to compare…*the timeless knowledge of unchanging eyes and loving hands!*"

"Who wrote that?" Trimingham asked.

"It escapes me for the moment…" McCarthy admitted.

"God's Teeth!" Fairchild gave more coins to the pot boy to find them a cab. "… Spare me the Friday night ramblings of romantics… I'll lay you odds it was Byron…"

"Well, 'twas not, that I do know…nor was it Shelley…" McCarthy put on his jacket and ran his hands through his dark curly hair. "Thank the saints I remembered to shave before I came tonight… I sometimes do not on a carefree Friday eve."

"In luck gents…" cried the pot boy, "Cab comin' around the corner instantly…"

Trimingham was allowing himself to be drawn into a hand of cards with men he knew from his own place of employment. "And remember…" he called to Fairchild as they moved off, "…you own the shoe emporium here in the town, the one located between the dispatch office and the public baths. I myself bought some fine hessian boots from you last month…excellent value, but the attitude of your staff leaves a lot to be desired…"

Fairchild swore at him and McCarthy laughed loudly…"Trim has a rare wit; it has to be said!"

"Does he not!" assented Fairchild. "He is indispensable at all festive occasions…"

McCarthy gave more coins to the pot boy while pushing Fairchild from the tavern before the coach driver became impatient and left without them. They boarded the coach-and-four to join two other passengers bound for a destination a few minutes along the road, and he pulled his scarf up around his lower face to obliterate the odour of alcohol then shut his eyes and pretended to doze. Careful of his reputation now when out and about in case meeting with parents or others who knew of him where he did not necessarily know of them.

"He has a bad toothache!" McCarthy explained to the middle-aged couple occupying the carriage with them and beamed his effusive charming smile so that they smiled too.

"I do!" muttered Fairchild through the scarf. He thought of his father's dismay, had he known of his often-inebriated states these days. The carriage sped into the darkness of the night and away from the town.

* * *

And so, lessons with the upper form girls took on a new level of attentiveness, laced with caution and antipathy thick in the air like a pungent spice. He did not care. He had attained an ease of the working day. In matters of learning, he was reasonable and patient and he knew that intelligence was not an indicator of how quickly children learned or even the way they learned. He had gleaned—in common with many other educators—that there was more than one sort of intelligence, several ways of assessing and absorbing information. He followed the work of experts in the field, from Austria and from Scandinavia. The subject was new to education but was gaining ground with the more enlightened in the profession. He was egalitarian in his teaching methods, but didactic in his expectations of conduct and application.

The demeanours of Melanie Petersham and Melissa Shaw had altered noticeably. Melissa Shaw still looked at him with pure disdain when she thought he did not see; a kind of extreme loathing which—if he caught her eye—she swiftly turned to indifference. They were careful in their behaviour and sought to placate him with a show of obedience to instructions. He was to them like a semi-tamed animal they were forced to tolerate that might at any time turn on them if provoked.

Melanie, Millicent and Melissa said nothing to anyone of what had transpired in the waiting room. Until Violet and Ursula, two recent newcomers to the upper form, were found guilty of having forged letters to excuse their lack of homework and were ordered to return at ten minutes past four. Melissa pinched Melanie hard on the way out of the class to deter her from saying anything to them, sensing that Melanie was eager to do so.

The next day before the lesson, Ursula and Violet began relating the punishment to the class, giving details of the waiting room exactly as they remembered from their own experience. Everyone was aghast. "I thought I would faint clean away," said Ursula dramatically, "When he told us what was going to happen."

Melanie yawned exaggeratedly and said, "I could have told you, you would not…"

Melissa kicked her on the ankle, but it was too late. "Has the same thing happened to you?" queried Violet in surprise.

"It has!" Melanie was not in the mood to deny anything. She began reliving her own thoughts and memories of the day for the enthralment of the assembled group and Melissa groaned loudly while Millicent put her head in her hands: their sacred privacy on the matter was shattered.

"It does not matter…" Melanie assured them. "We are all friends…and we should help one another!"

"You might have warned us yesterday!" moaned Violet, "So we would have been prepared."

"Would it have made things easier?" demanded Melissa. "Of course it would not! You at least did not have to spend all afternoon in abject terror."

"Perhaps you are right," said Ursula. "I prefer not to have had prior knowledge."

"I myself would have preferred to have known…" said Melanie, "But we did not have that advantage."

"Well, we all have the advantage of prior knowledge now…" asserted Elspeth.

"Imagine if Abigail were still here," cried Miranda gaily, "She might never have been out of the waiting room."

"I think not!" said the pragmatic Jane. "Even she would have learned to curb her argumentative ways."

A debate then ensued about whether they should see themselves as victims of his callousness, or as rebels who cared little. It was a matter for individual sensitivity, and opinion was divided. The dissection and discussion of the retribution was irresistible and morbidly fascinating, a little like the mysteries of childbirth or the marital bed…or other rites of passage.

* * *

Fairchild was satisfied at last with the way they saw him; draconian and implacable; a mere irritant to their weekday lives. They were a component of the means to his survival, until he could break free, and they knew the line they should not cross, separating them from suffering. Their flirtation with enmity and chaos was mostly dissolved. Though naturally he did not expect complete capitulation. Human nature might prevail.

On the verge of her final departure, on the last day of the last ever lesson, Melissa Shaw lingered in the empty classroom, committing to memory its colours and contours for a series of paintings she may later attempt. Fairchild returned unexpectedly to sort books and pack his voluminous satchel of books and entered as she made haste to leave. She ignored him, her eyes in that half-closed deprecating stare followed by the dismissive movement away from him, as always. Her eyes were quite stunning—the colour of grey doves in sunlight—and in a very few years she would most probably be beautiful.

"Goodbye, Miss Shaw…" he told her as she headed to the door. "I wish you well."

She hesitated with her back to him and he thought she would ignore him totally, but then she turned. "And to you, Mr Fairchild… I would like to say it has been a pleasure, but of course it has not."

She awarded him a fleeting glance, her face flushing at her own temerity in the remark. He remained neutral in expression and looked at her. She was no longer a pupil in his jurisdiction and he allowed her to have the last word. She left swiftly and he sat at his desk and took his ease, time to spare at the end of the working week. He put his feet up on the desk and permitted himself a full smile, his attention on the tree-line beyond the window.

Part Two
October 1844

High Teas and Low Tactics

And then their paths crossed again some four years later, at her home—a spacious and opulent residence of twenty odd rooms, plus servants' quarters, set in fifty acres of pasture and woodland. Having left the detested school, she seldom thought of Fairchild—he was part of her past, her childhood, an odious figure of male authority she did not care to mentally pursue. Then one day while returning from an outdoor painting excursion she saw him, descending the front steps and making for his trap. He had become associated with one of her brothers; Damien, an experimental chemist who kept his small laboratory in his own large room next door to hers. Anthony Fairchild was part of an educational reform organisation founded by a group of young men; Oxford graduates who deplored the state of education in its deficiency and inefficiency in Britain and consulted with government ministers and other officials. In this capacity he was tasked with various roles, and now had the responsibility of liaising with Damien Shaw, offering sponsorship to his projects in return for his speaking and demonstrating at various academic establishments.

Having alighted from the trap she shared with Damien; she handed it over to one of the grooms who took it back to the stables—the same groom having brought Fairchild's own trap to the front of the house. She took the hold-all containing her equipment from the groom, before he could carry it in for her; she preferred to carry it herself wherever possible, it was perhaps her proudest and most treasured possession. She loved the feel of it, and the substance it had, signifying as it did her worth in the world, rather than her privileged place easily given and received.

About to climb into his conveyance, and upon seeing her, Anthony Fairchild shielded his gaze from the bright September light to view her more clearly. Without hat, as always, his illustrious fair hair glimmered in the sun. Recognising her vaguely as she made for the steps down which he had just descended. He had been informed by her brother that she had once sat in his classroom and he had cast his mind back to try to recall her. Since her time quite a few girls had sat in his classroom and their faces were generally a blur—he forgot them as soon as he left the building, he generally detested tutoring them as much as most of them detested being tutored. These days as deputy head, he rarely had to teach the girls at all. Another male teacher undertook the duty while he was occupied with more important matters at the male academy.

He cast his eyes on the female crossing the shaled driveway and briefly recollected her, if a little hazily. Obviously, she looked quite different. Only her eyes were familiar—and perhaps her expression of self-absorption into matters not of the immediate moment. That she seemed bent on not looking his way did not help his memory. She moved with a swiftness of stride which did justice to her agility but not her status as a lady. She seemed practically to run, her skirts lifted in one hand, her pelisse thrown about her shoulders and askew. She was tall and willowy, elegant in stature, even in her outdoor and rather shoddy attire. Naturally he realised that persons of her heritage had no need to prove anything to anyone. He moved quickly and stepped in front of her. "Miss Shaw?"

She stared at him with astonishment and a face of impatience and—beyond that—one of abhorrence. He was quite wrong-footed.

"Well?" she demanded, rudely for any lady.

"You do not remember me?"

"Should I?" she enquired, her art equipment becoming heavy to hold while standing still. It was not apparent how he should take the reply.

"May I relieve you of that burden?" He was levelling her with his jade green eyes. They were unreadable but seemed to her to be full of a youthful candour she did not remember from before, and this somehow managed to reduce his true chronological age. Something in her jolted and shifted and moved like the unobserved fingers of a clock. He seemed almost boyish and she felt the reality of the past slipping from her. She grasped with her mind to hold on to it, the shade and mood of it. Covetously. She did not wish to relinquish it. Melanie and she—when the subject was allowed into their busy world—still detested him with a blunted kind of loathing. Melanie perhaps more so. He was waiting for her reply, his hands held palms upwards to accept her hold-all.

"No thank you…but perhaps you would let me pass so I may go into the house," she told him with a grandeur at odds with her attire…

She was, he felt, the strangest of creatures. Without any pretence to civility or without the usual vestige of pretension. He was not accustomed to women shunning his interest. "Of course…" He stepped to one side, his vanity being second to his excellent manners. He was not about to explain himself to a female who did not recall the first thing about him, or seem inclined to want to know him at all.

"Thank you!" Melissa said with marked dignity and felt exuberant at the slight she had given this perfidious tyrant from her increased worldliness since the days she had been obliged to know him.

And then her mother came around the corner of the house, carrying a basket of late summer blooms. "Oh…" she said lightly. "And who might this gentleman be?"

Melissa sighed; her irritating mother always interfering at the wrong moment. She thought to expedite matters and be inside. "His name is Mr Fairchild, Mama!"

"How nice…" Mrs Shaw moved to him and presented her hand, now removed from her gardening glove, and he accepted it into his own ungloved hand and bowed formally and briefly, moving his attention back to her daughter as if seconds may miss him the chance for better understanding. "Then you do recall me?" he said to Melissa with ironic inflection.

"Of course I do…though I am trying not to…"

"Melissa!" said her mother in mild admonition. "That is rather rude!"

So, it was not simply his own vanity or sensibility—she *was* rude. "I had the pleasure of teaching Miss Shaw at Barton Grange," he said.

Melissa laughed shortly and looked away from the proceedings. "I am glad you thought it so, Mr Fairchild…"

He smiled thinly. "Life places us often in difficult positions and unlikely situations…" he pronounced in his own defence.

"Does it really!" she muttered, her lips barely moving.

"And what brings you here, Mr Fairchild?" queried Mrs Shaw.

"I was visiting your son… Damien…"

"Oh indeed…he is certainly my son…" Mrs Shaw, whose first name was Marguerite, laughed prettily and took in Fairchild's pleasing countenance: his estimable appearance and manners and cultured air of confidence. "Perhaps you would care to take some tea?" she ventured.

"I cannot, I am afraid…another day perhaps?"

Marguerite glimpsed her daughter gazing at him rapaciously while his attention was diverted and she completely mistook the situation. "Sunday perhaps?"

"Splendid…" he said. "That would be very agreeable."

Melissa made an exasperated sound and they looked at her with differing expressions.

"That is settled then…" said Mrs Shaw, turning to leave and picking up her skirt in preparation for the steps. "About four?"

"Thank you, Ma'am…" He grinned more than smiled, covering it instantly by tightening his jaw. It jolted her back years, to seeing him on odd occasions (as rare as hen's teeth) make the same kind of facial movement, quelling it quickly as if it betrayed him.

Mrs Shaw disappeared towards the house, having accomplished her worst. Anthony Fairchild paused before moving to the phaeton and inclined his head to Melissa politely in farewell. "Until Sunday…"

She was beyond angry, beyond confused, she was incandescent with furious energy and she moved to follow him as he climbed in. "Do not bother attending!" she said. "My mother was simply being polite… I have no wish to see you."

He took the reins of the trap and then looked down at her. "And naturally, the world revolves around your wishes?" He smiled, but not with any pleasure, and she turned and hurried up the steps, dropping half the unsecured equipment from the hold-all as she did so.

* * *

"I scarcely believe it…" said Melanie the next day when they met in St Mary's Gardens. "How has he the gall to accept such an invitation? Knowing how much you detest him!"

"I know not…but I told him I do not wish to see him." Melissa paced alongside her as they pursued their separate thoughts, all lines of it going back years to the academy.

"How does he know Damien, did you say?" asked Melanie.

"He is associated with an educational foundation and they wish to sponsor Damien…or something of the sort."

160

"But I did not think Damien was so…so…" Melanie floundered for words, "So accomplished and legendary in his field…we always thought he was blowing his own trumpet."

"I know…but obviously he has some merit," Melissa said grudgingly—her brother being almost as detested as Fairchild.

Melanie began to increase her speed, incensed at the thought of this man stepping once more into their orbit, albeit professionally, and outraged at the thought of Melissa being vulnerable to him again. "He will be constantly at your residence now…"

"Matters not," claimed Melissa. "I shall revile him at every turn, if he dares to approach me."

"That may please him!" claimed Melanie, heading without pause for the exit to the gardens. "How did he look betimes?" she enquired, despite her ire.

"Well, he…he was… I did not really notice…" Melissa was lost for rightful words.

"You must have had some impressions…with your critical artists' eye…" complained Melanie. "Was he haggard or bald? Or fat and stooped? What?"

"Heavens above, Mel, 'twas only a few years back…he looked the same…perhaps a bit older…but somehow more youthful…"

"Older but at the same time youthful!" scoffed Melanie. "Quite an enigma…even for him!"

"I was too shocked to make an assessment… I was furious and not concentrating…" opined her closest friend.

As one mind they made for the tea shop; fancies and a hot drink being the only recourse for such a dreadful turn of events. "Well, if he is to attend on Sunday for tea, then I shall put in an appearance…" said Melanie as they took their seat at a window table.

Melissa looked distressed. "Is that wise?"

"Wisdom scarcely enters into it?" retorted Melanie with asperity. "Self-respect is everything."

"But you will be unable to contain your anger and displeasure."

"I shall try." Melanie picked up the written list of confectionery and decided which to choose.

"But if you do not contain yourself my parents will be extremely annoyed…my father hates any discourtesy to visitors…" Melanie's parents and her own were good friends due to their fathers' business exploits, and all would be shared knowledge if they were not careful.

"How dare the man!" murmured Melanie, scanning the menu while her thoughts were still on the social dilemma of Sunday. "What a nerve he has!"

"Well, 'twas my mother…she all but insisted! Annoying woman that she is!"

"Perhaps she would not be so eager if she knew how he had dealt with us on occasions," observed Melanie.

Immediately in agitation, Melissa dropped the cake fork she had been toying with onto the polished table, noisily. Neighbouring customers turned to stare. "You are not to say one word of that…" she hissed. "'tis unthinkable…and my mother would not be altered in her opinion…they would all find it amusing and say it served us right…they would simply dismiss it as whimsical childhood folly and retribution… I can just picture it! Are you listening to me, Melanie?"

"Yes, yes…" Melanie patted Melissa's hand soothingly. "Be calm, Lissy, I shall not mention anything."

Melissa was disbelieving. "Mel, I do not think you should appear."

"Trust me, my sweet, I will not do anything that cannot be justified or that might be seen as rude…" Melanie smiled winningly. And still Melissa was unconvinced, she did not trust her on this subject but could not deter her from calling if she so wished.

"He is still teaching at Barton Grange, is he?" enquired Melanie after some pause for summoning the waitress.

"Yes, but he is deputy headmaster now," said Melissa. "He told Damien, apparently…"

"For pity's sake! The power will have gone entirely to his head…" murmured Melanie, but with some less aggravation.

* * *

Melissa thought of ways to avoid the Sunday tea. The idea of it was mortifying for reasons she did not quite comprehend—it was a brain soup of mixed and terrifying possibilities and heightened reactions. But to not attend would annoy her mother and no doubt raise undue suspicion with other family members, and explanation then was unthinkable.

She entered the drawing room on Sunday afternoon at five minutes before four o'clock and found her father poking the fire, his favourite indoor hobby, and her mother poking at her floral arrangements. Damien sitting staring from the large windows in serious contemplation.

"Who is coming to this Sunday tea?" asked her father cheerily. "Apart from the family…"

"Only Mr Fairfax, dear," said her mother.

"Fairchild!" corrected Melissa. "His name is Fairchild."

"And who's he when he's at home?" queried her father.

"A friend of Melissa's," said Marguerite Shaw.

"He is no friend of mine…" Melissa informed the room.

"Well, of Damien then…" said her mother impatiently; the less said about her contrivance to romance the easier things might flow. Her daughter had already spurned introductions to several highly suitable men; local politicians, a couple of struggling aristocrats, a successful banker. Declaring she did not wish to wed, and was not sure she would ever wish it. Stupidity of the highest degree, in Marguerites' opinion. Her father seemed to indulge her in this, believing her wise enough to believe that only genuine affection should be the incentive.

"Damien hardly knows him…" Melissa was telling her father. "He knows him professionally that is all."

"Then if he isn't a friend of either of you, who the devil is he friendly with?" asked Giles Shaw, pausing the din of his grate rattling.

"I doubt he has many friends…" Melissa said a little peevishly, and her mother swung around from the vase of flowers. "Melissa, I hope you are not going to be rude and off-hand with him…he seems a nice well-bred young man."

"He is not so young, he must be now at least nine and twenty…he was four and twenty when he first came to the Grange," she claimed, and her father straightened his back, wincing a little, the poker held aloft. "There'd better not be any impoliteness to guests in this house!" he warned, his paunch sitting comfortably above his burgundy trousers. She thought about Melanie arriving and looked pained for a few seconds.

"No indeed…" chimed Damien. "I do not want my sponsorship jeopardising…"

"Exactly who is he?" persevered Giles, "I still don't have that fact."

"A linguist of esteem…but he had the misfortune to teach Melissa at school," Damien said.

Seizing the moment, she addressed her father. "He is a mere school master, Papa…no-one of consequence."

"He is not a mere schoolmaster…" declared her brother. "He is an accomplished academic with a growing influence, and now deputy head of Barton Grange…he lobbies parliamentary groups on educational reform."

"Lars!" said her mother. "Are we grand enough for him?"

She ignored them both. "You see, Papa, he is just another self-satisfied windbag…'tis why he and Damien get along so well." She looked at her father with aplomb; knowing he thought this of most politicians and government. Her father seemed bemused. "And what has he to do with you?" he asked Damien, seldom keeping abreast of looser family gossip. Damien entered at once into complicated explanations, with self-gratulatory asides thrown in, to which nobody listened. Eventually, Giles Shaw had the gist and held up his hand and stopped Damien in his tracks. "I see now, and that makes more sense."

"You also see then why my sister should not be present," Damien said importantly. "She may offend him."

Melissa made scoffing laughter in the midst of drinking lime water, and spluttering it back into the glass in her dismay. "*Me* offend *him*…?"

The three members of her family waited for her to give explanation of the loaded comment. She sealed her lips and assumed a superior expression.

"You are hardly fit for polite society…" Damien remarked. "With your churlish attitudes to people of our gender."

The phrasing of this criticism amused her more; soon she would be giggling too much and unable to hold it in.

"Tell her not to attend, Father…" Damien entreated in conclusion. "I do not want this opportunity going west."

"I do not wish to attend…" she said hotly. "'tis Mama's doing, not mine. I cannot abide him."

"You seemed quite taken with him the other day on the drive…" her mother said. "He is very pleasing to the eye…it has to be said."

"You are mistaken!" declared Melissa.

Her mother's attention was again on the floral arrangement. "And please try to be more biddable when he arrives…"

"I shall find that almost impossible."

"There had better be no impoliteness to visitors…" Giles repeated, but was interrupted by the entrance of her middle brother, Edmund, and his wife and their two young children. Giles was always heartened by his two grandchildren and forgot the subject of Fairchild immediately.

Marguerite was now telling Edmund and Geraldine of the guest they expected. Melissa sighed and made faces of disgust for them to see her feelings on the man in question so that there would be no further misconceptions about romantic allusions. "Melissa does not wish to be present..." said her mother cheerfully, "But it will look bad if she does not stay...she was present when he was invited, and indeed, I think she was the reason he accepted."

"Utter nonsense, Mama..." She was about to add more scathing denials and rebuttals when Damien jumped in.

"He will most likely be relieved if she is not here..." he declared. "He has perhaps had quite enough of her for one lifetime."

"That will do," said Giles from the hearth. "I will not have this squabbling in the drawing room...or any other room for that matter...and I do not want to hear it when this Fairfax man is here..."

"Fairchild," corrected Damien impatiently.

Geraldine, Edmund's wife, sat herself on the sofa nearest the oblong sideboard where cutlery and china and tea cups were laid in readiness, together with covered dishes of edibles. She gazed pointedly at Melissa with sparkling humour. Melissa stared her down and frowned, which did nothing to dowse Geraldine's curiosity.

At fifteen minutes after four, the outer bell from the porch was heard to clang and then Fairchild was admitted by the maid. He bade everyone a courteous good afternoon and looked directly at Melissa with a neutral expression. He sat on one of the large sofas, which seated five with ease, at the opposite end from her. So that she became, with the passing moments and without the use of her eyes, intensely aware of him; his inhalations of breath, his quiet throat clearings, the small incidental sounds of masculinity in repose. She largely ignored him, having bid him welcome in some slight and false way.

"How are you these days?" he asked her after a while, as if he genuinely cared, and she cast upon him a brief glance, her eyes slowly blinking as she muttered a reply. Then she looked away to convey her disinterest in his interest. Her mother stared at her; the rudeness being painfully apparent. Things were made more awkward by her sister-in-law's curious gaze upon them—just too intense for polite drawing room society. Geraldine must not become aware of anything amiss. She was like a dog with a bone where the personal doings of others were concerned.

Fortunately, Damien held sway with his pompous self-interest and began boring Fairchild, and anyone else who may listen, with his latest experiments and projects. There was an immense strain about the proceedings, they were somewhat unreal, and she looked covertly from the side of her eye at Anthony Fairchild, taking in as best she could his general visage. He appeared more mature in ways she could not fathom. His features more pronounced. His lustrous blonde hair well-groomed and a little longer, in keeping with current fashion; small tendrils of its loose curl clinging to his upper neck. His clothes were immaculate and spoke of expensive tailoring.

She thought again of how she might sketch him—his excellent bone structure and his almond shaped eyes and high cheekbones. He was perhaps very attractive to most women; her mother and Geraldine were almost drinking him in, unable to look away for long. She was suffused with confusion; the past opposing the changing present. She stared at the flames of the fire, high and colourful due to her father's ministrations, and then she became aware of his voice, low and even, just as she remembered it, bearing a tone she did not. "I am sorry…were you speaking to me?" she enquired.

"I was asking how long you have been painting!"

"Oh, a long time, since I was about twelve…but more seriously since I left…since leaving Barton Grange." She could not bring herself to use the word 'school'—it pained her to do so.

He nodded and kept his gaze on her. He was not one for wasting words. And then the dreadfully inevitable occurred and Melanie was announced by the butler, and flounced into the centre of proceedings, making her entrance in a flamboyant fashion, as only she could. She halted abruptly on seeing Fairchild and feigned surprise. "Had I known you had such a distinguished guest I would not have bothered to call…" she told Melissa. "But I was passing and thought to see how you are…"

"She is not changed since you saw her the day before last…" said Damien provocatively, and he gave one of his wide, unbecoming grins to Fairchild, as if the other might wish to share the humour.

"Be quiet, Damien," snapped Melanie in her newly confident woman-of-the-world mode, acquired since her engagement to a successful young lawyer. "You know nothing about it, as usual…"

"We'll not have any bickering today, thank you," enunciated Giles in a menacing low tone.

Melanie swept around and faced Fairchild and smiled: supreme satisfaction laced with malevolence. "Anthony, how are you these days?"

Geraldine suppressed a gasp and Marguerite sighed in muted horror at the flagrant use of this visitor's first name. Melissa waited for the floor to open and swallow her and willed an excuse to spring to mind that might extricate her from the room. None came.

Fairchild took this use of his given name in his stride, having remembered suddenly where it lay in the controversial script of their shared past. "I am well, thank you," he replied coldly, and it was as palpable as the fragrance of the cut flowers and the furniture polish that there existed bad feeling. Having risen on her entrance he did not offer to take Melanie's hand and sat again at once. His chilly reserve barely disguising his misgivings.

The infant daughter of Edmund and Geraldine had entered the scene, as Melanie seated herself between Fairchild and Melissa, and somewhat distracted the onerous mood by giving her doll to Melanie whom she knew from previous occasions would be interested in it. Melanie accepted it and cooed over the tying and untying of its ribbons for the little girl's benefit. "Are you fond of small children, Anthony?" she asked airily and was unsurprised by the long pause and the general silence as the assembled group struggled with their bafflement and mesmeric interest in proceedings most bizarre.

"I am not acquainted with many..." replied Anthony Fairchild after some thought. "Apart from my nephews and nieces."

Melanie smiled again with a sickly falseness and said, "Of course it would be a distinct disadvantage in your profession to be fond of children, I would imagine...although I thought perhaps small children might escape your disapproval."

There were muted sounds of anguished surprise from Marguerite and Geraldine, and a quickly suppressed bark of laughter from Damien.

"Really, Melanie!" sighed Marguerite.

Melissa felt she might faint, but she sprang to her feet instead, her voice a veritable screech. "Melanie, perhaps you would care to see the painting I did of the lake? I was thinking I may give it to you and Geoffrey for your wedding present, if you like it. We can go to the art room and survey it..."

"You will do nothing of the sort," said her father placidly. "Bide where you are, the pair of you? We're in the middle of Sunday tea and we don't need any such rudeness as that."

"Indeed not, Lissy…" echoed Melanie. "Anthony will think we have not been raised with manners or respect for others…or that we think life a mere folly for our own entertainment…"

Fairchild kept his counsel and steeled himself for worse to come. Melanie Petersham's appearance was obviously planned and timed. "Then he may think our parents remiss and that 'tis somehow their fault…" Melanie continued recklessly.

"Melanie!" hissed Melissa, and everyone stared. Geraldine with her tea cup perilously balanced between her lips and her saffron silk dress.

"What is it, Lissy?" asked Melanie blithely.

Melissa made scowling, venomous faces at her while Fairchild stared languidly at the far wall and the maid entered with scones and savouries and more tea. And Marguerite Shaw was thankful to have something to do besides fret over what she had innocently engineered in the way of calamitous social gatherings. While her husband absolved himself from responsibility by playing with his beloved fire grate.

"So, what position do you hold now at Barton Grange?" Melanie enquired of Fairchild, knowing already the answer to the question, but the resounding silence of the room bequeathing her full power.

"Deputy head," he replied obligingly in a flat voice.

"Deputy head! How nice! Isn't that nice, Lissy? And so laudable."

Melissa made no reply, her wits deserting her.

"And is Mr Frondley still head?" enquired Melanie.

"No, he died, shortly after his retirement," said Fairchild in the same bland tone.

"Poor man. And who is headmaster now then?"

"Mr Stevenson."

"Oh yes, I recall…the one who could never leave the women alone…"

There was further astonished stillness, during which nobody moved. Then Marguerite intoned. "Really, Melanie…" for the second time.

It was obvious Melanie was out to wreak havoc and savour retribution, but no-one knew quite what to do about it.

Melanie bounced back with equanimity. "Well, Aunt Maggie, I am only quoting what my father has said."

Giles, having followed the last bit of the conversation, commented. "That is untrue. Your father would not make such a comment in the company of women or children…that much I do know of the man."

"Perhaps I overheard him when he thought I wasn't listening?" retorted Melanie.

"More like it," concurred Giles, "Ears everywhere you women…"

Mrs Shaw intercepted in her gentler voice. "Even so, Melanie, we do not blurt out things of that nature in polite circles…"

The atmosphere and the tension had to break. The two girls exchanged glances and hilarity descended. Melissa, in a split second, overcome by amusement. She leaned forwards and covered her face with her fingers, emitting sounds that were not readily recognisable, her upper body shuddering.

"Are you ill, Lissy?" enquired her mother.

She was unable to speak, she fumbled for her kerchief and retrieved it from her sleeve and put it over her mouth. "Oh, you are laughing?" stated her mother.

A squeak of strangulated agony came from her throat as she nodded mutely.

"Then do it in a more open manner, not in that silly way, and let it be brief!" Mrs Shaw summoned the maid to bring more hot water for the tea.

Melanie succumbed next; holding her breath while appearing to gaze up to the ceiling, her face screwed into a strange grimace, her lips pursed and her eyes shut tightly.

Melissa's brother, Edmund, watched with a deadpan expression as they struggled with these comedic forces, no doubt connected in some way to the mention of the Stevenson fellow. Then Gerladine, a quiet amenable girl—despite her fervent nosiness—and a few years older than them, caught the vibration as if laughing gas had been released into the room. She released her own amusement in a tinkling cascade which was easier to listen to. Then looked at her mother-in-law who smiled thinly for politeness' sake.

It was all too entertaining; it might have been a heaven-sent opportunity earned over years of grudge-savouring. Melanie sprang from the sofa and paced towards the window to turn her back on the assembled company, before she fell to the carpet, overcome with the hilarity of it. "Is Gregory not here?" she enquired, recovering partial control of herself. She liked Melissa's cousin Gregory enormously, though Gregory did not return this compliment—preferring, in his own modest way, females less boisterous of character.

"He is playing at someone's wedding anniversary!" Melissa said and she half turned to Fairchild, deciding to be socially correct for an instant. "My cousin Gregory plays the piano like an angel...his 'Emperor' is superb. Is it not, Melanie?"

"Exquisite," agreed Melanie in a tight high voice of iron control.

"Is he professional?" queried Fairchild obligingly.

"He may be, once his father stops dictating to him!" declared Melissa. Being accustomed mostly to the kind of music played in inns and taverns, though familiar with fugues and classical arias from his childhood, he had to wrack his brains to remember what and who the 'Emperor' was. "How old is he?" he asked to cover his ignorance. "He's one and twenty but does not get his inheritance until he is twenty-five...from his paternal grandfather's estate!" Melissa informed, and then made further effort by enquiring. "Do you like classical music?"

He hesitated, being indifferent for the most part, although if Gregory played as poorly as some of the drawing room performances he had been forced to witness then he had had a lucky escape. But Melanie turned from the window and jumped into the breach. "Of course he does not..."

Fairchild looked at her for perhaps the second time only that day. "How do you reach that audacious presumption?"

Melanie spoke directly to Melissa. "One has only to look at him to see that!"

Melissa shot Melanie a fierce stare. Mrs Shaw had not heard the comments, being preoccupied with her granddaughter's request for trifle, but was alerted by another horrified general silence and looked across at them. "What are you talking about?"

"Cousin Gregory's piano playing, Mama!" Melissa said quickly.

Fortunately, only Geraldine, Edmund and Damien had heard the interchange. Her father had not, or else there might be awful consequences by now.

Melissa lowered her head and peered at everyone from beneath her frontal hair arrangement. Her brothers and Geraldine were watching her with varying expressions of unrest. Geraldine was looking delightedly scandalised. Her brother Edmund shook his head slightly in embarrassment. Damien might have said something but was aware of his need to tread carefully around the visitor whose solicitations to financial support he craved.

Surely Fairchild would remove himself and leave now; she would have done so when being insulted so readily. But he was obviously not going to move and in some ways, she began to admire his fortitude. Her amusement at this realisation grew worse in the encroaching quiet of the drawing room and she made muted coughing sounds which the others might recognise as merriment. These were the final bars of her mirthful orchestration she hoped—for she knew herself well—and she lifted her fingers from her face and saw Melanie again wearing her tortured expression and exhaling with an alarming sound like a hiccup. Melissa relapsed again behind her fingers.

Anthony Fairchild observed everything with some distaste and a little fascination; they could indulge their amusement as much as they liked now. He was immune to it.

"For Pete's sake!" said Giles from the hearth. "Sounds like folk in the last stages of consumption!"

This comparison was too much, Melissa fell forwards again and her shoulders shook so that she looked as if she were sobbing—and in less familiar surroundings anyone might believe her to be giving way to that much more acceptable form of emotion. The sofa vibrated gently between herself and Fairchild.

"You see why we feel it right to take ourselves out of the home so much!" said her father to the male company in general.

She was making soft noises, not unlike a stationary steam engine, into the folds of her dress.

"Giles dear, desist with those kinds of comparisons…you are making them worse!" Marguerite offered.

"I'll make them a lot worse if they don't control themselves!" muttered Giles.

Fairchild was reminded of his professional life; those were the kind of comments he would make to pupils. He displayed a swift grin then obliterated it utterly with his tightened jaw. Mrs Shaw noted it and said, "Of course, you might be familiar with these girlish outbursts, Mr Fairchild…do you have sisters?"

"I do not, Ma'am," he said shortly. "But I am familiar, from working in the classroom!"

"There's some might say you deserve a knighthood!" affirmed Giles.

Melanie snorted audibly, unable to stop herself. They were all now looking at her, waiting for her to completely over-step the mark. The mention of the classroom had sobered Melissa and she raised herself to an upright sitting position, placed her hand on her rib cage and in so doing inadvertently pushed her left breast above her low neckline. She made a tiny noise half way between a groan and a sigh, resonant of someone who has reached the end of an arduous hill climb…or a woman on the arc of descent from physical ecstasy.

Fairchild noted it all by glancing at her sidelong, the tiny movement of her small round breast having alerted him. She rolled her eyes and then allowed them to almost cross, releasing her breath and coming back into the practical dimensions of the room.

She felt his stare, and cast him a mutinous look. He was intrigued. She was in full womanhood now, and evidently a female with a deep sense of passion. In his not inconsiderable experience over the last few years, he had discovered it to be an improbability that a woman who enjoyed the range of her various senses with such enthusiasm would not also enjoy the pleasures of the bedroom. He began to see her with new eyes but gave no indication whatever of these reflections; his own drawing room control—like his classroom control—honed to perfection.

"Are you recovered now?" said her mother and then glanced at Melanie who was aloof and unreadable. "And you Melanie?"

Melanie turned and looked at Mrs Shaw, "Quite, thank you."

Melissa could not trust herself to speak. Though she did not quite know what she found so hilarious.

"Thank God…" said Giles taking up lumps of coal with the tongs to throw on the fire and add to the existing heat. "Our visitor will think he is come to some kind of musical theatre!"

Melissa spoke in her own defence. "Papa, do stop…you are so comical!"

Her father said nothing and eyed her with suspicion. She did not normally find him so diverting.

"My husband has a very dry wit," Marguerite said to Fairchild to alleviate any awkwardness.

"I'm not aiming to amuse anyone, Maggie…" Giles told her, and then seeing that the assembled group was generally in good humour he gave way to the demands of his pipe: the mystification of the feminine rabbit hole down which they seemed to have fallen was too much to stomach on a day of rest. "'tis as well my mother is not come yet…" he concluded.

Fairchild looked immediately towards the driveway, visible from the large windows, for signs of another of the Shaw relatives.

Noting this, Edmund said helpfully, "Our paternal grandmother often joins us for Sunday tea."

"I see!" Fairchild said.

"Yes, but she's away with the fairies mostly…" Damien offered. "So, we don't generally take much notice of her."

"Some respect boy!" said Giles through a sheath of tobacco. "That's your grandmother you're talking of!" Edmund addressed Fairchild apologetically. "She has days when she thinks the Napoleonic wars are still being waged!"

Unable to resist, Melissa roused herself from the self-imposed torpor. "Grandmama is the wisest of women…her age is simply against her now…"

Her father looked at her approvingly, he liked the way his daughter defended and adored his mother.

"…and if anyone is away with the fairies, Damien, 'tis you!" she continued.

"I think so too…" conjoined Melanie. "Spouting your fairy tale theories."

"Quite so!" affirmed Melissa, glad to have a sobering topic to earth them. "As in the one where we are all actually floating about here on a pillow of gas…"

"That is not what I have said…you are misquoting the theory…" objected Damien and looked at Fairchild anxiously. "Don't listen to them, they simply love the sound of their own voices…"

"Ha, ha, ha…" Melanie trilled. "Have you listened to yourself, Damien?"

"That will do!" said Giles in reproof and was not heard.

Fairchild stared steadily at the fire grate and cleared his throat. He was clearly above such wrangling.

"The only gas he floats about on is his own…" chirruped Melissa, and Geraldine and Edmund smiled wryly, while she and Melanie struggled to resist further paroxysms of hilarity.

Damien drew a noisy antagonistic breath through his teeth. "You see, Father, I do not know why you let them get away with this kind of insolent rudeness…"

Fairchild smiled to himself and Giles muttered incoherently and the grate rattling began again more vigorously. Melissa watched Melanie's lips quivering and felt herself undergoing a full relapse. She placed the kerchief to her mouth again.

"Stop all this bickering!" her mother warned.

"Yes, indeed…you are making a spectacle of yourselves!" Damien announced.

Melanie whirled round to face him. "Taking the limelight from you is what you mean, for if anyone likes to be centre stage, Damien, 'tis you!"

"Hark who's talking! I don't know what you are doing here…you were not invited."

"How dare you!" Melanie expostulated.

"I invited her," Melissa offered from her guarded position behind the kerchief. "Who do you think you are, Damien? You are being rude to a guest…"

"She isn't a guest…" Damien shot back. "She's an irritating perennial nuisance…like a wasp from the rose garden…"

"Boorish ill-mannered oaf!" rejoined Melanie.

Coming reluctantly into the fray, Giles practically threw the poker to the hearth. "That will now do… I don't want to hear another word… Maggie, give everyone some trifle!"

Damien was not fazed and turned to Fairchild. "Perhaps you'd care to come up and see my latest experiments?"

Fairchild looked pained but before he could decline, Giles spoke. "Leave the fellow be and let him enjoy his tea in peace…he doesn't want boring to death a'fore he can digest his scones! He's likely enjoyed enough diverting behaviour as it is…all this fidgeting and junketing about."

Fanned by the *fidgeting and junketing* of her father's quaint and colourful vernacular, she feared she may grow weak and be unable to move from her seat. A common symptom of too much merriment while wearing laces beneath her day dress.

Sensing that assistance was needed Melanie suggested. "Shall we take some air in the garden, Lissy? You might benefit…"

"No, you shall not," intercepted Giles once more. "As I said, there needs to be less junketing and more calm."

Mrs Shaw handed Fairchild a dish of trifle. He detested trifle but accepted it graciously and ate a tiny amount. Melissa watched surreptitiously. She saw about his features an unmistakable urge to good humour; he was amused by the domestic interlude, or perhaps he was laughing at them silently. Or perhaps he had a sense of fun and was, when out of the school, a different person. The artist in her wondered how she would sketch him. She noted every feature of his face, from his jawline to the slight stubble around his cheeks and chin—rendered almost imperceptible by his colouring.

In the main, his skin was peachy smooth, apart from one faint line beneath each of his eyes, symmetrically running from the outer tip by perhaps a half inch to just above his cheekbones. She was riveted by his pristine perfection of face and oblivious to the fact of his being not quite thirty.

From her own youthful age and vantage point, he seemed to her today to be quite young, quite personable, like any good-looking man one might see in society drawing rooms. And then just as she was about to look away—in case she became so enthralled she would lose her sense of perspective—he turned sharply and caught her looking, his gaze serious and steadfast upon her. It held in its depth confirmation that he knew of her scrutiny, maybe even her thoughts. She grew very warm and panicky. Now the ground should open and swallow her, but naturally it did not. She gave an indifferent smile and he slowly looked away.

He had seen all he needed to see.

She said to Melanie. "Come and sit down…ignore Damien, he is an ignoramus."

Melanie moved towards the sofa but did not reseat herself and Mrs Shaw said, "Would you care for trifle, Melanie?"

"No thank you, more tea will suffice… I had a very late luncheon."

Marguerite busied herself with the tea pot and the cups, telling Fairchild. "I hope you do not think badly of us because of the girls' behaviour…but then again, I expect you might be used to disruption of this kind…"

Melanie scoffed theatrically and hovered at the arm of the sofa, watched carefully by Melissa who sensed a dark prelude to battle. Fairchild had not spoken for long minutes and replied to Mrs Shaw, "Quite, Ma'am…although I always discourage disruptive behaviour in classrooms before I am obliged to become used to it!"

Melanie snorted loudly, incensed by memory. "Yes, that is very true…we can vouch for it, can we not, Lissy? We could write penny dreadfuls on the subject of his discouragement…"

Another ringing silence and Edmund looked directly at Fairchild and Geraldine raised her brows, while Damien smirked. Then Melissa leapt from her seat and grabbed Melanie's arm and shook it violently. Any moment now the topic of the waiting room would be aired and Melissa felt she might faint. The shaking displaced Melanie's headwear—a purple lace concoction with trailing white ribbon, so tiny it barely had gravity enough to rest on her hair. The pause among them was awesome, everyone was waiting for more information; Edmund, Damien and Geraldine staring at Fairchild to see his reaction. Even the children were quiet. Giles looked over at his wife as if she were to blame, as if she might offer explanation to the tangential course the afternoon had taken.

Fairchild discarded the trifle on a low table and sat back into the sofa and crossed his legs. He wondered whether they would now air their childhood grievances over their misbehaviour and the consequences it had given rise to. Well, let them! They had been children and he had authority in the school they attended. He would not dissemble, he had right on his side. But he could tell that Melissa, a wholly different character to her friend, was desperate to keep things private and to herself.

Melanie patted Lissy's hand soothingly and then loosened the claw-like grip on her arm and adjusted her hat. They exchanged glances conspiratorially as she said. "Calm yourself, Lissy! We will speak of other things…" She moved to accept a cup of tea from Mrs Shaw and then returned to her standing position next to the sofa arm.

Geraldine was looking in rapt fascination at Fairchild—unlike any school teacher she had ever seen, undeniably attractive to the female of the species. She began tentatively. "Mr Fairchild…?" They all gazed towards her, agog for what she might say to the stranger in their midst. "I hope you do not mind my asking, but you do not resemble a school teacher. Have you always wanted to become one?" She raised her brows even higher and waited to hear more details of the *penny dreadful* alluded to previously; she read a lot of them in her spare time and considered trying her hand at writing a few.

"No, Ma'am?" said Fairchild shortly.

"Why, Geraldine?" intercepted Damien sportively. "How many school teachers do you actually know these days?"

Ignoring her brother-in-law's sarcasm and her husband's pressure on her arm in an attempt to stay her nosiness, she continued. "Then what made you become one?"

"I am a linguist by education, but I made a bad business investment on leaving university and had to do something to recoup my losses very quickly…" Fairchild favoured her with one of his direct appraisals which betokened both sincerity and humility. "And I was offered a teaching post here, where I am from originally, so I took it."

"I see," said the amenable Geraldine, putting her fingers to her throat and smiling appreciatively at his luminous male charm more than his response.

"How sad…" intoned Melanie, "Especially for the pupils of Barton Grange."

Melissa, from her seated position, grabbed a handful of Melanie's skirt and tugged it like an errant five-year-old, but Melanie shook free of her grip.

"What do you mean, Melanie?" demanded Geraldine, despite Edmund's disquiet; for now, the 'penny dreadful' was bound to unfold.

"Yes, why don't you explain to everyone what you mean?" said Fairchild, unexpectedly catching her off guard, a challenging expression in his eyes directed at Melanie.

Melanie considered matters carefully. Of course she had Melissa to think of in any revelation of this sort, and Melissa may never speak to her again if she spoke out.

"Or perhaps, you prefer me to tell them?" said Fairchild evenly, throwing down the gauntlet.

Melissa leapt from her seat in an alarming manner. "Certainly not! Neither of you is to tell them…and stop goading her," she said to Fairchild.

Geraldine gasped voraciously and Marguerite swallowed tea the wrong way and coughed and choked.

"I think the shoe may be on the other foot, Miss Shaw…" he replied calmly, "When it comes to goading!"

Melissa was animated in a way no-one was accustomed to, almost shouting. "We must change the subject immediately… Melanie, sit down. I will move up to the middle of the sofa so you do not have to sit next to *him*."

There was another slight gasp from Geraldine, and her mother thankfully could still not speak. Realising her verbal crassness, Melissa amended. "I mean… I mean you do not need to sit next to Anthony if you prefer not…" and then she saw that the second usage of his first name may be a worse social blunder and looked at him swiftly. His green eyes became wide—the colour of ripe limes in the light from the window—a quizzical but nonchalant appraisal.

"We must talk of the dresses…tell Mama how you have changed the colour of the bridesmaids' dresses…tell her now!" gabbled the daughter of the house.

"'twill take too long," drawled Melanie, "And bore the men!" She resisted the offer of the seat on the sofa and then began again in a startling change of tack, and said to Fairchild: "Well, Anthony, perhaps Mr Stevenson will pop his clogs soon too, and then you will have complete power…for if ever a person knew how to use power, 'tis you!"

Fairchild marvelled at this change of direction; how they could move from childish spurts of humour to mature verbal manipulation. It was astonishing. He stared at Melanie, his eyes now betraying his deeper annoyance, glittering in a darkening opaque shade of green beneath his pale lashes.

He wondered what he was doing still here! Why did he not invent an engagement elsewhere and leave? Some obscure and perverse inclination was keeping him rooted to the spot. He barely recognised himself.

Noting the intense visionary exchange between him and Melanie, Melissa jumped up suddenly, feeling a little dizzy as the blood fought to reach her brain, and swaying slightly before getting her bearings. "Melanie, where is Geoffrey?" She could not take another minute of this charade and must stop Melanie's rhetorical flow immediately. Or at any moment, she would lose her modesty with her temper and hurl at him the loathing she had harboured these years and mention in passing the waiting room incident. She thought she may simply have to make herself faint if Melanie was not diverted by the question.

But Melanie was diverted, momentarily. "He is outside in the phaeton!"

Marguerite was at once appalled and croaked in her recovering hoarse voice. "What? You have not left that poor boy outside!"

Seconds passed, while this was generally imagined.

"He is not a *poor boy*," Damien remarked off-handedly. "He is already prosperous in London, if I hear rightly!"

"Be quiet, Damien!" said his mother in a harder and shriller voice than they had previously been treated to. "Don't be so impertinent, or you will leave the room."

Damien—used to these sorts of put-downs to his energetic temperament from infancy—said to his brother, "But I notice these two are exempt from condemnation when behaving in that vulgar giggling fashion."

Edmund tutted dismissively. "They are girls, Damien! That is what girls do!"

Sensing an offence to her own gender, Geraldine nudged Edmund with her elbow and frowned at him. He grinned at her and put his thumb and forefinger on her chin to pinch it playfully before moving closer to her ear and whispering for a few moments. Whereupon she grinned too and nudged him again more sharply and whispered in reply. Anthony Fairchild perceived, from his seat on the opposite sofa, that they were very much in love and he thought of Lottie and was at once filled with a plummeting sadness.

Mrs Shaw's voice cut into his reverie. "You see, Giles, we now have the vulgarity of whispering to contend with…" she told her husband.

Giles shook his head and concentrated on the fire flames, dusting off imaginary soot from his hands, dismissing the shortcomings of his younger family.

"How very cross everyone has become today. Mr Fairchild will think we have raised barbarians!" she proclaimed, and then to Melanie: "Why have you not brought Geoffrey in?"

She was not listened to as Melanie continued to stare venomously at Fairchild.

"I do not think barbarians whisper, Mama…" supplied Damien into the breach. "I rather think they bellow and roar…"

"As you do on the staircase unnecessarily, you mean?" Melissa remarked. "As when you summon the maid or someone else?"

"Why is Geoffrey still in the trap?" persevered Marguerite, much stressed about social etiquette gone awry.

Melanie floundered a little. "He is happy out there reading his notes for court tomorrow…and I was only calling in for a few minutes, Aunt Maggie."

"Which as usual becomes all afternoon…" announced Damien to the room.

Melanie continued her explanation with majesty. "Geoffrey is actually quite shy, you know, and he has a bad cold and does not want to give it to anyone! He is very thoughtful on these matters."

Damien looked sidelong at his brother. "Geoffrey Gillis, shy! Do you recognise the description, Eddy? You were at university with him!"

Edmund paused and said in a deadpan manner. "I do not…but perhaps there is another Geoffrey Gillis…"

Damien peered at Melanie with satisfaction. "At any rate, he will catch pneumonia out there if he already has a cold. I'll fetch him in…"

"Mind your own business, Damien…" Melanie was testing the heat of the tea tentatively with her lips. "You may know a lot about a lot of things…but Geoffrey is my fiancé, and I know him better than either of you two… Go and tinker with your potions or something, Damien, and stop interfering…besides, I am leaving directly I have finished this tea…"

She began to sip the tea hurriedly before replacing the cup in the saucer as if she had finished. Edmund, Damien and Fairchild rose in the customary fashion on hearing of her imminent departure. Only Giles remained seated, his privilege as patriarch. But then she lifted the cup again and her eyes glistened with merriment above the rim as they roamed around the assembled company. She took a sudden step sideways and lost her balance a little and lurched, so that the tea was hurled from the cup and onto the lower part of Fairchild's light grey trousers.

Immediate consternation amid the females: the maid was summoned and Marguerite hastily found a tea towel and handed it to him to dab at his trousers while a dampened cloth was brought. "Melanie, really! What is the matter with you today? Is it pre-wedding nerves?"

"I think it must be…" Melanie opined with grossly false coyness. "Anthony, I do beg your pardon. You must send me the bill for the laundering!"

"That won't be necessary," Fairchild told her evenly.

Melissa began pulling Melanie by her arm from the room. Melanie holding onto her frothy headwear with her other hand. "Goodbye everyone…thank you so much for tea…it has been utterly delightful!"

Melissa yanked her through the drawing room doors and accidentally banged them shut after herself so that a reverberating crashing sound echoed about the place. Mrs Shaw stood in the centre of the floor and shut her eyes and drew breath and then looked at her husband whose facial expression she knew of old; it told her he would not comment and that there was nothing to be done with the situation.

"Mr Fairchild, I do not know what to say…" she told the visitor with dignity. Fairchild replaced the damp cloth on the table amid the tea things. "Do not alarm yourself on my behalf, Ma'am… I am familiar with their behaviour from when I had the task of educating them."

Geraldine spluttered her restrained amusement and Edmund pinched her leg to no avail. Damien frowned and nodded like someone in Parliament listening to an attack on the opposition. Only Giles remained unaffected in the midst of his ministrations with the poker.

* * *

Once in the hallway, Melanie tottered weakly across the parquet flooring and leaned on the umbrella stand, stifling the final hilarity with her gloved hand. Melissa joined her and for several moments they were unable to speak. Eventually Melissa assumed a serious demeanour. "Everyone will know you did that on purpose!"

"Not necessarily…'tis in your fevered imagination!"

"I think not, after all the offensive remarks you made to him. And he will certainly know…"

"Excellent, but he cannot prove it…and besides I am leaving now."

At that point, the porch doorbell clanged and the maid scurried out of nowhere to answer it. Her mother's sister, Dorothea, was admitted, along with her husband. Melissa swept them a brief curtsy and said, "Aunt and Uncle, how nice to see you…do go through… Melanie is just leaving…but there is tea being served and several family members are assembled, including a new guest…"

"Oh!" said Aunt Dorothea with doubt, she was always wary of meeting new people "How delightful!"

"Some might think so," stated Melanie in a dour satirical tone. "Others might disagree…"

Melissa nudged her to silence but Dorothea knew Melanie of old and went on imperiously. "There is a young gentleman on the driveway, waiting with a phaeton, enquiring if you are ready to leave, Melanie…are you aware?"

"Yes…'tis Geoffrey…my fiancé. He is always impatient."

Aunt Dorothea and her husband were ushered along by the maid into the drawing room.

"I thought he was too shy for that!" Melissa said.

The hilarity overtook them again and several more minutes elapsed while they took themselves in hand. Melissia doing so first, with a face of exaggerated concern. "'twas like that incident with the inkwell," she said gravely. "Do you recall?"

"Do you think I am likely to have forgotten! That was an accident and not our fault at all…this exactly serves him right! Just a pity I missed his shoes…"

Their renewed giggling was like exotic and strange birdsong at dusk. Then the butler appeared, and sensing that decorum had quite flown he opened the front door widely to expedite Melanie's departure.

She went giddily along the driveway to where Geoffrey was pacing in some annoyance, his health sound and his shyness not in evidence.

Touche

Melissa wondered whether she could decently retire upstairs, but thought it would add to the list of less than decorous behaviour in her parents' eyes, so she went intrepidly back into the drawing room with a deadly serious countenance, not unlike a mourner at a funeral, and resumed her seat. Her father watched her darkly and her mother with misgivings. A boring conversation about the local council was underway.

Edmund was an architect and worked within his father's business and at other times on outside commissions. He was talking of the restoration of the old bridge across the river into the town and soliciting Fairchild's opinion on the disrupted transport flow and how it affected the boys' academy. Her aunt and uncle were enjoying fresh scones and tea. Her father had become more cheerful with their arrival; Gilbert, Dorothea's husband, was of his own age and they discoursed comfortably together. Her mother was similarly heartened to receive her elder sister. With any luck now, the circus of the past hour would be forgotten about.

They all stopped what they were doing and stared at her as she crossed the room, and Fairchild watched her with calm civility as she reseated herself. She was alone now, with the erstwhile school teacher who had re-emerged transformed into some kind of social icon but was perhaps still as lethally threatening in other ways. She was unsupported by Melanie and must now fend for herself. Melanie had set the scene but the finale was all hers, should she wish it.

There was an utter silence as she arranged herself and her skirts on the sofa. "I do not know why you are all staring at me," she said quite crossly.

"I wonder!" said Edmund facetiously.

Then in embarrassment she commented into the room. "Melanie is a little high spirited due to her impending wedding…"

"And what is your excuse?" said Damien.

"Does Gillis actually know what he's letting himself in for?" remarked Edmund.

"He is madly in love with her, *actually*..." she retorted.

"He would need to be..." replied Edmund.

Geraldine found this amusing and sniggered and Melissa shot her a furious look, traitor to their sex as she felt her to be.

"They always say love is blind," said Damien.

"In her case, it would need to be deaf as well..." added Edmund, and Damien fell back into the chair with laughter as Geraldine chirruped her higher pitched merriment.

"I suppose you imagine yourselves to be entertaining," Melissa said with heat. "But you are simply rude."

"Oh, *we* are rude!" intoned Edmund.

"It's as I said earlier, one law for them and another for everyone else," muttered Damien.

"That will do!" Giles warned. "The squabbling better not start again..."

"Have we missed something?" queried Dorothea of her sister, who shook her head and made a face which Dorothea knew meant she would get to hear of things later.

Then Edmund—feeling it incumbent upon himself to put their guest at greater ease after the tea debacle—began telling Fairchild more about the planning proposals for the town high street and Fairchild commented now and then. It was tedium itself. What was he still doing here after the tribulations of the afternoon! Surely, he had had enough now!

She risked a glance at him and saw about his expression traces of vague satisfaction, amusement even, but carefully guarded. He was not discomforted in the least, she thought, but perhaps enjoying observing matters.

Then Geraldine and Edmund said they must leave to take the children home. As soon as they had left her father and uncle immediately began talking of recreational things. "Do you hunt or shoot...or fish?" Giles enquired of Fairchild.

He hesitated and considered his words with care. "I do not hunt or shoot!" he replied.

"Oh...is there a reason for that?" queried Gilbert.

Again, he considered his words carefully. "Well, with the greatest respect, Sir, I do not believe in killing any form of life simply for sport..."

There was another awkward silence for a few seconds—the afternoon would become legendary for them—and she looked at him shrewdly. It was a sentiment she could appreciate as an artist; far too many people had no respect for life form other than human. But she resolved not to let it soften her opinion of him.

Giles rallied first and said, "No need to apologise, young fellow! We have met other men who feel the same. A man's beliefs are entirely his own affair…"

No-one spoke. She awaited his next response. Then he gave it. "My father was a clergyman…and towards the end of his life, a bishop…he taught us not to kill anything if we did not need to eat it, and I find I agree with the principal more as I age…"

She decided to disregard the philosophy in favour of his heritage. "A bishop! Your father became a bishop?" The speculation upon his personal landscape had taken on a wider perspective. He raised his brows to her quizzically. It was as if he had said his father was a circus clown.

"I had used to fish…with friends…when I was a boy, on the river close to the vicarage!" he told the two older men.

Her father was euphoric almost with some kind of relief, the potential suitor or sponsor or whatever he was had an interest he might understand. "You must come and fish on our lake…the trout are abundant…is that not so, Gil?"

Then Gilbert, much encouraged, began a summary of their fishing experiences of the last season and recounted calamitous incidents causing them to miss great catches. These were singularly boring but Giles and Gilbert roared with laughter as Dorothea and Marguerite chatted intermittently about people they knew and the high cost of coal. And so, it went on—monotony itself! Relieved only by the arrival of her cousin Rex—Dorothea and Gilbert's younger son—in the hope of seeing Edmund over a building alteration in his house. He had been delayed by the aforementioned roadworks. "Has Eddy gone?" he enquired, rubbing his hands against the outside cold and surveying the room.

"You have missed him by only a few minutes…" supplied Damien.

Rex was of a pleasant disposition, in his late twenties, singularly lacking in airs of sophistication or artifice of any kind. He nodded to Damien and his parents, bowed formally to Marguerite and Giles, then spotted Melissa. "How do you go, Miss Rembrandt…" he asked in a fond way, using the nickname he always gave her.

Of all her cousins, Melissa thought of Rex as a good soul with a kind heart. "I go well, Rex, thank you…and you? How is Philie?"

Rex's face fell, he could not dissemble, he assumed an immediately distressed countenance. "Not well at all, Lissy."

Marguerite took over the enquiry and spoke in sombre tones as everyone listened respectfully.

"Who is Philie?" Fairchild asked quietly of her, surprising her with his interest.

"Rex's wife, Philomena…" she replied, dropping her voice so he had to lean towards her to hear. She caught the fragrance of his cologne or soap, a pleasing waft of something subtly pungent. "She is in mid-stage confinement but things aren't progressing well…'tis her first child."

Fairchild nodded and said no more and looked over at Rex who was saying…"I do not know what more I can do…"

"Nothing," said his father. "These are women's' matters…"

"She weeps so much and the doctor says it will weaken her if she doesn't stop," continued Rex doggedly.

"Of course it will!" said Dorothea. "The silly girl."

"She cannot help it, Mama…she is very afraid…and of a fragile disposition."

Dorothea made a groaning sound of frustration. "She must summon fortitude…all us women must at these times…or else where would the world be!"

Rex looked at his mother with muted annoyance. "She feels unequal to what is to come…and I feel so helpless…"

"That is how we men feel…" said Giles helpfully, "In the midst of childbirth when we can do nothing but wait…"

"I have told him all that myself," snapped Gilbert, "But he does not heed me. Best to let things take their course and stay away more."

Rex was scandalised at this suggestion. "I cannot just stay away… I must console her. I have to sit with her and hold her hand or she weeps constantly."

Gilbert rolled his eyes to the ceiling and Dorothea sighed audibly. Marguerite laid her hand on her sister's arm and whispered. "You must remember, Thea, how much he adores her…"

In Marguerite's tone was a trace of regret and the implication, that neither she nor her sister had ever been so adored by their own husbands. Though Dorothea seemed as if she had never heard such lamentable nonsense and there was more uncomfortable silence. Melisa coughed loudly to break the heavy atmosphere and relieve her own tension. Gilbert and Dorothea were rather cold remote people, and she wondered often how they had begotten someone as loving and warm hearted as Rex. "I am sure she will thrive," she said to her cousin. "Try not to fret."

"I just don't want her to…" Rex began and then faltered, and stared again at the floor. "I just don't want her to…" he floundered a second time.

"To what?" demanded his father. "You don't want her to what, boy?"

Rex struggled with his emotions. "I don't…want to…think of her…to think of her…" His statement petered out gradually like the fading afternoon light.

"Don't want to think of her what?" echoed Gilbert with more emphasis. "Do you know what he's trying to say, Thea?" He looked over at his wife and she shook her head so that the side ribbons of her silk cap shuddered, and she closed her eyes to denote an end to the subject. Still the room was silent as Rex grew more morose and was unable to raise his eyes. Then into the verbal vacuum Fairchild offered quietly. "I think the gentleman is perhaps referring to his fear of her sinking into unconsciousness…"

Everyone turned to him. It was evident that he meant 'death' but had used a euphemism.

"Ah…" said Gilbert dully.

"Yes… I see," muttered Marguerite.

"For heaven's sake!" intoned Dorothea.

Rex became animated. "That is exactly it, my good Sir…that is what I cannot bring myself to say…"

Soft commenting and soothing murmurings began, now that the elephant had been named, and Melissa gaped at Anthony Fairchild. He was looking in desultory fashion at the fireplace, his features bitter with some inner feeling. She remembered the sadness of his soul and thought about the letter they had found to Lottie. Perhaps Lottie now had suffered a similar fate in the intervening years between then and now. She stopped herself from thinking in this maudlin way, for it would lead to her weakening her resolve. She rose swiftly and crossed the spacious room—big enough to hold a gathering of twenty or twenty-five with ease—and poured Rex a cup of tea, adding milk and sugar.

"Come and sit by me in this armchair, Rex," she said to him, handing him the tea, and Rex did as bidden, seating himself in the lightweight Hepplewhite chair positioned at an angle from her end of the commodious sofa. He placed his cup and saucer on the tiny circular table between the sofa and the chair and she reached out her hand to Rex's hand and squoze it comfortingly. A few more moments passed and he came from his morbidity and was genial again, sensing that he had brought gloomy despondency into a happy occasion and remembering his social obligations. He looked at Fairchild. "Who is your guest?" he enquired of Melissa. "I do not believe we have been introduced before…"

She became instantly defensive. "He is Damien's guest, not mine…" she said coldly. "He merely called in for tea."

"Oh, I thought…" Rex paused. "I thought… I imagined he was a friend of yours." He smiled genially at the other man and awaited information, his simple approach making Fairchild more aware of her abrasive manner. It was himself she had targeted with her colossal rudeness, obviously, for she was kindness itself to this male cousin.

"I scarcely know this gentleman…we have barely even spoken…" she added, rubbing salt into the wound.

"I do crave your pardon," said the modest Rex to both of them.

Fairchild, stung by her off-hand dismissal of him, frowned at her dangerously with undefined displeasure but remained silent. Perhaps she was merely eccentric, as were a lot of artistic people. Or perhaps he should anticipate this treatment—given their history. He left the answer open to contemplation. Then he heard her making an introduction in the same cold voice. "… I am remiss, forgive me… Anthony Fairchild, my cousin, Rex Mainworthy…"

Rex reached across and extended his hand and Fairchild took it and they inclined their heads to each other.

Rex said. "I am heartily glad to meet you, my dear Sir…and extremely grateful for your timely intervention in naming what I could not…it was most astute of you…and kind."

Fairchild made a slight throw away gesture with his right hand and inclined his head respectfully to Rex. Melissa spoke into the air in front of her. "Well, he is deputy headmaster of Barton Grange, after all…"

Fairchild cast her another dark look and Rex gazed at her for a second or two, unable to see how that was relevant. "I see," he stared at the other man, his impressions not relatable to his idea of headmasters. An occurrence Fairchild was accustomed to.

She made the most of this pause and continued. "Yes, depressing is it not? But I suppose someone has to do the job…"

Fairchild watched her ominously and Rex with more bemusement, wondering if she was jesting. Then deciding it was some unfathomable feminine logic he was unable to follow he moved swiftly on and changed the subject. He enquired of Fairchild where he had come from and what mode of transport he had used to get here. They fell into a conversation about horses, for they both liked horses immensely.

Damien, seated alone near the windows, could not hear properly what was going on in their section of the drawing room but thought he saw Fairchild assume a bleak expression. He rose and sauntered over to the fireplace and sank into a third armchair and waited for a gap in the discourse between Giles and Gilbert. "Father..." he began, sotto voce, "I am sure Melissa is reviling Anthony Fairchild...call her over here on some pretence, if you please..."

Giles and Gilbert looked at him with humour and irritation. Gilbert cast what he thought of as a subtle glance towards the three people in question. "He seems perfectly at ease to me..."

Giles then gestured to Damien to come closer, Damien rose and leant against the marble fireplace. "Stop whittling over nothing, boy! If he was discomforted by her, he would not be sitting alongside her...and especially after this afternoon's tea antics...it was not two hours ago you were telling us how accomplished and clever he is. He can fend for himself in this without your interference..."

"Indeed...just look at the cut of him! He's no slouch," said Gilbert.

"But he might be too polite to extricate himself..." objected Damen.

The two older men curbed their laughter and Giles muttered, "Few men are too polite for that."

Damien was deaf to reason, his aspirations foremost. "She is playing some game," he declared, so that Giles shushed him with his hand and Damien's voice fell to a hideously loud whisper. "What is she up to? Her and Melanie Petersham together!"

His uncle stood and pulled Damien around so that they were facing the fire and their voices harder to hear from across the room. "Harken now, lad," said Gilbert softly, "If you begin to cudgel your brain about what women are thinking, you might start at Christmas and be sat there at Easter...and still be none the wiser."

Giles hooted with laughter, which the others took to be caused by more fishing stories. "Seldom a truer word, Gil...seldom a truer word."

"But she might completely ruin my sponsorship..." opined Damien, his voice rising so that Gilbert gripped his shoulder painfully and shook it slightly to bring him to sense. "Mayhap he has more than your sponsorship on his mind just now...and he won't thank you for sticking your oar in. Whatever she may be saying or doing he's a man of the world, no doubt."

Damien was unconvinced, he moved away from his older relatives and walked past the sofa, pausing as he did so to listen in before lapsing into an armchair near enough to catch the old word.

Rex and Anthony Fairchild were still talking about horses. Melissa had ceased listening—it was almost as tedious as the town bridge and the fishing—and so she rose and left them, without excusing herself, and wandered over to the fireplace and took refuge in the third armchair vacated by Damien, and in the midst of her father and uncle. And neither of them paused in their own equally mind-numbing conversation to pay her attention. Fairchild observed her while listening to Rex. He knew now he had not imagined it: her rudeness on occasions was unparalleled.

At length Rex made to go, fearing to leave his wife for too long. He shook Fairchild's hand a second time and expressed his hope of meeting him again, glancing at Melissa over the room and wondering why on earth she should spurn such a gentleman, notwithstanding her views on never marrying.

"We shall come tomorrow to see Philomena and cheer her up," said Marguerite to Rex. "Shall we not, Thea? We can perhaps supply helpful tips on confinement from our own experiences."

Dorothea agreed with reluctance. "I suppose we could...her mother goes daily now...but if you wish to, Maggie."

"Perhaps you will come too, Melissa?" said her mother.

Melissa agreed hesitantly. "I will if you wish, though I know nothing of confinement."

"Nor are you likely to unless you alter some of your attitudes," remarked Damien skittishly.

"How dare you!" She took a deep breath in readiness for vitriol but her mother stole the moment. "Damien, we do not need such coarseness in the drawing room," she declared, aware of how Fairchild may perceive this remark.

"Ivy Farm's pigs have more refinement..." Melissa opined.

"Stop your gallop right there both of you!" said their father. "I will hear no more squabbling today; my dander is at its limit."

"These young 'uns!" Gilbert tutted complicitly while filling his pipe.

"Indeed, Gilbert!" affirmed Marguerite, though she smiled more now that harmony mostly prevailed, and not the contentious atmosphere of before Melanie's departure. "Lissy, perhaps Mr Fairchild would like to see your work…" she ventured and Melissa inwardly groaned; she had been about to excuse herself and retire upstairs. She drew breath and looked at him without enthusiasm. He returned her gaze noncommittally. "He may not like art!" she replied, speaking of him in the third person deliberately to repel him.

"Why not ask him!" snapped her mother.

"I do like art," said Fairchild. "I enjoy it quite considerably."

"There you are then!" said Marguerite, as if she had pulled off a minor miracle.

* * *

From Bad to Worse

In her art room—which was at the back of the house beyond the conservatory and rather chilly, being today minus a fire in the grate—he walked about without speaking and looked at her various works, complete and incomplete. She leant against the wall and watched him.

"Quite a talent you have, Miss Shaw…" he remarked after some minutes.

"That is good of you to say," she replied. "Though I do have an excellent tutor."

"Oh!"

"He was at the Sorbonne for many years and recently came to retire in the county with his English wife."

Now he would begin winning her over, she could tell. She was determined to resist. "But let me say right here… I do not play the piano, sing like a nightingale, produce wonderful embroidery, undertake riding and archery…or any of the other attributes ladies are meant to enjoy…just before you ask…nor do I waste time at society balls, drawing room soirees, church hall sewing bees for good causes or afternoon picnics by the river with gentleman admirers… I only paint, but I do it prodigiously."

He watched her without commenting, concealing his astonishment at the outburst.

"And I have not been presented at court…and am not a debutante. I eschew society and have not made the decision lightly."

"I see!" he said, for it was all he could think of. "Not that any of it concerns me."

She was brusque and quite beyond rude. How could he have forgotten her indifference to amenable manners back in the days of her schooling! He had been blind-sided by her physical attributes, of which there were many. Vivid memories of her from the classroom flooded back to him with an amazing clarity. But now…? Close up, and even from a distance, she had a stunning sort of appeal which would be obvious to most men. Not the mundane sort of prettiness, but the oblique fascination of a woman with something worthy to convey; a classical overtone which would mature well and grow more piquant. "Have you finished now, recounting your limitations?" he added. "May I continue surveying your work?"

She remained silent and turned to look in the opposite direction. He inspected a couple of the water colours drying against the old cracked table she used for rough work. Then he said. "I expect you could do with a lie down after all that excitement earlier?"

She did not reply.

"Tell me, was it scripted or was it impromptu?" Still, she was silent. She was not obliged to answer these sarcastic forays into her mind.

"'twas like to something from Moliere… I wonder if you are not worn out!" he continued idly.

Still, she said nothing. There was little she could say, except to say she was sorry for any offence, but she was not sorry, not genuinely, and she did not intend to make a liar of herself for the sake of convention. She never intended to do that, no matter how long she lived.

"Are you going to speak to me at all, beyond the list of the things you never do?"

"Only if absolutely necessary!"

He turned and watched her for moments as she traced circles in the coal dust on the flagged floor near the fire grate with the toe of her satin house shoe. "Do you not think 'tis time you and that friend of yours grew up?"

"Have you seen everything you wish to see?" she enquired with her gaze still on her feet.

"No, not quite! One cannot appreciate art in mere seconds…but you obviously know that!"

He walked back around the room and looked at paintings in minute detail. He was posturing, she thought; he could not possibly be so interested.

"'tis cold in here, so kindly hurry!" she told him.

He looked at her sharply, forsaking the artwork to do so. He had decided now where the route of all this lay. So, he played the odds, "Are you in the habit of bearing grudges with anyone who has had authority over you as a child? Or is it just myself?"

"Just you…" she said flatly.

"I am flattered."

"I would expect you to find it amusing."

"What else am I to find it? Apart from childish!"

She straightened her posture and came forwards a few paces. "How dare you!"

"How dare *I*? You jest! After the performance given in the drawing room! I seldom saw such deplorably bad manners."

"What did you think we would do, fawn all over you!" She was betraying her intention to remain mute but could not help herself.

"Certainly not! But perhaps to behave with a little maturity…a little less like silly girls…"

"I warned you not to attend…" Her annoyance rose and soared and then glided to safety again. "When you have done, we will return…" she said, but he took out his cigars and ignored her.

"May I smoke?"

"If you must…though surely we are not here for the duration!" Her annoyance took to its wings once more. She sat quickly in a chair near the easel and leaned back and tried not to show any reaction. He lit the small cigar and put the match carefully in a discarded pot that had once held oil paint. "You cannot seriously think I would let you off with some of your worst antics back in Barton Grange…do you?"

"You should not have come here today, under the circumstances…"

He drew on the cigar and blew out smoke. "So you keep telling me, but nonetheless here I am…"

"Indeed…is there something amiss with you that you cannot construe social situations correctly?"

She saw him bridle—she had at last pierced the posturing.

"Are you ever civil in your dealings?" he said quietly.

"Not with people who have ill-treated me."

His disgust was subdued but he did not move to leave the room. "If you are serious in that comment, then you are obviously very short-sighted or very spoiled."

"I do not wish to talk of it…ever."

"Why not? You opened the subject."

"Speak with Melanie…she will give you a good run for your money!"

"I have no desire whatsoever to speak with her. I will not waste my breath!"

"Then as my grandmother would say, *'save it to cool your broth'*..."

"It runs in the family, does it? this scathing tongue amongst the female members!"

She advanced towards him with tiny running steps, on the balls of her feet, her anger unleashed, and he moved not one inch but waited to see more. "You took an absolute delight in making our lives a misery."

He examined the lit end of the cigar. "And that was the reason for all the sporadic giggling, I suppose...because you were all in such misery!"

"You see, you think yourself so clever...with your sarcasm..."

"It has escaped your notice perhaps...during all this lachrymose self-pity...but you could just have behaved properly..."

"We were children," her own sanctimonious tone annoyed her but she could not somehow avoid it, "and children are mischievous."

"I had upwards of ninety pupils to educate in various grades in two schools, and I simply could not have my authority undermined in that way and do the job I was paid to do! What did you really expect?" His voice rose on the question by a mere decibel. He would not lose his cool; only his resolve to extreme civility.

She wanted to hurl something at him—the slurred contents of the water jar on the easel perhaps—but then thought twice. She did not have Melanie's temerity. "You did not have to do what you did?" she said, almost sulkily, saved only by lightly applied dignity. "What did I do?" he asked, hoping to hear more of her thoughts on the matter.

"You know quite well... I am not going to outline it."

"Why not? You evidently think of it quite clearly!"

"I will not give you the satisfaction."

"I presume you mean the waiting room?" He stretched his back a little as he stood, stiff from so much sitting.

"Yes, of course I mean that...amongst other things!"

"Which other things?" He smoked and moved about and then took hold of a painting he liked and placed it on the small table. She was losing the resolve not to speak; she hated it but could not gain the former inclination to silence. "Perhaps overall the other things are not very important...in the main..."

"Make up your mind...either they are or they are not important. Straighten up your list of grievances for pity's sake."

"I am quite clear on the main grievances."

He turned to the nearest wall to lessen the intensity and looked at a pen and ink drawing of the large church on the outskirts of the town. And she thought he had dropped the subject. He had not. "Miss Shaw, do you have any idea how many pupils I have had cause to chastise in my working life to date?"

"I do not wish to hear of it... I suppose you are now boasting!"

"Of course I am not... I am entreating you to not take it personally..."

She laughed, a fake unconvincing laugh. "How can we not take personally such a thing, 'twas horrendous."

He turned again and assumed a solid position, his feet wide apart, in that masculine way, preparing for anything else she might verbally throw. "Well, believe it or not, that is perhaps because 'tis meant to deter bad behaviour! Besides, I doubt it was as horrendous as all that...more of a sharp shock."

"How do you know? Perhaps you were never beaten when you were at school?"

He sank into the lone chair and looked away from her. "No, I was excused on medical grounds." She stared at him in some astonishment. Then there was a low sound of derision from behind the small cigar. "I attended an English boarding school. Of course I was beaten...quite frequently..."

She picked up the magnifying glass used for finer work and polished it on her skirt. "Then you must know..."

He placed his left foot over his right thigh and sighed with yet more derisive overtone. "Well, I always induced a mesmerised state so as to feel hardly anything at all."

For a moment she wondered if this were true, but erred on the side of scepticism. "You use your sarcasm to avoid talking of your truth."

"And yet 'twas you who said you did not wish to discuss it."

Two or three minutes elapsed in which she went skipping around the room, picking things up and replacing them elsewhere, in a kind of light brisk whirl. He watched in fascination, reminded of the first act of a ballet he had seen with Lottie. It caused him to become still and frozen, the opposite of her whirling nervous motion. Eventually he drew breath and spoke with a change of mood. "Let us leave the matter where it belongs, in the past. I am merely trying to build civilised bridges."

"Which I shall burn as you go." She advanced again to where he sat, unable to leave the momentum of her memory. "It was meant to make us fear you...to frighten us to death..."

"Well, perhaps not to the extreme of death…" he remarked. "That might have seen me hang…"

The sarcasm, she felt, was insufferable, adding insult to injury. She cursed and muttered under her breath, and noting this he uncrossed his legs and rose swiftly, a different voice required to terminate the subject. "Listen please to common sense… It was clearly what was required to maintain order and respect in the classroom…so it was expedient."

"It was nothing short of cruel," she concluded.

He drew on the cigar and subsided into his former indifference and exhaled smoke slowly. "You have obviously never seen much cruelty…or you would not make such ridiculous claims."

"You are a despicable tyrant…" she avowed, moving back to her table of equipment, hoping to dismiss his unwanted presence finally. "Notwithstanding your loathing of killing animals for pleasure…"

He feared now he may betray his amusement and aggravate the situation so resorted to simple logic. "Miss Shaw, I have witnessed cruelty that would make your toes curl…"

"Where?"

"It does not matter where…at previous educational establishments, so-called, that it has been my misfortune to work in…" She regarded the painting he had taken down but remained silent and it encouraged him to elaborate. "Had you been forced into one of these institutions as a child you would hesitate to call my methods *cruelty*…"

She leaned back against the wall again for support, pressing her palms on her stomach, too suffused with anger to utter a word. Her breathing was jagged and her voice ragged. "You may dismiss it easily…but you know very well it was cruelty!"

"I do not think so… I am experienced in these matters so I know what I am doing."

"Indeed, you took your revenge on us and knew exactly what you were doing."

"Revenge? Discipline has nothing whatsoever to do with revenge!"

"So you say!" She moved from her table with alacrity and in so doing overturned a small pot of emerald green paint which landed on the floor and spilled its contents. They both ignored it.

"I never allow my feelings to over-run my detachment on these occasions, no matter how annoyed I may feel," he continued, pacing about and gripped by some peculiar brand of his own annoyance.

"You may preach all you like but I am never going to forgive you…ever! Neither is Melanie, so you may save your fine words for the Foundation or whatever it is you call it."

"The Foundation exists to eradicate poor and badly run schools, where *cruelty* is often used as a means of control… I am not without compassion for the plight of people exploited or abused…but unfortunately that does not extend to overly privileged nasty little girls at higher class schools."

"What an utter hypocrite you are!" she cried and flew across the room towards him, like a light flightless bird as he stood his ground. She sensed that he might be genuinely offended. It gave her pause, and then she saw that it was utterly what she had intended. She shook out her untidy hair, causing pins to fly from its depth and land about their feet. He watched them land and did not venture his thoughts; there was nothing like a woman loosening her hair to kindle a man's ardour. She was panting slightly, her palms once again flattened against her stomach, and he saw in her the beginnings of arousal, the tremors of physical awakening, and he wondered whether she understood it or not.

He saw too, a young woman with the potential to a widening understanding and intellect. A heady mixture of allure indeed. He regained his composure. "I see also that however cruel I was, it has not improved your manners…"

"Do not turn this onto my behaviour. I am always at pains to be civil at least…but your…your dreadful actions, they are unforgivable. You are a self-opinionated, conceited hypocrite…"

An awful silence reigned loud in the cool space of her art room. He was meant simply to leave the room never to return, but he had not done so and instead had rendered her speechless. He shifted position restlessly in the abiding silence but did not break it with any sound. It was the second time she had hurled that word at him in the course of the conversation: *hypocrite.* He looked down at his feet and then raised his head and displayed an altered demeanour, a more entreating tone. "What was I supposed to do in such straits? it was a grave misdemeanour within the required conduct… I could hardly put you across my knee and use my hand."

She moved her lips to form words which did not arrive. Then the wrong words came, before she had properly considered them. "It may have been preferable…" she murmured, and saw too late that she should not have voiced the thought.

He hesitated for only a second. "I do not think so! It would have been too familiar an act…the prerogative of your father or guardian or some other closely related male…"

"I do not wish to discuss it any further."

He ignored this. "But you are telling me it is what you would have preferred as a method of chastisement?"

"Yes…no…of course I am not telling you that…"

"Oh, I thought you were stating it as a preference?"

"I am stating it as the lesser of two evils.…and you must know very well that is what I mean…"

He walked away from her and she did not know what to consider next in her arsenal of rebuttal. At length, he turned and addressed her from some feet away. "I scarcely know what you mean half the time… However, I am bound to say that if you treat me to much more of your unwarranted incivility, hostility or flagrant insults you may well see your…*preference*…delivered on this very day…and I give you warning."

There was a slow dawning recognition of his words before she flared. "How dare you! Do not even think of it."

He stubbed out the cigar in the same jar he'd used for the match and watched her steadily as it made the sizzling sound of dying heat. "But you have just told me 'tis preferable as a lesser form of cruelty…"

She wondered if he was serious, or simply playing with her finer feelings. "I hope you are not suggesting I would allow such a thing?" She was flustered and sick at losing command of the situation. A pause was given for his deliberations and she opened her lips to fill it with anything that came to mind, but nothing did, and he spoke first, "On the contrary, I am suggesting that in the eventuality your *allowing* it would be unnecessary…you would be unable to prevent it."

He came carefully towards her and she crept backwards in an involuntary movement of protection until he stopped a couple of feet away. No doubt, it had been a calculated move of intimidation. "Such staggering arrogance!" She looked at the door and gauged the distance between it and where she stood.

"Perhaps quite as staggering in its way as your rudeness! I should like to buy this painting…" he said, changing the subject rapidly. "As a Christmas gift for

198

my mother and stepfather…" He had chosen a small water colour of a hill top with a white horse in the foreground.

"I cannot sell it to you…"

"Cannot or will not?" he demanded.

"My father does not permit me to sell my work. He does not think it respectable…"

"Then I shall pay him for it."

"He will not accept that either…he has money enough."

"Money is not something you acquire only when you need it……but never mind, I shall find a way of compensating you."

"Do not bother!" she said coldly. "Take it, I give it to you."

"I do not know if I can accept such a gift from someone whose opinion of me is so low."

"Please yourself…leave an address with Damien if you wish and I will have it delivered."

He walked to the door first. "Let us return…" He stood away from the entrance and allowed her to go on ahead and they made their way to the drawing room along a different corridor, one that brought them to a door on the opposite wall to the door they had used to leave. The corridor was dimly lit and devoid of furniture or servants, or disturbance of any kind. Outside the door she said. "There is a way you can compensate me if you take the painting."

"And that is?"

"Not to bother coming to tea again, or approaching me when you call to see Damien."

He watched her with mounting dismay. "I might comply…then again, I am not accustomed to meeting demands of those kinds."

"I am sure you are not…with your love of power."

He retaliated instantly. "You and Miss Petersham seem obsessed by this question of power. Next to *cruelty* it seems to rank highly on your agenda of philosophical considerations."

"How dare you!"

"And don't, for the love of God, begin *'how daring me'* again, because you know nothing at all of what I might dare…you really know nothing about me."

"I do not wish to know you. I despise and detest you."

He stayed her wrist on the handle of the door, his grip too tight for her to loosen. "One thing you should know, Miss Shaw, is that I have never punished anyone, either male or female, who did not deserve it…and you may include yourself and Melanie Petersham in that."

"Release my arm, you are hurting my wrist!"

"Nonsense…" His fingers lightened their hold but did not release her. "Cease making these ridiculous claims of ill-treatment…" His voice was barely above a low growl to prevent the occupants of the drawing room from hearing. "Stop pretending you are made of glass and will break at the merest touch…fashionable though it may be! For you will not…"

"Take your hand off me…" she hissed.

"Desist with all this nonsense about being so delicate that life will not support you. 'tis as foolish and misguided as the act of crippling your body in the corsets you might wear. You are not a porcelain figurine produced in the Wedgwood factory! You are solid flesh and bone…sound of wind and limb. You will not suffer any permanent damage from a man gripping your wrist. No more than you will break in two if he smacks your behind…"

She swallowed twice, her throat dry and parched. She looked sharply away to her right, where the petunias and the ferns danced in an imaginary breeze on the flock wallpaper. Then he gave her back her arm, like something he had borrowed, shaking her wrist slightly to emphasise a point. "See, it is completely intact…but you have no doubt experienced enough *cruelty* for one day, so we will return to the safety of your family drawing room…when you are ready."

"Words cannot describe how much I loathe you!" she pronounced in the hoarse tone that her throat allowed.

He moved not one muscle of his face but shuttered his gaze with lowered lashes, which looked almost white in the gloomy passage, and stared ahead as if she had not spoken. She inhaled the faint smell of his shaving soap, his cigars, and again some other unidentifiable male fragrance which emanated from him. She was distracted for seconds trying to place it: a musky lemon smell which was probably something he used on his hair. Then she remembered the state of her own and took out the remaining pins and began sticking them randomly in her abundant chestnut hair, so that it resembled a small nest for birds. He watched her perform this task, unfazed, and it occurred to her that he often saw women with their hair disarrayed. He knew women in an intimate sense.

She flushed and became very warm and could not look at him. Her hair now was utterly changed from how it had looked before they had left the drawing room but he did not comment, he doubted anyone would notice. He straightened his shirt cuffs as she smoothed her hair. It was, he thought, as if they had actually made love. Though he had barely touched her. What had they made? War of some kind! He did not know but he felt differently than he had an hour ago. He was drawn to her like the proverbial moth to the lamp; her persona was luminous and light, palpable like an early morning mist, in the close confines of the passageway; he did not want to leave her presence. She magnetised him in ways beyond his physical desire. He felt he had kept company with her for a hundred years—time had become elongated—he had trouble recalling what day of the week it was.

He was wary of himself and his unknown urges. As she fingered her hair in this futile attempt at styling, he removed his timepiece from his jacket and checked it. They had been gone just short of an hour. It might look odd, but then again it might not. He had taught her in school, he had provenance of sorts and integrity in the fact. It may be acceptable to disappear with her for that length of time alone. "Are you ready to re-enter?" he enquired with due formality.

"You are an utter swine," she told him in a voice which perhaps held tears, though he could not risk discovery for they had dallied long enough. She recalled his threat and looked at him and saw his jaw tighten and his cheekbones become more etched and she could not tell if it was from satisfaction or anger. But they were outside the drawing room now so she cared little. In his even voice, he said. "So, I am a canting hypocrite, an utter swine, opinionated and arrogant…and a cruel tyrant! Is there anything else you would like to call me while you are on safe territory?"

"No," she said and knew she sounded sulky.

"You may find…" he informed her in a gentler tone of voice, "that I am none of those things. I am just a man like other men, but you have not yet experienced enough of the world to know that."

She stood like a stone statue, unable to take her eyes from the wooden door in front, afraid to look at him for reasons she no longer understood. He watched her and waited.

"Of course," she offered, dredging up words from tangled thoughts, "You could simply this afternoon have apologised for the incident in the waiting room…" She felt this would give her the final say. But he put his head back like someone about to laugh, and did not; he grinned a little and then tightened his jaw to disguise it. "I expect I could…though I perceive that my alleged hypocrisy does not go quite that far…"

She gasped with outraged defeat and flung open the drawing room door and entered in front of him, smiling pleasantly to fool the family. He sauntered in behind her and said, "Your daughter is a fine and gifted artist!"

Her father looked over. "That she is!"

Her mother's eyes went immediately to her rearranged hair and took on an interested glint. She smiled beatifically at them and slid her gaze to her sister seated beside her to see if she too noticed the difference. Dorothea had noticed and frowned a little, her lips pulled into a tight line of disapproval. Even so, Melissa had redeemed herself now from the social awkwardness of this giddy unpredictable afternoon. Her aunt and uncle would stay to dinner, served in perhaps an hour or so.

They always dined when they had arrived in the late afternoon. She wondered if he would stay also, and though her father extended the invite he declined, looking at her briefly as he made some excuse to be on his way. She felt she had achieved some slight victory or he would undoubtedly have accepted. She smiled at him for the benefit of the assembled company and inclined her head graciously; a perfectly executed but false smile of acknowledgment…and satisfaction.

* * *

She scarcely slept. The next morning, she sent the footman with a note for Melanie to meet her as soon as possible. They met in the tea shop in the town the following day, and then left quickly to walk in a park where they would not be overheard; the tea shop owner and her assistants were notorious gossips who eavesdropped on customers while they were preoccupied with refreshments.

Melanie pranced around the lawned area of the rose gardens of the park in her buoyant tread which accelerated when she was animated. "I cannot decide whether he was toying with you or whether he was seriously put out," she announced at length. "In fact, I can scarcely make head nor tail of the jumbled narrative."

Melissa halted, a stitch in her side from so much brisk walking. Melanie halted a few paces ahead and waited for her. "It happened so quickly… I cannot recall every word or sentence in exact order…" Melissa objected.

"Lissy, an hour is a long time to be discoursing with a man."

Melissa said nothing and gazed at the late autumn clouds. "It went by in a trice…or so it seemed."

"Are you sure that is all that was happening?"

"What?" She drew breath and felt the stitch release. "Of course, what are you suggesting?"

"I know how very modest you are in these things…you may not tell me even if he…if he…"

"If he what?"

"Tried to become amorous!"

"Out of the question," claimed Melissa. "Amorous was the furthest thing from our minds!"

"From yours perhaps, but I cannot understand how you even agreed to go in there with him…"

"I have told you, because my parents were very displeased with the reception we gave him and your comments… I was placating them by being amenable. Damien has much at stake with that Foundation and you can imagine the uproar if it goes wrong."

"Damien is an overbearing oaf. He and Fairchild are well matched in business," Melanie said.

"'tis not business they are involved in…'tis education of some sort…"

"Even more apt," said Melanie.

Melissa ventured a few more steps, thinking of Fairchild's comments on wearing corsets. "I would not call Fairchild overbearing exactly…aside from his arrogant insinuations."

"And what would you call him?" enquired Melanie, increasing the walking pace again. Melissa struggled to form words. She looked pained and stared at Melanie like someone half drowning and keeping afloat while awaiting rescue.

"Let us sit on a bench…" Melanie suggested, and they went to the nearest one and reclined a little. Melissa remained silent. "What I cannot yet see is how you came to broach the subject of the waiting room. You were so adamant to keep me away from it and to not talk of it…"

"'twas he who brought it up. He tricked me into it by…"

"By what?"

Realising this was not exactly the truth, Melissa fought with memories and sentiments. "He accused us of being spoiled and short-sighted for holding grudges against anyone in authority in previous years."

One of Melanie's snorting dismissive noises emerged into the morning air. "That is the kind of thing I would expect him to say…surely you were prepared for that kind of statement? But you must have led him to the subject… I cannot see him bringing that accusation from nowhere…"

"Well, he did! When he enquired why I would not speak to him and… I flew at him…" Melissa raised her voice to agitated levels.

"You flew at him?" Melanie's voice rose in unison. "Do you mean you launched yourself at him?"

"Not exactly, I just ran towards him in a temper…then stopped before I reached him."

"Good Lord! He must have thought all his birthdays had come at once."

"Oh, I do not know what he thought… He is silent for ages and then he plunges into monologues full of convoluted parenthesis. I cannot tell when he is being sarcastic or serious…and I lose the thread of what I am going to say next…"

"That is because he attended Oxford," said Melanie with aplomb. "Once they have been to that place, they are never the same. They proselytise and go on with themselves and cannot resist the sound of their own voice. Geoffrey is the same…you simply have to pick up every sixth word and gloss over all the sentences."

Melissa tutted and pouted and shuffled her feet in the gravel of the path.

"So, he has one of your paintings now?" persisted Melanie, hurrying the narrative along.

"Not yet. I told him to take it as a gift…and then—"

"Pardon me?" Melanie interjected and shifted position to stare at her best friend. "You gave him a gift of a painting?"

"Simply to get rid of him."

"Hardly a gesture of rejection."

"I also told him that I despise and detest him and don't want him to come near me…"

"While giving him a painting? Lissy, you are too complicated for words!"

"The painting was a way of getting him to leave me alone… I have said that he can have the painting in return for not attending Sunday tea again and for not coming near me when visiting Damien."

"And he said?"

"That he was not used to complying with those kinds of demands."

"Of course he is not…you do realise he is not Roger Braithwaite? He will not be placated by a mere painting."

Melissa thought of Roger Braithwaite and his mild gentle ways. "I told him he was a tyrant and a canting hypocrite…and I thought he would explode at the hypocrite slur; he was so quietly enraged…"

"Or quietly suffused with glee…" offered Melanie.

"Then it went from bad to worse."

"So it would appear…but how did it come to him gripping your arm?"

"I cannot rightly remember…except that he was suddenly telling me, as we were going back into the drawing room, that he had never punished anyone who did not deserve it, and that included you and I."

"Yes, and? There must have been something else for him to have held onto you."

"He said you and I seemed obsessed with power and cruelty…"

"This becomes worse by the moment…" Melanie rose and walked about. "Let us retire to the tea shop again…'tis growing too chilly. We must just keep our voices low."

The tea shop was now crowded, there was a rumble of general conversation and it was easier to talk.

"So you accused him of being cruel towards us…?" Melanie prompted and Melissa had a flash of consistent memory and lifted the cake fork into the air. "Yes! And then he accused me of being ridiculous and said that he could show me places where there was real cruelty, which he was trying to eradicate through the Foundation…but I was not so easily placated."

Melanie waited patiently until Melissa had fortified herself with another forkful of cake. "Then he said…he said…"

"Yes, what did he say? This is like pulling teeth, Lissy!"

"He said, *what did I really expect after undermining his authority so badly*…and that he could scarcely have put us across his knee as it was too familiar an act…"

Melanie was arrested as she bit into the Victoria sponge. "He used that very phrase…*too familiar an act*?"

Melissa paused and took a sip of tea. "But then I said something idiotic…something I have since regretted…" She had turned a delicate shade of pink and Melanie stopped eating and stared. "Well? What was it?"

"I was trying to give some quarter…" she opined desperately.

"Ha," Melanie made a loud sound of disapproval and several adjacent customers looked at them. "A fundamental mistake."

"I know that now."

"And what was this thing you said?"

"I said… I said, had he done so it might have been preferable…" she confided in a rush.

Replacing her cake fork on the plate, Melanie raised her brows and looked out of the window where the mid-morning traffic was busier: horses and traps and all kinds of conveyance passing amid pedestrians bustling about. "I cannot believe you said anything so foolish."

Melissa consumed the fondant rapidly to give herself something to do. "Nor can I! And then he misconstrued it…obviously on purpose…because what I meant was that it may have been less…less severe and…"

"Yes, yes…" intervened Melanie, "I am aware of what you think you meant…"

"And so I am sure was he…" said Melissa while swallowing the remains of the cake and steeling herself to continue. "And then…after some thought he said that if I continued being uncivil and hostile, he would deliver on this *preference*…and that he was giving me warning."

Melanie's features went through a range of expressions, her eyelids fluttering as she conjectured. Melissa gulped the last of her tea. "And when I said…" She stretched her lips into extreme annoyance and bared her teeth and went on doggedly, "…when I said, '*I hope you are not suggesting I would allow such a thing*'…"

Melanie leaned forwards a little. "Well? What then?"

"He said that my allowing it was irrelevant and I would not be able to prevent it." She clamped her lips shut as if the words were not to be countenanced.

"That is true in somewhere as remotely situated as your art room…" remarked Melanie blithely.

"It is not…for I would bite him and kick him…" Melissa argued in heated tones.

Melanie laughed in a scoffing manner and assumed the superior persona of one who knew much more about men and their ways since her betrothal. "He would soon overpower you…you are no match for him, my sweet…he is a man…"

"Besides…upon greater reflection I see he would surely not have dared," claimed Melissa.

"You scarcely know what he will dare!"

Melissa's shoulders drooped. "That is also what he said!"

"Because it is true!" claimed Melanie in too loud a tone, so that Melissa became self-conscious and refrained from comment in case they were overheard.

"And what if he had dared?" Melanie urged from behind the napkin daintily covering her lips as she viewed the situation with informed wisdom. "What then? What were you going to do? Run around the hallway crying *'help, help me! Fairchild has given me a hiding!'*… I think not!"

"Of course not!" objected Melissa, forgetting to whisper. "Perish the thought!"

"Indeed! Not with your love of privacy, not to say secrecy on these matters. It would be worse than my divulging the waiting room procedure. It would be all over the household in no time…and then the servants would talk in the town and soon the whole county would know."

Melissa was scandalised and her body drooped with despondency, her eyes furious and fixed on a nearby painting of The Haywain.

"You see…" Melanie paused for a moment to let common sense prevail before it all became too comical. "You cannot…simply cannot risk annoying him in that way…if you see him again you must refrain from these insults." She placed her napkin over her mouth once more and giggled, her notorious amusement unravelling as easily as her umbrella.

Melissa was displeased but felt better for airing things. "It was not amusing. It was…it was… I do not know! And then in the back corridor, before re-entering the drawing room, he told me not to think myself so delicate…and he gripped my wrist to stop me opening the door and went on with some other diatribe about corsets and fashionably assumed fragility and my being strong in wind and limb…"

Melanie waited and Melissa wiped her fingers delicately on the table linen. "Then he released my wrist, telling me that I had probably experienced enough cruelty for one day…and I re-pinned my hair as best I could and we went in and he behaved once more with perfect propriety and he complimented my art to my parents."

Melanie frowned. "How had your hair become unpinned?" she asked suspiciously.

"When I was running about the room… I always partially run…or skip…when I am flustered, as you should know."

"Yes…" said Melanie sceptically. "Highly eccentric behaviour, as I have often told you… Is that all of it now?" From her more relaxed position in the Regency chair—which the tea room prided themselves on providing for customers—she tapped her fingers on her lips.

"My family likes him and are fooled by his charm…my mother is certain we are taken with each other…and she is encouraging him…"

"Not surprising…gone for an hour, having given him a painting and returning with your hair rearranged! What is anyone to think? I am not even going to enquire how corsets came up in the conversation."

"Simply that we cripple our bodies with them or deform ourselves…or some such."

"You see, his thoughts were on your body the whole time. It will not end there you may be certain! He is definitely desirous of you."

"He cannot be!" Melissa stared at the other girl. "I think he wants me to agree to be civil with him and that is all."

"Civil my eye! Why would he want only that? He has plenty of people to be civil with…and they will not include women, you may be sure. He has ingratiated himself on your family and is in league with your brother…'twill end in wedlock if you are not careful. Your parents will press for it…"

Melissas rose suddenly in great agitation, unable to remain seated.

"Now, Lissy, do not begin running around the town square in your distress," said Melanie comically.

"But that is a shocking suggestion…enforced wedlock!" cried Melissa.

"Is it? I might say that you have brought it upon yourself… I might say a lot of things, but I do not want to distress you further."

"I need you to help me discourage him. That is what I need from you."

"Are you certain you wish to discourage him?" queried Melanie artfully.

"Yes, he is too frightful by far…"

"Frightful or frightening?"

"Perhaps the latter…though he is quite interesting in many ways…"

"And there we have it!" said Melanie with ambiguity.

Melissa seemed not to listen. "He says things which if someone else had said I would find absolutely hilarious."

Melanie sighed noisily.

"I find myself looking at him. I think of how I would sketch him…he is so enigmatic in persona and appears so agreeable in many ways."

"He does resemble one of Botticelli's angels from some angles, I grant you," concurred Melanie. "But that is simply a trick of the light… I can guarantee, he is not one in reality."

They stared off into the distance and pursued their own thoughts, until Melanie ventured, "Your sister-in-law's eyes were almost out on stalks watching him…did you notice?"

"Geraldine has invited us to tea… I forgot to mention that…on Saturday afternoon, if we are free."

"So she can hear more of the back-story, no doubt."

"It was your talk of penny dreadfuls…she reads them all the time," declared Melissa. "She has even said she may begin penning them in her leisure hours…"

"There you are then! She is seeking content for the first one…well, we cannot attend…at least I cannot."

"I know! It will be all over the family if we attend and you tell her things."

"I shall tell her nothing, for I will not attend. You might, I suppose."

"I shall not… I shall make excuses. I much prefer not to have to talk about him to anyone except you."

Melanie watched her with a muted and amused glint in her eye and then took out her purse to pay the waitress.

"No, let me pay…" Melissa said.

"No, please allow me," Melanie began counting out her money.

"I much prefer it if you allow me…since you have been good enough to meet me at short notice," persisted Melissa.

Melanie waved this away with her hand. "Piffle, I insist! And besides, we have heard quite enough of your *preferences* for one day."

They lapsed into the usual merriment and left the tea shop hurriedly, not wishing to attract too much attention.

Needs Must

A few days later, Melissa had decided she would see more of Roger Braithwaite. So, she sent him a note asking for his advice on an oil painting she was undertaking of gardenias for one of her aunts. Roger was a horticulturist. It was his passion and his family's commercial pursuit. He had nowadays inherited private means from his grandmother but loved to be involved in the business. They had played together as children. They knew each other well with the familiarity that childhood association brings. Not for a match of marriage or such, Melissa resolved, though Roger did not quite know that. She suspected that like herself he was still a virgin. He was a wonderful companion and friend and admirer…when she was in the mood.

She was quite mortified when a note came from him regretting that he was going to Hastings for three weeks to see his Godmother who was ailing. And then she decided she would invent things about meeting him and pass them on to Damien who would perhaps impart them to Fairchild, who would think she was in a love tryst of some kind. Not that she really believed Fairchild would care, or cared about her in the way Melanie had suggested, but it was perhaps best to err on the side of caution.

"I am going to see Roger…" she told Damien unnecessarily when seeing him on the lower staircase. "I shall be gone some time…"

"And I need to know this why?" asked her brother scathingly.

"I am just mentioning it in passing…" said she haughtily. "In case anyone wonders where I am."

"Surely that is why we have a butler! Tell him instead. I care not where you go and for how long," said Damien, still miffed about the shocking scenario in the drawing room with Fairchild present.

She returned in the hour, it being too chilly to linger outdoors and out of sight. She crept back to her room. But as she was going into her door Damien came out of his. "I thought you would be gone some while?" he said. "Don't tell me, your rudeness has repelled Braithwaite at this late stage of his infatuation!"

"Mind your own business!" she snapped.

"Then keep your business to yourself," he rejoined. Relations between them were as chilly as they had ever been. However, the day after this she heard voices in Damien's room. She detected the timbre and inflection of Anthony Fairchild and flew to the large window of the upper landing to look down on the side of the house where the stables were situated. Sure enough, his horse was tethered and grazing on fodder provided by the groom. It was the same horse they had watched out for in school. The dappled grey. She went quickly back into her bedroom where she listened at the wall adjoining Damien's, but could hear nothing beyond the low burble of male voices.

He was soon off again, she heard him and Damien in the doorway as he departed, and she went slowly down the stairs, hearing the clop of the horse's hooves as he turned the animal and slowly cantered from the stable area to the drive. On the large hall dresser, she found a wrapped box with her name on it. It contained a large expensive set of paints and brushes with his card and a scribbled message thanking her for the painting which she had sent on to an address he had given; a superior lodging house somewhere in the town.

Melanie was irritated that she had not retained the address so that they may go and look at where he resided. But inwardly, she knew that it was exactly why she had not done so—the idea of spying on him being too onerous for contemplation. And of Melanie suddenly having to invent one of her lavish ruses when he turned up unexpectedly in the street.

She knew she had little choice but to accept the gift. If she refused it and sent it back, her parents would hear of it perhaps and be furious with her. Or he would call in person and demand to see her for an explanation of the latest slight and a veritable saga would ensue.

Three days later he was back, with another man in tow. They went to Damien's room after partaking swiftly of tea in the drawing room. Obviously, this other fellow was someone from the Foundation wishing to see more of Damien's bizarre and morbid experiments. They were cloistered with Damien for some time, and eventually she could not contain her curiosity and took a glass from her bedside and held it to the outside of Damien's door and tried to hear more. She heard Fairchild clear his throat and was surprised that she knew the sound quite well, like an obscure instrument intersected into an orchestral piece which one listens to often and then forgets until the next recital.

Suddenly, of course, the door opened and she withdrew, turning sideways and secreting the glass in her skirt folds. "I do beg your pardon, Ma'am," said the stranger as he almost collided with her side-on.

"Not at all..." she said. "I had dropped something and was retrieving it." She set off along the corridor in haste, glancing back over her shoulder and casting him a beguiling smile and seeing just some dark bushy side whiskers and merry blue eyes. He cast a glad eye over her in a swift appraisal. He was about the same age as Fairchild and quite as worldly and debonair, but she did not linger to see more. She ran into her own room and banged the door shut.

Damn! She always managed to bang doors when he was about; he would think she did nothing else but inelegantly close doors after herself. She fumed and paced and hummed with impatience.

She got out the glass and listened again at the wall where she thought the brickwork may be thinner, and she heard Damien guffaw and Fairchild comment more softly, and thought they would be laughing at her. Then the stranger returned, probably having visited the recently installed lavatory along the corridor—the pride and joy of her father for its wonders of modern engineering—and she heard the door open and close again. She gave it up and lay on the bed. She understood enough about herself to realise she was curious to set eyes on him. And she also knew instinctively that lots of women may go to great lengths to set eyes on him; she was not so biased that she could not see his appeal to her own sex.

Meanwhile, in Damien's room, the new visitor rubbed his hands together briskly and said to Damien, "Is that your sister I have just seen in the corridor?"

Damien became nonchalant. "If she went into the next door along, then I imagine so."

"Captivating little thing, to be sure!" said Rufus Henderson, the visitor. "A lovely girl!"

Fairchild cleared his throat noisily. It struck him for perhaps the first time that she was now very eligible and would be prey for men of all types.

Damien considered the compliment; Rufus Henderson was a leading light in the Foundation and had a first-class degree from Cambridge in chemistry and the new sciences. A self-made man and the son of a wealthy corn dealer. "Yes, 'tis often remarked upon," Damien announced in a proprietary manner. "She is quite pleasing to the eye, I must admit…but she is as precarious as the cat and may give you a nasty scratch if you go too near…" He glanced at Fairchild, who according to his mother was very taken with her. He was stony faced. Henderson also glanced at Fairchild to see if he knew more of her.

"A gross exaggeration, Damien," Fairchild commented mildly. It was obvious that he disliked her being mentioned.

"Then again, 'tis often the way with the beautiful ones…" Henderson mused. "Women are an exotic land through which we wander without the map. Isn't that so, Tony?"

Fairchild cleared his throat again, even more noisily; a sound of primal aggression perhaps. He was less than thrilled and knew himself not. Given to enjoying festive occasions in the company of Henderson, beyond professional purposes, he knew him to be a worse philanderer than even Nicholas Stevenson had once been. The memory of Lottie mingled with the thought of the powerful fascination he was kindling for Melissa Shaw rendered him quite paralysed with unquantifiable anguish. And recalling her entreaty to leave her alone rendered it almost unbearable.

"Is she spoken for…your sister?" enquired Henderson of Damien.

"Yes, she is," Fairchild heard himself say flatly. He closed his eyes against their scrutiny.

"Oh!" said Henderson with some embarrassment. "You are obviously…you are hoping to… I beg your pardon, Tony… I did not mean to…"

"Think nothing of it, Rufus. 'tis early days yet," Fairchild interposed graciously.

Damien was staring at him in transparent surprise, and he kept his eyes shut and felt both men awaiting further comment. At length, he opened them and regarded his colleagues with tranquillity and smiled good humouredly and took a breath. "My apologies… I have a slight toothache. Perhaps we should get on with matters in hand…time is overtaking us."

* * *

Later on, finding his mother in the conservatory amongst her potted plants, oblivious to the world, Damien approached her. "Mama, I did not realise that matters were so far advanced between Tony Fairchild and Melissa…"

213

His mother discarded the small trowel and looked at him. "What do you mean?" she said in an alarmed tone.

Damien related the conversation with Rufus Henderson and Anthony Fairchild, and Marguerite frowned. "I was not aware myself…nothing has been said to your father or me…you must have it wrong."

"I do not have it wrong," asserted Damien, "I am not dull-witted. He told Henderson she was spoken for…and he could only mean himself…for who else is in the picture?"

Marguerite speculated and stared in a short-sighted way at the petals of a late flowering pot plant. "He might have just been protecting her from this Henderson, if he thinks him a rake or similar. He perhaps feels it his duty, seeing that he taught her previously."

Damien laughed softly but refrained from comment, his mother's ideas on gallant behaviour were not worth the price of contradiction.

"Anyway, do not make too much of it, for heaven's sake," said Marguerite. "You know how she is if being pushed towards romance or suitors…"

"I cannot think what he sees in her," said Damien. "Tony Fairchild, I mean…"

"There is no necessity for you to think anything," claimed Marguerite retrieving her silver-plated trowel—a gift from Giles on her last birthday. "You are not Fairchild."

* * *

He tended not to call often after this visit; things were arranged following Henderson's appearance, between Damien and the Foundation. Damien boasted of it endlessly at meal times until everyone was sick of hearing about it.

She did not see or hear anything of him between mid-December and mid-February, and she was quite relieved not to have to worry about it and thought she had seen the last of him, although Melanie refused to believe it. He was biding his time, she said. He could wait. They had all the time in the world, unless she became betrothed to Roger Braithwaite. Which seemed as likely as hell freezing over.

Then one Saturday in February she went off into the lanes painting wintry landscapes and arranged for Melanie to take her to a point in the countryside in her trap and then to pick her up again two hours later on her return journey—the groom being otherwise engaged on her mother's behalf. This kind of excursion was one she took often and was successful and made her happy as always. When she had set out the weather was clement for the season.

But by her return, when she reached the turnpike road, it had become dull and cold with occasional snowfall; the sort of February weather which creeps up from nowhere. She checked her timepiece and saw that Melanie was late. She walked about to keep warm, her hold-all with her equipment stowed against a stone wall. A further ten minutes elapsed and still no sign of Melanie. Melanie, whatever her other faults, was always quite punctual.

Then from around the corner of the opposite lane came a trap. She craned her neck to see who drove it. It was a male person she thought, clothed well against the cold and indiscernible from a distance, until they drew near…then she saw it was Anthony Fairchild. He wore a greatcoat and a woollen muffler pulled up around his ears, concealing almost all the lower part of his face. She stood still and pretended not to recognise him. He stopped the trap and looked at her. "Would you care for a ride to wherever you are going?" he enquired, pulling the muffler low to speak.

"You do not know where I am going…" she returned. "I might be going out of your way entirely." She noticed that even in these temperatures he wore no hat. He never wore hats, despite the male fashion for hats, except in the summer—a straw hat from foreign shores—for keeping the sun from his eyes as he rode. Whereas she this day wore an old cloth hat which she had found in the hall cloakroom, having belonged at one time to one of her brothers. It kept her very snug but looked unstylish. She was dressed in her oldest outdoor clothes, all barring her shoes which were flimsy and light and not at all suited for the winter weather. "It matters not…" he told her. "I doubt you can be going far in this weather." He stared at her shoes as he waited for her reply. "What in God's Name are you wearing on your feet?"

"It was a fine day when I set out…not that 'tis any of your concern!" she replied.

He ignored the rebuff. "My dear girl, 'tis February in England…anything may happen between dawn and dusk weatherwise, and frequently does."

She stared at him, his staunch resilience to her dismissal, as always, was disconcerting.

"Well?" he said at length. "Are you getting in?"

"No, I am not," she said and then added. "Thank you all the same."

215

"How are you getting to wherever you are going?"

"I am going home, and I have arranged for a conveyance."

He considered matters. "You do know that it has snowed and some roads are impassable? Who are you waiting for?"

She saw the perfect opportunity. "Roger."

"Who is Roger?" he enquired, obliging the lie.

She smiled into the distance. "A dear friend…a beau, one might say."

He surveyed her without expression. "He has obviously been detained." His gaze shifted to her strange headwear. He was fascinated. "You had better get in…you will freeze to death, especially in those ridiculous shoes…"

She turned and blazed her annoyance at him. "My footwear is my own business…" and almost added 'how dare you' but thought better of it.

"If your conveyance does not arrive, how will you get home?" he asked with enforced patience.

"I shall manage."

He took out one of his small cigars with the matches from the depth of his greatcoat. "I advise you to get in and allow me to take you. It is not the weather for lingering on roads like these…"

"No, I shall walk," she said and moved to her hold-all, hoisted it and tossed it over the stile, following it and descending into the field. "It is only a mile or two going this short cut…" she called to him from some yards away.

"I would not recommend it in those shoes!" he called back.

She ignored him and, carrying the hold-all, made her way gingerly into the field. It was soddened with recent rain and her feet sank ankle deep into watery grass, instantly soaking her shoes and stockings, but still she persevered. Then without warning her foot became entangled in undergrowth hidden by the surface water and she tripped and fell onto the boggy ground. She righted herself, unhurt, but saw that he was still watching her. She was now loath to carry on, she clearly would not make it without further mishap. She had no choice but to return over the stile. She decided she would walk along the road, where there was still no sign of Melanie. She picked up her hold-all and prepared to begin the trek.

"Get in!" Fairchild said impatiently, his lit cigar between his teeth.

She carried on walking and he flicked the reins so that the trap moved with her but a little way ahead. When she was level with him, he again addressed her. "Melissa, I am asking you to get into the trap."

She halted, astounded by his first ever use of her given name. "I do not need your interference. Leave me alone."

"And I do not want your demise on my conscience…you will catch your death if you walk the distance from here to the house…"

She shifted the weight of the hold-all and pulled her hat down over her eyes. His voice increased in volume. "Get into the trap… I am already late for an appointment. Or must I get out and throw you in?"

She said it then, despite her best efforts. *"How dare you?"* and she pitched the hold-all in before her and climbed into the trap.

"And do not begin again with your dares," he said as he waited for her to be seated. She looked at him with her intelligent grey eyes, the shabby hat pushed back for better vision. "You are the most odious busybody it has ever been my misfortune to meet…" she told him in a low furious voice.

"Am I really?" he said, as if receiving interesting news. "How fortunate you have been in your life to date then…"

"And your sarcasm is unparalleled…" she continued.

"I try not to boast," he replied in the same tone.

"You think yourself so clever in your educated superiority…" She began to enjoy herself while he looked at her calmly. This girl, who in the school had never uttered more than short staccato replies, letting her sullen expressions and insolent eye movements speak for her, was suddenly loquacious. He had decided since last December to allow her some leeway, understanding some of the misgivings she felt since their past skirmishes and her dislike of him.

She took his stare to be oblivion to her words or indifference to her feelings and continued in the same vein. "In your vast self-importance you imagine people are agog for your interference and intrusive opinions…when actually you are like someone's perniciously nosey maiden aunt who has nothing better to do but—"

He suddenly came to life; the last comparison being intolerable. "I suggest you stop there…" He put up his gloved hand between them, "Before you go too far! I warned you on our last encounter about your insults… I have heard enough of my faults for now, thank you…"

"Well, of course you have! You would much prefer to be telling others of theirs… In fact, should you not be in one of the schools now, terrorising pupils? Oh no, of course, I forgot, 'tis Saturday."

217

"I cannot imagine how you have been allowed to become so rude and uncivil…coming from the background you do." He was quickly losing some of the previous resolve to forbearance.

"And I do not know who you believe yourself to be, with your pompous warnings! Just be quiet and drive," she instructed, put out by events and so frozen and wet she could scarcely see straight. He continued to stare at her, holding the reins tighter so that the horse was stayed from its restless backing and shifting.

"I beg your pardon?" He assumed a tone of faked innocence.

"I thought for a moment you told me to *just be quiet and drive…*"

She wrapped her cloak around herself and shuffled up to her side of the trap, then she glanced sideways at him. "Obviously, the cold has affected your hearing. I was saying it is quite good of you to drive me…"

"That is better," he concurred, and flicked the reins so that the trap moved forwards.

Her teeth were chattering, she was numb with cold.

He did not speak for minutes and she gazed at the lane and hillsides in the opposite direction, cogitating on the fact that their last encounter was evidently clear in his mind.

"Is it wise to make these excursions at this time of the year?" he enquired, starting conversation again on a better footing.

"Is it really any of your concern?" she retorted.

"If I were your father, I would forbid it," he said.

She laughed scornfully. "Of course you would! But if you were my father, I would have likely run away from home by now."

He threw away the cigar butt into the road and watched her and then took his gaze back to the way ahead, pulling up the muffler around his ears. She smiled to herself and hid it by tucking her chin into her cloak collar. She could not assess him properly, muffled in that way, could not sate her curiosity and her need to gauge him since their last meeting, and therefore little was lost. Even so it came as an alarming self-revelation that she placed so much value on looking at him.

They reached the manor and he took them along the drive and stopped the conveyance at the front steps. She was frozen to the bone and her knees would not accommodate her feet, they were like rocks and did not want to move of their own accord. He began to lift her, speaking before she could, pre-empting the possibilities. "Do not say *'take your hands off me'* before you think of doing so.

You are stiff with cold and will fall if not helped… I do not want that adding to the list of cruelties…"

He lifted her down and the contact between them was unutterably close. She smelt his cigars and the soap he used, but not the lemony fragrance from his hair, which was obviously only for special occasions or indoor events. He set her on her feet and got out the hold-all, and she moved to take it from him. He resisted her pull on it. "I am used to carrying it and know how to balance it," she told him.

A small tussle took place which he naturally won. "I cannot allow you to carry something almost a third of your own size…do you imagine me to be uncivilised!" He carried the hold-all and held her elbow, as if she might run away, and guided them to the front door and pulled on the large bell.

The butler answered and appeared shocked at the state of her and then glared at Fairchild, as if he were to blame, and they entered the house. Her father came immediately into the hallway. He was unsurprised to see Fairchild with her— having heard from his wife the previous December the gossip related to her by Damien concerning someone called Henderson—but was shocked by her sodden state.

"I have brought your daughter home," Fairchild announced. "She met with an accident." Her father appraised her. "Good God, wench! What were you doing? And what on earth possessed you to go out in those shoes on a day like today."

"My sentiments entirely," agreed Fairchild.

"My walking boots were muddy and the footmen were engaged with your visitor's trunks… I could not be delayed any further."

"Surely you could have waited five minutes," said Giles Shaw. "Rather than wear those inadequate things, more fitted for the ballroom."

"I shall throw them out now…" she said blithely and knew that Fairchild was no doubt thinking of how spoiled she was in this wealthy environment. She glanced at him and his expression confirmed the thought as he looked away and towards the staircase, rather than give her access to his mind. Then her mother appeared from the depth of the mansion and was delighted to see the re-appearance of Anthony Fairchild, before she caught sight of her. "Good Lord, Lissy, what has happened? You are so wet!"

"When you have all finished stating the obvious and commenting on my wardrobe… I fell…in a field."

"Melissa, there is no need to be rude," said her mother.

Fairchild grinned slightly for his own benefit and gazed at the large gilt-edged mirror on the opposite wall. She dropped her sodden cloak to the floor and a maid was summoned to retrieve it and then to prepare for her a hot bath as a precaution against cold.

"What are you wearing on your head? You look like a gypsy or one of those vagabonds one sees about the town..." Her mother was much aggrieved at the thought of what Fairchild would think.

Melissa took on an arch expression, not displeased with this description for it would deter him from pursuing any of his amorous notions as suggested by Melanie. She pulled off the hat and her hair fell in bounteous tresses about her neck and shoulders.

He looked away from her. The action reminding him of Lottie when disguised in her brother's clothing.

"Anthony, it was fortunate you were about..." said Marguerite Shaw, helping herself to his first name now that he was acquainted with two of her offspring and had re-emerged after an inexplicable absence.

"We are indebted to you, young fellow," said Giles. "Perhaps you will take a drink to warm you?"

Melissa stashed her hold-all next to the commodious Welsh dresser. "He cannot...he has an appointment and is late!"

Her father frowned, looking at Fairchild. "Mayhap you'll let him answer for himself!"

"Melissa is right..." Fairchild said. "I am already very late for an appointment."

Her mother stepped forwards and said in her prettiest manner. "Well, Lissy, I hope you have thanked Anthony for his very timely assistance..."

She turned to him. "Thank you, Anthony...lest I did not mention it before, which perhaps I did not...but I am as always in your debt for your very solicitous attentions. I shudder to think what might have happened were it not for your timely arrival." Fairchild held his counsel and her parents exchanged glances at this gushing flow. It was a touch embarrassing, very out of character, a shade overdone; they sensed more of the bewildering undertones of the infamous Sunday tea. He inclined his head to her in brief acknowledgement, the stony expression in place.

"Perhaps you would care to join us for dinner tomorrow? Weather permitting…" said her mother: the foolish parent she had been lumbered with in this lifetime.

"He has an appointment then as well…" She glowered at him with a mutiny he had seldom encountered in women of his acquaintance.

"Will you let the poor fellow make his own replies!" declared her father testily.

The *poor fellow* carefully considered things, fingering his cleanly shaven chin—so much without any facial hair today as to look positively peachy from the brisk winter climate. "Thank you, Ma'am, I will check my diary…though I am almost sure I will be able to attend."

She made a sound of disapproval but no-one noticed.

"If I cannot, I will send word in the morning," he concluded. "If the weather and the roads have not worsened…"

"Wonderful! About six thirty then!" cooed her mother and her father shook his hand as he prepared to leave.

Fear of Blind Alleys

Reclining in bed after the bath and partaking of hot water and rum as a preventative to chills, she saw that she had brought it upon herself, again! With her foolish attempt at the hike over the fields. And no doubt Melanie would lose no time in telling her so. After breakfast the next morning, she purloined the trap and drove over to Melanie's home. Alarming the groom who told her: "Mr Damien has ordered it for mid-day, Miss…he especially requested it yesterday."

"'tis only fifteen minutes from ten o'clock now… I will be back by then," she protested.

The groom looked uncertain. Damien Shaw was the most irascible of the males in the household.

"He is not the only one with urgent demands…" claimed Melissa in her arch but mild manner. "I need it as a matter of the greatest urgency."

The groom relented. "If you say so, Miss."

"I do…thank you."

Melanie was only just risen when she arrived at the Petersham estate, similar in setting to the Shaw household but in a slightly larger acreage, consisting of several paddocks. Her father was in the business of trading in horses and donkeys and was firm friends with Giles Shaw, doing regular business with some of Giles' cousins in Spain who bred the animals. She was bidden to go up to Melanie's rooms on the first floor and Melanie met her at the door of her boudoir wearing her silk dressing robe and her lawn sleeping cap to keep her long curls in place. "Lissy! Whatever is it?"

Lissy was breathless from running up the path and then the stairs and looked haunted and somewhat afraid. She explained in a jagged and jumbled way as usual and Melanie was at once exasperated and rang for the maid to bring coffee. "If you will go haring over the fields like a lunatic," she said, as predicted, "Instead of calmly accepting his lift and then getting out on the drive."

"Yes, but he would still have insisted on carrying the hold-all to the door and then met my parents…" Melissa wailed. "And had you been on time it would not have occurred!"

"'twas not my fault, my love…the Lichfield Road was impassable. I don't know why you didn't realise that."

"It was sunny when I set out…"

"But Lissy, 'tis February…"

"Don't remind me of that fact…that is what he said…the pompous *know-it-all!*"

"Everyone knows it…'cept you, of course…and perhaps other creatures of the art world who live on a separate planet to the rest of us."

The coffee arrived and Melanie poured. "I told you he would not give up. What has he said? He is coming to dinner tonight or some such?"

Melissa stared open mouthed at her friend's astute assumption. "Yes, he accepted Mama's invite, even though I stated that he had a prior appointment."

"Did he tell you that?"

"Of course not… I thought I would save him the trouble of making his own excuse, so I invented it for him."

Melanie pulled off her sleeping cap and let out gales of laughter then sank into the low velvet chair while Melissa sat on the bed. "So, what has been said this time? Have you flung more insults at him?"

"One or two…but they were more like caustic observations…"

"Were they really!" said Melanie in a sceptical voice.

"He told me not to begin *'how daring him'* as I climbed into the trap. So, I merely said he was opinionated…and interfering, like someone's maiden aunt…and he disliked it."

"No, surely not!" quipped Melanie.

"He droned on about my rudeness, as usual…so I told him to be quiet and just drive…but then I retracted that on his threatening look and said no more."

Melanie drank the coffee in two gulps, burped, excused herself daintily, and screwed up her face to think.

"But I have brought in Roger…" offered Melissa.

"Brought him in where?"

"To the agenda… I told him it was Roger who was due to collect me."

"That will not be enough," declared Melanie. "He will perhaps relish the thought of that rivalry…and especially if he ever sees the milksop in person."

Melissa was pained. "Roger is not a milksop…"

"Well, he is certainly not Fairchild…" Melanie countered darkly.

"But that is a good thing! Is it not?"

"Some women may think so, I suppose…most would prefer Fairchild."

"Then let them have him," Melissa affirmed.

Melanie retired behind the screen, dismissed the maid who had brought her Sunday frock, and then raised her voice to be heard as she put on her camisole. "I cannot attend."

"Of course you cannot," said Melissa. "You must not. For one thing, Michael is at home, and Edmund has told him of the Sunday tea debacle and Damien has exaggerated things too. He will probably not allow you to even speak if you appear for dinner…let alone make your ribald remarks."

Melanie's head appeared from behind the Japanese silk screen. "Oh, will he not! We will see about that!"

Melissa was quite in awe of her eldest brother. Melissa was, in general, too much in awe of these didactic men. And how did they get to be so powerful if not by women simply accepting it!

"I suppose," ventured Melanie at length, "That Fairchild is to be praised for rescuing you…"

"No, he is not. I could have walked…but he would not hear of it."

Melanie appeared in her camisole and sat in the chair. "Of course you could not have walked. You may have died on the way…and no-one would have arrived to save you, especially in those clothes you wear…beyond shabby. Travellers may have simply driven past…that is if there happened to be any in the foul weather of yesterday. Only clergymen and robbers would have bothered with you."

"Perhaps he was just being dutiful."

"No… I would not put it past him to have been lingering on that road in the hope of seeing you."

"What? Ridiculous!" Melissa drank her coffee too quickly and coughed. "Too far-fetched for words."

"Is it? You are not fifteen any longer…and you scarcely know yet what men will do when in the grip of their passion."

"He must have women all over the place to occupy his free time."

"Yes, but he may be tired of that kind of thing…seeing them all simpering and falling at his feet. He perhaps likes something more…"

"More what?"

"Exhilarating," said Melanie and thought that as Melissa was not yet involved with any men—like Geoffrey Gillis—who were older and more assertive, she was still quite naive. "Of course, you could always invite the milksop."

"Stop calling Roger by that name."

"If you invited him to dinner, he would at least be some kind of a baffle..."

"I cannot at such short notice...my mother would not be pleased. She would know what I was up to. She thinks Fairchild the most eligible man to have entered my life ever."

"What, beyond even young Lord whatshisname from Durham?"

"She does not press that these days...my father dislikes these distressed aristocrats...he thinks them all dissipated and inbred and simply after money. He likes men like himself...men who are offering a contribution to the world. Your Geoffrey for example, and your father and my elder brothers...and possibly Fairchild..." Melissa stopped in her tracks and gaped at Melanie.

"Quite!" said Melanie. "You see where this is leading, I hope."

There was a mortified silence during which they drank the coffee and the stakes of the game were increased without effort.

"Has she actually said she thinks Fairchild suitable as a husband?" pressed Melanie, the cup held aloft.

"No, nor will she. She is guile itself...but that is what she most probably believes and she cares not for my views on life at all."

"Then I am at a loss. You must just endure dinner with him...and for heaven's sake try to drop the antagonism towards him... I do believe that is what is encouraging him...that combined with the lure of your now mature physical attributes...'tis likely an irresistible combination in his eyes!"

"But why?"

"Perhaps he is a virgin hunter," said Melanie dramatically.

Melissa jumped to her feet. "Stop it, I implore you."

"Lie on my bed while I dress," said Melanie, generously, "You can rest while I think... You look fagged out."

"Small wonder, I have hardly slept..." Melissa kicked off her shoes, another inadequate pair more suited to the ballroom, and studied the damask drapes around the four poster as Melanie hummed to herself and the maid returned and preparations for the day continued. And soon she dozed off.

It was fifteen minutes after twelve when she awoke, Melanie was gone to lunch with Geoffrey, leaving a note on the pillow to say she would meet her in the tea shop on the following day. She ran down the staircase of the Petersham abode and out to the stables to collect the trap and wondered what she would say as an excuse to Damien about the delay of the shared transport.

* * *

When he arrived for dinner that evening at around six o'clock, he had mistaken the time and was early by half an hour. He was shown into the drawing room which was empty, he thought, until he saw a figure in the chair by the fire. It looked like a life size doll or some kind of marionette, draped in dark shawls with lace veils around its head. It was indeed strange but he sat down on the sofa and fiddled with his timepiece to try and get it to work properly. And then the doll-like figure stirred and a sound came from it. Startled, he saw that it was a very old lady. She rearranged her heavy veils which were enmeshed with jet beads and other dark stones, and of a style not seen for many years.

"Here, Sonny…" she said in a tremulous voice, not quite feeble but lacking in the lower octaves of someone younger. "Whoever you are! Come near me a moment."

He stood and moved towards her. She was as thin as paper and probably about eighty-five or more. He thought that perhaps she was Giles Shaw's aged mother mentioned in the Sunday tea back in December. He bowed to her quite formally. "Do you need assistance, Ma'am?"

"I need my medicine…" she told him, "In the second drawer of that cabinet near the door."

Obviously, she expected him to get it for her. He wondered whether to summon a servant but then thought it quicker to just follow instructions.

"What does it look like?" he enquired.

She cupped her hand to her ear and frowned. He raised his voice. "What does it look like, this medicine?" He was opening drawers and rummaging, and he suddenly thought how indecorous this was in someone else's residence.

"Not that drawer…" said the aged person, "The one on the right…yes, that one."

"But what does it look like?"

"'tis in a bottle…" she said. "Who the devil are you betimes?"

"Is this it?" He produced a green glass bottle containing some kind of liquid. She ignored the bottle. "You're Ariadne's youngest, ain't you?" She screwed up her ancient eyes, like currants in her head, to peer at him.

"No, I am not Ariadne's youngest…" he replied with patience. "Is this your medicine?" When he turned, he saw that a large black and white cat had entered the scene and was settling on the old woman's lap, wobbling somewhat until finding its hold; the lap was not adequate for its size. She stroked it in a perfunctory manner and it purred loudly and then stared at him as if he were intruding upon a private moment.

He took the bottle towards the old woman and she squinted at it. Then she took some pince-nez from the folds of her shawl and adjusted them on her nose. "No, no, not that…the red bottle, not the green. I told you just now the red…"

He sighed to himself, and the irony of being reduced to the role of footman or dogsbody after his professional life status these days was not lost on him. He moved back to the drawer and said, "I do not see a red bottle…"

"What do you say? Don't mumble at me…" snapped the crone whose verbal delivery was impeded by sucking on a sweet. "Look a bit farther…you're in the wrong drawer for a start…the one below it…did you not hear me say that?"

"I did not," he replied with great tolerance.

And then Melissa sailed in, looking entirely transformed since her outdoor excursion the day before, and quite fit for purpose. She wore a green taffeta dress with silver lace trim at the collar and sleeves, finishing above her elbow and revealing her slender arms, The neckline cut low to show exactly the right amount of decolletage. He noted with satisfaction that although her skirts were fuller, she had not taken to wearing the voluminous size of garment rapidly becoming fashionable. He was much relieved; he hated the fad, for these women with lovely figures did not need them and others without looked hideous.

She wore a single thread of seed pearls about her throat and he recalled that the acceptable custom for girls of her age was a necklace of pearls and nothing more ostentatious in the way of ornament. Her hair was taken up and arrayed on top of her head in plaited coils of various sizes. Her features were much enhanced by the arrangement. She was not so much pretty as classically alluring. She would be very beautiful as she matured. He stared at her for moments, much taken with the transformation, and then adjusted his expression to seem as if he were indifferent. "Thank God…" he said, straightening up from the drawer.

"Perhaps you would get this lady her medicine…in the red bottle and not the green."

"That is our grandmother," she announced and then said to the person in the chair. "Granny, you cannot ask visitors to do your bidding and fetch things. You must ask the servants. The bell is next to you on the little table…" She swung around to address him, reducing the volume of her voice for his ears only. "Why are you early?"

"I mistook the time… I came on from somewhere and have a problem with my timepiece. I apologise."

"Matters not to me," she said. "'tis none of my doing that you are here at all!"

He sighed. "I hope you are not going to begin with your hostility the moment I…"

"Who is this young fellow?" interceded her grandmother, her croaky voice rending the air. "He refuses to tell me."

"I do not refuse to tell you, Ma'am. You did not ask me."

"Don't mind her," said Melissa. "She is a little deaf…"

"I realise that, but she has mistaken me for Ariadne's youngest…whoever that is."

"Ariadne is my aunt and one of Granny's daughters. Lionel is Ariadne's son, my cousin. She thought you were her grandson…there is a passing resemblance of sorts. Don't worry, she will think you someone else in a few minutes. One of Nelson's captains or some such. She knew quite a few of them when she was a girl…she was raised in Cornwall where the fleet docked. She is not so chipper this afternoon."

"Well?" roared Granny. Her yell was like a cracked bell at close quarters. "I won't be ignored…young people with no manners!"

He turned away in annoyance, one thing he did not lack was manners.

"Granny, this is Anthony Fairchild…you do not know him."

"Well, I do now…foolish girl," said Granny. "And that don't tell me who he is…announcing his name like that."

"He isn't a servant," said Melissa evasively. "So, he can't get your medicine. I will get it."

"I can see he ain't a servant…" Granny continued querulously. "I can see that by the jib of him. I ain't daft. Who is he? I don't recognise him."

"Because you have not met him before…he is an associate of Damien's." Granny pushed the spectacle contraption up her nose and scrutinised him. "Come here, Sonny," she beckoned with a twig-like finger. "Let me see you closer."

"Granny, he is a guest and you cannot address guests in that way…he is after all the deputy head at Barton Grange Academy!" she added. "So, a personage of importance."

He stared at her with an inscrutable face. "I can say as I like…" informed Grandmother in the demeanour of a malevolent child. "When you get to my age you have earned the right."

Fairchild said very quietly. "This is Granny of the quaint sayings is it? The one from whom you inherit your scathing tongue?" He moved closer to the old woman to allow her scrutiny.

Melissa turned on him. "And do not begin with your sarcasm."

"And what of your own?" he shot back.

"I do not know why you had to come at all."

"Because your mother was good enough to invite me…and because the world does not revolve around you, as I have pointed out before."

"What's he saying?" croaked Granny. "I won't be mumbled at in my own home."

"You are not in your own home, you are in Giles' home, your son," Melissa told her in a voice loud enough for her to hear. "Besides, he is not saying anything of any significance beyond his usual pompous pronouncements…"

"Well, if he ain't Ariadne's boy, who is he?"

"I have just told you."

"I ain't familiar with this Grange place…so what's the good of telling me that?" cried Granny scornfully.

"You should count yourself fortunate then," said Melissa in an undertone that he would hear and Granny would not.

Fairchild followed her as she walked to the window to fiddle with the curtains and have some objective purpose. "Are you intending to be this objectionable throughout dinner?" he enquired, seeing now it was a mistake to have accepted the invite.

She swung round on him. "Just because you saved me from dying of cold does not mean you can waltz in here and…"

"My medicine, Madam…" said the voice from the chair. "I am tired of asking for it."

229

Melissa paid her no heed. "You are making it impossible for me to avoid you," she told him.

"Exactly how am I doing that? And why would you want to avoid me?"

"Because…because…'tis too difficult to explain…" She wondered if his needing explanation was a man-woman difference and he was genuinely at a loss. "But you must use your common sense and think about it yourself."

He stepped nearer to her in a movement of bewilderment as she moved backwards and put out a hand to signal the need for distance. "And do not come so close to me."

Her grandmother had heard the last sentence. "Don't be starting those shenanigans in here, young feller! Take her into the garden and chase her round there…but get me my medicine first."

He was growing quietly incensed. Not in the household above ten minutes and she had put him in the wrong. He pulled open a drawer without thought and magically struck lucky, the red bottle was lying on top of a sheaf of papers. He took it across to the old lady who received it without thanks and peered up at him. "Ma'am, you have completely misconstrued the situation with Melissa and myself," he said.

"Now you take my point…so give me a wide berth," Melissa told him.

Granny's hearing was improving. "Take no notice of that twaddle…" and then to Melissa in a changed and wheedling tone. "He's a pretty picture, for sure…he's better than Meg's parrot when it comes to something to look at."

Fairchild stared at Melissa. "Is that another of her quaint sayings?"

"Of course…" said Melissa. "You don't think we sit about staring at caged birds to pass the time?"

He was about to lose tolerance when Damien entered and took in the scene: his barmy grandmother and his erratic sister upsetting his influential colleague. "Tony…" he began jovially. "I did not know you had arrived."

Fairchild smoothly changed the subject to deflect from the animosity. "I was remarking on your grandmother's cat…" he told Damien. "Quite a magnificent creature…"

Damien looked askance at the cat, purring still and kneading Granny with old blunted claws.

"She is actually the kitchen cat…" Melissa informed him, "But she rules the house…like all cats must…she likes to sit with Granny, as she and Granny are about the same age…" She smiled as if he should be pleased with this warmer address.

"A mangy old thing…" Damien said, moving to the windows to look along the driveway for signs of his lady friend—also expected for dinner.

"She is not mangy!" Melissa said with asperity. "Gertrude is cleaner than you and less smelly…she does not exude the odour of acid and bromide as you do."

"Take care not to touch her…" Damien was determined not to be overset. "She scratches and bites…"

"You perhaps…" said his sister, "but no-one else." Proving her point, she went to the cat and stroked her behind her ears and the cat became ecstatic with purring pleasure. "She dislikes Damien…but then who does not? Apart from his lady friend!"

"Melissa, be quiet!" said Damien from the window.

Melissa feigned oblivion. "And even then, it is debatable whether Estelle actually likes him…or is just keeping him happy while she learns more about his science experiments…"

"I am warning you, little sister," said Damien with his back to the room. "I shall be having words with Father about your vulgarity…in addition to your commandeering of the trap earlier."

"You can have all the words you wish…one day he might even bother listening to you."

"Is this bickering necessary?" said Fairchild lightly.

"You see, he is after all a vicar's son…show more respect on a Sunday," she told her brother.

Damien was immediately competitive. "Actually, Melissa. he is now the step-son of a bishop…is that not right, Tony?"

Fairchild was uncomfortable. "Perhaps we should leave my heritage out of things…'tis irrelevant."

The cat jumped from Granny and stalked over to Fairchild and rubbed herself against his leg, as if showing support. Melissa watched the cat and then had a refreshing thought. "How impressive…a bishop for a stepfather…surely if you changed profession, you could one day become the Archbishop of Canterbury… Think of the power then!"

He gritted his teeth and closed his eyes and she felt a triumphant lift of her spirits. Damien reacted instantly, afraid for his sponsorship. "Melissa, that is simply impertinent… I shall definitely be telling Father of your rudeness…"

Fairchild smiled slowly and found his spirit returning. "Do not trouble him with it, Damien! I am quite capable of dealing with her rudeness in my own way."

There was a silence and Damien stared from one to the other. It confirmed what he had told his mother about how advanced things between them were. She picked up Gertrude who disliked being so far from the ground and struggled. Damien turned to Fairchild and smiled back at him ingratiatingly. "I hope you have not been much put out by these two."

"*These two!*" Melissa rounded on him. "How dare you!" She dropped the struggling Gertrude and Damien simmered his annoyance and darkened his gaze. "You will be hearing more of this."

"I dare say I shall… I dare say you will not let it drop inside a week."

Before she could provoke further altercation, Fairchild said to Damien, "Your sister is fond of a good dare…next to painting it seems to be her favourite pass-time."

She gasped with annoyance, unable to quell it in time, thought of everything she and Melanie had talked of and flounced out of the room.

* * *

Dinner went off fairly peaceably. Her mother encouraged Fairchild to escort her into the dining room, while Damien took in Estelle, his lady friend, and her mother's two sisters were escorted by their husbands. Giles took in his wife and his youngest sister, Amaelia, who was permanently separated from her husband. Only grandmother was left behind in the drawing room; she had fallen asleep, added to which she never ate any later than five p.m.

Being taken into dine by him meant she had naturally to sit next to him. Her coldness and silence towards him was quite palpable and her mother threw her warning glances, while her father cast the odd look at them.

"Was all that necessary?" he remarked in a low voice as they sat.

"All what?" she enquired.

"That scathing tirade you delivered to your brother…rather inappropriate."

She turned and appraised him. "I hope you are not presuming to criticise my behaviour nowadays…especially when you are no longer paid to do so," she said, pleased with her response. There was a pause and she could not resist looking at him to see how he had taken it. He ventured a small smile and glanced at her sidelong. "Perhaps I will take on the responsibility as a mere act of charity…to society as a whole!"

Her face changed without her volition to a lighter and fascinated expression. She watched him and blinked rapidly; had he thrown down some sort of gauntlet within this sarcasm? It was impossible to tell! She assumed yet another stony silence and turned away, and several minutes passed while the soup was served and consumed. The question absorbed her and she memorised the words to relate to Melanie the next day, for Melanie would know in an instant. Meantime, she did not wish for tiring repercussions from her parents to her aloof behaviour, and she turned to him pleasantly half way through the next course and ventured a conversational topic, "Mary Hampshire died, you know."

His shock at hearing her address him made him turn to her sharply. He had seen many female pupils pass through the school since his first days and needed to dredge his deeper memory. "Yes… I recall her now," he said. "The one with the sleeping sickness."

"We went to the funeral, Melanie and I…in fact quite a few of us from school attended."

"I hope you are not going to blame me for that as well," he said. "This girl's demise… I did, if you remember, request a medical opinion."

She put down the fork and stared at him. "Yes, I recall… You do have that in your favour." He returned his attention to his food.

She went on. "Millie played Brahms on the church organ…it was very moving. Millie is a fine pianist these days…as good as my cousin Gregory, whom I have introduced her to. They are alike in their disposition and well suited, I think."

"Who is Millie?" he asked, giving in to perplexity.

"Millicent Bromley," she replied in astonishment. "Surely you remember?" And then he did, and he sighed long. But she had thought of another way to get even with him while still paying heed to the niceties of dinner table conversation.

"She was quite in love with you, you know, Millicent…" He frowned and flushed darker in skin tone—dismayed on hearing such a thing about someone then so young. He shrugged slightly and held up his hand in a gesture of bewilderment and shook his head.

"But you are probably accustomed to females falling in love with you!" she said.

"I most certainly am not." It was a quiet protest. "What a strange thing to say…what affords you that idea?"

"Something Melanie said."

"Oh well, there we are then!" He lifted the wine glass to his mouth and looked cynically at the ceiling.

"Millie is the gentlest of souls and the most obliging of people," said Melissa.

"Have I said she is not?" he enquired, worried now where this was going.

"No, no…but just look at the legacy you left her, for all her devotion to you."

"Which legacy?" He replaced the glass and stared at her.

"Your casual cruelty, of course," she said tartly.

He realised she was talking of that first time he took serious disciplinary action in the waiting room and his own surprise at Millicent's part in the escapade.

"*My casual cruelty…* I see! Not this subject again, surely?"

"Did you imagine it had gone away since last December?"

"I had rather hoped it had…'tis becoming morbidly persistent…and unless she is very stupid, which I do not think she is, she must have seen that admitting a part in such a thing could only bring dire consequences. If you have discussed it with her since your schooldays, then I hope she at least has seen sense."

Melissa dropped her butter knife quite hastily so that it clanged against her plate and everyone looked at her. She ignored them and they turned back to where they were in their own conversations. She continued, undeterred. "*Millie discuss that subject*? I think not! She is worse than myself when it comes to privacy and not discussing her distressing experiences."

"Really," he said with dignity.

"Indeed…but it was most unfair for Millie because she really had no part of it. The chalking of the names, I mean."

"Then I fail to see why she said she did…and do not tell me it was to gain my attention at any price, or some other such girlish nonsense, because I do not want to hear of it."

"I am telling you nothing more of it." Melissa felt her own subdued fury rising. "Least not here…least not in the presence of your flagrant callousness."

"*My flagrant callousness* now…" he echoed. "Well, I suppose we may discuss it at a later date." He held the kind of calm resistance to rebuff she could not help but admire. "Provided my *casual cruelty and flagrant callousness* permit me the generosity of spirit, of course…"

This from the mouth of someone else may have caused her hilarity. She felt braver; his sarcasm was also a kind of verbal reassurance. "Anyone would imagine that the use of your first name in those days was some kind of blasphemy…" she said.

He chewed and then swallowed the food. "Chalked on a board in that manner…along with Miss Madeley's name…it amounted to that!" he replied.

"She was another stupid female who fell in love with you…" she ventured next.

He forked some fish and ate it and remained silent. He would not be goaded by her in these circumstances, he could bide his time.

She ate more of her own food and then said. "So, you deny having ladies constantly falling in love with you?"

He arranged his expression and made allowances for her inexperience of life. "'tis something like the question, *'how long is a piece of string?'*…"

"But you do know ladies? Ladies who are desirous of you?" she asked, concentrating on her plate.

This was, as Trim would say, girlish conjecture and rhetoric and he was at a loss. He thought carefully how to reply. "I do occasionally have association with ladies…" he said at length in consummate honesty.

"Well, who are they?" she enquired foolishly. "Where are they?"

He laid down his cutlery, stroked his forehead with two fingers and turned, leaning closer to her and lowering his voice, almost whispering in her ear. "Melissa, listen to me…" He waited for her full attention and she tilted her chin in his direction. "You should never ask a man those questions, because if he is any kind of gentleman, he will not give you an answer…"

Her eyes opened wide and she stared at him, seeing a new facet. "And what of truth?" she said from her vast innocence.

"What of it? 'tis a different subject…you are confusing truth with privacy!" He waited for her to absorb his words before saying more. "In any case, there are three kinds of truth: there is personal truth, undeniable truth and widely accepted truth…which are you speaking of?"

This was intriguing philosophy, perhaps something one learned at Oxford University, but too complicated for her to digest with the food, so she stored it for contemplation later when alone. She concentrated on her own uneaten meal. "But...but you are not betrothed to any of these ladies?" she asked and heard him laugh quietly.

"No... I am not betrothed to anyone."

She looked up and saw across the table her aunt Amaelia, mother of Gregory, staring at them. Amaelia, everyone knew, was no stranger to assignations with men other than her husband who was minor aristocracy and known for his debauchery. It was as if Amaelia perceived their subject matter, but she could not possibly; their voices were too low and the general level of talk at the table too high. Amaelia's fan was positioned so only Melissa—and not Fairchild—might see her face, and for her niece's benefit alone she lifted her brows above her lively dark eyes and nodded briefly before lowering the fan. It was a signal of approval on Fairchild, as a man and a potential husband.

The assembled adult diners all knew far more than she knew at this time. She was trapped in a web spun generations before her and set like hessian with enduring threads. The eyes of other guests were frequently upon them; him in particular. He was a gentleman, and one they found interesting for his own sake and not simply as someone associated with herself. He was young and accomplished and pleasing to behold, with vast male charm which was understated but apparent. She smiled at her aunt and then turned again to him. He was spearing a potato with his fork but alert to her presence. "And what of marriage?" she asked him quietly. "If one does not know the truth, how is marriage ever to work to advantage?"

He chewed and swallowed a mouthful of food and dabbed his lips with the napkin before leaning towards her once more. "Marriage should only be entered into for the highest of reasons..." he hesitated, and she waited. "For love," he concluded and leaned away from her to resume eating.

She was quite transfixed in her seat. She had not expected these esoteric wisdoms to emerge from his mouth; he of all people. She wondered if he was making fun of her and she stared at him in a way which was not quite acceptable in the company of others.

Sensing this he cleared his throat and raised his voice a mere octave or so to normality. "Anyway, I am sorry to hear of Mary's death."

She considered this sentiment and despite her previous annoyance she allowed her thoughts to take her into confidential waters. "I cried and cried at her funeral… Lucinda cried too. We could not stop…" She gazed at the crystal glass centrepiece on the dining table—filled with small flowers and illuminated by the chandelier above—her eyes laden with the memory of grief, and then she realised her vulnerability in the words and bestowed upon him a loftier expression.

"That is understandable…" he said. "The death of people so young whom one has known and seen cut down in their prime is beyond distressing."

"Has it happened to you ever?"

"Once or twice…"

She waited for him to elaborate but he did not. She thought of Lottie and the letter. Where was this Lottie now? She nibbled a piece of the fish without appetite and then washed it down with water, and ventured, "Do you believe death is the end?"

"The end of what?" he said. "'tis the end of this life certainly."

"Yes, but I mean the end of everything…"

"It would seem impossible. I cannot think there is an end to *everything*."

"Neither can I?"

He lifted his wine glass, took a long drink and said, "Good Lord, we seem to have agreed upon something."

She smiled at him, slowly and with caution.

* * *

When the men had returned to the drawing room to join the women, it was proposed by Damien that they play billiards. He had recently had a table erected in the smaller room annexed to the library and he suggested that he and Estelle play doubles with herself and Fairchild. She agreed and they went off to begin while the other guests, including Granny, settled down to play bridge with the eagerness of those addicted to the game.

Damien was accomplished in billiards, as was Fairchild. Estelle not too bad, while she herself was a novice with only a rough idea of how to go about it. Eventually Estelle and Damien fell out over a rule of the game and Damien stormed off to cool down and replenish the drinks. Estelle soon followed and she was left alone with Anthony Fairchild. It was somewhat mortifying. She opened the conversation. "What do you think of Estelle?" she asked him.

He paused in the inspection of the end of his cue. "Estelle?"

"Yes…whom we have just played against… I see you like to engage her in conversation…" She saw that he found it difficult to reply. "Do you find her attractive?"

He thought of Damien's lady friend in her divided skirt and matching jacket, her masculine blouse and severe hairstyle. "I do not think she is interested in being thought attractive by the average man…"

She laughed, for that was completely in tune with her own opinion. "And of course my brother is not the average man…he is himself very odd."

"I cannot comment on that," he said in his diplomatic way. "I find her interesting…her views on education…her pursuits in ladies' colleges and so on…she is an educator like myself. That is as far as my interest goes."

"Do you think she dresses in that way to be taken more seriously in what she does in education?" She brushed the velvet cloth of the table with the soft brush meant for the purpose and did not look at him. He considered her question: it was an insightful observation, deserving of thought. "Quite possibly, yes…but then she would have no reason to do so when off-duty."

"Quite!"

"Perhaps Damien likes her to dress like that…he may have a…" Realising she was too young or sheltered to understand some of the quirks of male society he stopped abruptly.

"So, perhaps underneath all that she is a veritable femme fatale!" she suggested. "If she dressed as a feminine person."

He smiled. "Indeed…she might then be quite alluring…and perhaps on occasions she becomes that sort of woman."

"I have never seen it if she does…" Melissa offered, "But who knows what goes on behind closed doors when they are alone."

"No-one…" he began chalking the cue. "What goes on behind closed doors is entirely their own affair."

Discarding the brush, she smiled widely. His answer was much to her liking. She changed the subject, picking up her cue. "I wish I could play well."

"Would you like me to show you how to better hold the cue?"

"Yes, I would," she conceded.

"Take the ball and position it…" He came to stand behind her and placed his left hand on the table to steady himself and the other on her right hand which held the cue, so that he was encircling her. "Loosen your wrist slightly and use the strength of your arm." She potted a ball with success and then another, and was a little dizzy at the closeness of him, his upper body almost touching her back, the skin of her shoulders in the low-cut dress sensitive to his nearness.

The warmth of another human being, and the softening of reality it suddenly brought with it. He took his hand from her wrist and she dropped the cue and turned. He did not step back to allow her to pass, and she looked at him in mounting alarm. He placed his right hand on the table at her other side so that she was completely encompassed by him. Then he kissed her, his mouth on hers before she knew what was happening.

At first, she did not respond, her lips stiff and set beneath his own. He lifted his head and looked at her mouth and then at her eyes which were stricken with fear. He put his mouth on hers again, moistening her lips a little with his own and caressing them with gentle movements of his own lips. She tasted the wine he had supped at dinner and the cigar he had smoked and the vague flavour of the mint sorbet the cook served—after meals as well as between courses. She kissed him back then with ardour, wondering where she had acquired the art of doing so and knowing suddenly that it was instinctive.

He pulled back and watched her eyes and she moved her face to his and put her mouth on his. He kissed her ardently for a long time, placing his hands on her back. Her arms around his neck, she felt the softness of his hair in her fingers. She was becoming intense with a desire she knew not how to begin expressing. She nuzzled his chin with her own, the small hairs of his early beard growth tingling into an unknown feeling in the pit of her stomach. She could not settle on any definition for how she felt. She was lost in the newness of sensuality and its myriad forms of need.

He kissed her not like Roger kissed her—as if getting it over with as in a guilty act. Nor how her father's estate manager had covertly kissed her—as if his life depended on it and his tongue down her throat. But like someone who knew her and knew how natural and easy and eternal the act of kissing was. Then he drew back and said, "That is enough for now."

"For now?" she repeated.

He hesitated, his eyes not leaving her's and did not reply.

"Why can we not continue now?"

"Because we have reached a point where we must stop...for now."

"Why?" she asked. He smiled at her naivety and did not know how to answer. He did not know how much she knew of the facts of life and he was not at liberty to explain them to her. "Surely one cannot have enough of a good thing?" she said.

"Not always true," he replied.

She heard Damien and Estelle return, chattering and annoyed with each other. She dropped her arms guiltily but they noticed nothing on their entrance and went to place bottles and fresh glasses on a table in the corner of the library. In the lull and before they came close to the table, she whispered to him, "I still detest and despise you...it does not change that." He grinned, concealing it swiftly by tightening his jaw, the way she knew of from a thousand years ago.

"It might," he told her. "In time."

* * *

Back in the drawing room everyone was cheerful and relaxed. Melissa and he took seats, this time opposite each other. Her mother glanced at each of them in turn and then quickly away, her face a mask of feigned neutrality within greater awareness. The hands of bridge were paused and there was much conversation and some laughter. Granny had fallen asleep again and was snoring slightly. Geraldine had arrived alone after dinner—to play cards, she claimed, but obviously to observe more of the *penny dreadful* saga. She stared at them both unashamedly and caught Melissa's eye and made pouting movements with her mouth. It was a visual signalling of desire and feminine triumph all in one expression. A little like Aunt Amaelia's at dinner, but more clumsy.

Melissa remembered the spurned tea invitation and smiled quite warmly back at her, and it struck her then that she was somehow embroiled with a man who was potentially viewed with favour by half the women of the county. But still, she could not shake off the past so easily.

Giles said to Damien. "You will have to help me with your grandmother up the stairs, my knee is giving me gip and John has gone home to Derbyshire for the weekend and is not yet back..."

Damien looked at their father askance. "Can the butler not do it?"

"No, he cannot," said Giles testily. "Like me, he is too much of an old fossil."

Melissa was perturbed, she did not like Damien to become responsible for her grandmother. "I would not have him do it, Papa. Unless you want him to drop her half way…like the last time."

"I did not drop her…you exaggerate, as always, Melissa."

"You certainly let her slide and both of you nearly falling down the stairs…"

"What a liar you are!" Damien said.

"How dare you!" she claimed and heard Fairchild sigh lightly. "You have to own that you have not taken any exercise since before Easter…you are so indolent and not at all in the muscular way…" she continued to her brother.

Estelle shrieked with laughter and Damien was persuaded to almost smile at the truism. "At least I don't sneak into stables and purloin other people's transport," he remarked.

"I did not sneak anywhere. I left a message with the groom to say what I was doing."

"But you were then an hour later than you had said."

"Because I fell asleep and it could not be avoided."

"Fell asleep where?" enquired her mother in consternation.

"It does not really matter where, Mama," said Melissa.

"I believe it does," said her aunt Dorothea, who stuck her nose into everything. "Respectable young women do not just fall asleep at random. Where were you?"

"At the reins of the trap probably," said Damien. "She scarcely drives it properly at the best of times."

"I was in Melanie's boudoir," she declared, and heard herself sounding guilty, as if Fairchild would know that they had been discussing him. She noticed then his expression, as if he had something distasteful in his mouth he was obliged to swallow. No doubt he was loathing this exchange between her and Damien as being too rude to be endured.

"Why did you not stay here and fall asleep?" queried her mother.

"It is rather a long story, Mama…"

"Please do not encourage her to tell it, Mother," opined Damien. "'twill be as boring as Homer's Odyssey and twice as long."

"You had better stop this bickering…" said Giles. "A'fore it starts in earnest."

Fairchild stood suddenly and assumed a subtle control. "I will take up your mother, if you will allow me… I will carry her…" he told Giles Shaw.

They looked at him as one group, the men murmuring approval, and Damien said. "Bravo, Tony!" Melissa gazed at him in a semi-daze, while Geraldine made contrived eyelid fluttering and more faces of rapt appreciation.

"You do not mind?" asked Giles.

Rather than reply he stood and began removing his close-fitting velvet jacket, revealing his dark waistcoat and the sleeves of his linen shirt. He threw the jacket casually onto the arm of the sofa.

He approached the old lady "Allow me, Ma'am?" he said in a louder voice. She awoke and glanced at him and said, "'tis Ariadne's lad again, is it?"

He smiled, and Melissa told her: "'tis Anthony, Granny, he is going to carry you up the stairs."

All eyes were upon him. Marguerite had rung for the maid, who came at once. "My mother-in-law is going to bed…please assist her in the bedroom."

"I don't want any young women fossicking around me," said Granny, "I can assist myself."

"I will assist you, Granny. Polly can arrange your bed," said Melissa, then to Fairchild. "I will follow and show you the room."

He bowed slightly to the room at large. "Please excuse us!" Then he and Giles, one either side of her, helped the old lady to her feet and Fairchild swung her easily into his arms—as if she were the doll he had firstly mistaken her to be, and carried her from the room and went swiftly up the stairs with her, for she was no weight at all.

Amaelia immediately took up her fan, opened it, and made vigorous movements in the air for the sake of entertainment. Giles had returned, having watched the initial progress up the first few stairs. Amaelia addressed him in comic tones. "Giles, my dear, what an obliging and totally beguiling male personage you have gracing your drawing room tonight."

Giles smiled and nodded.

"Quite, quite divine…" agreed Geraldine, "He might have walked out of the pages of an Austen novel." She took up her own fan and imitated Amaelia's ostentatious movements.

"Where on earth did she find him?" Amaelia enquired.

"He found her," explained Marguerite, rather listlessly, "While visiting Damien…though he used to teach them at school…her and Melanie…languages!"

"You jest!" said Amaelia.

"I do not!" her sister-in-law replied tersely; for when did she ever indulge in jests of that nature!

"Well, if that has not put him off...then nothing will."

"It has put her off...somewhat..." Marguerite opined. "She and Melanie are full of grudges about it... I am hoping she won't repel him with some of her disobliging speech and churlish moods..."

"She had better not..." Damien declared. "There's my sponsorship to consider."

"I do not think somehow," said one of the male relatives, "That he gives a damn about that right now..."

"Certainly not," laughed Amaelia. "He is not so devoted to duty as to make that a criterion...he has other duties on his mind."

"Please, Amaelia!" Marguerite moaned and she and Dorothea exchanged glances, their faces like people forced to drink vinegar. The admonishment was ignored and a much older male relation pronounced. "What it is to be young and robust...with all your own hair and teeth...and have the ladies falling at your feet."

"Or onto your bed," Amaelia offered, undeterred by her sister-in-law.

The amount of wine and liquor consumed now had mellowed everyone nicely, except perhaps Marguerite and Dorothea, and there was laughter and good humour.

"'tis but a distant memory..." added another male guest, "Though I would settle for having all my teeth again."

"I do not think he will need his teeth until breakfast," Amaelia countered. She was quite the most outrageous of Giles' sisters and Marguerite tutted and glared, and several people laughed appreciatively.

"I think we might play another round of bridge..." Marguerite told them. "Rather than sit gossiping about visitors behind their backs...'tis too vulgar."

"At any rate," said Geraldine, "Let us hope she gets over her grievances and accepts his attentions."

"Grievances!" echoed Amaelia. "Why should she have any grievances? 'tis not as if he were eighty and covered in warts."

"Dear me!" breathed Dorothea to Marguerite softly. "I never heard the like!"

"But she does have grievances..." Geraldine quietly affirmed for Amaelia. "She and Melanie both...you should have been at the Sunday tea back in December..."

Marguerite stood abruptly and lifted two empty glasses from a small occasional table unnecessarily. "Do not bring up the subject of that Sunday tea, Geraldine!" she said warningly.

"Why?" Amaelia demanded. "What am I missing?"

Marguerite looked daggers at Geraldine and then at Giles who intervened. "Enough now, dear folk!" he said good humouredly. "He may return any moment and hear us from the hallway and it will embarrass the fellow."

"He has more about him than that, I'll be bound!" remarked his jovial brother-in-law, Raymond, married to the quietest of his sisters, Arabella.

"He will need to have, if he's taking on my sister," said Damien, put out by the easy dismissing of his projects.

Geraldine leaned across the arm of her chair and whispered to Amaelia on the sofa, and they began to savour the marvellous knowledge they had so far of the enigmatic Anthony Fairchild. Then Geraldine gave a shortened version of the tea hurling incident at Sunday tea in December, for Amaelia's benefit.

Being carried swiftly and safely up the stairs, Granny grinned her near toothless grin as they ascended and thought back to days she could barely recall when her late husband—a fine figure of a man—had carried her up myriad staircases. At the door of her room, she asked him. "Are you my grandson or not?"

"I am not, Ma'am..." said he and she let forth her cracked-bell laughter and said to Melissa. "If I were forty years younger, I would have *him* assisting me now...not you!"

"Granny!" Melissa said in mock reproof. "That is as improper as it is ludicrous. Forty years ago, he was not even born." The maid and she exchanged looks of sheer delight as Granny grinned shamelessly; time had ceased to mean anything to her. He waited for Melissa to open the door and he took Granny in and deposited her on the chair by the large bed.

"You must not mind her," said Melissa cheerfully. "She had her heyday in Regency, when people said whatever they pleased."

"Really? I perceive that some people still do," he retorted.

"And if that gibe is aimed at me," she said, "Then it is in poor taste."

Granny came somewhat to life and claimed. "I do not want to listen to any more quarrelling...'tis not seemly...have a little more respect in other folks' bed chambers."

Fairchild glanced at the old lady in astonishment and then at Melissa—the switch from ribald commentary to puritanical critique was quite startling.

Melissa giggled. "Pay no heed…she is full of these canting strictures on the behaviour of others. She is almost as accomplished a hypocrite as you are…"

He stared at her for long moments. She ignored his call for attention and kept her nerve while taking off Granny's ornate slippers, as if oblivious. It served him right for kissing her in the first place and then stopping without reason.

At length, he found his words. "Melissa, I do believe I have told you this before…but you will one day let fly at me one insult too many…"

She watched him begin retreating from the room. There was the *gauntlet* again! No mistaking it. "Anthony?" She waited until he had turned. "Thank you for this assistance."

His desire for her was still discernible in his eyes. "'twas the best way to cut through the hideous squabbling."

"Your modesty is overwhelming," she told him softly.

He hesitated a second time. "Do not think that a polite *thank you* for an unrelated matter compensates for your insults, for it does not."

He left the room. The maid had feigned deafness while pouring water into the washing bowl and Melissa had begun unwinding Granny's voluminous shawls. She smiled covertly with Polly, the maid; they were the same age and Polly had assisted her since their early teens. She rolled her eyes and made her face into a mock frown. Polly giggled softly, then pulled down her lips in a show of theatrical sadness. Oh, the pleasures of teasing and tantalising men who were clearly besotted with them! Whatever their cultural differences, they were sisters beneath the skin.

Not behind the door when it came to these kinds of things, Granny knew what was afoot. "Mind you don't go too far with your caustic comments to yon fellow…if you're serious about him…and you'd be a fool not to be…"

"I do not know what you mean, Grandmama!" she replied with pursed lips.

"O'course, you do," said her ancient relative. "Do you think I'm blind! If you set up again' him too often after you're wed you will not come off best…mark my words."

Polly and she began more giggling and helped Granny into bed and listened to her prattle about the unwisdom of provoking men unnecessarily.

She thought that now she had an equal stance in the dance of desire; his dislike of her rudeness and her dislike of his sarcasm. They had a buffer, a safe place between temptation and consequence. It gave her joy of some unspecified sort. The desire had crept up on her, sprung into view like a hare from the ground, enticed into the open by the kissing. She cared little now for his words and dismissed them as easily as flies in a summer pantry.

* * *

He rode leisurely away from the mansion by horse in a slow trot. He had taken the horse so that he could imbibe more alcohol on the way back if the fancy took him. The upkeep of the horse at the nearest ostlers from his lodgings and the occasional hire of the trap cost him almost half his salary, but he thought this expense indispensable to his life. He deliberated on the situation he found himself in. He was going deeper into some kind of dangerous quagmire of passionate exchange with Melissa Shaw, almost against his own judgement.

A former pupil and the sister of one of the newly appointed specialists for the Foundation. It was unwise. For one thing she was still quite young. Perhaps not yet twenty, and although that was not an improper age were he to take her as his wife, it was not an age where he could play around at the water's edge or entice her into some kind of erotic dalliance. He now had a position to keep and a public reputation. Though he did not intend to stay working within education forever he also did not see a time to leave Barton Grange in the near future.

She was leading him into a heady brew made up of some kind of fascinated disgust with his former power over her and her own power now as an eligible and desirable female adult.

He seemed to have lost all ability to impartial overview.

He slowed the horse and contemplated. The night was dark and without a visible moon and it was not yet quite ten o'clock. He decided on a whim to call on Trimingham as he passed by the vicinity of his home.

Trimingham resided in the family mansion in rooms of his own. The footman on night duty answered the door after a lengthy interval and he apologised for his lateness and asked for Trimingham.

Trim was in his shirt sleeves and socks, minus his neckcloth. "Tony! What a surprise!"

"Do you mean an unwarranted intrusion?" Fairchild inquired.

"Not in the least." Trim clapped him on the back.

"I was passing and I thought I could do with a nightcap and a bit of moral guidance…"

"Moral guidance! I scarcely believe it!" Trim indicated an armchair and invited him to sit. "I am having a brandy myself."

"Excellent! Susan is not with you, is she?"

"God no," said Trim. "She left an hour since… Monday is her busiest day."

"Splendid," said Fairchild. He had some affection for Susan whom he had known as long as he had known Lottie, but she would insist on trying to advise him from a female bias, and would probably put a damper on their nightcaps; they would need to stay sober out of respect for her as a lady.

In Trim's cosy parlour a low fire burnt in the grate, and by the time he had outlined the developments and dilemma of himself and Melissa Shaw they were both quite inebriated. Fairchild more so, owing to the generous amount he had drunk in the Shaw household. Fending off constant interruptions from Trimingham as he got the narrative tangled and the events out of sequence, he fought to order his brain.

"I remember saying that these waiting room measures would return to haunt you…" Trimingham said in a paused moment.

"You said nothing of the kind," argued his friend. "If I remember rightly, you told me I was some kind of tyrant…and McCarthy had to fight my corner…you not having the experience of teaching young girls where he and I had…it was the night I first went to his relative's evening soirees…" He paused and closed his eyes and just as Trimingham thought he had finished speaking added, "…and those measures as you call them will not return to haunt me on a regular basis because I do not intend becoming personally acquainted with any more of their fold…she is more than enough…this is an unfortunate twist of fate."

"I thought you did not believe in fate!" Trim said dubiously.

"'tis a turn of phrase, Trim! How can we make progress if you interrupt me every few seconds?"

"You are inebriated and waffling," Trimingham pronounced sombrely.

The irony of this statement from someone in the same boat was not lost on them and they collapsed into a feverish intoxicated laugher, until eventually they recovered. "Hogwash!" said Fairchild, and followed it with heavier cursing, "I am perfectly coherent."

"A delusion of the state you are in," said Trim and then he struggled to sit upright and stay alert. "Anthony, pay me heed!" he commanded officiously. "Let us be clearer…what is the exact problem here? If you like the girl."

"God's Teeth! I have told you all this, have I not?" Fairchild screwed up his face to recall what he had said so far. "Her offensive comments are the problem…which are at odds with her other behaviour…she tells me she detests me; she hurls insults at me on an ad hoc basis…or abuses me verbally when I am least expecting it…then kisses me passionately in response when I kiss her…and does not want to stop…then she tells me it does not alter her attitude of loathing towards me…"

"So, you began kissing her without invitation?" queried Trimingham. "Not knowing what her response might be?"

"Well, yes…one has to start somewhere…but I gauged it carefully."

"So, you must obviously know that she does not believe her own insults…or you would not risk kissing her in her parents' home on such short acquaintance…" Trimingham's head had begun aching from the effort of deeper thinking.

"No, I do not know that! Perhaps I was trying to find out."

"Sounds like a variation on female behaviour in general to me…are you not perhaps overstating the case on these insults? Are they perhaps meant as witticisms?"

"No… I am not overstating anything!" He moved to stand to reach his cigars but was incapable of it and collapsed back onto the sofa.

"And you have tried telling her that these insults are unacceptable?"

"Of course not, I rather enjoy them," Fairchild said facetiously.

Trim peered at him in the dim light of the parlour. "Naturally I have told her…'tis what I have been saying. She has had several warnings and does not heed them." He had his jacket twisted in the quest to find his cigars and was heaving and wrestling with it before finding them.

"Warnings of what…to what end?" Trim asked.

"Her rear end…" Fairchild sniggered a little at his own wit and then lit a cigar from the nearest candle, succeeding on the third try. "…her sweet little derriere…when I smack it until her teeth rattle…if she carries on in this vein." His vision was wavering as he kept Trimingham in view. "'tis her personal preference…did I not mention that?" He grinned drunkenly and Trim had to rewind the conversation to ferret out the meaning.

It was exhausting and he dozed off while Fairchild was inclined to join him. Both of them slept and snored and allowed time to march on. It was an hour later when Trim woke and began shaking him to rouse him. A Monday morning was to follow a generous bout of quaffing.

"Where the devil am I?" Fairchild said irritably and then recognised Trim's parlour. "Oh yes…we had better retire."

"Precisely my thought…" Trim snuffed out the lamps and gutted several candles. "Or we will not be sober by morning." He went into his adjoining bedroom and re-emerged, lurching quickly as a means to remaining upright.

"It does not do to attend lessons smelling of strong liquor…" Fairchild was saying and then laughed in a less than elegant roar before becoming serious. "Not too bad at the boys' place…'tis the henhouse where one needs to be impeccable…"

"I should hope so." Trim threw him a woollen rug to sleep under.

"I have to call there late morning on school matters and Judith Tongs imbibes gin prodigiously…if she smells it on me, she will make much of it and begin with her predatory remarks…odious creature that she is."

Trim attempted to relieve him of the cigar without success; Fairchild held it away from him, like a child with coveted confectionery. "Give that to me…" Trim ordered. "I will wake you with coffee no later than eight so that you can go home and change…but don't attempt to ride tonight."

"You sound like Rupert…that is what he always says…when I oil the wheels too liberally."

"No-one has better oiled wheels than yourself when festive, dear boy!" Trim said.

"Rupert under-estimates my ability to manage a horse when oiled…probably because he does not really imbibe…much like our father."

"Well, never mind," said Trim patronisingly. "You have imbibed their share already in your time to date."

"Kettles and pots, Timothy!" He heaved the rug around his shoulders while pulling off his boots and then slipped off the edge of the sofa in his efforts to remove them. "Is this the floor? What was I saying? Oh yes, damned insults… I have had enough of hers without your own!"

Trim snatched the cigar away in a paused moment so that the house was not burnt down after his departure, lurching even more in an attempt to stand still. "This preference of hers! Are you sure you heard her correctly?"

"I heard correctly something of the sort…but I may have twisted it a little…she played right into my hands and I could not resist." He flung a boot to one side and fell back onto the sofa and stretched out. "She denied it afterwards, of course, but it was too late…she had said it… She meant back when they were in school of course…"

"But you deliberately twisted her meaning…and pretended not to understand! when really you understood precisely," concluded Trim.

"Yes, I am qualified in the English language, you know… I teach it."

"So, she must know you have twisted her meaning?" Trimingham was snuffing out all but one oil lamp.

"She accuses me of that…but I am not admitting it to her…it better suits my purpose not to…" Fairchild began laughing in a subdued way, removing his other boot. "And I will tell you this, Trim…she labours under a misapprehension regarding this preference of hers…for it will not be preferable at all…" The other boot fell to the floor and he fell back into the sofa and closed his eyes. "Unless of course…" he faltered and then grinned.

"Unless what?" prompted Trim.

"No matter…disregard it," said Fairchild.

Trimingham hummed and aahed for a moment or two and watched him. "I am not sure 'tis such a good strategy…she may never speak to you again," he offered.

"'tis an excellent strategy…" his friend countered; the rug pulled up to his chin. "The more I think on it the better it seems."

"You see this measure as perfect because you are foxed!" objected Trim, searching for his dressing gown cord in the way a cat chases its tail.

Fairchild ignored him. "At the very least, it will deter her vitriol and insults on further occasions…"

Trim made a sound of scepticism. "But there may then be no further occasions…you need to think on it when sober."

"I will not become enamoured of a woman with such a sharp tongue and low opinion of me," he muttered into the woollen rug.

"We need more perspective upon her," said Trim with his usual disarming sincerity "She is goading you perhaps…or you are goading her…unless it is a mutual kind of goading!"

"Or unless I decide to leave her alone completely and give her a wide berth." He thought back to dinner and the ensuing passion. It was mutual, he was not mistaken. He had much to lose, but perhaps a lot more to gain.

"We will talk of it more during the week, no doubt," said Trim and made his way unsteadily in the comparative darkness towards his own bed, stumbling over discarded boots and items of clothing.

"By the way, how is Stephen?" enquired Fairchild in a lightning change of topic.

"He sailed for America last Tuesday…he said to say goodbye and good luck to you," remarked Trim, referring to a mutual school friend with whom he played chess. "He was always a staunch kind of fellow…even at school, if you recall…" He leaned on the door lintel and began outlining who Stephen intended to stay with on his arrival and who they were connected with over here. But Fairchild had succumbed to slumber before he reached the end of the narrative.

Illusions and Stark Realities

Melissa was collected in the Petersham's carriage the next morning at ten thirty and joined Melanie and her mother to be conveyed into town. Mrs Petersham was a homely woman with no pretensions to major sophistication but extremely winsome and bonny in her youth, growing stouter nowadays. "Melissa, my love…how are you fairing withal? Melanie tells me you are painting more and more…" she said first off.

"I am, Aunt Gwen…" replied Melissa sweetly. "I have just had a gentleman take a water colour before Christmas…for his mother and…"

Melanie gave her a warning nudge. They did not need to broach the subject of Fairchild until they were alone. Her mother would only pry, as mothers do, and read much into it. "Mama wants a likeness of her favourite spaniel! Do you not, Mama?"

"Indeed," said Mrs Petersham. "When you are next over let me know and I shall discuss it with you."

"By all means," said Melisa. "I shall look forward to it."

Mrs Petersham was ready to alight at the dressmakers and kissed them both on the cheek before doing so, and they carried on without her to the modiste at the other end of the town. It was not quite three weeks now to Melanie's wedding and the question of her hats for the trousseau loomed large.

Seated at the large dressing table in the corner of the room, Melanie inspected a collection of hats of various designs and colours and accepted the coffee delivered by the milliner's maid and said: "Well, do not keep me in suspense…what happened yesterday evening?"

"He took me into dinner…" announced Melissa, sombrely.

"Yes…and?" Melanie tried on the first hat but gazed impatiently at Melissa through the three-sided mirror.

"I told him of Mary's funeral…"

"And?" demanded Melanie.

Melissa paused and waited. She was quite dreading telling Melanie of the kissing, but also unable not to do so. The feelings it had left her with were urgent and terrifying. "I told him that Millie had played Brahms at the funeral…"

"I imagine he was agog with interest," Melanie discarded the second hat and began sipping her coffee.

"I also told him that she had loved him devotedly…"

"Oh, Good Lord! As if he is not conceited enough with his own importance…"

"I felt he had to know!"

"I cannot think why!" said Melanie with disdain.

"Because he…he pretends a cavalier indifference, even a cheerful veneer, but he needs to hear these things."

"Who are you now, his mother?"

"His mother is Scandinavian. He told my parents after dinner."

"That explains it," said Melanie, admiring the third hat of pale green tulle with lace trimming and putting it to one side for purchase. "He has only to grow his hair another three inches and wield a spear instead of a cane and he will resemble one of the Vikings stepping off a warship at Hastings."

"He has wonderful hair!" Melissa said vacantly. "If it were only thirty years ago, he might wear it long and tied back by a black ribbon…it would be marvellous."

Melanie decided to waive this preoccupation with male hairstyles and replaced her coffee cup in the saucer the better to peer at Melissa. "And suppose Millicent hears of this tittle-tattle? She will be mortified!"

"He will not say anything…he thinks it girlish nonsense…it embarrassed him. I told him that she had done nothing but be devoted to him, and to look at the legacy he had left her."

Melanie was impatient. "As if he will care! Was that it, this saga of Millie's unrequited love? Was that all that you spoke of?"

"No, of course not…but I have just realised that if Millie sees cousin Gregory more, he may bring her to the house and if Fairchild is there it may be very awkward."

"Phooey," declared Melanie. "If that happens, 'tis because she is taken with your cousin…she will hardly be worrying about Fairchild. Besides, if she is still the same Millie, she will sit quiet as a mouse and not dare to speak."

"Yes perhaps…" Melissa paused and stared into the mirror.

"Something has taken place! I can sense it," said Melanie. "You have not hurled more insults at him, I hope."

"No…none…except the hypocrisy criticism…but that was more a small jest while with Granny in her bedroom."

"Oh, that is very well then," mused Melanie with sarcasm. "I am sure he will appreciate the wit."

"Perhaps…" agreed Melissa with satisfaction. "Though he again made one of his veiled warnings…for the future."

"Warning of what?" enquired Melanie with mounting suspicion.

"The usual one, I imagine…the one made in the art room. He did not specify… Grandmama and Polly were present," said Melissa, as if discussing the menu at dinner.

"He probably thinks he need not specify…" said Melanie sagely. "He, like myself, is beginning to think you enjoy these warnings."

"That is untrue," contended Melissa with arch disapproval. "You are both mistaken."

"Are we indeed!" claimed Melanie, the next hat held to one side. "So, what else transpired? Before this latest warning?"

Melissa sipped the coffee and remained silent, watching an elaborate hat being carried to a customer further along the shop. But the silence and Melanie's expression were too onerous and prompted the worst in confessions. "He kissed me," she blurted with an almost touching modesty.

Melanie gasped and sat back in the chair and then looked about at the various staff; they were all absorbed with their duties and talking between themselves, not listening at all, unlike the tea shop assistants.

"And you let him! Where was this?"

"In the library…we were playing billiards and Damien and Estelle left for a while and he showed me how to hold the cue!"

Melanie waited in vain for more. "I cannot believe this progression!" she uttered at length. "But then, somehow, I can imagine it all too well… I hope you slapped him."

"Of course I did not…but I did not respond at first. I was utterly shocked."

"And when you had recovered?" Melanie prompted.

"He kissed me again and then I responded… I could not help it." Melissa had turned a deep shade of pink and was toying with a waiting hat, looking at it intently so as not to have to look at Melanie. "We were kissing for quite a while! Mel, I was… I was truly…it was so very…"

"So very what?" Melanie sat with a look which was horrified and not one that Melissa was able to make out.

"I did not want it to stop… I wanted it to continue for longer…'twas he who stopped it…he said it was enough for now…" She ventured a look at Melanie who arched her brows wisely. "But even had Estelle and Damien walked back in at that moment, I would not have cared…'twas he who became shy…"

"He's not shy, you ninny…" Melanie began trying on hat after hat without much thought or attention. "He was in a state of high arousal most probably."

Melissa sipped her coffee and gazed at herself in the mirror and then eventually at Melanie's reflection. "I do not fully understand this *state of high arousal.*"

"Remember, I tried to explain it to you…the other month, when warning you of that estate manager of your father's…"

"Oh yes…" said Melissa uncertainly. "He is odious… I never want to kiss him again."

"I suppose you want to kiss no man but Fairchild now?"

"Quite!" Melissa confirmed. "Though I scarce know why."

A long time passed, or so it seemed, and Melissa seemed to lapse into some kind of trance of bewildered remembering. She was supposed to be helping choose hats and offering opinion on them but she seemed to have forgotten why she was there. So, Melanie tried the hats with more concentration by herself, all the while glancing at Melissa to see when she might return to common sense and reality. It did not happen. "This is quite mortifying…this turn of events," she said eventually. "I scarce know what to say…when is he returning for the next interlude?"

"I know not."

"Did you not ask him?"

"No, because he left quite quickly, having carried Granny up the stairs… John was not on duty and my father wanted Damien to do it, but he is not to be trusted and may drop her, so I objected and Anthony volunteered."

"Oh, Anthony volunteered did he? He is very well in now then, I perceive. He can scarce put a foot wrong, having proved himself so indispensable. No doubt your parents think him the paragon of virtue!"

"I believe they do…and Granny adores him…she was making her improper remarks and alluding to his good looks. She was quite taken by him."

"She is not on her own it seems!" said Melanie.

"Geraldine came by to play cards…so she claimed…but she was really there to nosey. She was making faces at me, pouting and fluttering her lashes…obviously so I would catch her meaning about how splendid she finds him…good thing Eddy was not present."

"Indeed," concurred Melanie. "Although it was not Geraldine I was alluding to."

Melissa lapsed into her previous other-worldly repose and Melanie cast about for more words of warning, or more questions. Then Melissa said: "I have told him that this does not mean I have forgiven him. I have told him I still loathe and despise him."

Melanie gaped at her, as if not believing her ears. "And what did he say?"

"He says that nor is he overlooking all my rudeness."

"Nonsense…he loves every moment of it. It feeds his yearning for power…'tis some protracted game underway… I am completely shocked by this turn of events."

"As am I," said Melissa and smiled to belie the statement.

"No good will come of it, Lissy! You had better know what you are doing. He is not Roger. He will not allow you to say horrid things to him when the fancy takes you…or lose your temper and storm off."

"Good Lord, no!" Melissa purred, and seemed to shiver slightly with anticipation.

"I do not know what has come over you," declared Melanie in subdued dismay.

"I know not either," said Melissa. "I have never experienced anything of the same before…'tis like I have no control over my urges."

"Well, it had better stop before it goes any further. You do not want to end up wed to him."

"No, no…nothing is farthest from my mind. I only want to kiss him in the library…at least for a while."

"Yes but, my sweet, he is a man! He will want more than that…or else regret his actions on Sunday…"

"Regret them," Melissa cried in a loud voice. "Why would he?"

"Ssshh…for heaven's sake. We don't want the whole town knowing. What I mean is that he may realise he has overstepped the mark…he will bethink himself. Or he will…"

"He will what?" demanded Melissa.

"Well, I am unsure as yet, but it had better not continue, this dalliance…"

"I am powerless to stop it if it does," Melissa insisted. "And anyway, I do not want to stop it."

Melanie called to the milliner's assistant. "These four will do, thank you. Have them credited to my account and delivered, if you please." She rose rapidly and, observing that Melissa had sunk into another trance-like state, pulled her up and guided her from the shop.

Outside on the pavement waiting for the carriage to return, she tried again, in a whisper. "Melissa, listen to me! It cannot go any further…your reputation will be ruined and so may his be, if you are not betrothed. You cannot consider a relationship with him so casual…not for another few years at least. He either has some kind of plan or he will be at pains to forget it ever happened."

Melissa looked as if she would sink to the ground and Melanie could not believe she was quite in earnest, though she was not given to melodrama in the normal way. She watched her slump against the wall in an unladylike and unbecoming fashion and she tugged her upright. "Lissy, stop lounging against the wall like a Park Lane doxie…people will think you're drunk."

Returning to more normality, Melissa offered. "You would have adored the way he was dressed on Saturday for the cold weather. He was wearing a black greatcoat with capes and a woollen muffler around his lower face. He looked like a highwayman, minus the pistol and the mask. And I know how you love highwaymen…"

"Not in reality, I do not…" Melanie made a scoffing sound and gazed along the road for their carriage. "But mayhap that is a more suitable career for him…it would suit his blood thirsty nature and aggressive tendencies…"

Aggrieved, Melissa opened her lips as wide as her eyes. "You do not know he has a bloodthirsty nature…he is always calmly mannered and in the main never shows aggressive tendencies…"

"Not in public perhaps…but in private he might show another side of himself…and perhaps you only feel as you do because he has been in the past so harsh and now, he is at the other extreme and covering you with kindness."

"Do you mean he kissed me only to be kind?" shrieked Melissa.

"No, no… I meant he is being tender because he wishes to make amends for his past harshness."

"He thinks we are unrealistic in our grievances, you and I…that we are indulged and spoiled and mistake discipline for cruelty, when actually…"

"I do not give a fig for what he thinks," interposed Melanie with annoyance. "One would expect him to make those kinds of rejoinders, as I have said in the past when you told me all this. It saves him from having to see himself in his true colours."

Considering this concept for a few moments and seeing grains of potential truth within it, Melissa ventured, "He just wants us to be civil."

"Kissing him passionately in the library is not being civil, Lissy…it is being wanton."

Melissa began to giggle and Melanie was prone to joining in and they relapsed into their usual merriment. Until the carriage arrived and they took on a serious demeanour and tried to behave with dignity.

* * *

As Fairchild was returning to his rooms the following day after work, Mrs Anstey stepped out of her parlour and handed him a letter. "This came for you, Mr Fairchild," she said, smiling broadly at him as always since his generous wedding gift to her daughter and son-in-law a few years back. "A private carriage brought it! From 'High Lawns'." Mrs Anstey could not help but sound impressed by the knowledge.

He stopped in his tracks. 'High Lawns' was the Shaw mansion. He ripped open the letter which contained the Shaw crest and saw that it was from Melissa. Her handwriting was somewhat improved since he had taught her how to write neatly but was still difficult in places to decipher. She had scribbled that he should come to tea on Saturday afternoon. Her grandmother wished to see him again, as did she, and they would be having a few hands of cards. 'they'…who were 'they'? And someone with a name he could not make out playing a piano.

It was not Millicent Bromley, for the name began with a 'G'. He was certainly not walking into any more contrived scenarios with Miss Bromley, who may, since leaving school, have grown as outlandish and audacious as Melanie Petersham, for all he knew.

He would think about whether to attend later. He quaffed a couple of glasses of claret earned after a hard day—or so he told himself—and fell onto the bed and slept for an hour. When he awoke, he found his dinner on the hob of the grate in his small parlour; the communal dining room having closed for the night. But before he was properly back into his senses the maid knocked and told him that Mr Trimingham was asking for him downstairs.

Trim entered at length, wearing his customary broad smile—the most genial person he knew and would perhaps ever know. "Take off your coat," said Fairchild and drew the second armchair nearer the fire. "Did you ride here?"

"No…" Trim began unravelling his layers. "Susan brought me in her trap."

"Then where the devil is she now?"

"She has gone home…she wanted to come up to speak with you, but I deterred her… They are refusing funding for the alms school and she thinks you will help petition the officialdom…yet again."

He groaned and took a second glass from the corner cupboard for Trimingham. "I have tried to explain to her in the past that I can do very little… I can ask my mother to talk to the bishop, but that is all…" It was never-ending, this sad liturgy of failed and needy charitable ventures catering to the poverty and destitution of the poor. Susan was tireless in her crusade, as were others like her, and that was admirable, but it was never enough. It was left to the church and the philanthropy of the generous rich.

"She thinks you hold greater sway with them through your position as deputy head at the Grange these days…" said Trim accepting the claret.

"No, no…they are obliged to listen to me out of sheer politeness and respect for the reputation of the academy…but 'tis mere lip service. Is she calling back for you?"

"No, I will catch the last mail coach from the town at ten…they always let me aboard up top if there is no room inside…they even take a detour along the drive to our front steps, for consideration of course…" Trim looked pleased with this prospect, as if he were to ride in luxury.

"I knew that if Susan came in she would be here an age."

"Tell her I will do what I can… I will visit the school committee on another pretext and introduce the subject." The school committee, a bunch of self-important civil servants—with no knowledge or real interest in the welfare of those they were elected to serve—always gave him their time. Barton Grange was a feather in the cap of the borough and they dare not do otherwise. Though what they afterwards attempted to change and how hard they paid attention, he was sceptical of.

"I am possibly going to the Shaw residence on Saturday afternoon, so I can take a detour to see my mother and ask her to talk to the bishop. She may be able to better persuade him than me." Fairchild ran his hands through his hair and contemplated the tea invite. He had barely touched his dinner barring one potato and had no appetite.

Trim dropped into the armchair and discarded his coat to the floor. "'tis the Shaw residence I have called to talk to you about...more specifically, the daughter of the house," he said nonchalantly. "I have been thinking since Sunday night..."

Fairchild changed the subject. "Have you eaten, Trim?"

"No, I will eat later," said his friend.

He indicated the table. "Have my dinner, I have no appetite..."

"No, no, otherwise you will go hungry..." objected Trim.

Fairchild thought of their schooldays and of the food sharing they did. Trimingham had always the greater appetite, back then as now, eating almost anything put before him. While he himself preferred to go hungry. "I had mutton stew for lunch at the boys' place...and that always fills me for at least two days."

"Liar!" Trim said in an off-hand manner.

"'twill go on the fire otherwise!" declared Fairchild adamantly.

Trim relented and moved to the table and sat and began to eat and said through a mouthful of vegetables. "So, why are you returning so soon to the Shaw residence?"

"Because she has invited me..." Fairchild passed him the letter and Trim read it and then read it again to see anything he might have missed *between the lines.* "I do not believe I am in a position to refuse...given the Sunday library episode...my honour and integrity is in question if I refuse."

"Quite so..." concurred Trim. "The daughter of a prestigious family... You have opened proceedings now, without a doubt."

Fairchild cursed in a low voice and cleared his throat. "I should never have kissed her... I do not know what possessed me."

"Obviously you do not need me to answer that..." Trim remarked airily and he discarded the letter and continued eating. "This is why I deterred Susan from coming up...there is a time to put your own house in order and give priority to your own affairs...and that time is upon you, Anthony!"

Fairchild swung around from the fire and removed his left foot from the fender and laughed in the lightning way he had of showing humour, gone before it was barely seen. "What?"

"I awoke yesterday morning with many thoughts on my mind…pertaining to what we had been saying…while in our cups on Sunday."

"We spoke sense even so," said Fairchild.

"Yes, but with some exaggeration…'tis a serious subject, Tony. We were foxed, and therefore flippant!"

"Who, us? Surely not!"

Trim returned to his food to allow the flippancy a chance to pass. "You are now on the edges of betrothal if you do not take care…and that is a weighty matter…especially if you take any serious measures…as suggested on Sunday."

Fairchild refilled his own glass while Trim watched him: The drinking over the years since Lottie's death had increased three-fold. "We must try to not imbibe too much tonight…" Trim said in a lofty manner. "We must keep clear heads."

"Must we?" queried Fairchild, obligingly, and lit a cigar. "Which measures are you referring to?" and when Trim did not reply, he cast his mind back. "Oh, about her rudeness and her *personal preference*… Is it to that you refer?"

"Just so," said Trim. "What a damn fine cook your landlady employs."

"She undertakes the task herself, I believe."

"Anyway…yes, I meant just that…you were in jest of course…?"

"No… I was perfectly serious."

Trim paused and frowned. "I must once more caution you against it."

"Must you? Why is that?"

"Because obviously 'tis a very proprietary move. It betokens some authority over her you cannot yet claim, unless you are to wed her. And even then, at this stage 'tis risky…"

"Risky in what sense?"

Trim laid down his cutlery and sighed in some despair. "You simply cannot go about smacking the behinds of young women who displease you…"

Fairchild grinned and fell back into the armchair and put his foot again on the fender. "I am not about to adopt it as a main pastime, Timothy…'tis simply in this particular instance."

"She may complain to her father, who may then strongly object, it usurps his authority," rejoined Trimingham.

"Then his authority comes too late in the day…mine does not. Besides, I will take that measure only if she continues to rile me the way she is wont to do."

"If she continues to rile you, 'tis because she wants your attention." Trim concentrated on the remainder of his dinner but was unable to leave the thread of his thoughts. "I mean, aside from all this rudeness what are your intentions?"

"I have no intentions until I know what lies beneath her apparent hostility…"

"Sometimes 'tis best to just apologise to them…women, I mean…even if one does not believe oneself in the wrong. It saves a lot of bother."

Fairchild stared at the ceiling and sighed ostentatiously. "I am not doing it…they should simply have behaved themselves and that is all there is to it…"

Trim again laid down the cutlery. "Yes, but will it matter that much to you if you apologise?"

"Of course it will…what kind of a spineless fool do you take me for? She already accuses me of hypocrisy… So, if I apologise now, she will think I am completely in her thrall."

"So, you are gambling on her responding with the sort of acquiescence she was obliged to show you in school?"

"No… I am gambling on her being a woman with some widening perspective to rationale who will see the error of her ways, or leave the table…if we are to use gaming reference."

"I see," said Trim, who did not entirely see but thought more of it over a five-minute interval gazing into the fire, having moved to the armchair. "I don't suppose there is any pudding?" he enquired hopefully.

"Unfortunately, not… I never eat pudding as you know…but had I known you were calling…"

Trim returned to the subject. "I suppose 'tis a gambit of sorts…seasoned in the aeons of time."

"Of course it is," said Fairchild. "She has already had the warnings…"

"How many precisely?"

"Perhaps two. I don't recall specifically."

Trim took out his pipe. "How do you know they have been heeded? These warnings!"

"Because she backs away from me when she has made one of her incredibly scathing and offensive comments, as if she is preparing to take off and run…"

"Ah… I see," Trim said. "Unless she believes you to be full of piss and wind…unless she thinks you are bluffing."

"She knows I am not bluffing…'tis in her eyes, disguise it as she may…"

"And just supposing she likes that sort of assertive behaviour in a man and then goes on being rude? Have you thought of that?"

"Naturally I have thought of it. I am not quite an imbecile."

"Well, then?"

Fairchild looked faintly reluctant to speak for a moment or two. "Trim, this is a hugely mystifying field of human behaviour, but to illustrate my point…she protests when I as much as grip her wrist. So, I do not believe she will welcome it…and certainly not to the extent that she wishes to experience it on a regular basis."

Trimingham placidly smoked the pipe and Fairchild watched his face for a few moments to follow his growing understanding. "I do not intend to make a relationship with a woman who cannot remain civil towards me for more than ten minutes…" He thought about the previous Saturday afternoon and became animated. "Do you know what she had the gall to say to me when I picked her up in the trap in her sodden condition and warned against the perils of country walking in winter weather? She told me I was like to a nosey and interfering maiden aunt…"

Trimingham found this hilarious and laughed loudly and rolled around in the chair for a few moments, managing at last to advise. "The insult to any maiden aunt is greater than to yourself, dear boy!"

"You see… I do not intend to become a laughing stock for all and sundry…" declared Fairchild.

"You are taking her too seriously."

"Or not seriously enough…the mistake a lot of men make at this stage is to not take women seriously at all."

Lost in thought and clouds of tobacco smoke, Fairchild and Trimingham pursued their inner worlds, until Fairchild continued in the same semi-outrage. "And minutes prior to that she instructed me to *just be quiet and drive…*" he hesitated. "Can you imagine such damnable cheek! Who the devil does she think she is talking to? The groom or someone!"

Trim put his foot on the opposite side of the fender and waited for further information, anxious to not pre-empt the recall of the narrative. "So, I begged her pardon and asked if I had misheard…then she said the cold had affected my hearing and asked me nicely to take her home while shuffling up to the farthest end of the trap…well away from me."

The images conjured up amused Trim more but he contained it and became profound, his left palm extended in deliberation. "Unless of course, 'tis some sort of a game…"

"A game?" repeated Fairchild irritably.

"Indeed…or a plot," said Trim.

"Trim, get to the damned point!"

"It has occurred to me that the only other possibility here…besides her being attracted to you…is that they are leading you into a trap of some kind."

Fairchild sprang from the chair in an alarming way and paced.

"I mean…'tis just a possibility…but I think I should offer it…if their grievance with you is deep enough, they may be getting even with you in some way, Melissa and the Petersham girl!"

"By what means?" asked Fairchild, standing stock still in the centre of the hearth rug.

"That I do not know…perhaps to embroil you in a scandal…"

"God's Teeth! I did not think of that…you might be right," said Fairchild with venom. "I would not put it past them!"

"I am not saying I am right, of course…"

There followed more imbibing of wine. More ruminating and puzzling. But in absolute silence.

Eventually, Fairchild sat down and declared. "I still must return…in fact, I have more reason to do so now that this angle has been introduced…the kissing makes it imperative that I bring things to a close!"

"Or make matters worse…" suggested Trim ominously.

"My God, I cannot do right for doing wrong," claimed Fairchild in near desperation.

"I think you should broach this more calmly…" Trim stretched out in the armchair—a sign of more discourse to follow. "And there is one more thought I have…and I must share it with you…"

"Spit it out!" Fairchild said. "The mail coach leaves at ten…"

"I cannot help but see this girl's resemblance in nature to Lottie…"

Fairchild watched him ominously—talking of Lottie was always a minefield of sensitive reaction and Trim bit the bullet. "Miss Shaw sounds like a free spirit…both of them unafraid to speak their mind. Both of them with artistic aspirations, both quite independent in pursuit of their art forms. There seems to me to be a strong resemblance…"

"Are you saying I am trying to replace Lottie with Melissa Shaw?"

"Not deliberately perhaps…but the similarities suggest a pattern of sorts."

"I do not mind their independent spirit," Fairchild mused. "Though it has to be noted that Melissa rarely leaves her art room when painting, while Lottie…but let us not reprise Lottie's more dangerous ambitions…and, come to that, what of Susan's independent spirit? Her roaming of the countryside while gathering herbs and the like for potions! But there is no more loyal or steadfast female than Susan Darnley…"

"Indeed," Trim concurred. "And so may the Shaw wench be…we do not yet know." He smiled and looked at the other man. "We are both inclined to women with more than just pretty faces."

"But…" said Fairchild, lifting an index finger for emphasis. "I will not tolerate women who are scathingly offensive to me…which Lottie was not…unless we were engaged in arguments."

"Which you frequently were," Trimingham threw in. "And all that said, have you not considered the fact that you might see more of Lottie in this girl than you care to admit?"

"No-one can take the place of Lottie…" he replied in sombre tone. "No-one can replace her."

Trim quietly groaned. "Well, I have said it now…but if you will love no woman but Lottie, how can you settle with this girl? All supposing you are serious about each other!"

Fairchild considered the matter. Trim and he were different characters, very different men, for all their closeness in friendship. He could not rightly explain what he felt or meant. He knew that there were varying kinds of affection and longing. Love had not yet entered the equation for him. And despite various random encounters with females, Trim had loved only Susan and may not understand—a ravine of experience and suffering and introspection separated them in this. He chose to ignore the question.

Minutes passed and then Fairchild offered: "Any comparison is in their approach to life…and their type of beauty perhaps…but Melissa has a loving home and a family who care about her… Lottie had not… Still, I will admit they are of a kind, perhaps overall."

"I believe they are…" said Trim and smiled one of his warmest and generous smiles. "So, perhaps she will meet the criteria, Miss Shaw! God only knows 'tis time you had a steady love in your life…"

"There's that impenetrable word again…and really 'tis the most elusive quality in the world." He gazed at the hearth and the flames. In not too many years he would be forever poking the grate, like Giles Shaw, soothing himself with domestic habits. "But what if as you say, 'tis merely a scheme of revenge…"

"That is only a vague possibility…" Trim said in a throw away manner. "So, perhaps you must give her the benefit of the doubt."

"I must give her no such thing! You are the romantic here, Trim, not me!" An acre more of silence while things were further considered individually. And then Fairchild ventured: "She reviled me first off…'twas I who made the advances. She did not exactly fall into my arms…"

Trim pulled a wry face. "That is neither here nor there…women have subtle ways of seducing men, as you must know…"

"Hmmm…" murmured Fairchild, much fraught by these new worries.

"Nevertheless…" Trim was almost sorry he had raised the possibility. He might be ruining a perfect match in its infancy, "…you need more perspective upon the girl, before we jump to conclusions."

"And even if it is not a ploy to ruin me, a union is not a given if she cannot mend her ways… I cannot abide impoliteness and rudeness, you know that."

Trim stood and put on his coat. "Neither was Lottie the most pleasant female when in a temper, not as a child and not as a woman, if I recall…"

Fairchild smiled. "The devil she was! And there's another useful comparison for you, I suppose."

Trim thought about the strong love between Lottie and Anthony Fairchild as he wrapped himself in his outdoor clothes. "Odds on then…" he said as they trod the first-floor landing to the staircase. "The cards are dealt and must be played."

The hall below was silent and dark, one single oil lamp burning by the front door. They spoke in low tones as Trim made to depart. "I have an idea…" said Fairchild on the porch step. "Cards are what she proposes for Saturday. Why don't I collect you on route and you can accompany me to the Shaw mansion? Then you can see her for yourself…and deter me if necessary, from public ruination…or from forays into the jaws of precipitous wedlock."

"I hardly think you are serious…" said his oldest friend dubiously.

"Of course I am serious."

"I suppose it might be a diverting experience," agreed Trimingham at length with his usual joviality.

Ace of Diamonds and King of Swords

Trim and he rode together to the Shaw mansion at around two thirty in the afternoon on the Saturday, both elegantly and fashionably attired.

"Now, pay no heed to the eccentricities of anyone present…" cautioned Fairchild as they dismounted and handed the trap over to the groom. "For instance, Grandmother! Who will no doubt mistake you for one of the grandsons or somebody else…and ignore any rudeness on the part of Melissa!"

"Certainly…do not worry on my behalf," said the magnanimous Trim.

"And if Melanie Petersham is present or appears at any point, we are leaving…" added Fairchild.

"Really! I was rather looking forward to meeting with this infamous creature…surely, Tony, between us we can manage two tempestuous girls?"

"I have no inclination to managing her," said Fairchild, "And neither do I want more liquids hurled at me…"

"What I thought regarding the Petersham wench," said Trim skittishly. "Is that I could hold her while you pulled her hair."

"I know you think this is a huge joke, but you have not yet met her. 'tis like encountering Boudica in a stylish dress…and 'tis not you she will hurl refreshments on!"

"Well, if you notice, I am wearing my second-best suit today, not my best," Trim was about to make more comedic comments to lighten the mood when the butler opened the door and bade them enter and took their coats and then left them in the hall a minute or two.

Presently, Melissa came from the drawing room and stopped in surprise at the sight of Trim. She was wearing a chequered muslin dress in various shades of red and brown, decorated with an edge of white broderie-angle cotton at the collar and wrists, but minus the layers of petticoats required for more conventional dresses. Her hair was drawn off her face and lay in a single plait down her back.

She looked, Fairchild thought, like someone from a moving exhibition he had once visited in London showing settlers from the Arizona trail about to board wagon trains as pioneers of the New West. He was not displeased with the impression, it was refreshingly different and yet alluring, and no doubt it may be *a la mode* in some places he had not yet been introduced to.

"Who is this?" asked Melissa right away of his companion and he closed his eyes and gritted his teeth—her direct and acerbic manner catching him as always on the raw.

"Well, he is certainly not the bailiff…" he replied in some annoyance.

Melissa stared at Trim with an arch wariness. Trim smiled at her with his genial smile…

"Allow me to present my oldest friend, Timothy Trimingham… Trim this is Miss Shaw."

Trim stepped forwards and bowed formally. "Your servant, Ma'am…" said he, taking her hand and holding it a second or two before kissing the backs of her fingers. He could see at once how striking and attractive she was. Melissa bethought herself and made a slight curtsy, looking at Trim who loomed large in his considerable height of an inch over six foot, a little taller than Fairchild. "How do you do?" she said and then turning to Fairchild gave him her hand, though he did not attempt to kiss it. "I mean, what is he doing here?"

Fairchild drew a long breath. This was beyond rude in the ilk of manners he was accustomed to.

"We have been elsewhere and are travelling together…" he improvised. "So, naturally I could not abandon him by the wayside."

She hid her dismay as quickly as she could, unused to dissembling in daily life, then turned and said to Trim. "You are very welcome, Mr Trimingham…come this way." She flitted swiftly towards the drawing room doors and Fairchild followed at a distance, with Trim some steps behind, saying to him: "You see right off the sort of thing I mean?"

Trim grinned and raised his brows in a look of tolerant discovery to whatever came next.

In the drawing room Grandmama was already seated near a card table, and not far away seated at the grand piano was a young man of about twenty or so, with long dark hair loose about his shoulders and combed back over his ears. He took this to be cousin Gregory, playing very tolerably a Chopin prelude. He paused a moment with the shocking thought that Millicent might be present, and therefore who knew what might be in store in the way of past grudges and grievances revisited. The young man nodded to them and did not hesitate in his recital. Melissa bade them be seated and skipped away again while Granny seemed not to notice them at all, her eyes half-closed, listening to Gregory's music.

At length Melissa returned, followed by a maid with delicacies on a plate. Melissa gestured for them to help themselves. Trim lifted the plate of pastries and offered one to Fairchild who declined, so he chose two pastries and put them on a small plate. Trim loved to eat, more than any other pastime. Gregory finished playing and stood, and Melissa appeared from the other side of the room. "Gregory, that was delightful…" she said.

Trim murmured his agreement and Fairchild said, "Indeed." For it was a very proficient musical talent.

"Gregory, let me introduce Anthony Fairchild…and Mr? I have forgotten already his name…" she told Fairchild with more unthinking rudeness of address.

"Timothy Trimingham…" supplied Trim, discarding his plate for a moment and standing. Both men stood and Gregory gave them a highly formal bow, as to an audience, so that his luxuriant hair—the exact same hue as Melissa's—fell forwards over one side of his face.

"This is Gregory Montalbein, my cousin."

"An honour, gentlemen," said Gregory in dulcet and eloquent tones. He resembled, Fairchild thought, a young Franz Liszt, and no doubt the impression was not accidental, Gregory being of an age where looking the part would seem obligatory. Fairchild and Trimingham gave slight bows of acknowledgement and Fairchild said. "Very pleased to meet you, Mr Montalbein."

"Likewise," said Trimingham and they seated themselves once more.

"So, you are a close friend of Anthony's?" Melissa asked of Trim, who affirmed by nodding as he chewed a pastry.

"Yes, Trim is to me what Miss Petersham is to you," Fairchild told her, then added. "With the slight difference, of course, that he knows how to behave himself in company."

"You are so amusing!" Melissa retorted.

Her grandmother came to life and looked across. "Who is this now?" she asked.

"'tis Anthony…" said Melissa. "And his friend, Mr Trimingham… Mr Trimingham, this is my grandmother… Mrs Shaw senior…"

"Anthony…" croaked Granny. "What a wonderful surprise…and he's brought with him another comely example of manhood."

"Granny!" Melissa said reprovingly.

"What?" said Grandmother, scrutinising Trim through the inadequate pince-nez contraption she had found in her lap. "He is indeed…and he's tall… I like a tall man."

Gregory seated himself in a chair placed beside Granny's and took one of her tiny, gnarled hands in one of his. "Grandmama, they are visitors…" he said in his velvet voice which was as refined as the rest of him. "You must not make those kinds of remarks."

Stopping the irrepressible Granny was like stemming the tide at full flow. "Humbug," said Granny. "I can say as a I like…'tis the truth."

Gregory kissed her hand and informed them: "Our grandmother is very sociable, gentleman! And she forgets herself nowadays. I pray you will overlook her comments."

Granny took her hand away from her doting grandson. "Don't apologise for me, boy! I am beyond caring."

Melissa giggled and looked at the two men. "Once the tea arrives, we can play cards, if you wish."

"Yes…" said Granny, getting to her feet with some alacrity but gripping the sides of her chair before moving to the card table. "How do you fancy a hand or two of whist?"

Trim flexed his fingers expectantly—card playing was his second favourite pastime after eating. "Consider me in," he said sportingly.

"Very well," agreed Fairchild more reluctantly.

The maid, Polly, appeared with a loaded tea tray and set it down on the low table and began to arrange the cups. She smiled at Fairchild in a conspiratorial manner, obviously remembering the conversation he had held with Melissa before leaving Granny's bedroom the weekend before. He silently reproved himself for talking in a free manner before the staff. Young staff at that.

The tea was poured and cups of it partially drank, and Melissa refilled them and they all moved to the small card table.

"What stakes are we setting?" asked Gregory nonchalantly, also an enthusiastic card player.

"The usual," offered Melissa.

Fairchild shifted to make himself more comfortable in the chair. "Surely we are not playing for money?"

Everyone looked at him.

"Of course we are," said Melissa. "Where is the fun otherwise?"

Cousin Gregory sat back a moment and looked abashed as if he had given some kind of offence to the visitors, unsure of his ground.

"We always play for money," said Granny in sanguine manner, "And I always win...almost always to be more precise."

"She always cheats where she can as well..." said Gregory, smiling at her fondly. "I warn you now, so you must tell her when you see it happening." He once again took his grandmother's ancient hand and squeezed it.

"Do we need to play for money!" Fairchild claimed.

"Why ever not?" defended Melissa. "Do not tell me you are short of the stuff? I will lend you some if so."

"He is never short of the blunt," offered Trim, in what he thought an excellent character reference, "And never shy in throwing it around."

"That is not the point..." replied Fairchild. "I don't know if I can be comfortable playing cards for money with ladies!"

"Of course you can!" Melissa said gaily. "We are not pauper ladies, you know...and this is not the vicarage parlour..."

Trim coughed to cover his urge to laugh and looked at Fairchild who gritted his teeth and searched for patience before speaking. *It was possible she had forgotten he had been raised in a vicarage and was using it allegorically. He would give her the benefit of the doubt before taking it amiss, he decided.* He felt himself to be very old suddenly. Very boring. Surely, he was not so ancient in his ways? He was just thirty!

"Perhaps we could play a ha'penny a game," suggested Trim to him tactfully, accustomed to some of Fairchild's quite arcane values from his ecclesiastical upbringing, despite his urbane way of living nowadays. Nurture would always out.

"Oh phooey, Anthony!" croaked Granny. "I did not have you down as a stuff-shirt."

Trim laughed softly. "He is not a stuff-shirt, Ma'am...come, come, Anthony...you cannot disappoint the ladies withal..."

"No," said Melissa archly. "You do not want disappointed ladies, surely!"

Fairchild cast upon her a darkling look, detecting a double entendre, but then thought he laboured again under an illusion. "Very well then...a ha'penny a round." He pulled his chair closer to the table. "But I do not have change on me."

"Do not worry..." Melissa sprang up from her seat. "We always have plenty." She tripped along the room to a bureau from which she pulled out a money bag and took coins. Trim handed her a shilling from a side pocket of his jacket and she changed it into pennies and halfpennies, and he halved the coins and passed Fairchild his share. "I am sure we will need only a quarter of it," he said jokingly.

"Oh, are you?" said Grandmother. "You are very cocky, young man...what is your name, did you say?"

"Timothy Trimingham," said Trim obligingly. "But you may call me Trim, if you wish."

"And you may call me Jemima," said Grandmother as if she were twenty again, and smiled at both men with her near toothless beguiling smile.

"That is a very sweet name!" said the convivial Trim.

"Is it not?" agreed Melissa. She seated herself on the other side of her grandmother and took her hand as Gregory had done previously. It was apparent that both Gregory and Melissa adored their grandmother.

"But Greg..." Melissa cautioned her cousin, lowering her voice unnecessarily. "Michael is at home this week...if you see him ride past the terrace while we are playing, we must hide the stakes...he does not approve of card playing in the daytime and he will come in and make his presence felt...especially as there are visiting strangers here..."

Gregory nodded wisely, but Granny chimed in instantly. "He will not dare say anything amiss while I am presiding...unless he wants a clout round the ear..."

Melissa tutted and Gregory laughed soundly. "We will have to lift her up so that she can accomplish that..." he told the two men. "Michael is as tall as Mr Trimingham."

"Who is Michael?" enquired Trim.

Melissa spoke dismissively, as if the subject should be disposed of as swiftly as possible. "My eldest brother...he is seldom home, but when he is the world has to bow to him..." She glared pointedly at Fairchild to see if he recognised the trait. "He will perhaps not make adverse comment but he will manage to discomfort everyone…he scarcely knows when he is not welcome. He likes to know everything and hovers and meddles like an old maid…"

Gregory sneered. "Another blistering hypocrite!"

Melissa gazed across at Fairchild meaningfully, knowing he might remember her insult about maiden aunts and hypocrisy. He looked back at her with his penetrating green gaze. "Why?" he enquired politely of Gregory, "Are there more of them hereabouts, these hypocrites?"

Melissa declined to comment and Gregory said. "No, Sir, I was alluding to my father…"

"That windbag!" Granny offered with towering disrespect to one of her sons-in-law.

"Just so, Grandmama!" concurred Gregory, taking for granted the feminine allies he had to either side. "He too has an opinion on everything and everyone…most of them misinformed."

Fairchild frowned a little, he was not disposed to this kind of family tittle-tattle. Gregory caught his expression and said, "My father is the bane of my life."

"Fathers often are!" Trimingham said sagely.

Gregory flushed slightly; perhaps these two older men thought him spiteful and childish. Then Grandmother asked of Gregory: "Is he still interfering in your career?"

"He is, Grandmama…'tis his favourite hobby-horse…but I am intent on ignoring him. My mother takes my side more and more…she tells him he is jealous because he has no particular gift or talent of his own. Except for hunting and gaming and all the rest of it. He thinks I am effeminate…"

"Of course you are not," said Melissa with spirit. "You are simply artistic and cultured…which he is not."

"He is a positive philistine!" said Gregory with heat.

Fairchild and Trim exchanged covert glances, remembering not so long ago being Gregory's age and full of criticism about their fathers while courting the support of their mothers. It was a universal and timeless pursuit…but not in social drawing rooms with strangers.

"I don't know why your mother wed him…" said Granny next, growing worse than the younger members of her family. "…she could have had any one of a parcel of men with her beauty and charm. Why she had to choose that posturing, self-opinionated bore I will never know…and neither did her father. But she was one and twenty at the time so we could not prevent her…and off they went to Gretna one Monday morn behind our backs…and the deed was done. She has long regretted it…though she will never say so."

"Do you really think so, Granny?" asked Melissa, arranging her hand of cards. "Aunt Amaelia regretted marrying Montalbein?"

"Sure as eggs are eggs!" said Grandmama, perusing her own hand carefully. "I told her over and over that his money would not compensate for his lack of grace…and that he'd be dissipated and bullish a'fore he was forty…and so did Jago who was a shrewd judge of character…he'd pit his wits many times again' men like Montalbein, whose faults were all about him even when a young man…folk don't change that much!"

"I do not believe he is my real father," proclaimed Gregory dramatically in the pause of his grandmother's diatribe, his voice larded with feeling.

They all looked at him, the two older men quite briefly. Then Fairchild heaved in a long breath and rolled his eyes at Trimingham. Here was another popular myth-enhancing line offered by young men who did not wish association with their fathers.

"Then who was your father, do you think?" asked Melissa, giving credence to the theme and oblivious of anything else.

"I do not know, Lissy, but my elder brothers are certainly his, they look like him, whereas I do not. I look like my mother."

"That is nothing to go by…" said Granny sensibly, "Many folk resemble only one of their parents."

Trim paused in the arranging of his cards and said gently, "You must take care where you say things of this nature…or you may slander your mother's good name unwittingly…"

"What good name she has left…" remarked Grandmother, "With some of her foolish escapades. Jago would turn in his grave!"

Gregory ignored this and gazed at Trim with consternation. "You are quite correct, Sir… I did not look at it that way."

"Yes, 'tis best…for you may never know the identity of her lover…the one who may have sired you," said Melissa with passion.

Trim coughed to cover his imminent laughter and Fairchild sighed with disdain at the torrid dialogue but made allowances for their youth and inexperience and muttered something incoherent. "Shall we commence?" he said aloud in his quietly authoritative tone, having had sufficient of the melodrama threatening to unfold.

And so, playing began in earnest. It was decided that Gregory and Melissa play as one person, taking it in turns to partner Fairchild, while Trim and Granny opposed them. But no sooner had the first hand been laid when Trim stopped and looked at Melissa and Granny in turn, still absorbed by the preceding account of family history and the sort of saga he enjoyed. "Forgive my inquisitiveness, but who is Jago?" he enquired.

Melissa smiled. "He was our grandfather…"

"My husband!" said Granny, closely peering at her cards. "His rightful name was Diego Miguel…but in Cornwall they called him Jago…'twas easier…"

"I see," said Trim, much intrigued. "So, he was not English?"

"Indeed not," replied Granny proudly. "He was a Spaniard with the Spanish fleet. He was sailing with them in the seventeen eighties…a first lieutenant…when the ship floundered in rough seas and went down. He and two others survived and floated in becalmed waters…they cobbled together a raft of sorts and drifted out in the Channel to the coast off Devon…they were days without food or water and near to death, but then they were taken up by an English fishing boat…" Granny played her second card and Fairchild played his third. Trim paused to hear more and was prodded by Fairchild. He played a card and said: "So, he stayed here in England?"

"Oh, that he did…for a while…" said Granny. "He hid for a few months, badly wounded by debris and rough waves, and sick from lack of water…he'd been with the fishermen and o'course they'd been bringing the vinegar in the barrels. He'd no choice but to get embroiled, or be thrown back over the side. Him and the cabin boy both…for the third man had not lived above a day more…"

"The vinegar?" Trim said, confused.

"I imagine it was contraband," offered Fairchild to be helpful.

"I see," Trim said and neglected his cards to stare at Granny.

"Folk had no choice then but to smuggle," Granny asserted defensively, "Down off the Cornish and Devon coast…they were starving…taxed to the hilt, money going to the crown. They'd nothing. That's how the English treat their own, I fear."

Fairchild drew another deep breath to summon patience; now there would no doubt be a critical treatise on the history of the British Empire.

"What a colourful past you have, Mrs Shaw," said Trim and Granny removed her pince-nez and looked at him. "Well, I ain't really Mrs Shaw neither. I rightly be Mrs Cassada…my husband was Diego Miguel Cassada and I wed him as Mrs Cassada…the locals continued to call him Jago, and for the rest of his life he was known as Jago Shaw."

"Bless him!" Melissa said soulfully.

"And where does the name Shaw come from?" Trim asked, ignoring Fairchild's uncomfortable shuffling, hating as he did this kind of prying as the highest point on his scale of vulgarity.

"'twas my maiden name, my father's name…" said Granny, pleased to be so questioned. "Jago took my father's name for safety…though he would not wed me in that name…he was of the Roman church, being Spanish, and would not lie afore the priest and God…but we darest not keep his real name for any other matters."

"Of course!" Trim said in rapt fascination.

"My pa ran a tavern on the St Ives coast…my mother was a Frenchie…she'd come over with some aristos, she was their maid, and they landed at Penzance…they'd connections in St Ives and she stayed in St Ives when they moved on…she did not fancy going back to France, so she worked at the inn for my father who took to her strongly and asked her to wed him. My sister and me grew up at the inn…we helped when the vinegar came, we all did, the whole village. We formed lines on the beach and took it in turns to pass the barrels…all through the night we worked, til sun up…and then on one occasion off the ship comes Jago…he was three and twenty then and myself just fifteen."

"He hid in the hollow earth beneath the cellar for weeks on end, only coming out for fresh air and food and ablutions…the Excise men were all about the place like a swarm o'bees that summer…. I took him his food and we could barely speak a word a'tween us…him being foreign and me being English…" Granny continued to play her hand in a sterling manner, hardly losing any cards as she narrated.

"Yes…" encouraged Trim, to the annoyance of his friend. "What happened next?"

"Then Jago slowly learned our tongue…myself and my sister taught him bits…"

Melissa intervened in the story and placed her cards face down. "Imagine, if Jago had not adopted your father's name, I would have been Melissa Maria Cassada… Miss Cassada! How marvellous would that have been!"

"Think how well it would have looked on your paintings," said Gregory. "The name alone may have made you famous."

"I could use it now, I suppose…for art purposes."

"You could," said Gregory enthusiastically. "You should…but what about Uncle Giles? Will he have something to say about it?"

"Probably… I would just have to not tell him and hope he did not notice."

"He is bound to find out," said Gregory. "What a cursed nuisance they are, these fathers with their constant meddling…"

Melissa began musing on the new idea for a name, and Fairchild muttered, "Yes, they should confine themselves to putting a roof over your heads and educating you…and not have the gall to intercede in anything else going on in their own houses."

Gregory looked at him a moment or two to suss his meaning, and Melissa remarked: "Pay no heed, Greg, he is being sarcastic! When he is not being sarcastic, he is being facetious…and when he is not being either his comments are usually objectionable."

Gregory went back to his cards, uncertain of what to say. Fairchild exchanged glances with Trim, raising his brows to convey the reality of what he had already told him about her insults. Trim was disposed to laugh, but held it in. There was an awkward silence and then Gregory said. "If we have given offence, then I apologise, gentlemen…"

Fairchild turned to him. "You have given no offence…please be easy…"

"Not at all," sanctioned Trim. "We are neither of us fathers yet…not that we know of, eh Tony!"

Fairchild cast Trim a warning glance against this kind of ribald humour in mixed company, then smiled briefly at Gregory. "'tis merely my sense of humour…" he assured him. "It is at times caustic and is often misconstrued…"

Gregory was reassured and Melissa laughed in a mocking high sound, causing Fairchild to look at her with benign displeasure. The atmosphere was charged between them, the table separating them. Gregory eyed them secretly, sensing for the first time an unresolved tension.

Granny said: "What is being discussed here now? I cannot follow it at all…?"

Melissa let her gaze fall, moving it from Fairchild's calm and unsettling stare. She knew he had the better of her momentarily for she had broken eye contact first. It was hard to fathom from his frosty veneer that he was the man who had kissed her passionately only a week ago.

Trim quickly changed the subject back to the old lady and Cornwall. "What a wonderful tale, Mrs Shaw," he said with sincerity.

Granny made a face. "You can call me Jemima!"

Trim smiled and looked at Melissa who began dealing the next hand. "Yes, call her Jemima, she loves to be called by her first name."

"I do not think I can bring myself to such a familiarity," murmured Trim.

"You may as well…" quipped Fairchild quietly. "They help themselves to first names in here like sugar from the bowl."

Melissa cast him a haughty glance and thought of the Sunday tea and Melanie. "You are so amusing…"

"You told me that earlier," he replied. "Please do not overdo the compliments."

"And what happened next?" Trim prompted Jemima. "After Jago had hidden for months?"

"He went off again…" Jemima gathered her shawl around her and stared into space. "He said he had to go for he did not know how long…he would not say where…but some said 'twas to make things square with the Admiralty in Spain…" She paused for effect and leaned nearer to Trimingham. "Bear in mind he had not more than held my hand in all those weeks, but we knew we wanted to be together…"

Trim sat back in his seat and waited expectantly for more. Gregory smiled fondly at Melissa.

"You do realise I hope, Trim…" interposed Fairchild. "That she is telling you all this to distract us from the game!"

"But 'tis not working," said Melissa. "We are ahead."

Trim ignored them and Grandmama continued. "He said to me, *'Mimi'*…for that's what he always called me… *'Mimi, I hope to return and by then you will be old enough and we can wed. But if I am not back in two years to this day you must not wait for me…you must wed elsewhere, for I be dead and not coming back at all'…"* There was avid attention to the story, even though Melissa and Gregory had heard it before several times. "I cried for days. I could not stop. They called a doctor who gave me something to make me sleep and I slept for four days solid. Then my ma said to me *'don't be foolish, girl, you will not see him again. He has been entertaining himself to pass the days.'*…the French being a cynical lot!"

There was a pause and Melissa interposed. "Do you have French ancestry at all, Anthony?"

He ignored her.

"… I cried and cried, even after the long sleep…and no-one could console me… I was as thin as a rake through not eating…" Grandmama was saying, before she paused the narrative and took the current hand with a straight flush.

"But he obviously came back?" Trim prompted.

"O'course…these are two of his grandchildren! I was walking the dogs on the shoreline one early morn and my young sister called out to me that there was a small boat coming and a man waving and shouting my name… I looked and looked but could not see, the sun being too bright in the sky…nor hear for the sound of the waves…then as the boat came closer, I heard his voice… I waded out to sea and he jumped over the side and swam to meet me. He carried me up the shore and I thought my heart would burst with joy… I never since had quite such a feeling as that…"

Trim was riveted, and Melissa and Gregory enthralled—even on hearing the story for the fifth or sixth time.

"He had pouches full of gold by then, hung around his neck for safe keeping…" Granny was lost in reverie. "He had two gold teeth too, and a gold loop in his ear…" She fished into the upper folds of her clothes, today she wore a woollen dress with only one shawl about her shoulders and her veil replaced by a jaunty bonnet full of ribbons and bows. She pulled out the earring Jago had worn and which she wore on a long chain around her neck as the others followed its slow emergence from her clothing. "He was a rich man betimes…he bought the tavern from my father so my parents could take life easier…"

"And then you were wed?" Trim enquired.

"Not at once…my pa thought me too young, I was just seventeen…but my ma told him, *Joshua, you had best let them wed, unless you want her with child out of wedlock…for he's a Spaniard and he can scarce keep his hands off her…*"

"A heart-wrenching entreaty indeed!" muttered Fairchild.

Melissa was overcome with amusement and leaned forwards and began giggling, her face in her skirt. Grandmama wound up her memoirs. "…and my pa soon saw the sense of it and so we were wed…" More cards were laid.

"You began a family then, did you?" Trim asked, oblivious to Fairchild's long sigh of dismay.

"We tried for a babe but it wouldn't happen. So, he took me to the best doctor in Truro who said I had weakened my health through fretting and not eating…then Jago made sure I had everything to make me well again, and we moved to Bristol. He had started up an import and export business by then, using my pa's name. He wanted us to be respectable. It broke my heart leaving Corn'all but I did it…and we never looked back. I was three and twenty by the time I fell with child and I had a daughter, Isabella…our first born…she passed away, sadly, years ago now, just after her twenty fifth birthday…in childbirth…" Jemima paused to reflect and there was a respectful silence and only the sound of cards being arranged.

"Then I had Giles…he's my only son, you know, for then we had four more daughters," Granny laughed gleefully. "I don't think Jago was expecting that!"

"I am sure he was not." Trim sent her an apologetic smile. "'tis surely too much for any man, five girls! You should ask my own father. I am *his* only son, first born, then they had four daughters…"

"Each time I was delivered of a girl, Jago would say, *'Mimi, she is beautiful…and next time we have another boy'*…so we went on trying for a boy…and getting more practice…" added Jemima with a wry face.

"'tis wonderful," Melissa remarked, trumping her grandmother's card and causing the old woman to curse. "Think how well daughters look after you."

"And think how much they cost!" Trim said.

"Jago never needed to mind the cost, we had plenty of gilt by then…but he was relieved that Giles survived, his one son…for many babies don't o'course…"

Trim dealt again and enthused. "Mrs Jemima…that is a marvellous story…truly marvellous!"

"I have been blessed and I know it," declared Jemima. "Not everyone finds love…but 'tis the only thing worth finding…"

"Yes, it is," affirmed Trim.

Melissa said: "You are a romantic, Trim?"

"I own that I am," said Trimingham. "I cannot deny it."

"I am proud of you for owning it…" she replied.

"I think I need a cigar!" Fairchild said.

Gregory rose and announced: "I shall play a Strauss waltz now, to revive everyone."

"As long as we are not expected to dance!" remarked Fairchild.

"You see, there he goes again," said Melissa. "Pay no mind at all, Gregory. There is seldom any pleasing him…it stems from his professional persona and has now become his natural way."

"Forgive my asking," said Gregory, sitting again momentarily. "But which profession is that?"

"That of schoolmaster," Melissa informed him.

Gregory looked surprised and Fairchild knew that Gregory would now make comments he had become familiar with.

"We are both schoolmasters," supplied Trim. "We require the money to fund our more festive pastimes."

"But you do not look…you do not seem…" Gregory floundered.

"Old enough?" joked Trim.

"No, I meant only that you seemed too…too…"

"Dandified?" suggested Melissa.

"Melissa, not that!" said Gregory impatiently. "That is quite rude."

Fairchild glanced at him, laying down his cards. "What a surprise!" he said darkly, and then to Gregory. "Of course I am thinking of changing my vocation soon…to that of revenue official…or possibly, executioner! I have not quite decided."

Finding this banter hilarious Gregory threw back his luxuriant hair and laughed.

"Indeed," continued Fairchild. "I thought the comments I may receive then would be more complimentary withal…not quite so loaded with scorn and contempt."

"I am sure you are both excellent teachers…" Gregory remarked in overt flattery. "You have such good vocabulary and fine wit."

"That is because they attended Oxford," Melissa remarked, her arsenal borrowed from Melanie.

"I attended Cambridge, in truth…" amended Trim. "Though Tony is a headmaster too," he added, innocently fuelling the flames.

"No!" exclaimed Gregory in greater astonishment.

"'tis true…" asserted Melissa. "Discouraging is it not!"

Gregory flashed his cousin a look of consummate displeasure.

"Yes…" Fairchild affirmed airily, "Though as I keep reminding Trim, I am actually the *deputy* head only."

"That is a mere detail…" added Trim. "He is bound to become head before long."

"Not if I can help it," Fairchild amended.

"I can scarcely imagine the self-satisfaction and opinionation if it happens," said Melissa, not looking at anyone and staring at her cards.

"Melissa!!" exclaimed Gregory again, his discomfort barely concealed.

"I shall now take some air," announced Fairchild with dignity and left Trim to talk to Granny while Gregory played the Strauss and Melissa called for more tea, and the dealt cards lay on the table.

* * *

Trimingham saw that the flood tide was at its height. The dam was about to break. He sat back into the corner of one of the sofas calmly, tugging down the points of his stylish beige waistcoat and fixing the warmth of his light brown eyes on Melissa in perplexity. He parted his lips several times in preparation for broaching the question of her provocative attitude while Melissa noticed nothing, not knowing him well enough to gauge his mood. He was quite at home and enjoying himself in the affable surroundings of an informal drawing room setting—apart from the disconcerting remarks she was wont to make to his closest friend. But before he could form any coherent sentences, Grandmama and Gregory began politely questioning him about himself and his life.

They elicited his family history and his marital status. Trim replied to them with equanimity, only too willing to supply a fuller summary following their grandmother's disclosures. He informed them that he too taught in a boys' school, a lesser prestigious place than Barton Grange perhaps, at the opposite side of the town. His father was of the newer breed of prosperous men and detested the squandering of life and time in idleness. In common with Giles Shaw, he foresaw a brave new world where people contributed their talents towards progress and prospered by their merit.

He insisted that his son do something useful with his accomplishments, and so Trim had chosen education as a profession but, like Fairchild, wanted only to pursue it for a limited period of time. The Trimingham family-owned pottery sheds and Trim was not inclined to entering the business. Added to this, his finance had threatened to disassociate from him if he did not take up a useful profession of some kind on graduating from university. She was herself an industrious and capable young woman. So, he taught two languages and history to the sons of the relatively well-to-do.

"And why have you and your fiancé not wed as yet?" she enquired.

"We do not want to rush into anything," said Trim merrily. There was much amusement until Melissa said seriously. "People refine too much on the union of marriage…'tis not to be contemplated."

"Indeed," concurred Gregory, helping himself to the fresh dish of pastries.

"And Susan is not perhaps the conventional kind of young woman of her class," offered Trim.

"No indeed," agreed Melissa who knew of Susan Darnley's good work from her sister-in-law Geraldine. "She is a paragon of diligence and conscience within society…"

Trim made a noise of semi-agreement. Susan was not a paragon by any means, but he was too loyal to disabuse Melissa's belief.

"Pah…" said Jemima, sucking on a cup of tepid milky tea. "She is likely just a girl with a healthy urge to see a bit of life and do some good into the bargain. This modern fad for making saints of folk is beyond silly."

"I concur, Mrs Jemima," said Trim.

Within minutes, the plight of the alms schools was revealed and Gregory had suggested a fundraising event at which he would play for entry fee to be donated to the schools. Melissa then thought she would offer some of her paintings which might be sold or auctioned towards the cause. So, it was agreed that Trim would petition his mother for the use of their ballroom for the event and saw little obstacle to her agreeing, provided Susan and Melissa assisted on the day.

It was a fairly faultless plan and one which should take place in May, giving a few weeks to prepare and advertise the event. It was literally all *done and dusted* within a ten-minute conversation. And they sat back and thought their various thoughts and did not miss Anthony Fairchild's presence until Grandmama said: "Where is Anthony?"

"I believe he is in the garden smoking," said Trim, looking at his silver repeater. He had been gone more than twenty minutes now.

"He has most likely taken his leave," said Gregory.

"Of course he has not," Trim retorted with good humour. "He would not do anything so impolite…besides, he has me to consider on his ride home."

"What an odd thing to say, Greg," said Melissa. "Why would he do that?"

Gregory hesitated. "I think he disliked some of our comments..." he murmured at length, rising and returning to the piano. "...and your derogatory slurs upon his person," he added.

She gasped in mock surprise and feigned dismay and looked at their faces in turn.

"He does not consider those things beyond his management, I am sure," offered Trim in a placatory tone.

Gregory placed his fingers on the keys in readiness for play. "Some of my cousin's remarks to him were...well they were somewhat..."

"Were what?" demanded Melissa on her metal.

"Audacious and contentious..." stated Trim.

"Surely not!" She looked at him with fascination and Trim looked back at her, his good nature apparent in his eyes—almost the identical colour to his hair.

"Audacious how?" she enquired.

"I think you know how, Miss Shaw!" Trim said equably.

"Of course they were." Jemima replaced her tea cup and eyed the latest fancies brought in for their delectation by the maid. "I don't know what you're thinking, girl! Saying those sorts of things to yon fellow."

Gregory began to play a Chopin prelude softly and refrained from comment.

"Quite so, Mrs Jemima..." Trim cleared his throat and beckoned Melissa to seat herself beside him on the sofa so that he would not have to increase the volume of his voice. She sat and looked at him in ingenuous wonder. "Perhaps you would do well to refrain from your more strident remarks," he told her. "He much dislikes rudeness of any kind..." He waited for her to respond and when she did not, he continued, "I do not think it will progress any...any friendship between you..."

"Friendship?" she echoed in great distaste. "I have not said I wish for his friendship...nor has he expressed a wish for mine."

Gregory stopped playing and pretended to sort through his music, the better to listen.

"Whatever you might call it or wherever it might go, it will not be to your advantage to provoke him with the sort of comments you were making earlier," Trim told her.

"Good sense in that..." said Jemima, hearing every third or fourth word while chewing a pastry.

"And what if he provokes me?" demanded Melissa heatedly.

"But he does not, does he!" replied Trim with patience.

Melissa opened and closed her lips and could not properly form her reply. She perceived at once that they obviously conferred in the way she and Melanie conferred. "He simply makes fun of me instead," she announced with dignity, and blushed deeply. Gregory began to play diligently as the mood became silently one of sensitive and unspoken knowledge.

"Perhaps 'tis his way of defending himself," said Trim.

She knew at once then that Trim would know the root of the problems. "I suppose you mean my art room that day…and Melanie throwing tea on him," she said in a rush, then regretted the admission of the supposed tea accident.

Trim hesitated for a mere second or two. "Indeed…and other things hurled at him."

She had given over the advantage now by the use of the word *'throwing'*.

"Lissy, that is shockingly vulgar…throwing tea on someone…" Gregory could not prevent himself from voicing his reaction before beginning to play more vigorously.

"'twas an accident!" protested Melissa lamely.

"No 'twas not…" Jemima objected. "Geraldine gave me the account of what happened with great accuracy. She saw the theatricals…and how Melanie made it appear an accident."

Trim opened his eyes wider. "Then *she* certainly requires taking in hand, if that was the case," he uttered without thinking.

"Ha!" trilled Jemima with vehemence. "From what I've seen of her you are not wrong…*peas-above-sticks with herself*, that one."

"Granny, I cannot believe you are taking their side in this…" Melissa opined.

"I am taking the side of common sense!" said Jemima, licking her fingers one by one following the consumption of the pastry. Melissa was quite frozen to the sofa, mortified by the unexpected limelight onto her actions. While Trim was determined not to show his regret at having said out loud something, he had meant only to think in his own mind. He looked at Melissa, resolved to not worsen the matter with any dissembling kind of expression. There was a time to *grasp the nettle*.

"Do you not think he had it coming to him?" she enquired hotly. "Given what he made us endure in Barton Grange!"

"No, I really do not…" replied Trim with equanimity. "You had no business chalking names of staff on blackboards, did you!"

"Which names?" blurted Gregory, unable to stop himself.

"Never mind!" snapped his cousin. "'twas four or five years ago."

"My point exactly!" interceded Trim. "Time to let bygones be bygones and behave civilly...like young women of breeding."

"Well said!" chirped Jemima. "And I don't know what your father was thinking...allowing such behaviour in the drawing room."

"He was unable to prevent it...being unaware of the plan!" She almost jumped up from the sofa, inelegantly, as her temperature rose.

"So, it was a plan!" remarked Trim adroitly and stared at the mantlepiece.

"Have you anything else to add?" she enquired, too mockingly sweet to be other than acrid. Everyone was blurting out thoughts, it seemed, in an uncontrolled manner and the tension was breaking.

"'tis not my business... I am only telling you what I think..."

"Yes, but you are obviously very conspiratorial together...and 'tis obvious he confides in you."

"He does," concurred Trim, unable to deny the fact.

Melissa thought it best to laugh—the high and false laugh which she had now honed to perfection for difficult occasions. "I assume he has not presumed so far as to tell you I am interested in anything he has to offer."

Trim hesitated and Gregory—despite his best efforts at discretion—played wrong notes in his recital.

"And yet here he is, at your invitation," concluded Trim lightly.

Total silence in the room, except for the softest of the piano notes—insufficient to mask human voice. "And in any event, whatever he is or is not offering...and whatever you are of a mind to accept...'twill even so be a good idea to not provoke him anymore today!" added Trim.

"I see," said Melissa who was now between wishing to make a proud stance of indifference and wanting to know exactly what Fairchild had said to him on the subject. "I expect both he and you think women are silly docile creatures who need not have anything to say beyond *'good morning and good evening'* while pursuing their embroidery..."

Trim frowned, as he might frown at his youngest sister, with a pained and weary expression of greater tolerance. Then Grandmama interpolated. "Lissy, no man worth his salt won't tolerate being spoken to so rudely by a young woman he has more than a passing fancy for..."

"Well, I do not know what to say," she claimed in a neutral voice covering her confusion.

"That's right…better to say nothing," said Jemima. "You've said enough… He's not that other nincompoop who dangles after you…"

There again was the criticism of Roger they all felt it their right to give. "I am shocked by you, Granny," she said, without much heart.

"Humbug!" said Granny. "I don't know where you've found some of these notions…you and Melanie both…not fit for the real world."

Melissa looked at Trim who was now smiling omnisciently, like a benign Santa Claus unmasked on Christmas Eve. "I suppose you think we…we are of a mind to…" She could not finish and looked instead at the window, beyond which the man in question lurked unseen.

"I am sure…" interjected Trim hastily, "that it may be a long way from that… I am merely suggesting that this uncivil exchange is one which needs greater care…on your part."

"This sounds like another threat…are you both in the habit of phrasing your threats in such fanciful ways?"

Trim picked up a few cashew nuts for diversion, but did not at once attempt to eat them. "I perceive that his *'threats', a*s you put it, are far more prosaic than mine…"

"Of course, you are very clever and educated and used to dictating to people…the pair of you!" cried Melissa as the piano grew louder again.

"Cleverness has little to do with the matter in hand…" offered Trim, biting into a couple of the nuts. "People may be clever in different ways. Or they may be learned and not clever at all! Men the world over have likes and dislikes…merely differing means of expressing them."

"I am not in his classroom now," she said irritably.

"Knowing him as well as I do, I doubt he will see that as relevant!" Trim said off-handedly. "In fact, I am certain he will not. It will be of no consideration in the matter as it stands now…so I am simply warning you."

"Of what?" she demanded suspiciously.

Trim dusted his fingers on a napkin delicately and cleared his throat. "I perceive, Miss Shaw, as his confidante, that you already know of what!"

Gregory stopped playing abruptly with the sudden realisation that Fairchild had taught Melissa, and therefore Millicent, when they were in school. It threw him completely and needed thinking about.

"Are you quite concluded on this treatise?" she enquired of Trimingham majestically.

Trim smiled more widely. "I am! I was merely offering you advice."

"Oh, I thought it a dire warning…"

"Of consequences perhaps…but I cannot say, of course, how dire you might consider them withal…being cognisant of the fact that you are aware of the *consequences* implied…"

Melissa gasped, closed her eyes, and rocked a little on the balls of her feet. "Mr Trimingham, you are quite the most infuriating of emissaries."

"Good Lord!" opined Trim in bewilderment and looked over at Gregory who feigned ignorance of anything discussed by making his face into the kind of blissful appreciation of his own music as he resumed playing. "You must do what you will at your own peril," said Trimingham.

She gaped at him and did not know whether to laugh or to extoll her disgust.

"You have seriously overset the man!" said her grandmother, biting into another confectionery delight.

"Your remarks were quite mortifying, Lissy," added Gregory casually. "I don't know what Uncle Giles would have said, had he heard them."

She moved around in a small circle and deliberated as they watched her. "I shall go and see where he is…and try to bring him round," she said in a pacifying way, like a by-stander to all allegations.

"If I were you, I would leave him be for now…" suggested Trim. He was ignored and she went determinedly from the room via the window doors to the garden.

As soon as she had gone and breaking his current orchestration, Gregory began playing Mendlesholme's *Wedding March*. Trim laughed softly and Jemima chuckled, and no-one said another word.

* * *

Fairchild was in the rose garden, smoking his second cigar. Walking up and down and surveying the early rose buds and the spring flowers. He had rambled around the whole interior grounds of the house and taken in the lay of the land. Things were off to a bad start, it had to be admitted, though he did not know what he had actually expected. He turned when he heard her and then turned away and ignored her.

"What ails you?" she asked and he did not reply. "I sense I have offended you," she continued.

"You more than sense it," said Fairchild shortly, "You well know it."

"I do not…until you confirm it."

"Let us return!" he said and dropped the cigar into the large rose bed and covered it with soil by the toe of his shoe. "Tell the gardener I apologise."

"I shall. For your manners cannot be criticised at any point…unlike mine."

"Your lack of them is unparalleled, and you sport them like a badge of honour…"

She waited for him to join her on the path and then sank onto a stone bench. "Sit a while," she said.

"No, thank you."

"Please do not sulk in this way."

"I am not prone to sulking…that is your privilege."

"Anthony, let us be civil…as of your suggestion in the art room last year."

"Civil? I think that impossible for you."

"What then? What shall we be?"

"Come, time to return! 'tis too cold now to stay out here." He took her arm and pulled her up from the bench. She practically sighed her next words. "You must desist pulling me in this manner…"

A scathing noise of dismissal issued from him and he pulled her more swiftly towards the drawing room. "I do not know whether your disingenuous approach is sincere or calculated…but I am not about to discuss the matter. You are making me do something I dislike to do at any time…lose my temper."

She shook her arm free and took backwards steps away from him. "You are not a block of wood then…but prone to human frailty."

"Of course I am!" he said, waiting for her to see sense and accompany him back to the drawing room. "Come along…'tis too cold for garden sitting."

"Not until you talk with me…"

"I have said no…"

"You are a coward now as well as a hypocrite?" She posed lightly, brushing her palms along the material of her skirt as if preoccupied by the act.

He froze at once. "I beg your pardon?"

Her face flushed but she gazed in the other direction and feigned deafness. He took her by the wrist and now she watched him with a mingled reaction; fear and desire and other kinds of impulses. Just as suddenly he let her go. "Go inside…now! Before I actually do lose my temper."

"I perceive you have lost it already…and do not presume to tell me what to do in my own home!"

"Go inside," he repeated. "You will catch a chill, or something worse." He had resolved to erase her last statement from his memory.

"Let us kiss first," she said.

"Certainly not. I am not playing these games… I am not twenty if Roger is."

She was shocked by the mention of Roger but strove not to show it. "Poor Roger, so maligned by everyone…"

"I do not know if he is *'poor Roger'*…but I am not about to be managed and manipulated the way he is."

"How do you know this?" Her curiosity betraying her, she could not sustain her air of indifference. "You seem to know a lot about it."

He gazed over the length of the rose garden to the lawned area and considered his reply. "Damien…"

"Oh, of course! The family blabbermouth! And he is so well informed on these things, and such a good judge of character!"

In the grip of his intrinsic need for honesty, he heard himself confessing. "I asked him outright… I observed you walking out here with some mawkish youth a few weeks ago when I called to leave documents…"

"He is not a mawkish youth…he is twenty-one and a horticulturist…soon to become a botanist too!"

"I am pleased for him…now let us go inside!"

"And at least he is not an unfeeling *schoolteacher* and a coward…" She regretted the remark as soon as it was made. She felt him turn and stare at her. She could not take it back now; to do so was to put herself in an untenable position. It occurred to her that just weeks ago she had wanted nothing better than to use Roger as a deterrent to Fairchild's attentions. She wondered how she could have wanted that. How could she not have known how things would be!

"What did you just call me?" he demanded.

"You heard it the first time, I will not repeat it…"

"No, indeed…probably because you dare not."

"Really! I would not be so sure…"

The interchange had become heated within seconds. It was not what she had wished. She deliberated on whether to return immediately to the house. He would not now be amenable or receptive to her softer words.

"Out of interest, where are your parents this afternoon? I have not seen them," he enquired with nonchalance.

She inspected an early rose—set to perish in its precipitous beginnings. "They are neither of them at home…they are on their separate missions somewhere… I do not keep a journal of their comings and goings… Why? Are you thinking to tell them of my rudeness?"

"I would imagine they have observed it for themselves," he said in his caustic manner.

He began assessing her dress. He saw suddenly that she had very few layers beneath this garment. He could take her to the summer house around the corner facing the interminable stretch of lawn down to the lake; it was quite isolated and it was exactly the right time! Then when she had composed herself, he would bring her back into the house, and face any music—aside from Gregory's—and if she complained of matters, he would leave and return at a later time and explain the situation to her father before some dreadful scandal began brewing.

He would tell Giles Shaw that he was heartily sick of being insulted and toyed with and generally made to seem like a fool and that she had pushed him a little too far. Giles would either understand or he would not, but somehow, he thought Giles would understand. He would remember the infamous Sunday tea last December. Giles was elderly now but he was a man who had experienced the trials and tribulations of marriage and relationship.

By instinct, he knew that her father would take any such incident in his stride, the more so if he expected a match between them. "So, what was it you just called me again?" he enquired anew.

He watched her take small steps backwards, in the wrong direction for her own escape, and he followed her slowly. Yes, this was the time! There was none better. He saw her note his gaze along the length of her dress and he knew that she had read his mind.

"Do not even consider it…" Her voice quavered with trepidation, and no doubt with the cold. "I know what you are thinking to do…"

He reconsidered suddenly. "Then go inside now…" he heard himself saying, beset with an irritating sort of sympathy for her. "Go quickly, before I change my mind…" She was drawing him again with that magnetism he little understood, even in his dissolute frame of mind.

"I will not run away from you…" she said in hot jagged words. "I am not such a coward as you are!"

There was that word again—for the third time. It was insufferable. He moved swiftly and closed the space between them. She darted backwards in a longer stride but her skirt impeded her feet and he caught hold of her hand. "You see! You simply cannot help yourself. You have no self-control."

"Let me go…" she breathed and he felt her whole body trembling through her arm. She was afraid and it spurred him on.

"Let go of me…this minute. How dare you!" She realised she was shrieking and strove to contain her anguish.

"You had your chance a moment ago…but as always you do not know when you are winning and when you are losing…" He released her wrist but swiftly gripped her upper arm and began leading her forcefully along the path to the lower part of the grounds.

"I am sorry," she wailed in a pitiful attempt at capitulation. It was quite childlike and he reflected on it while pulling her forwards—without too much haste but just enough determination. "No, you are not. You are sorry for the consequence 'tis bringing…" He paused in his stride and changed tone to one of sarcastic patronage. "But it will be, after all, your *preferred method of chastisement…"*

"You are horrid…" she screamed.

"You knew that before, so you have only yourself to blame…"

Instantly she turned her body ninety degrees into him so that she could push at his arm with her free hand and attempt to release herself. He tugged her onward more doggedly. She began pummelling him with her fist, her dainty little fist, and he seized it and held both her wrists in one hand, stepping a little ahead of her to facilitate smoother movement along the path. They were only feet away from the corner, the small summer house positioned just beyond it. On a sudden tactic she launched herself backwards to delay progress, so that she hung low off his arm in an ungainly manner and he had trouble moving at all.

It occurred to him briefly how this scene would look to anyone peering from a window, but he was too resolute to retain the worry. She may sustain an arm or shoulder injury at this rate and he paused to consider matters. As he did so she lowered her body further to the ground, bending her knees, her skirt billowing out around her; now he could not easily pick her up or move her. "Anthony, no…please do not do this," she pleaded, and he felt like the villain in some melodrama. It made him almost grin.

"Someone will see this display…'tis inelegant…'tis shocking!" she wailed.

"You should have thought of that before you began with your insults." He gripped both her arms and tugged her upright and moved her forwards as he walked backwards.

"I am truly sorry," she cried.

"You are not, but you will be in a few minutes…"

She made more sounds of protest; squealing, mewing sounds—feminine and primal—and he absorbed them with detachment while she more ardently resisted him. And then her sleeve ripped at the shoulder seam and it disconcerted him; the sound of tearing material. It had become difficult to direct the progress to the summer house without letting go of her. He would have to pick her up and carry her. Or let her go completely and admit defeat. This juncture was perhaps the pivotal point of their present-to-future dealings. He could not admit defeat now. So, they struggled and heaved and gritted their teeth against their individual failure.

They had almost reached the corner bordering the lower grounds and he paused to consider the dimensions of the opening and the necessary manoeuvre, and his voice became matter of fact—it reminded her of her days in his classroom and his dominion over her life. "You should know, Melissa, from previous experience, that I do not make idle threats. I always see through on my intentions…who do you think you are dealing with? You unwieldy, thoroughly offensive little girl!"

"I am no longer a little girl," she gasped and pulled against his grip with the last of her strength and her arm felt as though it may dislocate from her shoulder. The rip on the dress opening further.

"You are vile!" she wailed. "Utterly without feeling."

"Do you imagine your insults are helping your plight?" he said angrily.

Then the drawing room doors opened and closed somewhat noisily. He looked around and saw Trim coming down the steps in a hasty tread. Alerted no doubt by her squealing and shrieking. "What are you doing out here?" he called genially, determined to make light of what was going on, for he had a good idea of what might be going on. "'tis freezing. The temperature has dropped and the wind is easterly."

Fairchild glared at him in annoyance and knew that his appearance was a hiatus which would save face, but would ruin the overall plan. Trim came nearer and then looked askance at her torn dress. His lips parted for speech and he shifted his gaze to Fairchild with concern. "Tony, have a care for how this looks…for your position and reputation…if anyone is watching…and her gown is ripped."

"Entirely her own fault…" Fairchild said. "She insisted on struggling."

"Did you expect me not to?" she cried and sank again to the path as he held onto her. She knew she must look idiotic to anyone observing. As if she had fallen or fainted and stopped herself inches from the ground. "You unconscionable tyrant!" she hissed.

This last insult striking Trim as quite hilarious, he spluttered with mirth which he tried turning it into a sharp cough. Fairchild cast him a withering glance to remind him of the brevity of matters previously discussed. Then Trim, his pleasant smile all about his features, put his hands under her arms and lifted her to her feet and manoeuvred her slightly away from Fairchild, finally relieving him of her entirely.

She gazed at Trim, who just minutes ago had tried to warn her, and he appeared to her like an avenging angel. She had unshed tears in her eyes. "He is…he is intent upon…he is about to…" she stopped and could not continue.

Trim said quietly, "I know what he is about to do…and I did try to warn you."

A silence dragged with the unreal quality of a bad dream.

"Perhaps you should come indoors…" Trim suggested. "Your grandmother is concerned that you have no shawl and 'tis too cold."

Fairchild was noticeably calmer and spoke evenly. "Divine intervention in the nick of time," he told her.

Trim had gone back on what they had agreed was expedient, but then he knew his friend's nature of old and understood him well enough to just about forgive the interruption.

"Let me have a moment and I will come…" she said to Trim.

"You must come in right away…" Trim told her gravely. "If you do not do so within the next minute, I will be obliged to carry you."

Her position was ignominious; she was hard pressed to not yell at him. She swallowed hard and closed her eyes. "I do not know where you two have assumed this huge authority suddenly to order me about in my own home…"

"Possibly to do with us having charge of children five days of the week…" said Fairchild in a sour tone.

"You see…" she said to no-one in particular, "His monumental sarcasm!"

Trim looked at Fairchild with raised brows to question his sense in antagonising her further. Even so, the situation seemed more comedy than tragedy.

"This is my home, you know!" Melissa emphasised with vehemence.

"To which we attend as visitors…" Fairchild retorted, "…into which you invited us…and as such we deserve to be shown some respect."

"Respect! How dare you talk of respect when you have just…"

Trim interjected swiftly. "I think that is definitely enough for now…come along!" He took her arm in a firm but gentlemanly manner and they walked back to the steps, Fairchild following a few feet behind.

"You imagine you rule the world, you men…" she said, addressing the garden in general and not looking at either of them.

"I think you may find that we actually do…" Fairchild commented.

Shaking off Trim's hand she moved to one side of the path and waited for him to catch up, and lifting her skirts an inch to facilitate fast movement if necessary, she said in a quieter voice. "All of this is your fault… I told you not to come near me last Sunday when you arrived. I asked you to stay away…but you would accept my mother's invites in a carefree fashion."

"And yet you then send a personally written invite asking me to tea this afternoon! Do you not think you are conflicted in this argument?" he said levelly.

"Only to clear things up…after…after you kissed me and then deserted me!"

"How can I have deserted you when here I am in the garden?"

"You know what I mean! You think you are the only person who can issue demands and orders but let me say…"

He cut her off. "*Do-not-say-another-thing*!" He was punctuating every word with a pronounced space. "Simply go indoors with Trim, as he and your grandmother wish…do as you are requested. I will not speak more on this matter at present."

"But I need to clear my tormented thoughts and speak more freely to you."

"In a while…" he concurred. "When this mood of hostility has passed."

"Neither of you say any more now," ordered Trim, growing irritated with proceedings. He took her arm again and they went back into the house. Being possessed of sisters and accustomed to the moods and tantrums of young

295

females, he was not overly concerned by what had transpired and took his seat at the card table, smiling pleasantly at Gregory and Jemima to put them at ease.

Fairchild followed Melissa along the polished wooden floor of the drawing room and she paused and entreated him in the lowest voice. "Anthony, I am aggrieved we are at loggerheads…"

He considered her words, staring at the ground, giving no indication of what they meant to him. "I think, Melissa, that you will get over it." He moved into the heart of the room where all was as he had left it.

Jemima was dozing in the chair but soon awoke. "We have been waiting an age to finish the game…" she said testily.

"My apologies, Ma'am…" replied Fairchild.

"Yes, Granny, I am sorry if you were concerned for my welfare."

"I was not in the least concerned for your welfare," said Jemima and looked at Fairchild pointedly. Melissa turned to Trim in bewilderment and he met her eyes with a defiant expression in the face of the white lie.

"Never mind," said Jemima. "These things happen…now let us finish…"

Fairchild hesitated before the card table and glared with subdued temper at Trimingham. "'tis bad manners, Tony, to leave a game of cards incomplete… Just another hand or two perhaps…" Trim was aware that normality needed to be restored before it was lost for good. Aware that a turning point had been reached. He felt like an avuncular presence, one which was required to bring harmony to a raw situation which might yet be avoided.

Gregory had seen her torn sleeve before she had time to pick up her shawl and he looked at Fairchild in pure astonishment, rapidly revising his opinion of the boring lives led by schoolteachers. But as she re-entered the scene with her silk shawl he rose from the piano and said carelessly. "Lissy, the middle c here is painfully flat…can it be remedied?"

Melissa looked at the piano and just as casually replied. "The piano tuner was due last week, apparently, but did not arrive…he sent word that he has been ill and is not coming now until next month."

"Oh, that is very well then…" said Gregory, and then to Trim. "Shall I need to tune the piano at your house or will that be a given?"

"I shall see that it's in order, don't worry…" Trim told him as he picked up his cards. "My mother and my youngest sister play all the time, so there will be little amiss with it."

"Splendid..." said Gregory and cracked the knuckles of his long flexible fingers in anticipation of yet another musical instrument with which to become acquainted.

Trim began informing Fairchild of the plan to raise money for the alms schools by Gregory's playing and Melissa's donated artwork and other monetary donations offered on the day. Gregory had now bethought himself to enlist the talents of a friend of his, a virtuoso violinist, and Fairchild listened as he sorted his cards in his customary attentiveness to the important words of others, nodding approval. "Yes, excellent indeed!" he concurred.

Card play commenced. He and Melissa glanced at each other frequently with expressions which the others could not properly read. It was as if nothing out of the ordinary had occurred; the curtain closed on the fractious interlude introduced by Fairchild and herself, as if they were on a theatre stage between acts. For a few minutes, she was filled with the ageless notion that she may have imagined it all or fallen asleep and dreamt it and perhaps not moved from the drawing room to the garden at all.

At the conclusion of the game, he said to her, "Do you wish to talk with me in the morning room or somewhere?"

"I do," she said and they rose and she led the way to the morning room which stood empty.

"Let us partake of a glass of wine," offered Gregory, as the only man of the house left to officiate, "Shall we, Mr Trimingham? I perceive you may need one."

"I do!" agreed Trim.

"My uncle keeps a very fine cellar..." Gregory assured him and rang for the butler.

"I will have sherry," said Grandmama. And then she shook her head in her summery hat with its furbelows and ribbons and pronounced in a tight voice. "I never saw goings on like it..." More for something to say than because it was true.

Gregory began to laugh a little, he could no longer help himself. "My cousin is very outspoken, you see, and a little unconventional at times..." he told Trimingham.

Trim began to laugh in similar vein, politely and with heed to discretion. "Women, eh!"

"Yes…" agreed Gregory in sanguine manner—scarcely knowing any besides Millicent and his mother and aunts but resolving to seem worldly. "What can a man do!"

"Not much you can do…" supplied Jemima. "For we rock the cradle…and at the end of the day you depend on us for it."

"We do!" conceded Trimingham.

Trim was somewhat on edge, and trying not to show it, in case the rowing began again in the morning room.

"You need have no fear…" Jemima told him placidly, swigging her sherry rather than sipping it. "Yon fellow will settle her ash once they're betrothed…a headstrong little madam indeed… I should know, I was one myself!" And she laughed her cracked-bell peals of laughter.

Trim seemed startled for a moment and then inhaled deeply. "Yes, but they must yet get to that stage, Mrs Jemima…"

"They will!" said Jemima with certainty. "Both of them strong characters…the question for now is who's to be in charge…" Neither man commented. "And my money's on him…" The chortling croak of her amusement came as fresh music to their ears.

They fell to conversing on a wider range of topics, relaxed and urbane in the *drawing-room-manner* of centuries.

* * *

As soon as the morning room door closed Melissa began as if they had not broken conversation. "You kissed me and I thought you enjoyed it…"

He turned a full circle where he stood and rubbed his chin with his thumb and fingers, the way she knew many men showed deeper deliberation. He seemed quite calm again, but she did not entirely feel secure in the thought. "…and then you simply ignore me…"

"I was not ignoring you…" he said adamantly.

"Then what do you call it?"

"I call it being busy with other things."

She sank onto the sofa, relieved to be resting. "Surely if we kissed it means something."

"It means that we needed to kiss… It does not have to signify anything more," he ventured.

"Oh, I see…so it was convenient at the time and…do you think I allow just any man to kiss me?"

"I am hoping not," he replied carelessly. "But it was only last weekend, Melissa…" He hesitated, with the realisation that this sounded like an excuse which gave room for future possibilities. The moment to declare himself free of her totally was now past unless he spoke immediately. He did not, and she watched him with wide eyes and construed the statement exactly as he had feared. "Then you must know that it meant something to me…when we kissed."

"It occasionally happens and it is good, but it is not a recipe necessarily for anything longer or more binding," he informed her.

"You are a dilettante…" she declared, despite herself.

"I am no such thing… We have recently established that I am the detested deputy head of a well reputed school. I cannot be both…"

"Of course you can… Nicholas Stevenson was, and he is now the head of the school…if you do it carefully and with discretion…"

He thought of Nicholas Stevenson who had indeed been something of a philanderer and much occupied with his romantic life, but in recent times had married a widow of beauty and societal position. Both he and Stevenson had laudable reputations. Any philandering was their own business. They were not part of a religious institution and their private lives were their own outside of the academy doors.

"So, that was discretion was it? Earlier in the garden!" he enquired next, arguing against his better judgement; he scarcely knew now which side he was on or where he wished to stand. She could tell that he was considering the weight of her accusation and was encouraged. "No, 'twas not…and 'twas your fault not mine…but that does not mean you are not a dilettante…you simply lost your temper…"

"I did!" he agreed. "You would try the patience of a saint."

She reverted back to the nub of things. "To me it signified a lot…the kissing!"

He was tempted to tell her that to most young women of her ilk it would signify a lot, but decided not to share so much of his insight lest it give her untold advantage in argument. "Yes, but it can be left there…" he said in growing desperation. "'tis not as if you will be with child."

She stared at him; he had guessed her unspoken and unacknowledged fear. "I actually did wonder if that may be possible…" she said softly.

"Who has told you that?" he asked sharply. "That kissing conceives children?"

She was embarrassed. "'tis just one of my aunts told me that passionate kissing may lead to the making of babies…though Melanie assures me it does not!"

He was between the need to enlighten her and the need to leave her in her innocence; her ignorance would protect them both perhaps. But protect them from what? He was completely at sea; he knew not what he thought or felt. He covered his confusion with a logical response. "What she may mean is that passionate kissing can lead to the act which begets babies…"

"Oh…oh, good!" She sighed. "You perhaps think me very stupid and ignorant…"

"You may rest assured you will not have a baby. Least not from our kissing…she may have told you that to deter you from being…from becoming…" he faltered, not knowing how to continue, or whether to say the word *promiscuous.*

"From what?" she queried suspiciously.

"You will not have conceived a baby!" he asserted.

"That is good to hear, for I do not want a child as yet."

"No more do I," he replied with grim irony.

"So, this revulsion to kissing me means you no longer find me desirable!" The question was posed craftily in the statement.

"It has nothing to do with revulsion to kissing you…though God knows your antagonism may deter the most ardent of men."

"Then if you enjoyed it and I enjoyed it, why can we not simply kiss more?"

"I do not think it that simple."

She felt the cold shift to the recent rift between them as a palpable essence, unavoidable and heavy, and then she hit upon an idea. "I should like to sketch you… I should like it if you would sit for me…you have archetypal bone structure!"

This mixture of naivete and sophistication in one female confounded him. This girl with the potential to salient womanhood took away his ability to breathe evenly.

"You need not seek to flatter me. I do not have that kind of mind."

"No, but I should like to do so…then I will give it to you as a gift."

"Out of the question," he said, turning away.

"Then I shall draw you from memory... I shall draw you whether you wish it or not."

"Of course you shall...you do only what you wish...and what you can get away with."

"I do not! You do not know me."

"No more than you know me. Though it does not stop you from reaching your outrageous conclusions. Why do you think 'tis different for me?"

She had discarded the shawl and her ripped dress was showing pale flesh at her shoulder. It was a reminder of how her whole body may look, it was more provocative than if she had sat naked. He wanted her. He felt the stirrings of longing in his throat and his groin. It overpowered him and he struggled to gain control.

While she gazed from the window to the far end of the rose garden, where the gardener's boy was wheeling a barrow for the collection of weeds and dead-heads. He had doubtless heard the fracas between them and would lose no time in telling the gardener, who was himself a little deaf. "Perhaps because you are a man and I cannot imagine what it is to be a man and think like one," she told him at length.

He smiled a thin sort of smile and paced about the room.

She was weary suddenly, weary to the bone from their physical struggle and the situation. She could almost feel her eyes closing. She brought herself to stronger presence in the moment, having made the decision. "I am ready to be civil...I am ready to be polite and amenable to you!" she announced.

He looked as if he did not believe her, he looked more suspicious than she had seen him look that day. He paced for several minutes as she sat and rested and let her eyelids droop. Eventually he came to stand in front of her and she opened her eyes on cue, sensing him without her vision.

"Are you listening?" he enquired in the softest of tones, so that she wondered if she had merely imagined him speaking. She nodded in case he had actually voiced the question, thinking of how softly he may speak if they were to become lovers. She recalled Melanie and herself laughing over Melanie's assertion that some men bellowed even when being intimate with a woman, and that was quite as repellent as if they did not wash; she had read of it in the kind of womens' journals that had to be subscribed to and were not readily available for purchase: Melanie's older sister read material of this sort and passed it on to Melanie. She smiled at the thought, her mouth moving ever so slightly to its wider contours, He waited to see more. "Are you sure you are paying me heed?"

She nodded again and glanced at him. His face from this angle was pleasing in the extreme in its symmetry. His expression of deliberation on matters sensitive, his calm resolve. It filled her with a strange sensation. Similar to knowing that chocolate was nearby to be devoured but not in plain sight. An insatiable inner emptiness outlined by memory of taste.

He changed his position and shifted his feet and assumed a solid stance some two feet from her. "I am telling you this for the last time," he said as his opening theme. "Do not ever accuse me of being a coward…because Trim will not always be there to save you…and even should someone arrive with a royal pardon, it will not save you!" He paused to see if she had anything to say; she did not and sat impassively gazing past him to the far wall. "If you hurl just one more insult at me…if there is but one more offensive and derogatory remark upon my person, I shall take you across my knee and smack you so soundly your previous grievances will pale into insignificance…"

She would not look at him, it was not within her power as yet. She shut her eyes and compressed her lips and arched her brows and made an elongated face which showed no discernible thought. Her features a tight mask of parody to the eternal surprise of life, like a mime from musical theatre. She could not risk giving away any of her thoughts; the blend of indignation, emotional confusion and some kind of relief were altogether too much.

The sensation was making her light headed. It was strangely close to making her want to laugh and even she—with her propensity to frank expression—knew that to be a dangerous reaction. She refined on the fact that he had alluded to the future, he had warned her of something she must avoid in a mysterious place beyond *now*. She pondered on what it meant exactly and whether she really desired it. He frowned at the ludicrous expression on her face. "Melissa, did you hear what I said?"

She contemplated her reply, flickering her eyes like someone sleepwalking.

"Have you understood me? Because this is absolutely the last warning I shall give you."

She opened her eyes wide, grey as polished pewter, and regarded him. "Of course I heard, I am not deaf!" she said with asperity—then she smiled a sweet but questionable smile—and rose and fled the room. Leaving him wondering what they had actually agreed and what they had left to chance.

Chance, the Fickle Companion

Sometime later, the two men left by the side entrance of the mansion for the quickest route to the stables. Passing the kitchen area and the low shrubbery bordering a small enclosed lawn for use by the staff, from the side of his eye Trimingham caught sight of three female faces peering over a bush, their full forms concealed. "We are being watched…" he remarked and they both halted. Then a child's voice piped from the unseen. "'tis him with the yellow hair and someone else…"

"Shush this second," said an older voice. And a tray of something metallic was heard to drop to the ground. Fairchild turned his gaze to the bush and waited, his stare measured and steady in the knowledge that all would be revealed, and at length Polly the maid appeared, pulling with her two much younger girls not above nine or ten years of age in voluminous aprons too large for them and caps of similar dimension.

Polly dropped a very elegant curtsy and nudged the little girls who followed suit. "Good day to you, gentlemen!" she said.

"And to you, Ma'am…" replied Fairchild courteously.

Trim was wearing a short stovepipe hat at a jaunty angle, which he lifted a little as he inclined his head to her. They walked on. "Come along now 'Yellow Hair'…" he said in great good humour. "Before you have any more of the female population trembling in your wake…"

Fairchild broke stride and punched Trim on the arm. Trim broke stride too and punched him in return. "You think I am in jest?"

Fairchild stepped aside and aimed another punch. They grappled a little, like schoolboys, as they moved towards the stables, stopping abruptly as a male servant crossed their path from the lawns. They proceeded in a dignified manner. "Just think…" continued Trim festively, "Were you to live with North American Indians that would be your given name on initiation… *'Young Brave Yellow Hair'*…and no doubt she would be *'Little Squaw Sharp Tongue'*…"

303

"I have had enough of your interference for one day," said Fairchild with an ambiguous air.

In the kitchen, the disturbance in the rose garden was the centre of the gossip. No sooner had Polly entered with the two little girls than the cook paused in the blanching of the peas and said: "Well, did you find out the reason for all the pandemonium?"

"No," retorted Polly, "This one dropped the cutlery and they saw us hiding behind the bushes."

"For pity's sake!" moaned the cook. "How will that look now! Supposing they give complaint about being spied on?"

"They will not," said Polly assuredly.

"'twas the gent with the yellow hair…" piped the eldest child. "I see'd him the other day…"

"You *saw* him," Polly corrected, swilling the cutlery. "He has beautiful manners…he addressed me as Ma'am."

"Did he now!" said the cook acidly. "Well, not all of us are taken in by these beautiful manners… It means little, as you may find out one day! And did you hear any more?"

"Nothing of interest," said Polly. "The cutlery noise silenced them too soon."

"She can't be that a'feared of him," offered the assistant cook, a raw-boned girl with the demeanour of someone twice her age. "She sent the invite for him to come today… John delivered it…"

"Of course she is not!" said Polly. "She likes him beyond the usual."

"And t'other feller with him was tasty…worthy of a bed for the night in any woman's book…" The assistant cook let out a raucous crude laugh.

"That will do, Matilda…" cautioned the cook. "We don't want no talk of that nature where there's children about. This ain't the kitchen of the Broken Broom."

"How do you know?" demanded Matilda, jealous of Polly's inside information and Polly's feminine charms in general. "And where was he dragging her off too?"

"I have an idea where…" said Polly, helping herself to a roast potato. "And my loyalty to her is unquestionable."

"Oh, *unquestionable*…" mimicked Matilda. "You're as hoity-toity with your fancy words as them…"

"She picks it up while fossicking around them all day…" the cook said; if anyone here should be addressed as 'Ma'am' it was herself, as befitted her

304

seniority in the kitchen. "I do so hate a tale half told...what was all her squealing about if she likes him?"

"I b'aint heard that part..." Matilda was chopping cauliflower. "They be too far along the path... I only caught a bit by accident, collecting the crocks from the old lady's room...lucky I paid attention."

"Have you told us the full?" queried the cook.

"I came to it as it was full tilt, I heard him say: *'what did you just call me?'*...then nothing til he seized hold of her...then her pleading with him to let her go..." Matilda broke off from the chopping to strike a pose she thought better depicted the scene: her head thrown back, her hand against her forehead and her voice tragic. "...'twas more like this... *'I beg of you, Anthony. I am at your mercy'*..."

"It was nothing like that," objected Polly, "...she does not speak in those ridiculous terms. The gardener told me what she said...'twas simply, *'Anthony, please don't do this'*...then him speechifying in a low angry voice and her squealing and demanding he release her...the gardener thought she may have called him a coward, but he isn't that sure...he only had it from the boy."

The cook made a wincing sound as if she had scalded herself. "The silly girl! You canna call a man that and expect it to blow over in two minutes...that's bound to have him in a rage..."

"She called him other things too according to the gardener, but his hearing isn't sharp and he doesn't know what for sure," Polly added.

The cook sucked in breath and tutted. "Foolish wench! She's set to lose him at this rate."

Polly straightened her lacy French cap with dignity. "Miss Shaw is very direct in her speech...although very private, she believes in moral honesty and speaking her mind."

Matilda barked a loud laugh. "Mayhap she spoke it once too often for his liking..."

"She'll grow out of that," said the cook. "You don't want to be telling a man your mind, whatever class he is...'t ain't wise..."

The youngest footman, John, entered the kitchen carrying empty cups and glasses left in the library from the night before.

"Do you know any more?" demanded the cook of him.

"No," said John flatly. "What more do you need to know?"

"Where he was dragging her off to for one," said Matilda.

John folded his arms and leaned against the large wooden table. "To have his wicked way with her, I would have thought...probably to the small summer house...or the boathouse...while the master and missus were gone!"

"Have some sense!" admonished the cook. "Gents of his calibre don't call on ladies in these kinds of houses and force themselves upon 'em...this ain't France."

"And why did t'other fellow come out and stick his neb in?" said Matilda challengingly.

"P'raps he's lusting after her too," said John; the question of male urges never far from his mind. "Nobody could blame him...a fetching little baggage such as her."

The cook bridled. "We'll have no more of them remarks, John...little ears are listening."

John took an apple from a bowl. "Didn't see 'em there," he said.

"And you'd best not let the master hear any remarks about his daughter such as that...or you'll be on your way quicker than the cat licks its ear..." admonished the cook.

"Anyway, they were all carrying on as if nothing had happened when I took in the third lot of tea...chit-chatting calmly," said Polly.

"O'course they were..." Matilda scoffed. "The world might have fell in and they'd be drinking tea and chit-chatting calmly...that's how toffs be..."

The cook moved back to the food on the stove. "She can't have been that much a'feared...or she'd have screamed the place down and we'd all have heard it."

"She wasn't a'feared..." jeered Matilda, "...the struggling and going on was but all a show for his benefit."

"I don't think so!" Polly was defensive. "She is not that sort of girl. Though I suppose she might be pretending to be afraid so as to excite him a little..."

The cook made a sound of derision. "*My eye and Peggy Martin!* What woman needs to go to those lengths when she has all the advantages of Melissa Shaw?"

"Who's Peggy Martin?" queried the younger child, and was ignored.

"And why would her being a'feared make him excited?" asked the elder one, carrying ingredients for the cook who was their aunt.

"Never you mind!" said her aunt. "Take no notice of these two...or they'll lead you down some leery paths you're best avoiding."

306

"What I wouldn't give for a jaunt down the path with a man so fine and fit as those pair…" mused Matilda.

"But not if you were a'feared of him?" said the younger child with awe.

"Mayhap even then…" replied Matilda, a ladle held aloft for paused perusal into fantasy.

The cook was exasperated. "Now see, we are ten minutes behind with the dinner preparations."

* * *

"That did not exactly go according to plan, I know…" said Trim after a little time on the ride home on the treacherous back lanes, still icy in patches.

"All thanks to your noble intervention," Fairchild remarked shortly. He was annoyed again and not fully aware of why: he felt two emotions at the same time; he should have cut loose from her once and for all and told her they had no hope of any relationship. But he was also glad that he had not. It was unsatisfactory— he liked at all times to know his own mind.

"But on the bright side…" began Trim.

"Is there one?" Fairchild interrupted.

"Yes…the Petersham wench did not arrive…otherwise it may have been you I was forced to rescue. I may have come out to find you lying grievously injured in the garden." Trimingham was a couple of glasses of wine into a festive mood so Fairchild ignored the comedy.

"All in all, it was a highly entertaining afternoon. They are quite wonderful people…" Trim was saying in his genial manner. "That resume from young Montalbein concerning his true parentage… I do not know how I kept my face straight."

"If I am right here, his father is Gideon Montalbein…a degenerate waster of noble background who has scarcely been sober since his coming of age. He would little know where his wife was on any evening. So, our young pianist may be correct…"

"I see!" Trim was fascinated.

"He's seen occasionally in company with my brother, Richard, and that tells you everything you need to know…"

"I see!" Trim said once more.

307

"And…" confided Fairchild. "One of Montalbein's former mistresses is reputedly Richard's current paramour…"

"You jest!" said the astounded Trim. "And whose before that, I wonder?"

"I expect they pass her around, as they do the claret!" Fairchild said derisively. "She's a veritable Jezabelle!"

"But what a marvellously hospitable bunch they are, the Shaw family!"

Fairchild stuck his cigar between his teeth, glanced at Trim sidelong and said, "Yes, they are very lively and colourful…but you were not there to enjoy an entertaining afternoon, if you recall! But to observe…you should not have intervened… I was on the verge of getting straight to the matter we discussed…"

"*You unconscionable tyrant!*" Trim said, repeating Melissa's term, but the humour remained unappreciated. "For some reason, I could not let it happen."

"Oh, could you not?" retorted Fairchild in sarcasm.

"She is quite adorable, Tony. She is quite unique and of a natural beauty which will perhaps never fade."

"I can see all that for myself!" came the reply.

Trim remained silent. Then after a few moments he offered. "I did not want to see her suffer…it seemed to be too precipitous!"

"Suffer!" echoed Fairchild. "She would not suffer over much."

"She is very taken with you betimes…'tis written in her eyes."

"And that gives her the right to behave with such a flagrant lack of manners and hurl insults, does it?" Fairchild removed his cigar to add. "What a hopeless romantic you are, Timothy."

"Perhaps, but I suddenly feared 'twas the wrong move… I suddenly felt sorry for her."

"How you do surprise me!" said the other.

Trim shifted uncomfortably as the trap increased in speed hazardously on the wintery roads. "I suddenly had the knowledge that she might have had too much of your severity…in the past I mean… It might have been the last straw."

Fairchild spoke louder now over the noise of the wheels. "The last straw was her unfounded bloody insults in the garden… I might have overlooked her earlier audacity… I might just have been able to not…"

"I tried to warn her, you know…" interjected Trim, and Fairchild pulled up his muffler against the wind. "When? What do you mean, you warned her?"

"When you first went outside to smoke… I sat her down next to me and gave her a gentle reminder of how not to behave. It was subtle but it was quite stark."

"Not stark enough!" Fairchild geed up the horse. "She does not understand subtlety…she requires something more practical…which I was just about to render her when you came along with your blasted chivalry…"

"Perhaps I should not have done so…but then I was glad I did. She looked petrified…"

"So she might…out there in that frock…with little beneath it…of course, I was just about to warm her up considerably when you came along…" The trap increased in speed yet again and Trim closed his eyes to see if the pace was merely temporary and contingent with the passing moments of speech. It was not and the speed increased.

"She called me a coward just minutes before your appearance…twice or three times. She was lucky I did not throttle her," Fairchild continued at length.

Trim spoke with closed eyes to ward off nausea as the trap hurtled round zig zag bends. "You see, had you sisters you would dismiss all this rhetoric and name calling…you would see it as simply girlish stuff. It means little…"

"I have no wish to dismiss it…she is not my sister…and even if she were, I do not think I would care to be spoken to in that manner. God knows she is bad enough with her brother, Damien! I have no wish to endure it."

"It may be simply her age…her inexperience…" offered Trim blithely.

"I care not what it is, Trim. I am not putting up with it."

There was little Trim could say; they were different people, he and Fairchild, and he could not further his viewpoint without provoking further argument between them. But then Fairchild went on with his tirade heatedly and without thought to the speed of the conveyance, and Trim remained silent for fear of causing an accident.

"I cannot just kiss her on demand…not without wanting her fully, so then I cannot concentrate properly on anything else. Without care, I will end up taking her in some moment of madness…and she is so inexperienced she will not realise what is happening and will not stop me…then there will be a dreadful mess…a wholly unthinkable situation…we are going around in circles now, thanks to your misplaced sympathies. She thinks it acceptable to hurl these kind of ridiculous insults…and you have stopped me teaching her otherwise in the short term."

"But I had the strong feeling 'tis your tenderness she requires at this stage…not more of your harsher strictures."

The horse veered to the left as Fairchild made a heavy groan of aggravation and Trim gripped the strap on the door of the trap to stop being hurtled out of his seat.

"You talk as if I beat them hourly every day… I did not. And I will not apologise for any of my actions…they should have shown better behaviour. I inherited the negligent results of former staff… Henry Stringer, Miss Sullivan, Henrietta Madeley…all of them too idle to maintain any discipline… I will not apologise."

"I am not expecting you to apologise…" Trim said through gritted teeth as the trap veered from right to left. "I am talking of the present day…no doubt you were somewhat justified in your actions back then."

"So kind of you to *somewhat* see my side of it!" his friend sneered.

Trim eased his tension by stretching his legs as far as they would go and felt his nausea and the reckless travel rise in conjunction. "Tony, reduce the speed of the trap or let me drive…your temper is getting the better of you. A stay in the infirmary is not going to change matters." The trap slowed and Trim breathed out before continuing, "If you offer her love now, or some tenderness, she may reveal herself differently."

"She has just earlier vowed to be polite and amenable…" Fairchild admitted in a sceptical tone.

Trim looked sharply at him. "Then the mission is accomplished," he said cheerfully.

"It might be…until she forgets herself and begins with her insults the moment she is displeased."

"You have to give her the benefit of the doubt…for now."

"I do not have to give her anything of the sort unless I choose to do so…"

"But 'tis what you wanted from her, is it not…to gain her more gentle acquiescence?"

"True!" concurred Fairchild, calming a little. "But I cannot be going through these dramas all the while… I have too much else to think about… I may be better leaving her be and cutting off the association."

"And cutting off your nose to spite your face?" Trim said wryly.

"Preferable to risking my good name…or a precipitous marriage to an unmanageable immature female who despises me and insults me whenever I see her…and covers it behind a facade of lustful passion…and as you have pointed out, her family are good people…her father is very decent… I do not wish them to think I am dishonouring her for my own advantage…"

Seeing a pause in the flow, Trimingham offered. "But of course, upending her and giving her a hiding is not dishonouring her at all!"

"No…'tis a different thing entirely…besides, I would allow her to retain her drawers…"

Unsure whether this was meant humorously, Trim tipped his hat forwards over his eyes and leaned back into the seat. "Why be so magnanimous!" He made huffing sounds of muted laughter and tried to light his pipe, unsuccessfully in the swaying vehicle. "So you employ this method with all your women, do you?"

"The devil I do," said the other. "They are generally older and more sensible…besides, my stamina is required for other matters…"

Trim gave up on the pipe and pushed it into the pocket of his greatcoat. "Then I will ask you the same question I asked the other night…what makes you think 'tis the wisest move?" Several moments passed and he thought he was not going to receive a reply, when the answer came. "Lottie!" Fairchild said in a gruff voice.

"Ah!" Trim left a respectable pause before pursuing the topic. "And was the outcome favourable on that occasion?"

"There were actually two occasions…and suffice it to say things improved considerably…"

Trim thought that here was another comparison brewing, but he kept his counsel while a reverent silence was observed in respect of the deceased Charlotte Fitzwilliam, as was always the case when she had been mentioned. Trim allowed him to speak first, which he did eventually. "I believe I am better giving her a wide berth withal…" he offered, the trap at a reasonable pace and he in a more reasonable mood.

Trim made a pained face. "I do see that she could be a handful perhaps…a little minx…"

"A little minx? She has the makings of the shrew all about her."

"No, no…she is young…she will learn."

"She may if someone teaches her…" Fairchild rejoined caustically.

"Perhaps she will now have realised…for she knew what you intended."

"Of course she did…she remembers the warnings I have issued and chooses to ignore them until the eleventh hour, when she pleads her innocence and her remorse… I am not about to be played like a fiddle…and next time I will not allow her to get away with it, no matter what."

"Oh, so there is to be a next time then!" Trim remarked.

Fairchild considered things, holding the reins in one hand and fishing out his cigars with the other. He stuck one in his mouth but did not light it. "In truth, I am expecting a letter from her in the next few days saying she does not wish to have any more to do with me."

"Then allow me to conjecture that you may be disappointed…" Trim struck a match for his friend's cigar. "I doubt she will be so easily discouraged…"

"We will see," said Fairchild.

They rode for some time without speaking, their breath icy white in the cold night air. At length, Fairchild enquired. "So, we do not need to call on my mother now…or do we? Now that you have this plan with the fundraising arranged? We would have a good supper if we called at this hour…"

"Your decision entirely…" said Trim amiably. "I never mind seeing your mother."

"Are you meeting with Susan tonight?"

"Yes, but she will know I have been delayed and dine with my parents."

"Then let us go to an inn and dine…and I will drive you back afterwards."

"I thought you had an engagement this evening…" Trim remarked, remembering a lady Fairchild had outlined who was staying in the same lodgings.

"I do, but it need not include dinner… If we go to the Four Horsemen it will leave us free to imbibe as we eat…whereas my mother will look askance on our second drink and make veiled references to the evils of strong liquor…"

"That is what mothers tend to do," Trim said. "Of course, they are wives too…and brides…and fiancés before that…and little minxes first off, perhaps." He waited for the reaction to his last comment and several seconds elapsed before he received one. "Trim, I hate to correct you here…but I am quite sure that *'minx'* does not have a plural…" He swore heavily and Trim erupted into laughter as the trap picked up speed again and swerved perilously on the icy roads.

* * *

Later that night Fairchild was with his temporary neighbour from two doors along, in her bed. She was a French modiste staying in the town only until the end of the month so that they had a mere few weeks in which to enjoy their amorous exchange. She was older than him, perhaps thirty-four or five, and extremely pretty with pale red hair like newly minted copper and the delicate skin to go with it; skin so fine he could see her veins beneath it. She had two children in Toulouse and possibly a husband, but the latter was a vague inference only and did not figure at all—she was transient and would be a mere memory soon enough.

Mrs Anstey's lodging house saw people coming and going all the time, for long residence or short, but rarely did one so appealing as Annette appear in the building. The convenience of their rooms was a boon and they were virtually undiscovered, except by a porter who carried up and down the heavier objects and luggage and brought the coal for the fires and the water for the hand basins. He was accustomed to such goings on and was tipped generously to remain oblivious.

Annette was representing a fabric merchant in France and was selling to some of the millinery establishments in the borough and a few lingerie manufacturers; applying her wisdom and technique for the fashionable ladies of the county harbouring aspirations to looking chic and fetching at great expense. While the milliners and manufacturers ordered quantities of the fabrics produced by her employers.

He had not needed to try very hard to entice her; she had set her sights upon him during supper in Mrs Anstey's dining room—where he was also at his evening meal—on her very second evening in the house.

Presently she had wrapped one of her slim shapely legs around his thigh and made noises of appreciation and longing. But he rolled over away from her, leaving his hand on her stomach and stroking it lightly with his thumb so that she would not feel abandoned. "I am not very… I am not so enervated this evening…" he told her in his deep and even tones. "I apologise."

"No need," she said and then reverted to speaking French (this was another bonus—that he was fluent in her own tongue). She told him not to worry about it, she understood that men were not machines, as neither were women. He was strangely inert and flaccid and unable to vouchsafe his manhood. He knew not what assailed him. Though suspected it had to do with Melissa Shaw. Annette had been very talkative at the start of the assignation that evening, not able immediately to do anything very strenuous herself owing to the amount of food she had consumed at dinner which needed better digestion. She fell to conversing with him instead, telling him that he was a naughty boy who had lied to her.

He struggled to understand some of her words due to the strength of her dialect and the rapidity with which she spoke, like most of the French. He gleaned that she had learned in passing from Mrs Anstey that he was not a banker as he had initially told her, but the deputy head of a prestigious educational academy for children. He admitted then that it was his older brother who was the banker, and that he was tired of people judging him on his profession and commenting that he was not typical of his role by mere appearance…or in any other way.

Tired of explaining that it was not his chosen vocation and that he meant to leave it in a couple of years. The longer he stayed in the job the more unconvincing he felt himself to be in this explanation, so lying to her had been easier.

She reverted to English to say that she understood now. She had thought it was because he might have feared her talking to people about their liaison. She elaborated on this theme, telling him of how she knew the English to be starchy and staid in their institutions: the clergy, and the lawyers etcetera. She went on for some time about the shortcomings of the English…fuddy-duddies and small-minded bigots and, of course, everyone knew that the English were hypocritical with their double standards about sex.

The use of the word *hypocrite* put him straight in mind of Miss Shaw and made him morose. Although he was disposed to accepting the 'third person' slight from Annette in a less sensitive way, as it was not aimed personally at himself. Even so, it affected him badly. Perhaps at heart he believed himself to be such a thing and was unable to own it. Maybe that was why he took such an aversion to Melissa's recriminations.

Annette noted his taciturn reaction and began to cheer him by telling him he was too handsome to be an Englishman; English men in the main were not usually handsome, though they had strong and entertaining personalities…which almost always at base proved to be not genuine but assumed as a pose. These were not sentiments he had not heard voiced before, but they made him even more morose, coming from a person of her gender.

The use of her words *hypocrite* and *pose* and her rebuke at his untruth about his profession made him question his integrity. Perhaps Miss Shaw was right.

Perhaps he was no more than a posturing dilettante! His state of detumescence was made worse and seemed likely to crown the night.

The last woman to occupy this single room had been Clara Anstey, daughter of the landlady, before she had wed her long-term fiancée. She had offered him comfort and succour through the first months of his arrival at the academy. She had cheered his life during the stressful time before Lottie's demise. And afterwards. She had been a diamond of the first water and he regretted that she was not still in residence.

After her, there had been an opera singer from Bucharest, again just passing through. She had been resident on the floor above this one—a mere flight of stairs away. Before that it was a female antique dealer, employed by her family business to scour the land for rare objet d'art, and accompanied by her aged uncle who saw and suspected nothing and was always asleep by nine o'clock at the latest. She was called Margaret and was twenty-seven and from another part of England entirely, but he forgot now exactly where.

He was a dab hand at the art of casual capers with females these days. He was not particularly proud of it but *'needs must'*…life dealt you gifts occasionally, amongst the blows, and you accepted the gifts when offered. Perhaps it was time he settled down and stopped hopping about the beds of transient women, all chosen mutually because neither party wished to enter into any permanent relationship.

He had until lately been prone to appease his unrest by the thought that had Lottie survived, he would be settled with her now and possibly raising a family. But that was paling as a baffle to insight; he was beginning to believe she may not have wanted to settle down once the theatre was strongly in her blood, with a selection of the male population at her feet: he might in time have been rejected for someone richer or more interesting, an actor or writer, someone more like herself in temperament.

He positively loathed himself this night. Until Annette began to arouse him with her erotic talk and her skilful delicate fingers, and he found it within him to satisfy them both, above once, and perhaps for the final time.

* * *

Melanie was only ten days from her wedding. She was nervous, in a way others were not used to her being. Excitable at the least thing. Melissa hesitated to say too much for fear of upsetting her unduly. It was a difficult balance of needing to confide and needing to be circumspect. Added to which, Melanie was as scathingly biased about Fairchild as he was about her.

She collapsed into her boudoir chair and blew her breath upwards to her dishevelled honey coloured hair which was falling into her face as she threw clothes about and searched for other items, all the while digesting the latest bulletin. "Lissy, you are quite beyond salvation… Anthony Fairchild is a force of nature and you will not curb him. I know because I am a little that way myself…"

"I do not know why you do not like him then," said Melissa petulantly.

"'tis impossible for two such people to like each other," Melanie snapped.

"But what about Geoffrey? He is quite a force of nature in the courtroom. I have heard it said of him."

"Yes, but," Melanie hesitated in order to think, "In a different way…he is more biddable withal."

"How do you know Fairchild is not biddable…in his private life?" demanded Melissa.

"One has only to look at him. He has that steely glare behind his eyes, and a jaw line that is utterly Teutonic."

"He has classical bone structure… I offered to sketch him if he will sit…but he will not!"

Melanie sprang from the chair and then rooted around in her dressing table drawers and came out with a pack of perfumed Russian cigarettes—her nerves required tobacco. "Of course he will not…it would rob him of control…and besides, he may be afraid you would paint him as a gargoyle or something."

Melissa shrieked with laughter as Melanie lit two cigarettes and passed one to her. "We have to open the window soon…even if 'tis freezing, for if Mother comes there will be lectures and frets about young ladies smoking, and I cannot stand any more on top of my present state of fright."

"What?" Melissa choked a little on the smoke. "What are you afraid of? Surely not Geoffrey! I thought you found him biddable?"

"Of course not Geoffrey…" Melanie shut her eyes. All men were frightening if one considered one's position as a wife. Women said they changed after marriage—they often became monsters of selfishness and unreasonable behaviour. "Geoffrey is the least frightening of men…" she countered, more to convince herself. "Whereas, Attila is another matter."

Melissa held the cigarette inelegantly between her thumb and forefinger, as she had seen the workmen at the mansion do. Melanie jumped up again to correct her and placed it delicately between her middle and index fingers, then went to throw open the windows.

"Why is he another matter?" enquired the languid Melissa, now unsure of her hold over Fairchild. It had sprung from some deep well of primaeval wisdom since his departure on Saturday. His proprietorial attitude and careful wording had shown her that he cared about his position more than he did about her, notwithstanding his dire warnings, even if he had alluded to future contact.

"You need to take extreme care..." Melanie said, ignoring the leading question. "I cannot emphasise it enough...stop antagonising him with these insults and remarks, if you must keep his acquaintance..."

"I cannot help it..." Melissa exhaled the purplish smoke in careful puffs and tried to blow smoke rings as she had seen people do. "It just comes over me and I cannot stop myself...he makes me very annoyed, and I do not trust him any better...but somehow, I want to be near him. I feel bereft when he leaves the room..."

Melanie expostulated loudly with words that could not be made out owing to the management of her own exhaled smoke. Unable to believe what she heard, she coughed for a few moments and then regained composure. "I knew how it would be... I said it. He has you under some kind of spell. I would not be surprised if he had not mesmerised you..." *Mesmer and his works were a favourite reading material for her.* "If so, you will not be in command of your own mind."

"Nonsense," said Melissa quietly. "If that was so, why would I still feel the need to become vexed and say things to him he does not like..."

"Because you are used to dealing with Roger Braithwaite!" said Melanie. "Old habits die hard."

"Fairchild called him a mawkish youth...he saw us walking together in the garden, apparently."

"He was spying on you!" said Melanie. "He may creep into your grounds and do it often without anyone knowing..."

Melissa found the notion hilarious and began giggling.

"Too ridiculous, Mel! He is far too busy and self-possessed for that!"

"He is jealous of you and Roger then...?"

"I cannot tell. I can never tell what he thinks on the subject of us…except when he is talking in general about my rudeness and bad manners… I dare not say one more offensive thing to him…not for a while at least…he very nearly…" She stopped abruptly.

"Nearly what?" enquired Melanie. "What did he nearly do?"

"I went too far…with my remarks…" said Melissa evasively.

"So, you do admit you provoke him?"

"I merely speak my mind…"

"And what did he *nearly do*?"

"I was rescued by his friend Mr Trimingham, in the nick of time."

"Rescued from what?" persevered Melanie.

The maid entered and Melanie instructed her as to various items needing repairing or laundering. The maid ignored the tobacco smoke—being herself partial to a cigarette—and left again. Melanie returned to the topic in hand. "What is he like…this Mr Trimingham?"

"He is quite delightful…very warm and genial. Tall and good to look at…"

"Then why not court him?"

Melissa looked askance. "I do not think we are drawn to each other in that way. Besides, he is engaged to Doctor Darnley's daughter, Susan, for a few years now."

"Oh yes…the parochial do-gooder who sticks her nose into everything. I hear tell of her often…she crusades for the plight of the poor."

"As does Fairchild, you may be surprised to hear, on educational reform and so on…and the need for the alms schools."

Melanie eschewed this glowing reference in favour of more personal issues. "What almost happened? Lissy, you had better tell me, today, before I go on honeymoon for a month. You will regret it if we do not discuss this…what did he nearly do?"

Melissa began to giggle; the subject and the caution it warranted was safely in the recent past and seemed just part of a longer more important picture.

"What? For the love of God," cried Melanie, out of patience. Melissa controlled her giggling and stubbed out her cigarette and then gritted her teeth and told Melanie of the rose garden episode and their struggle and Trim's intervention. And for a good few moments Melanie assumed a series of expressions, all of them contradictory. "Well, if you would insist on telling him it was your preference!" she pronounced at length with the satirical tone she had previously brought to the topic.

"I told him no such thing…he uses that as an excuse…he was the one who suggested it…in the art room…"

"Of course he did, to see what your reaction might be…and you gave him exactly the cue he needed, almost the permission to do it."

"I did no such thing," said Melissa with vehemence, her expression becoming mutinous. "I told him I expressly did not wish it. Then he said I would not be able to prevent it, if you recall."

"Boasting of his superior strength…so arrogant!" reiterated Melanie.

"His strength is not in question indeed," Melissa purred in a silky sort of voice and began giggling again, though she knew not why: little bursts of laughter which were painful owing to the wearing of laces beneath her dress. "It was a faux pas on my part."

"I am coming to think it was not… I am coming to think you will not be satisfied until he carries this threat out." Melanie paused and then suddenly enquired, "What were you wearing the other day in the rose garden?"

"My russet and red muslin…"

"What! That one from America?"

"Yes…the one I wear as a house dress and casually in the art room…"

"You were not meant to be casual; you were receiving guests."

"'tis quite respectable…if a little plain…" objected Melissa. "But I do not like too much formality of dress at home."

"Plain has nothing to do with it…'tis the fact that you wear practically no undergarments beneath it! Do you imagine he cannot see that with his own eyes! It was perfect for his objectives. He would not have to wade through yards of petticoats to find your ripe little derrière, would he? You practically enticed him into it."

Melissa gasped and looked coyly indignant. "That is outrageous, Melanie."

Melanie persevered. "You are fascinated by the idea of it now…and he will find a reason to carry out the threat, and you may then see that it is not a pleasant experience. It will be quite horrid…and painful."

"That is what he implied…he said my past grievances would pale into insignificance next to it…"

"You see…he is serious! He is not playing, as you are, and then it will become the first of many occasions on which it happens, in his uncontrollable lust for power…he will say he is justified and 'tis his right as your fiancée or husband…"

Melissa gaped at her and tried to think of all the nuances. "I think not!"

"You may think what you will, Lissy…but it will not alter what I am saying. Nor will you be able to stop him once you are wed."

"Perhaps I would not mind overall…" Melissa mused. "What is worse is that he refuses to kiss me now."

Melanie's mouth opened in horror and her voice became louder. "I think you will mind when it becomes more than an idea. Some men enjoy that kind of thing…and he will be one of them without a doubt. 'tis a safe form of domination…and whether you would want to kiss him afterwards begs a question…you will be glad to get as far away from him as possible, I assure you!"

Melissa sat and stared at the pile of garments discarded on the bed, and then she sat up straight in the chair and grinned. "You are speaking from experience, I can tell… Geoffrey has done the same thing to you…admit it!"

"He might have…" said Melanie with some uncustomary modesty.

"But still, you are marrying him?"

"Yes, of course!"

"There you are then!"

"I may admit that I do go a little far at times, and I may admit that he was not without justification," countered Melanie in a sudden change of tact.

"Then perhaps I should admit that too."

"Only to me, my love! Never ever to him…besides, Atilla is not to be excused so soon. He has earned your scorn and your scathing remarks." Melanie rose and tripped over to the window to close it. "Melissa, stop antagonising him, or stop the association. For if you cannot manage your temper, then you will be at his mercy. And if you insist on thinking yourself so taken with him you will be in too deep and not be able to extricate yourself. 'tis an infatuation of some kind, nothing more."

Melissa was very still in the chair—the intricacies of it all were too much to conjure with. It felt like her entire womanhood unfolding in slow motion. It would be like a secret battle of minds and wills and words and unknown outcomes. It might be dangerous…just a little…or overawing or beyond her ability to understand, but life would never be tedious or without challenge. "Why is he refusing to kiss me now?" she lamented, as if not hearing Melanie's last remarks.

"He has thought more of the consequences of the dalliance, as I said he might the other day...'twill take him some time perhaps," said Melanie.

"How much time?"

"I know not...until he thinks more about your verbal attacks, perhaps." Then from a different standpoint Melanie offered, "So, we cannot be sure it was not staged...this intervention? Perhaps Trimingham was primed to arrive in just the nick of time. That way Fairchild would not have to carry out the threat but still you would see how intent he was upon it. The threat would be perceived only and perhaps therefore remain more strongly in your mind..."

"I had not thought of that," Melissa replied. It was certainly persuasive reasoning, and Melanie's astute insight was worth considering. "But Trimingham did try to warn me...before I went into the garden. I doubt it was staged, or he would have encouraged me to follow him...instead he cautioned me to leave him be..."

"Perhaps not then..." Melanie concurred. "But it shows they have been speaking of it or it shows that they have discussed this threat and your *preference*...but they may be unsure whether you like the idea or not..."

"Stop calling it my *preference*!" Melissa snapped, then sighed herself into a more accepting frame of mind. "Trim certainly knew of the tea throwing incident. He thinks you are...never mind, you do not want to hear that now...but Geraldine had told Granny that it was deliberate, she had watched every movement...and then Gregory said it was vulgar...and it was clear that Trim was unsure until then whether it was an accident...then he was very disapproving of the action."

"I care not," said Melanie with spirit, "I would do it again."

"I think Trimingham felt sorry for me...in the garden!"

"He obviously knows of Fairchild's callous and cruel nature. Trimingham may be disposed to treating women with more gentleness," said Melanie glibly.

"You cannot know that Fairchild has a cruel and callous nature..." objected Melissa in sudden support of the man she purported to loath.

"What?" Melanie was near to giving up the argument. "After the waiting room incident... I know not how you can say that."

"Then after your admission of minutes ago, what of Geoffrey's cruel and callous nature!" Melissa announced in defiance.

Melanie paused, like a chess player who suspected her opponent of cheating, and Melissa continued on the advantage. "A lot of people might say Fairchild was justified back then…they may say that we were just errant school-children and that we deserved it."

"I do not want to hear all his canting rhetoric again, Melissa. You are merely quoting his logic."

"Yes, Melanie…even Geoffrey, when you told him of it recently…very ill-advisedly in my opinion…said it served us right. I remember distinctly you telling me he said that…and after all, he deals with injustices all the time, does he not!"

"Yes, but he too is a man, remember." Melanie fell back into the recess of the boudoir chair, quite defeated at last. A long silent interlude ensued while they gathered their wits and their various thoughts. The room temperature was arctic now that the window had admitted the cooler breeze and Melissa shivered. "I fear he has done with me…" she said dramatically after some time. "I fear he will not want ever to kiss me again. I think I have wounded him sorely."

Melanie's laughter was both comforting and annoying. "Certainly not! He is not Roger Braithwaite… I told you he would not allow you to say horrid things to him! He is playing you at your own game!"

"What game though?" cried Melissa.

"It has many names, my sweet! He may not know himself what game he is involved in…he may see only the need for rules to be set, which he then changes to suit himself, if you do not get ahead in it."

"I see," said Melissa, who did not see at all.

Frayed Ends and Floral Gatherings

Quite a few days after the incident in the garden Fairchild sent flowers to her. He owned to a growing regard for her, alongside his incipient desire. He did not wish her to think ill of him, although he really believed she was too young at this time, in ways which were hard to quantify. Their understanding of life differed dangerously. He was not patient enough with her, or she with him…the list was endless. But it was clear that she was not sending any letter to break off their liaison.

The flowers arrived in the form of a luxurious and expensive bouquet: roses and gardenias and gentler kinds of small flowers topped by an exquisite orchid, but the overall effect on her was not positive.

He had signed the card: *"With Best Wishes… A.F."* Could he be any more formal or aloof! She carried them through the house, firstly taking them to her bedroom then changing her mind and bringing them downstairs and along to her art room, all the while seething with frustration and uncertainty.

'Best Wishes'? Who wrote that on a card to a woman he had kissed intimately? Unless he regretted the action and was salving his conscience! Obviously, he meant to fob her off, while attempting to remain in favour in general.

It was beyond insulting. She worked herself up into a temper, alone and unwitnessed by anyone in the isolation of her art room, and spoke aloud to relieve her awful misgivings and anger to Gertrude, the cat, who had taken to following her that day, drawn by her dark mood no doubt, as only cats could be.

But the containing of her frustration was impossible. Her feelings required an outlet, and she bashed the bouquet of flowers against the easel and the work table and eventually only some of the roses and the smallest flowers had survived. The bouquet was a tattered mess. Less than a quarter of its original size. She gained comfort from the thought of wasting his money, and the fact that he would be in ignorance about it, even while she felt some sympathy for the flowers whose glorious innocence and purity pained her even more.

Then she picked out the surviving roses, a couple of miniature carnations and the sturdier orchid, and placed them in a vase of water on a table in the dimly lit passageway beyond the art room door where no-one would see them.

Polly spotted them sometime later and thinking they had been forgotten about carried them into the main hall and placed them on the large Welsh dresser beside the front doors. Wondering at their diminished appearance.

Her mother then caught sight of them on her entrance later in the day—an expert *par-excellence* on indoor floral decor—and she fished out the card which loitered in the mess of mossy fibres supplied by the florist in a small sunken container to give them longer life. This container fitted perfectly in the large vase Melissa had found but rendered the flowers the sort of miserable appearance of a woman dressed in a gown too large in a setting inappropriate; they looked quite pathetic and not up to the usual standard of arrangement on which Marguerite Shaw prided herself. Nevertheless, Marguerite managed to read the soggy card and its inscription.

"Look at this…" she said to Giles as he passed through the hallway, and Giles Shaw read the card.

"Not very warm, is it?" claimed Marguerite. "Not what one would expect…and such a paltry little bunch…"

Giles stared at the flowers, nonplussed at the state of them and the size and unsure what to make of it. Then he looked at Marguerite blankly. What did she expect him to say!

"Of course…" she said hurriedly, "I am just surprised she is showing an interest at all with her dislike of the idea of marriage."

"Then he can't have very high hopes for himself in that respect…" uttered Giles in conclusion. "If he finds her attitude satisfactory."

"No, no, Giles, you are quite wrong, my dear…so many couples have rows before they see reason and become betrothed," argued Marguerite.

Giles regarded her blandly. "I think you may be backing a lame horse there, Maggie…they were having a set-to last Saturday in the garden according to Philips…"

Philips was Giles' personal valet and told him things about the house activities that he may have missed and needed to be aware of.

"How does Philips know this?" asked his wife, rather miffed.

"The gardener told him in the ale house…and then he asked John who also told him." Giles pulled off his boots while sitting on the bottom stair, which Marguerite found annoying in the extreme when there was a perfectly good wooden settle nearby. "He was taking her off somewhere against her will…and she was appealing to him to stop…"

"Good God, Giles!" cried Marguerite. "*Against her will!* Why did you not mention this before?"

"I thought you'd heard… I thought she'd have told you…"

"She tells me very little, you know how secretive she is."

"Then again, Maggie, I have other worries a'sides her antics," said Giles.

"But…but…" She floundered for words. "That sounds serious…what was he about to do to her, do you imagine?"

"Well, it won't be anything causing a hanging offence…he ain't daft and he has his position to consider…"

"John is not trustworthy in these matters," she said tartly. "I will go and ask Philips myself…where is he?"

"Leave him be…he's pressing me a shirt for tomorrow. He's the only one does it as I like 'em done."

"Then I must ask your mother…she will know…she was with them playing cards on Saturday… I will drive over and find out what is going on between them."

Giles made noises of weariness and rubbed his hand over his face. "Not a'fore you've told 'em to hurry the dinner, I hope." He flung his muddy boots down on the shiny tiled flooring where anyone might fall over them or see them upon entry and Marguerite summoned the footman to remove them.

"Those flowers look to me as if they've been dragged through a hedge…" Giles remarked, pausing to give them a second glance, "And it looks as if there should have been more of 'em…not that I'm the expert!"

His wife studied them more closely. Why had she not gleaned this with her expertise! She tutted and shook her shoulders and then glided towards the kitchens, her second-best taffeta rustling like springtime leaves as she went.

* * *

The next morning, she found her mother-in-law of little help; perhaps deliberately, or because she was having one of her difficult memory days.

Marguerite suspected the former—she was constantly annoyed by Jemima's loyalty to Melissa and the reciprocation Melissa gave to it. Jemina and Melissa were two of a kind in Marguerite's estimation, except that Melissa had the benefit of a better upbringing and more social awareness of the niceties—when it suited her. But they were both self-willed and inclined to being a law unto themselves, as were some of Giles' sisters.

"Lars, Maggie!" moaned Jemima in the sitting room at her eldest daughter's home. "I can't be expected to remember what was said and when… I scarcely remember who was there…that good-looking young fellow with the blonde hair who carried me to bed… I remember him square enough…" Jemima grinned her wickedest grin and ruminated while sucking a peppermint and gazing out of the window. "He has a body like Jago's…slim yet solid…he has Jago's forthright manner too…"

Marguerite waited in great impatience for Jemima to release the more prurient memories of her late husband and his masculinity, and eventually she said. "He was not best pleased, the blonde feller… Anthony something! Yes, that's him…that I do recall…he brought some other young feller with him…tall and good to gaze on…but beyond that 'tis a blur… I know I took two good hands in the cards and Gregory played the Chopin for me…wonderful as always!"

"Yes, but what happened in the garden between Anthony and Melissa?" persisted Marguerite.

"How should I know that?" retorted Jemima and then fell back in the chair and rested a while to remember. "I think t'other fellow went out and fetched Melissa back…he was of a fret after she left for the garden…but what was afoot I don't know… I told 'em all about Jago…they wanted to know…they found it fascinating and had me tell the whole story…" Jemima smiled fondly.

"Good Lord above," muttered Marguerite below Jemima's hearing. The Jago saga was best left to history in her view, though everyone found it entertaining—if they were given the chance to hear it—and she did not dare say too much to deter the telling of it; Giles adored his mother and wanted only her happiness in her declining years. He saw nothing wrong with his parents' past and heritage. "How did they part? Melissa and Fairchild?" Marguerite asked. "What was the mood between them?"

"Melissa and who?" Jemima was slowly returning from the mists of time.

"Anthony Fairchild…the blonde gentleman," prompted her daughter-in-law.

"Seemed well enough…though he is very close and does not give much away…bit like Lissy, come to think…but with more gracious manners, 't 'as to be said! I think he finds her too rude betimes…from the bits I bothered listening to…t'other feller was saying something of the kind to her…advising her not to be so uncivil."

"Yes, just as I thought…" Marguerite's tone was anguished. "She is already in the business of deterring him with her unconventional way of going about."

"I wouldn't call it unconventional by rights," Jemima said in defence of her grandchild. "More like direct and homely."

Marguerite was gathering her belongings, not in the mood for time-wasting on useless missions. "Homely isn't what is needed now, Mother…he is an educated man of notability in the borough, not a tradesman…she has plenty of time to show him the homely side of herself when they are wed… She is like to some kind of gypsy…and a flibbertigibbet…her and Melanie both."

"Lars, don't mention her… Mr t'other-feller was put out by her tea antics… I can tell you that much…he'd been told of 'em a'fore hand, it was plain…and even Gregory had strong views on it…"

"We all had strong views on it," cried Marguerite. "Nothing short of flagrant…and that dress Melissa was wearing on Saturday! No petticoats to speak of…"

Jemima gave a croaking laugh and pushed the mint to one side of her mouth to speak. "That may be so's he can get at her better when they're alone…"

Marguerite was beyond words for a moment. Her mother-in-law was shameless in delicate matters. "I hope, Mother, he will not be *'getting at her'* at all, until he has a ring on her finger…"

Jemima sucked the mint fervently. "Come down off it, Maggie…we're not in a convent…and a man wants to know what he's buying for his blunt a'fore he lays it on the table. He'll know what he's about…a fellow like that. He'll have experience a plenty with women to know what's enough…he ain't that floristry lad she keeps company with…far from it."

Marguerite made haste to depart, shutting out the visions of her daughter and Fairchild in compromising situations. The way Jemima construed these things in her quaint Cornish style was unthinkable.

"I fear what Fairchild will say of it to other people," she said in dignified conclusion.

"Well, I'm saying no more…" proclaimed Jemima. "'t ain't my job…and a'sides, I have only my instinct to go on…they'll work it out themselves…if they're not interfered with." She stuck a larger sweet into her mouth, preventing further speech.

Marguerite climbed into the phaeton with the groom. The roads were perilous still and she never drove herself in such weather. She deliberated on the slow and careful drive home, hoping that Melissa was not going to turn out like Amaelia, Giles youngest sister—beautiful but wild and disinclined to the conventions, notorious now in her middling years for affairs outside of her marriage.

Melissa had the same European blood courtesy of Giles and saw life as an open road to discovery; her quite cool and reserved manner disguising it adequately except in matters of her need for freedom. Marguerite decided she would call next on her sister, Dorothea, and share the situation with her over tea and a sisterly chat.

* * *

Meanwhile, at the Shaw residence, Melissa and Melanie were on the first-floor balcony practising dance steps for Melanie's nuptial celebrations on the coming Saturday. This was done with a frivolous noisiness which was characteristic of all they undertook when together. They had decided they should learn the Gavotte—a boisterous and fairly new fashionable dance, and then they could teach it to the other guests who would follow and pick up the steps quite quickly. Melanie had brought a sketchy map of movement on the dance and perused the paper on which it was scrawled.

Having listened to it described, Melissa seized Melanie's hand in a fashion she thought emulated a male dance partner. This was not the way things should be done and Melanie was calling for her to lighten her touch as she guided her, but Melissa paid no attention and the resultant effect made the dance clumsy and inelegant. Peals of laughter rang out about the house as they cavorted. They were interrupted by Giles who told them to be quieter as he wrote letters in his study.

Giles was fairly tolerant of this kind of hullabaloo and did not see the giddy propensities of girls as the worst cardinal sin—having been raised with so many sisters—unless it was in the drawing room or the dining room or other formal spaces.

"Can you not do that in the library?" he called up from the hall and Melissa went to the top of the staircase and swept him a curtsey. She was always careful to show him due respect, and he was always placated by it. He allowed her egalitarian privilege that he had not allowed to her brothers. Melanie came to stand beside her and swept him a curtsey in her turn.

"Papa, dearest, we cannot use the library!" exclaimed Melissa. "There is cleaning and polishing taking place in there. But we must learn these steps for the wedding feast…"

"Then do it more quietly please."

"We are sorry to have disturbed you…" she said.

"Yes, we are very sorry…" echoed Melanie. "We will be more restrained."

"We will!" agreed Melissa and gave another brief curtsey.

"There's good girls," Giles sighed in a paternal voice, as if they were still ten, and disappeared again. He was awed by the importance of the wedding preparations and his long association with George Petersham, Melanie's father. The galumphing about continued.

Melanie had put on a silk stole which was to be passed between the female dancers as they moved. Melissa caught hold of it in an excess of enthusiasm to pull Melanie around in the opposite direction. The stole tore and was quite tattered and almost in half. They cursed and Melissa held together the two parts and inspected it. "I am deeply aggrieved…" she told Melanie, "And very sorry, but I will replace it, I promise."

Melanie stared in some sadness at the accessory as Melissa relapsed into giggles and leaned against the wall.

"Wretched, clumsy girl…" cried Melanie in mock rage and grabbed the stole from her and twisted it into a knotted rope and began chasing her along the landing, whipping her with it carelessly from the rear.

"Stop…that hurts…" She attempted to take the weapon back, without success, and they careered up and down the landing and staircase, shushing each other in vain; an unstoppable whirl of excitement and hilarity. Melanie whipped her harder. "You must become accustomed to it…'tis what will happen to you when Fairchild finally has you in his clutches…"

Melissa went again for the stole and missed and tripped down several stairs and grabbed the wooden stair rail then landed on her behind. Melanie flew past her down towards the first-floor landing. "Except he will probably use a riding crop…"

"Indeed, he will not," Melissa shrieked and dashed after her. Then she saw Polly ascending the first flight of stairs making shushing sounds. The laughter continued while the stole lay discarded on the floor and Melanie adjusted her clothing. Polly leapt the last two steps and came at them, waving her hand frantically. Melissa brought herself to a standstill and was silent. Polly gestured with her finger to the space below and Melissa moved to the balcony to look down.

Anthony Fairchild was standing in the hall. She let out a sound of dismay and Melanie scrambled to her feet and joined her. They instinctively shrank back out of sight and Melissa hissed. "How much do you suppose he heard?"

Melanie did not reply but stepped calmly to the balcony rail and looked down on him. He was gazing upwards with his customary neutral and dignified demeanour. "Anthony, what a charming surprise..." she trilled. He was not fooled and did not reply. Melissa took Polly's arm and pulled her through one of the vacant bedroom doors. "How much did you hear?" she asked and Polly said, "Enough...but he may not have heard, he was below in the hall."

She felt herself ready to panic and was light headed from too much fast movement and giddiness. "He is here for Mr Damien," said Polly. "I am about to tell him."

Damien's workroom was next to hers on the second landing and Polly continued up the stairs while Melissa went forwards again with more confidence and joined Melanie, holding her position with dignity amid his stony silence. "Miss Shaw..." he said on seeing her. "I trust I am not interrupting something important?"

"We were rehearsing a dance for the wedding feast," said Melissa.

"I see..." he replied.

Melanie felt her trembling beside her and put a hand on her arm. "Shall we come down to join you?" she enquired of Fairchild. He considered matters, his eyes not leaving Melissa. They were both of them quite locked in a shared gaze: two people stunned by sudden encounter. "It won't be necessary... I am here to see Damien Shaw but briefly..."

Melissa was without her faculties of speech. "I trust you received my flowers," he enquired next.

"They are in the hall..." Melissa told him, "Behind you on the dresser."

"I did not at first notice them," he said, having glanced at the paltry bunch.

"I split them to put them in several vases," she lied.

"I see." He was not sure what to believe.

"Say 'thank you'…" said Melanie in a hushed tone and Melissa stared at her uncomprehendingly.

"She is urging you to say thank you!" he said in his unruffled manner. "But never mind… I will take it as read."

"Yes…thank you…" Melissa stammered. "They are quite lovely."

"What little there is left of them," he muttered darkly.

"Though why you bothered, I cannot think," she blurted.

She allowed Melanie to pull her backwards, putting her fingers over her lips to stay her from more rudeness. "For heaven's sake, don't begin with your uncivil remarks…'tis some kind of an omen, my foolery! Do you not see?"

They stepped forwards to the rail of the balcony and gazed down on him in unison. "She will join you directly, I am sure," Melanie said.

"She need not trouble… I see that you have more important things to do."

At that point, Damien appeared and regarded them with disdain before descending into the hall. They went into Melissa's room and shut the door and stared at each other. Melanie had pronounced the bouquet to be a token of the fact that it was not the end.

Melissa disagreed; she could not see that the inscription of *'Best Wishes'* was anything but a plea for finality. Melanie stated that they had possibly cost him half a week's salary, if Melissa's description of them were accurate, and that spoke volumes. An impasse was reached.

"'tis some kind of reckoning time…him appearing just now…but whatever you do, if you must go after him, do not insult him…you are again wearing one of those dresses with little under garment…" The remark was said quite humorously and was meant to lift the mood.

Melissa looked down at herself in the casual day dress of fine blue linen imported from County Galway. Her need to have his attention on things unresolved, her longing for his physical presence…none of it was understandable. She paced in uncertainty while Melanie rested on the bed, watching her with tolerant resignation to foolhardy attachment.

Until Damien's heavy tread was again heard on the landing and his door opened and closed.

Melissa sprang up and out of the door and ran to the landing window and looked down to see the side of the house. Sure enough, he soon emerged from the front of the house and came around the corner in the direction of the stables.

She knew from the way he was attired that he had ridden there. She lifted her skirt and began to run to the back staircase giving immediate access to the side of the house, Melanie shouting to her to think carefully before she spoke with him.

* * *

She caught up with him as he was heading into the stables. He retraced his steps towards her and they regarded each other with the uncertainty of partial acquaintances. "I suppose you think me churlish and rude again? About your flowers?" she began.

"I am accustomed to your lack of graciousness…" he said without inflection.

"I could not understand what was meant by your inscription."

"Really! Did I perhaps write it in another language by mistake?"

She flared immediately. "You see! You must begin with your sarcasm…which is far more acceptable, it seems, than my rudeness…which is not rudeness at all, but my forthright manner…" She walked away, turning her back and then turning again. "*Best Wishes*'…what did you mean by it?" She swung around and began to move away; the question left to be rhetoric. He followed at a leisurely pace until she was at the border of the drive and the low stone wall embracing the manicured flower beds. "I do not know what you expect," she said, pausing her stride.

"I expect nothing," he replied with simplicity.

She was suddenly seized with the notion to climb on to the wall, a mere three feet in height, and then walk its perimeter slowly. He watched this absurdity in fascination. Unused to seeing females climb walls—apart from his nieces who were below the age of twelve. He stood still amid a small sense of fear. Where did the fear come from? What she might do next which he may not feel equal to dealing with! It was unnerving and he was impatient with himself. This latest antic, this towering over him, was probably her quest for power following on his show of strength in the rose garden the last time they had met.

She was balanced on the narrow stone wall, experiencing a heady sense of not being in the present. Then she took a small run and leapt towards him, placing her arms around his neck and wrapping her legs around him to perch on him like a lithe monkey, her face at the level of his. She kissed him ardently on the mouth and he responded for mere seconds. Then gripping her elbows, he lifted her and set her on her feet. "You must think of where we are…" He was completely overset by her actions and fell silent and stared at her. Her magnetism was working on him of itself and he was unable to form words.

"I am in the family garden… I feel quite at home," she said blithely.

His eyes were slanted against the sunlight. "Even so, you cannot just…"

"Just what? Begin kissing…the way you did in the library?"

"You cannot jump on men in that manner and not expect…"

"Expect what?" He had no answer and again she wrapped her arms around his neck, shorter than him now by three inches, and kissed him with more passion and held fast to the collar of his shorter coat worn for riding, rough to the touch and made for the weather. He could not easily prise her away.

But eventually he did so and put her at arm's length. His hair was slicked back with some kind of oil and darkened in colour, flattened against his head, as if he had just emerged from a lake after swimming. It changed him considerably; into someone she scarcely knew. A million miles away from how he appeared on social occasions.

"That is not what you said in the library that day…" she declared.

He was never going to be allowed to forget the library incident, whatever he did. "That was indoors and not out in the open where anyone might see us." He strove not to sound flustered—like the 'maiden aunt' she had compared him to previously.

"I care not for that… I do not care who sees or what they think… I am not…" she stopped abruptly before telling him she was not a hypocrite. She smiled a sly knowing smile and he waited, sensing her unformed insult. "Stay and take some tea…" she entreated.

"I cannot…" He was moving away from the situation, yet again. "I am due at the Grange for a tutorial with the senior boys at three thirty…perhaps in a few days?"

"You say that, but you will simply disappear again…" she claimed.

"I have not disappeared…" he asserted. Why was it that females of all ages demanded their requests be catered to immediately! He thought once more of his small nieces; requiring him to come and look at something they had made or discovered or were in the act of making: when he promised to accompany them after concluding his conversations with other adults, but then forgot, so that next time they pounced straight away and recriminated him, then he was obliged to restore his integrity by going with them to the fairy glade and sitting in it for ten minutes in case a fairy should appear, drinking milk from miniscule cups made especially for fairies, as they chattered to him more on the nonsense. Wasting his time and satisfying themselves with his full attention.

Melissa Shaw now was waiting for his further reply to her invite… She, like his nieces, had all the time she needed to take to entertain herself, she was not encumbered by a heavy schedule of duty. Possibly she would never understand his attitude to life. Of a similar class in society, they had diametrically opposed worlds. He looked down and turned to go—the notion about their worlds rivening the path he needed to follow.

"I thought we had mended sails…" she said. "After we discussed things that day…when you decided to forgive me…and issued your *last warnings*…" She pulled her mouth into a long thin line to show her contempt for his 'last warnings'. They stared in opposite directions, past each other, strangers on a temporary path. Then she looked at him afresh, with a new expression of hope and candour. "We do not have to kiss…" she went on hurriedly. "If you do not want to… I shall not try to make you…"

Turning his face away, his grin escaped for a second or two, out of his control. Her sincerity, her moral honesty, was a pin-prick of sharp light brighter than the sun and pierced his throat where words were almost born. It was painful and it shocked him. He had not felt anything like it, since Lottie. "I have not said I do not want to…" He hated prevarication but found himself at its mercy. "I am just not certain 'tis wise…"

She paused before blurting out her truth. "I do not see what wisdom has to do with it… I think I am beginning to be drawn to you…"

He was overwhelmed by self-consciousness, unbecoming to his manhood. "I thought you loathed and despised me!"

"Well, perhaps I do…perhaps I have both states within me."

"It is sometimes said that hatred can be an aphrodisiac…"

"I do not hate you," she said softly. "That is too strong a word!"

He walked some way towards where he was headed then turned for the last time. "Melissa, have a care how you behave…you take far too many chances with your welfare…"

"Do I?"

"You run around the countryside ill clad…throw yourself on men…when you know little of what you are doing."

"You are not just any man…and 'twas you who started the kissing, that day in the library."

He straightened the collar of his coat, the situation off at a tangent again before he had time to explore his feelings…"And I take exception to your saying I am ill clad… I acquire all my clothes at the best places…" She made the remark to delay him, knowing full well his meaning.

"I meant that the clothes are unequal to the weather…"

"And as for my being reckless!" She was beginning to feel emboldened. "I am sure you are far more reckless than me…when you are carousing."

"What do you know of my carousing?"

"'tis the sort of thing I can imagine you doing."

He thought of his private life. He could not make such a liar of himself to blatantly deny it. He had a sudden flash of memory of them in the classroom; Melissa always careful with her overt behaviour, her subtle ambiguous retorts. And all the while he had been mistaken, her character was bolder and braver and more honest than he could have possibly envisaged. She was waiting for what he would reveal next, but he shook his head in a final denouncement of the conversation and made a gesture of resignation with his hand. She noticed his deerskin gloves and stared at them with rapt attention, everything he wore fascinated her, and heard herself tell him, "I cannot say I care for your hair today…"

Then she feared for a second that he would construe it as an insult. He ran his hand over the side of his hair, securing it behind his left ear. "It needs attention and I have not had time to visit the barber…whereas yours, on the contrary, is beautiful."

Her gleaming chestnut hair, free and loose, streaming over her shoulders and framing her face with its youthful glowing skin. She cast her eyes downwards and to one side, modestly, and smiled. "Oh…so 'tis not a permanent change, that style?" His compliment had not distracted her.

"No, 'tis merely an occasional measure…"

"Good. I am relieved."

His self-consciousness was about to swallow him whole, his vulnerability a huge shadow of doubt.

"I expect there is not a tutorial at all," she said provocatively. "… I expect you are going to meet a lady…"

"I am not meeting a lady…" he said impatiently and turned with determination to leave once and for all. "And I shall return…"

Why in God's Name had he promised her that! He was losing what little control he had gained of the situation. He rallied swiftly. "What fanciful little madams you are…you and Miss Petersham."

She remained silent and looked wary.

"And on the topic of fanciful notions…" he intoned. "You may be assured… I do not own a riding crop…"

Struck by mortification, her breath seemed to lodge in her chest as she heaved it into her lungs.

"Perhaps you would *prefer* me to acquire one?" he said before entering the stables.

She retreated in haste so as not to offer any reaction.

* * *

Melanie was still lying on the bed. Melissa sank down next to her and kicked off her shoes and flopped onto her back. "He heard us…everything," she announced, levelling her breath. "Even your comment about the riding crop."

Melanie continued to lie with closed eyes. "Of course he heard. He always had eyes and ears like a midden rat, if you recall. What did he say about it?"

"Nothing at first, then he turned on leaving to assure me he does not own one."

"He would say that at this stage," said Melanie.

"Then he asked if I would *prefer* him to acquire one…being sarcastic."

"Or he wants you to think he was being sarcastic!" Melanie drawled. "You did not call him anymore names, did you?"

"No, I almost called him a hypocrite, but I stopped in time… I am mortified… I cannot believe the coincidence."

"I do not believe in coincidence…" Melanie objected.

"But what do you suppose he thinks now?" enquired Melissa.

"That we talk about him! How happy that must make him withal. Though viewing him today from the balcony, I am persuaded he is an extremely prime specimen of masculinity…and it has to be said…" She paused and considered her next statement, glancing sidelong at Melissa. "In fact my mother has heard gossip about him…He was invited to dinner by Lady Moncrief, wanting to introduce him to her daughter…"

Melissa resorted to wit. "Good grief! Not Lady Moncrief!"

Melanie laughed. "Lady M is on some charitable committee and came upon him at a meeting which also involved that Foundation he is so fond of…"

"Really!" Melissa said with feigned indifference.

"But according to Mama, he has declined the invite on the grounds of too little time…and Lady M cannot think why!"

"He smells match-making, most probably."

"Of course he does…there can be no other reason why the Moncriefs would wish to solicit his company."

"What is she like, their daughter?" She became tense for seconds in anticipation of the description she may hear.

Melanie took a sighing breath. "Frightful in every way, apparently…'tis even rumoured they are laying odds down at Almack's on which decade she may actually find a husband."

Melissa remained serious and rose and twitched the drapes.

"What is it that worries you so?" enquired Melanie.

"When I have been with him 'tis as if he is still present…I feel him close to me…"

"Dear God! You have it very badly for him…there is no doubt."

"If he leaves the room 'tis as if he has not gone at all. I see his face and the intense expressions he has when he is thinking. I could watch him forever, you know…'tis both exhilarating and calming…"

"And perhaps not such a good thing…"

"Why not? Does it not signify the deepest of attraction between people?"

"I am not sure 'tis wise to give oneself over so utterly to another person…"

This was a new Melanie; a woman Melissa was not accustomed to. A long pause took them to different mind places, then Melanie ventured: "I suppose the only thing to know now is whether he feels the same."

Melissa sat bolt upright and stared at her. "Do you suppose men feel those things?"

"Of course! They are the same species as us are they not! Simply with some appendages added."

337

The laughter came, as always, and carried through the upper stories and the opened windows. Until Melissa said. "We are leaving our girlhood behind…soon we will be matrons and our carefree days will be long gone…"

"Yes," concurred Melanie. "Though we must always strive to maintain our spirit of freedom and fun…" She reached for her friend's hand without looking, until their fingers clasped. They held tightly to each other's hands and the present moment, which was not filled with 'unknowables'. Safe behind the curtain separating their girlhood from the possibilities within marriage.

"We perhaps should rest…" ventured Melanie in a weary voice. "I have wedding preparation discussions with my parents and Geoffrey's at four…what do you have?"

Melissa was loath to focus but roused her vocal cords. "I am finishing the oil of your mother's dog. And I must start the painting I promised my cousin Rex…for his wife…'tis her birthday next week and I promised it him for Monday."

"Painting of what?" Melanie droned.

"A small pastel of lily o'the valley amid fern…"

"Sounds dreary and morbid…"

Melissa yawned loudly. "She inclines to morbidity…she imagines she will die in childbirth soon."

"Perhaps she will…" uttered Melanie in exhaustion.

"Especially if she imagines it…she…" Melissa finished the sentence in her head and not aloud and there ensued a dozing state as they floated on individual mind planes and drifted amid their concerns and impressions. Until they awoke almost simultaneously and Melissa returned to the subject of her emotional quandary. "Before I knew that he had heard everything, I did something very outrageous," she said.

"I know… I was watching from the window!"

"Was it very terrible?" She made a theatrical face which the other girl could not see from her prone position on the bedspread.

"'twas very impressive…'twas the stuff of strong and fearless women…your womanhood is upon you fully these days." Melanie's usual self seemed to be reinstated.

Melissa raised herself on one elbow and peered at her. "Perhaps you had better tell me again about this act of union…this thing that happens when men have the highest state of arousal and women succumb…"

The Wise and the Willing

Some nights later Fairchild joined Nicholas Stevenson and his wife in their home after dinner. The month of March was well underway, with the sort of deceptively clement weather it often brought, only to snatch it away again and return the land to winterish conditions. But for now, it was mild and tranquil with a clear night sky. And he pondered—having tethered his horse to a garden post for quicker get away—on what to say exactly to his superior. He had met Louisa Stevenson a few times since her marriage to Stevenson two years before. He was struck by how very at ease and homely they were together in their domestic setting. It was what he would wish for himself.

Louisa was tending the drawing room fire and Stevenson was trying to take over the task. Fairchild sat in an armchair and watched impassively. He wanted the meeting over; he wanted Stevenson to understand his decision. They had known each other a considerable time, it was Stevenson who had put him forward for the position of deputy head when he had become headmaster.

"Louisa, let me do it…" Stevenson was saying. "Give me the poker."

"No!" said his wife. "You do not do it rightly."

"That large slab of coal will choke it," he told her.

"'twill not…the fire will burn more slowly and take better, which is what I intend," she said firmly.

"Meantime, the room will be cold." Stevenson made a grab for the poker as she held it away from him. He reached around her and tried to take it and a minor skirmish took place in some private world of careless intimacy. "Stop interfering with me, Nicholas!" cried Louisa in semi-righteousness.

"Good Lord, woman, be careful using words like that when I have three large glasses of burgundy inside me."

"And cease with your ribald remarks…" she said, "You are just showing off."

"If a man cannot show off in his own home, I fail to see where he might…" retorted Stevenson. Their arms wrestled and she let him take the poker. "You will have coal dust on your dress…" he said in an ameliorative manner.

"And you will have it all over the carpet… I know more about fires than you…"

Fairchild thought of Giles Shaw, and consequently his daughter, then realised Stevenson was addressing him. "…you will be unsurprised to hear that she knows a lot more about a lot of things than me!" He gave her back the poker. "Have it your own way then…"

"Pour our guest a drink," she said. "I have been tending coals since I was a girl."

"What a strange claim, my love!" remarked Stevenson in majestic satire. "Anyone would imagine I took you from some mine in Yorkshire."

Louisa laughed loudly, while her husband lifted the whiskey decanter to Fairchild.

"No, thank you, Nick, I will abstain," said Fairchild.

Stevenson feigned great shock. "Abstain! What ails you?"

"I drank too much last night… I often have trouble rising in the morning these days."

"Imagine how you'll be at my age!" replied Stevenson wryly.

"You will gain no sense from him at this time of night…" Louisa told Fairchild, assured that he knew her husband's true self-from working closely with him day in and day out. "Having relinquished his role as headmaster he resorts to the role of clown."

"Of course! How else does one preserve the balance of one's sanity!" Stevenson said. "Tony, are you sure you will not partake?"

"Maybe a glass of wine," said Fairchild.

Stevenson poured him the last of the burgundy from dinner and sat and looked at him from his place of worldly whimsy and waited. Louisa poked the coals, and all was domestic bliss for a few moments. "What is it?" asked Stevenson, pinching the bridge of his nose to assume a more professional frame of mind. "Must be something grave or you would be elsewhere at this time!"

Fairchild drew breath and re-settled in the chair, taking a few mouthfuls of the wine. "I am letting you know in person that I will be tending my resignation…"

Stevenson paused with his glass half way to his lips and attempted to speak but was at a loss. Even Louisa stopped her labours to look across.

"Resignation?" said Stevenson. "You are not serious?"

"Quite serious…"

"But why? Tony, you cannot have thought this through."

"I have thought it through…"

"Has something happened that I am unaware of?"

"No, but 'tis time I moved on."

"Moved on! What are we suddenly, a group of roaming tinkers?"

"Nick, be quiet and let him speak…" said Louisa, rising from the hearth and shaking out her skirts. She seated herself in the chair nearest the fire and took up embroidery on a frame which she made careless stabs at with a needle. Fairchild watched her rather than her husband—it was easier; she had beauty and a matured grace which radiated from her in the gentle lamplight and the glow of the fire. Sensing his attention, she offered, "You are perhaps unhappy, Anthony?"

"I am tired of having to explain my choice of profession!" he announced, gathering his wit and fortitude.

"What?" exclaimed Stevenson. "You jest…"

"I do not…people constantly remark on how unlike a schoolteacher I appear…how unlike the usual image of someone typical of our profession. I begin to feel like a fraud."

Stevenson stood and wandered over the room. "What utter rot!"

"Shush!" said Louisa softly and kept her eyes on her needlework. "Allow him time to gather his thoughts and speak."

Stevenson gazed at her; her wisdom on professional matters was always sound, he smiled at her before returning his attention to his deputy. Her grandfather had been one of the founding members of the academy, and she held a position on the board of governors.

"'tis true… I do feel like a fraud."

"'tis pure nonsense… I never met a finer teacher…how is one supposed to look? At your age you are meant to look…to look…"

"Handsome and well attired?" supplied the headmaster's wife lightly.

"Louisa, don't make him more conceited than he is…give him a few more years and he will soon assume the appropriate guise…harrowed, stooped and with a paunch…it comes to us all."

"Nicholas, you are not amusing…" she said, "Though doubtless you imagine so, with the wine."

Fairchild smiled at Louisa and she smiled back. "I never meant to teach for over long, you know that… I fell into it accidentally."

"As do many men…" said Stevenson, "But that does not mean 'tis wrong as a choice. You are excellent at what you do. The curriculum results are excellent and the conduct of the school has never been better. We are a fine partnership, you and I."

"Agreed, but…"

"But what?" persevered the head.

"I am thinking of making a business venture with Trim and someone else."

"Oh?" said Stevenson. He was feeling aggrieved when he really had no right to. "What kind of business?"

"A translation service…interpretation and translation of documents…for export merchants and so on."

"Splendid!" said Louisa and nodded approvingly.

"Don't encourage him, Louisa!" sighed Stevenson and she glared at him. "Nick, he is a free man, he may do what he wishes when he wants."

Stevenson paced and Fairchild looked abashed. He flushed a little and cleared his throat.

"There is more to it than that!" said Stevenson, sobering rapidly. "I can sense it."

Fairchild raised his brows and showed an open expression of honesty.

"Are you moving away?" enquired Louisa.

"No, no…we will set up here in Barton…with one more office in Cheshire perhaps."

"Splendid!" she said again.

"I shall give you a term's notice and will not leave until you have a replacement…" he informed Stevenson.

"I should damn well hope so…" the head rejoined, then laughed to cover his abrupt tone. "I cannot just lay my hands on deputies of your calibre at the drop of a hat."

"Dominic McCarthy might do!" Fairchild said.

"I doubt he'll accept…he is looking to return to Ireland soon…which you well know. So don't fob me off with that! Will you not reconsider?"

"He does not wish to," said Louisa, adding: "The governors will be most upset…you are well thought of in every sense, by staff and parents and governors." Louisa was herself fond of educational reform; corresponding with people of influence and championing from the sidelines. "But you must live your life as you see fit…" she said.

"Yes, yes…we know all that!" Stevenson paced a little more and then turned and addressed them both. "And now that the homilies and platitudes have been dealt with, perhaps we can talk some truth…will you stay for financial inducement?"

"No," said Fairchild.

"A share of the equity perhaps?" The profits of the school were healthy and getting healthier and Stevenson already had hefty equity himself. "It would be a pity to waste your efforts. Perhaps you might consider working part time? Say as Head of Languages for the senior grade, the university aspirants?"

"I might…but I will relinquish the deputy headship."

There was a long pause and no-one felt equal to breaking it. Stevenson had helped him climb a ladder which many would envy in the profession. He heaved a heavy breath and drank more of the wine, then said. "And the other thing is… I have become involved with a former pupil."

Louisa made a sound which stifled her surprise and Stevenson stood still for a moment or two then swigged more whisky. "How *former* is this pupil?" He winced slightly for what he may hear.

"She is nineteen or twenty, no more, but not less…" said Fairchild.

"An excellent age difference!" declared Louisa from her chair in comfort.

"Probably too young," declared Fairchild almost inaudibly.

"No, no, you are not more than eight and twenty surely?" Louisa said.

"I am thirty!" he offered flatly.

"Well, then! We women live longer withal…"

"Will I remember this wench?" Stevenson asked.

"'tis Melissa Shaw!"

"Of the Shaw Land Company?"

"Indeed."

Louisa and Nicholas exchanged quiet glances and then both looked with appreciation at Fairchild.

"Quite a bit of wealth there!" Stevenson remarked at length. "Her grandfather was the Spaniard who started one of the larger shipping companies in Bristol, I believe…"

"Yes. I received the full history from his widow last weekend," Fairchild smiled. "Over afternoon tea and a game of cards."

"You *are* well in," said Louisa, much impressed.

"Her brother, Damien Shaw, is working a little for the Foundation…he's an experimental chemist…"

"Been busy on the social ladder, have you not!" said Stevenson.

"The Foundation tasked me with meeting him, then to introduce him to Rufus Henderson who is a chemist himself…it was quite accidental. I came into contact with her again when visiting their home."

More silence while this information was absorbed.

"So, all is well and set for a union?" trilled Louisa.

"Not entirely," Fairchild looked pained and shifted about in the chair.

"And you are leaving the school because of this liaison?" queried Stevenson.

"She indirectly helped me reach the decision within myself."

"How?"

"'tis hard to explain."

"Can you at least try?" Stevenson was determined to talk him out of it and it was not subtly done.

"She is scathing about education in general," began his deputy, but the head interrupted. "I never heard anything so inexplicable…that a girl of her social privilege should decry education is beyond belief."

Louisa kept her eyes on the embroidery. "Not everyone is an advocate of education, Nick. A lot of people feel similarly…they see it as an incursion upon liberty…you live in a cloistered world."

Stevenson was a first-class mathematician and wrote books on the subject. He was immersed in that side of academia and saw it as a gateway to a better dawn.

"Some of the more religious elements of society, for one…the puritans and the trade merchants amongst others," Louisa embellished.

"Well, those latter beggars see everything in terms of wealth!" Stevenson opined. "Melissa Shaw's family are not religious, are they?"

"Not that I have noticed. She is a painter…" Fairchild offered, as if religion and painting were not mutually inclusive. It caused Louisa to laugh in a carefree manner, and her husband to stare at her as he failed to see the amusement.

"And does she claim to have gained nothing from her time at school?"

"She thinks us tyrants and pedants," said Fairchild miserably.

"Does she now!" Stevenson was becoming less and less patient with this treatise of semi-romantic success and confusion. Louisa was laughing still, silently over her embroidery. There was nothing she had not heard before.

"Although she is sympathetic to the basic education of the poor…the alms school, for one thing."

"Magnanimous of her…" Stevenson muttered.

"She and her cousin, together with Susan Darnley, are organising a fundraising event for the alms schools in May…"

"That is much to her credit," said Louisa.

"She seems to think that once people can read and write they may formulate their own views of the world and life and be left to their devices…"

A master of sarcastic rhetoric in the best tradition of many teachers, Stevenson barked laughter and shook his head. "Does she also believe we should move back into caves so as not to have our freedom impeded by brick structures?"

Fairchild ignored this and said in dull tones. "She sees us as canting hypocrites…or at least she sees me that way…"

"Clearly she has addled your brains…" intervened Stevenson, "And romance has outweighed logic."

"I am confused in myself about what I think…and I would not call it a romance…as yet."

"Perhaps you should tell her to disappear and come back when she has grown up a little!" decreed the head.

"I have tried that…"

"And yet here she still is?" put in Louisa.

Stevenson sat down opposite him and assumed a look of scrutiny, "I am unable to understand any of this…do you?" he enquired of his wife.

"I think I may…they are inexplicably drawn to each other but unable to reconcile their day-to-day differences," offered Louisa.

Fairchild became more animated. "That is exactly it!"

"'tis not an uncommon theme… I expect a lot of it will have its roots in a struggle resulting from her being in his classroom and him having authority over her…"

"That is exactly it," Fairchild said again, relieved at gaining a female viewpoint.

"She cannot quite forgive you for being all powerful in her schooldays and at the same time wants to love you now as a woman…the dilemma must be painful for her."

"'tis painful for me too…but I suspect she enjoys it. In fact, I think she may see it as a game." He was quickly losing his former reserve.

"Ah!" said Louise darkly.

"Why does she not just accept that life changes?" Stevenson asked in tedium.

"Because she is a female…we are not as black and white as you are," Louisa threw back at him.

"She says she loathes and detests me," confided Fairchild. "Yet at the same time she…" He broke off, wondering if he should be this explicit in front of Mrs Stevenson.

"Yes? She what?" encouraged the lady of the house.

"… She kisses me with great ardour!"

"She does not loathe and detest you then, believe me!" Louisa strived not to laugh again for fear of him becoming further embarrassed. "She holds onto the past to have it over you, until she is sure!"

"Of what?" he enquired covetously.

"That you are not in reality these days some kind of tyrant."

He looked sharply at Louisa. "I have told her I will not apologise for those days…so we are at a stand-off."

"What have you to apologise for?" she asked.

"Ah well…" chimed in Stevenson, gazing at the ceiling. "Thereby hangs a tale!" He had remembered clearly the 'Henrietta and Anthony' daubing and the resultant consequences. He went on to outline the crime summarily for his wife.

"She thinks me overly severe in my reactions…monstrously callous…while they were just…just…" Fairchild stopped, again at a loss.

"Which reactions?" queried Louisa.

"His disciplinary measures, naturally…" supplied Stevenson. "'tis the hardest thing to gauge, putting a young male teacher in a classroom of teenage wenches. Bound to test his metal. When he arrived, they were accustomed to

Henry Stringer and Mistress Sullivan, both of whom allowed them to behave as they wished. Then in walks this fellow, the same age as their elder brothers…and they believed they could play him like a fiddle…and then discovered they could not…"

Fairchild looked at Louisa. "I merely made them pay attention and cease giggling."

"He introduced them to the meaning of classroom respect and conduct," Stevenson told her, "And what a shock it was for them…don't listen to his modest denials."

"I see…" Louisa said. "And this daubing of names led to…?"

The question hung in the air. Stevenson raised his brows at her to encourage the use of her imagination. "He is embarrassed about it… I will tell you later."

"I am not embarrassed about it," Fairchild protested. "I would own and defend the actions to anyone."

"Now he's boasting," claimed Stevenson with merriment. "No gainsaying him at the moment…"

"Pay no attention…" Louisa told Fairchild. "I warned you to not expect sense from him tonight."

Stevenson became grave and frowned with exaggerated intensity. "Nonsense, Louisa, I am merely making light of a heavy situation." They stared at him and he continued in a censorious way. "But let's make no mistake…the chalking incident was a huge piece of audacity and could not be left unchecked. He has nothing to apologise for. At the end of the day, they had a choice as to whether to behave themselves or not…"

"That is how I see it," Fairchild said. "But 'tis not the way she sees it."

"That is the only sane way to see it," said Stevenson in conclusion. "Your private life was none of their business! Where would it have ended, this flagrant use of chalk in the name of entertainment! And had you not acted then I would have done so as deputy head, as I told you at the time…"

"I tend to agree with Nick," Louisa said, "Having been that age myself and being very…very…"

"Do not say mischievous, please…"

"Teenage girls are not simply mischievous…they are often shockingly antagonistic," Louisa affirmed.

"Of course they are…the devil's own. Worse than lads when mismanaged," Stevenson intoned.

Then Louisa ventured, "I have not met her so I shall not say too much…but she may always hold this action, whatever it is, against you!"

The two men turned to her in disbelief, and Fairchild flushed darker. "Then that is it…we cannot go forwards."

"So, do not be hasty with the resignation," Stevenson said, his desperation rising again.

"Of course you can go forwards…" Louisa intoned. "There is a lot I could say regarding how a woman thinks, but I do not wish to do her an injustice or give away too much of the mysteries of our gender…"

"For pity's sake!" sighed Stevenson. "Can we have less of the mystery and more common sense?"

"She may even secretly respect you for your actions back then…with greater hindsight…"

He looked at Louisa with hope and she put a finger in the air to delay his comments. "But…she still may not forgive you…and even so, it may not stop her overcoming the past. Although she may not admit that, until she is sure you are no longer worthy of her former dire opinion of you."

"Yes, leave her to discover your worst side until you have her down the aisle," put in Stevenson.

"Nicholas, 'tis not a humorous matter," Louisa chided.

"Louisa, you will soon have reduced him to a self-abnegating wreck. He will be no good to us at all then…they will smell his contrition when he enters classrooms."

"Nonsense…" said Louisa breezily. "I am giving him a contrary perspective of the situation and he is astute enough to shape it to size."

Fairchild rose from the chair and crossed to the fire and looked into the flames for warmth. "That is the point as well…"

"What point?" sighed Stevenson wearily, losing the conversational thread. Fairchild cleared his throat and began like an orator at the start of a long address. "I carved out a role for myself in those first months… I assumed it like a costume on entering their presence. I still do…'tis a role, and I had to work hard to sustain it, but then it becomes actually a part of who I am…"

Lifting the whiskey decanter, Stevenson scoffed. "Do you imagine this is new? Very few of us are in reality the ogres children think we are… *'Falling into the job accidentally and assuming a false persona'*…what other unique and revelatory gems do you have to impart?"

"Nicholas!" his wife warned and glared at him with ferocious eyes. "Were he your age he might be familiar with cynical self-realisation…but he is not there yet…and not everyone is so adept at falsehood and posturing…"

"Posturing!" echoed Stevenson, relenting somewhat his dour mood. "How dare you, Madam! Are you accusing me of posturing?"

"Well, if the cap fits…" said his wife with delight.

"Hark, dear fellow…this is the kind of thing you will have to endure when married if you grovel and dissemble too much with her…"

"It will not reach that point," Louisa said. "Unless he acts with sensibility now…"

He was not listening to their banter but following his own thoughts. Husband and Wife paused to look at him and Louisa became earnest again. "Have you told her all that you have just told us?"

"Not in so many words…but I think she is coming to guess it and wants me to own to it."

"All is well then," said Stevenson with false heartiness.

"No, all is not well," said Fairchild. "She makes me question myself. I simply do not want to go back into dealing with female pupils for the sake of earning my living…"

Stevenson put his head in his hands and smoothed his forehead with his fingers, and then looked at Louisa, his amusement tinged once more by annoyance. "But you seldom deal with the girls now."

"No, but when Freddy Knox goes, for example, I shall perhaps be obliged to take them for French…and I simply do not wish to."

"But they are so much better these days are they not! They know of your fearsome reputation and…" Stevenson tailed off, aware of his faux pas.

"You see my point!" Fairchild said.

"I do not see it at all…" rallied the head. "'tis similar to saying that a surgeon may blunt his scalpel in case people become afraid he'll cut them accidentally…"

"Ignore him!" chirruped Louisa. "Being clever for the sake of cleverness."

"You see, this is what happens…they ridicule and overrule you at their whim," said Stevenson and Louisa raised her voice an octave. "You are doing it again, Nicholas, and making light of everything…"

Fairchild ignored the return of the banter, too aware of things between himself and Melissa that he had missed previously. He was between annoyance and optimism and could see no balance yet. "I see how she is dismantling a part of my character before my eyes..." he continued, staring into the fire. "She knows precisely what she is doing...and she may not be able to stop herself...even despite my warnings."

"Which warnings?" asked Louisa astutely. He ignored the question.

"Sounds to me like she is urging you to resurrect and strengthen that detested part of yourself," Stevenson remarked. "Goading you into adverse reactions."

"That is often what it feels like!" he conceded.

"She is doing both things," Louisa supplied omnisciently. "She desires to see both sides of him, but she wants the tender side to win out...then, she is sure."

Fairchild thought of Melissa at her most provoking, hurling insults at him in the garden and refusing to retreat yet pleading with him not to do what it was obvious he would do. He was wrought with confusion on a subject Louisa Stevenson understood very clearly as a woman. He saw in his mind's eye her blue linen dress of a few days earlier, her walking along the wall.

It was such a pungent memory she might have been in the room. He wanted her. The physical longing for her was in his throat, so powerful was her essence. He crossed to Louisa and took her hand and kissed her fingers. "You have helped me, Ma'am...you do not know how much. You have brought great clarity to the situation."

"God, how complicated you all are..." Stevenson was wearied by the sudden occurrence; the weakening and resignation of his deputy in a way he would never have imagined possible. "Don't go grovelling at her feet..." he told him gruffly, "In this fit of remorse or whatever it is. You can turn too much the other way, you know, and you will regret it. She will have you on your knees in no time."

"I am aware of what you are saying," Fairchild assured him, somewhat discomforted now by his own revelations. "I have warned her about crossing certain lines."

"What sort of warnings?" asked Louisa and again was ignored.

"Otherwise, you may end up like me!" Stevenson roared with laughter to overturn the awkwardness.

"Nicholas, you are back once more to frivolity...and 'tis not a frivolous matter." Louisa picked up the embroidery, pleased with her efforts and the outcome but concealing it. "Does he seem to you the type who will become a grovelling ninny?"

"No, but this is how the greatest and strongest of men are brought down…not by their enemies or their battles, but by the women they are in love with." Stevenson supped more whisky, pleased in his turn with his own oratory.

Fairchild drained his wine. "I have not said I am in love!"

"Not yet…" said Louisa archly. "Because you are still coming to terms with it and cannot yet admit to it…"

Stevenson massaged his eyelids and sighed. "Sit down awhile, Tony! There is the other matter of the resignation to sort out."

"And besides," Louisa continued, glossing over the professional needs, "any woman can see you are not callous or cruel…you are a man of character and strong integrity, determined not to be undermined by your sensitivities."

He bowed to her modestly and returned to the armchair. Stevenson was looking at him with the former mix of incredulity and irritation. Anthony Fairchild was alluring to women in the way he had once been himself when younger. Now his wife was succumbing to his appeal, despite their age difference; he was a little jealous and closed his eyes to conceal it. Fairchild sensed this and returned swiftly to the subject. "But if it turns out badly; I do not wish it thought that I select upper form girls for my own gratification…'twould damage myself and the school…"

"For God's sake, Tony! No-one will think that. I imagine we would have noticed it before now if it were the case!" said his superior impatiently.

"Even so there could be a scandal," he retorted.

"What kind of scandal?" said Louisa. "You are both free to love are you not?"

"Yes, but she wants to dally…she does not take it seriously…she wishes only to entertain herself and experiment. Whereas I see the danger in that. I think she is not even fully au fait with the facts of life yet…but she has elicited from me some kind of promise of continuation which I do not fully understand myself."

A further silence, the chiming of the ninth hour by the grandmother clock and the rattling of carriage wheels on the road at a distance. Then Stevenson dished up more humour. "Next I expect we shall have a visit from Dominic McCarthy, lamenting the perils of *his* love life as a reason for resigning…" He glanced at Louisa to see how she had taken the remark and finding her disposed to some quiet amusement, he added. "He, as you know, is the other dashing young blade about the place…though being Gaelic and a musician he will probably sit at the piano and set it out as an operetta…'twill be easier on the ear perhaps."

Louisa twitched her lips and put her palms together in a gesture of delight, like a theatre goer unsure whether to applaud. Fairchild ignored them and carried on in his train of new thought, staring at the fire's gyrating flames and allowing himself to be soothed by them.

Louisa eventually noted his absence of attention and looked directly at him. "Anthony, it strikes me she does not herself believe half of what she says…she says it either to keep you at bay for a while…or to create a sort of spice to the courtship…possibly both…you should not be too disconcerted by it…perhaps it acts as a kind of cementing of the relationship…" Her words tailed into a hallowed silence, a homage to her insights.

He was quite stunned by the illumination in her sentiments, almost blinded by the light—like Paul on the road to Damascus. He wanted to leap up and take her in his arms and embrace her. But of course Stevenson might take great exception to it: a man of strong passion and feeling himself, despite his cynicism. As it was, he had begun to nod off in the chair, content to let his wife deal with the matter at its pinnacle. "Do not worry about the resignation," she said at length. "Nicholas is too tired to discuss it sensibly…as long as he thinks you will not rush off precipitously 'twill keep for a few days. I will not let him forget you have announced your decision formally to him."

"I am obliged to you, Ma'am," said Fairchild and waited for her to dismiss the matter so he might leave. Which she did not. Three more minutes passed as she embroidered and he smoked a cigar. Then she said. "This is what I think you should do, Anthony…" and she discarded the embroidery frame and explained.

* * *

The next afternoon a further bouquet of flowers was delivered to her from him. This time with a card stating his intention to call on her soon and signed with his first name. She was heartened, and she put the flowers in the hallway in their entirety. Her mother saw them within minutes and called her father's attention to them. Giles smiled and said nothing, not wishing to begin a verbal saga which may go on for days.

In the kitchen, one of the tweenie maids informed other staff in the middle of a busy cooking period. "More blooms has arrived for Miss Melissa…and very handsome they be too…"

"Probably from that flower shop lad…" said Matilda, concealing her envy. "They be cheap as cornflour to the likes of him…mayhap even free…"

"Not if he ain't called Anthony," said Edward, the other footman, who had received the offering and read the card.

The cook paused her stirring of various pans and looked up. "He's made up with her then?"

"Seems like it," said Edward. "Ask Poll when she comes by…she'll know."

John made scoffing sounds. "*Flower Boy's* named Roger…" he said importantly. "He always announces hi'self fully when he arrives…"

There was an ominous silence; the prospects of a match for the daughter of the house and a possible wedding feast to be prepared.

"She was never going to make a union with that one, surely to God." Matilda announced.

John and Edward shared smutty laughter. "S'to be hoped not…" John sniped. "What's a fop like 'im to do with a comely parcel as 'er…he'd not know where to begin…"

Edward and John began sniggering more as the butler entered. "I hope you are not making disrespectful comments about one of the family…" said he, and the cook retrieved her long spoon from a large pan and held it like a baton. "I've told 'em, Mr Jarvis, afore now…if their cheek gets back to the master, they'll be sorry…"

"Go about your work," Mr Jarvis told Edward and John with menacing authority "the pair of you!" and he smiled unctuously at the cook who catered well to his culinary requests, and whose position in the household was beyond question along with his own.

* * *

Fairchild left his next visit to the Shaw household until after the weekend, which was the weekend of Melanie's wedding to Geoffrey Gillis. He did not wish what needed to be achieved to be minimised by the drama and trappings of a wedding celebration. He rode into the mansion at nine thirty on the Monday morning, having delegated his early morning duties to Dominic McCarthy, and he asked Jarvis whether he could see Giles Shaw on a matter of urgency.

Giles came out of the breakfast room in his shirt and minus his jacket. "Well, young fellow…" he said genially. "I hope this is urgent… I am not at my best until an hour after I've broken fast."

"I beg your pardon for the intrusion, Sir, but I needed to catch you at home, and alone."

"Come and take some refreshment while I finish eating," said Giles and then enquired over his shoulder. "Have you broken fast yet?"

"Yes, I have, thank you, but coffee would be welcome."

They entered the breakfast room which was empty except for a maid clearing various dishes. Giles indicated a chair at the dining table, asking the maid to bring coffee. Fairchild waited for the opportunity to begin and for the maid to finish delivering the coffee while listening to Giles Shaw talk of the problem of land drainage. He added milk liberally to his coffee so that he may drink and relieve his parched throat, dry from nervous apprehension. "I have come to ask your permission to pay court to your daughter," he said plaintively.

Giles raised his head from buttering toast, wearing an expression of surprise. "Stap me!" he murmured and stopped chewing. "I thought that is what you were already about…" He dabbed his mouth with the napkin. "All these garden shenanigans! I hear she jumped from a wall t'other day and began kissing you!"

"That is true." Fairchild reddened and felt even more inadequate than he had with Louisa and Nicholas Stevenson. "But that is the whole point and why I am here… I do not think she can be serious… I feel she is playing some kind of game…"

"Game?" echoed Giles. "Well, mayhap she is! They never stop playing games, far as I can tell…her and Melanie both… It may stop now that Melanie is wed to young Gillis…but then again, it may not."

Fairchild sat back and drank the coffee steadily. This was not going to be an easy exchange.

"So, you have feelings for her?" asked Giles at last, not looking the younger man in the eye.

"I believe I do," said Fairchild. "But she does not make it plain what she herself wants…"

"Beyond the fact that she kisses you in broad daylight and does not scruple to care who knows it!" said the girl's father with some irony.

"Well, yes…but as you have just said, girls of her age play games and I…" he tailed off, his embarrassment now obvious.

Giles suddenly laughed. "Ye Gods! You have my sympathy. I am not trying to make this hard for you…"

"'tis hard…very hard!" agreed Fairchild. "Do you mind if I smoke a cigar?"

"Not at all." Giles pushed his plate away. "I shall light a pipe…perhaps we should take a stroll in the garden…the subject is a delicate one and my wife will be in for breakfast any moment…best if she does not begin with her two penneth just yet awhile…"

Giles led the way through to the drawing room and pushed open the doors to the garden and they went into the mild early spring weather and descended the steps. "My daughter is not your average young woman," Giles offered. "But doubtless you may be aware of that!"

"I am!" Fairchild said.

"And you don't see that as a disadvantage?"

"It is partly the uniqueness of her character which draws me to her. I see that she is young… I see that she has many good qualities…and, of course, she is quite beautiful…"

The older man inspected the green fly on the most expensive roses still in bud. "She has declared an open dislike of marriage…she says she does not want it at any point. Her mother ignores the fact but I see it as something which may not change… I see in her traits of some other members of my family…my youngest sister for one…my mother for another. Both strong women with an inclination to their own beliefs…"

"I played cards with your mother the other weekend, of course," said Fairchild. "She is quite a colourful character…and she is obviously adored by Melissa."

"Yes, she is. No doubt you heard of her history with my father?"

"She regaled us with the story in detail."

"She does so when she has listeners… She has raised six children, as doubtless she told you…and she has done it because of her love for my father…my father and her were passionate about each other to the last. But without that my mother would have led an entirely different life. She would never have stayed with a man for the conventions…and so is Melissa the same way, I think."

Fairchild lit his cigar and Giles indicated for him to drop the match on the path; the gardener in evidence already in the clement morning. "That is very insightful...very helpful in many ways..." he said.

"I thought it might be," said Giles. "I think you gather my meaning."

"I do... I think."

"My wife is all of a dither about that garden escapade...she thinks only of the conventions...but my mother sees more natural occurrences brewing between the two of you...and I hasten to add, she is seldom wrong on these matters."

Fairchild refrained from comment. He was following the drift and seeing for himself the unfathomable side of their love as it may manifest between them. Struggling to not become overwhelmed by his feelings. "You are saying that Melissa may in fact have some affection for me?"

"I think she might...but whether she sees it as part of the game you referred to, I cannot say." Giles put a match to his pipe then inspected the bowl. "And then again, in many ways I wonder sometimes whether love and women and what they bring to a man... I wonder whether 'tis all a game!"

"Shakespeare thought so..." mused Fairchild and quoted. "'*Hanging and wiving go by lottery*'..."

Giles turned to look at him. "I am not an educated man... I did not wish it and my parents did not press me. My sons all went to university, they are all natural academics in some way. I was not...neither was my father...he was a naval man, as you have heard...but by God, he knew a thing or two about trade, a shrewd man...so I went into his business and learned from him...and from my Spanish relations...he was successful from a young age, my father....'tis now a family business."

Fairchild inclined his head respectfully; it was only recently dawning on him just how successful and prosperous the Shaw Land Company was.

Giles paused and gripped Fairchild's arm in a sporting manner then spoke a few words of Spanish. It was poor Spanish but he interpreted it and replied in like tongue, making Giles grin. "'tis the only other language I have a grip on, mind!" He told the younger man. "And only because I needed to...you on t'other hand are a man of letters...you have languages aplenty I hear."

"Five, besides English!" he replied with what he hoped was appropriate humility. "One being Latin, of course!"

Giles released his arm and clapped him on the shoulder. "Stap me! That's good enough for anyone…" Giles stalled for words. "A man of letters indeed."

"Does it make a difference in matters of the heart?" Fairchild queried modestly, walking a little faster to keep up with the older man's pace.

"No, I think not, overall…but you will need a wife perhaps who can keep the conventions…as seen by the governors of Barton Grange, for one thing."

"I am thinking of leaving there and going into business myself…" Fairchild declared and Giles turned to him in astonishment. "Are you by God? But you are so well thought of in that establishment…set for life…"

"That is the problem. I see my life passing by in a welter of curriculum and exam papers and changing classrooms…the same constant demands."

"I wouldn't do what you do…not even if I could…you should be proud of yourself, so young an' all when you started there…but you have earned the right to change direction."

"I never meant to stay in teaching as long as I have…"

He began outlining some of the business plans he and Trimingham were proposing and Giles listened with interest—loving enterprise and commerce and the new world opening to today's young men. He saw too that Fairchild's planned venture might be useful within his own and that the family empire may benefit enormously. A son-in-law with several languages at his beck and call in the new world was something to be considered seriously.

Fairchild drew the oration to a conclusion, himself taken up by his enthusiasm on the subject, and he stuck the cigar between his teeth. He would most likely enjoy having Giles Shaw as a near relation. A man of sound vision and values. And now he wanted to have Melissa consent to marry him with a certainty that was alarming.

"So…this possible game?" Giles repeated, bringing the conversation back to the moment.

"I cannot see any other way to discover her true feelings but to court her…if she will consent to it," he said, quoting exactly Louisa Stevenson's wisdom word for word.

Giles laughed. "I thought she already had consented to it…in her way."

Fairchild stopped in his tracks. "Yes… I suppose she has, but what I am saying, Sir, is that it may not get to marriage…and I don't want you to think that I will in any manner…"

Giles intervened swiftly, as delicacy demanded. "I suppose you can be trusted to honour her in the way it matters?"

"If I cannot," Fairchild said, "And I fall prey to temptation, then I must marry her and there's an end to it."

"There speaks a practical man!"

"I will try my best to honour her. I will not sully her in that way…though I think 'tis what she wants…to have an affair and no consequences."

"Then she must be disappointed," said her father. "She is too inexperienced to know what she is asking…"

"I agree."

They walked slowly and smoked and enjoyed the early sun, and were seen by Marguerite from the upper windows. "I never pretend to understand women…" said Giles conspiratorially after a minute or two. "And I do not believe men who say they do. Women are a different species…they have a logic of their own, but it defies my understanding. So, I find it best to just listen to them and see what I make of it and then let them do what they do best while I do what I do best."

"Sound advice in all," declared Fairchild with a lighter heart. "For anything else is liable to drive a man demented."

"Without a doubt!" said Giles and grinned up at the sky, then extended his hand and Fairchild took it. "You had best go and tell her what we have talked on," he said. "Then there can be no misunderstanding… She is in her art room, I believe… I saw her drifting down that way, wearing that smock thing she wears when she's painting…"

"Good day to you, Sir," Fairchild said and made a swift courteous bow. "Thank you for hearing me out."

"And to you, young man…if all goes well, I shall be happy to welcome you into the family!"

* * *

He walked to the art room in careful and considered tread. Between Louisa Stevenson and Giles Shaw, he saw a somewhat clearer path. Louisa had advised him to approach Giles and ask for permission to court his daughter—but not to promise marriage, yet. That way there was a safeguard in place which allowed them a certain leeway and gave them some surety of ground to discover each

358

other. He saw now why Stevenson had wed Louisa, why he had been able to relinquish his more profligate bachelor ways at the advanced age of his mid-forties. It was perhaps the best time to settle, when one had seen much of love and attraction, or lust and desire. It took one by its own force, this path of shared union with another person.

He knocked on the door and heard her call out to enter.

She looked around at him in surprise as he stood in the doorway and she smiled, but cautiously. "What brings you?" she queried in her matter-of-fact tone. "Do you require another picture as a gift for someone?"

"No."

"Do not tell me you have come to kiss me!" she said. "For I may not be in the mood…"

He walked with his head down and measured his first words; there were none that seemed apt, so he simply plunged in. "I have asked your father for his permission to court you…"

She dropped the brush she was priming with paint and stared. "I beg your pardon?"

"I have asked him if I may court you."

"You jest!"

"Of course I do not." He felt his former calm repose and certainty dissolving.

"How very presumptuous of you, Mr Fairchild," she said without expression.

"I think not, Melissa…you cannot keep…*we* cannot keep having lustful encounters in the garden for all to see…we must be more mature and sensible about matters."

She made a sound of contempt in her throat, like someone tasting a sour fruit. "That is the last thing I want…to be mature and sensible!"

He sat in the chair he had sat in on his last visit to the room and watched her. She turned to her paints and brushes and seemed to dismiss him—or was it that she knew not how to continue the game without the support of Melanie Petersham! Perhaps Melanie was the reason she played the game; to have an appreciative audience. Anything was possible and he was anxious to find out what it was. "How did the nuptials go?" he queried. "On Saturday between Mr and Mrs Gillis?"

"They were well," she replied, her back to him. "Melanie looked beautiful, the bridesmaids…of which there were three and of which I was one…wore apricot silk with tiny white rosebuds in their hair and carried small white flowers of various types."

"How delightful!"

She turned swiftly. "I suppose that is your sarcasm as always?"

"No…'tis me saying the only thing I can think to say. I expect it was delightful."

"If you like that sort of thing," she said carelessly.

"I thought you cared for Miss Petersham? Mrs Gillis now," he said listlessly, not wishing to talk overlong on the subject.

"Of course I do! I love her as my sister…but that does not mean I loved being a bridesmaid."

"I see." She was indeed of a philosophical mind; she was able to decipher the duality of life; quite an accomplishment for such a young woman. She painted for a few moments and he watched, with interest and some admiration for what was unfolding on the canvas. And eventually she spoke. "You had no right to approach my father in that way…"

"You had no right to leap from the wall and kiss me in that way…and to compromise my position…but you did so."

"Compromise your position? You cannot be serious!"

"I am serious, Melissa…the worry is that you seldom are…you are frivolous and think only of your immediate wants."

"Oh, do I?"

"You do."

"What makes you think I want your courtship?"

"You certainly want something from me…are you denying it now?"

"No."

"Well, then, what is it?"

"Intimacy of the usual kind between a man and a woman."

He was stunned, without the means to express himself. She allowed him to contemplate matters in silence as she painted.

"That cannot be…not without some formal arrangement in place," he said eventually.

She turned again and flared slightly, "I am only just twenty in three weeks. I have to be free yet."

"Then you need to be more restrained in your dealings with men."

"Do I?"

"Your father agrees with me…"

"Of course he would! He scarcely believes women should drive themselves in phaetons or go out alone without a maid…so he would think such a thing."

"I perceive he is a good man…and probably a very good father. Do you know how fortunate you are in that?"

"Yes…as a matter of fact I do… I pay him every courtesy and every respect. Not so my mother, unfortunately… I avoid her where I can so as not to cover her with disrespect and disdain. He would not like that."

"Nor should I," he said. "Were I witness to it."

"Oh well…you are almost as antiquated in your need for formality and etiquette as they are…despite your up-to-the-minute attire and fashionable shoes…or at least you pretend that way."

"If you are intending to call me a hypocrite once more, I would think twice."

She cleared her throat and ignored the comment. "So, did he agree to this courtship, Papa?"

"He did…provided I honour you in the most profound of ways…until there is a marriage on the horizon."

"Of course! A marriage! He likes you. You are a sound sort of fellow with excellent breeding and a position to boot. Who could want for a better husband? Until they might suspect your callous cruelty."

He left his cigar in the old disused dish and came to stand behind her, putting his arms around her and his hands on her stomach, feeling the warmth of her and kneading the roundness of her belly with his finger tips, his face in her loosely bound hair. "Well, yes…" he murmured, "We must not forget my callous cruelty." He stopped and pulled away, so that there was a space between them. She leaned back towards him, her body with a mind of its own. "I must leave in a few moments," he murmured, his voice thick and deep with arousal. "I have forsaken the schedule and caused disruption in order to catch your father at the best time."

She picked up the brush again, trembling inside and aching for the experience that Melanie had described to her; one not easily understandable but imaginable in a way, like unseen landscape described by travellers. "Yes, the precious schedule of the wretched educational mill must go on." Her own voice was quiet and soft, and he was tempted to tell her of his decision to leave education, but it was not pressing and his arousal was and he needed the ride back to clear his mind and his body of the all-consuming force of desire.

"I will think about whether to accept your courtship," she said tritely, without too much levity.

He made her a partial bow and before she could detain him for one more moment he had moved to the door. "As we have previously agreed, if you control your rudeness, I will control my sarcasm!" he said without looking back and the door closed after him and her work inspiration for the morning was entirely lost.

He walked briskly to the front door, and as he passed the breakfast room Marguerite Shaw sprang into his path, genuinely startling him from his reverie. "Anthony!" she gushed, clutching hold of his sleeve, her hair covered in a lace affair of some kind, her face devoid of any paint and her slight form looking even slighter in her morning gown. "I am so truly delighted."

"I apologise, Ma'am, but I am very late…" he said to soften his abrupt departure…

"But you will come to dinner on Sunday? We must celebrate!"

Giles appeared behind her, still in his shirt sleeves. "Maggie, leave the man be for now. He has a school to manage…there is nothing to celebrate as yet…" He raised his brows to Fairchild, a questioning expression expecting response. Fairchild smiled at him and gave a brief nod.

"But the formalities have to be…" Marguerite swung round to see what her husband had left unsaid. "We have to…"

"The formalities will wait," said Giles. "They are not yet formally betrothed and it will be kept as quiet as possible for now…"

"Well, that is extraordinary," claimed Marguerite in some annoyance.

"Be that as it may," said Giles, "'tis how we have agreed on matters…and we'll be glad of your compliance."

"Indeed!" Fairchild said, accepting his coat from the butler. "But I will no doubt be along for dinner…thank you, Ma'am…"

He left quickly and collected his horse and rode back to the school and too swiftly through the town, as was his habit, incurring annoyance in some of the residents who thought him irresponsible for someone charged with the instruction of children.

* * *

"But, Giles…" Marguerite was saying, trotting after him in low day heels as he strode back to the breakfast room, "He was seen kissing her by at least four people, three of them staff and one of them a visitor of yours on business…they should be betrothed!"

"Mayhap they will be!" said Giles. "But it can't be rushed…she is not of a mind to it yet."

"That is unfortunate, but 'tis not entirely up to her…'tis up to us to use some pressure. If she has a mind to kiss him so recklessly and chase about the garden after him in those inappropriate frocks, then she must consider the proprieties."

"I have said all I am saying on the matter," said Giles. "He is not a fool…he's an honourable man. He will not exploit her in that way…he has self-control."

"'tis not him I worry about," said Marguerite. "'tis her…what if she prevails on him until he weakens and then she decides she is not wedding him after all?"

"We will cross that bridge if it arrives, but I doubt she will do that," said Giles and put on his jacket and rang the bell for the footman. "I am not discussing this any further, Madam, so please trust me to have dealt with it."

Marguerite fumed and took a portion of grapefruit and a cup of coffee and sat at the table to eat alone. When he called her 'Madam' in that way, she knew not to pursue things further.

Sensitivities Like Harp Strings

Having rested for an hour or so Melissa wrote to Melanie at an address in Scotland—which Melanie had given her to use in emergencies—and apprised her of recent developments. Especially of Anthony Fairchild's refusal to agree to intimacy without some betrothal being in place; this was not the way things were supposed to happen.

She hastily sought the footman to take the letter immediately to the dispatch office. The footman was not to be seen, and the butler suspected he had gone somewhere in the garden to smoke, as was his wont at this quiet time of day. So, she ran from the side door and into the grounds, encountering her mother in the close garden gathering a bunch of small daffodils. "Melissa, I want a word with you…" she said, lacking the joy in her voice that she had shown to Fairchild.

"I am in a hurry…" Melissa told her, knowing what the topic would be.

"I care not," said Marguerite sharply. "Stop immediately and follow me indoors."

"I will be in directly!" Melissa said, not giving way.

"You had better be, young lady," said her mother. "I will not countenance this discourteous attitude to my wishes…come to the morning room when you have done."

"Very well," she replied. "But I have a lot of work to do for next month's fund raiser… I cannot be idly chattering for more than five minutes."

"And don't be so impertinent!" said Marguerite. "I will not countenance that either."

The two footmen were eventually located and she slowed down, quite breathless. Edward and John were standing together gazing at the skyline from the mount beside the lake overlooking the west side of the woodland, smoking. They looked at her in surprise, the mixture of deference and desire with which they always regarded her. She was after all their pier in age…and had she been a local girl of their own class they met about the town they would both have tried their hand.

John bragged to Edward that were that the case she would most likely have agreed to wed him by now and he would have given her two children by this time, had she been in his touch. Edward brayed with scornful laughter each time this was broached. He looked at Melissa now with the expression of an undisclosed joke about his features.

"I do not know what you find amusing..." she told him tartly. "I have been put to the trouble of racing around to find you..."

John leaned into his colleague and nudged him quickly, this statement kindling his delusion and seeming hilarious.

"John..." said Melissa breathlessly, addressing him as the elder of the two.

"Miss?" said John, eyeing her messy painting garb but not in any way repelled.

"Take this right now to the dispatch office and send it..." She fished in her commodious pocket for loose change, bringing out other items of belonging before locating the coins.

"I shall, Miss, but I must have the permission of Mr Jarvis first."

"No, don't bother with that... I shall tell Jarvis. Just do as I ask of you...'tis very urgent...come with me forthwith to the stable while we have the groom saddle a horse," she ordered.

John enjoyed riding the horses and he followed her flowing skirt and dropped his cigarette end to the grass, turning to give a backwards wink to Edward who wore a scathing look: doing her bidding was not in his estimation a sign of her reciprocated longing.

"And, Edward..." she called. "You had best return to the house...neither my father nor Mr Jarvis approve of you both absenting yourselves at the same time..."

"Yes Miss..." said Edward, making comedic faces at John.

The groom was not pleased, he was in the midst of brushing and grooming the only available horse, but he obeyed Melissa's instruction owing to her strident manner. "You come straight back, mind..." he said to John.

"Where do you think I wanna go at this hour?" replied the churlish footman.

"And less of your lip," said the groom, king of his own domain just as the cook and butler were of theirs. "I need this mare in three quarters of the hour, no more."

Melissa watched John ride out and returned to the house, ignoring her mother's instruction. Eventually her mother caught up with her in the art room. "I asked you to come to my parlour!" she said with mounting annoyance. "Why can you not just do as you are told for once!"

"I do apologise, Mama..." opined Melissa, not stopping her brush strokes. "It completely went from my mind."

"What were you giving to John...and where has he gone?"

"To post a letter for me urgently."

"A letter to whom."

"To Melanie..."

Marguerite sat in the chair, the only chair, where Fairchild had sat half an hour before. "I expect you have been appraising her of matters...before you speak with me about them?"

"She is my closest friend," Melissa announced, using her brush as a ruler against the canvass and closing one eye to gain perspective.

"You are such a sly little vixen..." said her mother, tapping her fingers on the arm of the chair. "I can't think where you get it from..."

She let out a swift squeal of sarcastic laughter and Marguerite rose quickly, understanding the noise to be one of irony aimed at herself. "I hear from your father that you are engaged to Fairchild..."

"Then you hear wrongly. He has agreed to him paying me court."

"Yes, but what exactly does that mean?"

"As it sounds," said Melissa unhelpfully. "Surely 'tis quite plain."

Marguerite advanced to the easel—a few inches shorter than her daughter, she stood and gazed at the canvas and squinted at it, recognising some half-finished people dancing, but she could not make out which were male and which were female. "What is not plain is why you do not go straight to a betrothal..."

"Because we are not ready for that... I am not ready for that!"

"So, you prefer to chase him around the garden, scantily clad and throwing yourself on him for the world to see!"

"That has occurred only once..." she replied calmly, her eyes focused steadily on the canvas.

"And once is too often...you were seen pleading with him the other week, and he pulling you against your wishes...these exploits are far from usual. They are quite indecorous..."

"But they are so much fun," said Melissa and smiled as she applied vermillion paint to the brush.

"What do you intend next?" queried her mother.

"I know not your meaning…"

"I mean, when do you suppose you will make your mind up about him…"

"When I know him better, of course."

"I would think you know him well enough, if you know enough to want to kiss him all the time."

"Surely that is quite different," said Melissa.

Marguerite was lost for words, her daughter's superior intelligence and cool wisdom had her at a disadvantage. She was, as Marguerite often suspected, cut from the same cloth as Jemima and two of her daughters: she liked men for the sake of liking them, for the pleasure they may give her. She was a woman more suited to being a mistress than a wife.

Marguerite thought in these extreme terms all the time, being of a strict and oppressive background and a narrow life experience. She and her elder sister, Dorothea, enjoyed nothing more than comparing the looser morals of the Shaw family relatives to their own strictures on how not to live. "'tis not different, Melissa! This is not Vienna, or Paris! Kissing a man, the way you kiss Fairchild is tantamount to saying you are betrothed to him," she told her.

Melissa sighed. "I will not marry a man whom I do not know…in every way."

Marguerite gasped in shock. The worst had been voiced.

"Melissa, if you give your virginity to him, you must wed him."

"Not unless I am with child by him, surely?"

Marching around the room, her low heels clacking against the floor tiles, Marguerite sighed and hissed like a low boiling kettle. "You do not even know the facts of life…" she declared at length, coming back to the vicinity of the easel and shaking her head so that her grey curls were loosened somewhat from her lace cap.

"Well, I do now, as a matter of fact… Melanie told me before she wed."

"I might have known…"

"Had I waited for you to tell me, Mama, I may have been an old maid, or a dried-up spinster… I expect they are both the same."

Marguerite clutched her daughter's arm, causing her to go madly off course in her painting. "Mother!" shrieked Melissa. "Look what you have made me do!" She grabbed a cloth with turpentine and began erasing the damage.

"Do you mean to say you have already lost it?" cried Marguerite, ignoring the protestations about ruined art when ruined honour was far more pressing.

"Lost what?"

"Your virginity! Have you already given yourself to this man?"

Melissa was extremely annoyed; two days' work almost ruined. She would have to paint over the damage and that would change the perspective completely. "Please just let me work, Mama... You are infuriating."

"I am infuriating!! *You* are infuriating! You thoughtless girl. Now answer me! Have you given yourself to Anthony Fairchild?"

Melissa sighed long and closed her eyes. "I think not."

"You think not? Do you not know?"

"I have not!"

Marguerite sank into the chair, quite weak with relief, fanning herself with the tassels of her thin silk shawl. "Nor must you...not until you are wed to him."

Melissa looked over at her with pity, a scornful shape to her mouth. "You cannot know a man until you wed him, in the sense you seem to mean!" continued her mother in calmer tone.

"I will not be at the mercy of any man," pronounced Melissa with dignity.

"What? What do you mean, *at the mercy?* What a stupid remark."

"No 'tis not...look at Aunt Amaelia..." declared Melissa. Her mother bridled immediately. "She is a wanton and foolish woman...she always was."

"Yes, and Montalbein is a boorish and overbearing tyrant."

"She should have thought of that before she wed him...enough people told her, including your papa and her own," retorted Marguerite hotly.

"Perhaps she had not worked it out herself from lack of experience! Which is why I shall be more careful."

"But Anthony Fairchild is not like Montalbein!" posed Marguerite as if waiting to be contradicted in the belief.

Melissa considered matters, raising her head from the canvas and staring at the far window. "He is quite callous when he wishes to be."

Marguerite sprang up from the chair. "What? Of course he is not."

"How would you know?" said Melissa.

"What makes you say that?" queried Marguerite, lowering her voice.

"Never mind. I do not wish to go into it."

"But I do mind," Marguerite's tone was becoming once more louder. "If there is reason to believe he is not a good man, your father and I will wish to hear of it."

"I did not say he was not a good man!" Melissa said, her eyes again on the damaged work; she could play these evasive word games all day and tie people in knots. "He taught us at school, so we should know better than you."

Marguerite laughed drily, not really a laugh at all but a mocking condemnation. "Not these old grievances again! The same ones which caused Melanie to hurl tea around like a fish wife."

Melissa returned her attention to the canvas, her mother's heels again clacking as she paced. She did not think fishwives drank tea in the first place, it was probably far too expensive, but she kept her thoughts to herself. "At the school he is different, no doubt…" Marguerite was saying, "He would seem callous because he has to maintain discipline. Anyone might be so, faced with a classroom of rebellious girls…"

"We were not rebellious…just high spirited," Melissa corrected.

"'tis the same thing!" screeched Marguerite, her voice rising to a crescendo of frustration. "Surely, he is the most polite and genial of young men. He has marvellous manners and wonderful breeding. Only think of what an excellent father he will be to your children! And of course, you will have splendid children, the two of you, with your combined good looks and talents… You will not do better for a perfect husband."

Why did everyone harp on about having children! No sooner had one left one's own childhood than one was expected to think of the next generation. What a repetitive whirligig of unrelieved silliness! Still, she kept her own counsel. Then Marguerite had a dreadful thought and turned with a harrowed face. "Unless you are thinking to accept that Braithwaite boy…are you?"

"I will not accept any man until I am ready," she said.

"Then you must be restrained and not see him alone."

"But I crave his nearness…and his kisses," said Melissa, forgetting herself momentarily.

"I thought his callousness was an obstacle?" intoned her mother, craftily changing track.

"That is only one side of his nature…" She closed her left eye to assess the painting. "His other side is sensuous and inviting…"

"'tis nothing short of reckless and brazen! I won't hear another word of it," cried Marguerite.

"Then do not talk to me of it," said Melissa in mounting defiance. "My father has given it his blessing and there is little you can do. So why do you not just let matters take their course?"

Marguerite stomped from the room, halting in the doorway. "I shall be telling your father all this."

"As you wish…" said Melissa without further thought.

* * *

She painted steadily for the fundraising event on behalf of the alms schools, and for other commissions already underway. The weeks passed and the time seemed to encrypt itself in a new period of life experience and almost lost meaning.

Often, he visited her, during the day and early evening, (they were not yet to be seen publicly together beyond the grounds of the mansion, as protocol dictated). He brought her flowers or confectionery, which she viewed with polite indifference. "I do not need these gifts!" she told him after the first couple of visits. It might have been construed as rudeness had he not known her well enough now to realise it was her manner of plain speaking. "It matters little," he told her, "I like to give them to you…and someone will enjoy them!"

"I did not say I would not enjoy them! 'tis your intimacy I desire."

Kissing her and holding her and continuing to sail as close to the wind as his own self-control would allow, he saw that to explain was futile; she was not a words person, she was a tactile creature with unfathomable wants and cravings that she little understood but seemed driven by. "That kind of thing at your age has a price," he murmured into her hair as he held her.

"You sound like a money lender…or a blackmailer!" she whispered, her face in his neck as they enjoyed closeness. He dissolved into laughter, which lost him his erection, which was useful as it was barely two in the afternoon and he had to take Latin with the younger form boys in less than an hour.

It changed the mood, but not the overweening longing, and she seated herself at the escritoire and began to place cards for a game of patience. He picked up his jacket in one hand. It was spun cotton of the finest material, light in weight, an oatmeal colour, befitting the spring weather. His wardrobe pleased her and she took stock of its varying contents whenever he called. "I mean that we must be wed for that kind of thing…" he explained presently.

"I knew what you meant," she said, "And I am not talking of it right now…it will sully my mood for painting."

"I will sully your mood if I linger…" he muttered, his voice deep and husky like the water as it fell from the dam into the deepest part of the stream in the lowland of their grounds—a burbling low torrent of sound. She knew now that this tone of voice denoted his high state of arousal. How she loved his high states of arousal. They evoked something similar in herself.

"How will you do it…tell me!" She sprang from the chair and followed him and leapt up onto his back and put her arms around his neck and sucked his earlobe, moving his hair aside with the tip of her nose, in control from her position behind him and cleaved to him—as agile in her sudden amorous movements as she was guileful in her words. "Tell me in detail how you will sully my mood…"

He shook her off and dropped her onto the sofa and then put on his jacket. "I hope you are not toying with me, Melissa…" he heard himself say.

"I am not toying with you, Anthony," she replied.

His glare continued for several seconds. She savoured this dark intense frustration and smiled at him slowly. "I cannot tell you of the outcome you wish for…but as far as feelings go, I am not toying with you…"

There was no answer to it, as yet. He left before he lost his patience and said something unpleasant or sarcastic in his confused state of mind.

* * *

A letter had arrived from Melanie in reply to hers some weeks since, delayed by the distance, but Melanie was also delayed and not yet returned from her honeymoon for another couple of weeks. Melissa read it yet again. Melanie had written…'*Lissy dearest, he is manoeuvring you now into a position which will be untenable. And he has your father's backing. Either make up your mind to wedding him and taking your chances—or do not let him touch you before you are sure. If he begets a baby with you, you will have no choice but to wed. (Although he will probably know how to avoid that occurrence). 'tis whether he wishes to avoid it or use it as ammunition…*'

Melissa read it through again and then decided at last to destroy it, lest she become careless with it and one of the family find it. She lay on the sofa after his departure that day drifting into a doze while thinking of everything and surveying the landscape through the high wide windows. She was awoken sometime later by Polly entering and announcing that Roger Briathwaite had come.

Roger rushed in, trying not to seem so hurried—and failing—he was always afraid that she would refuse to receive him on some pretext or another nowadays. And often he was proved right. He handed her a bouquet of roses which she did not really look at for more than three seconds. "Roger..." she kissed his cheek. "How good of you, but I have only a few minutes...the paintings are not yet done, and I have had a catastrophe this morning due to my mother's interference..."

"I am sorry to hear it," said the modest and ever polite Mr Braithwaite falsely; he cared less about her art works than she for his floral offerings. They were at an impasse, and he refused to see it. He had little or no experience of women elsewhere and it was evident by his fumbling and shuffling as he attempted to achieve closeness with her in order to kiss her or take her hand. He was as far from Fairchild's level of sure and subtle seduction than she was from becoming Fairchild's mistress.

He indicated a chair, ascertaining her permission to sit, while splitting the tails of his jacket in readiness to seat himself. "I need to speak with you immediately if possible...it cannot wait."

She assumed a wary expression, not ready for more rigours after the hour of safe and arousing romance shared with Fairchild. "What is it?" she began, perching on the edge of a seat so as not to look too comfortable and encourage him.

"Well...'tis delicate...you surely know now after so many years of our acquaintance..."

"Most of which we spent as children..." she interjected.

Roger was not to be deterred. "...you must know how deep my feelings for you are...and I need to know, for my own peace of mind, whether you anticipate ever...that is, if I... I need to know that I am not wasting my time in thinking of you in this way."

"Roger, I do not know how your mind runs...what am I to say?" She was being deliberately disingenuous and coy and it was mortifying to him, for he knew it portended little of good omen. "I need to know if you would ever consent to marrying me!"

Melissa coloured, despite her hard stance, and looked first to the left and then to the right, avoiding his eye.

"Roger, this is so precipitous."

"I think not! You must see I adore you, Melissa…and always shall."

She rose quickly and flounced her skirt with impatience. "Can we talk of this another time? 'twill disconcert me for the day and I have work to do…"

"I take it 'tis a no then?"

"Why are you pressing this suit just now? I have told you in the past that I have no wish to be married to anyone for many years…if ever!"

Roger decided to overlook this reminder of her past views; females were notoriously fickle on the subject of marriage: that much he had heard. He rose and paced the room, pausing to look from the window and watch the birds in the garden and the progress of the summer flowers recently planted by the gardeners. "Not to put too fine a point on it…it has come to my notice that there is another man…a rival paying you court!"

She turned and frowned. How had he found that out when there was so much secrecy and discretion exercised. She stared at him and waited.

"You do not deny it?"

"No, but I fail to see that it is your business. How did you know?"

Roger went on to explain that a girl assistant in one of their shops locally—knowing that he cared for Melissa—had told him that a gentleman customer had called several times and ordered bouquets meant for her to be delivered to the mansion. This person had opened an account with the shop and so his details had been easy to find.

"How very indiscreet of her!" Melissa said with more prevarication.

"Not really," said the truculent Roger. "She has worked in our business for some time and she…she…"

"Holds a fondness for you!" supplied Melissa.

"Well, yes…perhaps…"

"Then marry her!" Melissa said.

Roger allowed his face to drop and knew not how to continue. At length he ventured, "I do not think marriage is that easy. She is just a shop girl… I have not even thought of… I am not of a mind to do that."

"You are a snob," said Melissa without venom, but simply, in her direct way.

"I do not think so, 'tis nothing to do with that."

"If she thinks so much of you to betray a customer's discretion, then she must value you greatly. Imagine the customer's dismay if he found out about it."

"We own the shop," declared Roger imperiously.

Melissa turned, beginning to flare up in a sudden temper. "My family owns farmland which we rent to tenant farmers, but our estate manager does not go around talking of the ins and outs of the tenant's leases and latest profits."

"That is entirely a different thing," said the truculent suitor.

"I think not!" Melissa said, and then more majestically: "Now, Roger, I am busy and you must go..."

"So, this man..." persevered Roger, "This Anthony Fairchild, he is deputy head at Barton Grange?"

"He is!" concurred Melissa, walking to the door to open it and precipitate his departure.

Roger stood very still. "So, you probably knew him when you were a schoolgirl?"

"I did, but I hasten to add, he did not then pursue me in that way."

"I should hope not." Roger pretended to be horrified. "But no doubt he taught you?"

"He taught us languages."

"How old is he, for God's sake?" he demanded, envisaging some middle-aged professor with ludicrous pretensions to a bygone youth.

"He is thirty...not that it is any of your concern!"

"You were in love with one of your teachers?"

"Of course not... I loathed and despised him then."

Backing up to the chair once more, Roger dropped into it. This was growing more painful and more bizarre by the moment. "Then what has changed?"

"*We* have changed, of course...he is no longer my teacher and I am no longer fifteen."

"I see," he said, but did not see at all. It was the most incongruous and baffling thing. That a young woman could loathe and despise someone in charge of her at school and then go on to accept his advances. Melisssa did not expect him to understand; she barely understood it herself. They both stood in some consternation, and the clock ticked and then chimed. "You must leave now, Roger... I do not have the time to talk today."

Suddenly, Roger fell into a hopeless state of turmoil; emotions and logic vying and backbone deserting him. "Melissa, I beg of you to consider what you are doing...you do not know him the way you know me..."

"Stop it!" Melissa said in a strangulated tone. "'tis most unseemly...you do not know anything of what I feel or even who I really am...you are not..."

"Not what?" wailed Roger, advancing upon her and seizing her hands. "Not what? Old enough? Man enough?"

"Not experienced enough," said Melissa with dignity, "Not mature enough to know what you are saying."

The young man could not have been more affected had she slapped him. He was truly slighted. He reddened and looked as if he may cry and she averted her eyes and sighed. He bowed to her formally and left the room.

* * *

She told Fairchild on his next visit. "Anthony, I ask that you send me no more flowers...or at least not buy them from the shop in town where you purchased the last!"

"What?" Fairchild paused in the removal of his jacket.

"'tis upsetting Roger..." she said in haste, hoping to quickly dismiss the matter. She had left the art room to be with him in the small reception room that had now been designated for their assignations. He flung his jacket onto the chez long and stared at her.

"He owns the shop...or his family does...and the girl in there tells him of your bouquets."

"You cannot be serious!" Fairchild said, his eyes darkening and turning the shade of green betokening his extreme annoyance, his manner otherwise not seemingly changing. She turned away and smiled to herself before saying. "I am quite serious."

"Well, I'll be damned..." he remarked. "What interfering pernicious busybodying! Does this girl pry into everyone's floral acquisitions and then gossip?"

"I know not...but I think she likes Roger."

"That is no excuse...how old is she?"

"I do not know that either. I expect she is around the age of Roger and myself. Did you not gauge her age when ordering the flowers from her?"

He frowned and shook his head slightly, trying to remember. "The assistant who took the order was an elderly woman. This girl is perhaps in the back quarters seeing to the flowers and not the customers."

"I have tried steering him in her direction…she obviously adores him to do such a thing."

"How considerate of you! Although I perceive that he may prefer to choose a wife for himself."

"He cannot marry a shop girl, is what he implied… I told him he is a snob."

Sipping the coffee brought in by the maid on his arrival, he seemed to absorb himself in the subject more and then murmured, "That is something he will grow out of. Men when they mature care little for a woman's background or family tree. If she pleases him and he is enamoured of her and she is a decent woman, most men will overlook that kind of thing."

"Indeed?" What a superb philosopher he was proving to be, her erstwhile schoolteacher. It gratified her more than a little.

"'tis not of importance in the grand scheme, and men of intelligence know that…" he continued.

"I am not sure Roger is that intelligent withal," said Melissa harshly, "Or he would not believe I would want to settle with him."

"That is his age and lack of experience…but this flagrant indiscretion is something I cannot get over. I hope he has told her 'tis not acceptable, even if it did suit his purpose…"

"I doubt he has."

"Because he is no more than a boy…and she doubtless is of the same age and needs to learn some respect for the customer's privacy!"

"I expect you are right…pity you cannot order her to the waiting room for correction," she said facetiously.

He glared at her. "I perceive his upset has not upset you or you would not be jesting about your historical grievance!"

She began to laugh, and then to giggle. And soon she was leaning forwards with her face in her skirt, the better to vent her hilarity. Perhaps it was a good sign; he could not tell. "I have a good mind to make a formal complaint to his company about this breach of confidence…"

"I do not think you will…you do not have that kind of petty mindedness…and 'twould only bring undue attention to us."

He lit a small cigar and helped himself to more coffee. Then he straightened his spine as he leaned back in the sofa and allowed himself to relax while remaining upright. It was quite a bodily feat and one that only gentlemen seemed capable of. She smiled to herself and wanted badly to kiss him, but the display of his reactions was not done yet; they enthralled her in the way everything about him enthralled her.

His cheekbones had become more etched with his preoccupation on these profound personal matters, his nostrils flared and somehow flattened. His whole face a study in consternation—dramatic and intense. How she adored his brooding moments of introspective remoteness, his removal from the present into matters so complex that he was utterly immersed. It made him seem like a statue carved by Angelo, a monument to all things arcanely unfathomable and masculine.

"So, he has taken his leave for good now…has he?" he enquired at length.

"I know not! Perhaps so…after he proposed marriage!"

"What?" He sat forwards suddenly and the coffee in his cup looked as if it might spill, but he caught it quickly.

"Do not worry, I did not accept."

"Oh, did you not!" he replied in grave sarcasm.

"Naturally not…'twas perhaps only prompted by this information about you…he is worried you may usurp him."

Fairchild blinked rapidly and looked to the side of her, not seeking her eyes for fear he would become more enraged. He was in his shirt and waistcoat, and with a loosened neckcloth (tied today in a style she knew was called *a la Romantigue)* so that his throat was exposed, revealing hints of golden hair on his upper torso.

This was an unprecedented move so far, this revealing of more of himself bodily. She wondered if he was aware of it, or whether it was an involuntary action based on the need for greater familiarity, or even proprietorial possession of her. Although he was also perhaps over warm in the room with the fire stoked as always.

He set the coffee cup on the saucer and looked at her. "Melissa, this is not a game…feelings are at stake…if you continue to treat it with flippancy, I shall become very vexed. Boys of his age are wont to taking these matters seriously…often with lasting damage."

She had trouble controlling her mirth but saw it as expedient to do so. She rose and took her own deep breaths and attempted to regain calm. She smiled nonetheless and the more he watched her the worse it became. Until she said. "I know! But the whole thing has taken me by surprise and I need to absorb it somewhat…and do not tell me you are concerned for Roger! Do not say next that you fear he may call you out at dawn or some such." She circled the room, unable to be still any longer. "'twas not me who agreed on a private courtship…'twas you and Papa…so 'tis not my fault."

This could not be argued with, and he knew it. He sipped coffee while thinking how to proceed in the situation. If Roger Braithwaite wanted to make a fool of himself and ply her with his suit that was his look out. But if this shop girl and other staff were to talk of it at random in the town, then it became another matter. His hand would be forced and he would have to formally ask her to wed him.

Would that be so bad? It would if he, and she, had not complete faith in the move! And if she then refused outright how long could they continue playing life this way? But there again, how long could he keep from fully seducing her? Currently with no other females in his life he was in an agony of unfulfilled physical longing at times, which destroyed his concentration and his peace of mind. Perhaps Brathwaite's proposal was a good thing. "You must stop receiving him…" he told her at length. "'tis not seemly now."

"Anthony, he is one of my oldest friends."

"That might be acceptable were you both in your thirties or older…but not now, at your ages, with your young lives ahead…it must cease."

"Are you attempting to tell me to stop seeing him?"

"I am not attempting… I am doing so," said Fairchild in his even unruffled tone. "If you want my continued courtship."

She stood very still and stared ahead of her with unseeing eyes. The situation had become worse than she imagined. It had rebounded on her. She saw that this was a deadlock, a potential impasse which could not be dealt with easily. She needed Melanie's input, so it must wait. Melanie should return in a few days. She moved over to where he sat and sank onto his lap, covering his face with light butterfly kisses. At first, he did not respond, and she sat back to survey him. "You must not be cross…" she murmured.

"Must I not?"

"No…"

"And you must tell Braithwaite to cease calling on you…or I shall tell him…you cannot play these kinds of games, 'tis just too vulgar and without sensibility. I am aware that you see this side of life as a frivolous pastime, but I do not… I am older than you and I know the trouble it can bring. He must look elsewhere for a wife, or you must accept his suit…"

She gaped at him, aghast. "Do you want me to accept his suit?"

"Of course I do not… I am merely telling you what the protocol now dictates."

She recovered her composure and exhaled audibly. "Oh, I see…the protocol! If 'tis not you dictating, 'tis the infernal protocol."

"And do not turn this on to me!" he said, his mood dark and not amusing or enlivening at all.

"I shall tell him I cannot receive him," she said, more to placate him than for any more confirmed intention. She began kissing him again, this time fully on the mouth, until he put her from him and stood abruptly, aware that she was manipulating him with her wiles and seduction. "I must go…"

"Must you?" she said in her lamenting voice. "I am again bereft then…"

He moved to the door. "And cease speaking in that contrived manner…like someone in a bad novel."

He doubled back for his cigars left on the arm of the sofa. On route again to the door he smacked her once on the behind, causing a shock wave to her body, wearing as she did her chequered house dress with little beneath it. She made a slight sound of shocked pain between her teeth.

"Consider it a down payment on your favourite preference," he said and she closed her eyes and resisted reaction.

"I am leaving before you attempt anything else. I shall see you in about two or three days."

"I shall count the minutes and be heartsick until then," she opined, ignoring his reference to bad novels.

He was displeased by this sickly rhetoric; he suspected her of the game playing he and Giles had discussed. He glared at her, his almond shaped eyes the colour of pale jade in the light from the window. She was everything he desired in a woman. He was unsure whether she would make a good wife, but he knew that the wife role was secondary in importance to him than that of desirable and constant lover. He would have to marry her to hold onto her, there was no other way now.

Secrets, Lies and Modifications

Melanie called two days after she had settled into her new home in town. Geoffrey's law offices were in the town and it was a shorter distance to High Lawns than from her parents' house previously. "I have only an hour, my sweet..." she told Melissa. "Our groom is in the stables with your's, waiting for me, and Geoffrey needs him by four..."

Melissa nodded and looked sad—it was apparent to both girls how much their lives were changing. Gone were the carefree days of lounging about and pleasing themselves and indulging their needs every which way they fancied "How was Scotland?" asked Melissa quite formally.

"I did not see much of it..." said Melanie airily, "'twas very cold... I had trouble understanding what most of them were saying...and they play those hideous instruments every evening..."

"Bagpipes, do you mean?" asked Melissa, her tone desultory.

"Yes, those! Now tell me what has happened with Atilla in my absence?"

Melissa hesitated. She had as usual to warm up to the theme. She had not seen her friend for weeks and needed to grow accustomed again to the level and tone of their intimacy. "But what of your honeymoon? I want to know more of it."

Melanie sighed, her face screwed into a puzzled and ambivalent musing expression.

"Do not tell me it was disappointing...do not say you regret marrying him?"

"No... I do not...but let us say, the bedroom is the best part of it all."

Melissa could quite imagine how that would be the case. She giggled, then Melanie giggled, and the recent distance was broken. Melanie retrieved her cigarettes from her reticule and took a spill from the fire grate with which to light two. Melissa accepted one and inhaled and then divulged to her best friend all that she felt. Then the shock of Roger's proposal and Fairchild's ultimatum.

"My mother is as bad…" she declared finally. "She is practically forcing me to accept the idea of marriage…why can't a person enjoy the pleasure of being with someone without being chained to them?"

"Why indeed!" agreed Melanie. "Although, I perceive that you still might…he thinks he has you where he wants you now. You should not have told him of Roger's suit. He thinks to force your hand…if you refuse to be coerced and refuse to see Roger, he cannot advance his game."

"But he will not make love to me unless we are wed…and he has promised my father…"

"Then seduce him," said Melanie. "Until he is unable to resist…how many other women are in his life, do you know?"

"No, I have not asked him that…he will doubtless deny there are any."

"Then if there are none, he will be growing quite frantic with lust by now."

"As am I…" wailed Melissa. "I cannot sleep for thinking of his hands on me and myself wanting more…"

"Yes, but 'tis worse for him…'tis always worse for men. He will be distracted and like a bear with a sore head…it cannot continue…he must weaken soon. Have you found out about the Lottie person yet?"

"I dare not ask him."

"Why ever not?"

"Because then he must hear about how we read his letter that day when he left the classroom…"

Melanie found this hilarious. "We are not in the classroom now, Lissy! Just tell him we read it, as girls will…and then ask about her…he knows how much we despised him then so 'twill not surprise him and surely he…" She was interrupted by a knock at the door of the morning room where they were cloistered and Polly came in. "Mr Fairchild is in the hall," she announced in a voice that held a mild warning, knowing by now how Melanie and he disliked each other.

"He is not expected this day!" she told Melanie in some annoyance, though still yearning to see him.

"Even so…he is courting you now, my sweet. You must receive him…and I shall go."

"No," Melissa advanced towards her with her hand out to deter her rising. "That will look very odd…and you will have to pass him even so… Show him in, please, Polly."

Moments later, Polly re-entered with Fairchild who stopped abruptly on seeing Melanie and lost his customary confidence for a second.

"Shall I bring coffee and more tea?" enquired Polly, and looked towards him.

Having bowed quite formally to Melanie, he replied. "No, thank you… I do not wish to have it hurled at me."

Polly gasped a little and Melanie kept a poker-face. Melissa said. "Thank you, Polly. That will be all."

"Anthony!" Melanie rallied cheerily, "You do know that the Sunday tea incident was an accident?"

He tightened his jaw over what might have been a reluctant grin. "I know no such thing, Mrs Gillis!"

"Oh, the use of my married name! I still cannot grow accustomed to it," trilled Melanie brightly, and she beamed at him. "You may call me by my first name, you know, Anthony…"

He gave no comment.

"For I shall certainly continue calling you by yours…"

"I have no doubt you shall…" he said. "Especially as I am powerless to prevent it."

"And what a novelty that must be for you…being without your power!" responded Melanie evenly.

His steady gaze held hers and they exchanged the combative eye contact of equals. The one thing in common between them being their attachment to Melissa. "But then I am sure," continued Melanie, "That very soon today you may cane a few miscreants to reclaim it again…your power, I mean."

"No doubt a couple…" he replied laconically, determined not to be thrown by inflammatory rhetoric, "Since I will be going back to the boys' school."

"Why do these schoolmasters not do their own dirty work?" queried Melanie, replacing her gloves as she watched him pause to construe her meaning.

"They mostly do, but serious incursions are usually dealt with by deputy heads in schools like ours…these matters go on record."

"Very wise…" she replied sweetly. "'twould be a pity to waste such powerful talent…"

He drew a long breath. "I do beg your pardon, Mrs Gillis, but I am not in the mood to pursue your favourite theme of power right now." He shrugged off his jacket, revealing the sleeves and rolled collar of his pristine white shirt. Melanie laughed delightedly and gave him a warm smile to denote the fact that she was teasing. He perceived that if he lingered, they may make sport of him and demolish him with their sparkling repartee. He raised his jacket again and considered, "Perhaps I shall leave and call later…"

"Not on my account indeed…" Melanie also rose. "I must leave in five minutes anyway…so be at ease and have a seat. We were just talking about you…were we not, Lissy?"

"No, of course we were not…" said Melissa contrarily.

"I imagine you perhaps were!" he said, knowing that she lied.

"Not in a bad way…" she admitted.

"Then I am gratified…it makes a wonderful change."

Melanie laughed again, her drawing room laughter, full of innocuous overtones and mendacious intent, and she moved to the door. Melissa followed her and said over her shoulder. "Anthony, I will be back instantly, make yourself comfortable."

Melanie decided not to bid him a formal farewell. It would be a step too far in terms of false bonhomie. She sailed from the room swiftly before any further exchange might be broached. Walking with Melanie to the porch and the front steps Melissa said: "What shall I tell him if he raises the subject of Roger again…and whether I have deterred his visits? I feel 'tis only a matter of time before he enquires."

Melanie considered things. "Just tell him you have written but have not yet had a reply."

"But what if he then seeks him out in person?"

"He could do so whatever you tell him…but this way he will be inclined to believe you and give matters more time."

"Yes…yes," Melissa mused. "I think you are right."

Melanie turned on a whim. "You do realise, Lissy, that he is perhaps one of the most eligible and desirable bachelors within three counties?"

"Only three?" Melissa rejoined. "I perceive that he might have a waiting list…"

"Without doubt, and containing a range of females of perhaps dizzying variety. He is strikingly attractive; it has to be owned…but then you are strikingly beautiful."

"I am not," Melissa whispered, modesty and embarrassment mingling.

"Oh, but you are, my love…even if you do not allow the world to see it."

"I do not wish the world to see it…" She opened the front door herself, deterring the butler who hovered nearby. "As you know, I do not care much for the world in general…or its opinion of me!"

Melanie smiled and knew it to be the truth. They embraced and Melanie said. "I shall write to you tomorrow or the next day…if I have more thoughts on the matter…in case we cannot meet again until the end of next week." She skipped down the front steps and along the side border to the stables.

* * *

In the morning room, Fairchild looked at her with his well-shielded gaze. Waiting for her to speak first, determined not to comment on Melanie's visit, nor to pry into what they had talked of concerning himself—it was no doubt to do with Roger Braithwaite and the rivalry factor that would enthral them.

They were always left to themselves when he visited, with her father's consent and to the dismay of her mother. He rarely stayed more than a half hour or so, and it would continue that way until they had decided whether to marry or not. She sat down next to him, as close as she could, curling her legs beneath her skirts on the largest sofa. He was wearing a tight-fitting waistcoat, fashionable in the extreme, with small buttons all the way up to his collar—his neckcloth a stark black like the rest of his suit and contrasting with the whiteness of his shirt. "You are dressed very fine today…do you go to a wedding?"

"I had a meeting in town with colleagues," he told her.

"Other teachers, you mean?"

"No, men of finance."

She pulled away and stared at him. "Oh…why?"

"I am entering into business with Trim… I have decided to leave education."

She was so far amazed that her jaw dropped. She could not imagine him in any other professional setting apart from the school. "You are leaving Barton Grange?"

"That is obviously the result…yes…apart from certain tutorials with the upper form boys prior to university entrance."

"But why did you not tell me?"

"I wanted to be certain of the decision."

She fell silent and could think of nothing else to add.

"I thought it would please you…" he said.

"Why should it please me?"

"Because you dislike the educational profession… We are all hypocrites and pedants and tyrants…if you recall! Not forgetting monsters of cruelty."

Her previous words were familiar to her. "Well, I may have exaggerated a little…" she floundered under the surprise news and her more generous spirit. "I may have overstated my opinions somewhat…"

"No!" he said facetiously. "Are you sure?"

She stood and walked to the window to have something to do to disguise her misgivings. She was not interested in his educational career. She showed as much interest in what went on at Barton Grange these days as she might to the political system in Outer Mongolia. "Surely 'tis not simply for me that you are leaving?" she said.

"No, no…but you helped me come to the decision. If we are to wed, I need to seek better prospects…"

"Where?"

"We are opening a translation bureau… Trim and I and another fellow we know who will be a silent partner…'twill prosper I think."

She was astounded, having imagined she would be married to a deputy head or a headmaster all her life—if in the end marriage was to be the result. "But you are very well thought of at that place, everyone will be disappointed…and probably you do a lot of good there," she stammered.

"When I am not occupied in caning miscreants you mean?"

"Well, I…" she prevaricated again. "I expect even that does some good on certain occasions."

He stared at her. "This is a sudden change of tune is it not!"

"No, not really… I understand if 'tis the boys you discipline…they most likely have deserved it."

He laughed out loud. "What a very biased view…female children being beyond reproach at all times, no doubt?"

"Not at all times…but certainly less than you perceive…"

He wondered whether to change the subject before the past engulfed the present, or whether to put paid to the supposed grievance once and for all. He sat back and prepared words. "So…your accusations of my callousness and monstrous cruelty were also exaggerated, were they?"

"No," she said flatly. "They most certainly were not…"

"I see…well interestingly, I have recently thought that I could change my modus operandi at the girls' place for the remaining time… I thought I could employ instead your favourite preference…"

She turned from rearranging her hair in the gilt-edged mirror and flared. "Don't you dare!"

"Dare what? Refer to the method or action it?"

"The latter."

"I felt sure you would endorse the suggestion… I cannot see why you would not!"

"Because…because as you have previously said, 'tis far too personal a measure."

"And as you have previously said, 'tis a lesser form of cruelty."

"I have not said 'tis a cruelty at all. I used the word in connection with the waiting room…and this *preferred method* is a figment of your imagination!"

"I am somewhat confused," he intoned, his eyes on his expensive shoes. "Do you mean your *preferred method* is a figment of imagination, or the method itself?"

She was struggling to resist becoming angry but was unable to stop her words from flowing. "I have never said it was my preferred method."

"But you have just referred to it again."

"You know very well what I mean. You are being deliberately obtuse…and anyway, you are leaving there you say…so this method will not be required."

"Yes, but there is a way to go yet… I could for the time remaining easily experiment with your theory…"

He spent little time at the girls' school these days—his teaching there had been taken over by another male teacher, and he cared little as deputy head how this staff member-maintained order or protected himself from rebellion, as long as it remained within the constitution of the academy—but he was not about to inform her of that. She flounced her skirts more thoroughly and made some steps around the hearth rug. "You must not adopt any such method with those girls…" she said at length.

He took on a look of pretended displeasure at being told what to do in his own professional realm. She stared him down and her eyes blazed untold dangers. He relished the rising temperature but remained cool. "Why not? If it might have been good enough for you then why not the present females at the Grange? Surely you wish the cruelty to cease…"

She floundered more. If she seemed to in any way endorse the alleged cruelty, it would destroy her old grievance. She shook her skirts with agitated vigour and looked mutinous. "Do not make any such reform for my benefit…and do not tell me of it if you do. Or I shall refuse to speak to you. These girls must take their chances…as we all did."

He allowed a smile to dawn and she felt he had gained some advantage but could not quite see how. He looked towards the window, beyond which garden preparations were underway for a child's sixth birthday party. She was supposed to be organising games involving hiding and finding things but could not muster the enthusiasm. He thought of Lottie in years gone by; her jealousy over his teaching girl pupils, and he watched her carefully. "Hmmm…" he murmured; his meaning inscrutable.

Thinking his mind to be still on the question of the girls' academy, she thought that soon they would be arguing over old ground and picking up on pointless quarrels. No good progress could come from it. She approached him with a look of predatory intent and sat on his lap. "You think you can tie me in knots with your words and your clever reasoning…" she kissed him passionately, preventing his reply, and when she was breathless and knew him to be likewise, she drew back and surveyed him.

He took a deep breath. "I believe the shoe is on the other foot…" He waited and allowed his eyes to fathom her own with untold suspicion and ideas, darkening in hue and becoming more opaque. "'tis you, Melissa, who believe you can rake up the old bones of your ludicrous grievances and rattle them to detract from whatever you don't wish me to look at…"

"Meaning?"

"Just what I have said."

"All that aside, you know enough now to realise Melanie's wit is not to be taken seriously?"

"Oh, her wit? I see! Is that what she calls it?"

"It covers the depth of the anguish you caused us in the past…" she said airily, not meaning to be so cavalier and regretting it immediately. His amusement was not subtle, not disguised, he put his head back and laughed. "Good Lord…perhaps she should have Gillis serve me with a lawsuit…"

She thought of Geoffrey's dismissive attitude to Melanie's telling him their grievance and was suddenly filled with a temper born on the wings of other emotions. She placed her hands on his hair, gently at first, and then twined locks of it around her fingers and tightened them so that he winced with discomfort. "Let go…" he said calmly. She pulled harder. "Here is an appropriate form of cruelty…" she purred. "My own version…"

"Let go!" he said again. "Melissa, I am warning you!"

"What?" She lessened her grip on his hair but did not release it, kissing him again with greater tenderness and then spoke against his lips. "Another of your warnings… I grow tired of your warnings…" She pulled his hair tighter and he put his hands to hers and tried to remove her fingers. Her resistance was an aphrodisiac to them both, but his annoyance was as real as her disgust.

He manoeuvred her to the edge of his knees as she held fast to his hair. "So, you are tired of the warnings? I see!" With a sudden jerk, he dislodged her and she began falling to the carpet, still clinging to tendrils of his hair. "Well, then…obviously I have overdone the lenience… I shall show you the result of ignoring them…"

He jumped forwards and held onto her and the movement dislodged her hands. He seized one of them as he attempted to move her to a position of control. Then she performed her famous trick of falling backwards and toppled them both as she fell onto the floor. She lapsed into giggles and lay quite still. He was on his knees and splayed over her, his hands flat on the floor at her other side. He attempted to stand. "You are a little shrew…" he told her. "And I will not have it…"

"Surely you must see now you are defeated!" she taunted him, her laughter uncontrollable, worsened by the tension.

"God's Teeth…" He pulled her upwards, his breath jagged from exertion. "You delude yourself, wench…"

And then there was an unwarranted interruption as the door opened and her mother came in. They froze for seconds. He stood up first, smoothing his shirt and recovering his wits. "Ma'am…" he intoned. "This is not how it may appear…'twas an accident!"

Melissa was in the grip of her greater hilarity, her face upturned to the ceiling and screwed into expressions which Marguerite found hard to decipher. "Good Lord!!" cried the matriarch.

He attempted to explain further, clearing his throat in preparation, but the door banged shut as Marguerite disappeared. He helped her to her feet and surveyed her. "I hope you are satisfied now."

"Immeasurably so!" she said, and skipped quickly across the room and out of his reach. The mirror was the only destination, and she stood in front of it to arrange her hair. "But not as much as I wish to be…"

"Another divine intervention in the nick of time…" he mused. "But you do know that your luck must run out at some point?"

She looked at his reflection through the mirror and continued to smooth her hair as he smoothed his and muttered, "I suggest you leave these vitriolic eruptions until later…"

She turned. "Later when?"

"When you have my name and wear my ring," he replied. "Then you can launch as many attacks as you wish…but be assured, 'tis not something you will wish to do often."

"Such bragging!" she laughed, and he allowed her the last word; he had learned much in the past quarter hour.

Speaking normally, as if there had been no break in the previous conversation, she said. "Remember, we have all to get on together…for the future… Or how will it be at dinner parties and so on? You and me and Melanie and Geoffrey! And possibly Trim and Susan!"

He stared at her. "The prospect of you and me and Geoffrey and Melanie, with Susan thrown into the mix, positively fills me with delight," he said sagely. "Mrs Gillis is not an addition to my social life I wish to make…"

"You are very contrary today, Anthony! And you must stop calling her so formally…use her first name…surely you can manage it?"

He reseated himself and took his ease, while she righted her clothes. Then suddenly he surprised her as much as she had surprised him minutes earlier. "Have you told Roger Braithwaite to cease his attentions?" he enquired.

Startled, she wondered if he had followed her along the hallway and overheard their conversation. "You are changing the subject."

"No, I am extending it… I glean from that reference that you do consider such a future!" he said cunningly and she felt herself dizzying with fear and confusion. She remained silent.

"Have you told him?" he repeated doggedly.

"I have written to him but not so far received a reply."

He ruminated on this then remarked: "He is perhaps coming to terms with it and knows not what to say."

"Yes, perhaps…" She felt as if she were being liberated from an old life and propelled into a new one. "Let us walk in the garden, shall we?"

"If you wish to and need the air," he said compliantly. "I must go in fifteen minutes… I have been away from the school since eleven this morning."

* * *

The afternoon air was warm and the sun hazy. The ideal weather for outdoor activities. A new mood of tranquillity had descended between Melissa and Anthony Fairchild…based perhaps on mutually released tensions. They dallied by the terrace where several adults and one or two nursemaids sat watching the children. They stared at Fairchild with interest when it was not obvious he knew of it—though she felt that he must sense it, for women especially always stared at him. Everyone today was mostly informed of their love interest, so the scrutiny of him was not easily disguised.

"Let us go further into the wooded area near the lake," she said to him, then pulled him quickly towards the territory intended. He followed in his usual steady pace.

Under the ancient oak trees where the canopy of leaves gave them both breeze and sunshine in parts she leaned against the bark of the largest of the oaks and said, "Kiss me now…you must kiss me. For I sometimes think when you have gone that, I merely imagined you kissing me at all." She put her arms around his neck and on the back of his head and he pulled her arms upwards and placed her hands against the soft bark of the tree, pinning her there and leaning into her, then kissing her. "I will not pull your hair…" she said. "Indeed, I am sorry if I hurt you…it was perhaps spiteful of me…"

"I will get over it…" he murmured. "Your spite is not something beyond me to deal with."

"More boasting!" she declared, though in a tepid tone.

His eyes followed the curve of her cheek. "You are very beautiful," he told her and his compliments were so rare that it caught her off guard. "So, are you!" she replied.

He began to quietly laugh, which did not please her. "What? Do you not believe that men can be beautiful too?"

"No, I do not," he concurred.

"Because you are not an artist…"

"Or not a woman…" He gripped her wrists again and lifted them to the tree bark and held them there and kissed her for long moments. She wondered if he thought she would run off if he did not hold her in this way. It did not occur to her that it was so she could not touch him in any way and thus engender feelings and urges he was not strong enough to resist. Eventually, he stood away from her and looked at her with consummate desire. "We must return to the lawn."

"Why?" she asked and put her arms around his neck.

"Because people will know what we are doing. It is precipitous, until we are formally betrothed."

She tutted and turned her head from side to side. "Not this again…can we not just enjoy ourselves with my father's consent now?"

"No…not to the extent you wish…" He pulled her from the tree and led her to the path from where the lawns were just about visible. At the bottom of the front lawn where the drive began there was an enclave of ground, shaded by trees, still visible to passersby and from some of the windows of the house. An old wooden seat stood, without a back, meant only for the briefest of rest. "Let us sit a while…" she coaxed. "While I ask you something."

The bench was narrow and not comfortable. He looked at it without enthusiasm until eventually he sat next to her and then waited with some wariness.

"I need to ask you…who is Lottie?"

She felt him freeze, as if something had hit him or stunned him. Not daring to breathe she sat out the moments during which he assembled his thoughts. The shock it still rendered him when hearing Lottie's name spoken aloud by someone else was allayed by the knowledge of having only thought of her minutes previously. It occurred to him, as it had many times before, that thoughts were alive and took wings between people and places. "How do you know of Lottie?"

There was only the sound of the breeze at its strongest in the trees, and her father's dogs barking on the higher part of the grounds. "We read your letter…one day at the Grange… *'My dearest Lottie, I am so sorry that this letter is a day late.'…*" she quoted the opening lines to him. "You had left it on the desk and gone from the room, so we read it."

"Of course you did!" he said in irony. He was amazed that she remembered so accurately the opening words. Though he would never himself erase them from his memory.

"What else can I say! We were young girls…and girls are notoriously curious in matters such as private letters…you should have covered it."

"So I should…"

Perhaps three minutes elapsed, and they sat and watched several children play across the wide expanse of the grass. She feared that he might admit to Lottie being another woman in his life, a woman he could not bear to be without. What would she do? How would it change her decision? It became—in the passing seconds—a fear so real her heart began to pound. She had realised that she did not want to live her life without him. That she would eventually have to agree to marriage to prevent him leaving her.

At length, he found words. "She was my sweetheart, since childhood. She is dead now."

"How?"

"She drowned at sea, in a ship which floundered…returning from Ireland."

Her hand went to her throat and she felt the thudding of her heart, and then the sadness of his soul. "I am sorry…'tis indeed a tragedy."

He murmured something indistinct. The phrase *'I am sorry'* sounded hollow to her ears.

"When did she die?"

"Perhaps a few weeks after you saw the letter…"

"How old was she?"

"Three and twenty."

Turning to him, she kissed his cheek and then began covering his face with quick tiny kisses. He suffered this for a few moments and then lifted his hand and held her chin to stop her. Her tenderness added to his sentiments made for him a brew of untenable emotions, too much to deal with. "It explains the sadness I felt from you at that time…your terrible morose and cold essence."

He looked at her closely, unsure what to make of the disclosure. "You felt sadness for me in the classroom? How do you reconcile that with loathing and despising me?"

"Easily…" she replied, looking away. "They are different things."

"You discern what others think or feel without being told? Artistic people often do, I am told!"

"I know not…but I felt the sadness of your soul."

He considered matters carefully, his remote and intense inner world enveloping him utterly.

"But it does not exonerate my harshness and casual cruelty?" he asked too flippantly.

"No, but it possibly explains it." She left his side and walked about the small enclave.

"Disregard my last question…'tis not worthy of a man…my attitude would have been the same whether she was dead or alive," he admitted.

"I will disregard it," she said, "Though I do not entirely believe you."

She did not know how to express that she instinctively gleaned he still loved Lottie. It was not something she could phrase, nor something she could take from him. It was not her right to do so and it was not within her power. And yet, it needed to be dignified or addressed. "You still love her perhaps?"

"I shall always love her," he said plaintively.

He wondered if at this pivotal point of proceedings and on hearing the admission she might break off their association. He was pained by the thought but said nothing to deter her. She thought about the confession. His integrity shining as always so bright as to almost overturn the memory of her grievances. She thought instead of Lottie and her abiding memory. "Perhaps the dead have a place of their own in our hearts…in a different part than the living," she claimed. "We agreed on that first dinner we ate together last year that death is not the end."

"I think so," he concurred.

"So, perhaps she waits for you…or in another life you take up with her again…"

He turned his full attention upon her. He had before him a young woman of consummate insight and understanding, but also a child who still needed to play at life.

* * *

For her part, she did not think badly of him for his honesty. He was the most perceptive person she knew. His strength of character was perhaps what she loved most. It lent something to her where she felt her own to be as yet lacking. She was light with relief, giddy with hope and other strange notions that were almost palpable in the air. She needed to skip about. "I think I shall run back to the garden…" she told him.

He was taken by surprise and rose from the uncomfortable bench. "If you have the strength."

"I can run any time. I'll wager I can outrun you!" she said challengingly.

"I'll wager you cannot."

"How much?"

"You know I never lay bets with women… I can barely bring myself to play cards with them for money."

She lifted her skirts and took to her heels and began to run the length to the lawn. He gave her a few yards start and then chased after her. They ran around the corner to the other side of the house where she tripped over a toy rabbit lying on the grass. She fell to her knees, not bothering to stop herself, and rolled onto her back and lay looking up into the sky, and immediately two of the very young children fell down next to her and rested their heads on her stomach.

Her mother hastened over. "Good heavens, Melissa, what now? Are you hurt?"

"Of course not…just winded."

He was staring down at her. "She was trying to outrun me…"

Marguerite attempted a smile. "What a strange pursuit," she declared and Melissa thought that her mother had not run anywhere since she was perhaps as young as the children on top of her.

"Her falling was a ruse to avoid losing," he said in jest.

"Indeed it was nothing of the kind," she peered upwards, her eyes squinting into the bright light. "The only way you will outrun me is if you are on your horse!" she taunted.

He looked down on her with a humouring expression full of deeper urges.

"Prove it then…now!" She sat up from her prone position.

"Certainly not…time is of the essence!" he declared.

"Because you do not dare to risk failure…"

He sighed. "Melissa, do not begin with your *dares* at this time…"

"You should be organising the games you said you would oversee," said Marguerite, cutting into this preposterous scene.

"I shall do it presently, Mama…" She watched him steadily as she got back her breath. "You may challenge me any day, Anthony, and put it to the test…" she said graciously, peering into his eyes as they penetrated her own.

"Lissy, a gentleman does not require to know if a lady can outrun him," Marguerite admonished.

"This one does, he needs to hear it for when he becomes too aspirational in some of his intentions…"

Her mother was once more alarmed. "Which intentions?"

When she spoke, it was for his benefit, she existed in this moment for his benefit. "You forget how ancient you have become…" She put back her head to laugh, her neck and throat exposed to the sun. He saw himself in his mind kissing her throat and tracing the hollow down to the mound of her breasts with his tongue. Her body lifting and heaving towards his own. "…so you imagine yourself able to catch me…but then I suppose you must think that withal…" she was saying.

"You deceive yourself in this, as you deceive yourself on many things about me," he told her, her taunts flying to other of his senses.

"What are you speaking of?" asked Marguerite more abruptly.

He brought his mind from erotic excursions into the future. "She is talking only of one of her preferences…" he said smoothly.

"Hush!" she ordered in strident tones. "Or I will not talk to you for a month. She does not need to hear your pet theory."

Her mother sighed with vexation and he allowed his grin almost full exposure. While the children—perhaps five or six of them—shouted and danced with excitement as the atmosphere of interesting exchange rose in the air like the coming of mythical creatures.

"Which theory?" persisted her mother sharply, and was again ignored.

He lifted the two very young children off her and said quietly. "Even if it is a theory, do not delude yourself as to your capability in the matter, my dear girl."

"I am not your *dear girl* just yet, Mr Fairchild," she breathed, her eyes unfocused like someone a little drunk.

"Get up, Lissy, do…" implored Marguerite, "'tis most indecorous to sit about in that manner…"

"I am winded," she repeated, dizzy with emotion. "But I shall be able to run for a few hundred yards yet…if he dares to accept the challenge."

"Lord, how you do fool yourself. I shall bring you down within twenty yards…"

"You imagine so? You will be mistaken!"

Marguerite surveyed them for a few moments more; they were watching only each other and speaking in private riddles, as lovers do. There was no doubting they felt as lovers, and not just people considering a union.

"Yes…come along…let us have it settled…" Melissa scrambled to her feet and positioned herself for running. He was struck again by the potential foolhardiness of marrying a girl scarcely out of childhood, with privileges that held back the real world, an ignorance of demands and authority beyond the wealthy mansion. "Melissa, stop…" he said and caught her wrist and restrained her. "I must return to work…"

"We can race instead of games…can we not children?"

"*Run and race!*" The children yelled.

He put his hands on her waist and placed her inches away from him so that she was not so perilously close to him. But she backed up against him and leaned into him again, feeling his warmth as warmer than the sun. She had introduced the foolish play to partly dispel the subject of Lottie and lighten the mood, and partly to begin the seduction process—which could take a while, "Scaredy cat…" she said and the children shrieked with pleasure. "Afraid to be outrun!"

He put his face into her hair and nibbled her ear. "Cease now," he whispered. "I must return to work."

"Surely it can wait."

He groaned. "'tis a school…not a potato field."

Her small nephew, Wilfred, pointed at her with his small finger. "…*tatater feel…*" he echoed.

"You see, someone appreciates your sarcasm…even if 'tis only a tiny person."

"Tatater feel!" Wilfred shrieked. "Tatater feel…tater feel…'unning and 'acing…" He had a piercing shrill little voice which rent the air and scared the birds.

"Perhaps sing us a song, Wilfie!" she told him and within seconds a loud childish monotone began as he sang something indecipherable in his unmelodious tones. His slightly older sister, Florence, stepped forwards and put her hand over his mouth to mute him and he shrieked in a higher octave and held it as long as his breath would allow.

"God's Teeth…" Fairchild said. "'tis definitely time I was not here."

"This is what family life is like…" she murmured. "And 'tis you pressing for it…not me!"

Marguerite came close again and stood among them. The atmosphere between her daughter and Fairchild was intimately charged, a small wildfire kindling steadily and radiating sparks and likely to ignite an inferno. "Come children… Aunt Lissy will get herself to rights…better if we leave her…then the party games can begin." She took her top skirt of chiffon and held it in one hand and took her grandson's tiny hand and the hand of one of the other children and led them away, others skipping after them, ecstatic at the idea of games. Two or three of the children remained and tugged at her skirt to ensure she moved, impatient with delays and unfulfilled promises.

"You see what a wonderful mother you will make!" he informed her, his breath on her ear—the focal point for all sensation. She made a low growling noise of pure desire, enveloped in her deeper senses. "I have not even agreed to wed you as yet."

"The two points are not mutually inclusive," he said. "I was merely making an observation."

The idea of parting from him became an elongated misery, as if she may not see him again; a frightening and never-ending chasm. "I cannot wait for us to share a bed," she whispered.

He became exasperated. "Then you must marry me."

The frown she made was disconcerting and spoke of genuine fears he could not in honesty dismiss without resorting to coercion.

"But what if we are trapped?" she breathed. "In a never-ending spiral of my spite and your callousness…"

"Well, then…we will have to deal with it," he said. "We will have to take it as part of the union and accept it for what it is."

Straightening her back she pulled from him completely, "You are not serious? Are you?"

"Only as much as you are in the suggestion overall."

"Well, just look at you now, running off at the first sign of family life!"

He lifted her at the waist and twirled around with her and then set her down again. The children squealed for him to do the same to them and he lifted each one in turn and spun around with them before they cantered off and threw themselves about the lawn.

"I must return to work." He dusted himself down and then moved steadily backwards so as not to be tempted to linger with her. The children clamoured for more exuberant play and the adults stared from afar, as if at a seaside show.

Geraldine was watching the proceedings with an eagle-like stare. She saw Melissa blow him a kiss as he neared the side of the building and then the swift lift of his hand to the region of his heart in acknowledgement. She gave an intake of breath. "Did you see that gesture?" she asked of her sister.

"I did," replied Grace.

"Which gesture?" queried Edmund, who despite his quiet nature did not like to miss anything. Geraldine imitated the gesture and Edmund leaned back in his chair and remarked to his brother-in-law. "Could that fellow become any more appealing to the ladies, I ask myself?"

Geraldine seized his hand. "No, I think not…next to you, Eddy, he is the most desirable man in these parts."

"I have gathered that," said Edmund and kissed her fingers. "My sister is unable to sustain her usual indifference to male attention when he is around."

"But you forget his awful reputation," Geraldine whispered. "The *penny dreadful* we have yet to hear of. He has to atone for something in the past, if Melanie's veiled remarks that day are anything to go by…" She told her relations. "Putting two and two together, one assumes he was inordinately severe with them when they were in his classroom…"

"Really!" said Grace.

"He would have been a fool not to be," muttered Edmund. "Look how she and Melanie are when left to their own devices! Otherwise, he might have ended by throttling them."

"Doesn't seem to have done him much harm," commented Grace's husband.

"Of course not," Grace advised. "We do not want men who are weak-kneed and afraid of us."

"For heaven's sake, Gracie…" said Geraldine, "Do not be telling them things like that…'tis extremely dangerous…" Geraldine and Grace began to talk in low voices while their partners discoursed more casually…

Giles' sister, Lydia, watched too and commented. "What a beautiful couple they make…like to something from George Elliott."

Marguerite scoffed gently, a mixture of pride and annoyance. "You would scarce think so if you heard them rowing on occasions…"

"All couples do that…" said Geraldine to be helpful.

"I am not sure that is true…" rejoined Dorothea. "I am sure my husband and I never did…"

"I cannot wait to see them dance at their wedding feast," said Lydia, undeterred by the pessimism.

"But of course," went on Geraldine, "They must overcome their turgid history first."

"Which turgid history?" queried Lydia.

Marguerite was irritated. "Disregard the remark, Lydia! 'tis Geraldine being fanciful…she is as bad as the girls. We don't need it raking up now," she warned her daughter-in-law. "'twas most probably in their imaginations…"

"I think not…" argued Geraldine, whose own imagination had already placed Melissa and Melanie in her first novel.

"Yes, she has a lurid imagination," Edmund confirmed and squoze his wife's knee to stop her from more speculation.

"You may not say that, Eddy…" put in Grace, "When she is making a small fortune from popular novels."

"We will see," said Edmund. "As long as she uses her maiden name and not mine, I will have less fear of lawsuits."

"Good Lord!" said Dorothea to Marguerite. "Whatever next!"

And then around the corner of the smaller lawn came Giles escorting his mother slowly, her arm linked in his, having just met her from her carriage. They were closely followed by Gilbert from the other side of the lawn, arriving dead on three p.m. Marguerite checked her tiny timepiece with suspicion; *men who arrived simultaneously on the hour were obviously planning things.*

"You have just missed Prince Charming…" Geraldine told her father-in-law. "He left moments ago, leaving Cinderella glowing but bereft. I am surprised you did not pass him on the drive."

"And of course the next couple to tie the knot will be Gregory…will it not, Mother?" enquired Lydia of Jemima, the true matriarch of the dynasty now seating herself carefully. She looked blankly at her daughter who persevered. "You know, Mama… Gregory and that little pianist wench he seems so fond of… Mollie, I think."

"Millie!" corrected Jemima, coming into more fluent memory. "Her name's Millicent…and 't ain't no use asking me… I ain't exchanged above two words with the girl…she scarcely seems to speak…"

Gilbert had bowed briefly to the assembled company before sitting. "Stap me! Have you heard about this, Giles? That young nephew of yours has acquired for himself a woman who scarcely speaks! How far did he travel to find her, I wonder!"

Marguerite tutted and Dorothea shook her head, her precise curls like gun metal reverberating with the motion. "Very coarse humour, Gilbert," she commented, pulling her mouth into its habitual thin line of disapproval.

Geraldine was disposed to laughter, as were most of the younger generation of adults. Subdued merriment resulted and Gilbert sat with a nonchalant air and winked at Giles who allowed the wit to stand alone while he finished greeting the various friends and relations and patting the heads of children, then announced. "Betimes Gil, we had better be making a move…"

Gilbert had barely time to drink the coffee poured for him by the maid and attempted to do so hurriedly.

"Not worth you sitting in the first place!" snapped Jemima.

"Where are you going now?" demanded Marguerite of Giles. "You have only just arrived…"

"To look over some land…business, Maggie," retorted Giles, "These things don't wait, and Gilbert is the man to tell me from a distance the accurate measure of it on sight…ain't that so, Eddy?"

Edmund inclined his head respectfully to his uncle and father. "He is very astute in such matters…" he agreed.

Gilbert—a land surveyor for most of his adult life—took the compliment in his stride, gulping the rest of the coffee and rising. Marguerite stared at them and Dorothea remarked cynically. "I never realised I was married to a man with such amazing talents."

Gilbert buttoned his summer coat. "Well, my dear, it's what I've been telling you for over thirty years…"

Enjoying yet more of Gilbert's witticism, the assembled mood was jovial. Dorothea said to Marguerite as she watched them leave. "They are doing nothing of the kind, Maggie…they are leaving to go fishing…"

Marguerite waved her hand so that her rings jingled and shone. "Let them…they will only get merrier and become noisier than the children if they stay…" She smiled sweetly at the guests as Melissa joined the group in her self-contained manner and sat next to her grandmother and took her hand in her own. They were all trying to not so obviously stare at her, and failing. Emerged as she was now from her cloistered world and revealing both her womanly charms and private desires. It was impossible not to scrutinise her. *All the world loves a lover.*

* * *

When he next called a few days later, she was with her grandmother in the drawing room, keeping an eye on her; Jemima's skin was quite waxen and she was prone to dropping off to doze mid-sentence. She was in the midst of painting furiously for the fundraising event the next day, to get the last canvass finished.

"Come and see Granny." She pulled him by the hand into the drawing room. "Look who is here…" she told the old lady gaily. "'tis Anthony to see you…"

Her grandmother had dozed off. He looked at her closely and then at Melissa who was wearing her painting smock, her hair quite awry and blue and green paint smears on her face. She shook her grandmother gently. "Granny, continue with the story you were telling me…" She turned to Fairchild. "She was in the middle of telling me about Jago once masquerading as an English captain on a schooner and pretending to have voice loss so that the English sailors had to speak for him…but she keeps on falling to sleep…look at her face…'tis a poor colour."

He stepped forwards to Jemima. "She is fast asleep." He picked up the old woman's wrist and held it.

"What are you doing?" said Melissa.

"Finding her pulse." He took out his timepiece, then said, "'tis weak but that may be her age…"

"She is not dying, is she?" asked Melissa in agitation.

"I do not think so…but I am not a doctor… I think she would be better in bed…she is perhaps just worn out."

"She never admits to it…she fights it."

He was wearing casual clothes, not his highly formal attire, it being late Friday afternoon, and he began removing his jerkin—made of some kind of animal hide with a smooth but coarse pelt. She yearned to touch the skin at his lower throat where the loose shirt collar revealed its pale surface and golden chest hairs slightly visible. "I shall carry her upstairs, if you wish," he announced and removed his jerkin.

"Yes, please do…" She stepped to one side and allowed him to pick the old lady up. He did so in one swift movement again, as if she were a five-year-old child. She had lost more weight recently and was perhaps even lighter than before. They moved swiftly to the main staircase and a footman appeared and said: "Is everything alright, Miss?"

"'tis fine, Edward," she said. "Mr Fairchild is taking my grandmother to her bedroom…we will call if we need you."

In the bedroom, he laid Jemima carefully on her bed as she emitted slight snores.

"I am so afraid she will die in her sleep…" she told him, arranging blankets around Jemima, who as usual was wearing her nightdress beneath her shawls. It reminded him of someone surveying an infant and his expression melted into something she saw only now and then. He pulled her into his arms, kissing her hair and then her mouth, and then tried to erase the smears of paint from her face with his fingertips. "You look as if you are about to do a war dance."

"I do not want her to die," she said and when she looked up at him there were bright copious tears in her eyes.

He held her more tightly. "We spoke of this only the other day…remember? We agreed that death cannot be the end…'tis something we know little about…a great entrance to other things."

She began to cry, her breath sobbing out her sadness. "Yes…but she is one of the few people whom I truly love and trust…'tis for myself I weep. She wants only to be with Jago."

"Of course," he replied.

She thought instantly of Lottie. Was he waiting simply to join her? Knowing that his wait may be interminable! Was she herself simply a distraction! She changed the subject in her mind, quickly, and then the tone in her voice. "How do you know to look at this pulse you talk of? What is it?"

"It echoes the heart beat…"

"Oh, how do you know?"

"Information given to people in charge of children in better class educational establishments these days."

She gazed at him and her tears abated. They were drawn to one another as if by magnetism, she knew it and marvelled at it. It was the most compelling thing she had experienced in her life to date. She took her courage into her next breath and felt it throb in her throat. "Anthony, do you think that Lottie waits for you in the next world?"

An age passed and she felt his grip on her slacken but he did not let her go. "I do not know."

"Well, how will she find you? Or how will Granny find Jago?"

He smiled, his mouth in her hair, but he felt that he may also weep; it was a most disconcerting thing and he cast about for what to say next in his role as guide to this girl with her unusual ways and her striking beauty. "I think that there may be other laws governing the world beyond that we cannot understand."

"I think there must be…" she agreed, and her lithe slender fingers clutched his shirt sleeve.

"Or perhaps these meetings await other lifetimes here," he ventured.

She looked quickly up at him. "I often read the poetry of Christina Rossetti…she alludes to such a thing."

He murmured acknowledgement. And then after a moment she admitted, "You are the only person I know who understands and shares my spiritual views…the only person who seems to think about such matters…apart from Gregory and Granny! And occasionally Melanie, but she thinks it morbid and prefers this day and its colourful events."

"I see…" he said.

"And I think I might be starting to love you…"

"I see!" he repeated, but more softly.

"Of course, I may be mistaken," she added, embarrassed now for both of them. Making such a claim in the cold light of day without preamble was unnerving. It was more damning and more important than wishing to sleep with him. Although the latter should follow the former and everyone knew it, even if they did not believe it.

"Yes, you may…" he confirmed. "Or you may have reason to cease loving me tomorrow…or the next day, or some other time when I displease you!"

She took several moments to think about this and moved some distance from his embrace and still held his hand loosely. "Are you saying I am so shallow or fickle that I turn my affections on and off like a tap?"

"No, I am saying that I obviously please you in some ways but perhaps not in all ways."

"That is true of everyone who loves another."

"Well…" he hesitated. "If I recall rightly, you abhor some of my values when weighed against your own…"

She allowed her mind to conjure and her logic to meet her instincts and for both to confer. Seconds passed and still he waited patiently. She released his hand and moved backwards and sank onto the edge of Granny's bed while he watched her without movement or comment. Granny meantime did not stir.

Presently she knew how to respond and looked at him in his rustic clothes with his splendidly barbered hair. He was, as Melanie had remarked, one of the most eligible and attractive men of the shire. How many women would be foolish enough to hold childhood grievances against him when fate had placed him in one role and her in another. Many might say she was mad to think like that. He had not spoken of love to her, but then she perceived that in many ways he did not need to and might only very infrequently do so. Words were very cheap; she had been born with that knowing.

"But at times now I think my feelings are overtaking my loathing and despising," she announced into the silent room.

"I am gratified," he said, as Jemima moved in the bed and mumbled to herself. "But if you do not do as I ask in important matters, then you may have cause to say you do not love me."

"That sounds like a form of threat," she murmured and looked at her fingernails.

"No, 'tis merely an observation."

She shook her head and tutted and some of her hair fell from the scarf which held it. "I hate it when you begin with your subtle and not so subtle warnings...couched as observations or not..."

"That is just what I mean."

"There is no answer to it," she replied and frowned at the light lace veil which now partly covered her grandmother's face. Slyly placed there so that she could pretend to sleep while watching and listening to them talk.

"I will not be ordered around by anyone," she said, "Which is why I am so unsure about marriage...in marriage men often become..."

"Become what?"

"I do not know exactly...demanding! Or perhaps tyrannical!"

He sighed; there were no obvious or immediate answers to this. It was in general true but lacked a point of specific reference. He walked around the spacious room and looked with particular interest at one or two of the paintings on the wall. "Are these your work?"

"Only one of them...the one to your right."

"Excellent!" he said. Then looking at the sleeping form of the old woman, he asked. "Are you saying you think I may be demanding and tyrannical?"

She stood from the bed and paced. "I was speaking generally..."

"But generally, Melissa, 'tis only me we are talking of, is it not? There comes a point when you must stop talking generally and talk specifically," he said. "'tis part of the bonding of two people."

She resisted his attempt to propel her to the door. She turned to face him. His gaze upon her bore too much honesty and too much concern and she knew she needed to refute or dilute her previous words. "You are already issuing me with orders." She thought of the implications of love and jealousy and hurt and decided to be braver. "You are saying in some roundabout way that there will be consequences if I do not stop receiving Roger."

"I am saying it in a direct way…it cannot continue…you cannot receive his visits with the same innocence now that he has declared his feelings," he said at length.

"Roger is always declaring his feelings…it means very little."

"To him it obviously does." He stepped away from her and watched her. "So, now has come a point of reckoning… He knows I am a rival for your affections. You cannot go on playing with him. You either take him seriously as a man, as a suitor, or you do not. It becomes a moral issue and one of his integrity…and your own for that matter."

"If I accepted his suit, he would not know what to do with me…" she said impatiently. "He is, in a sense, play acting."

He frowned and pondered. He had never heard such nonsense, outside of novels and theatres. She saw it but knew not how to fathom it in a way which satisfied her. Here was an impasse reached. "And if I tell him to stay away from me 'tis a form of cruelty, is it not? He has relied upon my friendship for so long…he tells me of his concerns in general and I am like his sister."

He contemplated further and went to retrieve his cigars then remembered they were in his jerkin downstairs and that anyway he was in someone's bedroom. He could see the dilemma from her point of view—he was not without sensibility—but he saw also the point of no return they had reached. "Melissa, you are no longer like his sister. Unless he is…" he stopped abruptly, not knowing how to enter certain forbidden territory with her.

"Is what?" she demanded.

"I doubt he will see you as a sister," he affirmed.

"Well, that is how I feel."

"That is another matter."

She knew well what he said but preferred not to admit it. She felt insincere and moved to the nub of the issue. "And if I continue to see him and tell him besides that he can never have me as a wife or a lover? Would you agree to that?"

He was unprepared for this kind of emotional and moral conundrum. He did not know Roger Brathwaite, but he felt that if Braithwaite was a man at all he would demand her answer and then act accordingly. He would not beseech her and harrow her with his immature bids for attention. They were perhaps built on nothing but his own faulty impressions of what a man should be or do. On nothing but the need to keep what he valued in the way he valued it. Even so, he may go as far as wedlock, many men did without the armoury to survive within it.

"Would you agree to it, Anthony?" she repeated.

"I do not know…" he said finally. "Though I doubt it… I would have to end our association or put an end to his illusions."

This seemed to please her in some way—he could see it. But it was beyond his range of experience to date. Then she jumped suddenly into the breach and declared: "For certain, I do not wish to be married to Roger. Nor do I wish for Roger to take me to his bed."

"I want you to stop receiving him," he said with infinite patience and lowered his voice to an even gentler octave so that she would not accuse him of ordering her about or mistake his concern for tyranny. "Now let us go downstairs!" He took her arm and walked with her to the door. She knew he believed that she had not written to Roger. And he in his turn knew she had little intention of doing so, left to herself. She felt too that he knew her well now, and it made her feel vulnerable and comforted and accepted, and a whole host of other things that were seductively dangerous. She resisted his pull once more about a foot from the door. "But you see, this does not answer my fear of not being ordered around once married."

Now he was becoming impatient, and that again did not displease her. She looked at him for a reply and he took a deep breath. "This discussion does not constitute my ordering you around…'tis an outlining of what is acceptable to me and necessary to the conventions. That is not the same as me *ordering you around!*" He paused to see if she had understood the difference, and seeing her to be displaying an unreadable expression he continued. "I know you to be…among your other interesting qualities…a wilful little madam, disposed to doing what you wish to do and not in the habit of considering what others wish of you…and do not imagine that my love for you blinds me to that, for it does not."

She took in a breath unexpectedly and choked on it and coughed; he had used the word *love*. "But what will be next on the list which displeases you about my behaviour?" she enquired, clamping her lips firmly together to prevent her showing humour.

"I have no idea,...but I do expect you to take seriously such requests..."

"You mean you want me to obey you in all things?" she said. "I do not know if I can...or wish to..."

His expression changed slowly to a more grave mask of deliberation, so that his nostrils flared slightly and his eyes grew darker in colour. It thrilled her in that deeper and more unknown part of her body.

"In important things, yes...of course I do," he confirmed.

There were now two completely differing parts of herself at war, two very different aspects of her vying for conquest. She could not reconcile them or even bring them to align. "Well, you see..." she began. Then the door opened and her mother entered and the moment of honesty was lost, a curtain had descended to obscure the landscape. Marguerite looked askance at Melissa's dishevelled hair and the paint smears on her face and she barely disguised her distaste. "What is the matter that you are up here?"

"Anthony carried Granny up," Melissa stated in the cool and desultory voice she used to address her mother on most occasions. "She is exhausted...we were worried about her."

Her mother sighed and again barely disguised her chagrin at the attention demanded by her mother-in-law in her dotage. "Anthony, I am sorry you should be troubled by this."

"'tis no trouble, Ma'am," he replied. "I am glad I was here to assist."

Marguerite smiled her sweetest sickliest smile and patted his arm in a condescending manner and then looked sidelong at her daughter. "Lissy, perhaps you should see to your appearance...'tis most disconcerting."

"He does not mind my appearance...do you not, Anthony?"

He hesitated, looking at neither female. "I do not," he concurred, unable to lie.

Melissa flashed a self-satisfied glance at her mother and Marguerite turned and held the door open for them to exit, and he stood back and indicated politely for her to go ahead of them. Marguerite noted that Fairchild himself was dressed very casually that day. Very unlike his sartorial elegance. The two of them were a match in some way—they looked like country folk rather than persons of higher society. He perhaps had been riding or pursuing other outdoor activities, but there was no excuse for her daughter beyond her usual negligence to anything except her art.

Melissa flew down the stairs while he followed at a more dignified pace. Once in the hall she pulled him towards her art room and he walked more quickly to keep up with her. "Interfering old bat…" she intoned with some venom.

"To whom do you refer?" he enquired, as if misunderstanding.

"My mother, of course…certainly not Granny…my mother thinks she is the queen bee of the mansion!"

He grinned and said, "She is the queen bee of the mansion, Melissa… She is the matriarch."

"She is an annoying old witch… I detest her."

Closing the door behind them she indulged her frustration verbally on the subject. "And do not start next with your sermons about respecting one's parents or some such humbug, I implore you."

"Sermons are my elder brother's province… I am simply a linguist," he said. "I shall save my breath!"

"That is right…save it to kiss me…" She tore off her smock and cast it aside. He waited with apprehension to see if she would remove more of her clothing and wondered what he would do if she did. But she stopped at the smock. Wearing her better day dress beneath it she looked now quite transformed. She loosened her hair from the scarf which held it and then tied it back behind her neck in a more respectable style.

She took his arm and he allowed her to propel him into the one chair so that she may sit on his lap and begin kissing him, before he could raise the subject of Roger again—the other tedious fly in the ointment.

* * *

Riding home he was preoccupied by the question of Braithwaite, and then of childhood sweethearts. His own had met with an untimely demise; did he merely resent the man based on this. He doubted it but still questioned himself. He had thought of an Eastern philosophical treatise introduced to him while at Oxford. Whereby life was lived by mirror images. *The reflection one sees in outer life being the vision one holds inwardly.* It had held some sway with him at the time.

It was not that he feared Braithwaite's presence in her life; she had admitted that it was some kind of childish game he played as she humoured him within it. Even so, it was not to be dismissed lightly. They could not go on playing it while Braithwaite believed it to be a serious stage requiring the simulations of pre-matrimonial manoeuvres.

Then a worse thought struck him as he rode; had Lottie's own activities in the latter months of their association been no more than a childish game in which he humoured her? If so, he had refused her marriage until it was too late! The thought and the revelation were too much for him. He needed a drink. He picked up speed on the horse and turned down a lane which led to a tavern just out of the town. It was Friday night, so he could drink to his heart's content and then ride back in the dark, having imbibed enough to drown his sorrows but not enough to fall off the horse or drop off to sleep as he rode. He would be undisturbed in there, without much probability of being known or recognised by anyone, which was always the case these days in town.

He tethered the horse and mounted the steps to the 'Dog and Partridge'. But scarcely had he ordered the first drink in the quiet place when he was approached by Dominic McCarthy.

"Tony! What a surprise! How comes you in here?"

"I was hoping for a quiet drink…or three!" he replied.

Though a couple of years younger than himself McCarthy was already a senior member of staff and the one Stevenson would have liked to replace him as deputy. "What are you drinking?" he asked him as the barmaid pushed the ale towards him.

"The same as you…" replied McCarthy. "But I shall have only the one… I am with a girl…"

Fairchild nodded to the barmaid to fetch his friend a drink and then raised his brows and looked around to see the female mentioned. "A girl?"

"A young lady, I should say here in the English shires."

Fairchild wondered what manner of female met with a man in this kind of place unless being a jade or a married woman. "What time does she arrive?" he enquired.

"She is already here," McCarthy lowered his voice. "Upstairs…we have a room for the night," he added. "She will join me for a drink presently, before we dine and then retire…" He winked in a manner which was not so much lewd as conspiratorial.

"God's Teeth," said Fairchild. "I shall move off in case she is embarrassed."

"Ah no…she won't be embarrassed. Perhaps just a little shy… I have been seeing her a good while."

"So, that is why you have not been attending your cousin's weekend soirees?"

"Indeed."

"Is it serious?"

"'tis getting that way…" McCarthy quaffed the ale with a thirst shown only by men of robust constitution, then went on. "She is in service at one of the large country houses…'tis her one night off, so we have to make hay."

"In service?" Fairchild echoed before he could prevent himself. Knowing of the other's vaguely aristocratic heritage, he was not expecting to hear of such a portended union.

"You see, you are shocked," said McCarthy.

"No, just a little taken aback."

"'tis the same thing…let's not split hairs…'tis why if all continues well, I shall take her back to Ireland…they are not so faddy about class and status over there. 'tis merely religion concerns them… I can marry her and she can be anyone she cares to invent on becoming my wife."

Fairchild took generous swigs of his own ale and studied him. "Dominic, you're a dark horse…marriage and prodigal returns all in one breath."

"You have been enjoying them yourself, though? The soirees?" queried McCarthy.

"I have, yes…on and off…but it will stop soon, I imagine. Like you, I hope to settle down."

Dominic clapped him on the shoulder. "When you meet a woman you gel with, you should act… I am of a mind now to start a family…my papist upbringing, no doubt. She has no immediate family; she is an orphan…and Ireland is where my heritage is…so we can live happily there I hope…"

Fairchild clinked his tankard against McCarthy's and then raised it. "To your wellbeing and your intended family," he said and smiled widely. He liked people to prosper in their chosen ways.

"I expect we will go at summer recess…but I will not leave Nicholas in the lurch…he is wanting a deputy since your resignation, and cannot be without a history master as well…"

"That is considerate of you…" Fairchild was about to elaborate when a young woman he vaguely recognised approached the scene cautiously from his left, prettily attired and becoming to the eye.

"Dominic…" she said shyly, and Dominic turned and then put his arm around her waist. "Sweetheart, this is a fellow I work with…our deputy head at the Grange…"

As she stepped forwards into the lamplight above the counter he saw that it was Polly, the maid from the Shaw mansion.

"Polly Finch…this is Tony Fairchild," Dominic announced with pride.

Polly looked at him with some alarm and as McCarthy turned to her Fairchild smiled at her and gently shook his head, meeting her eyes with his direct stare and raising his brows; conveying to her not to let on just now that they already knew each other. He bowed to her formally. "Ma'am, I am delighted to make your acquaintance."

She offered him her hand and made a brief curtsy. "And I the same, Sir."

"Don't call him Sir," quipped McCarthy merrily, "he will think he is back at work."

Fairchild grinned and McCarthy laughed and Polly smiled demurely and said: "I shall not call him anything at all… I will leave you to drink. I must take a short turn around the green… I am in need of air."

"I shall join you presently," said her lover and Fairchild again bowed to her as she inclined her head to him and withdrew.

"A lovely girl!" he told Dominic as they finished the ale.

"Is she not!" said Dominic with softening eyes. "She should not be in service…'tis not the rightful place for her, though she works for decent people…she has a friend and ally in the daughter of the house, a girl about her own age who is uncommonly good to her…she will be sorry to leave. She has known her since they were in their early teen years, but…the time has come for me to take her to other realms."

"Where did you meet her?" enquired Fairchild lightly.

"The bandstand in the large town park…one Sunday on her day off, listening to the music and dancing, as I was doing the same." Dominic lifted his ale and finished it. "We danced together for quite a while…and that was it. I was smitten!"

"Serendipity!" declared Fairchild, and thought of Melissa as the girl who was good to McCarthy's future wife—it was a laudable testament to her character.

McCarthy checked his timepiece and said: "I will be off to fetch her so we will dine. She will immediately fall to sleep the minute she is in bed and then sleep for two hours…she has been working since early morning and is exhausted… I can only lie next to her and look at her."

Fairchild was mesmerised by this account told in Dominic's rich Celtic brogue, and he stared at him with a benign expression as he went on. "But you know, 'tis amazing how when they mean something to you 'tis enough just to hold them…do you not find?"

He thought of Melissa and of being unable to take her fully as a woman but being happy to hold her nonetheless. He smiled in sudden appreciation. "I do Dom… I certainly do!" The coincidence was staggering. The revelations today coupled with this coincidence, he needed more than ever to think in solitude. "Go and join her…" he told his colleague. "You have precious little time alone and cannot waste it…"

McCarthy drained the tankard. "I shall see you on Monday then, Tony."

"Indeed," said Fairchild and ordered himself another drink and moved to a table near the small window, so that he would not be the victim of more surprise meetings this night. He pondered the question of whether to tell Melissa of this meeting with Polly, and of what Polly was intending. Or did Melissa already know? He doubted it—it was the kind of item she loved to tell him. He became steadily more inebriated, but not incapacitated.

Eventually, on his ride home, he decided that he would acquaint McCarthy in the next week with the knowledge of how he knew Polly, in case he had put her in an untenable position where McCarthy may construe that they had both deceived him. Or that his wife-to-be was dishonest before the ring was on her finger. Or perhaps she would have already told him herself. But he would let Polly tell the Shaw residence in her own time. That part was not his concern.

On reaching his lodgings he fell into bed without too many concerns. *In drink life might always be viewed as a series of errors or happenstance for which one could not be held accountable!* This philosophy was of course a veritable refuge for people who imbibed and he was aware of it as he drifted into oblivion.

* * *

Later on, at the Shaw mansion, Marguerite moved about the bedroom she shared with her husband, readying herself for the night's sleep. Her face covered

412

in rejuvenating cream and her nightcap firmly tied beneath her chin to keep it from sagging while she slumbered. She was imparting information to Giles in fits and starts. "…and she was so unfit to be seen, 'twas unbelievable…"

"I doubt he takes much notice of that…" Giles said, removing his dressing robe.

"She looked like someone from the workhouse…or the pottery sheds, dressed in that old smock…and the worst of it is, he says he doesn't mind her appearance…" continued Marguerite. "Mind you, he was dressed very shabbily himself today…he is normally so formally attired…"

Giles climbed into bed. "Of course he is…how do you expect him to dress? He's a head of one of the best teaching establishments in these parts, so he has no choice…but that does not mean he likes to dress like that all the time."

"Yes, but she is nearly always dressed like a gypsy when he calls! What can be the matter with him that he finds her desirable in that way?" Marguerite demanded.

Giles yawned and settled himself into the large four poster—big enough to sleep five. "Nothing is the matter with him…he's a man."

"What?" Marguerite squinted in his direction, somewhat short-sighted in low lights. "What do you mean?"

"I mean he sees beyond her dress to what lies beneath!"

"He can easily see what lies beneath when she wears very few under garments with some of those frocks of hers…"

"Men like a bit of honesty in a woman… He's perhaps thankful to glimpse the concealed worth of what he's bargaining for…"

Marguerite snorted and threw her dressing robe onto a chair in annoyance. Giles was as bad as his mother for those kinds of remarks. "She goes about with that smug cat-like look on her face…with that glow women have…don't forget, Giles, how we were at that age!"

"I can just about recall…" said Giles, wondering where he found his stamina in those days. "Betimes, that may pass soon enough when they are wed a few years…not all unions are as fortunate as my parents."

Marguerite sighed ostentatiously; the references to Jago and Jemima's blissful passions were as tiresome as they were frequent in the family. "*If they are ever wed,*" she muttered darkly. "It had best be soon and you must make sure of it." Gazing sidelong at Giles's recumbent form, she dismissed the slight to their own marriage as accidental. That she did not possess the passionate natures

413

of Jemima, or his sister Amaelia…and obviously now her own daughter…was unfortunate. Giles had, in former years, taken mistresses, which she also easily dismissed.

Different qualities were required for wives and mothers than mistresses, and she had done well out of her marriage. "If he doesn't claim her maidenhead before they are betrothed, then I am the queen of Sheba…"

Giles turned over and pulled the eiderdown up to his ears. "You're the queen of somewhere, to be sure," he muttered.

Marguerite remembered something else and ignored whatever retort he had mumbled. "…and the other day they appeared to be involved in a struggle…yet again!"

"Perhaps you shouldn't listen at the door…" he said drowsily. "Leave 'em to court."

"Courting surely doesn't require them to roll about on the carpet! I heard him telling her to let go and then her squealing…which is when I paused to listen…"

Giles sighed—the bulletins on the progress of his daughter's courtship were endless, speculative and tedious. "It'll be the tomfoolery young 'uns indulge in when romancing…best they roll around on the floor now…a'fore they're too old to get up again unassisted!"

"This is not helped by your witticisms, Giles." She smoothed the lotion into her face and pondered—appalled at his libertine attitude to these kinds of goings on, herself helpless within them. "Have you no further thoughts on the matter?"

"None of merit," said Giles. "And don't forget to turn down the lamps a'fore you get in bed."

The Circular Motion of Life

The fundraising event at the Trimingham mansion was a huge success. Much money was taken by admission fee and by generous donation. Her paintings, ten of them, all sold within two hours, barring one—which she thought she might donate to Trim's parents for allowing them the use of the ballroom. But then Geoffrey Gillis arrived with Melanie and bought the last remaining painting himself, generously paying twice its asking price. Fairchild was not yet in attendance and she dreaded him walking in and Melanie beginning on her favourite repertoire and disconcerting everyone, but it mercifully did not happen and the couple left after half an hour. Geoffrey kissed her cheek on departure and said: "What a clever little bridesmaid!" And Melanie told him not to be so condescending, though in a gentler and less acerbic tone than she used with others who committed the same offence.

Gregory played the grand piano—brought in from the Trimingham's drawing room for the purpose—and was later joined by the solo violinist. A female opera singer, travelling with the violinist, sang two arias, accompanied by them. Both the singer and the violinist were from the Slavic states and spoke barely any English and seemed genuinely humbled by the rapturous applause, accepting it all with modest bows and then disappearing quickly. Although they really had little idea of what cause they had raised the money for—performing as a favour to Gregory who helped them since their arrival in England.

Gregory played steadily throughout the afternoon, repeating upon request Chopin's Nocturne Number One three times, whereupon the room fell very silent and sombre and people were seen to dab at their eyes. He took small interludes to stretch his legs and drink tea and talk with visitors who were eager to make his acquaintance. Millicent later entered the stage and sat at the piano with him and they played together—Brahms and Mendelshon. And then Bach's pastoral suite, where again their audience were immensely moved.

It was in the midst of this that Fairchild arrived, with Dominic McCarthy. They had come directly from participating in a school cricket match, an obligatory occasion that went with their posts. McCarthy was eager to hear what was left of the musical recitals and keen to engage Gregory and Millicent in conversation, as a musician himself. Much impressed with their performance, he recalled Millicent vaguely from one of the mixed school dances years before and remembered partnering her.

He and Henrietta Madeley always took it in turns to play the piano, as did her successor, Julia Archer, and himself these days. He perceived Millicent to be as shy today as she was then but much changed in appearance. It was hard to get a word out of her. Then he recalled also that her name had been linked to the infamous *'chalking incident'* which had caused Fairchild to almost resign. But she was so modestly retiring that he wondered if he had remembered incorrectly, for no-one of her disposition could surely have been so bold in younger years.

Susan and Melissa oversaw the refreshments—paid for by Trimingham and Fairchild—with the help of one maid and a footman. Susan engaged in the kitchen in food preparation, and Melissa pouring tea and coffee and serving the dainties and the pastries with the maid.

In the aftermath of the refreshment duties, Susan Darnley encouraged her into conversation and plied her with questions. "I hear you are not keen on education, Melissa!" she began. "So, this is exceedingly good of you."

What else had Susan heard she wondered, as she thought how to reply. Knowing that Susan taught at the alms school, and was therefore herself also a schoolteacher; a delicate balance was required. "I am not really an advocate of it," Melissa told her. "Although I do believe people should be able to read and write and do some mathematics, such as is taught in the dame schools and the alms schools…or else how will the poor ever fend for themselves in this awful world!"

Susan paused in sorting the cutlery and came across and hugged Melissa briefly, and Melissa was overcome by sudden shyness.

Susan was quite dainty in stature—much smaller than Trimingham—with petite features and an open countenance and lustrous black hair worn long and lifted back from her face. Frequently she put on little gold framed spectacles to see things close up, and they changed her face completely. Melissa was fascinated, always noting the smallest and subtlest of altered angles in others.

At length, she thought she had earned the right to question Susan in her turn, so she began by saying: "May I ask you, Susan?" she paused and Susan stopped work to give her attention to the question, whatever it was to be. "Did you once know someone called Lottie…beloved of Anthony?"

The other girl was silent for a moment, taken aback perhaps. "Yes… Charlotte Fitzwilliam…she was my best friend since we were little girls."

"Oh, I see!" Melissa faltered and Susan waited politely for what else might come.

"What was she like?" Melissa now waited.

"She…she was generous…and bright…and funny…a little wild. She was a person one wished to be with…life was seldom dull."

"A little wild?" Melissa repeated, hoping for elucidation.

Susan ignored this reference and said, "Tony was utterly broken when she died…"

"Why had she been to Ireland?"

"She was an actress with a theatre troupe."

"An actress?" Melissa was aghast.

"She was forced to make her living and she had the talent. Her father was pressing her into a marriage of convenience…she needed to get away." Susan's voice was a flat monotone.

"Why did Tony not marry her to save her from that?" Melissa asked, knowing that soon the questioning would be deemed impolite.

Susan opened and closed her lips several times and eventually said: "That is something you must ask him yourself…though I think he would have done so had she survived."

She knew she would not ask him. It was not her business. It was nobody's business but their own. "So, you all played together when you were young?" she said brightly, changing tack.

"We did…though Lottie and I played together more. Timothy and Anthony were away at school all week, they joined us some weekends and in the holidays," Susan gazed at the ceiling where black smoke smudges discoloured the paintwork from years of cooking. "Tony's father was the village parson at that time and my father was the local doctor…and Trim's father owned the nearby pottery sheds… Lottie's father was the local squire…but the less said about him the better…"

"How wonderful for you all," declared Melissa.

"When you are children, you think life will go on endlessly without change, do you not! You do not think how it will be in the future and what can go wrong..." Susan continued in a quiet voice.

They were interrupted by the maid who told them that a visitor was outside in the ballroom asking for the lady artist. Melissa followed her to the door and then turned before leaving. "One more question, Susan! What was Anthony like as a little boy?"

Susan studied the ceiling again, wrinkled her nose in thought and then grinned. "Much the same as now...only smaller."

Melissa's laughter was appreciative as she left to follow the maid. Near the refreshment table stood a lady sipping tea and reading the various literature and letters written from dignitaries about the origins of the alms schools. Tall, well attired, and carrying herself majestically. When she turned around she gave the warmest of smiles and held out her hand.

Melissa accepted it, her own hand being gripped with meaning. "Melissa...forgive me for calling you by your first name, I have forgotten your last, I'm afraid. Thank you for agreeing to see me..." Her voice had a slight foreign accent. "Allow me to introduce myself... I am Hildegarde Wyevale."

"Oh," Melissa was at a loss.

"Anthony's mother!"

Then she saw that the resemblance to him was striking; the same bone structure and the same texture and curl of the hair, except that his mother's now was a very pale silver. His same direct way of looking people in the eyes..."I am very glad to meet you, Ma'am," said Melissa.

They appraised each other with candid fascination. "He is here somewhere abouts...he has been playing cricket."

"Cricket?" repeated his mother.

"Yes, he has no choice, apparently," said Melissa.

Mrs Wyevale lifted her brows. "Really! I was under the impression he was the deputy head, not head boy..."

Melissa giggled. Hildegarde plunged on by exclaiming: "I wanted in particular to thank you for the painting you made...the one he gave my husband and I at Christmas. It hangs in our dining room."

"Oh yes," said Melissa. "'tis not one of my best, but he liked it and thought you might."

"We do, indeed."

"Is your husband with you?" She was eager to see his stepfather also.

"He is not, unfortunately," said Mrs Wyevale. "He is always engaged in matters of the church at weekends. I wanted to come to meet you…" she paused and allowed Melissa to draw her own conclusions. "William Wyevale is my second husband. My first, the father to my sons, died some years ago."

"Yes, yes… I did know," said Melissa. "Also, a bishop I believe?"

Hildegarde's shrewd humorous eyes took in her every detail and intuited her thoughts. "Perhaps you would care to call and take tea with me soon…if you can spare the time…and if Tony will bring you. Or if you have your own conveyance, you could come alone. Let me know your availability a few days before by letter and I will reply at once. I should like you to undertake a second painting for me…for my husband's birthday in the late summer. 'tis of his dog. Do you paint animals?" She fished a calling card from her reticule and handed it to Melissa.

"Sometimes, yes… I am not very experienced in animal portraits but I could certainly attempt it for you. I am detailed to paint one for my closest friend's mother…and if you did not like it I…" She broke off as she saw him approaching and waited for him to come close. He regarded his mother. "Mama, how are you?"

Mrs Wyevale kissed him warmly and then he looked at Melissa. "You have been introduced?"

"Of course," said Hildegarde in her confident tones. "We are capable of making our own introductions, you know. I had someone fetch her… I was telling her of the painting I wish her to make for William…"

His mother was one of the world's redoubtable people whom others naturally accepted and welcomed. "I trust His Excellency is well?" he said, the slightest tinge of sarcasm on his stepfather's official form of address, and before she could reply he asked, "Have you driven yourself?"

"Indeed, in the phaeton," she replied.

"Could the groom not have brought you?" he enquired lightly.

His mother paused and then glanced at Melissa. "'tis wearying the way men believe we cannot drive ourselves competently…do you not find?"

"I do!" Melissa agreed. "My father believes the same…as do my brothers."

"The roads are unsafe," Fairchild said, "And the lanes perilous!"

"Only for women perhaps!" said Hildegarde in droll fashion. "And I have been driving myself since I was fifteen! Anyway, I do not have Richard with me if that is what you are worried about."

He turned to Melissa. "Richard is one of my brothers, as I may have mentioned…we do not see eye to eye. He would be a step too far for you on a day like today…"

"Tony, that is unfair…she should make her own evaluations," claimed his mother.

Adopting a pained and set expression he looked past his mother to the rest of the room which was quieter now but still held visitors here and there. "He would be slavering all over her with his blandishments and inappropriate remarks. She has probably never met men like him!"

Hildegarde seemed to hold her patience with great effort and said to Melissa: "He is exaggerating, ignore his remarks. Richard is somewhat outlandish but he is not as bad as he is being portrayed."

"He is perhaps worse…" said her youngest son with asperity. "I am being charitable. He is like to someone walked off stage at the Adelphi…a flamboyant coxcomb from the last century. He and that painted jade he keeps company with."

Melissa was now enthralled. He never normally criticised people in this way, being too well-mannered. She stared at him and then at his mother.

"You go too far!" said Hildegarde in a low aggravated tone. "He is your brother, after all."

"Well, so you say, Mama, but are you sure he was not swapped with another infant while you were sleeping?"

She was quickly succumbing to merriment which she felt she must resist; she could not hope to contain it while wearing her laces beneath her dress, she would pass out.

"He is not like anyone in the family, near or distant, whom I have come across…except perhaps for Uncle Charles," he said.

"Who then is Uncle Charles?" Melissa queried, intrigued.

"My first husband's eldest brother…" supplied Hildegarde. "A rather unpleasant man."

Fairchild scoffed. "A vast understatement, somewhat like comparing a ravening wolf to a feisty pet."

Hildegarde tutted and grew paler of face.

"He was just the kind of person you like to refine upon…" he told Melissa in rising satire. "A callous wretch…a veritable monster of cruelty. He is dead now, thank God! But perhaps that is where I might have inherited my worst traits by your estimation."

Melissa drew in breath which caught in her throat between a squeal of protest and a hiccup. "I do not like to refine upon such people…how dare you!" She coughed for a few moments as Hildegarde watched them both separately.

Once she had controlled her breathing she eyed him with suspicion, encouraging his satire further.

"He used to beat us prodigiously…myself and my brothers…and our male cousins…at every opportunity…he had no children of his own."

Melissa looked at Hildegarde who shook her head with magnanimous disdain. "And his wives," he added, "He beat them too…all three of them." He held her gaze in a challenging way, softened by his overall expression of affectionate desire.

"You are inventing all this…" she claimed hotly.

Hildegarde had heard enough. "'tis true," she confirmed. "And my husband and his brothers were unable to prevent it if they were absent…and so was I, even when I was not absent."

She was between horror and respect for Hildegarde's honesty.

"But really, it did us no harm…" he interjected with heightened relish, "Though I cannot speak for his wives, of course."

"I would expect you to say that!" Melissa said sharply.

Hildegarde turned to him. "Tony, cease now! She does not need to hear all this. Are you trying to discourage her or court her?"

"No, no, Mama…'tis just the kind of thing she adores to hear."

She watched him with annoyance and considered whether to prolong the issue or not with his mother present. Hildegarde had gleaned for herself that some kind of subtle game was underway, and even so was displeased with this open summary of their family's *dirty linen*. She addressed Melissa directly in ameliorating terms. "Disregard his remarks, I think he has been in a tavern quaffing before coming here."

He gasped his outrage in theatrical manner. "Nothing stronger than coffee has passed my lips today…though I hope to remedy that as soon as Trim appears…"

Then Hildegarde continued for Melissa's benefit. "'tis true also, my dear, that Richard is more like to some of the men of my first husband's family, in being rather loud and given to excesses…but Richard is not like Uncle Charles."

"Not yet, perhaps…" said her son, "Give him a few more years."

"He is simply overly exuberant and careless," amended Hildegarde.

"He is beyond even that!" exclaimed Fairchild. "He may well have been taken up from a crypt in Transylvania…"

Melissa succumbed to paroxysms of mirth and dragged a nearby wooden chair to their midst so she could sit, aware that she might faint from lack of air to her lungs. "He and that torrid creature both…" he added, causing her to pause her giggling and look up curiously, another character having been introduced to the amusing saga.

"He refers now to his…" Mrs Wyevale attempted to elucidate but was intercepted once more.

"…his paramour!" Fairchild said, "…his harlot."

"She is known as Lady Caroline Wentworth…" explained Hildegarde. "She inherited the title from her late husband."

"That is who she claims to be…" he interjected. "She is in reality a failed actress…she assists him in all his unsavoury schemes. The pair of them are caricatures."

"But I love caricatures," declared Melissa. "I adore colourful people…they make life interesting! And that is the only reason I am interested in your Uncle Charles…" she told him censoriously. "'tis also why I love Melanie…"

"Who is Melanie?" queried Hildegarde quickly, glad of the diversion.

"A further example of garish human nature," he replied just as quickly.

"That is simply rude…" Melissa protested and he turned with fake amazement to look at her. "Rude! How you have the temerity to use that adjective after her vulgar antics, I fail to understand…"

She felt herself flush but decided to ignore him; it was perhaps his mother's unexpected appearance making him careless of speech. "She is my closest friend," she informed Hildegarde.

Fairchild was disposed to lighten his expression and smile. "Yes, but the Wentworth woman would make Melanie appear sainted by comparison. She is predatory and lurid."

"Predatory?" said Hildegarde, allowing her curiosity to overrule her discretion. "Has she tried her predatory ways on you?"

"She may have done…" came his response in the same light tone. "I do not recall."

Hildegarde took this as an affirmative, a dawning understanding lit her face and she became sombre at the thought of the female whom her second son had welcomed into his life also having her claws into her youngest.

"But what sort of schemes does your brother make?" pursued Melissa in semi-innocence, fanning the flames.

"He is a banker," retorted Hildegarde before he could imply more derogatory accusations.

"He is more like a vulture," said Fairchild, determined not to be undermined, "And Caroline Wentworth is Lady Vulture."

This last appellation was too much and Melissa leaned forwards, her feet on the staves of the chair so that her knees were raised beneath her skirts as she put her face into the taffeta folds and released the hilarity at its height. Hildegarde watched her with benign amusement. "I do not wonder she is in convulsions...your comments today are beyond ridiculous!"

"Even so, Mama, I do not wish Richard to be introduced to her...at least not yet...he will prejudice her opinion of the family and I shall end up hitting him. I can see it clearly."

"I do not think he will prejudice anything," Melisa recovered and rose from the chair with little confidence that the hilarity had left her, "And I wish very much to meet him."

"Of course you do..." said Hildegarde tolerantly, and then to him. "Do you know nothing of human nature? You have kindled her interest now!"

He arched his brows and paused for deliberation. The thought of Melissa being in any way swayed or charmed by his brother was insufferable. "However, she does not need to meet with Richard yet... Rupert, certainly, she will like him...and Bella..."

"She may like Richard..." said Hildegarde in defence of her most unprepossessing child.

"She may...but I somehow doubt it."

Melissa sought to regain diplomacy by changing the subject. "Have you finished with the cricket now?"

"Yes, it finished with us...out for six wickets."

"Crickets? Wickets?" repeated his mother. "Are these insects?"

"No, Mama...you have seen it often on the village green...'tis a game played with bats and balls in which I am obliged to partake for certain matches...'tis in my terms of engagement, when we play against certain other schools..."

"What purpose does that serve?" asked Hildegarde.

Melissa, seeing the strangeness of the query, began to giggle again, covering her mouth with her kerchief.

"She giggles like this frequently…" he told Hildegarde, "So, try not to let it worry you."

"Of course she does," said Hildegarde. "All girls do when we are that age…'tis one of life's great pleasures." She smiled winningly. "And now I must be leaving. I must be home for this dinner with the diocese people…'tis very boring, but I always think of other things while they are prattling on with themselves."

Her accent had short vowels and long sibilants and Melissa wondered how she had not lost it in all this time in Britain. Perhaps it was a point of pride with her.

In the midst of these musings Mrs Wyevale leaned towards her and kissed her on both cheeks, warmly, in the way she had kissed him. "Is Eleanor hereabouts at present?" she asked suddenly, referring to Trim's mother. "I should have liked to see her before I leave."

"She was about earlier, listening to the music…" he replied. "Shall I have someone summon her?"

"Not at all…simply give her my love if you see her and tell her I shall see her at the Groves' anniversary dinner on Friday." She turned again to Melissa. "Goodbye, my dear… I look forwards to when we next meet."

"As do I," said Melissa, thinking how easily she had sent love to Eleanor Trimingham and not just stiff regards. She watched him escort Hildegarde to her phaeton and she knew without a moment's doubt that she would like his mother a lot better than she liked her own.

* * *

Returning to the kitchen to help with the last of the clearing process she found Susan humming to herself as she recounted the money from the day's takings for the fourth time. "There is a veritable fortune here…" she announced, her eyes behind the tiny spectacles gleaming. "I could not be more pleased, Melissa…"

"I have just met Anthony's mother," she told Susan, dismissing the financial triumph.

"A splendid woman!" affirmed Susan. "She is on the orphanages committee so our paths often cross at Parish Council meetings… Melissa, we could perhaps host another event for the orphanages, in a while, if you were willing."

Melissa inclined her head in acknowledgment. "Yes, by all means. Our own ballroom will be refurbished in a couple of months. My parents closed it for lack of use. It houses old unwanted furniture at present, but my mother dislikes that. She would rather have it intact, even if it is not utilised…though I shall need some time to produce more paintings."

"Of course," agreed Susan happily.

"So, you know Hildegarde?" Melissa queried.

"Indeed. I knew her in childhood too, naturally."

"Do you know Anthony's brother, Richard?" she asked of this newly acquired useful mine of information. "Did he play with you when you were children?"

Susan paused from the engrossing sight of the money—enough now to see them through the next year at least.

"No, he did not…he is a few years older. He is quite an odd and dubious character…"

"Anthony cannot bear him, it seems."

"With good reason," said Susan.

"And what of Uncle Charles…" Melissa ventured. "What do you know of him?"

Susan lifted her head from the cash tin and pondered. "I know only what Tim told me of him…he was cruel and tyrannical to the boys of the family… I remember Timothy once telling me when we were about twelve or so that he went to call for Tony who appeared at a window and said that Charles had beaten them so badly he could not walk well enough to leave the house."

Melissa sat abruptly on a chair near the table, feeling sick at the thought. "That is quite dreadful…who could do that to children!"

"Many people, unfortunately!" said Susan. "Charles Fairchild was a tyrant of mammoth proportions." She chewed on a pastry thoughtfully. "Every family has one somewhere along the line, I suppose…an *Uncle Charles!*"

"I do not think ours does…" Melissa said quietly. "Does yours?"

"Actually, no…we should consider ourselves fortunate, should we not!"

"Indeed…" Melissa concurred and considered the work she knew Anthony Fairchild undertook with the Foundation outside of his professional duties. "He jests that he has inherited the traits of Uncle Charles," she offered uncertainly.

Susan tossed her hair from her neck and made a pained face. "He is simply *jesting*, Melissa."

"I would hope so," she replied softly.

"Of course he is…'tis perhaps the way he copes with the memories of that appalling man." And then Susan swiftly changed direction. "I would ask you if you'd care to attend at the two alms schools now and then…but I perceive you will not agree."

Melissa shook her head, aghast at the thought.

"I thought you could perhaps draw or paint with them…they would adore it and most of them will not get a chance like it in their entire lives."

"I could not," said Melissa. "I would be too nervous…they may eat me alive. I would not be any good with them…"

"I know not why!" Fairchild said, appearing suddenly in the kitchen. "They have no idea about manners, are often unwieldy and tend to say the first thing that comes into their heads…you may feel quite at home."

She gaped at him, about to say *'how dare you'* for the second time and then refused to give him the satisfaction. "I hope you have done with your outrageous remarks today!"

He put his arm about her waist and kissed her neck. "Perhaps you simply dislike being played at your own game," he said into her ear.

"I would be in the classroom with you…" Susan went on, as if they had not been interrupted. "I would not throw you to the lions in that way."

"Why do you not volunteer?" Melissa said to him. "Once you leave the Grange you will have more time…and you may miss teaching…you and Trim!"

He looked askance at her and then at Trimingham who had entered with him. "I doubt it!" Trim said. "We do not teach for pleasure."

"Just so," Fairchild claimed. "Besides, I do not have the patience with those kind of children…for all the reasons I just gave you."

"Tony, for heaven's sake!" objected Susan. "They cannot help their background…'tis not their fault."

"I am aware of that, Susan…but it does not change matters!" he replied.

"And yet you care enough to campaign for them," Melissa stated lightly.

He smiled. "That is altogether different than working with them. I claim no credit in that…"

The enigma engaged her for a moment and then she thought of their classroom grievances yet again. She refused to be charmed by his smile. "Though on further reflection, Susan…" she said. "If you wish these children to keep attending you should perhaps not be inflicting *him* upon them." She pointed her thumb at him without looking his way. He pretended to fall backwards, hitting his chest with his fist as if fatally wounded. Then Trimingham said: "You asked for that!"

"And what they fail to include in their list of paltry excuses," continued Susan blithely, "when I suggest they perhaps take the Saturday morning classes, is that it may get in the way of their Friday night quaffing."

"There is that, of course, Susie…" Trim confirmed with shameless candour, picking up a couple of dainty sandwiches left over from earlier. "Speaking of which, Anthony, let us retire upstairs!" he concluded.

There prevailed almost a festive mood, all present had found a level of easy kinship.

"You see, they show no remorse at all…" Susan told Melissa airily. "And the states of inebriation which ensue beggar belief…"

Fairchild moved to the doorway. "Miss Darnley, I beg of you to keep a civil tongue in your head… Trim, time to retire! Your good lady is becoming a shrew."

Susan threw at him a tightened ball of damp cloth with which she had been wiping the wooden table and Fairchild dodged it by turning sideways. Then she went on smoothly. "Tim, I have to leave in half an hour so please do not have more than a couple of drinks before then… You will need to lift some of the furniture between you. I promised your parents all would be restored…and Melissa and I certainly cannot be lifting heavy furniture…" She had one eye on Fairchild, anticipating any retaliatory moves.

"Of course you cannot!" said the happy-go-lucky Trimingham. "We would not dream of leaving that to you. We are far too well-bred!"

"Yes, but 'tis the point when you are far too *well foxed* that is of most concern to me…" said Susan and Melissa trilled her laughter. Fairchild moved towards Susan and kissed her cheek. "We will be down again shortly…we just have some minor business details to discuss…"

"Of course!" retorted Susan. "Which of the brandy to consume or whether to have the rum instead…you will be incapable of heavy work by six thirty if I do not set a deadline."

"And Susan…" Trim turned to her with a serious expression, "Do not even consider taking that cash tin with you into the trap…give it to me and I will put it in my father's safe for now."

Susan sighed and clutched the tin possessively. "'twill be safe enough… I can go to the bank first thing on Monday…"

"No, Susan… It is not safe to be riding about back lanes carrying that amount of money," said her beloved emphatically, his patience tested. "You do not know who might see you with it and follow you. There are some unsavoury characters lurking about the lanes."

"I never see any," said Melissa in innocence. "And I am in the lanes quite often, sketching and painting."

"That also is not always safe," said Fairchild.

"Bad enough that you drive the phaeton when the groom could do it," Trim said to Susan, underlining Hildegarde's previous sentiments. Melissa began to giggle, though it was not apparent why to either Susan or Trimingham.

"You waste your breath on this issue…" Fairchild said to his friend. "None of them will listen."

Trim took the tin from Susan and a slight disagreement ensued which she knew she would not win. Fairchild stepped towards Melissa in the interlude and kissed her. "I am very proud of you…and you look very fine today." She reached her face to his and they began kissing, reluctant to release, kissing more ardently by the second. Trim coughed politely and Susan stared. "Come along, my dear fellow…" Trim said to him, carrying the tin. "While the going is good."

"Yes, off you go…" Susan began again washing the table top. Her apron and sleeves dusted liberally in icing sugar and butter; she looked more like the Trimingham's resident cook. "Or the time will fly by…and do not forget to return… I shall drive Melissa home if you wish, Tony, since I will be passing High Lawns on my way…and then you and Timothy can move the furniture with the footman. In fact, I shall come for you before I leave, to make sure you have not forgotten."

Melissa and he came apart. "Yes, thank you, Ma'am…very good, Ma'am…much obliged, Ma'am…" mumbled Fairchild.

They jogged to the back staircase hoping not to be detained elsewhere. "Trim, I swear Susan grows bossier by the month."

"I am used to it," said Trim blithely. "I do not notice it…"

"Obviously not!" retorted Fairchild, but then bethought himself that next to the likes of Caroline Wentworth women like Susan Darnley were the *salt of the earth*.

"When there is a serious issue at stake, I always stand my ground…" Trimingham shook the cash tin and Fairchild thumped him lightly on the shoulder and grinned, reminded again of the deceptively mild quality of Trimingham's nature, shielding the metal beneath.

* * *

They were about to mount the back stairs when they were intercepted by Gregory Montalbein, carrying his satchel of music and accompanied by Milicent Bromley. It was the last thing they needed but they were obliged to stop and Trimingham said heartily: "Gregory, thank you, dear boy. A very good show…we are obliged to you." He turned to Fairchild. "Is that not so, Tony?"

"Indeed. People have been most entertained and hopefully you will receive more engagements from this," Fairchild supplied helpfully.

"We already have several…" enthused Gregory. "Do we not, Millie? Gentlemen, may I present formally, Miss Bromley, my accompanist and dear friend, Millicent Bromley! Timothy Trimingham and Anthony Fairchild, Millie!" Gregory looked at her and saw nothing amiss in her usual shyness as she clung to his arm. He took it to be exhaustion and her delicate constitution and fear of strangers. To outsiders Millie might seem about to faint and her air of tremulous uncertainty was disconcerting. These days she was quite transformed: mostly because her former mousey brown hair was lightened to a pale almost flaxen colour—obviously the result of her hairdresser—and it suited her pale complexion and her light translucent eyes.

Gone was the female of insipid countenance; she bore now a subtle beauty of her own which defined and enhanced her for her musical appearances. She had grown a little taller, of course, but had still the same timid personality (within a silent strength, fostered and not impeded by her reserve). Fairchild saw all this in a trice with his honed instinct into her gender and what they brought to the world. He was tempted to smile at her more widely but thought better of it. It was best not to look so directly at shy women, he had discovered, but to allow them their privacy at close quarters.

Gregory, however, was gazing at her as if she had fallen from the heavens, and Fairchild—remembering Melissa's statement about her having loved him during her school days—became hesitant in his own way. Accentuated in a list of those pupils who detested him, the contrast was almost insufferable. Then Trimingham bowed and said, "Delighted to meet you, Miss Bromley!"

Fairchild brought himself to look at her and lifted her free hand and kissed it briefly. "We are already acquainted! Miss Bromley, how good to see you again...and how beautifully you play these days... Miss Madeley will be gratified..."

Millie's cautious smile faded at the mention of Henrietta Madeley. She stepped back and leaned harder on Gregory for support as he looked at her with some concern. Her frailty was always a concern to him and he knew it always would be, but was not yet aware that it was the main part of her allure for him. Her usually alabaster skin had turned a delicate peony pink. "I do not... I fail to see how she will...how she will come to hear of it," stammered Millie. "But 'tis good of you to say so."

"Oh, she will hear of it!" Trim said enthusiastically. "Her father is vicar at St James' and my parents attend quite frequently...so they will tell him the news of today by way of conversation..."

"Oh!" was all Millie could think to say. "Please send her my fondest regards through them." She was heartened to hear of Henrietta whom she had loved dearly. She glanced swiftly at Fairchild and he read her mind. "She is wed now..." he said in matter-of-fact tone, "To a clergyman in Scarborough, I believe..."

"I see!" breathed Millicent in wonderous tone.

"Yes, Trim keeps abreast of these matters..." continued Fairchild evenly. "Do you not, Timothy? He loves these parochial chronicles and follows them avidly...that way he does not need to waste money on popular novels." The humour in this statement was a gamble, it might have gone either way, but Gregory grinned and Millie almost smiled. Trim briefly closed his eyes in tolerant good humour and said obligingly. "According to my mother, she just a few months ago was delivered safely of her first child...a little girl."

Millicent gasped with awe and looked at Trim with shining eyes, as if he were one of the three wise men arrived at Bethlehem. She looked next at Gregory who was bemused, having no knowledge of who Henrietta was. "She taught us music, and she paid particular attention to me…" Millicent informed him.

"As well she might!" remarked Gregory adoringly.

"So, you see…" Fairchild interjected. "All's well that ends well…" This was further irony under the circumstances and not lost on Millicent. She blushed more deeply and Gregory felt he had missed vital pieces of the history so far. Another awkward silence fell and Millie cast her eyes to the ground and all present noted her trembling. Fairchild could stand no more and leapt into the breach. "Melissa is in the kitchen, I believe…should you wish to speak with her."

Millicent peered at him with consternation and attempted to form words which did not materialise.

"I think we will just," began Gregory, but then Melissa came tripping along the hallway with several forgotten shawls and fans and gloves in the way of lost property. She hurried over to them, dropping the items onto a nearby chair. "Millie, how wonderful to see you…" She pulled Millie from Gregory's clutches and embraced her, stroking her back soothingly while moving her gently out of the fray. "Do not be alarmed…" she told her softly.

Millicent looked at Melissa with a childlike wide-eyed confusion and whispered. "I am simply overwhelmed."

"Of course you are…" Melissa turned to the men. "Greg, we must bring Millie to the kitchen and I will make her strong tea. She is a little faint perhaps after all the exertion and excitement…"

Gregory was torn but Fairchild said: "Yes, that is the best thing…"

"Perhaps give her some brandy too…the maid will acquire it for you if you ask her," Trimingham added.

Fairchild nudged Trim forwards to the stairs, bowed again to Millie and shook Gregory's hand. Melissa took Millie by the arm and led her off, with Gregory loping behind them.

Once upstairs in Trim's parlour, Trim enquired: "What was all that about…with the pianist wench?"

"You do not wish to know," said Fairchild, reluctant to enter into explanation.

"Is she by chance one of your former pupils, at school with Melissa?" pursued Trim.

"Just so!" replied Fairchild.

"That would explain all the quaking and trembling," Trim quipped. "You being the veritable ogre you are over there!"

"Yes, but Miss Bromley is without doubt a die-away heroine of the first water…she will be fortunate to make it to thirty years…so do not take too much notice." Fairchild sank thankfully into an armchair.

"She seems to be a timid and shy little creature to me…wait a moment!" Trim paused at the small table containing the alcohol. "Wasn't she the third girl in the chalking of your names on the board? Yours and Henrietta's?"

"Indeed, she was!" Fairchild said with heavy patience, sighing out the words.

Trim made a noise of self-satisfaction on having his good memory validated.

"You are quite right, she is a timid little thing…and she was quite the model pupil." Fairchild added, seeing that Trim had not moved towards pouring the drinks and was effectively lost in thought. "But then she became embroiled with Melissa and the Petersham girl in the *grand chalking scheme*…although the intricacies of her part remain a mystery due to my not paying due diligence perhaps…and when I tried to get to the root of it back then she would not speak out. Then when I tried again recently with Melissa, I was met with the hostilities of which you are already familiar…'twas all my fault, as you know, and nothing whatever to do with their misconduct…so I prefer to let sleeping dogs lie…and what else can I say to you?"

Trim was pouring brandy into balloon glasses and looked over in preparation to comment, but Fairchild went on. "And 'tis made more awkward now by Melissa having informed me that she was in love with me back then, or some such girlish notion… Millicent, I mean, not Melissa! Damn embarrassing… I wish she had not told me."

Trim paused in the act of stoppering the brandy decanter. "Melissa perhaps did so to make you feel bad about your actions. Girls conjure up these kinds of illusions all the time…"

Fairchild sat upright and groaned. "Not alongside my terrible cruelty, surely?"

"Especially alongside that," said Trim with consummate wisdom. "They need to sweeten their plight and find you more tolerable."

"And here was I hoping to be more than just *tolerable!*" Fairchild said with whimsy.

"Yes, so you were," agreed his friend.

"Trim, the brandy!" snapped the other. "You are as bad as they are with these morbid imaginings."

Oblivious to this order, Trim followed his train of thought doggedly. "Good God, you should pen your memoirs…they could be in the window of bookshops right now and making you a fortune."

"Trim, enough!" Fairchild beckoned impatiently with his left hand for the liquor. Trim held the glass aloft a moment and then did as bidden. "It strikes me, you know, how many varying types of women there are to the differing tastes men have for them…"

"Yes…how fortunate we are!" Fairchild replied, taking the brandy and swigging from it.

"There are perhaps as many different sorts of couplings as there are fish in the ocean," added Trim, falling into his favourite chair.

"You are not about to lapse into one of your philosophical diatribes, are you? 'tis barely past six o'clock… Though I have myself been pondering recently, on the state one falls into…the satisfaction of just being near them. Despite their various charms and methods of seduction, there is a mood or an essence which descends, if 'tis the right woman, which defies all explanation…and 'tis enough just to be with them. Dominic McCarthy remarked on it the other week."

"Quite!" Trim said. "The difference between being in love and simply enamoured of them…'tis the way you know you have found love."

Ten or fifteen minutes passed in silence, then Fairchild offered: "But you know, Trim, I doubt I will survive another month without ravishing her…'tis sometimes more than I can bear. I have to leave her presence before I give into temptation…"

Trim opened his eyes and stared. "And does she feel the same, do you suppose?"

"She is the most tantalising little witch withal…she is always suggesting we do what she calls *'the act itself'*…if I have to go much longer without having her, I shall expire."

Trim opened his eyes even wider. "You will just have to think pious thoughts then!"

Fairchild glared at him. "I think you are confusing me with my brother, Rupert, are you not? Although his pious thoughts have not helped him…the vicarage is overflowing with his offspring. Pious thoughts are only good in

433

solitude…and you forget, I do not have any other female around me now to relieve the agony…"

The door flew open and Susan entered, attired in her cloak and bonnet. "Who is having pious thoughts? Not you two I'll be bound!"

"God's Teeth, Susan!" exclaimed Fairchild in mild shock, and then he froze at the thought of what she may have heard.

Susan said: "What kind of agony do you suffer, Tony? I may have some herbal remedy for it…" Her expression was contrived into concern but loaded with irony. Trim and he exchanged glances and then Trim grinned. "That is doubtful, my love… I expect he wishes to hang onto his manhood, not jeopardise it…" And his laughter saw the breaking of any tension.

"Susan, do you need to creep about in that fashion and listen at doors?" Fairchild commented off-handedly.

"I was doing no such thing," she replied with false contrition. "Now come along…the time for supping has passed. Follow me."

She received no reply and neither of them moved immediately.

Scoundrels, Saviours and Sensible Folk

Riding home in Susan's trap, Melissa felt great satisfaction. She had scarcely done anything so meaningful in her life to date as help raise so much money for needy causes. It was a heady feeling.

Susan eventually said: "I cannot tell you how pleased I am, Melissa. I am truly indebted to you…we all are!"

"'twas not hard!" Melissa said. "My father knows so many people, and I expect Mr and Mrs Trimingham do too…together with your connections."

Susan skipped past the comment and went on. "I suppose you will be engaged soon to Tony?"

Melissa turned to her, "Well, I… I really am not sure…"

"Not sure!" Susan laughed briefly, and her temperament not being one of great discretion, said: "But the way you both kiss! And the way he looks at you!"

"That is not a recipe for marriage surely!" Melissa said. "Not on its own…"

"A very modern and, some might say, bohemian viewpoint," Susan replied, "But I think he will want to wed you… I overheard some of his remarks as I entered Tim's parlour before… I think he is quite mad for you!"

"Really!" Melissa flushed a little and smiled. "What was he saying?"

"I could not possibly repeat it," rejoined Susan primly. "Though you must know, Melissa, they are not like we are…they are suddenly overcome with their urges and nothing can stop them. 'tis better you have an agreement in place…because you may end up with a child before the time is apt."

Melissa made a face. "Oh, how awful a prospect. I must make myself ready for that with the passing of more years yet."

Susan smiled to herself omnisciently—as her father's daughter she had assisted at many births with women who had told themselves that story before succumbing to untimely seduction and bodily instinct.

"And…" continued Melissa, as they rounded bends on the road which Susan took quite recklessly, "if he does not prove his greater tolerance more yet, I may not agree to marriage at all."

Susan slowed the trap and gazed at her.

"I shall be on the lookout for traits of his uncle Charles," said Melissa with brevity and Susan, unable to tell if this was a witticism, drew the horse to a stop completely. "What? You are not serious?"

"I am quite serious," she replied.

Susan gathered up the reins and held them in her hand and turned to her, shuffling in the narrow seat to see her better. "Melissa, I shall tell you more now of Uncle Charles and his history, which I do know something about…but you are to promise me not to tell anyone I have told you…"

Melissa nodded; her eyes dark with concern.

"Charles Fairchild was the worst kind of scoundrel and blackguard…" Susan began. "Legend has it that he always wanted Hildegarde for himself, from the moment Joseph Fairchild brought her home to the family. You can only imagine how lovely she would have been back then…and Charles hoped to take her from Joseph, but he could not succeed…and so Charles' long terrain of jealousy began…he became besotted with her, despite his own marriages. He was jealous of the sons she bore Joseph, he believed they should have been his. He could not make any of his wives with child, and even if he could have done so would perhaps still have detested her sons to his brother…especially Tony who resembled his mother in all but gender. He terrorised them, and Tony particularly."

Susan paused and Melissa waited, the sun going down slowly and the wind growing chill on the hilly road. "One day, as the story goes, he came to the parsonage when Joseph was acting as temporary curate in the next county. Hildegarde saw him riding down the lane and she could see he was drunk and knew he meant no good…she locked the boys in an attic room so he could not get to them, except for Rupert who was already fifteen and as tall as Charles…but Charles knocked Rupert out with one blow and demanded to have the younger boys fetched. She refused to give up the key and he chased her about the vicarage for an hour or more…and when she became exhausted, he became less than gentlemanly…" Susan paused for breath and Melissa stared past her to the beauty of the countryside with the old church lit and dappled by the weak sunlight and resplendent as a monument.

"Yes?" she urged. "Go on."

"Have you not heard enough?" enquired Susan, readying the trap to move again. "'tis a harrowing story and becomes worse…"

"No, there must be more…" Melissa gaped at Susan; the intrepid herbalist and reformer, beloved of Timothy Trimingham. Not to be underestimated. The trap began to move forwards and Melissa clutched Susan's arm. "What happened next? That cannot be the end of the tale!"

"Well, hear me out…" Susan rejoined, "But I need to rest my voice and piece together the parts of my memory, to have it right…and I do not wish to shout above the noise of the trap…"

"We are near the house now…" Melissa said. "Please come in for some tea and tell me the rest…you cannot leave me in suspense."

"Well, only for ten minutes. I must be home to assist my father with his notes…his clerk is gone home to visit for the weekend," Susan declared.

* * *

At 'High Lawns' Susan entered with Melissa and blinked at the opulence of the mansion. On the scale of grand country houses it was indeed impressive. It appeared to be staffed better than most hotels and Melissa hurried her to the breakfast room and ordered tea urgently from two passing servants.

"What a magnificent house," Susan said. "'tis as nice as the Trimingham mansion, but bigger…"

"Yes, perhaps…" Melissa concurred. "So, you must have heard by now that I am from a privileged background…and 'tis why I am rude and spoiled and mannerless. Surely Anthony has told you that!" she said facetiously. "Or Trim at least?"

Susan took a moment or two to construe her tone. "Timothy will not say much, they hold each other's secrets in the way they have since being boys," she said airily. Not being one for delicate airs or docile complicity herself, she had no wish to waste time. "I did not overly believe it…so do not concern yourself… Tony expects the alms children to say things like *please excuse me* and *I do beg your pardon*…when they can barely string a grammatical sentence…so I did not take it too seriously."

Melissa felt her merriment begin but controlled herself—aware of the pressure of time. They took seats at a small table near the windows where visiting guests often preferred to eat first thing in the day. And within minutes the tea arrived—along with her mother. "And who is this young lady?" enquired Marguerite.

"This is Miss Darnley, Mama," said Melissa. Susan inclined her head to Marguerite and smiled. "Doctor Darnley's daughter…"

"How nice," rejoined her mother sweetly. "We all know of your esteemed father, my dear. How good of you to honour us…"

"She has only minutes to spare and we must talk privately, if you do not mind."

Marguerite raised her brows at them both. "Oh? What about?"

Melissa busied herself pouring the tea. "If I disclosed that it would no longer be private, would it?" she replied patiently.

Marguerite kept her more bitter retorts to herself and smiled again, as if she had taken this to be a witticism. Susan had in the meantime removed her cloak, revealing her grubby kitchen smock and the sleeves of her blouse smeared with butter and flour and icing sugar. Marguerite averted her eyes from her disheartening appearance, wondering why Fairchild and his friend Trimingham, with their sartorial elegance, seemed to be attracted to young women who ran around looking like the serving classes. Perhaps it was a growing fad with men of their ilk. The thought was quite worrying and she pondered it as she left them alone.

Susan sipped the tea, too hot to swallow, and then began to chuckle deep in her throat, her lips compressed, as was her habit when inconveniently amused, and the sound grew like a distant flock of high-flying geese.

"My mother is incipiently nosey. I do beg your pardon," said Melissa, then erupted into laughter, having used the same phrase Anthony thought appropriate for alms children.

Susan thought she beheld before her a girl who may rise to great heights of influence in society. All the panache of a lady with the common sense of a woman. Anthony Fairchild might use her to oil the wheels of a better and fairer society if he were clever enough, and if she would consent to mix in the right circles. "So, where had we got to?" Susan asked, the tea cooling enough to be drunk in mouthfuls.

"Rupert had been assaulted by Uncle Charles…and Charles had behaved less than courteously to Hildegarde."

"Oh yes…well, upon recovering Rupert apparently ran for help to the verger's house and they gathered men and came back and between them overpowered Charles and locked him in the cellar until the next morning… He was beside himself with rage and threatening to kill them all… When Joseph heard of it, he confronted Charles, but he was not a fighting man, not an aggressive man, certainly no match for Charles who broke his arm in two places…"

"Could nobody stop this monster?" opined Melissa.

"Men like Charles Fairchild are not easy to stay…but of course, had I been around, I would have known which herbs to give him secretly, to keep him more calm…" declared Miss Darnley with a ludicrously innocent belief in her own powers, and Melissa pondered briefly on how Susan would have gained access to Charles, much less been able to slip tinctures into his food or drink.

"Was he insane, do you think?" she asked next, her own tea grown cool in the cup.

"My father thought he was…and in need of treatment…anyway, as legend has it, that is when the other Fairchild men called time on Charles. They had had enough of his depravity and cruelty and gambling and bad debts…they knew he would bring catastrophe to the family if not stopped. So, they organised a riding accident…one night when the moon was not too high…" Susan looked at Melissa to see how she was taking this history.

"And did it work?"

"It did…eventually. They were hoping that the accident would be fatal, but it broke his legs, not his neck, and he never walked again…which made him less of a menace. He lingered for another year before he died."

"Good God!" Melissa held her hands to her throat. "His legs would not mend, I suppose."

"They might have done so had he had medical assistance in time…but it was not the case. The Fairchild brothers, and Charles's brother-in-law, had approached the two local physicians to beseech them not to attend him swiftly in the event of him surviving the accident…and miraculously they agreed. They knew what Charles was capable of…they saw that he had to be stopped…especially on hearing of what he had done to Hildegarde. Assistance came eventually from the next town, but 'twas too late to ensure correct treatment to his legs…"

Melissa was very still for a while, gazing at Susan who allowed her to look fully into her eyes to gauge her sincerity. "When you say, *'legend has it'*...and *allegedly*...where did you acquire the knowledge?"

Susan took her tea and drained the cup, deferring her reply for several moments. While Melissa raised the tea pot and offered more, which was declined. "One of the local physicians was my father!" said Susan at length. "He refused to attend...and he told me of it several years later. He attended Hildegarde the next day, after Charles had tried to...had attempted to..."

"Force her into the act with him...?" supplied Melissa quietly.

Susan looked at her, amused at the phrasing, and nodded agreement.

"Does Anthony know all this?"

"I think he must...someone will have told him...perhaps Rupert...and if he does not, then he does not need to."

"I agree," said Melissa.

Susan nodded again slowly. "But, Melissa, you must swear not to tell Tony I have told you...not at least while my father lives."

"No," concurred Melissa. "What an evil man, this Charles..."

"Indeed," Susan looked at the clock nearby as it chimed and she stood. "But Tony is nothing like Charles...he is not a cruel person...nor a tyrant..."

Melissa gazed towards the window with a disdainful expression. "That is a matter for conjecture..." she remarked casually, "His not being a tyrant..."

Susan paused in the putting on of her cloak. "What?" She waited for the other girl to speak and when she did not, she flicked through various possibilities mentally. "You cannot be referring to his classroom regime, can you?"

"I might be!" Melissa said with dignified indifference.

Susan resumed the fixing of her cloak. "I cannot believe you would see that as relevant...or hold against him the fact that he was doing his job."

Melissa turned swiftly with rising annoyance and Susan held her eye curiously, until Melissa found the neutral response which would not jeopardise her newfound friendship with the doctor's daughter. "Oh yes...doing his job!" she said with ambiguity and a slight smile. "Silly me..."

At length, Susan had construed the meaning of these remarks from her memory of brief conversations with her fiancé who had imparted a little about the historical grievances and the rows they caused, and she ventured carefully. "There is of necessity an expected standard of conduct and behaviour in classrooms you know, Melissa, which must be maintained if our jobs are to be done effectively…and a choice about those, even in children…"

Melissa sighed extravagantly to defer argument. No doubt Susan was a tyrant herself—in female form—in the classroom. They were probably all of a muchness these teaching folk. But she reserved her further comment, not wishing to offend the other woman—or indeed to appear foolish and immature. A silence engulfed them and Susan allowed this impasse to go unremarked. "I must be off before the dusk falls…my father will worry otherwise." She picked up her reticule and bonnet…

Melissa watched her without comment and thought of all she had heard regarding the history of the Fairchild family. Then Susan sat again and took Melissa's hands and looked directly into her face, her round dark eyes as intense as any Melissa had seen. "You and I may have a long association if you wed him…because of the friendship between our men…and I need to know you will not tell anyone I told you all this… I promised my father and I cannot betray him…it was a hard decision for him to make…his oath and his reputation…but I am telling you so that you will be aware of what Tony alludes to when he talks of Charles Fairchild…"

"I swear not to say anything!" Melissa said solemnly, and there came then the realisation that it was perhaps the first major test of her integrity. She could share this with nobody, not even with Melanie. "What a terrible world it is in parts," she lamented.

"It is indeed," agreed Miss Darnley, "And my father and others in his profession know that only too well…as Shakespeare wrote: *'to do a great right, do a little wrong.'*…"

* * *

At dinner in the Shaw household the following evening she said to him, "Susan thinks we will marry soon…"

He set down his wine glass carefully. "'tis not Susan's opinion that matters here…'tis your's."

"She is very worldly," Melissa added, ignoring this last wisdom.

"Hmm," he murmured. "She is also very opinionated!"

441

"What a shocking occurrence…someone having opinions and also being female!" she said provocatively. "She is learned in many ways…and her work is commendable."

"It is!" agreed Fairchild. "She is a virago of pioneering…but at times an insatiable little busybody!"

Melissa disliked this slur upon her latest ally. "And your mother is adorable… I find her fascinating." He picked up the glass again and drank and did not speak. "But what of this brother of yours, Richard? And Lady Vulture? Why can I not meet them?"

"'tis unnecessary!" he replied. "Since I do not intend to socialise with them in the future…nor shall I allow you to do so."

She drew a loud breath and fell back into her chair to recline. "Do not talk of what you will and will not allow me, I implore you! I find it disconcerting."

"I cannot help that," he said in a quiet voice. "I will not have you as my wife associate with them…"

He had bought her a small pearl pendant in filigree silver and she fingered it around her neck. It was the first piece of jewellery he had given her. "I have not agreed yet to wedding you and already you are ordering me about…"

"I am not ordering you about. I am telling you what I will not allow."

"Whatever you call it, I have a mind to leave you at the table alone."

He leaned into her and put his mouth to her ear and said, "If you do, I shall come and find you, and I shall be very vexed…'tis extremely rude…we have not finished dining."

"I care not…so do not issue your threats just now." She turned her face to his so that their mouths were almost touching. It might be to her advantage, she thought; if he were vexed, he may become enraged enough to forget his self-control and claim her fully in carnal knowledge. The way Melanie had described to her. She flung her napkin to the table and stared at him, her eyes betraying her desire along with her intent.

"I am warning you!" he said softly. "Do not dare to behave in such a vulgar way."

"I do dare…" she said, and rose. He grabbed her hand and pulled her back down into the chair. She stared at him, ignoring the interest other guests now gave to them. Her mother was looking daggers at her. Her father: oblivious to what was happening. Damien, seated opposite to Fairchild, smirked and awaited more, while Estelle—seated next to Damien—pretended to see nothing amiss.

There were fourteen people dining in total, but the far end of the table held five or six people who had not noticed anything at all.

"I noted that your mother too thinks your attitude to Richard unreasonable…" she said, goading him into comment.

"My mother has the peace to keep…" he replied, "But she knows full well what I am saying, and is not surprised."

"What is it they do, this woman and Richard, that is so off with you?"

"Never mind!" He lifted his glass once more as the butler came to refill it.

"I do mind, Anthony…what is wrong with him being a banker?"

"That is what he calls it…but in truth, he is also a usurer…a money lender!" he said in a low voice.

"Susan told me that Lottie was an actress. So, what is wrong with Lady Vulture being a failed actress?" she continued ingenuously.

He turned to her, his fury under control but near to the surface. "Lottie was a theatre actress…not a harlot."

"I see," said Melissa. "But what does she do, the harlot?"

"What do you think harlots do?"

She considered this for several moments. "Even so, she is hardly likely to turn me into one, is she?"

"I do not know what she may attempt… Richard will smell your family's money and that will be enough to set his mind working."

She laughed quite freely. "But I have no access to my family's money! What an idiotic suggestion."

"Melissa," said he in his normal and audible voice that might be heard by anyone round about. "I am not discussing this any further."

Geraldine caught her eye from across the table and made gentle tutting noises with her tongue so that Edmund pressed her ankle with his foot. Geraldine smirked and made other faces at Melissa. Geraldine was always making strange faces these days, following the progress of their romance assiduously whenever she could. Melissa ignored her.

"I will not be dismissed in that way," she told him, "As if I am a child!" She adroitly moved her hand to above her waist so he could not easily grab it and then stood swiftly and left the table, going hurriedly from the room.

He continued to eat his second course until the plate was almost empty before excusing himself and leaving the dining room.

As soon as the door had closed on him the mutterings rose to a crescendo. Her aunt Dorothea was the first to comment. "Oh dear…trouble in paradise, I perceive."

"We have all been there of course…" said one of Melissa's uncles, and Giles raised his glass to his brother-in-law and said: "Just so Raymond…just so!"

Marguerite said to Raymond: "Well, I have not been there! I was never so rude. We were never allowed to be, were we not, Dorothea!"

"Certainly not!" agreed Dorothea.

Geraldine began to giggle and said to Estelle: "What a carry on it is when one is not yet betrothed but nearly so…"

"I am glad I shall never be betrothed," said Estelle cheerfully, and she glanced at Damien who laughed freely. Estelle was a young woman of a new order, wearing stark blouses and dark jackets over divided skirts which simulated male trousers. She smoked cigarettes in public and wore no adornment and taught chemistry and controversial doctrines at a lady's college. Marguerite had grave doubts as to whether Estelle was actually a woman at all. She was almost worse in outre attire than Melissa with her paint smocks and her frequently dishevelled appearance. Or Dr Darnley's daughter in her grubby apron on a Saturday evening.

Shocking to think what the world may be coming to. Marguerite cast Estelle a filthy look which included Damien in its radius. Her two youngest children—Damien and Melissa—seemed to her to be eccentric with little interest in convention. While her eldest son, who worked as a journalist and biographer, was a dark horse but very formal in his manner and did not openly court comment. Marguerite sent a little smile of approval to her daughter-in-law, Geraldine, married to her middle son, Edmund, gratified that they seemed content to live normal lives.

"I think the success of yesterday has gone to her head…" Marguerite then announced to the table in general.

"Too much going on for her to cope with well…" supplied Amaelia from her undeniable worldly experience of all matters social. "She is normally living such a reclusive artist's life…"

"Until Prince Charming appeared…" offered Geraldine.

Jemima was present, eating only fruit and saying little, watched over by Amaelia. "They will sort it out a'tween 'em…" Jemima said, as if expected to reach an overall summary as retired matriarch.

"No man wants that sort of behaviour in a wife," offered Dorothea in a dispassionate tone.

Jemima waved her forefinger in the air at Dorothea, like an orator at a rally. "He ain't a duck egg! He'll no sooner have a ring on her finger than he'll bring her back in line…mayhap even afore then!"

Some discreet amusement among the diners. Geraldine giggling ardently behind her napkin as Edmund squeezed her leg beneath the table to deter her, and a couple of the men raising their glasses in Jemima's direction.

"Disgraceful behaviour…" said Marguerite loudly, and then covertly to Jemima. "How do you know this about him, Mother?"

Jemima had the question repeated to her by Amaelia and frowned at Marguerite. "Common sense and experience o'course! Would you not if you were him!"

Marguerite looked away from her mother-in-law, while Geraldine and Amaelia—both devoted to the nuances of romantic desire for their differing reasons—caught each other's eye and smirked like cats with the cream. Everyone awaited more from Jemima and Marguerite feared more tiresome reminiscence about her younger life with Jago. But Jemima closed her eyes and assumed the look of the elderly *Cheshire Cat,* as the other diners returned to their various conversations. Giles leaned behind his sister and squeezed his mother's frail hand. "You are very right, Mama…better to leave them to it."

Dorothea sighed and Marguerite commented: "That is what you say to most of these domestic upsets, Giles dear."

* * *

Having gone to the art room and found it to be empty, he moved to the stairs quietly. He found her in the bedroom—he perceived that nobody would be so shocked or outraged if they saw him enter at this stage when they were more and more involved. But he looked about the corridor firstly and saw no-one. He knocked on the door and received no reply, then trying the door found it locked. "Melissa, open the door!" he called.

Several moments elapsed and he waited. "Melissa, open the door now… I am not playing these games!" he said through the wood panelling.

He waited a little more and the door opened, as he had anticipated it would. He stepped into the room and saw that she had removed her dress and wore only her silk camisole. She had obviously not been wearing laces beneath her dress, but she was slender enough for it to go unnoticed. "Are you planning on retiring to bed?" he enquired levelly. He smelled a contrived situation of some kind. Perhaps she was trying to precipitate *'the act itself'* as she liked to call it.

"Yes..." she replied truculently.

"Then perhaps you should reconsider..." he told her.

"And perhaps you should consider taking yourself off again... I did not ask you to follow me!" She seated herself on the dressing table chair.

"Put on your dress and let us return to the dining room," he said. "This development will be remarked upon downstairs..."

"Certainly not...here you are once more, ordering me around!" She stared at the closed curtains of the window recess.

"So I am," he agreed blithely.

He turned the lock in the door and pocketed the key. She began to watch him with a growing trepidation but with something more brewing inside her, something awesome in its unfathomable and disturbing quality, leaping and roaring furiously. Now she was trapped. The situation had become critical in its potential for change.

"I will ask you only once more to dress..." he said with an assumed languor, "And if you do not do so I shall take you across my knee and spank you... You cannot behave in this way."

She rose swiftly and crossed the room and considered her options. There was no-one about. Not even Polly, who was making up beds for guests elsewhere. She watched him with pursed lips and kept her feelings guarded.

"Well? Are you going to dress or not?"

She watched him remove his jacket and place it with care around the wooden frame meant for her own blouses and jackets. It was, as Melanie would say, *a nice piece of theatre.* Though she knew that his threat was probably not idle.

She went over to him and stood a little way removed, her face a few inches below his own so that his cologne assailed her nostrils. "You had better take me across your knee then!" she told him. "If you are equal to it...and if you can."

He raised his brows and almost smiled. "Oh, believe me, I can! And I shall! Whether it is your actual *preference* or not...and Trim is nowhere around to save you..." He thought of some of Louisa Stevenson's words and discussions with Trimingham and wondered if it might be what she actually wanted. He half

446

expected her to ring for a servant or try to run, but then remembered he had locked the door.

She was not moving, standing back some yards like an opponent in a fencing match with one arm behind her back. Perhaps she had picked up some lethal type of weapon with which to defeat him—but he couldn't discover it without losing ground. "You have only about ten more seconds to reconsider…" he told her with more theatricality and then moved to the small chair upon which he intended to sit to carry out his threat.

But before he could sit, she had sprung onto the small velvet chair and put her arms around his neck and jumped onto him, her legs around his body, cleaving to him. He was undoubtedly surprised, though not unduly so, and she allowed herself to slide down him as she had done some weeks ago, leaping from the garden wall.

She had a firm hold on his shoulders; how she adored his shoulders and the solid feel of his upper arms beneath the fine linen of his shirt. She moved one hand and took hold of his crotch, her fingers feeling for the shape and mound of him. He gasped in one long rasp of anticipation and stared at her with annoyance and longing and a plethora of assorted urges. And his carefully constructed control caved in, one huge shift of momentum and he toppled her onto the bed and began to take off her drawers.

"I want you inside me, Anthony…and I cannot wait any longer…" she told him.

He began removing his trousers. "You had better be sure, Melissa."

"I am sure," she said.

He was rapidly going beyond good judgement with no inkling of how to reverse things. "I mean, sure that you want to wed," he mumbled into her neck as he manoeuvred her. She did not reply and he was too far into the process of sensuality to think of what her silence might mean.

She smiled into his hair, her lips tasting strands of it, as she appreciated the skill he used in undressing her and himself at the same time. The years of experience it betokened. She did not mind his years of experience, was glad, thrilled to be in the hands of a man who knew what he was about. She lay still, watching his face, her breath coming in little pants of excitement, sighs of anticipation. He moved back from her and she looked for the first time at his semi-naked body.

She made a small sound of amazement at the sight of his erection and wondered at how it had looked different in her imagination. She went to sit up and he pushed her down again in one long movement. She arched her back and did not know what was causing her lower body to rise in such a way. He fell onto her and began kissing her, sucking and nibbling her breasts. Her nipples coming to life in an extraordinary way she had not previously known about. He was pushing the camisole this way and that, pulling it impatiently so that it tore in the centre.

"I want you to enter me!" she said with emphasis and he momentarily stayed his ardour and closed his eyes. He was into some kind of rigid control again; he had schooled himself for so long and could not bring himself to the point of penetration just yet. She moaned in disappointment and made an agonised face. He stroked her inner thigh and then used his fingers to pleasure her and she writhed and went to touch his throbbing erection.

He held her hand away and pleasured himself a little before returning to the increasing wetness between her legs. He would not enter her; he would simply bring her to a climax and allow her to understand the feeling of being possessed by her strongest needs.

She held onto his hand as he massaged her and pushed it into her so that she could feel the most sensitive areas of herself become more and more responsive. He kissed her and licked her nipples, until she was a shivering mass of sensations within a beautifully formed physical arrangement of flesh.

Eventually she climaxed, shuddering in a scream of delight. He propped himself onto one elbow and put his hand over her mouth to mute the sound. But still he continued to pleasure her—until she lay still—and then he pleasured himself. Eventually he lay down next to her and pinned her almost lifeless form to the mattress with his hand on her belly.

An age seemed to pass and he rolled off the bed and stood and looked down at her. Her eyes were closed and she was making little sounds in her throat, like someone beholding a vision beneath closed lids. At the wash stand, he bathed and then put on his clothes. He returned to the bed and held her hand and stroked her belly. Until suddenly she sat up and her eyes were glazed. He smiled at her. "Are you quite well?" he enquired.

She emitted a small laugh. "Yes, I am quite well."

He rose again and went to her dresser and found her hairbrush and began brushing his own hair in preparation to return downstairs. Then he heard her exclaim in horror and he turned quickly to look at her. She was examining her fingers with fear. "I am bleeding," she said in anguish.

He sat on the bed and took her into his arms.

"What is it?" she wailed.

"'tis your virginity…" he said. "You have just lost it."

"Oh…" she held her fingers to her inner thighs and watched him in terror. "How long will I bleed?"

"Not long…a few minutes…or on and off for a few hours…you will not bleed to death…do not be alarmed."

"You have seen a woman lose this before?" she asked in awe.

"Only once before!"

"When?"

He was about to deny her an answer but saw that she would be disturbed if she did not receive one. "With Lottie," he said and his voice was that of someone in a confessional.

"So, 'tis not like my monthly bleed?"

"Nothing at all like it…though 'tis possible it may bring that on." He began to walk about the room, and then he took out his cigars and lit one, ignoring the protocol of the bedroom, anxious to regain composure.

"What does this mean?" she asked, like the child she still was.

"It means we must wed."

She sat up at once. "But supposing I do not wish to?"

"Then I must go to your father and tell him what has happened."

"You cannot do that! He will be embarrassed and so shall I." She became quite frantic and looked about for what next to do.

"He is a man of the world, Melissa…he has sired children and is wed to your mother. He will not be so embarrassed, he cannot understand."

"But he will try to coerce me into marriage."

"Of course he will…" he said sardonically. "He is your father."

Tears trickled down her face and she swiped at them with her fingers. "I need time to think…" she told him.

"Stay there… I will tell them you are indisposed and have them send Polly to you."

"No, I do not want anyone in here."

He grew impatient. "Melissa, you must go through with the act of being unwell, while you think on what you want now for the future…at least until the morning. Otherwise, we have to tell your father what has happened. We cannot appear again in the drawing room as if nothing has occurred. It is either that you are ill or we have been talking seriously and are now betrothed."

Her eyes wandered the ceiling. "Yes, I see you are right."

"I shall go down and tell them you are feeling faint and I will sit in the drawing room and make polite conversation and you must come to the rose garden in half an hour and we will talk."

"Very well," she agreed.

He pointed to the small ormolu clock on the dressing table so that she would note the time, then he unlocked the door and replaced the key on the inside of it and left the room, relieved to see she was not prone to hysteria or regret.

* * *

They were all back in the drawing room when he returned, sitting or standing about and chatting, preparing to play cards. They looked at him at once and did not avert their faces, though their expressions varied from mild curiosity to cautious disapproval.

"Melissa has been near to fainting…she is recovering now and lying down."

He could see that Marguerite and her sister, to name but two, did not believe him and he realised that his neck wear was re-tied in a different style than before he had left the room. But he was not so concerned.

Giles Shaw watched him with a questioning and patient look of enquiry. Fairchild smiled at him vaguely and some understanding passed between them, one man to another. Giles did not comment, his trust was complete, and it was not misplaced. All the men present may smell seduction on him, the way men did, as one feral breed. He studied the ground, the carpet at his feet, and felt the eyes of the women probe him with the fierce and piercing look of females in the knowledge of timeless and universal sexual events. Marguerite unfroze and announced to the room. "I will summon Jarvis to send Polly up to her."

It was the right thing. Polly could fetch her whatever she may need now; who else could be privy to it! Polly was the same age and they were more than just mistress and maid, but friends over years of growing up. Besides, Polly had probably lost her own virginity at some point—at the very least recently to Dominic McCarthy. She would know how to handle the situation.

450

The butler was informed and went off to summon Polly. He saw then the disparity and coolness between mother and daughter, for any other mother he knew would have ascended the stairs herself to minister to her child. It was why perhaps she liked his own mother so much on first acquaintance—she sought a more proficient substitute.

In the absence of maid or butler and to have something to do, Marguerite began clearing away coffee cups and placing them on the sideboard. She was joined quickly by her sister, Dorothea, and they spoke in very hushed tones. "I hope to God this faintness is not because she is with child..." Marguerite opined.

"Yes indeed," Dorothea sympathised, "'twould not be surprising the way they are at times when they think they are unobserved."

Marguerite shivered and felt Fairchild's eyes upon her. She turned to meet them and he smiled at her calmly and with consummate reassurance. "Mind you, 'tis not the end of the world..." she told Dorothea. "He can be trusted to do the right thing...or so Giles tells me."

"Oh my dear, I am certain of it...the breeding is all about him. He is far better mannered than she...wishing no disrespect," Dorothea assured her.

Marguerite sighed. "I know that, Dorothea... I blame Giles...he has allowed her to get away with far too much."

"The old lady is right," Dorothea added in a lower whisper. "He will bring her to heel once they are wed."

Dorothea then shifted her gaze to her brother-in-law, and Giles felt it and assumed a weary and disgruntled expression. Dorothea was never subtle in her facial expressions and everyone always gleaned her every suspicion and notion without her being aware. "I am glad in one sense that I have had only sons," she said to Marguerite.

"Let us be seated," suggested Marguerite, "Lest they think we are gossiping."

This remark was picked up on by Amaelia and Jemima—seated immediately to their rear—and Jemima let out one of her ad hoc squawks of amusement to show that she had heard the last comment and had succumbed to the irony.

Edmund began engaging Fairchild in conversation about the latest town centre bridgework and how it may affect the boy's school, feeling it incumbent upon himself to put his potential brother-in-law at his ease in whatever situation had arisen and away from awkwardness. Damien joined in and then Dorothea's husband, and soon there was the familiar sound of men talking together, oblivious of anything else. While the women still awaited news of any outcome from upstairs and exchanged quiet remarks.

Polly entered the room after some fifteen minutes and went over to Marguerite and spoke to her in audible tones. "Miss Shaw is recovered now, Madam…nothing to worry about."

"I wonder if 'twas the fish at dinner," said Marguerite in trite and clear tones so that normality may be resumed; even if there was now a worse suspicion to be considered regarding the halibut.

"O'course it was not…" said Jemima in a caustic voice. "Otherwise, we would all be bent double in agony."

This sent Geraldine into peals of laughter and Amaelia joined in. Marguerite shook her head in an offended manner as Dorothea tutted and drew in breath. The lack of social nicety in Jemima's family was too torrid to be countenanced.

Polly passed Fairchild closely with empty glasses on a tray and slowly closed one eye; a careful wink. He knew she knew. Melissa had felt the need to tell her, for she would need to deal with blood on sheets or personal garments. He raised his brows to her and inclined his head. Polly kept his secrets now, as much as he kept hers.

At length, Melissa re-entered and sat by his side with an expression of consummate satisfaction. The women marvelled at it and the men were unsure.

He scowled at her. "Are you sure you are fully recovered?" he enquired.

"I think so, but I may need a little air…" she told him.

He rose and bowed briefly to the group and they made their way out of the drawing room windows to the garden.

"She looks decidedly pale!" exclaimed Marguerite to emphasise the charade. "I hope she is quite recovered."

"She looks right as ninepence…" declared Jemima contrarily, not about to add fuel to the posturing. "She is positively glowing."

* * *

In the garden, they strolled leisurely to the first bench. There was only dim light from the windows illuminating everything, barely enough to see each other.

"What a little monkey you are!" he said. "I asked you to enter the garden discreetly….not make an entrance into the drawing room in peach

452

condition…they will know nothing was wrong with you and be suspicious of the time we spent alone upstairs!"

"I am not ashamed of anything," she said.

He lit a cigar. "Melissa, you have to care for the conventions sometimes…for the sake of others more than yourself!"

She knew he could not see her look of perplexity but gazed at him anyway. "I know not why…"

This was a fundamental difference in their characters which worried him, it signalled a huge gulf between them that might or might not be detrimental to marriage.

"Because 'tis a matter of sensibility," he said.

"How fond you are of these values," she replied.

"'tis not a case of how fond I am of them…more of seeing them as necessary."

"Well, I do not think we will agree on it."

"Perhaps not, but 'tis why you must do as I ask in certain matters, not as you wish…"

"Why? Unless we are married."

He pulled deeply on the cigar. "And there we have it! You will not agree to wed me simply because you resent the fact that I may *order you about!*"

"Yes…perhaps." She saw that he was too clever for any kind of ingenuous prevarication in this respect and saw right through her flimsy objections. But not wishing to be manipulated and ordered around was not a flimsy matter.

"We are at an impasse…" he declared and stood quickly and paced the length of the path. "If we are to make progress you must get beyond this…or we cannot go forwards."

She cleared her throat and placed her hands on her stomach and took a long breath. "Or you must stop thinking you can order me about…and see that I have a mind of my own."

"Of course you have a mind of your own…everyone does. That is beside the point!"

"Then you must trust me to use it."

"And you must accept the consequences of my vexation when I do not," he declared.

"Do not begin again with your threats and warnings…"

"Then do not force me to express them," he said.

"So, the circles decrease endlessly…" she concluded.

He stubbed out his cigar on the path and she jumped into the verbal gap, not wanting to end on this perilous note. "And when were you going to tell me of Polly?" she asked, "And her intended migration with whatever it is he's called? I cannot recall."

"Dominic McCarthy…"

"Yes, him!"

"I did not think it my place to do so…'tis their business, and her choice to tell you when she wishes. I presume she has now done so?"

"Just now when we were alone in the bedroom… I cannot think why you kept it to yourself!!"

"I have just told you…'tis a matter of discretion…and integrity."

"Oh, I see…more of your cherished values! But I perceive I may not be allowed any discretion in my friendship with Roger!"

He halted and froze. "'tis an entirely different thing…you surely see that!"

"You know how I value Polly. She has been with me since we were both children. I shall miss her dreadfully."

"Obviously, but she has a life of her own to lead and opportunities such as the one he is offering will not come along often."

"I understand that, but we are talking of you not telling me you had seen her with this fiancé and knew of it all."

"You are talking of that… I am declaring there is nothing more I can say on it."

"Perhaps I will declare there is nothing more to say on my friendship with Roger…other than it is at my discretion."

Was this childish obstinacy or was it something deeply entrenched which went down into the bones of her? He bit the bullet. "If you cannot decide on whether to marry me, we must go to your father and inform him that you have lost your virginity."

"Why must anyone know? 'tis my body, my virginity that is lost, no-one else's."

"Your father deserves to know. He has allowed us great licence in courtship. 'tis a matter of respect…how you cannot see that I do not know."

"I do not see it. He wishes only for me to be married!"

"'tis a question of my integrity as a gentleman, and my respect for him as a gentleman."

"And if I do not wish to marry you?" She peered at him in the darkness and waited.

"I do not know yet!" he said.

"Can we not go on as we are?"

Circling the path and returning to her after several seconds, he ventured, "You know that what we just had was simply a taste of what we could have?"

"Yes, I imagine it was…'twas not the full act…"

"By no means!" He sat next to her with a swiftness that startled her and took her cold hand and kissed it. "You surely cannot want us to share only odd moments of intimacy? You cannot think that enough, surely?" He began squeezing her hand between his hands to warm her cold fingers.

She did not reply—to do so now would weaken her stance. "Have you ridden here?" she asked instead.

"Indeed! I have had a good bit to drink over the day, and I never drive any sort of conveyance when that is the case."

The dogs were barking, which meant that either someone was exercising them nearby or there were visitors at the main door. It was doubtful there were visitors at this late hour. They both listened carefully for sounds of approach and minutes elapsed.

He gave her back her hand but then changed his mind and seized it again on an impulse and trapped it beneath his elbow, taking off his garnet signet ring from his little finger and pushing it on her third finger left hand. It was a near fit, if one size too tight. She snatched her hand away in annoyance. "I know what you are doing…you are sizing my finger for wedding rings."

"Melissa, I am asking you to marry me."

"I know…" she said, "But you are not down on one knee, so it hardly counts."

With difficulty she prised off his ring and gave it back to him, and felt his anger in the air like a change in temperature. "What will happen if I do not consent to marry you?" she enquired. "Will you abandon me? Will you give up on us?"

"I think I may have little choice…at least for a year or so until you are of age."

"And then?"

"How the devil do I know?" he said, a callow and desperate note she had never heard him use before creeping into his voice. "Do you want that? To not meet?"

"Of course not…and if you gave up on me so easily 'twould say a lot to me about your true feelings."

He rose and looked down on her, aggravation and frustration the flavours of the dark. "Is this some sort of a test? You holding out in this way!"

"Indeed not! I would go upstairs and make love with you now if you would have it."

"I cannot have it," he said, his voice rising despite the potential closeness of listeners. "My position is untenable, you silly girl. So do not taunt me with it."

Immediately, he braced for her reaction to his insult. His frustration was at a tipping point. Her face was an oval pale glow as she looked up at him, her brows—darker than the rest of her features in the dim light—dipping towards the faint outline of her nose. Then she rose too. "I do not taunt you with it… I want it as much as you…'tis worse for me…you perhaps have other women you can go to for…for comfort…"

He stopped in his new bout of pacing and faced her. "To which other women do you refer?"

"I do not rightly know…" She was in some agitation. "Mistresses or ladies of the night!"

He was speechless for seconds and then laughed. "I cannot afford mistresses…and I…"

She cut in on him. "… But you would have some if you could afford it?"

"*Some*? *Some mistresses*? Melissa, who do you think I am?"

"A gentleman extremely attractive to ladies of all kinds and ages…" she returned.

"I am flattered." He wanted to laugh but saw it as inappropriate. "And as for *ladies of the night!* Do you know what a lady-of-the-night does?"

"Not fully… I expect they flit about after dark or something, like moths. But Melanie holds that men of your ilk always have women somewhere along the way…even when wed. She fears as much with Geoffrey."

"I see…well much as I hate to contradict the font of all knowledge, Melanie Gillis, men like me, or Geoffrey Gillis, do not always have women on hand so conveniently. We have enough to do holding down our daily work and keeping one woman at a time happy…we usually do not wish to reprise a life from 'Arabian Nights' once we are affianced…"

She did not know whether or not to believe him. She did not have enough information on life as yet. He went on and broke her introspection, "… Of course, if men are unhappily married, they may well seek solace elsewhere…although usually not *ladies of the night*…they are…they are…"

"What?" she demanded impatiently.

"Not always clean…not desirable to men who are not lecherous for the sake of being so."

"Do you mean they don't bathe?"

"No, I mean they are riddled with disease very often…"

"What kind of disease?" she asked in fascination.

"Never mind…we cannot have this conversation just now…'tis not relevant…but rest assured, I have no other women presently."

She felt untold tension leave her body, and they held fast in silence for a full three minutes before she had an idea. "What if we had a long engagement?"

He turned slowly to regard her. "So you can break it off when you have experienced the fullness of love making…or tire of me after a while?"

She sprang up and moved quickly into him, putting the full weight of her body against his. "Anthony, I would not do that… I would… I would…" She came away from him and paced. "I would perhaps try to delay the marriage, but I would never want to be apart from you…not ever. I know that now!"

"Then why do you not want to marry me?"

"I have no answer…except some innate loathing of the prospect of marriage…to anyone…try not to take it so personally."

He found this hilarious but contained the laughter. "My dear girl, how can I not take personally your refusal to marry me…'tis a preposterous suggestion. You cannot care for me enough if I am simply an object within the prospect of marriage."

"That is not it at all…" she cried and mounted the lawned area around the rose bushes and tripped about in a state of greater agitation. He went after her and caught her by the arm so that she was obliged to turn to him. "And you are not the one to talk of not caring…you have never talked of your love for me," she said.

He lifted her easily onto the path from the grass which was sodden and soaking her hemline and her satin slippers. "I am an Englishman…" he said in his own defence. "I do not talk of love, I show love…"

"What an easy way out," she retorted.

He pulled her to the bench and they sat. "Melissa, I do love you."

"I know not whether to believe you under these circumstances."

"Just as I know not whether to believe the suggestion of your long engagement."

Then her mother emerged from the other side of the rose garden, carrying a small lantern. It was obvious she had been listening as best she could. "What are you doing now?" she demanded, her skirts rustling and her neck jewels jangling softly as she moved.

"I think that is our business!" Melissa said abruptly.

"We are talking of marriage…" he told Marguerite to appease her.

Marguerite stood very still suddenly and was obviously thinking.

Melissa exclaimed in a loud snort of annoyance, but realising it to be the truth said: "Yes, 'tis the only place we can be assured any privacy…"

"Then come in and use a reception room…'tis unseemly to be out here in the dark."

"Ridiculous!" said her daughter with indignance. "What is unseemly about the darkness of the garden?"

He squeezed her hand, pressing the small bones of her wrist so that she would be silent. A fight with her mother was the last thing they needed. "We will be along in a moment, Ma'am," he said in his deep smooth tones which Marguerite could not argue with. Her skirts rustled off the way they had arrived and she disappeared.

They regarded each other again in the rapidly deepening darkness, sensing without their eyes and gleaning more of what lay beneath.

"The day after tomorrow!" he said eventually, leading her by the elbow in a manner she could not deflect. "We will talk more then…but a decision must be reached by the end of that day and we can tell your father…whatever you decide."

"Very well." She moved with him in the swift strides he was taking to the drawing room windows.

"I will say goodbye for now…" he told her and she clung to him, like someone about to lose a loved one. He read a lot into it and knew that she would not risk their parting for a year or more. He would have wagered money on it if pressed. It was a safe bet that she would not want that. No more than he wanted it.

Serious and More Serious

"But what am I to do?" she wailed to Melanie as they sat in the usual park in the centre of the town. "I am not ready to wed."

Melanie was growing exasperated and tried not to show it. She put her fingers to her belly. She was quite certain she was with child now but loath to jinx it by speaking precipitously. The thought made her more mellow and patient and she sighed. She had listened very closely to a highly detailed account of the proceedings of Sunday evening. Nothing in it surprised her. "Lissy, you knew this point would come…you must decide now whether you want him for a husband or not."

"Is there no other alternative?"

"Your period of getting to know each other *was* the alternative…and now you cannot bear to be without him, so you must take the plunge or risk losing him."

"Why does he want me to wed him? He surely knows I am not a wifely commodity!"

"He knows nothing of the sort. He will be determined to fashion you into such a thing. It will thrill him to do so, I am sure."

Melissa was near to tears, but also close to laughter. It was ever thus when she and Melanie were trying to talk about serious concerns. "I know not what you mean…"

"Think of last night. He adored having to come after you and issue his threats to attain your compliance," Melanie said.

"I am not sure he did…adore it I mean," objected Melissa. "On first entering the bedroom, he was very vexed."

"Yes, but he loves being vexed…that is my point. He craves that kind of contest. I have always told you that."

There was a pause while three well-dressed matrons passed with small dogs on leads and Melissa thought about Melanie's statement. "I am not sure you are right," she said with reluctance. "And I often make him worse in his vexation."

"Because you love it too…though you don't admit it. You both love it…so what could be a better match? The game could go on forever."

"Could it?" Melissa wrinkled her nose and looked up at the trees, magnificent with foliage and birdsong. "After we are wed?"

"Certainly!" asserted Melanie. "'tis the stuff of which the union is made. He issues his instructions, or requests, or whatever he chooses to call them, and you defy him, or imply that you are doing so…and he comes after you and then…"

"Then?" coaxed Melissa.

"Well, that depends on who gives way first I suppose…and that might differ from occasion to occasion…just to stop things from becoming stale and predictable."

At this point, Melissa relapsed into merriment and fished out her lacy kerchief to cover her mouth, then spent a good few moments enjoying the release of hilarity. Having recovered she said. "And what of the occasions when I do not give in? When I am in the throes of my worst obstinacy!"

Melanie became pragmatic and took up her white kid gloves and smoothed them. "Then he will no doubt deliver your *preferred method of chastisement…* I am, I admit, quite surprised he has not done so already!"

Melissa became overly serious. "Well, he has not… I always manage to defeat him…and for the hundredth time, it is not my *preferred method of chastisement.*"

"Oh, have you chosen another one betimes?" trilled her closest friend.

Melissa made a face of wry amusement to acknowledge the wit. "And surely, he cannot be doing that when we are quite old…in ten years or so? For I shall fight him, you know."

"Lissy, in ten years he will be forty and you will be thirty…hardly rheumatic old fogies."

More people passed them in the clement weather for walking and Melissa's kerchief was now quite damp. Absorbed with getting herself back to sombre normality, she hardly noticed Melanie's serious mood enshrouding her like a mist, but then stopped blowing her nose and gazed at her friend with guilty and doleful eyes, awaiting a further announcement of some kind. It was not long in arriving. "You must decide now…as he says." Melanie smoothed her blouse sleeves with dignity. "You are entrapping him…and really you are as guilty of seduction as the most callous seducer…"

"I do not think so!" expostulated Melissa.

"Of course you are! Think on it…often 'tis men who lure women into situations such as the one last night."

Melissa gaped at her and then stood and walked about in front of the three fountains; they made her think of lovemaking and bodily stimulation.

"Are you denying now to me, your oldest friend, that you lured him to your bedroom with one of your freakish bouts of sulking?"

"Well, I…" Melissa paused and considered things, her hand raised to her eyes to shield the sun's glare, and peered into the distance. "I did not exactly lure him…but I suppose I knew he would follow."

"Of course, who but a feeble sort of man would allow you to leave him at a table with lots of people watching on and not come after you! 'twas beyond rude. You tested his resolve deliberately…some may say, his authority."

"Do not use that word. That is what we had the fight about."

"Indeed, because that issue is the cornerstone of the seduction…" Melanie assured her.

She was unsure now of her own motives, her own moral compass. She turned to look into Melanie's face and beheld Melanie at her most responsible, her most righteous, her most upstanding. It was rare and it was unmistakable. "You lured him into taking your virginity…" she said, her brows arched and her mouth set in a straight line, ageing her by ten years.

She derived some of her more serious stances and statements nowadays from Geoffrey as she watched him go through the scripts for his court briefs. She even played the opposing side for him. She was a very helpful aid to his career in that sense, and she was intrigued by some of the cases he outlined for her.

"I did…" conceded Melissa. "Though I did not know exactly how 'twould be. I am too inexperienced and I…"

"Needed to discover more…" Melanie concluded.

"Yes." Melissa sank to the bench and her body sagged, her hands gripping the edge of the seat to keep her upright.

"Well, now you have discovered…and so has he…he knows he wishes to wed you…and unless you wish to lose his admiration and respect for you… I may even say his love…you must agree to it."

"Must I? Simply because of convention?"

"No…because 'tis what he wants…and you always knew that from the start of all this. That is why he is taking the course slowly and waiting for you…"

"But what about what I want?"

"You want him too, but on your terms…yet you scarcely know what those terms are…"

Melissa stood again, and Melanie stood with her and took her hand and held it loosely. "'tis perhaps what we conjectured on months ago…and I never thought to be in his corner then…but you are not far from making a fool of him…and if you do, he will not forgive that…there will be no turning back."

"Come!" Melissa pulled her towards the path to the gates and then released her hand. "And what of his overarching thrust for authority…his warnings?"

"You mean the *preferred method of chastisement?*" Melanie enquired in a voice of feigned concern.

"Do stop calling it that!" Melissa stamped her foot as she paused and Melanie tutted with fake disapproval. "'tis just the stake with which you play the game…the rules of the house, were you in a gambling room."

They picked up pace and strode more swiftly, the subject and the passing of time demanding it. "But really 'tis neither here nor there…" Melanie continued. "'tis like a beloved old chair near the hearth…you may keep it forever, re-upholstered, or consign it to the attic…'twill be always there somewhere if you wish it to be…for now, you cannot bear to see it go…for his part he may not wish to risk repelling you at this stage so he may defer any such action until after the wedding…but be assured, the game in the immediate future will almost certainly entail this *unfortunate slip of your tongue,* as you call it."

They both began giggling and Melissa fell against Melanie clumsily as hilarity inclined her sideways.

"As long as 'tis nothing worse than that…" She breathed deeply into the final stages of self-control and moved in a very upright way.

"Worse than what?" asked Melanie cunningly.

"The *preferred method,"* said Melissa carelessly and Melanie turned, her eyes glittering. "You see, 'tis your preference."

"It is not...'tis simply a term of reference for convenience's sake." She pulled at her skirts to straighten them and regain dignity. "What has Geoffrey done to you so far...?" she ventured, "When you displease him greatly...as you surely must, knowing you."

"Well, only last weekend he..." Melanie paused and thought twice. "No, I will not elaborate, I do not wish to make you more reluctant than you are towards matrimony."

"You cannot do that!" squealed Melissa. "Introduce that note, then not continue...tell me!"

In a bid to derail the conversation, Melanie changed tack recklessly by saying: "Lissy, you must not tell anyone...no-one yet...but I think I am with child!"

Melissa was suitably distracted and gasped and then took Melanie into her embrace. "I could not be more pleased for you."

"'tis not definite...but I am hoping."

"I will hope with you!" Melissa said earnestly.

They linked arms and continued to the front gates where the carriage from the Shaw mansion awaited them to take them both home. Melanie's new house being first en route.

"I may call on Granny, she is always wise in these matters," Melissa said as they parted company.

"She will say to wed him, naturally..." Melanie pronounced, "Just to have him around more often to carry her upstairs...but do ask her opinion...she will have played a few games with your grandfather the Spaniard, for sure!"

Melissa was prone to more merriment at the remark and was propelled quite forcefully into the conveyance by John, the footman—who was acting as groom that day—for fear she fall from the steps and he would get the blame. Having delivered Melanie home safely, she instructed him to turn back towards her aunt's dwelling; a fashionably large townhouse some three or so miles away.

However, Jemima had decamped to stay with Aunt Ariadne for a few days, according to Gregory, who promised to bring her over on the following Saturday so that they might play cards and spend time with her.

So, she carried on back to High Lawns.

"Had quite a jaunt this morning, haven't you, Miss?" said John cheekily as he assisted her into the conveyance a second time, more sober this time in her demeanour now that she was without Melanie's company. "I expect you got plans to make…"

"'tis absolutely none of your business!" retorted Melissa tartly, and John sealed his lips and took the unaccustomed rebuff from the usually equable daughter of the family with a pinch of salt and drove home.

* * *

She had painting commissions ordered at the fundraiser to finish, plus Mrs Petersham's spaniel portrait which she had not yet started. She was near to suffering from creative overwhelm and determined to get on with things and not be harrowed by these emotional climaxes until tea time, when shortly afterwards she could expect Fairchild to arrive. But on her way to the art room her father intercepted her progress. "Lissy, come into the study, please," said he and led the way without preamble.

Melissa followed him, unused to being summoned in this way by her father on the spur of any moment.

In the corner of the room under the window sat the estate manager, writing up documents, and she looked at him briefly as she took the armchair nearest her father's impressive rosewood and oak desk on which he prepared papers for a business meeting that afternoon. The summons could not bode well. "Leave us, Croker, please!" said Giles to the estate manager.

Mr Croker rose and on passing Melissa, made her a flourishing obsequious bow. He was the same estates manager who had on two occasions been bold enough to kiss her. An earnest young man, his longing and liking for her was not disguised behind any discreet expression. He widened his eyes as he passed her and smiled and held himself more upright. She batted her eyelids in acknowledgement of him and then turned her head away to signify indifference.

Mr Croker flushed and left the room. He would never again be allowed within two yards of her of course, and she wondered how she could have even contemplated allowing his kisses, except for the purpose of experiment.

"Now then, young lady…" began Giles in his patient paternal tone. "What are you intending about this dalliance? Has it not gone on long enough?"

"Which dalliance, Papa?" she said artfully.

"Good God, girl, don't go all coy! Anthony Fairchild, of course! How many dalliances do you have going just now?"

She blinked in delicate confusion as if bemused.

"Your mother tells me he was asking for your hand in the garden Sunday eve…and you were refusing him."

"That is not quite accurate…" extemporised Melissa.

Giles looked up from his stack of documents. "What are the intentions?"

"I… I am unsure still…though I have tentatively agreed to marriage." She was between a rock and a hard place, and floundered in discomfort.

Her father continued filling a leather satchel with papers. "Stap me! You cannot be seen kissing a man and disappearing from the dinner table with him for long periods when there is no clear intention."

"But why not?" asked the ingenuous Melissa. "What harm are we doing to anyone?"

Giles summoned tolerance, preparing himself for unfathomable and tiresome prevarication. "He is a man of position in the community, Melissa…not some lad you've met at a fayre…you must see that he will not be played with in this way forever."

"I am waiting to be sure we like each other, Papa." She thought of Melanie's strictures earlier and wondered if everyone saw her as shallow and fickle.

"What?" Her father rose from his seat with horrified alacrity. "You like each other for certain, far as I can tell…you hang on his arm and his every word and make the kind of faces that might shame a courtesan."

"Do I?"

"You certainly do." He paused once more; perhaps she was not aware of her behaviour. "So, let's not go round in these circles. I have an appointment in the next county in an hour… I can't be sitting here engaging in romantic parlour quizzes."

Melissa sighed and crossed her ankles neatly beneath her loose house dress, donned for painting. It was warm in her father's study, the fire stoked high by his own ministering and love of the poker. She removed the shawl she wore to stave off the cool atmosphere of the art room and draped it over the arm of the chair. "Naturally, I am enamoured of him…" she began.

"Then what is the hold up?" queried her father.

"I am not sure."

"Of what?" he snapped, his concentration on his pipe and tobacco pouch. "How much surety do you think you're going to have this side of the wedding?"

She looked pointedly in the other direction, perceiving that her mother had not perhaps heard all of their last exchange in the rose garden. "There is more to marriage than bodily desire, surely?" she said, causing her father to flush slightly; his plaintive daughter never failing to surprise him with her comments. He rose and lit the pipe with a long spill retrieved from the holder in the hearth. "There is indeed…but which part is it that worries you?"

She thought about Charles Fairchild and the conversation with Susan Darnley, then pushed it from her mind. *Melanie had pointed out that there were various sorts of tyrants…harmless ones, vindictive ones and downright despots…but Anthony was decidedly not one of the latter.* "The day to day, I suppose…" she improvised. "I fear he may become less than attentive to me and I may grow bored." It was an absolute lie, but her father smoked and ruminated. "That is not impossible, but neither is it a reason to overlook his suit…'tis a risk marriage brings with time. He's a fine fellow, you won't get many of his sort to the pound."

Melissa smiled and partly closed her eyes and exhaled gently and slid the tip of her tongue around her upper lip; ingenuous signs of innate desire. "Yes, I am aware!" she purred.

When she regained focus and looked about her, Giles was out of his chair and pacing around the Persian rug in front of the fire grate. Her lascivious comment and expression had thrown him off kilter. "I think we need your mother into this discussion…'tis a delicate subject after all…"

Melissa rose too. "No, no. I will not speak with her on it…she meddles far too much…she is a veritable busybody."

Her father froze and then turned. "I shall pretend I did not hear that!"

She ignored the rebuke. "She cares not for the truth of matters…only for the appearance, and she cannot appreciate the depth." She sank into the chair again.

Her father waved his arm, the pipe extended like a smoke signal of distress. "Melissa, I will not allow this dalliance…or romance, or whatever you care to call it, to go on for much longer. There was obviously a stage reached on Sunday night that had him of a dither and caused you to behave badly…your mother is the woman closest to you in blood and you must be honest with her and tell her what is afoot."

"I will talk with Granny!" she said firmly, "I called this afternoon but she had left Aunt Amaelia's house for Aunt Addy's."

Giles billowed smoke, his face obscured within it and his voice emerging as a disembodied growl. "Your granny is old now..."

"But wise..." she interjected, "Which my mother is not..."

"Melissa!" said Giles in exasperation. "Your grandmother is apt to mislead the situation with random facts and memory meanderings concerning my father."

"She understands what it is to love deeply and be in confusion, Papa..." she paused again, having realised that the remark was tantamount to saying her mother did not love her father deeply. She glanced at her father who seemed to have heard nothing amiss.

"So, you do love him then, Fairchild?" he asked.

"I adore his every facet," she pronounced. "He pleases my senses utterly, but I am not sure if that is love..."

A small bark of laughter then Giles murmured, "For most women that would suffice." He thought that perhaps some of her phrases and sentiments were coined from novels or poets, or the kind of fashionable journals women read, and decided to look beyond them.

"Perhaps it would," she concurred, "But they may then regret the step later...look at Aunt Amaelia with Montalbein!"

"Oh, don't bring that up..." he said testily. "I am sick of hearing about it...every month there is something new on his debauchery."

"'tis a case in point, surely?" she protested.

"Everyone knew what Montalbein was becoming twenty odd years ago...and 'twas only Amaelia could not see it... Fairchild is a different kind of fish...an educated and well-mannered man. He is not some braggart who thinks only of pleasure and trades on his ancestral title...he knows the meaning of hard work and responsibility and respects the rest of society."

"As far as you know! But you know nothing of what he does when out carousing..."

"For Pete's sake!" Giles said in simmering desperation. "Most young men do that sort of thing...'tis you he wishes to wed, not any floozy he meets when out carousing."

"How do you know?" Melissa asked.

"I do know..." countered Giles, faltering a little at the thought of further explanation. "I have been young myself..."

"And you went carousing?"

"Of course!" confirmed Giles, losing control of the conversation. "I was normal in every way…as yon fellow of yours is…"

"And you never met any woman while out carousing whom you wished to love and settle with?"

"I did not!" he said conclusively. "A man does not meet that kind of woman when out carousing."

"Why not?" she queried. "Supposing he meets a woman he likes better than me when out carousing one night?"

Her father watched her carefully; he suspected her to be arguing simply for the sake of delay. He sighed and said: "Don't be ridiculous, Lissy, a man does not offer suit for a woman with no more than five minutes' consideration…and women in taverns and such are not the class of lady a man like Fairchild would wish to marry."

"I see," she said and became lost in introspection. While her father collected himself and cleared his throat and rose and came around the desk with a purposeful tread. "Do you think he will wait forever? Do you imagine a man like him will be dallied with and just accept it?"

"No, I do not."

"Well, then! See sense! Unless you think to make a suit with the Brathwaite boy?"

"I do not," she said flatly.

"Good, because I can tell you now that it would not have my blessing…he is by no means a suitable match."

Poor Roger, maligned as usual, she felt duty bound to defend him. "I do not see why!"

"Doubtless you might one day, but he is not about to meet with favour as a potential husband, should he approach me on the matter."

"You need have no fear on that score, Papa…" she said, and satisfied by that at least, Giles returned to his satchel of papers and a silence fell, until she ventured: "I notice you do not push Damien to wed Estelle…they dally and get away with it."

Giles looked up, frowning. "I do not particularly wish to have Estelle in the family…not with some of her peculiar beliefs and ways…any more than I would wish to welcome young Braithwaite… Estelle is just…she is just…"

"Odd?" supplied Melissa to be helpful.

Giles cleared his throat again. "She is indeed a strange young woman…and your mother is not taken with her…betimes, never mind all that…'tis different for Damien."

"Because he is a man?"

"Precisely."

"And he is as odd as her, so they are well matched…if free to do as they choose…" she added with emphasis.

"Melissa, your dalliance with Fairchild has to be brought to a conclusion!" pronounced Giles with purpose.

Not wishing to enter any further into the argument and incur his wrath, she said in a near whisper. "I know…he wishes it too… I am to give him an answer."

"Good," Giles was relieved. "And you intend to say yes, do you?"

"I am intending to say yes…but I am unsure when," she concurred with more definition in her voice.

Glies came around his desk and sat on the edge of it facing her. "Then let me be sure for you! You will say yes to him by the end of the week. Or let him go with his self-respect intact…do you understand me?"

She rose and smoothed her painting smock and put on her shawl and assumed a quiet majesty. "I cannot bear to let him go…" she said in a faint voice.

Giles looked at her sharply. "By the end of the week, Melissa! Do you harken?"

"Indeed, Papa…do not let me detain you further." She dropped him a curtsy and he smiled. "That's a good girl," he said in a conciliatory tone which annoyed her greatly. She moved to his side and kissed him on the cheek to disguise the annoyance she felt.

"Be off with you now, you little besom…" he said airily.

She carried on to the art room and felt her mood not conducive at all to creative matters. She decided to say nothing of this conversation to Fairchild when he called that evening and to speak of marital matters only by the end of the week, as her father had ordained. Her father's authority was as yet greater than her lover's.

* * *

Early the same evening, Fairchild met with Trimingham in a tavern on the outskirts of the town and they began drinking, promising themselves moderation.

469

He told Trim. "I have gone too far… I must now marry her or go to Giles Shaw and declare the state of affairs."

Trim swigged a large portion of ale and then paused to digest the words. "You have taken her virginity?"

"I have…'twas unavoidable. She took me too far on an edge and I have proposed…"

"And she says?" queried Trim politely.

"She is unsure…'*can we not go on as we are?*'…she wants not to be committed to wedlock yet."

"Then why must you marry quickly?" queried Trim.

"I have promised Giles Shaw… I have said that if I take her virginity by accident or design, I will wed her, if she will consent."

"But if she does not want to?"

"I am not sure she does not want to…though neither does she want to relinquish our relationship. And nor do I."

Trim quaffed the rest of the ale and ordered more from the barmaid. It was not in his remit now to advise. He had enjoyed one of the longest engagements in Christendom, he was not in a position to talk. But then Susan's position and age were different to Melissa Shaw's.

"I have told her that she must decide by tonight…or I will go to her father and tell him of the development!"

"Is that wise?" Trim asked.

"Perhaps not, but my reputation and honour are at stake, Timothy, and suppose she tells someone of the loss of her virginity and it gets back to him? I cannot have that."

"No…no indeed," said Trim. "But she is surely disinclined to telling anyone?"

Fairchild almost choked on his ale. "God's teeth! She is a female; they change with the weather…she will tell Melanie Gillis for certain…and her maid knows…'tis open season now."

"Out of your hands then, dear boy!" Trim said as he paid for the drinks. "You cannot force her to marry you…though obviously Giles might do so."

Fairchild pulled a face. "I cannot countenance coercing any woman to wed me…'tis unthinkable. Marriage is for life."

"Indeed," concurred Trimingham, lifting a tankard. "Though at the end of the day, 'tis only a piece of paper."

"Well, I… I do not…" He was unable to express his full armoury of thoughts. He wondered what he really felt and thought and the conundrum grew worse in the confusion. He felt the room almost spin. "I am not sure I agree with you on that point," he concluded.

Trim widened his eyes and grinned. "You shock me, Tony! And then again, there speaks the vicar's son…*give me the child until he is seven…*"

"That is not helpful…" said Fairchild, but sought the possible wisdom within the words.

* * *

As soon as he entered the reception room they had been exclusively allocated for their private courtship meetings, where a fire burnt brightly in the grate as usual, she remembered that he had said he wanted her answer this night. In her confusion and overwhelm with life, she had forgotten the days of the week. It was Tuesday, two nights after Sunday's heated exchange and the loss of her virginity. The loss of that was the overriding focus of her mind since it had happened.

He sat on the ornate velvet sofa which was not made for any zealous activity beyond lounging. A larger more commodious chesterfield sofa stood invitingly at an angle and fully available, seating six people if necessary and deeper in depth than was perhaps practical, unless one was lounging flagrantly or lying. Doubtless he had chosen the flimsier one so that she could not begin any amorous antics before the serious discussions had happened.

"'tis like the hobs of hell in here…are you not near to fainting?" he opined, removing his jacket.

"No, I am used to it. My father orders the fires lit winter and summer, except perhaps in a great heat…so that no-one is cold indoors. We douse the embers if we are near to passing out…though my father is never that. He is forever complaining of his rheumatics and the chill and so on. Perhaps 'tis his Spanish blood…"

"Perhaps!" concurred Fairchild cryptically. He was less interested in Giles Shaw's heritage at present than his own predicament.

"Why are you dressed as if still in work?" she queried.

"I had business to attend to straight afterwards and did not have time to change."

She sat next to him and snuggled into his side, then sniffed delicately. "Business that involved the quaffing of ale no doubt?"

She was already speaking like a wife, though not yet agreeing to engagement. He smiled to himself; perhaps it was a good sign. "I had two ales. I met with Trim in a tavern to collect documents."

She curled her legs beneath her skirts, her feet up on the sofa, and leaned on him cosily. "It does not matter to me. I quite like the smell of beer…as long as 'tis not overpowering!" she added meaningfully. "As long as you are not drunk."

"Good Lord…" he looked at her sidelong, quite mortified. "I would never be drunk in your presence…nor in the presence of any lady."

"Of course not…" she said, "But if we were married?"

"Yes? What, if we were married?"

"Perhaps you might become so then…drunk on occasions…and not so ceremonious about showing it."

"I assure you I would not…my upbringing is entirely against it," he said flatly.

She murmured in satisfaction. That was one thing in his favour, if he could be believed. She perceived that he probably could, he was usually truthful. "Should we take a glass of wine?"

"Certainly," he agreed.

She poured a large glass of claret for him, decanted and delivered by the butler on his arrival, and a smaller glass for herself.

"Well?" he asked, having sipped for several seconds at the wine and kept himself from downing it in one. "Have you come to a decision?"

"A decision?" she said.

He was again on his metal. Surely, she could not have taken Sunday's talk so lightly. "Wedlock!" he said in some vexation. "You cannot have forgotten…"

"Oh that."

"Yes, that!"

"No, I have not forgotten."

"Well, then?"

"My father is insisting I make the decision by the end of the week," she admitted, seeing no other way forwards but to talk of Giles' intervention.

He sat away from her and stared. "So, you have talked of it with your father?"

"Yes, he forced the issue…the old witch must have listened to some of our discussion in the garden and told him. He says I must decide by the end of this week."

"Yes, but I told you I wanted a decision by tonight!"

She drank her own wine and thought. "I cannot listen to both of you," she said ingenuously. "Which of you must I obey in this *ordering around process* of my own life?"

He was speechless. Her artfulness was beyond belief.

"What is the difference between tonight, which is Tuesday, and the end of the week on Friday…two or three days hence?"

Naturally she had no reply. He wondered if it was simply the way her mind worked, or because she felt trapped and needed time. "Well?" he demanded. Still, she did not comment. "What else has your father had to say? Does he know of the loss of virginity?"

"He is saying that we cannot go on forever in this way…that is all."

"And he is correct!" He put down his glass on the side table and gently pushed her off him and then rose and stood before the fire looking at her, in much the same way her father had earlier. "So, what is your answer?"

She tutted, as if this were a minor irritation and not a proposal of marriage, and then said. "I will agree to be your wife…but only if we do not actually marry for a further six months at least!"

He was between two extremes: the fact that this topic seemed to afford her no pleasure at all and the logical answer she had given. "Six or eight months is probably a good time length. Any sooner and people will imagine you are with child and marrying only for that reason."

"Heaven forfend!" she said facetiously. "Though I think that Melanie is with child."

"That is different…she is already wed."

"You must not tell anyone. I should not have said anything. She swore me to secrecy."

"Her condition is of such little interest to me as to be already forgotten."

"And that is another thing…" she said, bringing her feet from the sofa and sitting up. "Your horridness regarding Melanie. I do not want it to carry into our future…"

He was taken aback, here was unprecedented table-turning, even for this inflammatory subject. "Oh, I see, my *horridness*…which is not an actual word, incidentally…and not her's to me? Perhaps she should modify her *horrid* tongue in my presence…either that or do not bring her into my presence at all."

She paused to consider his correction of her grammar over her complaint; should she remark upon that for further deflection? She decided against it! "And what if I said the same to you of Mr Trimingham?"

He refilled his own glass with claret. She was beyond exasperating. "Trim does not make hostile remarks or create vitriolic atmosphere via imaginary grievances from history."

"What?" She stood and moved in her stocking-feet for more wine. "Are you now saying that we have invented the experiences in Barton Grange waiting room?"

"No… I am saying they are not grounds for disreputable behaviour and vituperative conversation in the drawing room in present day!"

She swigged the wine too quickly and the room spun. She quickly sat again on the sofa and clutched her glass, taking time to compose herself. "All you have to do, Anthony, is apologise…or show some contrition."

Unable almost to believe what he was hearing, he felt he should remove himself before more damage could occur. He retrieved his jacket and put it on.

"Melissa, let me assure you…for what hopefully is the last time…that it is not going to happen. I have nothing to apologise for. And if all you can talk about at this point in our relationship is your's and Melanie's futile grievance, then I am leaving…"

"Simply because you lack humility…'tis a matter of the greatest arrogance."

He finished buttoning his jacket and stared into the far corner of the room, unable to look at her for his mounting anger. He ran his tongue around his teeth and then bit his upper lip, as she watched him calmly. "And all you need to do now is to call me a hypocrite and the advantage is mine…" he said, his voice the low and husky growl she so loved.

"I shall not… I shall not fall into that trap," she said, "Though doubtless you would love me to do so."

"I would love you to behave in a mature and suitable manner…that is what I would love…and to not harp on about your school days as if we were still back there."

"I do not harp on about anything," she said, finishing the rest of the wine but not risking her feet in case she fell back into the sofa. Her heated emotion was fuelling her dizziness when added to the drink. "I simply will not be made to feel as if we…as if I…were at fault in the matter and not you."

He closed his eyes and chewed his inner lip and then sighed and said: "I had authority in the classroom…you were children…'twas your insolence and misbehaviour where the fault lay…"

"Of course…and not at all your callous intolerance of the nature of young girls!"

He took in a deep lungful of air through his gritted teeth and she almost giggled. "I will bid you goodnight and allow some time so that you can see the dangerous absurdity of this continuing subject."

She did not speak and watched him vacate the room and then missed his presence immediately but praised herself for her fortitude under attack. Not to mention the time she had bought on the question of the proposal.

She was too overwrought to sit and relax so she allowed a few minutes for him to depart the building and then went to the art room, where she fished out the charcoal sketch she was making of him. It was the next best thing to being with him. She looked at it objectively and tried to detach from the recent argument sufficiently to gauge how the likeness was coming along.

It was early in the process still but she perceived that it was good. In a mood of frustration, she began drawing over lines she had previously made and changing the slightly elevated angle of his face. She succeeded in making him look angry. Less handsome and decidedly unappealing.

Clearly, he was now seething about her lack of a decision on marriage, and her audacity in raising again the subject of the waiting room. But it was always going to come between them unless he paid some homage to contrition or regret. Or unless she climbed down from the moral high ground. Should love conquer this resentment, or should the cause be understanding of love? That was the moral dilemma. One she could not answer.

Fifteen minutes later, she had made his face on the paper look like something from the Roman Empire; too draconian, too intensely fierce, lacking his usual calm expression as he went through his days. His almost—as Melanie had once remarked—deceptively angelic persona. But he was just a man, as he had told her outside the drawing room after that first notorious Sunday afternoon tea; not anything very extreme or remarkable at all.

She threw down the brush and was about to leave when her mother entered the room uninvited.

"Why has he left so soon?" she enquired.

"Who?" said Melissa unhelpfully.

"You know very well who… Anthony Fairchild!"

Melissa snuffed out the oil lamps and opened the door to admit the light from the passage, then held it open for her mother and herself to depart. "He has translations to complete in a hurry…" she said at length, pleased with this excuse.

"Not in such a hurry that he cannot spare more than ten minutes of his time with you, surely!" said Marguerite. "Are you sure 'twas not because you have argued with him?"

Melissa groaned; the door held open but her mother still on the inside of the room. "Do you mean you were unable to hear what was said when listening outside the door?" she replied with cool temerity.

Marguerite made a rasping sound between her teeth and bridled and pulled herself up towards her daughter's height. "You are so insolent…and rude!" she said in a low anguished tone.

"It has been pointed out before…" agreed Melissa with patience.

"Are you sure you have not caused him to have done with you for good?" said Marguerite, betraying her underlying concerns in her quivering voice and manner.

"And what if I have?" cried Melissa as she closed the door finally after them. "'tis our right to argue…and our business."

Marguerite was almost as vexed as Fairchild had been. She lifted her skirts, voluminous and fine for the receiving of evening guests, and swished her way to the end of the passageway leading to the main hall before turning. "You are the most vexing of creatures…antagonistic and provoking…" she hissed at her daughter. "It is my business! I am your mother. He will not tolerate all this prevarication and deceit for much longer, you know…"

"There is no deceit," Melissa interjected. "I am perhaps all the things you say, but I am not deceitful."

"Not by direct means perhaps, but by implication you are quite the most deceitful of people!"

"Says the woman who creeps around in gardens and hides behind hedges to listen to other's private conversations…the one who then reports them wrongly to her husband to create conflict where there is none…"

Marguerite moved towards her and went to slap her, but Melissa caught her wrist as she raised her arm and then dropped it and stepped back. Marguerite took steps towards the main hall. Furious beyond measure. "I am warning you! He will not wait much longer. Do you think you can live under this roof forever?"

"'tis my father's house," said Melissa. "So, I will not move until he tells me I should."

"He has told you to accept the offer of marriage," said Marguerite. "I have heard it from him."

"I intend to accept…but not to please you."

Marguerite went quickly up the stairs and retired to the bedroom to calm herself and have Polly brush her hair, again, and re-pin it. It always calmed her. She knew nothing of Polly's engagement to Dominic McCarthy and her intention to move away, and Polly smiled at her in a pleasing manner as she worked, watching Marguerite's reflection in the dressing table mirror. "You are agitated, Madam," she said.

"Nothing to worry over…" Marguerite removed imaginary fluff from her sleeve. "Just my vexing daughter, as usual. She is so impolite and ungrateful…she always has been."

Polly said nothing. Melissa was never impolite to her, and seldom in her hearing to other members of the family. Except perhaps Damien Shaw, who was vexation itself. But the hostility between mother and daughter was quite marked, and quite well known, though not often referred to. Polly wondered whether— had she known her own mother for more than her first two years of life—they would have had such a relationship. "I am sure she does not mean to be…" Polly said at length and smoothed Marguerite's hair upwards with her hands in the most gentle of ways, so that Marguerite closed her eyes and almost drowsed.

Presently, as Polly was making sure all the pins were secure, Giles entered the bedroom and paused in his customary hesitant and considerate manner to see if there was something going on that he should not see.

"Thank you, Polly!" said Marguerite and Polly left the room, curtsying to Giles swiftly as she passed him. He smiled at her and inclined his head. He was the most genial and amenable of men, and Polly felt she would miss him almost as much as she would miss Melissa.

Marguerite rose from the chair quickly and followed Giles to his dressing room, stopping at the threshold. "Our daughter is beyond rude to me, Giles! She has accused me of listening behind the hedge and spying on her."

Giles heaved a breath and chose a fresh waistcoat to wear, saying nothing whatever.

"He has left again… Fairchild…after only ten minutes in her company."

"So, you were spying on them?" said her husband.

"I was doing no such thing. I happened to be in the hall when he arrived and, in the hall, when he left…that is all."

"Of course!" said Giles blithely.

He was quite as annoying as Melissa. Quite as disparaging of her maternal concerns and her moral values. She went back into the bedroom and rifled noisily through her large jewellery box.

"She says now she is accepting him…though he looked none too pleased when he went. I do not know what they find to row about."

"You have not eavesdropped thoroughly enough then!" said Giles jestingly.

Marguerite was beyond exasperation. She picked up a heavy silver bangle and hurled it across the room in his direction, knowing it would miss him by yards. He looked at her with a curious expression, not deigning to comment. He was not about to enter into the political situation between his wife and daughter. Melissa had hardly caused him a moment of unrest until this business with Anthony Fairchild. She was a sensible and intelligent young woman, if somewhat headstrong. Two of his sisters and his mother were headstrong women and he had grown up with them and was accustomed to it.

It did not faze him. He was happy to have Melissa as his only daughter. Her presence in the house caused him no bother at all. Though of course he could see that she may be better married. Single women might be happy when young, but whether they remained so later in life was questionable. He wanted her to marry someone she cared for, and that she cared for Fairchild was not in question. It was written all over her when in his presence. He saw too Fairchild's undoubted ability to manage her in her more headstrong times, which he considered expedient to their happiness.

"I suppose you think you know better than me on this matter." His wife threw at him soon after the bangle had been hurled.

He did not reply.

"If you ask me, Giles, they have done the deed already and she has now lost her virginity to him…"

Still Giles remained mute, fastening his neckcloth in the mirror behind the door of the dressing room, in the absence of his valet.

"I expect too, that you are going to say they will sort it out and that they should be left to it…"

"Then you will not be disappointed," said Giles and left the bedroom before the neckcloth was fully tied so as to avoid further argument.

* * *

By Saturday, she had heard nothing further from him. She was slightly concerned, but not overly so. He was letting her stew no doubt. So that she would not in future press this grievance which Melanie and she shared, and which in some way united them deeper in friendship…and perhaps made her connection with him more interesting. Though she seldom pursued that notion for long, it was too loaded with disturbing imponderables.

She was climbing the stairs wearily after a painting excursion in the nearby countryside on the Friday afternoon late on, when it occurred to her like a flash of lightning—supposing that was the only thing that had attracted her to him; this need to sate their past grievance, their insurmountable wounding of schoolgirl dignity and pride! It brought her to a standstill at the turn of the staircase where the wide window showed a view of the side lawns and surrounding grounds—she stared at her own faint reflection thrown back from the glass in the mild sunshine. Surely not!

She went on up the stairs and then into her bedroom and she flopped fully clothed onto the large bed and stared at the drapes and the painting over the fireplace of a lakeland scene by another local artist.

If that was the only thing that had kept her so enamoured of him then what would happen when it was finally allayed! Or done with! When he either apologised or she let it go? What would be the cement holding all together?

That concept could not be right—and was this the reason she would not let it go?—surely not! No, this was just a mere freak of her avid fears since the row on Tuesday and his absence. It was her lurid imagination.

* * *

On the Saturday afternoon, Gregory arrived with Jemima, and had brought along Millicent too. Melissa was surprised to see Millicent who rarely ventured into society except to play the pianoforte or the harpsichord, and was altogether a ghostly presence in Gregory's new life, only talked of in her absence. Millicent the third culprit in the childish chalking of names on a blackboard! Or so Millicent always believed, when really, she was barely involved at all.

She could not concentrate on the cards for thinking about it and she glanced at Millie now and then, who played indifferently and kept her own council, occasionally smiling at Gregory when he sought her eye and smiling sweetly at Granny, who thought her someone to be tolerated but not engaged with for fear she dissolve like tissue paper in damp weather.

"Your eye is off today, Lissy!" reprimanded Granny after a few hands. "What bothers you?"

"I know not..." said Melissa apologetically. "I am sorry... I have bad concentration today."

"Why?" demanded Jemima sharply, her gaze on her cards.

"I know not," said Melissa once more.

"Nothing to do with the absence of young feller-me-lad then?"

Melissa paused and could not lie. "Yes, it is... but Granny, he is not so young, you know, in reality...he is thirty now."

"A grand old age!" quipped Granny.

She would have spoken out about everything, but Millie's presence stopped her. Millicent had been in love with Fairchild, they all thought, though she never admitted it. Even so, it was obvious to everyone when they looked back with the hindsight of more maturity.

"Your father tells me you have rowed with your mother and with Fairchild too..." persevered Jemima intrepidly.

"Do not talk of my mother!" snapped Melissa. "That viper in our midst."

Gregory snorted with laughter: Melissa's colourful turn of phrase amused him greatly. What with his own father and his aunt there were saboteurs all about the family.

"I have told her not to meddle in my affairs and she does not like it," Melissa announced next.

"No? Truly? She does not like it?" echoed Gregory in facetious amusement. And even Millicent tittered at this.

"She follows us and creeps about listening behind doors and hedges."

"'tis the only way she can gain information..." said Jemima airily.

This last amused Gregory so much that he fell back into his seat and guffawed. Millicent looked more entertained than Melissa remembered seeing her and a tinge of colour came into her pale face. Then she surprised them all by tentatively saying: "Lissy, is it true? Forgive my curiosity... Greg tells me you may wish to marry Mr Fairchild...is that so?"

"Well...yes, Millie...but I really prefer not to have to wed him so soon...except they are all pressing me to it."

Millie became pale again and stared with her luminous eyes at Melissa and Melissa could not for the life of her read Millie's thoughts.

Several more hands were played, Polly brought in tea, and Melissa could stand it no longer. She said: "Excuse us please, Greg and Granny... Millie, I should like to speak with you privately..."

Millie rose apprehensively from her chair and Melissa took her arm and guided her from the room, Gregory rising too and bowing to them informally. Jemima exclaiming loudly at the interruption in an already poor spell of play.

For lack of any more private and secluded place Melissa took Millie to the art room, where they could be sure of privacy. It was cool and lit in patches by the sunshine through the windows—dappled on the walls and the various canvases. Millicent looked about her in some awe before taking the one chair which Melissa indicated to her.

"Goodness, Lissy, you are so talented..." she said as she sat. "All these paintings."

Melissa smiled. "But so are you, Millie...look at all the people you entertain nowadays with your playing."

Millie sighed almost contentedly and uttered, "Yes. I am thrilled by it...and 'tis mostly due to your cousin and his encouragement."

"You will be wed to him one day, I expect."

"I suppose I might be..." said Millie in her modest manner. "But I never look that far ahead. Besides, I am happy the way we are."

"Ah yes! *The way we are!*" echoed Melissa. "If only people could leave others to be *the way they are* and not interfere."

"You are speaking of the coercion you feel to marry Mr Fairchild?" said Millie, and Melissa—heartened by this introduction to his name—perched on the table near her. "Indeed...and 'tis about him I wish to speak..."

Millicent seemed to shrink into the chair and assumed an alarmed expression. "What about him?"

"Well...'tis not an easy subject to broach...but I have qualms, you know, as any woman does before accepting an offer of marriage. So, I wanted to gain your insight..."

Millie was frowning with trepidation, her hands folded and her thumbs twiddling furiously. Melissa plunged in headlong. "Millie, have you forgiven him now?"

"Forgiven him?" echoed Millie in confusion. "For what?"

"You know! For his overly severe attitudes at Barton Grange."

Millicent stared at her and then moved her gaze to one of the nearest paintings and opened her lips once or twice before eventually saying: "We were in his classroom then…as school-children."

Melissa picked the little collection of cigarettes Melanie had gifted her from the drawer of the table and offered one to Millie. Millie shrank further back as if being offered hemlock and looked entirely shocked, shaking her head. "No…thank you."

"I smoke, I am afraid…now and then…but not many people know…especially not my mother and father…scandalous is it not!" She lit one of the long-perfumed cigarettes which she adored and blew out smoke. "I mean in particular, Millie, the incident in the waiting room…you remember?"

"Yes, I do!" said Millie quickly. "As if I would ever forget."

"And that is exactly my point. 'twas quite an unprecedented and unforgettable ordeal…so I wondered whether you could forgive him that?"

Millie breathed deeply and closed her eyes and laced her fingers over her velvet bodice. "We were very audacious to have chalked his name with Miss Madeley's and—"

"You did not chalk it… Melanie and I did that."

"Even so, I was responsible for telling you his name and prompting the whole thing…"

"I know you *think* that, Millie, but in actual fact you—"

"I *know* that!" interposed Millicent in a strongly defined statement, closing her eyes against alternatives. "I was entirely to blame…"

Melissa saw that argument was useless, and was anyway beside the point now. "Yes, but…have you forgiven him for the cruelty of what he did to us?"

Millie opened her eyes and looked back at Melissa without speaking and Melissa suddenly felt that she was being ridiculous, or worse, inappropriate. She hurried on. "You see, Melanie and I have not forgiven him…in fact, Melanie is…well, never mind, that is irrelevant…but the point is that I—"

"Then how can you consider marrying him if you have not forgiven him?" interjected Millicent again in her quiet tone. "Surely that can bring nothing but sorrow and resentment to the union!"

"Exactly!" Melissa said and felt herself redden and regretted having brought her here for this kind of sensitive interrogation. "That is what he says. It is what we row about…'tis why I need to know what you think…"

"I am not the one he wishes to marry," said the now emboldened Millie. "So, it does not matter."

"But it does because…because…"

"Because what?"

"I need to know if I am being overly critical or childish… I need a different view on matters…" Melissa drew deeply on her cigarette and was somewhat calmed, while Millicent remained silent, staring at the painting of the old church. The one he had stared at when he first visited her art room. Until Millie broke the silence. "I shall not give you my thoughts on it, Lissy," she said finally. "It has nothing to do with your proposed union with him."

Melissa was abashed and blinked rapidly. "Millie, I am asking you as a friend…"

"I know…but I cannot speak against him. I let him down badly by revealing his name."

"Good God, Millie, you cannot be serious! 'twas his ridiculous reaction…the trifling issue of his first name, as if it mattered…and everyone knew he was walking out with Henrietta Madeley. He was being self-righteous…and cruel."

"No, not cruel," said Millie. "Severe, as you said in the first instance…and I think he had a right to be angry…and severe…"

"Yes…perhaps…" concurred Melissa suddenly, in a conciliatory voice, "But it did not give him the right to thrash us as if…as if we were boys…"

"I think…" said the precise and deep-thinking Millicent, "That had we actually been boys he would have thrashed us much more severely…and without all the ceremony."

"Yes, I know that but—" Melissa began.

"It was most probably Miss Tongs' doing. I believe she encouraged him. Odious creature that she is!" declared Millicent.

"Yes but, Millie, he has a mind of his own."

"Certainly, but she was fanning the flames…for her own gratification no doubt."

"No doubt! She is just above my mother in my list of despised women."

Millie shut her eyes and took on an impish look. "The on-dit is that she tries seducing all the male teachers who enter the doors of the girls' school…the handsome ones…not the likes of Mr Frondley or Mr Stringer, obviously."

Melissa giggled. "I have heard that too…and perhaps Anthony was bedding her at first…while walking out with Miss Madeley."

"Perhaps he was afraid not to…" ventured Millicent. "Possibly he feared for his job otherwise…perhaps they all do."

Melissa grimaced; it was hard to imagine him being afraid of anyone. "Perhaps…but he had better not be bedding her now."

"He will surely stop once he shares your bed…between you and her there is no contest."

"It is kind of you to say so…" said Melissa modestly. She took in a large inhalation of smoke and felt her head spin. "He has bedded many women, you know…" she said carefully. "It is implicit in the answers he gives to certain questions I pose."

"But that is not unusual for gentlemen of society…'tis considered quite normal…" said Millicent with aplomb. "Especially while they are unmarried. 'tis different for them than us."

"'tis unfair…" Melissa asserted.

Millicent's eyes opened widely. "Do you wish to bed many men?"

"No, I do not…but I should like the option if I chose to do so."

Millicent was giggling in her quiet more decorous fashion. "I can think of nothing worse…" she said softly.

"Well, you do not know for sure…until you have tried it," Melissa asserted and studied the end of her cigarette—the way she had watched her future husband study the end of his small cigars—in a detached and preoccupied manner.

Millicent was overcome by merriment. Her skin flushing in a pleasant way which warmed her countenance and enhanced her. "No…perhaps not." She began to play an imaginary keyboard on her lap, sketching out musical notes with her finger tips from memory and humming to herself, then pausing to say: "Melissa, you should not judge Anthony for doing what is normal for most men… I do not think he will want other women after he has wed you…he will think you enough for him…unless you cease to care for him."

She was utterly wrong-footed, taken aback. She knew not how to reply to this girl who might become family one day, with whom she would share dinner parties and other occasions. This girl, who had in her own young innocence loved him, and who might be present in the future when he was also present. She knew not what to say next, but Millie saved her the trouble by pronouncing, "And, Lissy, I do not think him a cruel person. As I perceived him lately at the fundraising, in my adult years, out of the classroom. I think he has a generous character…and kind eyes. I think he was just a young man who felt out of his depth with schoolgirls who sought to ridicule him and hold him in the greatest contempt…"

Melissa stubbed out her cigarette in the old dish he used when smoking.

"I think we hurt him that day…in some way he could not properly understand himself," continued Millie.

"I see," said Melissa. She thought about Lottie and her sudden death in their last year at Barton Grange as Millicent went on with her assessment. "I imagine from what I have heard about him…his work in educational reform and so on, his association with the alms schools and so forth… I imagine that he may be a good person at heart, and simply believes in upholding authority."

"Oh, he certainly believes in that…" Melissa jumped from the table and skipped about the room in some agitation, smiling grimly and picking things up and putting them down again, ineffectively trying to lighten the mood, as if she had not spoken of the matter.

"Besides, 'twas not the physical pain that was greatest that day…'twas the indignity," said Millicent.

"Of course," retorted Melissa with asperity. "But that is almost worse."

"No, no… I disagree," said Millicent. "The ordeal was perhaps not as bad as we thought it at the time."

Melissa paused in her speedy flight around the room and stared at Millie who suddenly looked back at her with arched brows and a gentle set to her lips. "Next to the atrocities visited on girls in some institutions, 'twas not the worst example of retribution at all."

"You sound just like him on the subject," Melissa remarked flippantly.

Millicent shook her head, dismissing the comment, and Melissa waited a moment or two and then enquired. "So, you think it all a fuss about nothing?"

"Well, I… I hesitate to trample on your finer feelings…'tis not my place to say," said Millie with consummate diplomacy. "You are entitled to your feelings, and I respect them."

"But still, you think it a fuss about nothing?" persisted Melissa.

There was an acre of awkward silence.

"You may speak your mind, Millie, 'tis what I have requested of you."

Millie heaved a sigh. "I think 'tis a poor reason to turn away from what might be a lifetime of happy marriage with someone you care greatly for! Does that answer your question?"

"Not entirely…" said Melissa, skipping back with a small painting of a young woman sitting at a harp. "But 'tis helpful…" She held the painting out to Millicent. "This is for you…"

Millie looked at it and examined it as if it were a piece in an auction.

"'tis fitting perhaps…although you are a pianist and not a harpist, you may one day play the harp too…" She looked at Millie imploringly. "I hope you will accept it."

"Thank you. 'tis beautiful… I should like to learn the harp, I said so to Gregory only last week…" She smiled, briefly, and then became sombre again. "Lissy, you must think hard now…about how much you care for him. Do not marry him if you cannot forgive him the past. You will break his heart…and whatever you think of him from the past, he does not deserve that!"

Melissa stared at her own hands and her third finger left hand where her rings of marriage may yet sit—if he had not done with her forever.

"Perhaps you can pretend you have forgiven him…" suggested Millie, examining the painting. "Sometimes if you pretend things hard enough, they become reality…"

"Good Lord, Millie! What wisdom you have! 'tis perhaps why you play so beautifully…" Melissa said.

Perceiving that Melissa was still agonising over the matter, Millicent put her hand on her wrist and looked into her face.

"If I cannot forgive him, I cannot wed him…and if I cannot wed him, I might lose him…and I do not want to live life without him," Melissa opined.

"Of course not…" Millicent adopted a bright tone. "For one thing, he is so good to behold…you would be always delighted when looking upon him."

"Would I?" Melissa said wondrously, like a child at a Christmas grotto.

"Indeed…he is quite splendid in feature and form…and has a deeper arresting quality which is evident in all his ways withal. He is almost as attractive as Gregory."

Millicent was evidently in love now with her cousin Gregory and it was safe to accept her words for what they meant. Melissa swiped at her eyes swiftly with her fingers, annoyed at herself and her lack of maturity. She would have to write to him today and entreat him not to keep away. "How fortunate Gregory is to have found you!" she said and led Millie to the door. "Let us return… Granny will be fretting for loss of card playing and Gregory will be missing you! Time is precious."

"Indeed, it is," agreed Millicent and they linked arms back to the drawing room.

Tides Turning and Winds Changing

Fairchild made his way to the stables to collect his horse. He had just heard that Dominic McCarthy would be leaving at the next term end, persuaded by his family to return to Ireland with his fiancé to wed while his grandfather was still alive. Dominic was heir to his estate in Wexford. But there was still no sign of a replacement deputy head and Fairchild could not in all conscience leave Stevenson without at least McCarthy's replacement being in sight. Dominic McCarthy stepped in as deputy easily when he was absent, on top of his own teaching rota. So, he felt he had little choice but to wait—his loyalty and friendship to Stevenson demanded it. His mind ran between this latest news and Melissa. He had not seen her since last Tuesday and it was now the following Monday. She had sent a note by a footman on Sunday to his lodgings asking him where he was. He had replied that he was extremely busy and told her it would be mid-week before he could spare time. It would do her no harm to think on her constant resurrection of past grievances. Not to mention the dismissive and almost insulting evasion of a decision on his proposal.

The translation bureau was up and running, and Trimingham was retiring from education in less than two weeks to give it his full attention. He was intending now to head for the Trimingham household to give Trim the latest news of his own delayed resignation. He had just crossed the lawn towards the stable-yard when a figure loomed from the surrounding trees and accosted him, grabbing his arm from behind and pulling him back. "Mr Fairchild, I presume?"

Fairchild was caught off guard and tried to shake the man off, but he held his sleeve and would not let go. He looked to be no more than a youth, perhaps a senior pupil, although he knew all his pupils well and had no recollection of him. Clad in a large coat, his face partially obscured beneath the upturned collar, the stranger stared at him with simmering hostility. "Take your hands off me!" Fairchild said in his low even tone and pushed him away with the flat of his hand.

The man struggled to regain his former stance, releasing Fairchild's sleeve. "Of course you don't know me...though you will know *of* me."

"Who the devil are you?" he demanded.

"Roger Braithwaite!" announced the florist, only moments ago having ascertained Fairchild's identity from a distance, acquired from the boy who assisted the groom.

Fairchild smiled briefly and then looked the other in the eye, the smile gone. "What do you want?"

Roger Braithwaite hunched and shrugged his shoulders, uncomfortable in the heavy greatcoat in the humid weather. He propelled his head above the collar, straightening his neck with a proud expression.

"Well?" snapped Fairchild. "I do not have all evening."

Braithwaite was engrossed in examining him, every detail of his face and his general demeanour. He was not the bespectacled, dull academic he had expected to find. "I want you to stop pursuing Miss Shaw. I have known her a very long time and you will not just step in and take her from me!"

Fairchild thought it best to say nothing; the statement was quite pathetic coming from this undernourished young man who looked no more than a boy, and he turned away, giving himself time to think. Braithwaite jumped forwards again and grabbed his arm a second time. "I am warning you, Mr Braithwaite," said the deputy head with cool disdain. "Take your hands off me... She is not being taken from you because she was never yours to begin with. She has now told you by letter to cease your visits and suits, so accept it like a man and let her be."

"What letter?" Braithwaite yanked his top coat buttons open to reveal his colourful neckcloth and feel cooler air on his feverish neck. "I have received no such letter from her and she has told me nothing of the kind."

Fairchild hesitated; he was about to make a fool of himself with rhetoric containing no substance. She had lied about writing to Braithwaite. He clenched his teeth and allowed his lids to shield his gaze, staring at Braithwaite through his lowered lashes, glinting pale in the sunshine. "Perhaps not...but she has told you she does not wish to receive you..."

"She has not!" emphasised Braithwaite. "You are quite mistaken, and you are intimidating her into wedlock...you taught her in your classroom and no doubt have some unhealthy dominion over her...or so you think, and..." He got no further, as Fairchild seized him by the lapels, pulling him almost off his feet.

Roger Braithwaite's resistance was minimal, his body weight being so slight as to offer virtually no resistance in any struggle. Fairchild shook him so that his head wobbled, and fearing the lad's neck may snap he loosened his grip without letting him go. "She has chosen to accept my courtship and her presence at Barton Grange has nothing to do with things now."

"So you say…" Braithwaite's voice sounded strangulated under the pressure of the hold on his collar but he remained undeterred. "I have met your type before…"

"I doubt you have met *my type!* I doubt you have met many men at all…or you would not be accosting me with this ludicrous complaint…now go! And leave Melissa alone."

Braithwaite stared at him balefully.

"Do I make myself clear?" said Fairchild, relapsing once more into quiet solemnity as if addressing one of the upper form boys.

Braithwaite was bettered but not broken; he squared his shoulders beneath the greatcoat and then was distracted by another man entering the scene as Dominic McCarthy approached from the rear. "Tony, I have been seeking a few moments with you for the past two days, to tell you myself…" He stopped abruptly on seeing the stranger and sensing the tension. "My apologies. I did not realise you were engaged in serious conversation…"

"This young man is now leaving," said Fairchild.

Braithwaite appraised McCarthy disdainfully. "Here is another of your clan, I perceive… No doubt he also prays on young girls in his classroom."

Fairchild groaned and closed his eyes. McCarthy stood for a second or two in shock. "I beg your pardon! Did I hear you correctly?"

"Unfortunately, you did, Dominic!" Fairchild said. "Mr Braithwaite believes that we…myself in particular…select girls, while teaching them, for gratification in our private lives…"

McCarthy looked at Fairchild, wide-eyed and openly horrified.

"He refers in particular to Miss Shaw, of course…he claims I have taken her from him under duress. He believes he has the dubious honour of being her long-time sweetheart…"

McCarthy turned to stare at Braithwaite and his face moved through several expressions.

"I do not *believe* anything…" cried Roger Braithwaite, incensed at their joint scepticism. "I *am* her childhood sweetheart and I…"

"Then you are deluded," interrupted Fairchild. "For that is not my understanding when talking with her on the matter."

"No, because you have intimidated her into believing otherwise and she no longer knows her own mind."

Fairchild again seized Braithwaite's lapels and peered into his face in silence, not trusting his words and allowing his eyes to make the intention clear.

"You are the same…all of you…" stammered Braithwaite. "You are unable to attract women of her ilk any other way so you enter a profession where…"

"Say one more word…" Fairchild broke his own silence, "And I will lay you out where you stand…"

McCarthy moved forwards and prized Fairchild from him. "Tony, not here…" he said quietly.

Fairchild hesitated but then released Braithwaite. He stumbled backwards and bent double to recover his breath.

"You witnessed what he just said?" declared Fairchild in an anger McCarthy had never heard from him before. "I cannot have that kind of accusation go without retaliation."

Dominic McCarthy held onto him, keeping him back by several feet, and addressed Braithwaite. "Hark lad, you may think you are justified, and you may think this is a personal issue…but you have just slandered this gentleman and myself, as well as maligning this establishment. So, I suggest you take yourself off before I bear witness and we seek the redress of law on the matter. You cannot go about making those kinds of accusations at your whim…you will get yourself into serious trouble."

McCarthy raised his brows to Fairchild and nodded emphatically to solicit his agreement. He was somewhat tempted to laugh at the idea of himself and Fairchild being short of female attention but curbed his reaction from shows of vulgar male egotism.

Fairchild took out his cigars while regaining self-control. Both men were accustomed to handling trouble; it was a boys' school: fights, bullying, vendettas, uprisings of one kind or another…an endless list of youthful folly. McCarthy viewed the incident in a similar way, and he allowed Braithwaite a moment or two to recover then went on in his loquacious manner. "… What is more, this is private property…so unless you vacate the land immediately, I will have the constabulary summoned to remove you…"

491

Braithwaite looked pitiful, aggrieved at being addressed as 'lad' and without recourse to restore his self-respect. He pulled himself upright to his proudest position. "You have not heard the last of it!" he told Fairchild.

"There is very little else to be said…unless you would like to call me out at dawn…" Fairchild retorted laconically.

Braithwaite leapt forwards again and Fairchild grabbed him by the shoulders and pushed him to the ground, where he lay for a while. The caretaker was to be seen suddenly, striding across to them and they needed it to be done with. "Mr Fairchild…" he called. "What is the matter here? Can I be of assistance."

"No, Mr Peverill, thank you…this gentleman was just about to leave. He has mistaken a matter, that is all."

The caretaker looked askance at Braithwaite and waited for him to rise. They all waited. Then Fairchild turned on his heel and went to the stables as Braithwaite dusted himself down and, limping slightly, headed for the main gates where he had tethered his horse. He had done his best, he had put up the best fight he could, but these people were smug and unaccountable in their ivory tower of self-importance. He was sick at heart in his defeat but had acquitted himself to his own ability, which he knew to be inadequate at best.

Meanwhile, it was obvious to Mr Peverill that something serious had taken place in the exchange of words bordering on violence, though he felt it prudent to dismiss the matter without pursuing it. McCarthy's and Fairchild's private affairs were better not brought into the realms of this higher-class establishment. They were bachelors of society and prone to the kind of delights and pursuits of their age and ilk; there was no telling what may emerge to sully the calm waters of genteel education when stirred.

McCarthy caught up with Fairchild as he brought round his horse.

"Thank you, Dominic. I am indebted to you. You saved me from making a calamitous error of judgement and conduct."

"Who was that little jackass?" McCarthy laughed. "He puts me in mind of James Harcourt! You remember him and the tea dance escapade with Miss Madeley, several years back?"

Fairchild blinked in acknowledgement. "A similar sort of clown but less robust withal and a few years older. He is Roger Braithwaite…the family of flower shops around the county. He has grown up with Melissa…"

"I feared you were going to pulverise him into the infirmary," said McCarthy.

"I almost did, but it would have felt like injuring a woman…he is as fragile as one of his own blooms…"

McCarthy looked at Fairchild in a morose manner. "I take it Miss Shaw did not put those unsavoury ideas into his head?"

"No, I perceive not…he has reached those gruesome conclusions by his own tortured imaginings."

"Thank Christ!" McCarthy ran his hands through his dark curly hair. "I was never more mortified than at the thought."

"She has simply failed, in her charming duplicity, to tell him of current events. I shall be having words with her." Fairchild began mounting his horse and McCarthy pulled a wry face. "How colourful these women make life…"

The horse was becoming restless and moved impatiently back and forth. "I must leave to see Trim and tell him of the resignation delay," he said. "Have no worries. I understand about your departure. We shall talk perhaps tomorrow evening in the Royal Oak…?"

"Certainly," said McCarthy pleasantly and they parted to go their separate ways.

* * *

Trim was philosophical on receiving the news of yet more delay to Fairchild's fuller immersion in the new business. It was of no great importance. He was busy gathering a staff of people, fluent between them all in seven languages. The commercial requests had begun to come in steadily and he could manage for another couple of months single handed as long as Fairchild put in some work of his own at weekends in languages Trim did not have in his arsenal.

Though generally, Trim was more than pleased with progress and could not stop talking about the plans for a full twenty minutes in the cosiness of his private parlour. He went into the minutia of what he had said to whom and how they had responded in the last few days, in his usual informative style. Fairchild was monosyllabic in response, which was not unusual. Until Trim sensed his unrest. "What the devil's the matter now?" he enquired, pouring more wine, "Something is off."

"I have today had a run in with her childhood sweetheart, so-called…" said Fairchild and Trim paused to take in his meaning.

"Melissa's, you mean?"

493

"Of course…who else would I be a target for?"

"By God, I did not know she had one."

"She doesn't…except when it takes her fancy to pull him out for a verbal airing…"

The explanation of Braithwaite's arrival and onslaught was succinctly outlined in two or three sentences, and as usual it amused Trim greatly. "I never was so entertained as since you took up with the wench," he exclaimed, "There is no end to the goings on…what's he like, this lovelorn swain?"

Fairchild smoked his cigar and considered his reply. "He looks to be about her own age…the best way I can describe him is that he might be mistaken for one of the male pupils…he is like a thirteen or fourteen year old who's undergone a growth spurt."

Trim guffawed and almost choked on the drink. "You are not serious?"

"Perfectly! In fact, I am not certain he is a male at all…he could be a female in boys' clothing."

"She cannot have been sincere in her intent towards him!" declared Trim. "Can she?"

"No, I think not…she has grown up with him and is fond of him, and he is devastated that I am taking her from him. I am to leave her alone…" At this, Fairchild emitted a short laugh of his own and then curtailed it.

"Poor fellow!" Trim said. "One feels for him."

"Just so…though I cannot enter into that sentiment. He has accused me of using my teaching role to procure her!"

Trim widened his eyes.

"And then Dominic entered the scene and he was similarly maligned…we are all the same, you see, according to Braithwaite. We enter the profession for just that one purpose."

"Good God!" uttered Trim. "What confounded slander."

"Dominic threatened him with the law…constabulary as well as civil…damn good job he came when he did, clear thinking and objective about the issue. I was ready to do him an injury."

"And imagine were he actually not a male and you had attacked a female in disguise," suggested Trimingham.

"'tis unlikely that is the case, Trim! But even so, an unholy thought to contemplate."

"'tis not impossible…" mused Trim. "History is littered with such examples. Stranger things happen…" He cleared his throat and became animated. "Let me tell you a little story about one of our relatives…a family skeleton…" His tone was the one he used on settling in for a long and complicated yarn.

"Oh, God's Teeth!" opined Fairchild. "Is this going to last all night and rival one of old Jemima's tales of curious adventure?"

Trim ignored the comment and went on. "I had a female cousin…still have, as a matter of fact…went about dressed as a lad for quite a good few years in her young adulthood…"

"Lottie used to dress as a lad, remember…borrowing her brother's clothing at night for riding out and meeting me, to avoid being recognised," intervened Fairchild sombrely.

A candle guttered and went out and Trim moved to replace it, thinking the timing rather eerie but saying nothing. "Yes, but on closer inspection anyone could see that Lottie was female. Whereas my cousin went undetected for a long time…she was quite the plainest of creatures…anyway, she became caught up with a gang of undesirables…footpads or armed robbers or some such…they took her to be a male, until eventually they were all apprehended and put into the same cell…"

With the glass to his lips, Fairchild paused for reflection on the predicament posed and frowned. He had not before heard of this cousin and wondered if Trim had just invented her to distract and amuse him. "So, what happened when these men discovered her true gender?"

"What do you imagine would happen to her with men of that ilk? She was in the infirmary for quite a few weeks… I think they raped her, though it was obviously never named as such in our midst…"

"What an enlivening little anecdote?" intoned Fairchild.

"Of course it went in her favour at the trial…" Trim continued. "Her barrister advocated that they had forced her to do these criminal deeds dressed as a man. The judge looked more favourably on her and she was transported to Australia and served seven years labour, whereas the men were hanged."

Fairchild gaped at him in the low light, still unsure whether this was all made up for the purpose of entertainment, the way they used to tell each other ghost stories as children.

"I can see you don't believe me…but you may ask my father if you doubt it," said Trim. "Only do not ask my mother, whose direct relation this is, the daughter of her eldest brother…it upsets her dreadfully!"

"You surprise me!" said the other with sardonic humour.

"'tis a wonder you can't recall her, this girl…she came to birthday parties when you were there too…she always wanted to arm-wrestle with us… I often obliged to keep her happy, and let her win…but you would not agree to it."

Fairchild gazed at his best friend for moments, agog with incredulity. "Of course I would not. I was not raised to engage in arm-wrestling with girls…imagine the uproar had my father heard of me doing such a thing!"

"You do not remember her?" Trim asked in innocence.

"I do not!" came the reply. "Perhaps my male pride has erased the memory in case I might have one time given in to temptation and lost the contest," he added.

"I can see you do not believe me in any of it," claimed Trim a second time with some remorse.

"Trim, if you tell me 'tis true then your word is good enough for me."

Trim resorted to laughter which Fairchild joined him in; the vagaries of memory and childhood exploits!

"And the funny thing is…" Tim claimed cheerfully, "She survived the ordeal in Australia and resumed her male identity and stayed over there…doing quite well for herself in the haulage business…calls herself Laurence, apparently. Her real name is Lavinia…married now as well, to a woman she met in Adelaide…happily it seems."

Fairchild rubbed his eyes wearily. "Do not tell me, let me guess! They have three children!"

Trim looked at him in surprise. "No, two actually, the lady wife had been wed before and the children are from that marriage…though everyone assumes they are Laurence's…"

"All's well that ends well!" Fairchild said, quoting one of his favourite sayings in an avuncular tone. "And your point to all this is?"

"The point is that life is often not what it seems. Do you suppose Melissa would know as she matured if this Braithwaite character was a female?"

"I do not know," Fairchild said. "I know not sometimes when she is lying and when she is exaggerating and when she is telling the truth… I am still trying to fathom how her mind works."

Trim barked with laughter. "Better take on something straight forward…like the Pythagoras Theorem…"

"What I do know is that I warned her of this. I told her that she must tell him his visits should cease. Especially when he proposed a suit… I told her emphatically that feelings were involved and that it would lead to trouble…but as usual she ignored me."

Trim made himself more comfortable and stretched his feet out onto a footstool. "Although, I perceive that in general she behaves much better towards you than of months ago?"

"She has stopped hurling insults and abuse at me, if that is what you mean…but that, I suspect, is because she simply dare not and not that she does not wish to at times."

"That is better than nothing, surely?" Trim said. "It surely matters little, the reason she has ceased, just that she has done so."

Fairchild stared at him across the dimly lit circumference of the hearthrug. "I am heartened you think so, but I have to say I would prefer it that she had ceased because of a genuinely heightened opinion of me…perhaps that again is my own vanity at fault," he added caustically.

"But she is much more obliging and tender now, I have no doubt," Trim remarked encouragingly.

Fairchild continued as if he had not heard. "She is so devious and evasive on some matters…I scarce know what she is up to or what she is thinking. She has clearly lied about Braithwaite."

"Perhaps not," said Trim, sensing the need to play peacemaker. "Perhaps she did write and he is denying receipt of the letter. He may be unable to stomach the truth…or perhaps the letter became mislaid."

"And perhaps I am descended from one of the kings of Denmark!" pronounced Fairchild, swigging half the glass of wine in one and rising.

"That again is not beyond the bounds of possibility, given your heritage! Where the deuce are you off to now?" Trim asked. "Not to have the matter out with her at this time, surely! 'tis well after eight and it will take you another half hour to ride there."

"To the lavatory!" he replied. "So, you may calm yourself… I will see her in the course of the week. By which time I will be less annoyed…marginally."

Trim sank back in his armchair and let out more sounds of merriment and Fairchild grinned and wondered why he also felt the need to laugh. He was about to become engaged to one of the craftiest and wilful of women who thought little of ignoring his requests and flouting the niceties which made life bearable. He made his way to the latest example of indoor plumbing and convenience installed by Trim's father, similar to those installed by Giles Shaw. He thought he would put it from his mind—already overloaded—until he was with her in person.

* * *

On the following afternoon and across the town, Melanie was with Melissa in their favourite tea shop. Melanie was trying as always to make full sense of the garbled report of recent progress, which was not progress at all but a catalogue of calamitous and badly botched exchanges of words. "What do you mean when you say he has disappeared?" she queried in the first pause in the diatribe.

"How much clearer must I be?" said Melissa in a stage whisper so that people around would not hear; they were mindful of the fact that the eavesdropping here was without equal in the whole of the town.

"What? Without any trace?" enquired Melanie.

"No, no…he sent a letter saying he would be back this mid-week."

"Well, then! All is not lost!" Melanie now felt nauseous a lot of the time due to her expectancy and placed her hand over her mouth to quell the sensations.

"He cannot usually go more than two days without calling. And I have said I will marry him…do you suppose he is having second thoughts? He was angry when we parted last…he would not stay above five or ten minutes," persisted Melissa.

"Angry about what?" said Melanie, sipping peppermint tea for the nausea.

Melissa did not want to reveal that she had told him of Melanie's up-coming motherhood, she had promised not to say anything. But some explanation was necessary. "I was telling him about his unreasonable attitudes…before he stormed off…"

"Did he actually storm off…or leave in haste?"

"He always moves with the greatest calm…but you know what I mean! I was explaining how uncharitable is his frame of mind on the question of the past…the past as in when we were at school I mean."

"Of course! I wonder why he does not just fall to his knees and beg forgiveness," Melanie said facetiously, between sips of the tea.

"I told him that all he had to do was to apologise and all would be well…" Melissa bit into her cake and let her tongue savour the rich butter milk cream and spoke amidst the deliciousness of the confectionery. "You see, we need…to see peace…in this war, Melanie…because he is not tolerant of our friendship…he is scathing…he does not speak so well of you…"

"Why? Does he actually imagine I like him?" scoffed Melanie in response.

Melissa swallowed a couple of times and disposed of the cake…"I think, Mel, that if I am to wed him, both of you must try to see the good in the other."

Melanie let out a shriek of laughter which attracted undue attention, and then she covered her mouth with her napkin.

"Geoffrey and I get on…" continued Melissa blithely.

"Of course you do, but Geoffrey was never in a classroom teaching us at school was he!"

"But supposing he had cross examined me in court or something similar?" Melissa countered.

"Highly unlikely!" Melanie put her hand to her side at a sharp twinge.

"No, but just supposing… I would have to look beyond it."

"And I suppose the next analogy might be… *'imagine you were sentenced to death by his inept attempts to defend you'*…" said Melanie pithily and Melissa gasped and coughed for several seconds as cake crumbs lodged in her throat. "That is a dreadful analogy to make."

"Well, 'tis the nearest one I can think of, Lissy! And really there is no comparison to be had between you and Geoffrey and me and Attila…" She let the cup drop into the saucer clumsily and more attention came their way. They assumed trite and superior expressions and waited for other customers to return to their own affairs.

"If he apologises, I might see my way to doing the same…" claimed Melissa in a stage whisper.

"What?" Melanie was beyond shocked. "You have nothing to apologise for…"

"Perhaps not…but 'tis a token, is it not, of trust and harmony for the future?"

Melanie made a sound of consummate derision. "'tis more likely to be an invitation for him to display his cynical nature in the future…"

Melissa paused and stared at her. She had not thought of that. Possibly it was the truth. Between Millicent and Melanie, she was very confused. "Do you really think so?"

"'tis a great likelihood," said Melanie.

Melissa poured more tea into her cup. "Millicent, on Saturday when I spoke with her, told me she has forgiven him. She says she can sympathise with his position and why he might have done what he did…or words to that effect."

"Naturally she would! She was saying that kind of thing before we had left school."

"She is really rather a deep thinker. She made me feel as if I were being foolish…she—"

"Pardon me…" interjected Melanie, "But what has she to do with his disappearance?"

"Nothing…but Millie thinks he is a good person…"

"Does she?" purred Melanie, treacly disdain dripping from her voice.

"His work in educational reform and so on…and his association with those people at the alms schools."

"A mere *sop to Cerberus*!" scoffed Melanie. "If you ask me—which is what you are doing—those who are guilty of major character flaws always try to deflect from them by seeming to want to correct similar behaviour in others!"

They continued to sip their tea.

"And besides which…" said Melanie at length. "Millie is prone to being a martyr…she loves the idea of suffering. Women with those die-away airs generally do."

"I like her, you know, she is gentle and good. She played voluntarily at the fundraiser, with Gregory."

"I have not said I do not like her," Melanie argued, "But for heaven's sake, Lissy, she is not you! She would be a meek little wife for any man and not give him a moment's trouble…"

"Whereas I would?" queried Melissa archly.

"Of course you would…because you have character and spirit."

"Perhaps he would be better off marrying Millicent then!" retorted Melissa rather petulantly.

Melanie's peals of laughter brought yet fresh looks from round about. "For heaven's sake! You're in love with him yourself for one thing…and for another, why would Millie want to wed Fairchild? He was suitable for her girlish romantic notions when she was fourteen but would now be a nuisance to her glorious musical career! And added to all, he does not want to be married to her…he would be bored to death with her in no time…"

"Millie is beloved of Gregory…" said Melissa randomly, and then the thought struck her that Melanie might be jealous of that, since she had herself once been covetous of cousin Gregory's attention.

"I am pleased for them!" said Melanie. "They may be well suited."

"I think so…but I do not think she is the faint-hearted creature you make her out to be. She is just shy…and she still even now sees herself as having created the whole situation that day, with the chalking of his name…"

"Of course she does! 'tis perhaps her one bold claim to rebellion in her girlhood."

Melissa put down the cake fork and became solemn in demeanour. "She thinks we provoked him, all of us, she thinks he was suffering at the time…and maybe she is right, because of Lottie and the tragedy."

"That did not grant him the right to make others suffer," Melanie murmured.

"She thinks we ridiculed him and held him in contempt and it was…"

"I have heard enough of her drivel…" interjected Melanie impatiently. "She is set to become a latter-day saint at this rate. She was not responsible for the inkwell fiasco though was she! Think on that, Miss Shaw…before you hand out any more posies of forgiveness. That incident was entirely unfair and unwarranted…an accident! It was me who placed the inkwell, not you…he could have left you out of it."

"But I used the inkwell where it stood and he knew that. So, he could not just reasonably punish you. I was as much to blame…"

"Now you see, you are sounding like Millie…the pair of you are too pious for words. 'twas his anger over his precious shoes…that was simply the top and bottom of it…" Melanie stared in great annoyance at the window, reliving clearly the second expedition to the waiting room.

"But are you sure that there is not a grain of truth in Millie's overall philosophy?"

"I am quite sure…" Melanie said and summoned the waitress for fresh tea, and then it was obvious from her sudden smirk that some piece of fresh humour was imminent. "Or perhaps Millie is just some kind of devotee of corporal punishment."

This brought on Melissa's giggling and it bubbled forth with relentless ferocity. She lowered her head into her hands as Melanie watched and gave in to a small burst of her own amusement. "The gentle, biddable woman's visage might crumble once she and Gregory are wed and she produces a whip…" continued Melanie shamelessly.

"Stop…stop…" Melissa heaved breath into her lungs. "I am about to faint…"

Restored by seeing things from the humorous angle, Melanie sat back in her chair and changed the subject. "I have a doctor's appointment on Friday…the first of the expectancy…"

"How marvellous!" Melissa looked up in greater composure. "Would you like me to accompany you? Or is Geoffrey doing that?"

Melanie was aghast. "He certainly is not! 'tis too delicate and sensitive an examination, not the place for a man, apart from the doctor, that is. I would love it if you would come with me, Lissy. My mother will do it, but I prefer it were you…"

"Then I shall," said Melissa. "Gladly…and I shall be with you at the confinement too if you wish."

They smiled at each other and clasped hands for a moment. The throng of people beyond the window at which their table was situated had now thickened, the time being four thirty-five. Melanie gazed at the passersby as Melissa studied the menu on which the latest cakes and fancies were shown, for consumption next time they visited. Suddenly Melanie made a rasping sound of shock, and Melissa looked at her and then followed her line of vision. On the street outside a horse had slowed and the rider looking in at them was Anthony Fairchild. Melissa let her jaw drop but checked herself, closing her mouth as it flew open. "He is there…"

"So he is…" demurred Melanie and lifted her hand and gave him a tiny wave. The horse disappeared to the side of the road and out of view, no doubt while he found somewhere to tether it. "He is coming in…" said Melanie in a hushed voice.

"Oh damnation!" Melissa said. "I am not ready to see him."

"But he is your future husband," trilled Melanie. "What could be nicer! First you complain at his disappearance and then you complain when he re-appears. How contrary you are!"

Melissa adjusted her skirts beneath her. "Not a word of what we have talked on…" she said needlessly.

The tea room door opened with the jangling of the little bell and he entered and crossed to them. He bowed informally and said: "Mrs Gillis…" letting his

502

eyes sweep over Melanie before dismissing her and looking at Melissa. "How are you?" he began.

"Where have you been?" said Melissa, ignoring the niceties as always.

"May I?" He indicated one of the vacant chairs in the window recess and without waiting for a reply sat in it, pushing it back some way from the table. His legs as usual were shod in close-fitting trousers which accentuated his thighs and calves as he crossed one leg over the other and Melissa gazed at them appreciatively while Melanie smiled omnisciently. "Anthony..." she said sweetly. "We are taking tea...would you care for some?"

"No, thank you," he replied and continued to look at Melissa with equal appreciation of her form and face, before closing down any visible expression which might be too easily read. The attraction between them was palpable, the air positively charged around them.

"You have been gone for days," opined Melissa. "I was worried."

"I addressed your concern in my letter in reply to yours," said he and loosened his jacket buttons at the collar, revealing the immaculate neckcloth and the onyx pin securing it. "Did you perhaps not receive it? Letters do have a habit of going missing," he added meaningfully, and fixed her with his calm and penetrating green eyes and appraised her without relief.

Something was amiss. She stared back at him. "Yes," she concurred, "But you said only that you were busy."

"And so I am. I teach all day and mark work in the evening...and occasionally sleep. I saw you as I passed and—"

"Where are you going?" she asked nosily, cutting into the rest of his sentence.

"To the printers. I must leave in a few minutes or they will close."

"Will they?" said Melanie, suddenly coming to life. "'tis only twenty minutes off five."

He turned his eyes somewhat reluctantly away from his wife-to-be and gazed at Melanie with the lack of immediate response which she knew well; as if he had no need to reply but may do so if the fancy took him. "They close their doors to customers at five..." he said at length "What they do then I have no idea...perhaps they carry on printing without unwanted interruption."

Melissa acquired her arch expression and he stood.

"I must bid you goodbye. I will call later...about seven-thirty. I need to speak with you."

"What about?" She felt her nerve crumble, her confidence waver—he was having second thoughts. "I would have hoped you would call simply to see me…" she said. "Do you mean regarding the proposal?"

Melanie stifled a cough of surprise and looked away; a delicate issue had been broached.

"Yes, but apart from that…" He paused and she waited, her eyes upon him with mixed shades of emotional intensity. "I have no time to explain now…and besides, 'tis sensitive," he added, knowing without a doubt that Mrs Gillis would hear of it in no time at all.

"I will do my best to make myself available," said Melissa with dignity.

He levelled his gaze on her as he re-fastened his jacket. "You will kindly be sure to make yourself available, Melissa…'tis of importance."

He moved from one foot to the other, his thigh muscles—strengthened and primed no doubt by all the horse riding—enthralling her. Then he summoned the waitress. At length the waitress appeared and, perusing the table to assess roughly what they had consumed, he handed the woman coinage to cover the bill. "This should suffice," he told her. "Keep the change."

"We can pay our own bill…" Melissa objected and Melanie kicked her foot beneath the table, saying: "Thank you, Anthony…that is most kind."

"'tis my pleasure…'tis nothing any gentleman would not do," said he and then to Melissa. "I will be there at seven-thirty…"

"Certainly, my lord!" Melissa said with the smallest amount of disdain. "Whatever you wish."

He ignored the remark and bowed again. "Good day to you both!"

The waitress hurried to open the door for him—the last generous tipper of the day—and he went out to collect his horse being held by a passing urchin to whom he now owed remuneration. The heads of several women of assorted ages turned to watch him as he left and Melanie whispered. "You see what a stir he causes…you will be the envy of three counties…"

"I have no wish to be!" retorted Melissa. "And I do not like to be so high-handedly paid for…even if I am to be wed to him…which I may well not be if he does not stop being so…so…" she fought for clarity. "You see how autocratic he is…too bossy for words!"

"No, really!" Melanie felt better now, the nausea disappearing. "Have we been talking of the same man all these weeks!"

"If he does not stop all that, I shall not wed him," Melissa added ineffectually.

"But my dear, the allure of his legs and thighs may obviously sway you…" Melanie crooned.

"Was it that obvious?"

"Perhaps a touch…"

"I was thinking how I would sketch them."

"Of course you were…"

"He is annoyed over something…" continued Melissa. "And really, 'tis I who should have that prerogative!"

"When is he not annoyed over something?" said Melanie. "Perhaps someone has again dropped an inkwell on him… I wonder, does he ever manage to smile?"

"Oh, he does," said Melissa. "And it enhances his face marvellously…"

"Good Lord," Melanie sighed. "Thighs, calves and a smile worthy of an angel…what else could be desired!"

"I would not go that far…" retorted her friend. "If he does not agree to being less autocratic, I shall not agree to marriage…"

Melanie sailed through the door, again held open by the waitress. "And I shall perhaps give birth to triplets!" she claimed as they saw their coach and hastened towards it.

Sofas and Solicitude

It was almost eight by the time he reached High Lawns.

"I thought you said seven-thirty!" Melissa said at once as they entered the room they always used for their assignations. "I rushed my dinner to oblige you and now I have indigestion…"

He drew breath and arranged his thoughts. Exhaustion was rapidly overcoming him, he felt seriously unwell. He had been up marking books until the small hours, having lingered discussing the new business with Trim until gone midnight, then rising early as usual to work at the school. He had no time to sit in tea shops gossiping and eating cake: he had so much on his plate there would be no room for cake. He was almost dead on his feet; double lessons with the middle form boys that morning, then scarcely any rest at lunch as he made the first visit to the printers for the new venture, and an inadequate amount to eat.

Followed by a tutorial with the upper boys, and then the interview with Stevenson. All on a few meagre hours of sleep. He was aware of pushing his health to perilous limits. To add to problems, he had twisted his left ankle somehow, possibly in the altercation with Braithwaite, and it slowed him down.

He turned onto her by way of response his most censorious expression. "Do you realise how much I have to do of late?"

She tripped lightly to the fire and gave it a poke to liven up the flames, not thinking the question worthy of a comment. What could be more important than their forthcoming nuptials? Then she noticed his slight limp.

"What have you done to your foot? You are limping."

He looked at his foot as if it would speak for itself. "I must have twisted it getting off the horse."

She looked at it also. "I expect you were drunk at the time," she commented in off-hand manner.

"Contrary to your colourful imaginings and Miss Darnley's exaggerations, I am not always drunk, Melissa… I am seldom so in actual fact," he wondered as he added this whether it was an outright lie or merely a dilution of the truth. She made a scoffing sort of noise which annoyed him more and then brightened. "Are you not going to kiss me?" she enquired in a silken voice, her expression cat-like in its seductive and covert desire for attention.

"Not at the moment," he said flatly.

She reacted immediately and stepped back from the mantlepiece. "What on earth can be the matter with you now!" she snapped; her head turned away from him so as not to be made more nervous.

"Sit down," he told her.

"No thank you… I will stand."

"Melissa, sit down," he said in a quiet and decisive tone.

She sat, her insides quaking with apprehension. She did not want him to call off the marriage. She knew of late, had known since a fortnight ago, that she wanted to be wed to him. "What on earth is the matter?" she repeated in a louder voice.

He took out his cigars and a match and struck it in the chimney wall, then stood with his injured foot on the fender. "The matter is Roger Braithwaite."

She was quite frozen. "What about him? I have told you I have no wish to accept his suit and that I agree to wed you."

"I thought you told me you had written to him telling him to desist from visiting you?"

"I did."

"Which? Told me you had written, or actually wrote to him?" He was too clever with his words. Perhaps it came from interrogating recalcitrant pupils. He and Geoffrey Gillis were on a par: the courtroom and the classroom. But she could not bring herself to dissemble. "The former!"

"So, you lied to me about having written to him?"

"Yes, to spare any feelings."

"His or mine?"

"Both."

He kicked back from the fender furiously with his booted foot and then limped about the room.

"Have you seen him?" she asked in a tiny voice.

"Oh yes… I have seen him…he came to the boys' academy yesterday and accosted me…he accused me of taking you from him…and much worse! Then McCarthy joined us and was similarly maligned, witnessed by the caretaker who the next day told Stevenson…"

She was at a loss and stammered a little. "Are you certain…are you…certain it was Roger?"

"Of course I am certain. He announced himself…a reedy voice and the physique of a badly nourished teenage boy."

"What do you mean?"

"Simply that he is puny!" he said eventually. "Had he not been so I would have pulverised him into oblivion."

Poor Roger, always so maligned and incongruous.

"Did he hurt you?" she enquired anxiously.

His laughter was curbed almost at once; to vent it would sound vulgar or conceited. "Of course not! I doubt he could hurt any man…he got the worst of it."

"What? You hit him? I hope you did not seriously injure him!"

"I was sorely tempted… I merely pushed him backwards and he fell over and lay awhile on the grass…"

She walked around the room too and they virtually crossed each other in their perambulations, rendering the situation ridiculous. She was ashamed—for Roger as well as herself. "Well, there is no harm done then!" she claimed.

He wheeled about to glare at her. "No harm done! Stevenson has now issued him with a writ forbidding him entry to the grounds and from casting slanderous insults."

"What?" She took small steps of frustration towards him. "Surely that was not necessary!"

"Yes, Melissa, it was necessary…" His voice grew louder on each word until it held the cutting and searing tone that contrasted from the usual even and quiet one. "He cannot go around saying we procure young girls for our own advantage… Stevenson had little choice…" He was growing more angry and she felt she may any second regurgitate her dinner. "… Mr Peverill will likely tell people in three or four taverns… Dominic's good name and my own will be banded around… Braithwaite will be humiliated in the town…but as you say, no real harm done!"

She was near to tears and trying to stem them. It was a calamitous turn of events, and it was perhaps due to her. "I am sincerely sorry… I meant to write this week, I truly did."

He disclaimed in disgust. "This is all down to your vanity…" he said vehemently.

"No, no, 'tis not…'twas my bid to retain independence."

He paused for a beat and then turned back to the fire.

"Well, then!" he said, his voice dropping ominously, "If independence is so valuable to you, I know not why you wish to marry me."

"Because I love you," she announced simply. "And you won't have it any other way but marriage."

He moved to the largest sofa and sank onto it. He was weary beyond words. Work, worry and too little rest. He felt he may collapse any moment with fatigue.

"You look all in…" she said. "I will fetch you something strong to drink…brandy or whisky."

"I do not require brandy or whisky."

She hesitated on route to the door and began to gabble. "My father knows I am accepting your hand in marriage so he wishes to see you when you can spare the time. He is offering us a modest house on one of the estates and we may start off there…though you might not think it large enough. I do not care about that but it will have room for three servants perhaps and other staff can come in from the village… Or we can stay here, in rooms of our own, if we wish, until we—"

"Melissa, cease your prattling…'tis giving me a headache," he interjected.

She had thought he would be pleased, but she saw that he may not now marry her at all. "There is no need to be so rude!"

"No, no…" he returned. "That after all is your prerogative."

"I am merely offering soothing conversation so we may be calm…" she countered.

Making the greatest effort to revive, he sat up a little. "Yes, but 'tis not your usual style is it! Do you think I do not know what you are doing with all this diverting chatter? Do you imagine I have never seen these feminine wiles before?"

"No, but I am surprised you admit to it—the celibate life you claim to have led."

"I have never claimed any such ludicrous thing."

509

"I clearly remember the conversation over dinner that first time, when I asked you which ladies you met with."

"I clearly remember too… I said you should never ask a gentleman that question…does that reply suggest I led a celibate lifestyle?"

"Well, you change your attitude to suit your mood, so I do not know."

"I do no such thing…you are attempting to steer away from the subject of Braithwaite, and you imagine I am too dull-witted to see it." He fell back against the cushions and looked at her.

"I shall bring you some cold food if you have not had time to eat…"

"I do not require anything to eat, thank you. I require merely to rest awhile…"

She opened the door hastily to find her mother scurrying down the passage, obviously having listened outside. She pretended not to notice and went hurriedly to the dining room for brandy.

* * *

In the main drawing room Marguerite looked over at Giles, deep into his reading matter. "I thought you said she had agreed to the proposal? But they are arguing again…and he sounds very angry."

Giles turned the pages of his broadsheet in silence. He was used to these homely bulletins. So, she went on. "They are always rowing…they are never harmonious for ten minutes together. I fear he must see her as a challenge at best…or as a harridan at worst."

Giles cast his paper to one side. "Maggie, hark! I will explain this again, so we may get some peace… Melissa is not a run of the mill young woman…she's not interested in balls and gewgaws and tea parties and so on. She's clever and talented…and he's a man who wants such a woman by his side…so they'll need to get the measure of each other…and mayhap they will argue and row until they do. 'tis best they do it now, under this roof, to avoid a serious falling out and a parting after they are wed…"

Marguerite scoffed but stared at him with curiosity. She almost wanted things to go awry so she could be proved right against the seemingly superior knowing of Giles and Jemima. "I heard young Braithwaite's name mentioned. I hope she is not considering that popinjay as a husband…"

"She is not," said Giles. "She knows full well his shortcomings... See, now we have Melanie wed to Gillis...another clever and accomplished fellow with a reputation to uphold...and that helps matters...and just look at their long courtship..."

"Only because Melanie was barely seventeen when she met him," interposed his wife. Giles ignored her. "Both of them are strong women and they need men of strong calibre to bring 'em in line..."

"Little madams, the pair of them," Marguerite put in pettishly. "They are too spoiled and indulged." She stared at Giles pointedly and waited for a reaction which did not come. "I feared Fairchild would have had enough after the infamous Sunday tea, but here he is with a proposal of marriage."

"He doubtless saw the spirit of them in his classroom and was not fazed by the tea incident," Giles counter-claimed, scanning the broadsheet news again.

"He has probably left in a hurry now...as he does when she upsets him..." Marguerite glared at her husband who avoided her eye, encouraging her to continue in a calmer voice. "Mind you, I should not like to get on the wrong side of him...in his classroom or any other place for that matter..." She closed the curtains and jangled the heavy rings over the wide expanse of the windows, "You can see, despite his manners and charm, that he is not a man to be toyed with..."

Giles made a low sound of agreement. "He has doubtless put them in their place back then in a way which caused them to regret their behaviour, whatever it was...that would be the reason for the performance on that fiasco of a tea party you gave...their attempt to get even with him..."

"'twas not a tea party," claimed Marguerite in aggravation. "Merely Sunday tea."

Giles waved his hand, dismissing the niceties of which social occasion was called what. "And if you recall, he was not one to divulge what he knew then either...he's a man of principle and integrity...he's apace with her and knows her...he won't whittle too long on anything she has to throw, and she'll yield to him eventually. Better she wed him than some fop of an aristocrat without a bean to bless himself. She needs a man of the world with character and common sense."

"He is a good match for her, I agree...of course there is no money there..." Marguerite said, settling back into default marital mode and twiddling the leaves on her flower arrangements.

"Not yet…but they'll make good in this new venture…him and t'other fellow whose name I forget…"

"Trimingham!"

"Another accomplished fellow of good family… They will make good, mark my words…" Giles paused and lit a pipe, watched by his wife who waited for more. Then seized by the next valuable piece of information he leaned forwards towards her and went on in a more conspiratorial manner. "And Maggie, he'll be an asset to our business with his knack for foreign tongues… Spanish being one of 'em…now that we've acquired these land rights in Andalusia…the laws over there are tricky and things need to be just so in written documents…"

Clouds of smoke swirled around his head and Marguerite listened more closely to what emerged from the fug. "Eddy struggles to make himself plain enough with the Spanish surveyors…has a hard time making himself clear when describing his drawings in detail… I'll give Fairchild shares soon enough in return for those services…" He sat back as the smoke clouds subsided and waited for her to follow his meaning. She stared at him; his business acumen was never at fault and she marvelled at the shrewdness with which he viewed their potential son-in-law and said nothing.

"He'll more than pay his way for the return I make on the marriage will yon feller of her's…"

He felt her stare and sensing that something more personal and homely was required in the way of reassurance, he cleared his throat and softened his tone. "See, these educated clever young men are the future…my father arrived here with very little and look what he made."

"According to your mother he came with pouches of gold, the second time…" Marguerite said provocatively. "But best not to enquire too closely where that came from…"

"It came from a floundering Greek cargo ship in exchange for rescue," asserted Giles, "And originally from a Turkish vessel."

"Piracy on the high seas, most probably," said Marguerite, not for the first time.

"Well, it don't matter now. He put it to good use, and he bought my grandparents a better life and gave jobs to countless men."

Marguerite sighed; one could not fault the chronicles of Jago and Jemima without censor for doing so. She watched him calmly smoking. He again felt her stare and cast the broadsheet finally to one side. "And here's some'at else to think on…if it goes wrong a'tween 'em and it's called off, it may be many a year afore she meets a man she does settle with…now they cannot keep their eyes off each other when they're together, those two…nor their hands oftentimes… I seldom saw such a seductive match…"

"How vulgar!" Marguerite remonstrated and moved to give the curtains a final aggressive pull.

"Truth often is!" retorted Giles. "So, if you want more grandchildren sometime soon leave 'em be and it will sort out for the best…"

"I adore the way you always expect the best!" she concluded in a tone that might be construed any way he wished.

* * *

Melissa returned with the brandy and looked over at him. He had removed his boots and his jacket and was lying in his cream linen shirt and fashionable trousers, horizontally on his side at the very edge of the large sofa, as if trying not to take up too much room. She tiptoed towards him. "I have brought brandy, 'tis my father's finest. He has it shipped from France…so really, I expect 'tis cognac."

He made no reply and she saw that he was almost asleep. "Of course, there is also a Spanish variety, should you prefer it…'tis also very good…his cousins send him a large crate of it every year from Cadiz…" She drew up the small footstool and placed it in front of the sofa so she could sit and watch him. He looked even better in repose; his well-etched cheek bones, his well-shaped mouth and his straight nose. His features were symmetry itself. And that—Monsieur Tisserand had told her—was the hallmark of beauty and the thing artists always yearned to draw. His lashes looked almost non-existent in the dim light but shimmered golden now and then from the low fire glow. She stroked his hair from his brow and he opened one eye for a second and then closed it again.

He had succumbed now to near exhaustion and cared little for anything. She grew stiff from the uncomfortable stool but refused to move, only the time moving on—the ormolu clock on the mantle already showing thirty minutes past nine. She held aloft the balloon glass into which she had poured a quarter bottle of brandy. "'tis very good… I have sampled it… I could take to drinking brandy myself… Anthony, do drink a little."

"No…" he murmured.

513

"Yes, you must… I fear you might be unwell…you work too hard… I know it and I am not unsympathetic, whatever you may think…'tis just that I am so anxious about the future decisions and—"

"Melissa, do not begin with your chattering again. I have to sleep a while."

"Yes, you must do that…" She dipped her finger in the brandy and then traced it around his lips. He took hold of her hand and put it to one side.

"I know not what to say to you…" She sipped generously from the brandy glass.

"Say nothing."

"I cannot keep quiet… I am too wretched."

The next breath he took was a deep preparatory one. "Melissa, were I not so fatigued I would render you your preferred method of chastisement…you may be sure of that."

"I can understand how you might wish to…and because I feel so wretched about things, I might have allowed you to do so."

He could have hooted with laughter had he not been so weak. "At the risk of repeating myself, you would not have a choice in the matter."

She ignored the arrogance and ran her fingertip around his lips, and his tongue was unable to resist the taste of the brandy. She demurred in a tiny almost inaudible voice. "Of course…you would have to lay hold of me first, I move very swiftly, as you have witnessed."

His eyes had closed and they flickered to look at her. "I would lay hold of you…you would not get very far…be under no illusion." He became silent and she placed the glass on the floor and watched him fall rapidly towards sleep, then she whispered faintly in his ear. "That is very well then, for I should not want to be wed to a man who could not catch me when I run…"

She knew he had heard from the tiny movement of his eyelids but doubted he would remember it afterwards; it would be lost in his bleary state between waking and sleeping and remain unclear so that she could deny having said it at all. She began to gently hum and waited for him to object to the noise. He did not.

He was gone from consciousness. She sat—the little stool becoming more inadequate and she scarcely noticing. She curled tendrils of his hair around her fingers and heard his breathing deepen. At length, there was a tap on the door and thinking it to be her mother she ignored it. Eventually the door opened a little and one of the footmen put his head around, a young boy. "Begging pardon, Miss… I've brought a fresh scuttle of coal."

"Good…bring it in please, Thomas…" she said and the lad carried in the bucket, glancing briefly at the male visitor on the sofa and looking away hastily as if he had seen something too shameful for words.

"The gentleman is unwell temporarily from fatigue," she told the boy. "He is my fiancé, so do not be alarmed…have you more coal in the passage outside?"

"Yes Miss."

"Then bring in another scuttle for the night…and please tell them that we are not to be disturbed. If I require anything, I shall come myself."

"Yes Miss."

The scuttle was deposited by the hearth and followed presently by a second scuttle. Although it was now early June, the capacious rooms of the mansion in the evenings were prone to becoming chilly after dark and her father had the fires banked low in all seasons.

He had roused a little and enquired blearily in a groggy manner: "How old is that boy who just attended?"

"About twelve or thirteen, I think…"

"He sounds younger…"

"'tis merely that his voice has not broken…my father will not employ them if they are younger than thirteen…he does not agree with child labour."

"Gratifying…" said her fiancé in a thickening drowsy tone. "But you know they lie, these children, often at the behest of their parents."

"Or because they need to survive…"

"Indeed…" he murmured. "He should be in bed at this hour and in school tomorrow…not hauling coal…"

"Perhaps in your perfect world, my dear! I shall inform the butler that in future he is not to be on duty beyond eight in the evening, if it pleases you… Schooling, of course, is a step too far."

He smiled slowly, his generous mouth curving in a way which delighted her. "I have a godson called Thomas," he informed her in a weaker tone, trying valiantly to hold on to a waking state.

"Oh…you never told me!"

"There is perhaps a lot I have not told you…we barely know one another," he whispered.

She gasped then coughed for a moment or two and drank more brandy. "That is not a very encouraging thought…"

"We have all our lives to tell each other things."

This was a more heartening statement and she took from it that he intended to wed her. "Do you have other God children?" she enquired conversationally, thinking to keep him awake and in this world. She thought he had not heard but then realised he was forming thoughts or words.

"Perhaps three…some of my brother's children…" He was moving again towards oblivion.

"Perhaps three? You have lost count?"

"No, I am certain 'tis three," he uttered faintly.

"How splendid…all boys?"

"No, there is a girl…"

"And what is her name?"

He frowned with closed eyes at the effort of remembering. "I have forgotten momentarily, I am afraid."

She made a tutting noise and pretended dismay. "That is quite shocking!" she scolded. "Irreverent in the extreme to one's God children."

His smile curved his mouth once more. There was a faint scar at the corner of his lip, no more perhaps than a third of an inch in length. It looked as if his lip had been split, long ago, then healed. It was the only flaw in his perfect features. She placed the tip of her forefinger on it gently. Monsieur Tisserand had told her that true beauty was always a little flawed, to prevent it from becoming boring. She put more brandy on his lips and he took her hand and kissed her fingers. She leaned over and placed her mouth on his and kissed him so that he responded slightly. She was extremely worried; he was always so alive and strong.

Perhaps he would die before she had even received his betrothal ring. People died all the time for inexplicable reasons. The thought brought tears to her eyes and she steeled herself against morbid thoughts. She held the brandy glass carefully to his mouth and he drank from it and then shook his head against more. "I shall write to Roger tomorrow and make a plain statement. He has to stop this or their business will suffer."

He shifted in agitation and said: "He is love sick, Melissa."

"He has a delicate constitution," she replied pathetically, in her own defence. "Which is why I did not want to hurt him…he talks as if he will not survive us parting…"

Fairchild fought the oblivion pulling him down into regions beyond the room. "Young people often imagine that kind of thing…but life is not that easily left behind before the time is right…take it from someone who knows."

She stroked his forehead and began humming again and she waited. An interminable length. Time had ceased to matter. Eventually his sleep was so deep that she could move his arm to a more comfortable position without him knowing. If he was no stronger in the morning, she would summon the doctor to the house. Her eyes were weary and her body so stiff she feared she would not be able to stand upright and walk.

The little clock said a quarter before midnight. She took off her satin slippers and her top skirts and turned down the lamps and climbed carefully over him and settled in behind him, fitting neatly between his incumbent form and the back of the sofa. Cleaved to him, unable almost to move, as if they were already wed, and soon she was dozing as he slept soundly.

* * *

She was awakened at some minutes after six o'clock by Polly shaking her. Polly was leaving the following week and now at the end of their unequal association they talked freely and openly about their futures nearly every day. He was still sleeping and she peered into his face in the morning light and saw him breathing and felt relief flood through her. As Polly and she whispered, he awoke and struggled to stand, but he quickly fell back into the recess of the sofa and shut his eyes. She exchanged terrified glances with Polly who looked pained and at a loss. "Is my father about yet?" she asked the maid.

"I believe so…though he has not yet gone into breakfast. He may be out with the dogs as he mostly is at this time." Polly was adjusting the curtains so that enough light shone in without the glare of the early sun.

"I will go and change my dress and then return…and pretend I have just risen…" she said, putting on her skirts. Her father was always an early riser whatever the season. He enjoyed the fresh raw morning and then lingered over his breakfast. Not so her mother, thankfully; she was never about before nine.

"That is best. I will come to assist you," concurred Polly as she ran out of the room and along the hallway to the back staircase, Polly following behind.

They were back in fifteen minutes. She stared down at him and shook him gently. "Anthony, how are you?"

517

He looked startled as he opened his eyes and remembered where he was. "I shall rise now…" he said, and attempted yet again to stand, swinging his legs from the sofa. But as soon as he tried he fell back into an incumbent position. Little beads of perspiration dotted his lower brow and his upper lip. "Allow me a few moments…" he muttered, and then his eyes closed and he slept. His breathing deepening with every passing second.

"He is not well," said Polly, covering him with the thin woollen blanket.

"I fear not," she replied. "I will summon my father."

She found him, just seating himself in the breakfast room. She was breathless and quite distraught. "Papa, you must come with me at once!"

"What the devil is it now?" demanded Giles, flinging down his napkin and rising in haste.

"'tis Anthony, he is unwell…he cannot stand…"

They went swiftly to the reception room. "Has he spent the night in here?" enquired Giles as they entered.

"He was beyond exhausted…so I left him to sleep, but this morning he is no better…" she improvised, omitting her full vigil while lying beside him all the night.

"Not surprising…the workload he carries now…" Giles peered down at Fairchild. "He is sound asleep, that is all…though he is feverish by the look of his skin…" he said in a pacifying voice to Melissa who was clutching his arm. "I will summon a doctor to see him," he asserted.

"Fetch Doctor Darnley, if you would," she requested. "I believe he is the only one he trusts…and he has known him since a boy."

The footman was enlisted to ride for Doctor Darnley and Melissa again sat on the small stool and watched over him. Polly brought her coffee and a plate with bread and butter covered in marmalade. Then she too peered down at him; the gentle anxious look which females adopt towards sick people.

At length, he sensed Polly's presence. "Are you thinking of bringing in many people to gape at me?" he asked mildly, his vision unable to focus for more than seconds. It annoyed him, all this being peered at. He forced his eyes open wide, the light causing him pain, and peered back at Polly with a ferocious comical glare. She laughed and stepped away. "I somehow think he will live," she told Melissa.

"He had better," rejoined Melissa. "He has not yet given me a ring."

"This is but a ruse to save me money," he said softly.

They began to giggle. He groaned and turned away so that he might find oblivion. She shook him and offered him coffee. He declined but accepted a small drink of water before relapsing back into a slumbering state, from which he could hear them still whispering. He struggled to follow their words. "Let me see it again…" he heard Melissa ask.

Then some gentle tinkling of metal. He flickered his eyes open to see Polly bending towards Melissa, having unbuttoned the top of her dress and revealing one small full breast and a nipple the colour of pale plums. She seemed to be wearing very little underwear—it was obviously a fad they shared. She brought forth a chain with a gold cross and a jewelled ring next to it. A betrothal ring, he supposed, given to her by McCarthy.

"'tis beautiful!" Melissa affirmed, bending close to Polly's exposed breast to examine the ring. They had become oblivious to him in his slumbering state. He shut his eyes tightly; the sight of a woman's breast was too much at this time. He was succumbing to arousal and too weak to control it—the only part of his anatomy seemingly in working order.

"Dominic wants to buy me a larger stone…" Polly was saying. "When we reach Dublin…but I like this one so much. 'tis very dainty and suits me."

"He could do that and then you may wear this one on your other hand…or have it made for your little finger," Melissa suggested.

"That is just what he says!" exclaimed Polly delightedly as if the suggestion were some genius thinking pulled from the ethers. Their whispering had grown to normal volume. "I have told him we should save money. He is very careless with money…he is quite a spendthrift."

"There are worse sins…besides, he will have money aplenty soon, will he not!"

"He says I must not worry about money, now or in the future…for apart from his other inheritance he can carry on teaching… I suppose because I have never had any money I do not really understand how it works…"

Melissa gazed at Polly and tears came to her eyes; she knew not why the statement was so touching.

"Do not cry…" said Poly in hushed tones, "Or I will start too…"

"They are tears of happiness," said Melissa. "Just think, Polly, you will be a grand lady in no time."

"No, no…never that…though I might be a lady of some means…"

He followed the conversation loosely from afar, as if in a different room. Then he heard rasping breaths, which he knew to be their sobbing. Between the giggling and the weeping, he knew not which was worse. He slipped into oblivion, unable to prevent it. He floated and dreamt, or was it a kind of travelling! He was running through a wooded area he recognised and could not place. He squinted into the hazy distance and a girl appeared, yards away, out of the thicket. He moved towards her and saw it was Lottie. He picked up speed to reach her. She was dressed in men's clothes as usual for efficient riding, and she was waving and saying something he could not hear. He halted abruptly, afraid to approach. She glided nearer and then stopped. "I am glad you have come…" she said. "I wanted to see you one last time."

"Lottie, where are you bound for?" he called and he moved forwards as she backed away.

"Tony, don't come any closer…you must go back…"

"Back where?"

"To your girl…to the life you have…you cannot follow me now…" Then she was telling him other things but her voice was low and inaudible, only her lips moved and the sound was lost in the rustling branches and the wind in the clearing. He hastened to follow her as she moved with incredible lightness…then she was gone, dissolved into mist. "Lottie, stay a moment… I am sorry for everything…"

He peered in vain to see her, waited to see her appear from behind trees and shrubbery, as she always loved to do. "*Lottie!*" he yelled. And as he came to consciousness, he knew he had said her name out loud. He opened his eyes in alarm and looked at the two women by his makeshift bed. They had ceased chattering in a second and he sensed it. Tears of sadness oozed from his eyes and he shut them against questions and his own embarrassment.

"Who is Lottie?" Polly whispered.

"His childhood sweetheart…" Melissa told her in a matter-of-fact voice. "She died some years ago." She placed her cool hand on his forehead. "He is in and out of delirium, I think…he burns up."

There were no further queries from Polly. She looked at Melissa thoughtfully and there was a reverent silence which he did not witness due to sleep.

"'tis a sign of delirium…" Melissa said, "Dreaming of the dead!"

"Or seeing them!" said Polly with solemnity, and she made the sign of the cross quickly.

Melissa rallied from morbid thought. "I did not know you were a Catholic…"

"I am not, 'tis a habit. I was raised by nuns in the orphanage."

"'twill please Dominic…" Melissa offered.

Polly shrugged. "He won't care one way or the other…he thinks religion is all nonsense. Though his family are Catholics. So, it may please them to think me so…"

He seemed to doze for hours, and when he surfaced again, they were still chattering. About families. His lachrymose utterances had not disturbed anyone it seemed. "…the one who is not happy with our union is his great Aunt Feonnuala…" Polly was informing Melissa. "She is the sister of his grandfather and something of a gorgon…"

"Why is she not happy?"

"Simply because I am English. She dislikes the English…even though she has never met any. She cannot see why he does not choose an Irish girl…she has scarcely left the town in which they live and has never herself married."

"What does his grandfather say when she objects?" Melissa wanted to know.

"Dom went home last term end, and according to his mother his grandfather has said…" Polly lapsed into a fake Irish accent and a deeper voice. "'*Nuala, for the love of Christ! Any sane man knows that a woman is a woman wherever she hails from'*…"

This brought forth fresh giggling and they clung to each other while it passed. For the life of him, he could not see what was so amusing; the vagaries of things they found comical continued to elude him.

"As long as I get along with his mother 'twill be well," Polly stated.

"Indeed," agreed Melissa.

"Imagine if you did not get on with your mother-in-law!" Polly proclaimed.

"Then I suppose one must just pretend," concluded Melissa. "Fortunately, I have met my future mother-in-law and I like her."

"I could not stand to live my life in pretence," said Polly.

"Nor me! Remember though, Polly, if you are unhappy you must write to me and I will send money for you to return. You must not be unhappy."

There was an interminable silence and he fought to keep awake as the fatigue closed in on him.

"He has told me that too," continued Polly at length. "…'*Poll,*' says he, '*you know that if you do not like being in Ireland with me, I will escort you back to*

England. You know I will never force you to be a prisoner...even if it means giving you up'..."

"Oh, Good Lord...that is so beautiful...so selfless."

"If he means it! I hope he is who I think he is... I hope he is trustworthy and good withal...men are such strange beings..."

"I think he is, Polly... I think he is a man of integrity... Anthony speaks well of him and they are often out together..."

"Do you recall Dominic from your schooldays?" enquired Polly, now quite at ease and sitting on the arm of the sofa with Melissa on the stool near her, and he like an oblivious sleeping infant they must watch over.

"Not really. He never taught us, except for music, on rare occasions when Miss Madeley went absent. I recall him playing the piano at the dances we attended now and then with the boys in social decorum classes...beyond that I seldom saw him. He did not have to put up with us in classrooms. Luckily for him..." Melissa paused for effect and Polly waited eagerly for more about her fiancé. "Because you know, we were such dreadful children...ill-mannered and unwieldy...according to this one..." She indicated his recumbent form, "...we turned him into a perfidious tyrant..."

"Surely not!" claimed Polly.

"Oh certainly! Do you not recall my mentioning it to you years ago when I was at the school?"

Polly dredged her memory and stared towards the window, rubbing her fingertips together thoughtfully.

"We were so indulged and spoiled and generally naughty, you see, so he had little choice..." Melissa was using her most sarcastic tone and caused Polly to laugh loudly, for she could imagine the truth in it. It woke him sharply and he caught the gist of the conversation—they were on the subject of her pet grievances. "Ask Melanie, she will tell you, she adores talking of it...whereas I can barely bring myself to discuss it..."

He drifted in and out, their voices an ululation of sound and soothing comfort.

"...and will you tell his family your history and about your working since being a girl?" Melissa was asking.

"Dominic says to tell them whatever pleases me... I shall say I was orphaned and went to live with nuns...and then became a seamstress. It sounds better than being a housemaid…though he says it will not matter to them what I was. They are not so snobbish in Ireland…"

"But you are indeed an excellent seamstress if need be…" Melissa assured her. "Look at all the dresses you repair and alter for me…"

"'tis for his sake I will tell them that…to save him being ashamed for me…"

He lost track of the conversation and drifted. He was back in the woods, pursuing Lottie who was nowhere to be seen. Susan had appeared with a large wicker basket and was picking berries and flowers from bushes as she always did and looking as she had when she was twelve. She began telling him his mother was searching for him and if he did not return at once he would be in trouble.

* * *

Sometime before Doctor Darnley arrived, he struggled to wake and in his confused state thought he was on Trim's sofa after a heavy night. Through closed eyelids he said. "I must take a piss…" There was no reply from Trimingham and only silence, followed by tittering. He opened his eyes in alarm. "I beg your pardon… I meant I need to relieve myself… I must use the lavatory…"

"Bring a chamber pot please, Polly…" Melissa instructed and Polly hastened away.

"I will go to the lavatory…" he argued.

"You will not make it…" she said firmly. "You will collapse…you must use the chamber pot…" She helped him to sit upright on the sofa, and he managed with difficulty. He was as weak as the proverbial kitten. Polly returned with the required receptacle and they helped him up and stood behind him with their backs to his, propping him upright while he unbuttoned himself and urinated. He was overcome by embarrassment; though they struggled to keep their giggling muted he felt them suffused with merriment as he leaned against them. "Good Lord, we are to be husband and wife!" claimed Melissa. "I am sure, there is no need for such coyness…"

"We are not wed yet," he complained and she and Polly spluttered the worst of their amusement, unperturbed, as he relapsed once more into near oblivion.

Doctor Darnley finally arrived. He was nearing seventy now and took life at a more sedate pace, always driven to patients by his groom in the phaeton. He was the most popular and sought after physician in the borough, assisted nowadays in his practice by a young doctor who learned alongside him. But for his long-standing patients Doctor Darnley always tried to attend himself. Fairchild was barely his patient at all, though his mother and his eldest brother and their large family were. The patient himself had not been in need of medical attention for as long as Darnley could remember.

He entered the room, bringing the fresh outside air and his hearty soothing manner, accompanied by her father—her mother preferring not to make an appearance due to her fear of contagious diseases. The doctor was wearing a light frock-coat which had been fashionable perhaps thirty years ago, with a hat of similar era.

Melissa recalled Susan saying that her mother had died giving birth to her youngest brother and that he had never bothered marrying again; it was evident by his outdated attire, for no wife would surely allow him to go about with such unfashionable clothes. "Anthony, my dear boy…what seems to be the problem?" said the doctor in his sociable manner.

Fairchild rallied a little at the sound of his greeting and stared at him and then at Melissa. Melissa grinned carefully and he knew immediately that it was Darnley's wardrobe amusing her. "And this charming young woman is your fiancé, I take it?" The doctor looked at Melissa more closely. "Very charming indeed…"

Giles nodded. "My daughter, Melissa…"

Melissa swept the doctor a curtsey.

"Ah, yes, and an accomplished artist, I hear…young as she is…"

She flushed under the compliment. "Well, I am as yet perfecting my skills…"

"A very wise and modest approach, my dear!" said Darnley, smiling at her in his warmest manner. "I believe Susan has told me a lot about you…"

"I am sure she has…" concurred Fairchild in a monotone.

"Well, you know how the females of the family can be relied upon to keep one abreast of events…" claimed the doctor, taking in both men in turn. "Even when one has not elected to be kept informed…"

Doctor Darnley's wit was as legendary as his medical expertise and Giles, thinking of his wife's daily bulletins, laughed quietly.

The maid who was to take Polly's place entered with a tray of tea for him and Darnley removed his coat and hat and helped himself. "Perhaps you would take a pot of tea to my groom, if you would be so kind. He has had no refreshment since we began at seven-thirty and we came straight here on receiving the summons…" He took out a pair of tiny spectacles and perched them on the end of his nose and peered at her over the top of them. The maid turned to Giles, who said. "Bring the man into the kitchen and tell them to get him whatever he would like. Perhaps you would care for something to eat, Doctor?"

"Not in the slightest, thank you! I never eat before three in the afternoon. I grow too stout as it is…or so Susan tells me."

Fairchild groaned at the thought of Susan's freely given opinions on everything and anything, while those around took the sound to be due to his ill health. The doctor looked at him shrewdly. "Lord, you have sprouted since I last saw you medically…you were knee high to a grasshopper then."

"I was sixteen, I think," said Fairchild patiently. "'twas fourteen years ago!"

"Surely not? How time flies!" remarked Darnley affably.

"He is fatigued beyond anything," supplied Melissa and the doctor turned to her, assessing her with his well-versed eyes sparkling with lively interest and identical almost to Susan's.

"He has been like this since last night…" she added.

"Only since last night! Well perhaps we should let him tell us himself…" Doctor Darnley's style was that of someone who had seen people with all kinds of ailments and conditions over the long years and thought it best to treat them all with the pleasant and almost whimsical touch of a musician about to render an impromptu piece of music; they might or might not be pleased with the result but it was his pleasure to offer his best. It worked well and his bedside manner was second to none.

Fairchild had closed his eyes again, so Melissa ignored the last remarks and offered: "He has been sleeping and falling into oblivion…"

"Chance might be a fine thing, with all the chattering and giggling and general interruptions…" he remarked and Darnley erupted with laughter, causing him to wince—his ears had begun to give him pain as well as his eyes.

"He is exaggerating…he forgets he slept a good few hours in the night…" continued Melissa at length. "And there have not been that many interruptions."

The doctor meanwhile had opened his medical bag, a commodious and cunning piece of luggage containing all kinds of implements and bottles and sinister looking equipment. Fairchild had succumbed again to slumber so she took the opportunity to whisper to the doctor. "He was talking to Lottie earlier!" She paused and the doctor froze for a few seconds, staring at the far wall, recalling eventually that she referred to Charlotte Fitzwilliam.

He reprised the tragedy, the heartbreak and devastation his patient had suffered, as told to him by Susan. He had heard reports of such communing with the deceased many times from people near death, or narrowly swerving death, and had without effort become convicted of the belief that life did not stop at the grave. It was not his province, however, and he regarded it as part of the mystery underpinning life itself. He unfroze and exhaled. "That kind of occurrence is not uncommon in delirium…" he said after some thought and smiled at her sympathetically. "It means little in medical terms…certainly not what you fear."

She smiled back at him with relief and he took from the bag a small metallic instrument with bulbous glass at one end and shook it. It gave off a sort of phosphorus glow that illuminated small areas. Melissa was intrigued, she had never seen anything like it, though she had seen the glow before on Damien's workbench emanating from a larger contraption. He lifted Fairchild's eyelids and held the light near and looked into his eyes.

"How is your dearest mother?" he enquired of him, not expecting an immediate reply. "A lovely woman, your mother…always was… I hear she is wed again…to an arch-deacon or some such." He prised his patient's mouth open and looked inside, holding down his tongue with a metal implement so as to peer into his throat.

"A bishop," coughed Fairchild. "She is married to a bishop."

"Another bishop!" echoed the doctor with theatrical incredulity.

"A friend of my father…she knew him from years ago…the beggars are everywhere…can't move for them," croaked Fairchild.

Darnley laughed, this time quite loudly, and Melissa was tempted to giggle but the situation was too intense. She recalled Susan telling her of Charles Fairchild's riding accident and her father attending Hildegarde; she wondered if Doctor Darnley had himself been in love with Hildegarde back in the day. It was quite conceivable: as Susan had remarked she would have been very beautiful then.

"Had I known your mother was in the way of remarrying I might have offered for her myself…" Darnley said, fuelling her ponderance on the matter. She studied the doctor shrewdly and tried piercing his thoughts. Although his address was light and almost whimsical, and hard to penetrate. He was a learned entertainer—distracting his patients with vivacious rhetoric. It was always best, he thought, to divert them from the ins and outs of what he was doing before he had reached his diagnosis, or they pestered him with questions he preferred not to answer.

"Just imagine that!" Melissa was again perched on her little stool at the foot of the sofa so as not to miss anything. "Susan would have been your step sister and Trim your brother-in-law as well as your closest friend..."

Fairchild sighed. "What joy!"

Melissa tutted and said to Darnley. "My fiancé is much given to sarcasm...it saves him from revealing his true feelings."

"No such thing!" said her fiancé in mild aggravation.

The doctor inclined his head graciously in her direction. "I delivered his eldest brother, you know..." he told them conversationally. "Rupert! He was a tiny scrap of a mite, arriving prematurely...we feared he would not survive the night...and then he would not feed properly for days...but look at him now—a fine strapping fellow."

Fairchild adjusted his bodily position on his makeshift bed, his left arm cramped and painful. "He is the tallest of us, certainly..."

The medic was feeling his neck with finger tips. "Then her next children came easily...needing only the midwife..." he informed them. "Your fiancé included."

Fairchild moistened his lips and grinned slightly. "Well, in the case of Richard, I would imagine he was ushered in by Beelzebub personally..."

Darnley again displayed his amusement and she began giggling, her face in her skirts to conceal it. Her father was somewhat mystified and Darnley told him in a soft voice. "They do not much care for one another, I believe." Giles nodded.

"An understatement!" declared the patient.

The doctor cleared his throat and rummaged in his bag and changed tack. "Speaking of infants and parents, when is Trimingham intending to make an honest woman of my daughter? Have you any notion?"

"We do not speak of such personal matters very often..." Fairchild lied.

"They have been betrothed for close on seven years, would you believe?" Darnley announced into the middle distance. "They are fooling no-one..."

Giles was leaning against the mantle and watching the fire, enjoying the rhetoric more than was perhaps seemly—now that it was apparent Fairchild was not about to die.

"Perhaps they are better off that way," Melissa commented. "People are not happy unless they are pressing others to marry in haste…" She gave a sidelong look to her father.

"The devil roast him!" declared Darnley to Fairchild. "You may tell the bounder, I'll be after him with a shotgun soon…"

Giles found this quite hilarious and lifted the poker to distract himself from too much frivolity. Meanwhile, the doctor had taken out a long steel implement and he lifted Fairchild's shirt and jabbed him with it in the region of his side. He let out a screech of anguish and Darnley chuckled and looked at Melissa as if she might applaud. "Best to surprise 'em."

"Why the hell did you do that?" cried the patient.

"An excellent response to the test!" said Darnley in good humour. "Now what about Trimingham and my daughter? And don't tell me you know nothing of it. You and he have been close since you were breeched."

"Not quite…we met when we were seven or eight."

"Confounded hair splitting…seven or eight is a year or so after you were breeched…" More rattling around in the medical bag and it was evident that a serious response was not expected and that this was mere banter, but Fairchild relented somewhat in his weakened state and uttered, "'tis really none of my business… I think it may be Susan…she is always too busy for marriage…he is waiting for her to make the decision…"

The realisation came to him suddenly that in this respect he and Trim were in the same boat—waiting for women to condescend to wed them—the only difference being the time scale. He drifted off to sleep for a few seconds and was brought back abruptly; another instrument had emerged from the bag and the doctor put it to his chest and listened with one ear to the top of it, before straightening his posture. "In my opinion, he leaves too many decisions to her. He has no-one but himself to blame when in years to come he is not master in his own house."

"I have said such things to him myself…" said Fairchild, weary now of all the prodding and poking.

"Perhaps…" began Melissa, "he sees the good she brings to the community and allows that to have priority. Trim is the gentlest and sweetest of men…"

Her fiancé coughed out some kind of disdainful sound. "Well, he likes to yarn like an old boy and wax philosophical and take things at his own pace…"

He realised too late that both Giles Shaw and the doctor were themselves 'old boys' and added. "No disrespect, gentlemen!"

"None taken...*yarning and wool gathering* are the remaining indulgences for us *old boys!*" said Giles and he and the doctor laughed merrily.

"Besides, none of it is accurate concerning Trimingham..." Melissa said with marked forbearance. "He simply has the soul of a poet." It grew worse in lachrymose hyperbole and Fairchild groaned loudly while the older men chortled, causing her to become more adamant in Trimingham's defence, annoyed at being made fun of. "He is tolerant of the world and fully understands human nature."

Fairchild gave a sound between a laugh and a growl.

"Good God!" remarked Darnley. "We may need the services of your stepfather and his cathedral when this paragon finally consents to join the family..."

Giles guffawed and then smothered it to respect the mood of the sick-room.

"Gross exaggerations!" Fairchild said. "She is exaggerating."

"No, I am not... Look how he saved me from you that afternoon in the rose garden!" she declared hotly.

There was a sudden silence within the jollity and she regretted her words at once. Doctor Darnley glanced across at Giles who frowned slightly. "Saved you in what way?" enquired the doctor lightly.

"What do you mean?" echoed Giles.

"Nothing...'tis private," she said.

Fairchild conjectured even within the vacuous haze befallen him that they would now imagine all kinds of lurid things. "She means from my wrath..." he murmured and felt the silence thicken.

"Shush..." said Melissa. "'tis not something they need to know of..." No-one spoke and the two older men found themselves drawn into the lull, into the intrigue of young romance and its darker mysteries; both of them with due diligence to daughters. They waited patiently for more information.

"I was set to throw her into the lake..." Fairchild offered at length.

"Yes...that was it," Melissa agreed hastily, and the older men viewed her with suspicion. It was obvious they were not hearing the truth.

"Trim simply likes a quiet life," Fairchild added in what he hoped was the last of the matter.

"And who is he to demand such a thing?" exclaimed Doctor Darnley, reviving his jovial manner and rooting in his bag. "He must move to matrimony like the rest of us…'tis sheer selfishness. I should like more grandchildren while I am still able to enjoy them…"

Melissa looked away in disdain; how anyone could talk of selfishness while voicing their own desires over that of the people concerned was beyond anything reasonable. She wondered if he was in jest, and then he looked over at her and winked. He was quite the wag! He turned to Fairchild and began his professional summary. "Well, 'tis not consumption…" he pronounced.

"Thank God," said Melissa.

"Nor is it typhus or diphtheria…in fact 'tis not contagious at all…"

"Then what is it?" enquired Fairchild with his eyes closed.

"I am unsure as yet…be patient while I finish the examination…" It was often like shouting into the wind, asking patients to be patient. "'tis some kind of fever…internally caused…scarlet fever is rife in schools, as you are aware no doubt, but 'tis not that either…"

Darnley looked at him keenly, "I expect you have been overdoing things…and burning the midnight oil with Trimingham…as he pickles his *poet's soul* for safekeeping."

Fairchild said nothing but found this wit amusing and his lips curved slightly with his habitually tightened grin. Giles was heard to laugh as he bent over the grate and rattled the poker.

"That is just what they do all the time!" pronounced Melissa softly.

"No, we do not…" objected her fiancé. "Not all the time…"

She ignored him. "According to Susan they imbibe a prodigious amount when together…"

Jumping to the opposite side of the argument, Darnley took a more balanced view. "I would not put too much store by that, my dear! Susan is inclined to believe anyone taking a glass of sherry before dark to be on the road to ruin…unless 'tis Christmas Day. She is quite the zealot…and they are young men and that's what they do."

"I have told her that myself," said Giles.

"But they are not so young any more…" she pointed out. "They are both of them turned thirty now!"

Doctor Darnley and Giles Shaw exchanged amused glances. "What would I not plan for the rest of the week on a mere six hours sleep in four days, were I but thirty again!" Darnley expostulated and looked at Giles.

"Indeed!" agreed Giles.

"And you see what a good wife she will make!" the doctor told Fairchild, his cheerful but steady gaze falling onto Melissa. "She has all the right values."

Giles and Darnley shared more merriment while Fairchild saw nothing amusing.

"Doctor, what exactly is wrong with him?" demanded Melissa impatiently, to bring matters to a salient point.

"A feverish condition, perhaps glandular…brought about by exhaustion, or strain of some kind."

"'twill be my fault…" she opined. "I am worrying him by not agreeing to the wedding date and…" she halted and Doctor Darnley intervened to spare her any embarrassment. "I don't know what the world is coming to…young women shying away from marriage…it never happened that way in my day…boot on the other foot a lot of the time…" Then he became serious as he looked at Fairchild's inert and drowsing form. "He needs to rest for a few days…or even weeks."

She put her hand to her mouth in an anguished manner.

"I cannot rest for more than a day or two…" argued Fairchild. "I have things to attend to and the school to consider for now…"

Darnley straightened and peered over his spectacles in a clinical manner. "Dear boy, that is your choice…but do not say I have not warned you. If you fall off your horse and break your neck, I cannot be held accountable. Or if you collapse in one of your classrooms. You are in an extremely weakened state…that is what I know up to now…" He turned to Melissa. "Perhaps you would be kind enough to acquire for me a basin of warm water to wash my hands…while I ask the patient questions and carry out further examination." He smiled on her benevolently.

"Of course!" she said and dropped him a slight curtsey.

"Thank you for your ministrations, Doctor."

Giles hastened to acquiesce to the obvious need for doctor-patient privacy and put his arm around her and guided her to the door.

"You will tell me the truth of what the doctor has said?" she enquired of Fairchild, stroking his hair with her fingers in passing.

"When do I not tell you the truth?" he replied.

"When talking of what has been supped, for one thing!" she quipped, and hastened in the wake of her father.

"A bonny and witty young wife indeed..." said the doctor after their departure. "The girl has your greatest interest at heart. I foretell a veritable happy marriage here..."

"We will see..." sighed Fairchild. "She is at times almost as difficult as your daughter."

Darnley smiled and entreated him to turn onto his stomach. "All I can say to you, Tony, is that they have strengths of their own. In many ways they are stronger than us...they carry the burden of procreation...if they make us content and are faithful that may be all we can ask."

Fairchild tolerated Doctor Darnley's thorough and searching examinations and remembered Giles Shaw's similar wisdom to him in the garden several weeks past. Men in their greater maturity learned the sense of not expecting too much of relationship, it seemed. He began to slip into oblivion again, until the doctor's voice brought him back into the room. Darnley was preparing some kind of tincture from two glass containers into a smaller bottle for dispensing. "We have both lost women we loved far too early..." he was saying, referring to Susan's mother as well as to Lottie. "Although I at least have the blessing of our children...but you now have the chance to love again...do not waste it, would be my advice to you... It would be a travesty."

* * *

When Doctor Darnley left the room, he sought out Giles Shaw in his study. "He should not be moved today, for fear of accident...he certainly cannot walk without collapse...some kind of virulent fever waits in the wings and it may be hastened by precipitous effort of movement," proclaimed the doctor. "But tomorrow perhaps he can go up to one of the bedrooms? With some assistance."

"Yes, of course..." Giles stood and indicated for the doctor to sit in the armchair. The doctor declined on the excuse of a large caseload. "I will be back the day after tomorrow. I have given him something quite strong to lessen fever...he will sleep extremely deeply now; you will not be able to rouse him. He will need more of the medicine tomorrow. 'tis on the little table by the sofa. He will need to take fluid when he wakes...water preferably, and some milk perhaps, but he will not require food until I return, unless he demands it, which is unlikely… I am glad you fetched me when you did, any later would have been too dangerous a delay…"

Giles looked at him as if not comprehending.

"There may have been organ failure," said the doctor.

"What in God's Name ails him?" asked Giles in some consternation. "He seems so hail and healthy normally."

"He has pushed himself to his limits, I would say…he has anaemia too…which is curable if treated sooner rather than later…" Doctor Darnley buttoned his coat and hesitated, to prepare his words and not be misconstrued. "It has caused a form of nervous exhaustion bordering on collapse…happens when the body or mind is driven beyond normal tiredness for repeated periods…but he is young, he will recover with rest."

Giles sighed and shook his head. "The sooner she weds him, the better…her reluctance to do so has obviously not helped him."

"No, it has not," said Darnley. "In fact, what I will say to you man to man, is that often in young men—when over stimulated in the bodily sense—it can create a glandular imbalance precipitating illness."

Giles exclaimed in exasperation. "In other words, he is frustrated in the bedroom?"

"I would say so…though he is reluctant to talk of it, so I am not certain how right I am," Darnley chuckled delicately. "Not the end of the world, but coupled with his extreme work load and exacerbated by worry, it has possibly had deleterious effects…"

Giles breathed out, releasing tension, and gazed at the window. "We are grateful to you, Doctor. Give me your bill, I will discharge it."

"No hurry. I shall be back a couple of times before I am done. I am glad you understand me."

"I understand you only too well," affirmed Giles and escorted the doctor along the hall to the main doors. "I am thankful I am not that age again with all the brooha about marriage and courtship…waiting for her to say yes or no or change her mind."

"As am I!" concurred Doctor Darnley with his usual good humour, allowing Giles to open the front doors for him in the place of the butler.

* * *

Visitors and Variants

By the next mid-day, letters had been written and dispatched, to Stevenson, Trimingham, Mrs Anstey and to Hildegarde Wyevale. Melissa had written them herself at her father's desk, using his stationery. She added a further letter to Roger. Sealing it with the wax her father used for business purposes, in the tradition of important correspondence, to give it more validity. Her father looked at it as he perused the parcel of missives. "What's this? You are not still encouraging that coxcombe, are you?"

"No, Papa, I am discouraging him. I am telling him formally that he must not call anymore." She decided further that she might as well apprise him truthfully of events. "Roger took it upon himself to visit the Grange…and he attacked Anthony!"

"What?" Giles turned in great surprise. "Braithwaite attacked Fairchild?"

"Indeed…" She picked invisible fluff from her sleeve to distract from the sensitivity of the matter. "But it did not turn out well for him…"

"I would not imagine it did," said Giles.

"He apparently made slanderous statements about Anthony, which then involved Polly's fiancé. Now Stevenson has issued a writ warning him of a lawsuit for slander…" She paused, satisfied with this succinct overview of the situation, not too lengthy or too detailed.

"The witless boy!" said Giles.

"Anthony was angry with me last night because I had not written to Roger as he wished me to."

"I see…" Giles paced and looked at the collection of letters now being wax sealed by his daughter. The black diamond he wore on his little finger and given to him by his uncle and Spanish godfather on his coming of age glistened as the sunlight caught it. "When you marry him, you must understand that he will have authority over you and you must do as he asks…"

Melissa stared at him. "That is what he believes too…"

Giles remained patient. "Of course! Because 'tis the natural way of things."

"Yes but 'twill depend what it is he is asking of me," she countered.

Her father assumed even more tolerance and sighed. "He will not ask anything of you that is unreasonable, I am sure…"

"We shall see," she said airily, and replaced the seal next to the wax.

"Melissa, when you wed, your husband, whoever he be, has complete authority over you…"

"This is also what he believes…"

"Yes, because as I have said, 'tis his right to believe it." Giles paused to ponder. "I presume he knows you question this fundamental rule of marriage?"

"He suspects as much." She sorted the letters in her hand by priority of urgency. There was a rattling sound while her father poked the low burning embers in the grate, losing patience suddenly with this verbal maize. "All I can say is that if you go about disobeying him on matters of importance you risk his wrath…and you must answer for that…"

The poker was heard to clang to the hearth and Giles groaned noisily on straightening. "As for example, the other week in the rose garden when this Trimingham fellow had to intervene…" he said sagely, and he turned to look at her and waited for the fuller story of that day, "and saved you from some consequence of his wrath!"

She trilled a burst of light laughter and stood up from the desk. "Papa, dearest, he adores me to incur his wrath."

"Does he!" said Giles in huge scepticism.

"Besides, I do not fear his wrath… I am perhaps cautious around it, but I do not fear it…"

"Then why was he attempting to throw you in the lake?"

"He was not…he made that up."

"I thought so…then what was it?"

"I cannot possibly say…" She tiptoed around the room, as in some kind of slow dance. "'tis extremely personal."

When Giles looked at her again, he saw upon her neck the flush of deep pink—not of modesty, but that which women display when desire is upon them. He turned away to inspect the fire. The information he awaited was not to be forthcoming. He was left to conjure with his imagination. "These games will have to stop…once you are married," he said, for lack of any other thought.

"Papa, 'tis nothing for you to be concerned about…if you ask him, he may explain it to you in his words…"

Giles watched her move to the door so as to escape further questioning. He was not about to petition Fairchild on the matter: he might well be embarrassed by his own inability to understand. "I am done with these conundrums; I have better things to do! If you know what you are doing…or think you do…then so be it. I will send Phillips once he awakes and is stronger, to help him bathe and shave…and you must stay out of his bedchamber…"

"Why?" queried Melissa "He needs me now more than ever…" But she knew what the answer would be.

"*Because* 'tis *not seemly*…" obliged her father on cue. "He is flesh and blood when all's said and done…and the quicker you wed him the better for all concerned."

"He is certainly flesh and blood," she said in her new woman-of-the-world voice which disconcerted him. "But I have only just made up my mind to trust him."

"Trust him how?" her father demanded.

She hesitated and made small sounds of uncertainty. "With my welfare…"

Giles moved in front of her and blocked her exit from the room. "Hark wench! If there is any reason you cannot take him as a husband then tell me now… If he mistreats you in any way, you must say so…"

"He does not mistreat me…besides, I adore him."

"Then I am at a loss…" claimed Giles. He knew not how innocent she was still or how experienced, but his instinct told him he could trust Fairchild.

"Do not concern yourself, Papa. I shall willingly wed Anthony Fairchild," she said sweetly.

He stepped out of her way and allowed her to pass and made for his chair at the desk. He thought of his own father, raising five daughters; an exhausting labour of love. This kind of conversation was one she should be having with her mother, but it was plain that Marguerite and Melissa had ceased to communicate on all but the vital minutiae of life, and that his wife may also be out of her depth. Then he thought of his youngest sister, Amaelia. Given her chequered past, there was perhaps little in the way of romantic and intimate encounter that she would not understand.

"I am certain we shall make each other content…" Melissa was now assuring him, cat-like in her covert satisfaction of all things inexplicable to him.

"Not if you argue all the time," he murmured, already mentally wording the letter he would write to Amaelia.

"We do that only some of the time…and 'tis something we cannot…or perhaps will not avoid." She tripped back to where he sat. "Please cease worrying." She kissed him delicately on the cheek and picked up her skirt and just as delicately tripped swiftly again to the door.

* * *

Fairchild had moved to an upstairs bedroom by the end of the next day, walking unsteadily up the staircase with Phillips, Giles' valet, and a footman, both following behind in case he collapsed. He would not have them assist him bodily and refused their help to the lavatory or in taking off his clothes. Preferring to lean against the bedpost for whole minutes while recovering strength, as they waited on his convenience. He was not someone to be overruled in matters of his will and the excursion from reception room to bedroom took a quarter of an hour. "Leave him…we must bide and be patient…" Phillips told the footman who was overly anxious to have the job done. "I served such men as him in the army…he will not take kindly to interference."

Melissa watched from the foot of the stairs, afraid the whole time that he would collapse and die. Then she instructed the two servants to wait outside a few moments and went in and closed the door. She approached him as he stood leaning weakly against the bedpost in one of her father's nightshirts. "Anthony, I will come to you the second you send for me if 'tis necessary…"

This caused him to grin and he raised his brows and looked at her. "So, I must be almost on my deathbed before you show such concern and acquiescence?"

She stared at him, her eyes huge and haunted. "Are you teasing me?"

"Well, you may have heard the saying… *'many a true word spoken in jest'*…"

She moved to him and put her arms around his waist.

"I love you… I love you dearly…" she whispered.

"I am aware, do not fret." He held her briefly then put her away from him. "Phillips and the other fellow are outside, Melissa! Have a care. You should perhaps stay away from me while I am indisposed!"

"That is what my father has said…"

"He is quite right! We are not yet wed."

"Phooey!" she said. "I shall ignore both of you!"

He groaned a little but was too weak to argue. "How you do surprise me!"

Already she could see his weight loss. His eyes were darkly shadowed and his cheekbones etched sharply like razors beneath his skin, his lustrous hair lank and darker with sweat. But his male beauty was not diminished, she thought, and if anything, it was enhanced. Even so she was alarmed. "And if you pay scorn to my attentions in this way, I shall jump into bed with you," she said to deflect the grimness of things.

"You shall not!" He sat carefully on the side of the bed. "I am not strong enough at present and you will take advantage of me…"

She smiled in a way which began his arousal, soft but pressing. He inhaled and retired into his own thoughts, as lascivious as her own. '

"My father is insisting we bring forwards the union for when you are stronger…" she said.

He nodded, unable to formulate thoughts on the matter but in agreement with the proposal. She sought to cheer him and distract from the aura of sickness. "He is concerned too about our rows…unless I understand your authority over me."

"I hope you have reassured him…"

She began assisting him into the bed, his fingers too clumsy and weak to pull back the sheets. "Yes, do not worry, I told him you adore being infuriated by me…"

"I am perpetually at a loss to know where you derive some of these peculiar notions…" he said through closed lids.

"I know not myself…somewhere deep in my inner being, I expect," she said blithely, "But we need not argue now about any of that until you are yourself…"

"If I survive…if I leave my deathbed…"

"You must not say such things…this is not your deathbed."

"It might be as near as damn it…short of actual admission…"

She took his hand and held it and the tears stood on her lashes, tiny crystal formations like the droplets of thawing icicles. It was quite unbearable and he changed the subject and sighed, "So, have you told him you intend to do as I ask in all things?"

She blinked to clear her vision and frowned seriously. "Well, no…because I may not always do as you ask…"

He looked intently at the top buttons of the nightshirt and muttered something, losing strength and wind with every second and sinking low into the bed. She pulled the sheets up to his shoulders, seeing the perspiration on his throat and forehead. "But if that is much to your displeasure, you can refuse to wed me at this point…" she said, like a gambler for high stakes, aware of a strong motivation in her own words, an honesty which could not be silenced. He turned his eyes to her, staring hard to keep his concentration and his eyes open. "God's Teeth, girl! Do you imagine I will simply back away in the face of such a challenge!"

She smiled slowly and then began to giggle, but was interrupted by Phillips entering, with John the footman close behind and trying not to smirk while carrying a bowl of water and drying cloths. "We will help him now, Miss…" announced Phillips in a heavy respectful tone. "You may leave him in our hands…'tis what your father has instructed."

"I will look in again in a few hours…" she told her fiancé. "No-one from outside is permitted to visit you for three days on Doctor Darnley's instruction. I have written to all the relevant people."

He called to her as she left in the thin voice which sickened her. "Melissa…could you please see that they tend to Flossie…" She stopped abruptly, before remembering that Flossie was his horse. "Tell them she is accustomed to being ridden most days and needs exercise…"

"I will have the stables notified…" she told him, but Phillips was already onto the matter. "The head groom is out riding her as we speak, Sir," he reassured, with the satisfaction he always displayed when referring to the overall efficiency of the mansion.

* * *

The first caller was Trimingham two evenings later. He was obstructed in the hall for a few minutes by the butler who had been informed of the 'no visitors' ruling. He had Melissa summoned and being already so fond of him, she told the butler that he was an exception and had urgent need of conversation with her fiancé on pressing financial business. "You are only allowed fifteen minutes, Mr Trimingham!" she said with an impish grin as she led the way up the stairs.

Trim entered the bed chamber and Fairchild roused himself from the constant slumber overtaking him now at all times when he was not distracted. Trim fished out a box of his favourite small cigars and put them on the bedside table. "I thought you might be in need of more of these."

"I shall be, once I am allowed to get up…" Fairchild said. "I dare not attempt to go downstairs yet…your father-in-law has legislated!" Then he began informing Trim of Darnley's warnings on his own overdue marriage. Though he had doubts about how serious those had been during Darnley's *bedside* repartee.

"I am ready for him if he calls me on it," replied Trim cheerfully. "I am waiting for his daughter…and he knows it full well. So, what precisely is his problem?"

"He seems to want more grandchildren…" retorted his closest friend.

Trimingham groaned. "Her elder brother has just supplied him with another one a few months ago! How many does he want at any one time!"

"As many as he can get, I expect…you know how they are at his time of life when it comes to infant progeny…they seemingly cannot get enough."

Trim rubbed his hands together for warmth, it was drizzling outside on a damp and chilly summer evening. He dropped into the bedside chair, his long legs unfolding before him, elegantly shod in close-fitting trousers of a light-coloured weave. "I suppose there is nothing decent to drink?" he enquired.

"Of course not…some lime cordial over there if you have a thirst."

The visitor grimaced. "Well, it just so happens…" He retrieved a small flask of whiskey from his jacket pocket and held it aloft like a trophy.

Fairchild stared at it a second hopefully. "I dare not have any of that…the tincture Darnley has given me will not sit well with it…"

"Perhaps a small taste then?" Trim said as he rose again. The glass from the bedside containing water was emptied into a pot plant and the cup which had contained tea was purloined while he poured generous measures of the whiskey. He decided to rouse his friend from the doldrums of ill-health with some cheerful banter. "I tell you, Tony, on the subject of infants… I will lay odds that you'll be cradling your first born sooner than I will mine…in fact, within nine months of your honeymoon…now what do you say to a little wager right here?"

Fairchild swore and sank back onto his pillows. "Utter nonsense! Susan and you with your perfect arrangement so far, there can be no odds! Unless you have an accident one day soon!"

Trimingham laughed merrily, then eyed his friend critically while trying not to appear to do so; Anthony Fairchild was never ill, barring over-indulgences of the festive kind. "Melissa informed me in her letter that you are now *officially betrothed*…" he said, his voice larded with solemn comedic overtones.

"Apparently! I had to be near death, of course, before she came remotely close to accepting... I suspect it might have been born of her pity," Fairchild uttered.

Trimingham laughed loudly again, refusing to take the sentiment seriously. "Yes, but 'tis agreed now?"

"I believe it is," said Fairchild.

Trimingham diversified as soon as he had imbibed some of the whiskey. "Lot of business in for us already...the demand bodes well! Luckily, I have found another translator...and a scrivener...so no need for you to worry...and of course I am free to be fully present next week."

"Gratifying," said Fairchild and fought the need to sleep and continued. "Her father visited me yesterday and proposed to grant me equity in their business in return for translation services...and those will eventually convert into revenue and save on my salary..."

"Excellent news!" pronounced Trimingham. "The least of it being your salary reduction and the best of it being his interest in our business. You are off to a flying start now, my boy!"

Fairchild sighed like someone twice his age. "If I live now, I suppose I may prosper..."

Trim turned abruptly. "Of course you will live! What hare-brained waffle...obviously the medication talking..."

An inestimable time went by and he knew not how long. Next thing he realised was Trim rising suddenly. "Tony, you must rest...you are sorely over-strained..."

"I know it," he agreed. "I hope to be right again soon enough."

Seeing that his friend's whiskey was barely touched, Trim picked up the glass. "I had best remove this...or there will be an uproar and I will get the blame..."

"Possibly because you are to blame..." said the invalid sportingly.

Trim held aloft the glass Fairchild had sipped from in a cursory toast and drained it himself, and then took out a pristine handkerchief and wiped both the glass and the cup thoroughly before partially refilling the glass with water from the carafe. Finally remembering the packet of restorative herbal lozenges Susan had sent and tossing them onto the eiderdown. "Console yourself with those..." he said and looked towards the pillows for a reaction, but Fairchild was already asleep.

Downstairs in the hall he met with Melissa and took her hand and kissed her fingers. "You have agreed to the proposal! Let me be one of the first to say how glad I am."

"Certainly…" she said in a dignified manner. "Did you imagine otherwise?" She sniffed at the odour of liquor emanating from Trimingham's clothing. "I hope you have not been giving him alcohol…" she muttered in a vaguely censorious tone. "He is not allowed it yet."

"I offered him a drop but he declined!" replied Trim in a similar voice. "He is obeying the doctor in all matters."

She smiled, which turned into a grin. "I would hope so…or there will be trouble." She began to giggle softly, despite her best efforts, and Trim chuckled with her. He accepted his riding cape and gloves from the butler and looked at her with his benevolent warmth, his straight brown hair flopping over one eye and making him appear rakish. "And you are going to be a good girl in the future, are you not?"

She was about to make a tart retort and then remembered that he was her fiancé's confidante, the way Melanie was hers. "I am considering the matter…" she retorted.

"What a little minx you are indeed…" he told her as the butler opened the front doors for him, and she shut her eyes to allow this fond patronage to wash over her.

"How is Mrs Jemima, by the by?" Trim paused to enquire.

"Gregory is bringing her on Saturday afternoon, if you care to join us for a hand or two of cards… Anthony may be up by then and in need of diversion," she said.

"I doubt he will, least not without Darnley's permission…though I think I might accept your kind invitation."

"You could bring Susan, if she is free," Melissa offered tentatively.

Trim turned back, one glove on and the other off. "Susan is never free for such frivolity…"

"No, of course not! She is always so busy with important matters," agreed Melissa with due respect for her new friend and associate.

"However…" Trim intoned for effect. "We should not allow that to deter us lesser mortals…" He gave a lock of her hair a brief fond tug so that she began giggling again, and he left with a lighter heart.

Next along was Nicholas Stevenson, the following afternoon, a little before the visitors' curfew lifted officially. The new maid came to tell her of his arrival as she painted in the art room. "I thought you would want to know, Miss!" said Polly's replacement, a woman in her early thirties and much more staid and sullen than Polly.

"Thank you, Agnes." She put down her brush. "Could you take him upstairs to Mr Fairchild please?"

"Mr Fairchild was sleeping like a babe when I went in with his tea…and I dare's not wake him," Agnes told her. "Mr Jarvis says not to… It may be more than my job's worth!" The maid looked stricken and Melissa wondered for a second whether Agnes actually thought Jarvis the butler owned the mansion rather than her father. "Where is my mother? Perhaps she can deal with Mr Stevenson?"

"She's out with her sister," said Agnes mournfully. Her mother and Aunt Dorothea were always going out: to nearby towns, looking at dress material or furnishing fabrics and other goods they had no real need of; silly vacuous errands to fill their lives. She vowed never to become like them. She thought of her wedding gown, which her mother was anxious to have started, though she had already notified the dressmaker that she would be in urgent need of a cream silk dress of simple design, and the first fitting was next week. Her mother would demand something extravagant and ridiculous in which she would feel uncomfortable.

She returned to the question of Nicholas Stevenson. "Very well, I shall be there when I have washed my hands and righted myself," she said to Agnes. "Ask Mr Stevenson to kindly sit in the morning room." She removed her smock, underneath which she wore one of her casual day dresses. Her hair was awry and loosely bound with a scarf. Her appearance was not one for receiving people like Stevenson whom she disliked naturally, owing to his association with the school and her time there.

She walked to the morning room and he stood on her entrance. "My dear Miss Shaw," he began in his smoothly effusive manner. "You may not remember me…"

"I do…" she said and invited him to follow her. "How could I forget!" She had not given him time to take her hand and perform the usual flourishes of exchange required from gentleman to ladies.

Stevenson followed her as bidden, unaffected by her cool reception. "I hear you will wed soon?" he said sociably.

"Indeed…" she replied over her shoulder. "If he is well enough and survives."

Stevenson paused on the lower stairs and looked at her askance. "Of course he will survive…a healthy robust young fellow such as he. How is he now?"

"He is drained and exhausted…" she replied and waited for him to catch her up on the first-floor corridor. "Which is mostly your fault…"

Stevenson was aghast and amused at one and the same time and allowed his eyes to travel down the front of her dress. If he was not mistaken—and he seldom was where these things were concerned—she wore very little beneath it. Naturally he appreciated the female form as a gourmet appreciated the menu and she saw this in his expression. He was undressing her mentally, his lively humorous blue eyes betraying little animosity at her comment and everything of gladness at looking her over.

"You have been too long in finding his replacement…" she continued. "Indeed, Mr Stevenson, I do not believe you have tried hard at all…and so he is at the end of his strength, with you presuming on his diligence and sense of duty while he is getting to this state…"

"Surely not, my dear…" Stevenson said mildly, as if receiving an erroneous comment. He had strong patrician features and an aquiline nose, and apart from his hair which was now silver he looked no different to how he had looked when she was fifteen. She scrutinised his face with a detached interest, imagining him in a charcoal drawing. All of which he mistook for rapt attention. "As it happens, I am interviewing a fellow tomorrow who may prove suitable for the position of deputy…"

Melissa continued to the required bed chamber and paused again outside. "Then let me put it this way to you… If this person can read and write and is not a complete dolt he will have to do. For Anthony cannot continue with the new business in addition to his workload at the school and representing the Foundation…so something must be done! Please wait a moment, while I see if he is able to receive you."

Stevenson was unfazed, disposed as he had been all his life to taking even a rebuke from a beautiful woman as a compliment. He blinked rapidly as he apprised more of her personal virtue and then waited outside when she disappeared into the room.

Fairchild was dozing peacefully in the bed. She admired him from the doorway, taken as usual by his pleasing male features in response. She tiptoed to him and kissed him lightly on his forehead and then on his lips. "Sweetpea!" she murmured.

He stirred and opened his eyes and smiled. She took his hand and held it, noting with pleasure that his skin was no longer clammy. "How are you?"

"Improved…" he replied a little hoarsely. "And please stop calling me by that ridiculous endearment."

"But you are a sweetpea!" She kissed him again. "Nicholas Stevenson is here to see you, the wretched man!"

He struggled to sit upright in the bed. "What has he done to deserve that epithet?" He reached for the glass of water.

"He is lecherous…the signs are all about him, though he masquerades as a respectable member of society…"

"Somewhat harsh! And it may have a lot to do with the dress you are wearing…"

"I am sure I may dress as I please in my own home without being subjected to his kind of appraisal…" she said with sincerity.

"Well, the man is only human like the rest of us! But show him in," said Fairchild, unequal to such discussion at this moment in time.

Stevenson entered and Melissa left immediately, promising to send up tea. "Not for me, my dear, I have other calls to make elsewhere. I shall stay for only a few moments," said Stevenson.

"As you wish!" she concurred. "And do not tire him more than you must."

He bowed as she left and then turned to Fairchild. "Ye Gods, Tony, she is a little firebrand is she not!"

"I told you she was extremely direct… I told you that night when your wife suggested I approach her father to get to know her…if you recall."

Stevenson had forgotten much of that conversation. "I have just received the most severe roasting on the way upstairs."

"About what?" queried his deputy.

"Making you work too hard and exploiting your good nature…or some such…" Stevenson smiled widely and looked as if he had been awarded an accolade. Fairchild read his mind and cleared his throat. "Do not take her too seriously."

"Lord above, Tony, after my long and industrious career with females I am not about to begin taking them seriously on trifles such as that…but you have your hands full there…" Stevenson sat in the comfortable chair placed for visitors.

Fairchild smiled omnisciently. "I know how to manage her now."

"If I had a guinea for all the I times I have heard that from prospective bridegrooms!" pronounced Nicholas Stevenson and he gazed about the room where her paintings hung in several places. "Her artistic persuasion might explain her temperament, of course…and it has to be said, the girl is quite beautiful. One can see why you are so smitten. I do not mind a strong woman, if she is intelligent withal…being wed to one myself these days… When I was your age, Tony, I thought I knew all there was to know about the opposite sex! Good God, I had only just begun to open the book," Stevenson continued in this vein on his favourite topic of women and Fairchild—accustomed to these monologues—closed his eyes and let himself drift while he went on about various females he had courted or bedded or almost married by mistake.

Following it with an update on what was happening at the Grange and how Rodrick Doyle, the geography master, was now retiring: he was not only losing his two best men in himself and McCarthy but Doyle as well.

He had fallen almost to sleep when there was a knock on the door and Stevenson called on his behalf for them to enter. He came too quickly and saw Phillips standing inside the room. He rubbed his eyes and paid attention.

"Begging your pardon, gentleman, but if you want shaving, Sir, then I must do it in the next twenty minutes before I leave on a business journey with the master of the house overnight!"

"I am quite alright without, thank you," said Fairchild. "I shall shave on your return…although I may have done so for myself before then…"

"Now Tony, don't go cutting your throat by accident," said Stevenson comically. "Better wait for this good fellow to do it, until you are stronger."

"Indeed, Sir," concurred the obliging valet; Fairchild was the easiest of people to serve, his manner and attitude to staff was respectful and satisfying. And likewise, they assisted him in any way they could. Phillips left again and Stevenson began to get to the point. The school governors were prepared to pay him fully to the end of the month if he wanted now to resign, in return for his stalwart service to the school. But would he honour his avowal to deliver senior tutorials twice a month into the foreseeable future—once he was in good health again?

Fairchild agreed; he was ready to relinquish the Herculean schedule he carried, but no longer ready for death. He was stronger and for the first time saw his mortality as a thing he might become responsible for with greater care. Darnley had told him to cut down his alcohol intake, it was liable to permanently damage his liver, as he aged. He doubted if he could accomplish this without motivation, but perhaps his forthcoming role as husband might encourage him.

Stevenson rose to leave. "I have left a basket of fruit below with the butler! Louisa sent it for you. I told her you would perhaps prefer a bottle of something, but it fell on deaf ears, naturally."

"Kind of her…please thank her. Betimes, I am not supposed to imbibe, so she did rightly."

Stevenson found this hilarious in the extreme and left the bedroom, the amusement dying away as the door closed behind him.

He fell immediately back to sleep. Darnley was keeping him doped, it seemed, with his potions.

* * *

Minutes after Stevenson's departure (or so it seemed) Melissa re-entered. She crept to the bed and watched him. The hollows of his cheekbones were still pronounced but his skin looked to be a healthier colour. She smoothed his hair, which felt coarser with the need of washing. He opened his eyes and looked at her warily. "You again! Do I not recall you from somewhere?" He reached for her chin and pulled her to him to kiss her cheek. "I am not exactly fresh…" he lamented. "I might have been in a desert or tramping for days… I need to bathe."

"I care not," she said and put her fingers beneath her father's borrowed nightshirt and stretched them so that the buttons opened to half way down his chest. Golden hairs protruded in little clusters and she massaged him with her finger tips. He squirmed a little, his arousal instantly appearing. "Don't!" he cautioned.

She ignored him and shucked off her slippers and hoisted herself onto the bed. He watched in mortification, supine and unable to resist.

"No-one is about…" she whispered, "To interrupt us…no-one of any significance anyway…and I have locked the door…" She lifted the skirt of her

547

informal day dress under which she wore few undergarments, as usual with this attire.

"You really must not receive visitors, especially males, while wearing so little," he told her.

"How was I to know he would call when my mother was absent?" she said blithely, and she straddled him and he found she was without even her drawers. He moaned involuntarily as his erection increased in size and she became empowered and pushed him back into the mattress. "Melissa, this is unwise…"

"Why? I have agreed to wed you, as you and my father wish…"

"You have also to wish it…" he gasped. With any luck, he would release his passion quickly and she would lose the strong intention to what he imagined she was going to do. He was wrong. She began stroking him with firmer and firmer hand movements, her finger tips pressing him in places which took him beyond earthly reason and to heights he enjoyed the more because the rest of his body was so limp and inert. It was as if all his senses had dropped to his male organs and nothing else of him remained.

At what she judged to be the maximum of his tumescence she lowered herself onto him, until he was inside her. Concentrating hard, remembering instructions, she guided him into her vagina. He watched her face pass through a series of expressions; fear, surprise, delight and finally gratitude of some kind. He was exalted and fearful at the same time. He had known she was passionate from the moment he had looked at her sidelong during the famous Sunday tea, when her laughter had left her sensually drained. "No…" he cried thinly, his head thrown back and his neck muscles tight with desire. "Have a care, or we shall beget a child…"

"We shall not…" she breathed. "Melanie has told me exactly what to do and not to do…but if we conceive a child 'tis too bad."

"Christ alive!" he exclaimed. The thought came to him that if he did not better manage this reckless sensuality at her youthful age, gratifying as it was, they could well end up raising a family of seven or eight…or more. He was unable to sustain the thought. His own desire left him bereft of his wits. She began to ride him with steady and confident movements, increasing the pace and gripping his penis with her inner reflexive muscle—a shock of inestimable delight to them both. She thought back to what Melanie had described to her; how to pull away at just the right moment to avoid him pouring his seed into her.

She propelled herself upwards as she felt him climax and then shifted swiftly away from him and flopped onto her knees beside him, watching his face with interest. She was a goddess in her own powerful realm. This was what women knew and seldom talked of perhaps…except in close friendship, such as her's with Melanie.

"I cannot fully satisfy you…" he said in a hoarse voice, "Not right now, I am too weak still…"

She propped herself on one elbow and laughed. "It matters not…now I have had my wicked way with you!"

He sighed long on an outward breath, calming and refreshing, weeks of tension dissolving in some miraculous manner. "What a little jezebel you are becoming…" he said, grinning a little and then tightening his jaw to control it. "That is not a failsafe method…it only takes a slip of two seconds and you are pregnant."

"Do not tell me you did not enjoy it…"

He laughed without sound, his eyes shut. "I may be a hypocrite but I am not a liar."

"When you are well…" she uttered in a silky tone, "I shall remind you that you said that."

"I would advise against it. I am not presently myself," he replied in a similar sort of cadence.

She lay next to him and heard him breathing deeply, exhausted and sated. Sometime later he awoke and looked at her, remembering what had transpired, his eyes full of trepidation. Her own eyes were waiting for him. "It is not as if you have not already taken my virginity…" she whispered.

"No, but you do not even have my ring on your finger…or the assurance of an announcement."

"What a boring old fogey you are becoming!" She placed her hand on his stomach and his hand on her thigh. "Not at all what a *jezebel* like me requires in the least."

He ignored the remark, "In fact…" He became alert and pushed her away so that he could struggle to sit up. "You must wear this one for now…" He began to take off the small garnet signet ring he wore on his little finger.

"I cannot take your ring, 'tis yours and you always wear it."

He took her left hand and her wedding finger. "All the better! You can return it when you have a betrothal ring…" He manoeuvred it over her knuckle with some difficulty until it fitted. They looked at it together.

"I like it," she said happily, "'tis resonant of you… I will be aware of you as I see it, even when we are apart!"

* * *

The next morning, she went with Melanie to the doctor where Melanie was to have an examination to see if she was increasing as normal. She was very anxious and not her usual confidant self-and Melissa had to calm her as they waited for the doctor to return from someone else's premature birth procedure. She entertained her by regaling her with the events of the past few days. Telling her sadly of Polly's imminent departure with Dominic McCarthy.

"'tis quite an interesting paradox…" Melanie commented. "Polly and Atilla's colleague. Like to one of Shakespear's comedies. The mistress and the maid! Your house is becoming an enchanted garden for romance… Gregory and Millicent…you and Atilla…and then Polly and Dominic McCarthy!"

"Strictly speaking, Polly and Dominic met in the park at the bandstand months ago…" Melissa pointed out, leafing through a journal on maternity wear.

"I hope he is more fun than Atilla. Certainly less didactic and tyrannical…though he is in the teaching profession too so 'tis doubtful…"

"But they are both fond of a good time…" Melissa said. "When not in that damned school. Dominic is Irish and they are less prone to being starchy…" She fell again to worrying over her fiancé's health and Melanie dismissed it, to ease the concern, but also because she knew instinctively of Fairchild's core strength—it was akin to her own; it would take more than some fever to see him off at barely thirty. "'twill be good for him," she pronounced. "Being so much at the mercy of others…and especially yours in the bedroom!"

They began giggling, so that the female clerk who managed the waiting room looked over at them curiously, accustomed to all kinds of hysteria from expectant females. "…and his illness is not the only thing to occur in the bedroom… I took your advice and followed it to the letter…" Melissa whispered. Then she described the seduction. "God, it was so enjoyable!" she declared. "Taking him by surprise on the bed and having my way with him."

"Such a little strumpet you are these days!" claimed Melanie in her musically trite tone used for reprising satire.

"That is what he more or less said...he called me a jezebel..." Melissa proclaimed with pride. "But I do not want him to stay in this state for much longer...'tis not the way I want things to be."

"Of course you do not," rejoined Melanie. "Because you actually like his controlling ways..."

"You phrase it wrongly..." She smiled covetously, "Though perhaps I like him to be as strong as he usually is in all ways."

"I'll wager you do... It has always been the case, though you have denied it," Melanie said, her nerves much lessened. Then the doctor arrived and she was examined and eventually pronounced to be quite well, and told to stop wearing any kind of corset and to cease riding. She loved riding and was desolate. "Geoffrey will be gratified. He is telling me to give up riding now too," she opined once they were in the open air.

"I should think he is! What a foolish pursuit for a woman in your condition," chided Melissa.

They went to their favourite tea shop but could only spend minimum time as it was now well past lunch and they had been so long in the doctor's surgery.

"I have to get back to see how he is. I simply cannot bear him to be in the bed alone with no-one to comfort him," Melissa lamented, her cup poised at her mouth to hide her amusement.

Melanie's high-pitched laughter attracted attention as always. "I imagine you cannot...you are just hoping for the chance to seduce him again."

Melissa began giggling and put her napkin to her lips.

"You will have him in his grave before he gets you to the altar..." Melanie added.

Melissa spluttered into her napkin, already quite sodden with moisture. "I somehow think he is able enough..." she managed to say, "In the normal way of things."

"Yes, but he may never have the chance to be back to normal if you ride the life out of him now..."

Melissa was pink from the effort of restraining her mirth, and from some slight semblance of modesty, and Melanie looked satisfied, while people roundabout looked quizzical and disapproving. *What did these two young women of good society find so amusing whenever they convened for refreshment?* All the customers today were mostly elderly, so perhaps they had never seen life as amusing to begin with. Melanie pitied them. "We have only five more minutes before the carriage arrives," she warned, and helped herself to another chocolate round bun in celebration of the good news on her expectancy.

"Well, quickly tell me what I should do next..." Melissa said.

"Next?" repeated Melanie through a mouthful of cake.

"In the bedroom! How should I best pleasure him? he being so out of sorts and everything..." Melissa insisted.

Melanie swallowed the cake, dabbed her lips daintily and moved her chair nearer to Melissa's and began to speak very quietly into her ear.

* * *

Back at High Lawns, Hildegarde Wyevale had arrived, following the letter a few days ago informing her of her son's ill health. She sat in the drawing room near the expansive windows. "I have been away with my husband, you see, for three days in Gloucestershire. So, I only received the letter last night."

"That is not a problem," said Marguerite, studying her and taking in her every facet. "Your son has been well cared for here."

"I am sure...and I cannot thank you enough," said Hildegarde.

"There is no need," said Giles, adjusting the curtains so that the sun did not shine in too fiercely on them. "He is to be our son-in-law...and a fine young man he is indeed."

Mrs Wyevale smiled modestly. "'tis a good match...your daughter pleases me also. She is a splendid young woman, and vibrant of character...she will suit him."

"But they argue so much!" lamented Marguerite and re-positioned the tea tray to give herself something to do. She was somewhat overawed by Mrs Wyevale in all her fulsome glory. "Though I perceive it may be my daughter's fault...she is very headstrong..."

Hildegarde paused, holding one of the delicate meat paste sandwiches—made hastily in the kitchen on her arrival—and looked thoughtful. "It merely indicates perhaps a passionate nature."

"That is what I think," concurred Giles.

"And I tend to disagree," said his wife.

Both Giles and Hildegard looked at her and then looked quickly away again, unwilling to spoil this joyous uniting of two families before it had properly begun.

"Anthony has a strong character himself…he does not need some simpering silly girl as a wife. When I met Melissa…just the once," continued Hildegarde. "I perceived her to have humility as well as confidence…she is a very compassionate and genuine person, I think."

Marguerite felt wrong-footed. She glanced at Giles who was staring appreciatively at Mrs Wyevale.

"She may well be," said Marguerite. "She and I do not always see eye to eye…she ignores me and shows me her worst side very often."

"One always tends to be overly critical of one's children," Hildegarde said. She pronounced it 'shildren' in her slight accent. "Or else overly protective…"

"That is true," agreed Giles, again staring at Mrs Wyevale with overt fascination. He had seldom met such a charismatic and handsome woman of her years. No wonder Doctor Darnley spoke so glowingly of her. Her foreign origins adding to the appeal.

His wife looked at him sharply, sensing his thoughts, and he shifted his gaze to the windows guiltily. Mrs Wyevale stood a good three inches taller than Marguerite, had flawless skin and bounteous hair, the same texture and type as her son's. Obviously, it had been blonde like his originally but was now as white as new snow and beautifully upswept and arranged. She carried herself majestically and was a striking female whom one would not believe to be married to clergy. Marguerite felt herself to be dowdy by comparison, even though Mrs Wyevale's clothes were not of the highest fashion and were unadorned by any frills or jewels. An elegant but plain dresser.

Hildegarde sensed Marguerite's unease and went on urbanely. "It is just the same as being told one should not have favourites! One cannot help it, I think."

"Oh indeed…" enthused Marguerite despite herself, relieved to hear someone be so honest on the subject. "I strive very hard not to favour my second born son, Edmund…he is everything I find satisfying as a mother, and my eldest is my second favourite…"

Giles coughed and shifted in the chair; his wife was airing too much of her feelings on first meeting for his liking. "Perhaps Anthony is your favourite?" Marguerite persevered with a provocative smile and Hildegarde became a little coy, a demeanour which was suddenly incongruous amid her obvious social confidence. "Perhaps equally with Rupert, my first born!" she said with diffidence. "But Richard, my middle son…he is not to be countenanced on some occasions. I do not know how I tolerate his goings on…" She turned down her mouth in disdain and closed her eyes in what Marguerite considered to be a very *foreign* manner; dramatically expressive and almost theatrical. "Although Anthony will endeavour to keep him away from you, do not fear…for he cannot abide him. They cannot abide each other, if the truth is to be told."

Marguerite was now enthralled and her initial resentment dissolving. "Really! Why is that?"

"Jealousy!" said Hildegarde shortly. "Richard was horrid to Tony from the minute Tony could crawl…he was cruel to him and Joseph, their father, he—" she stopped abruptly, realising as Giles had that too much was being said on too short an acquaintance.

"The poor boy!" said Marguerite sympathetically to encourage further disclosure.

Hildegarde shook her head with its enviable hair and curved her lips downwards again for a moment or two. "Indeed, Tony has known quite a lot of cruelty in his younger life," she continued in a lighter but solemn tone, "…one of his uncles from his father's side treated him brutally, when no-one was around to intervene…again from jealousy! Although he treated all his nephews badly too…but not as badly as he treated Tony…" Mrs Wyevale paused and seemed to emerge quickly from a dark moment of reverie.

Marguerite was rapt. "Oh dear…" she lamented, like someone listening to a recital. Giles cleared his throat tactfully—the family skeletons should remain silent for now—but his wife ignored him. "What a dreadful thing for you to have to bear…"

Mrs Wyvale went on in an uplifted voice. "'tis, I believe, why Anthony has taken up with this Foundation he belongs to…to campaign against the badly run educational establishments of the lower kind…"

"Yes, I see!" said Marguerite in reverent mode of deliberation. "Much to his credit."

Giles murmured ascent in an undertone but did not comment.

"So, sometimes good comes of these tragedies…" intoned Hildegarde in the soft voice she might use to pray communally in church, as she thought of Charles Fairchild.

"Indeed…" concurred Giles, wishing they could talk of the weather.

"But please do not tell him I have told you of this…" Hildegarde entreated. "He would not like it. He does not like pity or sentiment of that kind…he is stoical in all senses."

"Of course not," said Giles. "We will forget we have heard it." He glared at his wife to stop her prolonged morbid fascination with the subject. But Marguerite was entranced now by the topic of children and favourites and family jealousies, and wanted yet more verbal stimulus; it was refreshing to have enlivening conversation in the afternoon before anyone had touched even a drop of strong drink. "Giles holds Melissa as his favourite…'tis plain, but he will not admit it." She looked at her husband challengingly.

"She is my only daughter," he confessed, "So I do have a soft spot for her."

"You see!" declared Marguerite triumphantly. "He knows it… That is why he has spoiled her."

"I have not spoiled her, Maggie…" said Giles in growing annoyance. "I have afforded her more lenience than the boys perhaps…"

"That is what I am saying," interjected Marguerite, her tone exaggeratedly pragmatic, honed over many years of wifedom. "You simply dress it up another way."

Then Hildegarde laughed in a beguiling manner; soon there would be the understated and classic dispute common in wedlock which she had heard too frequently as a clergyman's wife not to recognise the signs. "I can honestly tell you, Mrs Shaw, that I may have many faults but spoiling my children has not been one of them. I have never spoiled any of them…" she dropped her voice mischievously. "Not even my favourites!"

Marguerite was delighted by this and laughed with her. The ice was now broken. "You must call me by my first name, Marguerite! And I can see that you have not spoiled Anthony…his manners and conduct are exemplary."

Hildegarde inclined her head graciously; as women and mothers-in-law they must see eye to eye whenever possible. "Melissa does not appear spoiled to me!" she claimed diplomatically, appeasing both of them she hoped, so that the conversation continued in similar harmonious vein while Mrs Wyevale enjoyed her tea and sandwiches and intermittently admired her surroundings: the gardens and the mansion; sating Marguerite's vanity in subtle ways.

When Melissa arrived, she noticed the stately looking carriage with the fancy insignia which she did not understand. It was standing at the front steps with its coachmen hanging about talking with the younger groom. She hurried into the house and spoke with the butler. "Jarvis, whose is that coach outside?"

"A Mrs Wyevale's, Miss," said Jarvis. "Mr Fairchild's mother, I believe!"

She bounded up the stairs and entered his bedroom without preamble. He was dozing, emitting slight snores every few seconds, which amused her. She had heard that all men snored, and some women, but certainly all men. And she did not want to be married to one who was not normal in that sense. She kissed him gently on the forehead and he opened his eyes. "Your mother is here…" she told him.

"My mother?" he repeated in a bewildered way, coming around from several worlds in which he floated during the last days, due he thought to Doctor Darnley's tincture.

"Yes…you know, the lady who birthed you!" She giggled and sat down next to him on the bed. "'tis a dreadful shame, because I had planned to give you more pleasure while everyone was lounging or otherwise engaged."

He half smiled and half groaned. How much pleasure could a man in his state of health take? "'tis perhaps as well then…" he muttered.

She looked immediately offended and he took her hand. "We cannot indulge in these frivolities in your father's house, while I pretend to be ill and you take chances with your fertility…"

"I do not see why not!"

"Melissa, I am a man of my word… I have promised your father not to take your honour before we are wed."

"Too late for that!"

"Perhaps, but we do not need to over-egg the pudding."

"Over-egg the pudding! Am I a confectionery enjoyment now as well as a wife-to-be?"

"You are indeed an enjoyment!" he replied in a deep husky voice.

She was exultant. He clearly found her irresistible and desired more of her. The omens boded well for their union. "You are freshly bathed, I perceive, and shaved… I will fetch your mother imminently."

"I will dress and come down."

"No, you are not to get up until Doctor Darnley has been later," she commanded. "I forbid it."

He sank back against the pillows. "Oh, do you! I expect you are enjoying your little foray into power and control," he said softly. "And well you might…for I will be back to myself in no time." He paused for her retort and when it did not come, he looked at her. She was waiting for him, her eyes full of unfathomable lights. "Of course you will, my love…" she purred in a tone he could not properly read. "I am not ignorant of the fact."

He thought about it for several minutes after she had left the room: what she might mean and how much of it was innocent of any undertone. He could not tell. Just thinking about it tired him out and he drifted to sleep again.

She went downstairs on light feet and paused outside the drawing room door, which was slightly ajar, to listen how the conversation was going.

"…and we could hold the wedding breakfast and the celebration here," her mother was saying. "Our ballroom will be completely refurbished by the month end…"

"Yes, that would be splendid," replied her future mother-in-law.

There was a little pause and then her father enquired. "I suppose your husband, the bishop, would like to perform the ceremony?"

Hildegarde cleared her throat softly and said, "He might, but I suspect Tony may want Ruper to officiate. Rupert is a vicar as you may know…he and Tony are very close as brothers…but of course, he will need to discuss it with Melissa."

Melissa entered the room and Hildegarde rose and met her half way across the floor, taking her hands and kissing her cheeks in the continental style. "Melissa! How are you, my dear? I am truly delighted by the news…of your wedding that is, not of Tony's illness!"

They smiled together and Marguerite could see that they would get along better than she herself got along with her daughter.

"He is almost better now, but weak still…" she told his mother. "He's been working too excessively hard."

"He always has…" said Hildegarde with some pride and a little remorse.

"Nothing wrong with that…" remarked Giles calmly, hunting about for his pipe.

"There is if it kills him, Papa…" She looked at her father with spirit. "I have told the same to that Stevenson man when he called yesterday." The satisfaction she gleaned from referring to the head of Barton Grange in such a way—who in their day had been merely deputy—was unparalleled.

"I do not think you should have done that!" Giles claimed. "'tis for Anthony to speak for himself."

"He cannot though, Papa…he is too weakened. We should always speak up in defence of those we care for at times of need," she told him. "'tis our moral duty to do so, Granny always tells me."

"Ha!" trilled Marguerite and glared at her husband as he glared back; a fierce eye battle ensued.

"Besides, the wretched man is always too busy eyeing the ladies to actually listen to what they are saying," Melissa added.

"Not this indelicate subject again!" said her mother sharply. "Please Melissa!"

"He is not changed then… Nicholas Stevenson?" queried Hildegarde, unperturbed.

"I doubt it, even though he is wed to a most beautiful and charming woman, I hear," said Melissa.

"I know her well. Louisa Stevenson and I are both involved in the orphanages committee, so we often meet," Hildegarde informed her. "I think she takes him with a pinch of salt…she knows how to manage him." And then, perceiving that she might have made a faux pas, as there was a male person present, Hildegarde pursued a different topic. "I can take Anthony home with me if you would like."

"No, no…" Melissa replied hurriedly, "He is fine here…he cannot travel yet…and he is no trouble, we have plenty of rooms and many staff. Do we not, Mama?"

"Indeed!" confirmed her mother with grace and self-satisfaction.

"Doctor Darnley is adamant he must not exert himself yet…the journey may prove too much for him." Melissa sounded already to her own ears the epitome of the caring wife.

"Benjamin Darnley!" echoed Hildegarde fondly. "What a treasure he is to the larger community!"

"He speaks well of you too," she said and was tempted to giggle but kept her face composed.

"Bless him! I remember him when he was just a young medic, newly qualified…he delivered our first son, Rupert, who came very early. My husband called on him as the nearest doctor to be found."

"He told Papa and I so himself while attending Anthony…did he not, Papa?"

"I believe he did…" agreed Giles who had dismissed the information as soon as learning it but dredged it up now in his memory to be obliging.

"He was very inexperienced in those days and quite unsure of himself," Hildegarde went on. "But since, of course, we became friends. He was the village doctor and Joseph the parish parson…our children played together…and Timothy Trimingham, whose father and grandfather employed half the district…and Charlotte, her father was the squire…but the less said about him the better…poor, dear Charlotte!"

"How wonderful for them all," said Melissa with feeling.

"Has he told you of Lottie?" queried Hildegarde, feigning nonchalance…

"A little…"

"Who is Lottie?" Marguerite intercepted.

"I will tell you of her another time, Mama…" she replied. "Come, Mrs Wyevale, I will take you to your son."

They ascended the wide staircase, Melissa leading the way. Then Hildegarde suddenly noted her hand on the banister rail and saw his ring on her third finger. She exclaimed in a small breath and Melissa paused. Hildegarde put her finger on the raised shank of the ring, a thick and embossed gold shank containing the garnet. "His ring?"

"Yes." Melissa raised it to her lips in an unconscious gesture. "Just until he can take me to a jeweller for one of my own."

"We gave him that on his coming of age, his father and I… Joseph died not long afterwards!"

"I hope you do not mind my wearing it?"

Hildegarde smiled somewhat sadly. "Not in the least…a very romantic gesture."

"I think so too…'twas his idea."

Hildegarde moved to the top stair to join her and they looked at each other in the glow of unquantifiable love for another human being shared by both; Hildegarde, she perceived, was as keen to welcome her into her family as her own father was to welcome Anthony Fairchild into his. They smiled and Hildegarde put her arms loosely around her and kissed her cheeks again.

Melissa tapped on the door of the bedroom then entered with Hildegarde who crossed to his bedside. "Darling boy, what have you been doing?"

He roused from semi-slumber with effort and pushed himself to a sitting position. "Mama…how good of you to come…"

Hildegarde looked at Melissa and raised her brows in humorous irony—she never ceased to be amazed at the way the English overstated the expected in their stiff formality. "I am your mother, Tony! Did you imagine I would stay away?" She stroked back the hair from his brow for a second and then sank into the visitor's chair.

"I shall leave you to talk," Melissa announced.

Hildegarde said a few words to him in her native tongue, which he understood easily, and they began to converse. He was one of the few people with whom she could enjoy speaking her own language. She watched her son with concern but lightened her expression as he turned to her. "I came in the bishop's carriage, in case you needed to return with me. 'tis such a comfortable conveyance…but they tell me you cannot travel until Doctor Darnley says so."

"Indeed," he replied wearily. "My life is not my own at present…nor my will…"

"That will not harm you for now," said Hildegarde.

"I suppose not…as my father and Rupert would say, it will no doubt teach me humility…"

"Yes…" agreed his mother. "For there is no doubting you have a lot of power these days…"

"Over children!" he added with levity.

"Power is power…" argued Hildegarde. "And no matter who 'tis over, if 'tis not tempered with humility it is dangerous."

"My future wife would no doubt agree with you…" he laughed, and thought of Melissa and Melanie's obsession with the subject. Hildegarde gave him a searching look. He went on before she could query the statement. "At any rate, I shall go back to my lodgings as soon as I am stronger, which will be in a day or two." He looked at the medicine bottle on the table next to the bed. It still held a little of the tincture. He had neglected to take any today, purposely, to see if he was any less drowsy. He discovered he was, marginally.

"Is it wise to go back to the lodgings until you are fully recovered?" his mother enquired.

"I have everything I need there…maid service and laundry service…meals provided."

"Home from home!" said Hildegarde succinctly. She knew he did not feel at ease in her house, the 'Bishop's Palace' as it was formally known. Though it was in reality nothing like a palace and more like a small manor house. Nor did he feel at ease with her second husband, although the bishop tried his best to make him so. Of all her sons he was the most resentful perhaps of the man who had claimed her for his wife, and he strove to disguise it by staying away. She suspected the bishop's daughter felt similarly about her. Children always imagined life revolved solely around themselves where their parents were concerned.

"I keep on falling to sleep," her youngest son informed her, bringing her from her reflections.

"The medication! Darnley is known for giving people very potent tincture to keep them sedated while they heal," she said. "He believes they heal better when they sleep."

A long silence ensued, or so it seemed; an immeasurable lapse of time as befell him now with all his visitors as he drowsed, whether it was imagined or real.

"I cannot say how pleased I am…now that she has accepted your suit…" Hildegarde was saying to him in a lightning change of subject and still in her native tongue. "…and I think we shall like each other, she and I…"

"Gratifying!" he replied.

"Her parents seem nice…particularly her father…" Hildegarde reverted once more to the English language. "Genuine…sincere and down-to-earth."

"He is indeed those things!" replied Fairchild.

"And I think Melissa takes after him in that respect…she is a level headed girl…but captivating and sweet."

He laughed softly. "I do not know about her sweetness so much…"

His mother stared at him, replacing the tiny Oriental ornament she had been examining from the small table next to the chair. "You do not find her sweet?"

"It depends how you mean it…but then I could not do with too much sweetness, it would irritate me. Sweet women are invariably too false!"

"Precisely!" said Hildegarde.

"And God knows she is crafty enough without that…"

"As women we sometimes have to be…" remarked the bishop's wife with years of experience in communities.

"If you say so, Mama."

"I do…and I hear the wedding is to be brought forwards quite considerably?"

"It is… I have sent for Rupert to come, to see about the bans and so on."

Hildegarde prevaricated a moment or two before risking the ultimate question. "She is not with child, is she?"

Mildly taken aback, he hesitated, thinking of time spans and trying to piece them together. He had lost all sense of time. "I sincerely hope not, though she could be, I suppose," he said, too tired to think of diplomatic responses.

"So, you have already…you have been…?" Hildegarde let the words trail off. Then receiving no answer went on. "Anthony, what on earth were you thinking? She is to be your wife and is still quite young…"

He fell back against the pillows and found it impossible to dissemble. "You know very well, Mama, that most men are not *thinking* at those times…their sense is not in their heads…"

Hildegarde tutted. "Not that paltry excuse…there is something called self-*control…"*

"Yes, but I am as weak as a kitten. I could do nothing about it," he claimed in his own defence.

Hildegarde laughed in an unamused way. "I suppose she overpowered you and had her wanton way with you!"

He closed his eyes and groaned; was he really having this conversation with his mother! "It was her idea… She gets these notions and will not be deterred easily… I believe she was anxious to see if…to see how suited we are in the bedroom."

"And are you? Suited?"

He grinned, not bothering to disguise it. "Indubitably."

Hildegarde decided to accept this scandalous excuse as the more palatable. "What a naughty girl…" she said facetiously.

"She is headstrong in the extreme."

Hildegarde sighed and thought of Charlotte Fitzwilliam, also headstrong in the extreme, but said nothing of it.

"Her sweetness is only a facet of the whole," he added.

His mother, having long been in service to the parish at large one way or another, was not easily shocked. She retrieved a kerchief from her reticule and daintily blew her nose to gain time, then offered. "I am sure there are many men who would be counting their blessings regarding such ardour…but does her father know of this eventuality?"

"I certainly hope not," he declared a second time.

"Servants talk, Tony, and they tend to know everything."

"Indeed…but she is often a law unto herself," he sighed.

"Are you saying she displeases you?" persevered his mother.

He contemplated the mirror on the opposite wall which gave back no reflection of anything remarkable, being placed too high up. "No, she does not displease me...she infuriates me!"

Hildegarde remained silent. Courtship was a maize, especially in the young, and she was at a loss to understand these insights. "In what way?" she asked.

"In various ways...but she will think twice once we are wed... I shall take measures to assure it..." He grinned and then tightened his jaw to conceal it.

"What do you mean precisely? I hope you will not be unkind to her," cautioned his parent.

"Of course I shall not!" He became more animated and looked at his mother with intensity. "This ridiculous fad women have for believing all men wish to ill-treat them...'tis beyond reason..."

Hildegarde heaved a long sigh. "Believe me, my dear, many men do ill-treat women."

"And I am assuredly not one of them!" he asserted.

"Then what did you mean when you said *you will take measures?*" His mother turned her light blue eyes on him and held his own for a few moments.

"Never mind..." He adjusted his pillows and rearranged his hair with his fingers. "Though she may tell you if you ask her. If I say too much, I will be hauled over the coals for being indiscreet..."

Hildegarde took her small mirror from her reticule and gazed into it, giving herself time to reflect on more than her face. "So, she is aware of some kind of intended *measures* on your part, is she? When indulging in her more *headstrong* ways?"

"She should be...she has had enough warnings."

Mrs Wyevale wondered if Darnley's potion had affected his mind and thought whether to pursue the matter. "It sounds very ominous all of this," she countered. "I hope whatever you contemplate does not repel her, or you will have a frigid wife on your hands."

He placed his arms behind his head and perused the ceiling, which he now knew very well in all its detail from lying in bed. "Whatever she may become, *frigid* is not among them...you may trust me on that!"

Another silence ensued and then his mother remarked. "You say this now...but if what you do is not to her liking, she may turn away from you."

"'tis not about her liking it..." he affirmed, unable to stop himself. "You cannot confuse enjoyment with liking..."

Hildegarde sat very still and held back her musings until she had tried penetrating the notion. "I do not pretend to understand what you are saying."

He wondered whether he had said too much, in the grip of Darnley's tincture, and he smiled generously to comfort them both. "I am saying she may *enjoy* not liking it…"

"I see." Hildegarde felt herself to be disconcerted, it was similar to a dizziness, as if she had inadvertently left her seat and was floating around the room; the ways of young people in love had passed her by in her encroaching old age. "'tis far too deep for me…this erotic rhetoric, or whatever it is…but then I was never at Oxford University!" she added caustically.

He turned to look at her to see how she meant this but it was impossible to read her expression.

"There again," he mused, "Perhaps I, in my turn, enjoy being infuriated by her while not actually liking it!"

Hildegarde assumed a vague expression amid her mixed feelings. "What a very dark and perverse train of thought we are pursuing…"

"Not in the least…'tis as old as time!" he said.

She watched her son for a while, the realisation dawning that his philandering—in the years since Lottie—had led him to avenues of life and passion that were beyond her understanding. Rupert assured her now and then, briefly and with tact, that his youngest brother did not want for female company, and was not becoming a misogynist or a monk. Therefore, it was obvious he knew how to seduce women in the right way. But now her curiosity had the better of her she thirsted for greater knowledge.

"These convoluted rituals between men and women are best left to the privacy of each marriage…" she ventured encouragingly, but no response was given. "You are at the stage where game playing is intertwined in romance…you will tire of all that once you have children…there will be other priorities."

He was not to be drawn: he made a sound of dreary resignation; this constant litany of children and grandchildren was tiresome. Nothing was further from his mind. "I have had enough of children in the last few years…" he said wearily. "I need a rest from them."

"Yes, but those were other peoples' children!" exclaimed his mother in astonishment.

"Is there a difference?" he enquired.

"Of course there is! Good heavens, Tony!"

"Are there not enough children in the family now…with Bella and Rupert's small tribe?" he entreated.

"That is the most ridiculous remark," she exclaimed hotly. "I shall not give it credence! Surely Melissa wants children?"

"I do not know," he said frankly. "But I expect it will be hard to avoid having them…if her current habits are anything to go by…" He closed his mouth abruptly, thinking he had said too much far too indelicately.

His mother now smiled to herself and examined her lace fingerless gloves. He was the physical image of her eldest brother at that age. Her brother had been a bachelor with philandering ways. Women threw themselves at him wherever he went. He had died a lonely old age—never able to make the final choice before it was too late, overwhelmed by female attention. But that was not England. Her youngest son had more of the English character than the Scandinavian, inherited from his father's ancestry; he held his intimate matters in great privacy and was self-containment itself.

She gazed on him as he seemed to doze, suffused with pride at this specimen of manhood she had managed to produce and rear. "I shall go to see your little madam and say goodbye to her," she announced.

"She will probably be in her room…three doors along to the right, lying on her bed contemplating her latest artwork…as she tells me she does at this hour," he said drowsily.

* * *

Finding the correct door, Hildegarde tapped on it and heard Melissa respond. She entered and discovered her as he had described—reclining on her bed situated opposite the south facing window and secluded behind silken brocade drapes which separated it from the rest of the room. The bedroom was exquisitely arranged: armchairs and rugs and a hearth with a tiled surround, wardrobes of oak along one wall and a small dressing table and several other ornate pieces of furniture. In her time, Hildegarde had seen—in impoverished places—families of five or six existing in spaces smaller than this whole room. "Melissa, my dear, I have come to bid you goodbye for now…" she began, with no intention yet of leaving until she had investigated more of the mystery only half told.

Melissa rose from the bed and approached her.

"What a delightful boudoir," the lady claimed, looking around her.

"Thank you for saying so," demurred her son's fiancé.

Hildegarde pretended to be absorbed by one of the wall paintings, not one of Melissa's own. Then she turned to her. "You will miss this opulence surely? For Anthony will not as yet be able to keep you in such a manner."

"I care not about that!" claimed Melissa. "We will live in a smaller house owned by my father, if Anthony likes it well enough…or reside in rooms here…and that will suffice for now."

"Splendid!" said Hildegarde.

"He will quickly make great strides in life. He is so educated and clever…and industrious!"

"Yes, he is," agreed Hildegarde and moved tentatively to sit in an armchair. "So, you are sure you wish to make this step of marrying him? You have overcome your reservations now?"

"Yes…my reservations were about being married at all…and perhaps some of his ways."

Hildegarde paused, immediately alert to the subject avoided by her son. "What do you mean by *his ways*?"

"His claim that I should obey him in everything," she responded.

Hildegarde smiled. "Men of most cultures and nationalities believe that to be their right."

"Yes, but I do not think I agree with it."

"Few of us do," said Hildegarde lightly. "And you have told him this?"

"Oh yes!"

"And what is his response?" she enquired, not looking directly at her future daughter-in-law and holding her breath somewhat.

Melissa assumed a whimsical expression which was guarded and amused all at once as she considered her words. "He believes he will prevail."

Hildegarde sat more upright in the chair and turned her translucent eyes upon her. "You obviously must know by now, Melissa, that he rarely says things he does not intend?"

"I am aware… I would not marry him otherwise…but neither do I say things I do not intend…"

"I see…" said Hildegarde, the strange disembodied floating sensation descending upon her again. "And what do you think will be the consequence of you both having these *firm intentions*?" She was unsure whether Melissa knew even what she was alluding to.

"A major battle of wills, I expect," Melissa said.

Hildegarde watched her take on a sultry and hungry look. Her intelligent grey eyes calming to an expression of lazy longing. She reminded Hildegarde of a painting she had once seen of Salome about to dance for John the Baptist. "As long as you know that a man's will is not just a question of his mind…they usually have greater physical strength than we do…" she said, in what she hoped was not a patronising tone.

"I am aware of that too!" claimed Melissa, assuming a cat-like stare of neutral and vague satisfaction.

"So, you are aware that his annoyance over your…your more headstrong ways may result in consequences that might be…"

"Might be what?" she enquired sharply.

"Distressing…or discomforting," affirmed Hildegarde with delicacy.

Melissa gazed at his mother with a face of innocent yet sensory awareness. Mrs Wyevale was sounding like Melanie on the subject, or Trimingham before the rose garden incident. She frowned and lost her hungry look as her gaze roamed the far wall for inspiration. Then she recalled her father's entreaty of last week about husbands claiming authority over wives. Mrs Wyevale was obviously possessed of similar doubts and reservations about their union. They may even have conferred on the matter together in the drawing room prior to her arrival earlier.

She smiled a more open smile, but still one of guileful and arcane knowing, as she looked directly at her potential mother-in-law. "You need not be afraid for me…he will not harm me."

"No, of course he will not." Hildegarde was appalled at the notion, and annoyingly out of her depth. "Although the concept of harm differs from person to person…" She paused and waited, in vain, for more detail. "I mean, it depends what measures he may adopt to…to make you less headstrong, shall we say…"

"I could not possibly talk about it," stated Melissa, in much the same way as she had said it to her father.

Hildegarde perceived she was no more to be drawn on the subject than her son, so she gave up the project as hopelessly entangled with too many imponderables and rose and moved to Melissa and kissed her on both cheeks, before moving to the door and lightening her voice. "As long as you are somehow in agreement about the limits of your disagreements, I am sure all will be well."

"I am certain all will be well!" Melissa said with what Mrs Wyevale considered to be charming naivete. "I think I shall make him happy."

Mrs Wyevale paused; there was more to life than being happy—happiness was a very temporary state usually, but she did not wish to dampen any illusions at this point. "When he is up and about once more, you must come to us for dinner… William is eager to meet you."

"William?" echoed Melissa.

"My husband," clarified Mrs Wyevale.

"Oh yes…certainly! The bishop."

Mrs Wyevale laughed and put on her bonnet, which was tiny and allowed her plentiful hair to remain undisturbed. "He is indeed a bishop, but first and foremost he is my husband…and Tony's stepfather," she said. "That is really all I care about."

Melissa perceived that she was telling her she did not put much store by hierarchy or position or religious prestige. Her values were more personal and more human and the rest was dressing. Melissa gleaned it instinctively; her own were the same. She smiled broadly at Hildegarde and Hildegarde inclined her head, her eyes conveying the message that they understood each other.

Hildegarde left the room and went in search of her coachmen, who were no doubt below stairs drinking tea in the kitchen and having dalliance with the younger maids, as was their wont given half a chance, and one of the perks of the job. She asked the butler to fetch them and then sat in the copious hall chair.

Later that night, she would enjoy reprising today's beguiling conversations for her husband, the bishop—a broad minded and worldly man with whom she might discuss anything under the sun. It was the cement of their second marriages: their shared thoughts and curiosity about people and life. Apart from being a man of the cloth, he was a skilful and imaginative lover, even in his later years, and she was a passionate woman herself.

The Levelling

When Polly left the next day, Melissa felt her world to be changing before her eyes. Polly had served her and been her friend since they were thirteen or fourteen.

Dominic McCarthy came to collect her early after breakfast to take her to the ferry bound for Ireland. Her one meagre trunk was waiting to be collected and Polly was arrayed in the dress Melissa had given her as a parting gift. A dress she had worn only once herself but that she wished to see Polly wear. It was more her colour.

McCarthy put his head around Fairchild's door—he was up and sitting in a chair, dozing, a book discarded on the floor beside him. McCarthy gave a piercing whistle and he came to life, startled. McCarthy grinned and stepped a little way into the room. "I hate farewells when they are final…" he said.

"As do I!" Fairchild said…

"I have just come to bid you goodbye and to wish you well."

"Yes…to you also." He attempted to stand and McCarthy put up a hand. "Do not get up on my account, Tony… I much prefer you do not…"

"Where is your fiancée?" queried Fairchild.

"With yours in her bedchamber…they are weeping, I fear."

"You should prise them apart now, Dominic, or you will be late for the crossing… God go with you!" He thought of Lottie sailing from Ireland and into disaster, and he looked pained for moments as he tried banishing the visions.

McCarthy made a comical formal salute of some sort in his entertaining manner. "A pleasure having your friendship and a privilege serving with you, Anthony!" he said, and before Fairchild could form a response, he had left and closed the door.

"I shall never forget my time here…" Polly was saying to Melissa as they stood in Melissa's bedroom for the last time.

Melissa took Polly's hand. "Will you write to me once you are wed? Will you tell me about the wedding so I may envision it?"

"I shall for sure…"

Melissa attempted several replies but did not voice them, her lips parting and then closing. "We may never meet again, Polly…"

Polly looked dismayed. "I was hoping you would come over to see us…after all, Dominic and your fiancé are good friends."

"Yes but," Melissa held back her tears, "'tis a long way and we may not make that journey for many a year…and perhaps never." She thought of Lottie dying on the way home from Ireland and he not wishing to be reminded of it in a sea voyage, but she did not allude to it. Why sour their happy voyage with frightening memories.

"Yes, you are right! Life takes people on separate journeys, and with the best of intentions people lose contact," cried Polly in a deflated manner and blinded by tears.

"No, no, we shall always write. Send me your address when you write to me after the wedding, tell me exactly what you wore," said Melissa.

Polly brightened a little. "Dominic says we may even have one of those new daguerreotypes they have now…which capture your likeness. Perhaps I can send you one!"

"I would adore that! And I shall send you one of those too, when we are wed."

"Yes, for you will wed soon, no doubt."

Melissa sighed. "My father wants the marriage brought forwards and imminent. He fears…he thinks…well, never mind."

"I know what he fears," Polly said and looked at the diamond ring she had now placed on her third finger. "I heard him talking with your mother when I was outside their bedroom. He is an astute man, your father…" She became diffident. "He has a strong idea of what has taken place…'tis a risk, is it not?"

"I believe it might be…" Melissa flushed and looked at her hands. "But I also believe we were careful."

"There is no perfect safeguard," Polly said. "Whatever you do…"

Melissa gazed back at her earnestly for a few seconds and then began to giggle. It was a little like being with Melanie in the tea shop or other places of tete-a-tete. Polly giggled too; life was nothing if not an exciting gamble. Then there was a knock on the door. The new maid entered. "Begging your pardons…but your bridegroom is asking that you come down now. You are making yourselves very late for the ferry crossing."

Polly stood and Melissa followed her, and they went along the corridor to the staircase. "I had just better say goodbye to your man!" said Polly.

Melissa knocked on his door and then entered and Polly stepped into the room a little way. "Goodbye, Mr Fairchild," she said. "May things go well with you!"

He was much stronger—thinner and paler—but certainly stronger. "And to you Mrs McCarthy," he replied in his usual calm and level voice. "My greatest felicitations to you both."

Polly laughed at the use of her new name and Melissa said: "'tis bad luck to use her married name before she is wed."

"Only if you believe in such superstitions!" he replied.

"And I do not myself!" affirmed Polly.

Overcome by sadness and other mixed fears and feelings Melissa waved to Polly from an upstairs window until the carriage took them down the driveway and from sight. Then she retired to her bed to weep and recuperate and finally fell into a doze.

* * *

She rose immediately upon waking and went to look in on him. He was sleeping again, sitting in the chair, emitting the little snoring sounds, some of which were more like small groans from deep in his throat. He awoke and peered at her as she moved silently about the room, then he saw she had been crying. "Melissa, what ails you now?"

She turned away. "'tis nothing…"

"Then why are you looking as if the world is about to end? Is it about us?"

"No, 'tis not about us…" She turned and went over to him and knelt beside the chair. "'tis because Polly is gone."

He breathed in deeply and put his head back against the chair. He was wearing a borrowed woollen robe from her father over the linen nightshirt. In other circumstances, he would have entertained her in this unstylish garb. "People must move away sometimes…" he said softly. "They come and they go… Dominic is offering her an opportunity she might never have again…and they are in love."

571

"I know, but Polly has been a good friend to me. We were children when we met."

He took her hand and held it. He smiled at her, a different smile than the one she was used to prior to his collapse. It was as if they were getting to know each other anew. She saw him quite differently now so she sought familiar things in him that would give her reassurance. "Were you not sad to see Dominic leave?"

He cleared his throat and remained silent for an age. "Yes, very reluctant to lose him as a friend," he claimed at length. "But 'tis perhaps not the same for men."

"Why not?"

"I cannot answer that, for I do not rightly understand what women share in friendship. I know only that they feel differently than men."

She began wiping her eyes swiftly with the back of her hand. "Imagine if it were Trim," she said, and he laughed quietly. "Or Flossie, your horse."

"Now that I can make comparison with."

"That is quite shocking." She stared at him and he looked at her without qualm. "Or perhaps not, for the horse serves you unquestioningly and obeys your every command," she said. "Unlike me."

"Most of the time, but if I urge her to do something she dislikes she rebels and refuses…"

"Just like me then!"

"Let us not get onto this subject at this precise moment. I recall that was the problem the night I collapsed."

"But I perceive you have already broached it with your mother." She watched him from her side vision.

"Have I?"

"I believe so, from the intimations she was making about your strong will… I thought you had told her of your *preferred method.*"

"You mean your preferred method?" he amended.

"No, yours! You only say 'tis mine to suit your purposes. Did you tell her of it?"

He became whimsical. "I was rambling a lot as a result of Darnley's medicine…and you know how mothers are!" He had voiced his thoughts out loud yesterday with his mother, he realised, but he could not recall the whole. "I do not think I have told her of it," he concluded at length, "Though I might have said something along those lines."

She changed the subject before it could become quarrelsome. "They want us to talk about the wedding arrangements…my parents."

"I have sent for Rupert…he will arrange the bans for us."

"I do not mind about all that…'tis the whole fuss I fear."

"Then we will say we do not want a fuss."

She watched him forlornly. She did not know this man she was marrying—not now that the former version of him was evaporating in certain ways—no more than he knew her. Not in truth. They knew only their desire for one another, and their limitations and weaknesses, and those things were not the full truth of them both; her stomach churned. "But our parents…they will be so disappointed if we do not have a large wedding."

"Well, perhaps we can have a large church gathering and a small celebration afterwards?"

She felt unsure.

"Or a small church gathering and a large celebration?" He raised his brows and nodded emphatically so she would know he was only partly serious.

"Why can we not elope?" she asked.

"Because people only do that when they are ashamed or not approved of and we are most definitely approved of."

"Yes…" she agreed. She thought of Melanie and how she had enjoyed her wedding and all the attendant fuss. "You are right."

He stood and walked around the carpet to test his strength and increase it by exercise, a little unsteadily but gaining in certainty at every step.

"Anthony, you must not overdo things…?" she counselled. "You were very weak. In fact, I feared…" she faltered and could not finish, and he finished for her. "… I might turn up my toes?"

"Yes, and then it would have been my fault."

"Your fault? You poisoned the brandy or some such?" he jested.

"No, but I caused you worry and…extra strain…not agreeing to the wedding and being evasive…and…"

"Yes, yes." He waved his hand dismissively. "The list of your shortcomings is endless…but I shall cure you of those soon enough…and that is what I perhaps told my mother."

She turned to stare at him, her lips compressed and her impatience under control. "I trust that is the medication talking? Or your dark sarcasm, as usual!"

His eyes were quite humorous but his gaze on her unwavering. She sighed and looked away, her qualms resurfacing.

His turn to change the subject rapidly. "I shall be well enough to travel in a few days according to Darnley."

She moved over the room to him and he pulled her into his arms. "We need to discuss a honeymoon too," he said.

"Yes…think of all the things we have not yet done together! We have never strolled in the park or danced or ridden in a carriage through town…or taken refreshment in the tea shop…"

"I think we have ridden," he murmured. "Just the other day if I recall rightly…" It took her a few seconds to see the covert meaning of the remark, then she began to giggle.

"Disregard that comment…'twas vulgar of me."

Her giggling subsided slowly, like the kettle when it had been taken from the heat. "But I love it when you are vulgar."

"I am never vulgar with females…and certainly not with you."

"That is why it makes an interesting change…"

He ignored this, wishing his previous comment to be forgotten totally. Darnley's medication was a double-edged sword. "We shall do all the things you mention, Melissa. There is time for it all…"

"But you know I do not wish to mix much in society…" she ventured.

"I have heard you mention it, yes."

"And it will not bother you?"

"No…"

"But you will need an escort by your side…at formal dinners and so forth…"

He deliberated. "This is true…perhaps I could take one of my mistresses in your place!"

She gasped and walked across the room, creating space between them, and stared at him with horror.

"I am teasing you," he said. "I do not have any mistresses. How many times do I need to say that!"

Her expression showed mistrust; it would be a while before she believed this, he saw, if ever.

"But you might…in time…take mistresses."

"Might I? Why?"

"Because…because you may become tired of me…or dissatisfied."

"Well, I might…but I could say the same to you!"

She had no real answer and he jumped into the silence. "This dislike you have of society may change… I have heard it said before, from people who then saw what they were missing and were never out of society."

"And how can you know that will be me?"

"I cannot, for sure…but for every action there is an opposite and equal reaction."

"Is there?" She stared now at the window and contemplated on what she would be like as a socialite. "How do you know?"

"'tis a natural law of the universe!" He turned away to denote that he had said all he could. "And betimes, there is the honeymoon to discuss… We could go to Denmark if you wished. Or Norway…but you may not like the sea voyage."

"I should not like it," she said, thinking the same things as with Polly's suggestion of visiting; the memories might be too much for him and therefore ruin their honeymoon. "I am seasick in a rowing boat on the lake here…and I have only ever once seen the ocean."

"In truth?" he asked, surprised.

"When I was much younger and we went to visit one of my father's sisters in Brighton. Have you seen the ocean?"

"I have! In England and in Scandinavia."

"You have been to Scandinavia?" She pulled back to look at him, her eyes widening.

"With Rupert and my mother. Before Rupert attained his parish and had children and was besieged by responsibilities…we took her after the death of our father to visit her relatives and distract her from the grief."

"I have hardly ever been away from High Lawns," she admitted. "And really I have never much wanted to be."

"But you are the granddaughter of a Spanish sea captain and you have seafaring blood in your veins."

"He was not a captain…he was a first lieutenant…and your ancestry is Nordic and they are even more seafaring."

"So, we should neither of us fear a sea voyage," he fleetingly thought of Lottie's death and ploughed on to dispel it. "But perhaps we should go to France…dock at Diepe or Callais…a relatively short trip."

"Or we could just take a train to the coast. I should like that immensely. I have not been on one of those either…" She turned to look into his face. It was unreadable, she did not know whether from indifference, weariness, illness or something else. "But I could not be too long away from my easel…"

"Surely you could take a sketch pad?"

"I am at one with my art room…"

"It will be our honeymoon and I do not intend to compete with your easel for your attention."

"Because the easel might win…"

"Do you imagine I will allow that to happen?"

She sighed. "The list of what you will and will not allow is endless…you must modify your expectations of me, I fear."

He moved his fathomless green eyes to her own. "Only in some respects, Melissa…not in others."

The former version of him glimmered a little in the background—the idea of whether it was welcome tantalised her. His silent thoughts were a vast glade of unknowable revelation which made demands on her senses, so that her body was an orchestration of inner music. "Or, of course," she offered, "We could just move into our new modest house and spend the time in a comfortable bed…"

He thought of years to come in the comfortable bed; he would get little done. And if they had the consequential family, he would get even less done. Unless he and Trim made a huge success of the new venture and he could afford many servants. He searched about for his cigars, her hand still in his, then remembered he was not supposed to smoke in the bedroom. He kissed her hair and she moved in as close to him as possible, moulding her body into his, so that his arousal began immediately.

"Polly's full name is Paulette, you know," she said, to ground proceedings. "Her mother was French…they shortened it to Polly in the orphanage. The nuns said it was more fitting."

"Yes, I believe Dominic mentioned it…"

"That name will be more fitting if he inherits his ancestral title… Lady Paulette McCarthy…though I think she will always prefer to be called Polly." Her tears were drying. "I will think of them on their voyage and wish them God speed. The sea is a perilous place."

Lottie was immediately before his eyes again and she felt him tense. She knew he would often think of her for as long as he lived. And she knew too that it would not matter: the dead having a place of their own in the heart where they resided forever, enshrined in a different space.

The clock chimed into the minutes of the mid-afternoon. The dogs barked beneath the window and the footmen laughed as they carried sundry items along the landing to and from sundry places. Time moved on beyond the room and stood still within it.

"We should fear nothing, you and I…" she told him eventually. "For we are both very resolute and clear in our convictions…somewhat self-indulgent, both of us…we are two of a kind."

He sat in the chair, much amused, and then pulled her onto his lap. And wondered if she was right.

"I think I might like to visit London…" she told him. "I expect you have done so."

"Many times…"

"Is it nice?"

"In parts 'tis very grand and impressive…but also 'tis dirty and squalid and distressing."

"That is also what my brothers tell me."

"But as an artist you should see it at least once…so perhaps that is what we shall do if you wish, for one or two nights…and then we can go on from there to Kent and the coast…we can take a train for part of the journey."

"Yes, that is what I think I should like best…we can travel farther in the future perhaps."

They gazed together at the low fire and she wondered whether time changed people, and whether time altered the attraction between them. Or whether—when the bond was close and ephemeral—time was actually irrelevant.

* * *

She needed now to get on with her painting, having been delayed by several days, and she went after lunch the next day straight to the art room. She had been painting for not more than five minutes when there was a tapping at the window behind her. She turned to see her aunt Amaelia beckoning to her. She went across and pushed at the lower sash. It would not budge more than a couple of inches in its ageing frame. Her aunt began mouthing something to avoid raising her voice. "Come outside…" Amaelia was saying and began pointing to her right and the vicinity of the drawing room doors. Then she made off quickly before Melissa could argue.

Aunt Amaelia was petite, like Jemima, and very slight in figure, with pointed features and eyes black as midnight like her father's, and dark hair streaked now with silver. She looked more Spanish than English. She had inherited her mother's forthright character and direct manner and her father's warmth and generosity. And the passionate natures of both.

She wore floating blouses adorned with exquisitely embroidered and colourful shawls, and large picture hats which enhanced her piquant face and kept her olive complexion from becoming too swarthy in the summer. She held onto her hat with one hand in the breezy weather of the day and guided Melissa forcefully with the other along the path of the rose garden. A small brocade reticule hung from her arm.

"Where are we going, Aunt?" Melissa was hurrying to keep pace with Amaelia who moved rapidly, loping along at a gazelle-like pace, when not taking her dainty feminine steps and being observed.

"Somewhere private, where we may speak alone…the small summer house perhaps… I am requested by your father to speak with you, in the absence of your mother's intervention, which I believe you do not wish…"

"Indeed, I do not!" confirmed Melissa. "She understands nothing of the reality of love at all…"

"Yes, that is somewhat true…" agreed Amaelia cattily, not being over fond of her sister-in-law. "But even so, she is your mama…and we do not wish her to be offended by my visit."

Once in the summer house Melissa sat on the wooden seating running around the sides and back of the structure and thought of what would have happened in here had Trimingham not intervened for her that day. Amaelia closed the door, even though the weather was warm.

She looked at her aunt who was arranging her skirt beneath her and removing her hat so that she could turn more comfortably to see her niece. "Whatever is the matter?" Melissa asked.

"Your beau! This rather attractive and irresistible male personage whose heart you seem to have captured…" her aunt began.

"What of him?" she said, suspicion in her eyes.

"You need not look like that, my dear! One may admire clothes in a shop window even if one knows they are unsuitable," said Amaelia, taking out her slim cigarettes, similar to the ones Melanie smoked. "He is the son of a bishop, I hear."

"Yes, and now the step-son of another bishop!"

"Good heavens!" said Amaelia with a match to the cigarette. "Imagine if the stepfather becomes the Archbishop of Canterbury!"

Melissa tossed back her loosened hair. "'twould be like Anthony becoming the minister of the Education Board in England…or even the head of Barton Grange Academy…the power is unthinkable."

Amaelia exhaled smoke. "I think the Archbishop of Canterbury takes precedence over the head of Barton Grange Academy, my dear!"

"Well, good… I was simply making a comparison."

"'tis this question of power we need to discuss," mused Amaelia, "Leaving aside the fanciful imaginings."

Melissa frowned. "Anyway, he is leaving education to go into business…" she remarked, hoping to derail the subject. "And not before time."

Amaelia ignored this. "Your father is worried about the ambivalence you seem to show towards him."

"Ambivalence?" she repeated. "What ambivalence?"

Amaelia made twirling motions between her thumb and index finger as she pondered. Her plentiful rings clinking gently against one another on her left hand. "Lissy, in one breath you say you adore him and cannot live without him, then in the next you talk of your reluctance to his having authority over you and adhering to him…do I have this right?" She paused with the greatest diplomacy and tilted her chin upwards towards her niece who was a head taller than herself, and waited—to no avail—for confirmation.

"Your papa thinks you may speak to me more easily…but naturally he does not wish your mother to know I have interfered, hence the secrecy…and here I am…" Amaelia tailed off and wondered if she were on a fool's errand. Perhaps Giles had completely mistaken the situation, in a male way. "Your roses are beautiful this year, are they not?" she offered, to break the silence.

"They are!" Melissa said and began to hum to herself as she adjusted the smock-like garment she wore, at which Amaelia looked askance from her side vision. "Ours are pale and dreary by comparison…" extemporised her aunt, impatient by nature: this could take all afternoon. "Melissa, tell me the meaning of all the shrieking and arguing that day in the rose garden, which everyone heard…what was he threatening?"

Melissa sagged on the bench; her feet stretched out before her. "He was bringing me here…but I can say no more…"

"For what purpose was he bringing you here?"

"To triumph over me, of course!" she said unhelpfully, "To prove his power."

"In what way triumph?" snapped her aunt. "Which power?"

Melissa played with the pearl pendant he had given her and remained silent, so Amaelia added philosophical pearls of her own. "Many men want power, Melissa…some covertly and some more overtly. Much depends on how they use it. What is it about his *power* you do not like? Tell me now… I promise to be discreet… I will say nothing to your father…unless what I hear is simply dreadful, of course…"

Melissa was on the very edge of her own dilemma and about to fall through to the next level of the game and expose convoluted parts of herself, were she not careful. She remained mute.

"You have no need to be coy with me…you must know by now that I have a notorious reputation for romantic dalliance," her aunt was saying quite proudly. "You will not shock me whatever it is."

"'twas nothing…"

"If 'twas nothing why did his friend Trimingham feel the need to save you?" Amaelia played her ace with a vocal flourish and looked up at the sky through the windows of the summer house.

"Because…because Trim is a different temperament…he is more…more tolerant of shortcomings," she replied.

They were getting nowhere; Melissa would take them around in circles; she was cunning itself where prevarication was concerned. Amaelia shuffled about on the bench and made sounds of exasperation. "That is by the by, and you know it…we are not talking of Trimingham…what were Fairchild's intentions that day?"

"He gave me a warning which I ignored."

"Warning of what?"

"Not to make insulting remarks to him…" Melissa said tentatively, and then watched from beneath her lashes as her aunt sighed and rolled her eyes and showed utter dismay. "Why would you do such a thing to a perfectly suitable beau? How vulgar! I wonder he is still in your vicinity!"

Melissa's prevarication deepened, like a complicated crochet pattern on the third line, but she plunged on with indifference. "He lectures me on my behaviour…and it incenses me."

"Well, having tea hurled upon him by your bosom friend may not have improved his opinion of matters…"

"That was an accident!" declared Melissa for perhaps the twentieth time.

"Of course it was not an accident…" Amaelia rejoined in the kind of voice she might use to a trying child. "Do you imagine we were all born yesterday? And not content with that you then hurl insults at him! I wonder he did not take to the hills."

"The only reason he did not was because he would not see himself defeated…" her niece said in a rush, quoting one of the opinions delivered by Melanie.

Amaelia turned her face slowly for effect and raised her brows and levelled her gaze. "No! I suspect the reason he did not is because he has some genuine feelings for you."

The atmosphere in the summer house was warm from the outside heat and redolent of other more indefinable qualities. Melissa let out a sighing breath and emitted light sounds from high in her throat. Soothed beyond words by what she had heard.

"What is it he threatens?" Amaelia said, reverting to her brisker mood of persistence as Melissa walked about the summer house, gazing through the glass of the doors to the garden. "I cannot possibly tell you…"

Amaelia took out her fan and played with it, partially opening it and then closing it with a snap. The moments rolled on and the impasse yawned like a ravine in the road. Melisssa now wore her sulky pouting expression which Amaelia remembered seeing when she was a child—aggravating everyone by not saying what was bothering her, until slowly after an inordinate length of time, the sulk would always give way like leaden winter clouds allowing admittance to the sun. She could not be cajoled out of these moods then and she would not be cajoled these days.

It was unacceptable in a young bride, of course. It was a recipe for unholy alliance. But perhaps Fairchild liked sulky pouting females; there was no accounting for varied male tastes. Perhaps shock was the best ploy. "Have you given yourself to him fully?" she demanded into the midst of this sullen obstinacy.

Melissa blushed deeply. "I do not think so…" she lied.

"You do not think so! Do you not know?" demanded her aunt.

"I... I have been very close to him and we have shared very intimate moments..."

"Have you given your virginity to him, is what I mean?"

Melissa frowned intently at the red floor tiles and decided to lie. "I think not...not from what Melanie describes to me...she gives me advice on these matters."

"I am sure she does!" retorted Amaelia in a breathless sort of voice. "Of course she is wed now to Geoffrey Gillis, I hear...so she will know! How does marriage suit her?"

"She says the bedroom is the best part of it," Melissa confided, relieved to talk of her best friend rather than herself.

"Wise girl! If one is happy in the bedroom all is well elsewhere...with the right man, of course...if 'tis the wrong man, then the bedroom can be hell!"

Melissa looked at her sharply, shaken from her sulking by more pertinent fears.

"Men can be frightening at first in this respect, until one is used to them...they are so...so different from us," Amaelia announced carefully. "They are so very eager...it can be terrifying..."

Melissa brightened a little and viewed the rapidly moving sky. "He is never frightening in that respect...he is considerate and tender...and..." Unable to finish she sealed her lips and subsided.

"Then in what respect is he frightening?" Amaelia folded her hands in her lap and waited. "With these *authoritarian ways* of his...?"

"I have never said he is frightening!" she replied in a haughty manner. "When I annoy him with certain remarks, he becomes fierce...but even then, I am not really frightened...just a little wary..."

The sun was disappearing behind white and silver clouds and she watched it—losing the comforting presence of it, like a quiet friend vanishing into the distance.

"And what sort of remarks are these?" Amaelia asked dully, doggedly chewing the same bone to retrieve the marrow.

"Well, I... I...for instance, during arguments I make accusatory comments about the past, and about his character in general... I allude to the traits in him which—"

"Very foolish, Lissy..." intervened Amaelia in the same monotone. "Provoking a man in that way can never end well!" she sought to bring a finale to the whole interlude. Melissa would take them round in circles all afternoon if she allowed it. "I need more details before I leave here. I need at least to know about that day in the rose garden…"

Melissa made a hissing sound of annoyance but remained mute.

"My dear…" said Amaelia with yet more enforced tolerance. "I think you should tell me…or I cannot recommend to your father that you go ahead and marry him… I am wed to a complete bastard in Gideon Montalbein, even though we are separated…and I ignored everyone's advice not to wed him. So, I simply cannot see you go to the same fate…and I shall understand most things you may tell me."

"I do not want to stop the wedding," Melissa cried with vehemence, running a few steps forwards to nowhere in particular and throwing open the door to the stifling enclosure, not caring who may be around to hear. "I love him and cannot now be without him, Aunt Amaelia…"

Amaelia was a little stunned by this sudden emotional exuberance. "But sometimes love in itself is not enough," she mused. "There has to be mutual respect and trust. Tell me what he has threatened you with…you are being deliberately obdurate and difficult…we are both women, and you can tell me."

Melissa's silence persisted; it was about to engulf them in some irreversible deadlock.

"Does he threaten to lock you in attics? Or submerge you in cold water…or tie you to the bed and force himself upon you?"

"Of course he does not!" cried Melissa in horror. She was suddenly frozen to the spot by the thought that those kinds of methods might be common in disgruntled husbands. "Is that what men often do?" she asked in a small voice.

Amaelia closed her eyes, shaking her head slightly, and saying nothing. It occurred to Melissa that her aunt may have experienced some of these horrors at the hand of her despotic husband and she knew not what to say to offer comfort or elicit information. The world abounded with fiendish men it seemed: Gideon Montalbein, Charles Fairchild; the list might be endless. She looked at Amaelia as Amaelia pursued her darker thoughts. "Some men do…" she replied eventually in a near whisper. "Though I do not personally believe your fiancé to be one of them…now tell me what he does threaten, you silly girl, before I lose my temper."

Melissa brought herself confidently into the moment. "He threatens nothing like that. Otherwise, I would not marry him."

"Then there is very little which can be unutterable…" claimed her aunt, rallying back to her usual self. "So, what else can be the matter?"

"He is at times overbearing with his attitudes…" Melissa claimed, once more toying with the question. "He does not wish me to go into the countryside alone, when sketching…for one thing…and says he will forbid me doing so."

"Well, of course he does not want that!" said Amaelia. "'tis not safe for any young woman."

"I do not see why not. Nothing bad has befallen me so far."

"Then you have been fortunate. He is to be your husband and naturally seeks to protect you."

"From what?" Melissa queried.

Amaelia was running out of patience. "From all kinds of woeful experiences…"

"You mean like falling into boggy ground…which he once witnessed me do and has likely not forgotten…" Melissa scoffed.

"Not just that…"

"What then?"

"From unsavoury people…disreputable tramps and nomads and other characters… *From robbery and rape!*" declared Amaelia finally in a strident tone and *grasping the nettle.*

Melissa seemed somewhat stunned and paused to reconsider her view point. "And he doesn't like me seeing Roger in friendship."

"Who?" Amaelia turned in confusion to look at her. "Oh, the flower shop boy!"

"He is not a flower shop boy…he is a horticulturist and a botanist," she corrected.

"He's a fop," said Amaelia dourly. "And why you want to be bothering with him when you can have a man like Fairchild, I fail to understand."

"We are merely friends, Roger and I."

"Yes, but Fairchild will be jealous…of any man."

Melissa frowned and then made her inscrutable face of satisfaction mingled with impatience which some saw as haughty, and others saw for what it was.

"Anyway, never mind that now…what is it he threatened you with in the rose garden that day? What was it that necessitated such a struggle and an indecorous scene?"

Still there was no response and Amaelia thought she may have to display her temper, which was considerably larger than her; she would not disappoint her brother, whom she adored, on this errand. He had always been there for her throughout her own travails in marriage and had on a few occasions fought with Montalbein over his mistreatment of her.

"I have had enough of this prevarication! Will you write it down?" Amaelia demanded and began taking a small tablet and pencil from her tiny reticule which seemed to be bottomless despite its miniscule size, dropping her voice to a mutinous hiss, "Or must I go and find the gentleman and petition him to tell me himself?"

Melissa stiffened and assumed near outrage. "No indeed…he is not to be disturbed. Doctor Darnley has instructed…"

"Phooey to Doctor Darnley!" declared Amaelia. "I will not be usurped by him on the topic…or any other medic."

"Besides, he will not tell you…" Melissa said. She knew this to be a lie; he would almost certainly tell Amaelia now if Amaelia staged an intervention on her brother's behalf. He would honour her father's enquiry as one gentleman to another. It was her own need for privacy on the matter, not his. But she persevered on her course. "He is not someone to be easily intimidated…nor is he inclined to disclose secrets…he is not that kind of person."

Amaelia smiled to herself—now they may get somewhere. "Which secrets?"

"Our secrets, of course!" she said. "All lovers have secrets, I believe."

"I am not leaving until I have more details about these secrets…" Amaelia legislated. "At least, write what you know of his intentions that day in the garden…and hurry. I have an important meeting at five o'clock…"

Melissa gave way with a groan of deep remorse. "Very well…just to pacify you, Aunt." She seized the tablet and pencil and sat and thought for a minute while her aunt gazed in the other direction and lit a second cigarette. The perfumed smoke permeating the air in the summer house and lending to it a surreal and exotic quality, resembling a mountain shrine or a fairy grotto. "And I hope it has nothing to do with these silly grievances from schooldays you and Melanie apparently hold against him…because I shall not be sympathetic to that at all and you will simply waste everyone's time and patience! That has no bearing on the present…"

Melissa made her mulish face and stared at the ground. If Amaelia did not want her time wasting, why did she not just mind her own business! And how did she know whether those days had a bearing when it had not been spoken of? She began to scribble and cross out and scribble more. Eventually, she finished writing and then tore off the small sheet of paper and handed it to Amaelia who read it, raised her brows, then read it again twice over to make sure she had not missed anything between the lines. She then assumed a distant look, which made her appear myopic, as she tried to remain serious. "Is that it? Is that the whole of it regarding these threats and warnings?"

"Yes…" said Melissa with petulance. "Is that not bad enough?"

Amaelia resorted to casual merriment, quietly, and then with more effusive laughter, finally turning to Melissa with a patronising expression. "Oh, my dear! That is quite a normal measure many men favour…and quite acceptable. You will not be granted a divorce on those grounds, let me assure you."

"Do not tell anyone, please!" Melissa snatched the paper from her aunt's grasp and tore it to shreds so that no-one could find it and read it.

"My lips are sealed," Amaelia said indulgently and then rose, still alight with amusement. "You are marrying an utterly desirable man. Many women would give their eye-teeth for him…you must think to please him as much as you can."

"And what of him pleasing me?" Melissa claimed, feeling foolish.

"I am sure he shall… I am sure he already tries…besides, 'tis not difficult to please men…they require little to make them happy…rather like small children." Amaelia picked up her hat. "You will just have to make sure you are a good girl…" She turned and looked at her niece, attempting a prim face until her humour broke through. "Or not! As the fancy takes you!"

Melissa stared at her. Her aunt was too savvy in these matters and she could not dissemble. "I must fly now, my sweet," said Amaelia, "Having spent half a day on this *mountain from a molehill*…"

She watched Amaelia make her loping strides back to the house—a protracted dance almost, in forwards motion, not unlike herself when excited and beyond words.

Upon the departure of the visiting human, the black and white cat slid through the open door and jumped onto the bench next to her. She stroked the cat's ears in a rhythmic way, soothing to them both. "Good Lord, Gertie, how they do rattle on, these interfering busybodies…" she said softly. And Gertrude—differing only in species and perfectly aligned in wisdom—closed her eyes and purred. Her face turned like the daughter of the house towards the generous rays of the sun.

* * *

Amaelia waltzed into Giles's study and threw her exquisite hat onto the nearest chair. "Just a flying visit, Giles dearest! Is that madeira in the carafe over there, or sherry? Actually, it doesn't really matter, I need a drink of something."

"Sherry!" Giles replied succinctly and looked up from his paperwork. He watched her pour a vast amount of sherry into a glass and swallow a quarter of it; her capacity for strong drink might shame many men. "Have you discovered much?" he enquired casually.

She sank into an armchair "Certainly, though 'twas like drawing teeth…'tis nothing to worry about…in fact," Amaelia began again to laugh and Giles cleared his throat tolerantly. "Well, what is it?"

"I regret I cannot say…" She hiccupped after more hasty swigs of the sherry. "I have promised not to. She is mortified at having told me…but you need not be concerned."

Giles flung down his nib and leaned back in the chair. "For heaven's sake!"

Amaelia twirled the glass in her fingers. "Let us just say, he threatens a minor incursion to her dignity…just as Mama predicted when at dinner here that night she stormed off…think back!"

Giles reached for his pipe. "I can scarcely recall what was said at dinner last night, Maelia…how do you expect me to recall any of that!" He gazed at the oil lamp hanging over his desk. He was not famed for his memory or his imagination and he gave up after a few moments.

"Aaahh…" Amaelia exclaimed, swallowing the last of the sherry and exhaling delightedly. "I was never so amused… I will tell you perhaps after the wedding…or next year…or the year after that…when I am sure 'twill not matter to her."

"Have it your own way…" replied Giles in resignation to things beyond his remit.

She rose and refilled her glass—a little more modestly this time. "'tis my sneaking suspicion, Giles, that she cherishes these threats and takes great enjoyment from the notion. Girls of her age often do, until things become reality…in fact, I think she subtly encourages him in his quest for supremacy…she dangles it before him like a wager to an inveterate gambler…and he cannot resist the odds…"

Giles tamped tobacco into the pipe. "I said to yon fellow weeks ago, when he first approached me about her... I told him not to look to me for guidance as I've never understood women."

Amaelia finished the sherry in a hurry. "Do you really still believe we wish to be understood? 'tis to our advantage not to be."

He put a spill to the pipe and lit it. "As long as she is not repeating your error..."

"She is too astute for that, Giles. She is deeper than that lake out there...and he knows it...despite his refinement and modest demeanour I think he knows quite a lot about women...he has had experience enough, I am sure, and he..." She was interrupted in her assessment by the door opening as Mr Croker entered. He bowed to her stiffly and said: "Good day to you, Lady Montalbein..."

Amaelia inclined her head politely and then sprang up and put the empty glass on her brother's desk. "I have to be away...a meeting with Gideon and his accountants... I need to be rested and fortified."

"You will be alright in that, will you? said Giles as the pipe gained momentum."

"Perfectly, thank you. Jasper will be with me...he always thwarts his father's attempts to do me down..."

Giles nodded—his nephew, Amaelia's eldest son, was a shrewd character, already with business interests of his own in London, whom Giles felt should take his place as head of the business finances when he retired.

Mr Croker did his best to listen for more as he went to his own corner of the room and collected certain documents—but nothing else was said on the subject of finance and Jasper.

"Do you think it will thrive; this proposed union?" asked Giles as Amaelia stood at the wall mirror on tip-toes to pin her hat.

"Without a doubt...she would have refused him before this if she disliked all these warnings. She has been merely playing for time...and, you know Giles, I believe they are farther on in the courtship than you perceive...'tis as well you are bringing the wedding forward... I think they are already joined in the Biblical sense."

"That is my suspicion too..." opined Giles. "She has your *passionate* nature...'tis why I called on you to question her."

"Indeed! They may become legendary in the family, like Jemima and Jago." Amaelia smiled into the mirror as her brother also smiled. Both proud and heartened by the love story of their parents. "Many strive for it but do not find it… I wish I would have found it…" Amaelia lamented.

"As do I," said Giles softly.

She kissed his cheek. "I am glad my insights have been helpful."

"Thank you, Maelia…though they are hardly insights…more insights into the fact that there are insights to be had…"

Amaelia emitted a strong smell of gardenias as she drifted round the desk. "If you knew what these insights were, Giles…were I at liberty to divulge them, you might split your sides laughing."

Her brother disappeared behind a hefty cloud of tobacco smoke. "What a pleasant change it would make…" he said in a world-weary voice and Amaelia's peals of laughter went with her through the door.

END

Book Two Out Soon … 'The Entitlement' … following the lives of Melissa and Melanie.